Agee on Film

VOLUME TWO

BY THE SAME AUTHOR

PERMIT ME VOYAGE
LET US NOW PRAISE FAMOUS MEN
　　(WITH WALKER EVANS)
THE MORNING WATCH
A DEATH IN THE FAMILY
AGEE ON FILM

AGEE

On Film

VOLUME TWO

Five
Film Scripts by

JAMES AGEE

Foreword by John Huston

The Universal Library
GROSSET & DUNLAP · NEW YORK

Universal Library Edition, 1969

Special Contents © 1960 by The James Agee Trust
Noa Noa © 1959 by Mia Fritsch Agee
The Bride Comes to Yellow Sky © 1958 by Theasquare
Productions, Inc.
The Blue Hotel © 1958 by Theasquare Productions, Inc.

Library of Congress Catalog Card Number: 58-12581

Manufactured in the United States of America.

Designed by Alfred Manso.

Acknowledgments

Acknowledgment is here made to Horizon Pictures, Inc. for permission to include *The African Queen* in this volume; to Mr. Paul Gregory for *The Night of the Hunter;* to Mr. Huntington Hartford for *The Bride Comes to Yellow Sky* and *The Blue Hotel;* to Mrs. James Agee for *Noa Noa.*

Foreword

by

John Huston

It's all to the good that so many of you now know James Agee's writing—his novels, his criticism, his poetry. (In a sense it was all poetry.) I wish that you could also have known Jim himself.

Let me begin by describing him physically. He was about six-two and heavy but neither muscular nor fat—a mountaineer's body. His hair was dark brown, his eyes blue and his skin pale. His hands were big and slab-like in their thickness. He was very strong, and except for one occasion, which I only heard about, when he stove a *Time* editor against the wall, he was always gentle towards his fellow humans with that kind of gentleness usually reserved for plants and animals.

His clothes were dark and shiny. I can't imagine him in a new suit. Black shoes scuffed grey, wrinkled collar, a button off his shirt and a ravelled tie—he wore clothes to be warm and decent. Jim's elegance was inward. I doubt whether he had any idea of what he looked like, or whether he ever looked in a mirror except to shave. Vanity wasn't in him.

He held his body in very slight regard altogether, feeding it with whatever was at hand, allowing it to go to sleep when there was nothing else for it to do, begrudging it anything beneficial such as medicine when he was sick. On the other hand, he was a chain smoker and a bottle-a-night man.

You who didn't actually know Jim might wish that he had taken better care of himself and lived longer to write more novels and screenplays . . . more poetry. But we who did know him recognize the fact that his body's destruction was implicit in his makeup, and we thank heaven that it was strong enough to withstand for so many years the constant assaults he leveled on it.

I was with Jim at the time of his first heart attack, and while he did obey the doctors' orders over a period of weeks—out of respect for their profession—and never asked any of his friends to get him a drink or even give him a drag off a cigaret, he let it be clearly understood that once the crisis was past he intended to resume the habits of life that had led up to it. I can hear myself uttering some nonsense about doing things in moderation, like sleeping eight hours every night and smoking say half a pack of cigarets a day and only having a drink or two before dinner. Jim nodded his head in mute agreement with everything I said, or if not agreement, sympathy. And he went on nodding until I faltered and finished. Then he smiled his gentle smile and, after a decent interval, changed the subject.

His regard for other people's feelings was unique in my experience. I don't believe it was because he was afraid of hurting them, and certainly it had nothing to do with gaining in anyone's estimation. It was simply that his soul rejoiced when he could say yes and mean it to something someone else believed in.

He never attempted to win anyone to his way of thinking, far less to try to prove anyone mistaken or in the wrong. He would take a contrary opinion—regardless of how foolish it was—and hold it up to the light and turn it this way and that, examining its facets as though it were a gem of great worth, and if it turned out to be a piece of cracked glass, why then he, Jim, must have misunderstood—the other fellow had meant something else, hadn't he . . . *this,* perhaps? And sure enough Jim would come up with some variation of the opinion that would make it flawless as a specimen jewel. And the other fellow would be very proud of having meant precisely that, and they would go on from there.

I can see him sitting on the edge of a chair, bunched forward, elbows on knees, arms upraised, the fingers of one of the slab-like hands pointing at those of the other and working as if they were trying to untie a knot. His forehead is furrowed and his mouth is twisted in concentration. His head is nodding in sympathy and understanding. He is smiling. Gaps show between his teeth. (Jim only went to the dentist to have a tooth pulled, never fixed.)

He is smiling. It stops raining all over the world. A great discovery has been made. He and another are in complete agreement. We who beheld that smile will never forget it.

Contents

Agee on Film

VOLUME TWO

Noa Noa

"Noa Noa"

James Agee began writing Noa Noa *in 1953, under contract, with David Bradley as the director. The completed scenario, which was based on the life of Paul Gauguin, was read by his son, Emile, who was delighted by it and who felt that a true understanding of his father's spirit and courage had been achieved. Negotiations for the film production of* Noa Noa *were interrupted by the death of the author.*

FADE IN

BLACK SCREEN—Over which ALL CREDIT TITLES will read left to right, gradually appearing until ENTIRE FRAME IS FILLED. Storm sounds o.s. will slowly build to loud climax. FADE OUT

FADE IN

BLACK SCREEN—

"Except a grain of wheat fall into the ground
and die, it abideth alone: but if it die,
it bringeth forth much fruit."
John, 12, XXIV.

FADE OUT

FADE IN

EXT.—THE MARQUESAS ISLANDS—LONG SHOT—NIGHT
The islands viewed from the rough sea. On the beach can be seen a light from Gauguin's home, model framed to the right of center frame.

DISSOLVE

MED. LONG SHOT
Same setup but closer. The storm is subsiding . . . We are aware also of Tioka's hut.

DISSOLVE

3

MED. SHOT—GAUGUIN'S HOME AND TIOKA'S HUT—DAWN

We no longer use a model. Gauguin's home stands among palms. An o.s. wave spills water into f.g., and withdraws it, as TIOKA, an old native, crosses medium distant towards the home; delicately picking his way through the devastation of the expired storm. He starts up the steps to the door.

INT. GAUGUIN'S HOME—MED. SHOT—CENTERING THE DOOR

Tioka enters and pauses at door, hesitantly concerned; he is flanked by one or two paintings, reproductions, European and native objects.

TIOKA (softly) Koke . . . Koke . . . ?

He looks towards center-screen, below-frame; he advances, shyly, into CLOSEUP; and we see that his cheeks are ornately striated by heavy-ridged, blue tattoo-scars. As he advances, realization of death grows in his face. He pauses in this realization. Beyond him, KA-HUI, a young Chinese half-breed, appears in doorway, advances, hovers at Tioka's shoulder, also watching the still unseen Gauguin.

TIOKA (without turning) Fetch M. Vernier. . . . Hurry.

Ka-Hui hurries away. Throughout this scene, the brash cheerful sounds of early morning and after-storm persist o.s. Tioka now advances as we pull back slowly and downward, disclosing, very close to us, at the bottom of frame, the prostrate dead profile of Gauguin, which chokes the breadth of the frame—and, beside it, a small table, carrying medicines, a hypodermic, and a smoky, lighted ship's lantern. This profile is based on Gauguin's bronze self-portrait (Becker's frontispiece), used prostrate. The dead eyes are half-open; the nose is large and proud; the slight smile is at least as enigmatic as that of the Mona Lisa.

Tioka advances more and more slowly; he squats beside the head; he looks at it with intense concern and politeness; he is a fine old man. Then abruptly and simply, he leans forward and, with a cannibal's teeth, nips at the scalp, to test death. Getting no reaction, he again squats erect, gazing at the head, with deep emotion and a certain reverence. He is aware but does nothing about it when VERNIER, the Protestant pastor, enters, breathless, followed by Ka-Hui. Ka-Hui stays in b.g. Vernier, a tall, rather intelligent, melancholic man, walks slowly and straight to the body. Tioka makes room for him.

Vernier lifts one dead eyelid; then closes the eyes; then extinguishes the lantern, from which black smoke crawls and fades. He kneels as, past them, THE TRADER, THE GENDARME and THE PAINTER enter and advance with less courtesy, more curiosity. With their advance we bring up the Camera, losing Gauguin's face, into which all gaze downward. Silent pause.

GENDARME (with hatred; quietly) So he got away. And in the nick of time. (he looks contemptuously around the room) Well . . . I pity his creditors.

Over the latter, CUT TO

PAN SHOT

around the studio: paintings and sculptures by Gauguin, various native objects of great beauty and strangeness, photographs of great works of his time, and of the past; and a wheezebox organ.

PAINTER'S VOICE (o.s.) *I* pity *him*; all that effort, and not a grain of talent. Over this we, CUT BACK TO

THE GROUP SHOT

All, except Tioka, are looking about: summing up a man's nature, through what he has left. Tioka keeps looking at Gauguin.

TRADER (an American) You've got to hand him one thing: he had all the *courage* in the world. The way he kept jabbing in the old needle, and painting right ahead, morning to night. I never saw a man work so hard, in pain so bad.

All but the Gendarme nod.

GENDARME He was out of his mind; that's all.
Past them, a PRIEST and THE BISHOP enter, businesslike; a few natives behind. The group makes way; the natives hang back.

VERNIER (courteous; not friendly) Father; Monsignor . . .
They nod to him, advance, and look down (we don't see Gauguin).

BISHOP (in Latin; making a Cross) May the souls of the Faithful, through the mercy of God, rest in peace, and may light perpetual shine upon them.

GENDARME Faithful . . .

TRADER (to Gendarme) At least he always set up drinks when he had them; and paid his women.

VERNIER He kept his *own* faith. (a moved pause) I've never seen him look as he does now . . . He makes me think of Christ.

All glance at him in silent surprise.

GENDARME (slavish but sure) Antichrist would be nearer it, wouldn't it, Father?

The priest glances towards his Bishop, who says nothing.

VERNIER Very well: the look, then, of a man who has endured great suffering, with great courage, for a great purpose; and who has won a great victory.

GENDARME (contemptuously) *Victory*!

HEAD CLOSEUP—GAUGUIN—DOWN SHOT
Seen from this angle, the smile is even more remarkable, as if he overheard them.

VERNIER'S VOICE (o.s.) Yes, *Victory*. It's clear in his face. And that one thing, nobody can take from him, ever, whether in heaven or in hell.

Over this we slowly PULL CAMERA DOWN along the body, which is sheeted as high as the waist, nude above, and fantastically streaked, almost mangled-looking, with brilliant paints. We pause briefly above a hopelessly messy palette and an equally inchoate painting beside the dead left hand.

GENDARME'S VOICE (over this mess) A *painter*. (he snorts contemptuously)

VERNIER'S VOICE (o.s.) He was losing his sight, you know.

GENDARME'S VOICE He never had sight worth losing.
Now the CAMERA CROSSES the body slowly and again hovers, in a close downshot: a family photograph of Gauguin, Mette and their five children in the time of their prosperity; beside the dead right hand.

TRADER'S VOICE Why, I never knew he was married . . .

VERNIER'S VOICE Oh yes . . .
Now the Camera returns to the center of the body.

NEW ANGLE—SHOOTING STRAIGHT DOWN
past the body, a little to the left of the feet. Gauguin's last painting, the Breton village under deep snow. (N.B. The Camera is so moved and cut as to make the sign of the Cross over Gauguin.)

PAINTER'S VOICE (genteel and patronizing) Why . . . that must be France.

VERNIER'S VOICE Brittany.

PAINTER'S VOICE And rather pretty, too.

Now the CAMERA PANS to point straight down the axis of the body, past and between the bare and piteously swollen and wounded feet, at the great, bruised painting of sunflowers.

PAINTER'S VOICE *Sunflowers?* What on earth . . . ?
The Camera travels slowly towards the sunflowers: body in lower frame.

VERNIER'S VOICE I don't know. I remember when he ordered seeds, from some friends in France—

GENDARME'S VOICE (across him) O, don't tell me he had *friends*—

VERNIER'S VOICE . . . and grew them . . . but I never knew he had made a painting of them . . .

By now, the CAMERA MOVES BETWEEN, AND LOSES, the ruined feet; then MOVES SLIGHTLY toward the painting, hesitates, swerves sharply to right and down, into the family photograph, and we—

DISSOLVE TO

INT. CORRIDOR—BERTIN'S FIRM—DAY
colored and lighted a la Daumier. An office boy approaches as we PAN onto gold-lettered door:

PAUL GAUGUIN Liquidateur

He knocks.

BOY Monsieur? Monsieur Gauguin?

GAUGUIN'S VOICE Well, come in.
The boy enters and we DOLLY. GAUGUIN sits with his back to us at a desk littered with heavy ledgers and with papers.

GAUGUIN (not turning) *Now* what?

BOY Monsieur Bertin. He would like to see you, Monsieur.
Gauguin turns and looks up on "Bertin".

GAUGUIN (with extra meaning) I think perhaps I'd like to see M. Bertin.
Gathering up papers he walks into CLOSEUP, precedes the boy into the corridor. We PAN him to Bertin's door, which he opens without knocking.

INT. BERTIN'S OFFICE
A more sumptuous office. BERTIN, a decent enough man of 50, is clearly boss. He nods as Gauguin enters, continues writing, looks up.

BERTIN What are the total assets for Pierret?

GAUGUIN Not better than 30,000 francs.

BERTIN Too bad. I thought we might clear 5,000.

GAUGUIN Pierret knows how to conceal his discounts.

BERTIN But not his liabilities.
He laughs at his own little joke; Gauguin does not. Laughter dying, a short pause.

BERTIN Something wrong, Paul?
Silence. This is very hard for Gauguin.

GAUGUIN M. Bertin, I'm leaving.

BERTIN You're. . . ?
Gauguin's speechless nod.

BERTIN You're joking.
Gauguin shakes his head.

BERTIN Why, may I ask?

GAUGUIN To paint.

BERTIN You have your Sundays for that.

GAUGUIN I have my life, and I've already wasted too much of it.

BERTIN Sit down, Gauguin. (he keeps standing) Then listen. You're tired. Badly out of sorts. I've been noticing it for some time. Why don't you take a couple of weeks off?

GAUGUIN I'm leaving, Bertin. That's all there is to it.

BERTIN You're a man, Gauguin, not a schoolboy. A *businessman*; and a gifted one. You have a wife and children to support. And here, out of a clear sky, you begin to blather about painting pictures in a garret. Of course. I understand. We all get fed up at times. But—what can we do about it?

GAUGUIN Act like men, if we've got it in us to.

BERTIN Exactly.

GAUGUIN That's why I'm leaving.
Pause; Bertin brings up heavy artillery.

BERTIN Listen, Gauguin. Who are men who do the world's work? Who holds civilization together?
Gauguin's reactions to "world's work" and "civilization" are quiet, but ferociously contemptuous.

GAUGUIN (calm; smiling) The cowards. The fools. The rabbits. Those who have no talent to betray, and those who lack the courage to be true to it.

BERTIN (guiltily flaring) Courage? You've *lost* all courage and all responsibility.
Gauguin just smiles, tightly.

BERTIN (sincerely) What has brought you to this, Paul? So suddenly?

GAUGUIN Suddenly? Eleven years of finding enough courage (with detached warmth) Good-bye, Bertin.
He puts out his hand. Bertin does not take it. Gauguin bows ironically, turns and walks out, stripping off the black alpaca coat of his profession.
DISSOLVE TO

INT. GAUGUIN'S HOME—EARLY EVENING
A comfortably rigged-out front hallway, or the Parisian equivalent of the period—wherever eagerly waiting children, who love their father, greet his return from work.

GROUP SHOT—GAUGUIN—CHILDREN—METTE
They swarm him as he stoops to embrace them, with shrill ad lib cries of "Papa! Papa!" "Did you bring me a surprise?" Etc. They are in their night clothes. He is nicely and very conventionally dressed, well-shaven and shorn. They are charming little children, wild and trusting and loving in their embraces. He is clearly devoted to them and delighted by them. He lifts Aline, aged 5, high in his arms. It is clear that something very grave is on his mind. Aline senses something. He lifts her close to his face as we TILT to CLOSE SHOT, METTE entering behind.

ALINE (sensing; enquiring) Pa*pa*?
Suddenly moved beyond words, he holds her very close. We PAN to favor Mette, behind—a strong, noble, disciplined woman.

METTE (sensing it too) Paul?

GAUGUIN (moved; quiet) Later, dear.   DISSOLVE TO

INT. GAUGUIN LIVING ROOM—NIGHT
Prosperous, bourgeois furniture, and, in odd contrast, an early Gauguin (his first self-portrait?), and a small Cezanne on wall in b.g.

CLOSE SHOT—METTE
A strong, stricken face. As WE PULL AWAY, bringing in Gauguin.

METTE (quietly) It's a catastrophe, Paul.

GAUGUIN Come, Mette; you're no coward.

METTE A catastrophe.

GAUGUIN I'm not an amateur, you know: I'm a man of talent. All I need is time to develop it.

She is listening, but her face is dead.

GAUGUIN Before we use up our savings; I promise you: I'll be supporting us through my painting.

METTE And if you fail?

GAUGUIN I won't fail. Have I *ever* failed you?

METTE But if you do? Will you go back into business?

GAUGUIN If I fail, I'll keep working until I *don't* fail.

METTE That's what I was afraid of.
Gauguin puts his hand over hers.

GAUGUIN (quietly) You're my wife, Mette. You couldn't love a man who betrayed himself.

METTE No: you must do what you must. But—*why,* Paul! Painting is all very well, and I want you to be at peace with yourself, but—*why?*

GAUGUIN (tenderly) My dear, I'm afraid that's something you'll never understand. And for that, I revere your bravery all the more. We'll be well, I can promise you—so long as we both keep faith with our courage.

METTE *We'll* be well: it's the children I'm thinking of.

GAUGUIN (quietly) They'll be well too, Mette: for they'll never have to be ashamed of their father or their mother . . . How many children in this delightful slaughterhouse of a world, can be sure of that?

METTE (deeply moved) Paul . . .

GAUGUIN (almost a whisper) My wife . . .
They gaze quietly and proudly into each other's eyes, with deep love, courage and respect.

METTE Whatever comes of it, Paul . . .
They continue their quiet, intensifying gaze.

SLOW DISSOLVE TO

INT. A STUDIO—PARIS—DAY

A wretched and bare room. An easel in mid-floor; one straight chair; a mattress on the floor; beside it, torn bread and a wine bottle. Rain streams on skylight or window. A washstand.

CLOSE SHOT—GAUGUIN

Gauguin, at mirror, finishes shaving. His face is hardened and thinned by inward and outward privation. He snips at his overlong hair with scissors (or cuts with razor). He gets on his shabby coat and trims also at a frayed cuff. He cases himself bitterly in the mirror. He walks to center as we PAN and looks at his painting on the easel as if he were saying good-bye forever; then walks out and closes the door on the dismal room. DISSOLVE TO

INT. BERTIN'S CORRIDOR

PAN UP from close shot of Gauguin's old office door on which the gold letters now read:

ALPHONSE LATOUR Liquidateur

. . . TO CLOSE SHOT—GAUGUIN

He is drenched; he is bitterly aware of his years of captivity here, and of this return. He takes off and shakes his hat; dries his face with a ragged handkerchief; straightens his hair; arranges the handkerchief carefully in his breast-pocket, and, with the walk of a condemned man, moves on to Bertin's door as we PULL AWAY. Hesitation; then, with desperate resolve, he lifts his hand to knock. He can't bring himself to. Over his agonized face we hear his mental voice, very low.

GAUGUIN'S VOICE Mette. Mette.

Abruptly, as he brings himself to try again, Bertin comes out. Gauguin, as shocked and frightened as a caught thief, turns and ducks, to hide his face; then, with great bravery, forces himself to turn slowly, meet Bertin's eyes, and smile cooly; then turns on his heel and walks away as Bertin gapes after him; and starts down a stairway.

PULL SHOT—A STREET—WAIST SHOT OF GAUGUIN

Head high, hat in hand, he walks swiftly through the drowning rain, in anguish and in almost an ecstasy of pride in having done the right thing. We know he will never weaken again. He overtakes our pull short and we PAN and he strides proudly away down the rain-emptied street; a man as poorly dressed as he is, huddled and humbled in his poverty, pauses to watch after him in puzzlement. FADE OUT

FADE IN

CLOSE SHOT—THEO VAN GOGH

. . . losing Vincent, then the sunflowers. Theo is paying out money o.s.

THEO (apologetically) Of course, it's a shameful price, but—

GAUGUIN'S VOICE (o.s.) I'm used to shameful prices—when there are any.

During these lines we PULL AWAY to background Theo with the kind of paintings he would have dealt with: in later shots we also show art supplies.

WAIST SHOT—GAUGUIN
He is in his late thirties: shabby, weary, powerful, immensely proud. He counts the money (we can see paint at his nails), and pockets it.

THEO'S VOICE (o.s.) . . . but I think it covers your debts.
Gauguin nods; and waits; not making things easy for Theo.

TWO SHOT—GAUGUIN AND THEO

THEO (shyly) I do hope you'll see your way, now, to accepting my brother's invitation.

A pause.

GAUGUIN (like a cold bargainer) If I went down to Arles to live with your brother, it would be at *your* expense; wouldn't it, Van Gogh?
A motion of embarrassment from Theo, and a gentle smile.

THEO Vincent sets great store by your having been a sailor; he's sure both of you can manage on what I send him.

GAUGUIN And suppose we can't?
Another shrug and smile; then, gently:

THEO Don't . . . trouble Vincent, if that should happen.

GAUGUIN I don't—care—for the emotion of gratitude.

THEO He is very lonely, Gauguin, and his whole dream of establishing a community of artists—a—(shyly)—brotherhood—depends on you.

GAUGUIN (sardonic) Why *me,* of all people!

THEO (tenderly but with difficulty) You're a man. Vincent is a child.

GAUGUIN (embarrassed) I'm the last man to believe that *artists* should breathe each others' breath. Leave that to the bourgeoisie, and the unions, and the Churches.

THEO (very sad) Then you won't even consider it?

GAUGUIN I've been considering it—for months. I can't afford to go where I want to: so I'll go to Arles. (Theo grabs his shoulder impulsively) If he can establish "brotherhood" with *me,* anything is possible.

THEO I'm so glad you're going, Paul. So very glad. It's going to do wonders for both of you. You'll see.

GAUGUIN We'll see.

THEO Only one thing; please: my brother is increasingly . . . nervous, you know; excitable; and frightened about it. His . . . his religious ideas mean so much to him. (inarticulate pause, then) Be gentle with him.
A painful silence; then, from Gauguin, a short nod; then he breaks the prolonged handclasp.

GAUGUIN Good-bye, Theo.
He turns, and starts for the door; then stops; looks back.

GAUGUIN (rigidly) Thank you.

THEO Good-bye, Paul. And good luck.
He watches after Gauguin. We hear the door open and close o.s.

DISSOLVE

EXT. ARLES STATION—DAYBREAK
In the last darkness we shoot close from behind a smallish, jug-eared man in a fur cap—VINCENT VAN GOGH—as, close in b.g., with grinding and sighing, a train comes towards a stop. Vincent's head is flicking left and right as eagerly as a bird's. As the train stops we   CUT TO

CLOSE SHOT—GAUGUIN
. . . as, over the o.s. sound of expiring steam, he steps from the train with light personal luggage and heavy artist's equipment. He glances to right and left.

CLOSE SHOT—VINCENT
—from the front, the small, close-set eyes darting eagerly. He sees Gauguin o.s. and his bony, nervous face is transfigured.

VINCENT (shouting) Paul! Paul!
As he starts running we,   CUT TO

CLOSE SHOT—GAUGUIN
He smiles—rather warmly, for him—in recognition, and starts walking towards Vincent.

MED. SHOT—DOLLYING INTO CLOSE TWO-SHOT
. . . as, respectively walking and running, they converge. Vincent embraces him and slaps his shoulders and all but prances, looking up at him with incredulous delight. Gauguin, though more reticent, is pleased and fond.

VINCENT You really came! You really did it! God *bless* you! I'd almost given up hope. Why, you . . . you . . . (words fail him).

GAUGUIN (mussing his cap) It's good to see you, Brigadier.
Now words fail Vincent still worse. He claps him on the shoulders repeatedly, and exclaims like a child:

VINCENT O! *O!*
The train whistle whees shrilly and the train starts moving past in b.g.; both catch the resemblance, and laugh.

VINCENT (sporty) How about a rum! How about two! Eighty! There's a good cafe—marvelous place—very sinister—I painted it—place fit for a murder.

GAUGUIN Let's save it. I want to see that house of yours, that's going to start the world turning around the *right* way.

VINCENT Well good. Come on then.
He grabs up some luggage; Gauguin grabs it from him.

GAUGUIN No thanks, Brigadier; I'll take care of myself.
They bevel out of the shot as the train pulls out.

EXT. STREETS OF ARLES—DAY
A series of shots between station and Vincent's house or one LONG TRACK-ING SHOT down Street, as we walk Gauguin and Vincent through the streets. The awakening town as daylight strengthens, using b.g. where Vincent painted. Finally they arrive in front of Vincent's house and pause.

VINCENT (quietly) I know how good everything is going to be, because it's just the right time of day for you to come.

He gestures towards the sun o.s. Both look.

FULL SHOT—REVERSE ANGLE POINT OF VIEW—THE SUN
It has just risen in maximal splendor.

CLOSE SHOT—SUNFLOWERS—(STOP MOTION)
Two great sunflowers lift their faces towards the sunlight.

CLOSER TWO SHOT—GAUGUIN AND VINCENT
Profoundly moved, still gazing into the sun.

VINCENT And now look here.

We PAN as he and Gauguin turn, and first see the yellow blaze of his outside wall. As he swings open his door and ushers Gauguin in and follows we,   CUT TO

INT. VINCENT'S HOME—DOLLY SHOT

They walk through the house which is freshly painted in Gauguin's honor. As they move through the house we see paintings of Vincent, a gloomy Gauguin self-portrait, reproductions of other contemporary artists, etc. The room is very untidy—

VINCENT (almost ad lib quality) You see? You see? Your bedroom, my dear sir . . . and that very worrying portrait you sent me; we've got to get the melancholy greens out of that; get you back to Martinique, and your Negresses. Here's mine. I like to live like a painting inside a painting . . . Here's our studio, where all the great work is going to be done . . . and here's our kitchen—all it needs is a woman—You see? You understand? I painted my house just for you. All through my house, the color of the sun. Of joy. Of God. To bring light to everyone. We'll draw others to us —now that *you're* here; we'll all live here and work in the peace and the harmony and the holy happy poverty of Jesus Himself and His disciples, and we will bring joy and light to every dark, suffering creature in the world. You see, Paul? You see?

By now they are in the kitchen. Gauguin doesn't know how to adequately reply. A painful pause, then for him quite warmly:

GAUGUIN Of course I see, Brigadier. How could I help it? It knocks your eye out. More to the point, this is the right light for you. I always admired the things you did in Belgium—But I must say, you've broken loose down here like a—a hemorrhage.

VINCENT You'll brighten everything here, too . . . like the paintings you did in Martinique.

GAUGUIN Well; we'll see. I want a sun that blinds me. But what I want to get to with you is: I may like to call myself a savage—but that doesn't mean I like to live like a pig. *Look* at this! (Vincent looks around uncomprehending) Look there! (pointing to littered floor) You see? You see? Man, do you *ever* do anything cleanly, except paint? (Vincent looks sheepish) Do you ever wash a plate?

VINCENT (confidently) Of course. When they're all dirty.

GAUGUIN Or scrub a floor?

Vincent looks as if this were a new idea.

GAUGUIN (fingering a hole in Vincent's shirt) Or mend your clothes?

VINCENT The girls at—(he blushes) The girls at Madame la Rosa's take care of that.

GAUGUIN *Do* they! Well I'm glad they take care of *something!* Come on: get a big kettle of water while I build a fire.

Vincent hesitates, a little bewildered. Gauguin, as he passes him towards the stove, smacks his rear as he might a child's.

GAUGUIN Get a move on.
Vincent, grinning, starts for water obediently as Gauguin looks after him, amused, shaking his head.   LAP DISSOLVE

DOWNWARD TWO-SHOT—THE STUDIO
They are on their hands and knees, scrubbing the floor; barefooted, trousers rolled up, etc., in a sea of suds.

GAUGUIN By the way, where do you keep your money?
Vincent starts to put his hand in his pocket.

GAUGUIN (amused) *Dry your hand!*
Vincent obeys—drying it on his shirt—and fishes out a pitiful tangle of bills and coins.

GAUGUIN Mm-hm; looks like an old, tired salad that died of a broken heart. . . . How much have you got?

VINCENT Let's see, now . . .

GAUGUIN Don't bother: I just wondered if you had any idea. Look here: from now on let's put all we have in a box, and budget it.

VINCENT What a good idea! (he starts away) I think I know just where there's a . . .

GAUGUIN Hold on. One job at a time.   DISSOLVE

THE KITCHEN
The place is immaculate; the floor is almost dry. Vincent sits stripped to the waist, watching Gauguin with respect, as Gauguin with a sailor's proficiency, is mending Vincent's shirt.

GAUGUIN Another thing. Have you the faintest idea how much money you waste by leaving your paints and brushes in such an unholy mess? It's bad morals into the bargain; unforgivable, in an artist. Get a little bit of order and common sense into your living and you'll have twice as much time for your work.

He finishes sewing. As he crosses to the stove, he tosses the shirt to Vincent.

GAUGUIN There you are.

He lifts the lid of a simmering pot and tastes contents.

GAUGUIN Better set the table.

Vincent, impressed and pleased, hops to it; still getting into shirt.

DISSOLVE

THE KITCHEN—NEW ANGLE—A WINDOW IN B.G.—TWO SHOT

A kerosene lamp glows, in the fading daylight. During scene night falls and lamp glows increasingly brighter. They are at the end of a satisfying meal, tired, and in fine spirits. Vincent sighs with pleasure.

VINCENT That's the best meal I've eaten since I can remember.

Gauguin looks pleased with himself, like a purring cat.

VINCENT How did you ever learn so much!

GAUGUIN I've had to take care of myself, that's all.

VINCENT But you were a rich man. A wife. Servants.

GAUGUIN I was a sailor before that, don't forget.

VINCENT How could you give it up, for business?

GAUGUIN I didn't know I was an artist. And I got married.

CLOSE SHOT—VINCENT

VINCENT (bemused; admiring) You're so much I've never been . . . never *could* be.

CLOSE SHOT—GAUGUIN

He watches Vincent with a kind of tenderness.

VINCENT'S VOICE (o.s.) The father of a family.

A spasm of sorrow touches Gauguin's face.

VINCENT'S VOICE (o.s.) How many children?

GAUGUIN Five.

VINCENT'S VOICE (o.s.) Tsk! Think of that!

Gauguin is thinking of it, all right.

VINCENT'S VOICE (o.s.) And a successful businessman.

GAUGUIN O yes—a young man of shining promise. When people couldn't meet payments on mortgages, it was my business to slit their throats and to catch every drop of the blood.

TWO SHOT—VINCENT AND GAUGUIN

VINCENT Tsk-tsk. . . . but—after all, you had a wife and children to support, Paul. People have to do all kinds of sad, difficult things, for the sake of that, don't they.

GAUGUIN (with a bitter smile) O yes indeed.

VINCENT But you really were very *good* at business, weren't you?

GAUGUIN "Good?" It's just a machine for making money. If you're a part of the machine you make some of it; that's all; and if you get caught between the rollers, you get the life crushed out of you.

VINCENT (shyly) You're like me and Rollins, the postman, aren't you: a bit of a Socialist.

CLOSE SHOT—GAUGUIN

GAUGUIN (contemptuously) *Perpetuate* all this filth? Make it easier for *everybody* to smear himself with it? No thanks. Civilization nauseates me. To make it a little better is only to make it a little worse. All I want is to be free of it.

VINCENT'S VOICE (o.s.) But *Science,* Paul! Machinery! Progress! Just imagine what the world will be like in fifty years!

GAUGUIN (dryly) I can imagine; that's why I want to be free of it.

CLOSE SHOT—VINCENT

VINCENT (gently) But you can never be free of it.

CLOSER SHOT—GAUGUIN

GAUGUIN (ferociously) O, *can't* I!

TWO SHOT—VINCENT AND GAUGUIN

VINCENT I'm so sorry, Paul; I didn't mean to make you angry.

GAUGUIN (angrily) I'm not angry.
A short silence.

VINCENT Could I ask you a question?

GAUGUIN (stonily) Ask ahead.

VINCENT How did you ever find the—courage—to leave all that?

GAUGUIN My dear Vincent: I was perfectly sure that within a year, I'd be earning as much *or better* by my painting.

VINCENT But . . .

GAUGUIN (with quiet, intense bitterness) O *yes*; how mistaken I was! Of course, if I'd painted pretty breasts, and rich men's gargoyles (said so as to mean wives), and other pious subjects—

VINCENT *O* no! But when you found out your mistake; when it meant—

CLOSE SHOT—GAUGUIN

GAUGUIN You mean, when I was using Mette's tablecloths, for want of canvas—

VINCENT'S VOICE (o.s.) O *did* you!

GAUGUIN *Mmm*; failing my family; leaving *them*. O yes. That *was* a bit more difficult.

VINCENT'S VOICE (o.s.) What gave you the courage?

GAUGUIN It wasn't a question of courage. I had no choice, if I wanted to paint.

VINCENT'S VOICE (o.s.) Of course, Paul, but—why?

GAUGUIN *Why?*

HEAD CLOSEUP—GAUGUIN

GAUGUIN (flounders, intense) *Why?* Years on end of Sunday painting; of loathing my job and the whole world it was part of; loathing myself, for denying everything in me that meant most to me; for being so tempted to give it up, for the sake of those I loved, and felt responsible towards . . . What do you mean, *why!*

CLOSE SHOT—VINCENT

VINCENT (quietly) I mean the *final* reason why, Paul—the *only real* reason.

TIGHTEN TO HEAD CLOSEUP on this

VINCENT Deep beyond our love for painting and our duty towards it. Mine . . . mine is to lose myself in God's love; and to be His instrument. Can you—will you tell me, what *your* reason is?

A pause.

CLOSE SHOT—GAUGUIN

Further silence. Gauguin is thinking hard; his eyes are out of focus.

GAUGUIN Not to *lose* myself, anyhow . . . To find myself. Or perhaps
. . . my source. To find the thing I value more dearly even than I love my
children or their mother or my life (by now he is talking only to himself).
An image I carry in me . . . of the lost innocence of the human race. The
beginning of the world. Don't tell me it doesn't exist, outside my wishes.
(intensely) Look here: I'm only half a Frenchman. My mother was
Peruvian and I lived there in my childhood and I know the blood she
gave me. Moorish blood; the blood of the Incas. So I know it exists: because it's a memory and a torment in my blood. And somewhere I'll find
it; somehow: a place in this world where human beings live like all the
other plants and the animals under the sun—purely, and serenely, and
generously, without the poisoning of money, and without knowledge of
good and evil. And when I paint it, everyone in his right mind will
understand; and will seek out what gives him health; and will destroy
what destroys him.

Hold on Gauguin a moment in the ensuing silence, then,   CUT TO

CLOSE SHOT—VINCENT
Continue the musing silence a moment. Then,

VINCENT (quiet; rapt) The Garden of Eden!

CLOSE SHOT—GAUGUIN

GAUGUIN (cold; sardonic) The Garden of Eden was infested by a forbidding God, and a tempting Serpent.

VINCENT'S VOICE (o.s.) But God exists.

GAUGUIN (sarcastic) *Does* He!

CLOSE SHOT—VINCENT
Very quiet and sure.

VINCENT He exists in your Garden. He *is* your Garden. He gave men the
choice, between eating of the Tree of the Knowledge of Good and Evil,
or living as He hoped they would——and as you hope they still do: in
perfect innocence.

CLOSE SHOT—GAUGUIN

GAUGUIN Hm! . . . He wasn't either wise or kind, to trust human beings
with such a choice.

CLOSE SHOT—VINCENT

VINCENT He gave us that choice because He loved us.

CLOSE SHOT—GAUGUIN

GAUGUIN And people think that in matters of love, *I'm* cruel and ir-responsible!
Short pause; then he relaxes and abruptly shifts gears as we PULL AWAY, TO CLOSE THE SCENE, FRAMING THE INITIAL TWO-SHOT.

GAUGUIN Speaking of Love: Why don't we go comfort the girls at Madame la Rosa's?

VINCENT (a little shocked) But—we were discussing theology.

GAUGUIN Were we? *I* was discussing *in*nocence.

VINCENT (laughing) So you were.
He gets up and starts to get on his coat.

GAUGUIN (rising) Huh-uh-*uh!*: we wash the dishes first.
They start clearing the table as we,   DISSOLVE

FULL SHOT—A ROAD OR STREET NEAR VINCENT'S HOME—GAUGUIN AND VINCENT—MOONLIGHT

Gauguin and Vincent are walking home, slightly tight. O.s., the lonely, hollow barking of a dog. The men come into MEDIUM CLOSE, talking.

VINCENT But Paul: the poor girls are *out*casts—like us.

GAUGUIN I *said* they were good girls.

VINCENT But—you have no *tenderness* towards them.
Gauguin stops walking, close to us; so does Vincent.

GAUGUIN (cold contempt) What do you want me to do—fall in love with them? After all, I'm a married man.

VINCENT Why, I thought you'd—given up your family.

GAUGUIN Are you out of your mind?

VINCENT How's that?

GAUGUIN I'm sorry, Vincent. The truth of it is very simple; and very shameful, if you like: (wearily and ironically reciting) My wife and children are living in Copenhagen, with my *in*-laws, until I can get a decent price for my work. (with fierce, deep feeling) And until then, *every day* is . . .

He can't go on.

VINCENT (quietly) Forgive me, Paul.

GAUGUIN (shrugs) It doesn't matter.
Pause.

GAUGUIN (gently) We had a good time, didn't we.

VINCENT Wonderful.

GAUGUIN Let's get to sleep; we start work tomorrow.
They walk past us as we PAN them on to Vincent's door in silence; o.s., we hear the lonely barking of the dog.   DISSOLVE

INT. GAUGUIN'S BEDROOM—LAMPLIGHT
Gauguin, in nightshirt or underwear, is unpacking. O.s., we hear the sound of knees striking the floor. In Gauguin, a sardonic, half tender smile of recognition as he looks toward the partition wall.

INT. VINCENT'S BEDROOM
Vincent is on his knees by his bed, forehead buried in his hands on the coverlet, praying like a good child.

GAUGUIN'S ROOM
Gauguin is still smiling as he brings out his family photograph. As we PAN with him he lies down on his bed and looks at it. Sound o.s. as Vincent gets from his knees, blows out his lamp, gets into bed, and settles down. Gauguin registers affectionate recognition, still gazing into the photograph.   DISSOLVE

HEAD CLOSEUP—ALINE, ADORING   DISSOLVE

HEAD CLOSEUP—DOWNSHOT—GAUGUIN
. . . in somber, hopeless sorrow. Sound, o.s., of Vincent's breathing in sleep. Gauguin smiles tenderly.   LAP DISSOLVE

CLOSE DOWNSHOT—ALINE
asleep . . . Gauguin's large hand hesitates to touch her.
                    CUT TO

CLOSE UPSHOT—GAUGUIN
as her father, leaning above her crib; he turns as we lift and PAN; Mette stands in the lighted door (the room itself is dark), her finger to her lips, smiling.   LAP DISSOLVE

GAUGUIN AT VINCENT'S
He glances up at his melancholy self-portrait on the wall—which we glance at from his distortive angle. Then, after a grimace of distaste, he blows out his lamp and lies back as we PAN INTO A DOWNWARD HEAD

CLOSEUP. His hands are locked under the nape of his neck; he looks straight up into the darkness, and his eyes are white and hard in the vague light. O.s., very faint, we bring on the sound of a Peruvian Indian lullaby, as sung by a woman.   SUPERIMPOSE

CLOSE SHOT
Gauguin's mother, much as he painted her.
A MELANGE OF FAINTLY CLASHING PALM LEAVES MAKING SHADOW OUT OF BRILLIANT SUN.

AN INCAN ARCHETYPAL PROFILE—LIVING OR SCULPTURED—RESEMBLING GAUGUIN; BLURRING; BEGINNING TO SUGGEST ONE OF THE POLYNESIAN ARCHETYPES OF HIS LATER, DREAM PAINTINGS.

Through all of this, as we thicken and enrich, rather than much loudening, the sound of the song, we see his eyes close as he lies on the bed. Then as we go silent, we clarify the screen to his proud, sad, sleeping face, which suggests to us, though it is far less matured, the dead face of our opening scene.   FADE OUT

FADE IN
MORNING—EXT.—A FAMILIAR VAN GOGH LANDSCAPE—OVER GAUGUIN AND VINCENT
Both artists are hard at work; their bodies block their work from us. O.s. is heard the distant singing of an ordinary field bird.

REVERSE ANGLE—TWO SHOT
We watch their faces over their easels. Gauguin is sidelong observant of Vincent. Vincent is aware of it. Their easels are parallel and they stand shoulder-to-shoulder, easily able to see each other's work.

CLOSE SHOT—VINCENT
We watch his special, intense, way of working.

LONG SHOT—THE LANDSCAPE
Vincent's subjective viewpoint and manner. Yellowish filter.

CLOSE SHOT—GAUGUIN
His more detached approach to work. Gauguin paints as a hypnotist, imposing his will on it.

FULL SHOT—LANDSCAPE
Gauguin's point of view, using darker colors via filter.

TWO SHOT—VINCENT AND GAUGUIN
They are sharply aware of each other. Vincent is more disturbed about it. Each glances at the other's work; at the landscape; back to his own

canvas; again at each other; then again each gets to work, each intensively aware of each other. Vincent always comparatively sensitive and vulnerable. Gauguin always detached.   DISSOLVE

TWO SHOT—ANOTHER FAMILIAR VAN GOGH LANDSCAPE—PAST BOTH ARTISTS
Now their easels are angled so each has to crane to see.

CLOSE SHOT—VINCENT
He is hard at work, aware of being watched. A new field bird to above is heard o.s., more cheerful than above scene.

CLOSE SHOT—GAUGUIN
Like Vincent, past easel. Hard at work, unconcerned that Vincent watches him. Aware of Vincent's unease, Gauguin glances toward Vincent.

CLOSER SHOT—VINCENT
Working hard, he is becoming more uneasy . . . pause . . .

VINCENT Well? What's wrong with it?

PULL BACK INTO CLOSEST POSSIBLE TWO-SHOT. Pause.

GAUGUIN Nothing.

VINCENT *You* think something is.

GAUGUIN No: It's very good.
Pause.

VINCENT Paul: be honest. I can't stand all this silence.

GAUGUIN I haven't asked *your* opinion.

VINCENT Give me your opinion and I'll give you mine.
They exchange places, each examining the other's canvas. Pause.

GAUGUIN Very well. You paint as if you were using a dagger; or making love.

VINCENT You paint as if you were using a fan; or seducing.

GAUGUIN Why do you copy Nature so closely?

VINCENT Why do you distort Her so?

GAUGUIN Why don't you just tint photographs?

VINCENT Why do you ever bother to come outdoors?

GAUGUIN I wonder why, myself. I don't like these landscapes; they're cheap and pretty, like the people.

VINCENT (deeply hurt) Oh? *I love* the landscapes here. I *love* the people.

DISSOLVE

TWO SHOT—NEW ANGLE—BOTH MEN—NEW VAN GOGH LANDSCAPE
O.s. a new bird sound.

VINCENT They're what God gave us: why not serve them?

GAUGUIN I make my subjects serve *me*. Painting is decoration. Raphael knew that. (Vincent politely flinches) And Ingres. (Ditto from Vincent) Whoever tries to make it more, makes it less.

VINCENT Painting is the love of God.

GAUGUIN O, forget religion for five minutes and tend to your business as an artist. Do you want to know the real trouble with you?

VINCENT Thank you; do tell me.

GAUGUIN You're a hopeless sentimentalist. Your work's all emotion—hysteria. Don't you *ever* stop to think?

VINCENT What has painting to do with thought!
A harsh cold laugh from Gauguin.

THIRD NEW VAN GOGH LANDSCAPE—VINCENT AND GAUGUIN
Another o.s. bird sound.

VINCENT Do you want to know the real trouble with *you?*
Gauguin shrugs. Then, with his underlying respect:

GAUGUIN As a matter of fact: yes.

VINCENT For all your bragging about being, "primitive," you're afraid of everything really primitive.

GAUGUIN (stung) *Am* I!

VINCENT Yes you are. You're afraid of Nature, and afraid of your emotions.

GAUGUIN (with reckless cruelty) And you're afraid to use your mind because—(realizing, he goes silent)

VINCENT Well?

GAUGUIN Nothing, Brigadier.

VINCENT Go on; say it.

GAUGUIN It's unimportant.

VINCENT You were about to say, that I'm afraid of *losing* my mind. That was it; wasn't it? (silence) Wasn't it?

GAUGUIN (after silence) You're a man of talent, Brigadier. . . .

VINCENT Don't call me Brigadier.

GAUGUIN You're a man of talent. As matters stand, just now, you're a long way ahead of me. But—how can you *dare*: not to use every gift you have?

VINCENT (after pause) So are you a man of talent. Why do you insist on using so little of all *you* really have? You're much more intelligent than I am, in spite of your low forehead. (Gauguin laughs slightly) But why worship it; Why not submit to your heart? You have true greatness of heart.

GAUGUIN Ahh, you and "the Heart." All this nonsense about "God," and "feeling," and "Brotherhood"—it's bad for your work; and it's bad for *you*.

VINCENT *Nonsense?* You can *dare* to . . .
They fall into a silent deadlock. We hear the bird clearly.

VINCENT Just—one thing please: don't speak of my *mind,* again.

GAUGUIN I think we'd better stop arguing *altogether*.
They look at each other in silence. Gauguin is concerned; Vincent is painfully disturbed—beyond Gauguin's perception.   DISSOLVE

FULL SHOT—STILL ANOTHER LANDSCAPE, OVER THE PAINTERS—LATE AFTERNOON
The easels are still more at an angle towards privacy. They work in silence. Then Gauguin steps back to appraise the end of a day's work; then he starts to clean brushes and put away paints. No bird songs.

GAUGUIN Come along, Vincent; the light's going.
Vincent works a moment longer; then, rather stiffly:

VINCENT May I see?
Gauguin shrugs.

GAUGUIN May *I*?

VINCENT If you like.
They cross, and examine each other's work, as we,   CUT TO

FRONT TWO SHOT—NEW ANGLE

GAUGUIN Hmm. Now that's more *like* it.

VINCENT (across him) Why, Paul! You disagree with me but . . .
They look at each other and laugh a little.

VINCENT AND GAUGUIN . . . You're learning from *me!*
They laugh again.

GAUGUIN Now those colors belong to *you* . . . not "God." Don't you like them?

VINCENT I like this of *yours.* I *love* it. It almost makes me think of Millet.

GAUGUIN (sardonic) Really! Don't insult me, Vincent.

VINCENT (astounded) Insult you? Millet? *The Angelus?*

GAUGUIN *The Angelus* turns my stomach. Every time I see it on your wall, I'm amazed how a man of your talent can put up with such garbage.

VINCENT Let me tell *you,* my good friend: that painting has touched more hearts than any other of its time!
By now, Gauguin is ready to leave and Vincent gets ready too. During the rest of this scene we DISSOLVE them through THREE LANDSCAPES as they walk towards home through the dwindling light . . . never interrupting our dialogue.

GAUGUIN And a very pretty penny he made of it. No thanks, Brigadier: I abominate this idea of using Art, of all things, as a kind of wet-nurse for all the lonely hearts and pious old women and slobbering idiots and simple souls in this world. An artist's only message is the message of beauty. And the only people who are fit to look at his work are those who are capable of *perceiving* beauty.
Vincent, by now, is terribly agitated.   DISSOLVE

EXT. NEW LANDSCAPE SCENE

VINCENT Hah! So there's no beauty in *The Angelus!* I suppose Meissonier was no artist! Or Ziem!

GAUGUIN You can call those fourth-raters Artists? Can't you see they aren't even fit to clean the brushes of a man like you?

VINCENT (raging, desperate) *Fit?* What's *fitness!* What're you "fit" for! What am *I!* We're *brothers, all* of us artists. Every man does his best. Why, even to try to be an artist in the middle of all this sorrow and smugness and blindness and cruelty . . . O, how *can* you sneer at them, Paul! How *can* you!

GAUGUIN (humorous) Calm down, Brigadier, calm down. You're right; I'm sure in the eye of God, you're right. They're all your brothers, every one, if you insist, and so are the members of the Academy. And you're welcome to them.
They walk in silence and trouble. Then:

VINCENT (quietly) You make me so awfully nervous, Paul.

GAUGUIN I'm sorry, Brigadier.

VINCENT I'm afraid I—get under *your* skin, too.
Pause.

GAUGUIN We just can't seem to help it.

VINCENT I'm sorry I was so angry.

GAUGUIN Think nothing of it.

VINCENT Only—*please* don't speak of people so unkindly.
They walk on in silence out of the slowing pull-shot and we,
CUT TO

FULL SHOT—REVERSE ANGLE
They walk away from us, towards Arles, as, in rough approximation of Vincent's painting, a great moon rises over the town and the fields. A harsh crow o.s. is heard. DISSOLVE

INT. VINCENT'S STUDIO—CLOSEUP SHOT—VINCENT
A soft crumpling of thunder o.s. Vincent stands on a chair, hammering a nail into the wall. Startled by o.s. sound of opening door he looks towards Gauguin, bitterly, timidly hostile.

MED. CLOSE SHOT—GAUGUIN
He comes through his bedroom door, finishing dressing; a look of cool, sardonic surprise; a salute to match.

CLOSEUP SHOT—VINCENT
He turns, stoops low in the shot and straightens, with his photo of *The Angelus,* which he hangs. He looks again to Gauguin, in silent challenge. Gauguin walks into shot.

GAUGUIN Come on, Brigadier, let's have some breakfast.
He walks on out of the shot. Vincent gets down from the chair he has been standing on and looks after him, puzzled, timid, hostile.

GAUGUIN'S VOICE Looks as if we work indoors today.
Vincent, puzzled and tentative, nods. DISSOLVE

PANNING SHOT—THE STUDIO
The sound of rain continues less strongly, and the entire scene runs with gray, rainy light.

We PAN from a CLOSE SHOT of disheveled, heavy sunflowers in a vase on a table; past Vincent's easel (we don't see his painting), into a MEDIUM CLOSE TWO SHOT: Vincent at work; and Gauguin, at another easel, at work in b.g. *The Angelus* is on wall behind Gauguin.

A short silence of hard peaceful work; the closed stillness of a rainy day; their unspoken tensions. Then:

VINCENT You—don't seem to mind.

GAUGUIN Mind what?
Vincent indicates *The Angelus*.

GAUGUIN (cool and friendly) Why should I? He's *your* God. If I had Millet himself, I might hang *him*—(he indicates opposite wall)—over there; by his heels.

CLOSE SHOT—VINCENT
He reacts painfully, but is silent.

CLOSE SHOT—GAUGUIN
He looks to Vincent, sorry for what he has said; but is silent. He looks to his palette, below-scene, and reacts calmly.

INSERT—GAUGUIN'S PALETTE
A largish, delicate insect—such as a may-fly or a daddy-long-legs—is fouled up in some fresh paint. Gauguin's hand, with brush, comes into the shot, picks him up, and drops him, as we PAN, beside his shoe.

INSERT—GAUGUIN'S SHOE
. . . moving, about to crush the disabled insect.

VINCENT'S VOICE (in soft anguish) No—*no!*

FLASH CUT—VINCENT IN CLOSEUP
as he gets up.

FLASH CUT—GAUGUIN
surprised, a little of the look of *"now* what!"

TWO SHOT—NEW ANGLE

VINCENT (stooping) Let *me* have him.

INSERT: He picks the insect up very carefully.

CLOSE SHOT—GAUGUIN
watches him as he returns to his chair.

CLOSE SHOT—VINCENT . . . as he sits down.

VINCENT (tenderly, to the bug) *Ho.* Were you hurt? Let's just *see* now. He puts his palette on his knees, and holds the bug close to his small eyes. We tighten, centering the bug. NOTE: In all this, Vincent is wholly unconscious of Gauguin.

VINCENT Well, well . . . poor fellow. Come in safe out the rain, and what happens! Let's just see, now.
With a match dipped in turpentine he begins delicately to clean paint from the bug's legs.

VINCENT Ver-y gently now; very careful. I know those legs are very *delicate;* I don't want . . .
CLOSE SHOT—GAUGUIN, watching.

GAUGUIN He's lost two, in the paint.

CLOSE SHOT—VINCENT AND BUG

VINCENT (abstracted) I know . . . We don't want to lose *any more, do* we? But we've got to get this miserable *paint* off, or you'll be *crippled* by it. There.

GAUGUIN He's crippled already.

VINCENT There. He'll live, though . . . I think.

FLASH CUT—GAUGUIN

GAUGUIN Who wants to live, crippled?

CLOSE SHOT—VINCENT AND BUG

VINCENT (to the bug) Life is a sacred gift. *Isn't* it. *Isn't* it, my dear. Yes. *You* don't want to die, until God tells you it's time. *No* indeed. Now let's see.
He turns his palette upside-down on his knees and puts the bug gently on the clean surface.

VINCENT Now. Just try your legs. *Careful* . . .

CLOSE SHOT—GAUGUIN
He is watching Vincent, then the bug, with deep interest.

INSERT: THE BUG
He is polishing off one foot after another, between others; then he begins a spindly, invalid's walk.

VINCENT'S VOICE (over him) Yes yes; that's it. If it's too wretched, we'll take care of you; we'll kill you very quickly and there'll be no pain. (FLASH CUT CLOSE SHOTS of Vincent and of Gauguin, who is watching Vincent as much as the bug.) No pain at all. But if you *can;* there now; *try;* try your very best; because if you can, you want to live. *Don't* you. *Yes.* I wish you had *crutches.* But you're all right. You're going to be *all right.*

The bug limps off the palette onto Vincent's hand; thence to his knee, and to the floor.

CLOSE SHOT—VINCENT—OVER GAUGUIN
Vincent looks up to Gauguin, smiling, radiant.

VINCENT *He's* well.

CLOSE SHOT—GAUGUIN—OVER VINCENT
Gauguin looks at him, deeply touched. Short silence.

GAUGUIN Do you know, Vincent?

PULL around into a TWO-SHOT as Vincent looks enquiry.

GAUGUIN I want to paint your portrait.

VINCENT Really?
Gauguin nods.

VINCENT Well. Well. I'm—very much flattered. But we'll have to wait till I finish my sunflowers; I'm sorry, but—

GAUGUIN Go right ahead with them. That's how I want to paint you.

VINCENT Why . . . very well; but—*why,* Paul?

GAUGUIN (very reticent) I've seen something that interests me; that's all.
DISSOLVE

THE STUDIO—DAY—MED. TWO-SHOT—VINCENT AND GAUGUIN
Gauguin is at work on Vincent's portrait, while Vincent is working on his sunflowers. Gauguin's eyes and general manner are "surgical"; and Vincent's reactions correspond. DISSOLVE

CLOSER TWO-SHOT—NEW ANGLE
Vincent is keenly aware of Gauguin's close scrutiny, but hard at work. We intensify Gauguin's detached, intent, "surgical" manner, and Vincent's

strain. Vincent is tempted to glance at Gauguin, but looks to his subject instead; fills his brush, leans a little forward. Gauguin grunts. Vincent glances towards him.

GAUGUIN (abstracted) Just a second . . . Back a little.
Vincent obeys; glances enquiringly.

GAUGUIN Little more . . . Good. Now.
Gauguin applies paint very carefully. Vincent is intensely self-conscious.

GAUGUIN Good. (no motion from Vincent) All right.
Vincent comes to; leans forward again.

CLOSE SHOT—HIS SUBJECT
The vased sunflowers are a little farther gone than in our former look at them. Dead petals on the table, at the foot of the vase.

DISSOLVE

CLOSE SHOT—VINCENT
. . . over Gauguin, as at start of foregoing scene. Vincent is working hard; he is clearly under greater strain. After a moment, quietly, to himself:

GAUGUIN *Now* it's working.
Vincent glances up to him.

GAUGUIN *No* . . . keep still . . .

HEAD CLOSEUP—VINCENT
He is under great strain, between his own work and Gauguin's X-ray scrutiny. His eyes sidle towards Gauguin, o.s.

GAUGUIN'S VOICE Ahh. That's—*that's*—

CLOSER SHOT—VINCENT: NOSE AND EYES

VINCENT What is it, Paul?
No answer. Pause.

CLOSE SHOT—GAUGUIN: NOSE AND EYES
Pause, as he works intently; then Vincent's question reaches him.

GAUGUIN (abstractedly) Quiet.
He works still more intently.

GAUGUIN (again remotely) I've got it, finally . . .

SAME CLOSEUP—VINCENT
looking worried enquiry. Pause.

GAUGUIN'S VOICE That left eye.
Pause; Vincent struggles not to ask. Then:

VINCENT Can't I see it?

EYE CLOSEUP—GAUGUIN

GAUGUIN (abstracted) Shut up.   LAP DISSOLVE

EYE CLOSEUP—VINCENT

There is sweat on his forehead; he wipes it off with his sleeve.

GAUGUIN'S VOICE Hold still.

VINCENT I'm sorry.

EYE CLOSEUP—GAUGUIN

GAUGUIN All right . . . but keep still.
Tighten on his eyes. They are very cold, intense and busy, between
Vincent, palette and canvas.

EYE CLOSEUP—VINCENT

Tighten the shot, and his expression, which is now full of terror. Pause;
tension.

VINCENT Paul . . . I'll *have* to rest.

GAUGUIN'S VOICE Not yet . . . just . . .

VINCENT Paul . . .
A sharp hiss for silence from Gauguin, on a flash cut eye closeup. Back to,

EYE CLOSEUP—VINCENT

He waits, sweating, and suffering deeply. We PULL VERY SLOWLY AWAY TO
HEAD CLOSEUP. His face is desperate. Pause.

GAUGUIN'S VOICE (casual; altered) All right.
Again, Vincent stays frozen.

GAUGUIN'S VOICE Vincent?
Vincent loosens a little, glances up at him.

CLOSE UPSHOT—GAUGUIN

He is smiling, coolly, looking to Vincent. He too is sweating.

GAUGUIN All right; if you like . . . (he gestures that Vincent may look
now)

CLOSE SHOT—VINCENT

Vincent slowly rises as we PULL BACK and PAN INTO CLOSE TWO SHOT with
Gauguin. A timid glance to Gauguin, then he looks down at the portrait
(still unseen by us); then as we TIGHTEN SHOT:

VINCENT (very quiet and brave) It's me, Paul. (Gauguin in cool, complex gratification) It's me, all right . . . But it's me, already gone insane.

HEAD CLOSEUP—GAUGUIN
Gauguin in deep quiet consternation; glances from Vincent to Portrait.
INSERT: THE PORTRAIT OF VINCENT PAINTING SUNFLOWERS
HEAD CLOSEUP—VINCENT
Vincent smiling strangely, mouth trembling, eyes intense and ambivalent looks into Gauguin's eyes O.S. PULL AWAY TO MAXIMAL TWO SHOT to include Millet's *Angelus*. Pause. Vincent holds a strange smile, looking with deep intensity into Gauguin's eyes. Gauguin is a little appalled: then:

GAUGUIN (a hand to Vincent's shoulder) Come on, Brigadier; it's been a hard week for both of us. Let's have some fun.
Hold the shot after this line; then TIGHTEN on Gauguin, losing Vincent; then PAN to Vincent (losing Gauguin), still smiling, his lips dry; he tries to moisten them; nods twice . . .

VINCENT (in a dry voice) Let's.

CLOSE SHOT—THE SUNFLOWERS
Still more petals have fallen; now they look really devastated.

DISSOLVE

MADAME LA ROSA'S—INT.—NIGHT
. . . manner, roughly, of a provincial Lautrec. Gauguin is telling a story. It is not important that we hear Gauguin's whole account except for its spirit of cold, false stridency and the general reaction. Girls are close around him, and like him fine.

GAUGUIN Then there was the time I delivered a letter from the pilot I replaced, to Madame Aimee, Rua di Oudivar, in Rio. Now Madame Aimee! You girls ought to have gone to *her* school! Ohh yes! There was a true scholar! (hee-haw from the girls and Madame) There's an old saying, you know; when bad little girls grow up and die, God takes them to South America. (more hee-haw) Madame Aimee took the letter and gave it just one look, and then she looked into my big, big eyes—(giggles) —and said, "Oohh—so handsome—and only seventeen!" (giggles) And that, my dears, is how I became a man. (hee-haws) Oh, you never dreamed of a month like that! *Everybody* loved her; *everybody*. But I had one serious rival: the son of the Tsar of Russia. (incredulous murmurs) Oh, yes. He was. (with double-entendre) On a *Russian training ship*. (laughs) He was a very promising *midshipman*. (howls) He was spending so many thousands of rubles on Madame, that it became an international incident. His Captain tried to get the French Consul to intervene, to call off the dog: the dog—(modestly) was Yours Truly. (haw haw) He had his nerve. After all, the son of the Tsar of Russia; and little Paul Gauguin; it was too hot for *any*body to handle. (laughs) Except of course, Madame, who was so expert at handling hot stuff. (laughs) (soberly) It cost the Tsarevitch half the Crown Jewels. All it cost me, was the hangovers.

DURING THE ABOVE STORY-BACKGROUND, THE SHOTS AND CRUCIAL ACTION ARE AS FOLLOWS:

FULL SHOT—THE PARLOR—AT MADAME'S
A piano player is going full blast at the rear and, towards the rear, two small tables are set end to end, with Vincent relatively isolated. Over our cut, an outburst of laughter.

CLOSE SHOT—VINCENT
Isolated, eyes very bright; brooding over a glass: semi-false laughter dying on his mouth. Gauguin's voice across him and he starts listening, admiringly; bitterly. He is drunk.

CLOSE GROUP SHOT—CENTERING GAUGUIN—VINCENT'S VIEWPOINT
. . . among girls, Madame, and a quietly soused customer. Gauguin gets into his story. We PAN LEFT, THEN RIGHT, THEN CENTER him again, as story goes on. THEN TILT UP as in b.g. Marcia comes downstairs.

CLOSE SHOT—VINCENT
He smiles, above them, at Marcia o.s.

GROUP SHOT—MARCIA ADVANCING IN B.G.
She ignores Vincent. Gauguin continues talking. Marcia is a thin blue-white, rather pathetic girl. She slips her arms aroung Gauguin's neck. He glances up, and interrupts himself.

GAUGUIN Get away; you're Vincent's girl. (she withdraws, hurt) Vincent? (he salutes, a-la-Brigadier, and clicks his tongue) Brigadier: watch out for deserters. (laughter)

CLOSE SHOT—VINCENT
A forced smile, a piteous, absent-minded salute, he is more concerned for Marcia.

GAUGUIN'S VOICE Let's see; where was I? *O* yes.

CLOSE SHOT—GROUP
He resumes his story while Madame sharply indicates that Marcia join Vincent. As she unwillingly starts to, another girl, Zizi, appears in b.g.

CLOSE SHOT—VINCENT
Marcia glumly enters the shot and sits beside him; Gauguin's story continuing o.s. Vincent concerned, puts an arm around her.

MARCIA (snapping) Leave me alone, you *half-wit*.

VINCENT (flinching, bravely recovering) But my poor child—you're unhappy.

MARCIA What do *you* know? Ahh, *sure;* you're a *gentleman;* you're *educated;* you want to save everybody's *soul.*

VINCENT Marcia. Dear.

MARCIA (a little drunk) You think you're so smart, because your ears stick out, like a fox.
By touching reflex, Vincent raises both hands towards his ears.

VINCENT (puzzled) My ears?

MARCIA O yes; fine. (she grabs his ears) But all you *really* are is a *goose,* with no ears at all.
Vincent looks at her, hurt and bewildered, as Zizi sits at his other side.

ZIZI *Hell*-lo, sweetie; what're you going to give Zizi for Christmas?
Tight pause.

VINCENT (to Marcia; calmly) I'll find—something for *you;* don't *you* worry.
Then he looks hard at Gauguin as both girls watch him, puzzled.

CLOSE SHOT—GAUGUIN: VINCENT'S VIEWPOINT
He is finishing his story; suddenly, in a blur, his ears vanish from his head.

CLOSE SHOT—VINCENT
Vincent watches him, sharp and strange, with a queerly mean little smile.

VINCENT You think you're very smart, don't you.
He throws first the liquor, then his glass at Gauguin.

CLOSE SHOT—GAUGUIN
His face is wet with liquor. Brief pause of amazement; then in a cold killing rage he jumps up and dives across the table for Vincent's throat.

CLOSE GROUP SHOT—NEW ANGLE—CENTERING GAUGUIN AND VINCENT
Vincent, half-rising, is forced into his chair. He doesn't fight but tries feebly to loosen the grip. His eyes are those of a sacrificial lamb. Madame and the girls, expostulating ad lib, are trying to get Gauguin off him.

GAUGUIN Why, you sniveling little *maniac* . . .

This cruel word brings him to his senses. He relaxes his grip and, as we TIGHTEN, they gaze, astounded, into each other's eyes. Then, as we PULL BACK, Gauguin gets up from the table, sets up an overturned bottle or so, swabs spattered liquor from his face and comes to Vincent's side as we MOVE IN CLOSE.

GAUGUIN (quietly) Come on, Brigadier; it's time you got home.

No response. He puts a hand under Vincent's elbow and Vincent stands up, dazed. We PULL BACK a little more.

GAUGUIN (to Madame) Cognac.

Nobody budges.

GAUGUIN Cognac, I said! Haven't you got any *ears?*

Vincent again vaguely reaches toward his ears; Marcia registers vaguely. Someone hurries to Gauguin with a bottle and glass. He offers the bottle to Vincent.

GAUGUIN Here.

Vincent makes no move of hand or eyes or mouth.

GAUGUIN *Drink* it.

No move or realization. Gauguin gently forces the bottle mouth between his lips and tilts it so that the liquor spills down Vincent's chin.

GAUGUIN Come *on:* (Vincent automatically starts swallowing) *Keep it up!* . . . The sooner *you* get to sleep, the *better!*

Short, intense wait; then an overpowering lassitude—comes over Vincent; he looks at Gauguin and says, like a small child:

VINCENT I want to go home.

GAUGUIN Come along then.

Vincent starts, obedient but very weak.

GAUGUIN Can you navigate?

Vincent nods; Gauguin supports him strongly as they walk towards us and out of the shot.

REVERSE ANGLE—GAUGUIN AND VINCENT

Just now Vincent would fall flat, but for Gauguin; who now in an experienced manner lifts him in his arms and walks away from us as Madame bustles past them and opens the door and closes it after them. She turns and looks at us.

MADAME Go home.

REVERSE ANGLE—THE GROUP
All look bewildered.

MADAME'S VOICE *Go home,* I said.
The Drunken Customer begins to realize she is talking to him.

CUSTOMER *Me?*
Madame enters the shot.

MADAME Who else? Now hop *to* it. We're closed for the night.
Customer and girls look to her, surprised, as she snaps down a glass of
cognac and we,   DISSOLVE

VINCENT'S KITCHEN—AFTERNOON—CLOSE SHOT—VINCENT AT TABLE
A large coffee cup, held in trembling hands, hides his face as he swallows.
He is half-dressed, fresh out of bed.

CLOSE SHOT—GAUGUIN
He sits in a chair away from the table, watching Vincent quietly. He is
dressed for travel.

CLOSE TWO-SHOT—VINCENT AND GAUGUIN
Vincent puts down his cup and rests his cheekbones in the heels of his
hands, his elbows on the table.

VINCENT Ohhh. I've got *such* a headache!
Gauguin shrugs. Vincent puzzled, looks all around.

VINCENT What's wrong with the light?

GAUGUIN It's doing as well as can be expected.

VINCENT What time is it?

GAUGUIN Past four.
Vincent drinks some coffee. Gauguin watches him.

VINCENT Paul . . . You're angry about something.

GAUGUIN No; I'm not.

VINCENT There was *something* . . . I did something . . .

GAUGUIN Forget it.

VINCENT Something about ears.
Gauguin looks mystified.

VINCENT What'd I do, Paul? I did *something* wrong.
Pause.

GAUGUIN (quietly) You threw a glass at my head.

VINCENT O no. O *Paul. Why!*
Gauguin shrugs.

GAUGUIN How do *I* know?
Vincent drinks more coffee; then warms his hands against the cup and looks at Gauguin, ashamed and pleading. Pause.

GAUGUIN Don't you remember a thing?
Vincent looks at him helpless, and first realizes Gauguin's mode of dress.

VINCENT Paul: Why are you dressed this way?

GAUGUIN Because I'm leaving.
Vincent merely breathes a kind of shocked "You're le . . ."

GAUGUIN I'm going back to Brittany.

VINCENT O. But you can't. You can't Paul.

GAUGUIN I'm going, though.

VINCENT O Paul, forgive me: forgive.

GAUGUIN There's nothing to forgive. You didn't even know what you were doing. But I can't put up with *that* sort of thing. And neither can you, for that matter.

VINCENT But—the *Community*—the *Brotherhood!*
Gauguin just gives a sick, slightly disgusted shrug. Suddenly in a,

NEW ANGLE—TWO-SHOT
. . . Vincent falls hard on his knees beside Gauguin, who reacts with pity but still more with disgust and a desire to be gone.

VINCENT (almost crying) Paul: if *we* fail, *everything* fails. *Everything.* The whole world goes black. No sun. No light. No artists in this *world!* O don't go away. I'll do anything. I'll be *so* careful not to offend you. I won't drink, Paul. Never another drop. I won't talk about religion if you'd rather not. We don't even have to speak to each other if it makes you nervous. Only *stay. Stay on here.* Just even give it just one more chance. *Please,* Paul. *Please. Please. Please* stay.

GAUGUIN (after long pause) All right. It's against my better judgment but—let's give it one more try.
Vincent flings his arms around him. Gauguin controls reaction.

VINCENT O *bless* you Paul! You are a true Christian!

GAUGUIN (sick; controlled) Oh . . . get up off your *knees*.

Vincent rises, shyly. Both try to smile, a little, they laugh. Abortive, friendly gestures towards each other. DISSOLVE

INT. VAN GOGH'S KITCHEN—NIGHT

Exactly like the first supper scene in SET UP. Later in year. Vincent is eating dutifully. Gauguin has finished.

GAUGUIN How does it go?

VINCENT Like eating a mattress; but it's doing me a world of good.
Vincent eats some more.

VINCENT (peaceful and sad) It's amazing, isn't it, how much we've learned in these two months we've been together; that we didn't want to learn; never dreamed was so.

Silence from Gauguin.

VINCENT I was so sure, that Brotherhood was to be found through joy. But how could I ever have supposed so! How could you! (he chews)

CLOSE SHOT—VINCENT

VINCENT Now we begin to know, what the only good is.

CLOSE SHOT—GAUGUIN

He watches with increasing pain and impatience; he waits.

CLOSER SHOT—VINCENT

VINCENT (with peculiar tenderness) The only true good is through suffering.

CLOSE SHOT—GAUGUIN

Over the word *suffering,* cut to his pity, disgust, fury and hopelessness—which he is trying to constrain and conceal.

CLOSE SHOT—VINCENT

Vincent watches him, tenderly, knowingly.

VINCENT I know you don't like me to say that, because you don't like to admit it's so. You're so afraid of your heart and your soul. But it's so; it's so; and now you're beginning to learn it, too.

CLOSE SHOT—GAUGUIN

Near violence, he restrains himself only by getting up abruptly. He walks over as we PAN and picks up his hat.

CLOSE SHOT—VINCENT

VINCENT (an almost shrewish touch of panic) Paul: where are you going?

MED. SHOT—GAUGUIN—FROM VINCENT'S VIEWPOINT

GAUGUIN I'm going for a breath of air.

MED. SHOT—VINCENT—FROM GAUGUIN'S VIEWPOINT

VINCENT (gently desperate) But . . . I was—*talking* to you.

GAUGUIN'S VOICE That's why I need air.

We hear his footsteps o.s. as we watch Vincent half rise, gasping; then we hear, o.s., the opening and slamming of a door. On the sound of slamming, ZOOM or FAST DOLLY into:

HEAD CLOSEUP—VINCENT

His face is paroxysm as his mind explodes and he leans forward on stiff arms, knuckles to table, like an ape.   DISSOLVE

EXT. TOWN—A NARROW STREET—NIGHT

Gauguin walks slowly, in melancholy, anger and exhaustion. We hear his slow footsteps; then o.s. we hear short quick stealthy footsteps. Gauguin advances into CLOSEUP, then stops and slowly turns as we,

CUT TO

HEAD CLOSEUP—SLIGHTLY UPWARD—GAUGUIN, REVERSE ANGLE

. . . as he turns his head, his face is framed by a black slouch hat. His eyes have cold intensity.

MED. SHOT—VINCENT

Another few steps, slowly, brings him MEDIUM CLOSE; then he falters to a stop. His eyes and an open razor glitter, with intent to maim or kill. His lips bloom into a strange, shy little smile, showing his teeth.

GAUGUIN—EYE CLOSEUP

His eyes paralyze in their intensity.

MED. CLOSE SHOT—VINCENT

After a moment, with a kind of gasping sob, his tension breaks and he tucks his chin tight against his chest and turns and runs away as fast as he can.

CLOSE SHOT—GAUGUIN

He watches after Vincent until the dwindling sound of running dies o.s. Then he takes off his hat. His forehead is streaming with sweat. He dries it off with his sleeve, and looks around . . .   CUT TO

MED. SHOT—VINCENT'S HOME

Sobbing and out of breath, Vincent hurries into the shot (we hardly see his face) and into his bedroom, whose door he slams in our face, and bolts, as we center the door and very slowly DOLLY IN on it. Meanwhile, o.s., we hear him drop to his knees and we hear his frantic, half-whispering voice:

VINCENT'S VOICE (o.s.) O God forgive me! *Forgive* me! *Forgive* me! Forgive us our trespasses! *O* no. *O* no. *O* no.

Then we hear him get up suddenly; then a frantic scrabbling of metal and hard objects. Then dead silence. We stop dollying. Silence. Then a queer, shrill little animal cry, of amazement as much as pain. Silence. Another little cry. Silence. Then a much more dreadful cry. Silence. Rattling of paper. Silence. Quick footsteps and fast unbolting of the door and Vincent opens the door, close to us. He holds a towel tightly around his head, scarf-like, with one hand. Between the towel and the right side of his head a rag is caught; even so, the towel is somewhat bloody. His breath shakes almost as if his teeth were chattering. He leans for a moment against the door frame. In his trembling left hand he carries an envelope which he now brings to his mouth. He licks the flap, and presses the somewhat bulky envelope against the door frame to seal it. Then for an instant he seems to catch sight of us, staring at us. He looks quickly away —or even raises the envelope to conceal his face from, us—as he hurries from the shot. CUT TO

SIMILAR SHOT—FRAMING MADAME LA ROSA'S DOOR—EXT.—NIGHT

Vincent, back to us, knocks clumsily with the hand which carries the envelope; he still holds the towel tightly. Pause; silence. He knocks harder.

MADAME'S VOICE (o.s., angry) *Just a minute! Give me time!* (muttering) Never knew a man *yet,* could take his time . . .

She opens the door.

MADAME (fairly friendly) Why *Rusty!*

VINCENT I want to see Marcia.

MADAME Come in, sweetie.

VINCENT No. I'll wait here.

MADAME (bellowing over her shoulder) *Marcia?* (she peers at Vincent in the darkness) What've you done to yourself?

VINCENT I'm all right. Where's Marcia?

MADAME Now Lop-Ears, give a girl *time*. After *all,* you were a *bad boy* last night, you know; Marcia didn't *like* that . . .
Marcia appears beyond her.

MARCIA Who *is*—? O. You.

MADAME (across her) It's little old Rusty. He's come to apologize.

MARCIA Huh! What do you want *now?*

VINCENT I want—(interrupted, he stops)

MADAME (across him) Why, to kiss and make—(she too stops)

VINCENT I want to give you the Christmas present I promised you.
He offers the envelope which, after a moment, she takes.

MADAME *Well now,* ain't that *cute* of you! I always said it: there ain't a bit of real *meanness in* him.

MARCIA (across her) Why, Rusty, that's real sweet of you. And I thought you was just joking.

Short pause. Vincent shakes his head slowly, once.

VINCENT (quietly) No. It wasn't a joke.
Pause.

MADAME Well, *open* it.

MARCIA 'Tisn't—Christmas yet.

MADAME O don't be a *fool,* you're a big girl now. Besides, Rusty wants to be here when you open it *don't* you honey?

Marcia looks at him; he nods.

MADAME *Sure.* Rusty wants to see your face light up. Again Vincent nods.
Marcia, quite eager, starts opening it up.

MADAME Why just look—all done up in pretty paper inside, so dainty and nice . . .

Throughout this scene we shoot over Vincent, never seeing his face; and his body blocks any clear view of the envelope or its contents. But as Marcia starts opening her present we LIFT THE CAMERA A TRIFLE—as if going on tiptoe—and DOLLY SLOWLY IN ON HER, LOSING THE OTHERS, so that she is in HEAD CLOSEUP at the moment when she sees the ear and shrieks like a maniac.   DISSOLVE

INT. CAFE DE LA GARE—FULL SHOT
In vivid approximation of Vincent's sinister painting. Gauguin and Theo sit far back along one wall. Throughout the scene, softly, o.s., the clicking of billiard balls.

CLOSE PROFILED TWO-SHOT—GAUGUIN AND THEO
They sit at a small table over untouched drinks.

THEO Paul, for the last time I implore you: come with me to the hospital.

GAUGUIN Haven't I done *enough* harm?

THEO If only you understood how terribly he needs you now.

GAUGUIN If only you understood how much he hates me.
We begin to hear the approaching train o.s.

THEO Vincent is incapable of hatred; he needs love; desperately.

GAUGUIN Perhaps the trouble is that I'm incapable of—sufficient love—for anything. Except my work.
He gets up; then Theo too; train louder o.s.

THEO (desperately) Wait over even just one train.

GAUGUIN Theo, I'd wait over ten thousand, if I could believe there was any good in it.
Both take their luggage and leave the shot.

EXT. TRAIN PLATFORM—GRAY AFTERNOON—CLOSE TWO-SHOT—GAUGUIN AND THEO
Train in b.g. Theo, trying to smile, puts out his hand.

THEO *Well, Paul* ...

GAUGUIN In case you hear from your brother that I despise him ... (Theo shakes his head for "o no!") ... all the while I was painting that portrait, what I saw, was Christ on the Cross.
Theo's eyes fill.

GAUGUIN One more thing, while I'm about it: I have a higher regard for Christ on the Cross than you may imagine. I learned it through your brother. But there's something else I'm learning to venerate, perhaps even more: the Cross itself.
He touches Theo's shoulder and hurries aboard the train.   DISSOLVE

INT. A HOSPITAL WARD—LATE AFTERNOON—CLOSE TWO-SHOT—THEO AND VINCENT
Vincent, very gentle and quiet, lies bandaged, in bed.

VINCENT Theo, please tell me very frankly: am I a maniac?

THEO *You?*

VINCENT (trying to joke) Am I "wrong in the head"?
He pantomimes with circling forefinger at temple.

THEO Of course you aren't.

VINCENT If I should . . . lose my mind . . . my painting won't be any good.

THEO Vincent: if you love me, you'll go on with your painting as if nothing had happened.

VINCENT (ardently) O I *want* to! I was learning *so much* these past weeks. It was so exciting. Painful, but . . .
His face works; he dissolves into quiet weeping.

THEO (heartsick; helpless) Vincent . . . Vincent. . . .

VINCENT (sobbing) O Theo . . . *why did he go away.*

THEO He thought it was best for you, Vincent.

VINCENT (sobbing) He—he never—even—came to see me!

THEO He thought you wouldn't like to see him.

VINCENT Like to? If only I could beg his forgiveness! Then we could go on just as before!

THEO He felt he had done you great harm.

VINCENT But he doesn't understand.

THEO No: perhaps it isn't in him, ever to understand, *enough* . . .

VINCENT (serene and exalted) O: there you're mistaken, Theo. Paul has the greatest courage, and patience, and devotion, in the only things that really matter. It may take him many years, and terrible suffering; but he'll learn. *O yes! I believe in Gauguin's victory!*

FULL SHOT—THE WHOLE WARD
A nun moves from one bed to the next. Theo is the only visitor. The gray daylight is profoundly tender and pure—suggesting Vermeer. The low murmur of one sick voice. And o.s., the harsh cry of a crow. Over this cry we,   SLOW DISSOLVE

INT. THEO'S PARIS SHOP—CLOSE PULL SHOT—VINCENT'S PAINTING OF CROWS

THEO'S VOICE (o.s.) It was quite soon after he painted that, that he . . . found life too much for him.
We PULL BACK INTO CLOSE TWO-SHOT—THEO AND GAUGUIN

GAUGUIN But—in an *institution!* How on earth did he manage to get a revolver!

THEO What does it matter now?
Silence.

THEO He asked me to give you a message. (he looks in his coat pocket) I wrote it down: "Dear Master: after having known you and caused you pain, it is better to die in a good state of mind than in a degraded one." Silence.

GAUGUIN I don't want to live in a world where such a man . . .
He can't go on.

THEO (a touch of bitterness) What *are* your plans?

GAUGUIN To find a *better* world. A new one. Or a much older one.
He puts out his hand for Vincent's message; Theo holds onto it, folds it; puts it away. Each honors the other in this.   FADE OUT

FADE IN
INT. A ROOMING HOUSE STAIRCASE IN COPENHAGEN—DAY
A rather gloomy staircase and corridor in the kind of building where both flats and office space are rented.

DOWNSHOT—GAUGUIN
Carrying luggage, he climbs the last few steps into CLOSEUP as a man enters shot, studies him, and they pass with a minimal nod. Gauguin turns the stairhead and walks down the corridor away from us as we PAN. He stops at a door, leaning to check the door card.

INSERT—BELL PULL AND CARD
The card reads:

Mme Paul Gauguin
Translation
Lessons in French

His hand, hesitant a moment, pulls the bell; jangle o.s.

CLOSE SHOT—GAUGUIN
He waits, in deep, sad anticipation. In b.g. a glass-paneled door announces:

NAME COMING*
PHOTOGRAPHIC STUDIO

*Get the name from Emile Gauguin.
We hear the door open; he is deeply moved as he sees Mette.

METTE'S VOICE (o.s.) Paul!

GAUGUIN (across her) Mette!

CLOSE SHOT—METTE
She, too, is deeply moved; after a moment she closes the door behind her as we PULL AWAY into a balancing TWO-SHOT. They look at each other hard. A resolve to keep her distance and her bitterness, dissolves in her; the same with his own shyness and pride. Suddenly in deep love and sadness they embrace and kiss; then, still embracing, study each other.

METTE My husband.

GAUGUIN Mette.
They kiss again; again study each other.

METTE You've changed, Paul.

GAUGUIN (smiling but meaning it) For the worse?

METTE (after pause; sincerely) I don't know. But I know I love you—try as I will, not to.
Moved, he makes to kiss her again.

GAUGUIN My darling Mette . . .
She evades him.

METTE We mustn't keep them waiting.
He smiles, both impatient and agreeing. She opens the door.

CLOSE SHOT—GAUGUIN—NEW ANGLE
Stunned, in the doorway, as he sees his children o.s.

INT. METTE'S FLAT
An inexpensive living room, but with elements of middle-class furnishing.

GAUGUIN (making talk) Why, you've made it very comfortable, Mette . . . at worst it's better than staying on with your mother.
He goes helpless again, his eyes on the children, grave and unsure.

FULL SHOT—REVERSE—OVER GAUGUIN
The four children wait in a row, across the room; three boys and a girl. Their demeanor blends shyness, estrangement, intense curiosity. Mette hurries to join them. The two youngest come close to her. She nudges the oldest, a tall boy in his teens. He steps forward, does a military bow and heel-click, kisses his father on the cheek, does a dry, curious take, and withdraws.

GAUGUIN Well, Emile! . . . Quite the Copenhagen cadet, isn't he!
Mette smiles. She nudges the next boy. He does as Emile did, more
childishly, and hurries back to his mother. She nudges the next; after
hesitation he buries his face in her skirts.

CLOSE SHOT—GAUGUIN
Smiling, shrugging, he dismisses it. Then his eyes shift to Aline o.s. and
he becomes deeply grave.

GAUGUIN (very shy) Aline . . .

CLOSE SHOT—ALINE
Lovely, moved, very shy, about thirteen, she stands her ground.

PANNING SHOT—NEW ANGLE
We PAN with Gauguin as he crosses to her into close TWO-SHOT; Mette and
the others watching in b.g. He pauses, a pace from her, helpless: then unconsciously puts out his hands; bursting into tears she flings her arms
around his neck as he stoops, and kisses her.

ALINE O Father! Father! Never leave us again!

TILT UP TO GROUP SHOT
The children watch, curious and a bit hostile. Mette is complexly moved.
                                                                    DISSOLVE

SAME ROOM—EVENING—MED. TWO-SHOT—METTE AND GAUGUIN
She sews (clearly as a guard); he smokes and talks.

GAUGUIN I sold my Cezanne and my Pissaro; along with the sale of my
own paintings, it amounts to about 9,000 francs.

METTE (sewing) So you found buyers for some of your own.

GAUGUIN (ignoring it) And I have letters from the Ministry of Public
Instruction, entrusting me with an "artistic mission," and asking the
authorities to give me every kind of help.

METTE Oh?

GAUGUIN The Ministry promises to buy enough of my paintings, when
I come back, to pay my traveling expenses.

METTE (sewing) Then they're paying you nothing for your "mission."
Silence.

GAUGUIN You don't seem to realize, Mette, that a good many people in
Paris think very well of me, and of my going to Tahiti. Mallarme, and

Verlaine; Octave Mirbeau; Degas: . . . . there's to be a banquet in my honor.

METTE (sewing) I'm quite aware there are others like you.

GAUGUIN (flaring out) There's nobody else "like" me.
They exchange a restrained but amused smile. Pause.

GAUGUIN Half my paintings, I'll send you. You arrange for their exhibition and sale; the money is yours.

METTE (looking up) And the other half?

GAUGUIN They go to Paris: to develop my reputation, and to take care of my own needs.

METTE (dry) A very equitable arrangement.
She resumes sewing.

GAUGUIN Mette . . .
She looks up at him, moved, and fighting it. Pause.

METTE Why are you going to Tahiti, Paul?

GAUGUIN My dear: I'm afraid it's useless to try to explain; it always has been.

METTE Why are you going?

GAUGUIN Simply—for various reasons—Europe has become unendurable.

METTE Some artists you respect seem to "endure" it . . . M. Renoir; Degas; that vile little Count Lautrec.

GAUGUIN (dry) Possibly because they enjoy independent incomes, Mette; but I doubt that I would, even if I were Monte Cristo.

A silent, ironic assent.

GAUGUIN Surely you understand that I would never go, unless it was absolutely necessary to my work.

METTE So much has always been *necessary*—to your work.

GAUGUIN I'll bring back something new to the world; it's going to make all the difference.

METTE To whom?

GAUGUIN To us. As a family. Then we can be together again.

METTE How often I've heard that.

GAUGUIN But it's true. This is only temporary. Only until my work proves itself.

METTE (heartsick) Can you still believe that, Paul? You've done your best —so have I—but obviously your painting is no good: it doesn't sell.

GAUGUIN Mette: never say that to me again. (in obsessed fury) *Selling*—

METTE (near tears) O *please,* Paul; I can't bear to hear it all again!
He reaches forward fiercely yet tenderly, taking her by the shoulders, as WE DOLLY FAST into CLOSER SHOT.

GAUGUIN (quiet, intense) Now stop it, child: You're a woman of courage: I'm a man of courage. You know very well what I have to do, whether you understand it or not. You *know.* That's *all!*

METTE It isn't all: the rest is, I'd come with you, wherever you might go —whatever you might do: if you and I were alone in this world . . . We aren't . . . I have my duties: all the more, since . . .

GAUGUIN Since I *shirk* my responsibilities.

METTE No: I know you're true to your duty as you understand it; and I know the cost to you. I wouldn't have you do otherwise, if it seemed to you wrong.

GAUGUIN (gentle; hopeless) Not "wrong"; just impossible.
They gaze at each other in deepening love and respect.

GAUGUIN (very quiet) You're all a woman *ought* to be.

METTE You're all a man *has* to be.

GAUGUIN (whispering) Mette . . .
She shakes her head.

METTE My mother feels we mustn't risk having another child.

GAUGUIN Your mother won't bear the child: you?
She shakes her head in sorrow. Pause.

GAUGUIN (quiet) In that case I agree with both of you.
He looks at her hard, considering; then laughs quietly.

GAUGUIN Yes. *Indeed.* After all, we're a little beyond a "love affair": we're a family, or nothing.
He gets up; then she does.

METTE (indicating sofa) Stay with us.

GAUGUIN Thanks; I'll find a hotel ... Wake Emile, will you? ... I'll need company—if *not* a chaperone ... Meanwhile ... I have a few apologies— call it explanations—to make.

They part, for opposite ends of the room. As Mette opens a door in b.g. we,
CUT TO

INT. ALINE'S BEDROOM
With a soft knock Gauguin opens the door from the lighted hallway into her dark room.

GAUGUIN (softly) Aline?

ALINE'S VOICE (softly) Father. Come.
He hurries towards her into:

CLOSE TWO-SHOT—GAUGUIN AND ALINE
... as she sits up in bed and he kneels on the floor beside her. Hands on each other's shoulders, they look at each other. Pause.

GAUGUIN (broken but restrained) I *have* to go, you know.

ALINE (passionately) If I could only go *with* you!

GAUGUIN (incredulous) You *mean* that?

ALINE Of course I do!
She looks at him with adoration. For a moment he is wildly tempted to take her.

GAUGUIN You can't my dear ... I'm not—very good—at taking care of my children. (pause) But it's only for a while. The time will come when we'll all be together again. You'll see.

ALINE Till then, I just want to be with *you*.
He is very deeply moved. Pause. Then wonderingly:

GAUGUIN You really do understand me, don't you!

ALINE You're the bravest man in the world. And the greatest artist.
He is tremendously touched and heartened by this childlike absoluteness. Pause.

GAUGUIN (tenderly) Aline: ... my daughter: ... I'm going to begin making a little gift for you. A little book I'll write. Just my thoughts about living. Just—fragments; like life itself. Because we two understand things in the same way; so we're bound to be very lonely in this world.

ALINE O! Send it to me soon!

GAUGUIN No, my dear: it'll be for a grown woman, not a child, however brave and lovely. I'll make it for your twentieth birthday.

ALINE But that's so far!

GAUGUIN O . . . only too near!
He very tenderly lays his hand along the side of her face.

GAUGUIN Child . . . child . . .
They gaze at each other with love as we: DISSOLVE

INT. A SMALL PARISIAN CAFE—NIGHT—GROUP SHOT—GAUGUIN, MONFRIED, MORICE
Monfried, after paying off his drinks, gets up.

MONFRIED Well, my friend . . . I'll see you off in the morning.

GAUGUIN You've gone to too much trouble already. Both of you.

MONFRIED (smiling) *Trouble?* After all, you and I are old sailors, Paul. And we're both "on the beach," most of the time.

Their eyes meet in the warmth of deep friendship.

GAUGUIN I'll see you at the train, then.

MONFRIED Good night. (nodding) Charles . . .

MORICE Good night, Daniel.
Monfried goes out; Gauguin sits down again, and fingers a glass. Morice looks at him happily.

MORICE So at last your struggles are over. In Tahiti, you'll be able to work at leisure. Money will mean nothing, there.

GAUGUIN (with humor) It may mean enough that I'll thank you not to forget that little debt of five hundred francs.

Morice looks embarrassed; Gauguin grins.

GAUGUIN When you can, my friend, when you can; there are friends who owe me more than you do.

They drink. Gauguin looks at Morice long and hard. Then abruptly covers his face with his hands, and cries quietly.

GAUGUIN (through his hands) Charles, I've never been so unhappy.
Morice is astounded and embarrassed.

MORICE But—why *now,* of all times!

GAUGUIN (very quiet) Listen: I have never known how to keep both things alive—my family, and my thought. Up to now, I haven't even been able to keep alive my thought alone . . . And now that I can hope for the future I feel more terribly than ever before, the horror of the sacrifice I've made. (pause; then in a new, simpler intensity of knowledge and sorrow) I will never have my wife and my children with me again! Too late! Too late!

Pause. He tries to put on a brave smile.

GAUGUIN (cool and brisk) Now let's call it a night. If you come to the train tomorrow, perhaps by then you can forgive me for having cried before you. He smiles, the harder, and snaps his fingers for the waiter. PAN to lose him, and center Morice's soft, complicated face.   FADE OUT

END OF PART ONE

Part 2

FADE IN

EXT. NEAR MOREA AND TAHITI—LONG SHOT—A SMALL TRAMP STEAMER—
DAYBREAK

It approaches on water as calm and limpid as the light.

MOVING SHOT FROM SHIP—THE CONE OF MOREA IN THE DAWN

O.s. and throughout scene, soft trudging of ship's engine.

CLOSE SHOT—GAUGUIN AT THE RAIL

He watches in deep excitement. A light breeze stirs his hair. The SHIP'S
DOCTOR strolls up beside him; Gauguin nods.

DOCTOR Good morning. Did you rest well?

GAUGUIN I was up here, all night.

DOCTOR I know; I used to feel so, on my first voyages.
An extra puff of breeze; Gauguin inhales deeply, wonderingly.

GAUGUIN Hours out, I could already smell it . . . The richness. The wildness. I've never known anything like it.

DOCTOR Nor I . . . *Noa-noa*. (Gauguin looks enquiry) The Tahitian word
for fragrance.

GAUGUIN (shy) It's a fragrance fit for . . . an Earthly Paradise.
The Doctor watches him, touched.

DOCTOR Don't expect *too* much. (Doctor points downward) Now.
Gauguin looks down too.

MOVING DOWN SHOT

Just below the clear water, jagged reefs, near us.

ANOTHER MOVING DOWN SHOT

Other reefs, dangerously closer; we move very slowly.

CLOSE TWO SHOT—GAUGUIN AND DOCTOR

FAVORING Gauguin, who drags deep on a cigarette or stogie, looking to
shore. O.s., the beginning of the rattling of an anchor chain.

CLOSE DOWN SHOT AS THE ANCHOR PLUNGES

Over the plunge, and sound,   CUT TO

MEDIUM LONG SHOT

A small boat, rowed, approaches us; ship in b.g. Throughout scene to dissolves, roosters and gulls heard o.s.

CLOSE TWO SHOT—GAUGUIN AND DOCTOR, ON BOAT

Sound of oars. Again, Gauguin drags deep on tobacco; if inhaling earlier, he exhales now. The doctor is sympathetically aware of his intense excitement. Now Gauguin looks aloft in two directions, then down, registering ironic displeasure, then pleased irony. The doctor is quietly amused.

MEDIUM SHOT

As the CAMERA HEAVES GENTLY (the boat) the Tricolor is jerked the last two pulls up its pole, and hangs idle against palms. A loud rooster is heard o.s.

MEDIUM SHOT

A cross, atop a church; we PAN, centering another cross, as boat heaves, and grates gently o.s. against stone pier.

DOWN SHOT

A rope is made fast to a cannon which is sunken among flowering weeds.

HEAD CLOSEUP—GAUGUIN

. . . as with deep emotion he steps from boat to shore, Doctor following, pauses and looks about him, Doctor, behind, watching him. Then they walk towards us out of shot and we   DISSOLVE

INT. GOVERNOR'S OFFICE—CLOSE SHOT—LECASCADE, THE GOVERNOR—DAY

O.s., throughout, odd squawks of local birds, and yammering of hens; palm-leaves at window. He is a corrupt and brutal Negro. As we pull away into GROUP SHOT, with his officials in b.g., he is impatient with a native flunkey who hurries him into an official white coat with gold buttons, and he sits down fast into his chair behind his desk, just as we hear a door open and, o.s., a servant's voice in wild accent:

SERVANT'S VOICE Monsieur Paul Gauguin.

His face is fouled by a quick pseudo-smile.

TWO SHOT—GAUGUIN AND LECASCADE—OTHERS IN B.G.

. . . as Gauguin walks into the shot. Lecascade and Gauguin bow, put out their hands, and shake like honest men.

LECASCADE Monsieur Gauguin.

GAUGUIN (across him) Governor Lecascade.

Lecascade indicates a horribly bourgeois chair. They sit.

LECASCADE (with naive urbanity) This is indeed an honor, Monsieur. Won't you join me in an iced absinthe?
Gauguin nods thanks; both sip their drinks.

LECASCADE And what do you think of our little Capital?

GAUGUIN (with bald irony) Monsieur: words fail me. It's—Paris!
Lecascade looks for irony; then swallows it.

LECASCADE Ah, Monsieur; you flatter us! Still . . . it isn't quite what a Parisian might expect, out here among the savages.

FLASH CUT
Interchanges between the very correct native flunkeys and Gauguin.

GAUGUIN (deadpan) Far from it, your Excellency.
He sips his drink, comfortably, waiting the next move. An uneasy silence.

LECASCADE And now, Monsieur; your . . . ah . . .
Gauguin leisurely extracts an envelope, fancily sealed.

GAUGUIN This will explain my mission, Monsieur.
Lecascade takes it. Beaming.

LECASCADE Splendid.
Lecascade opens the letter and reads while Gauguin sips his drink and watches.

LECASCADE (suspicious) An *artistic* mission?

GAUGUIN Precisely; I am to become the first painter of the tropics.
Dead pause. All the others look at each other.

LECASCADE And what is—so—interesting—about these—natives?
Silence.

LECASCADE You mean to tell me that the French Government has sent you all the way to our Islands—for *that?*
Gauguin nods.

LECASCADE On what salary, Monsieur?

GAUGUIN If it is any of your business, Your Excellency, I'm travelling entirely at my own expense.

The Governor's disbelief of this is now total. He looks this disbelief at Gauguin, and he and his associates exchange similar glances; several begin to smile. In Gauguin a cold rage intensifies as he watches them.

GAUGUIN (cold and level) Evidently such an idea is very strange to you gentlemen. And it's quite true, that only an artist would work so hard, and risk so much, for nothing. But obviously you've never heard the meaning of the word "artist."

LECASCADE (with a nasty smile) I think I know the meaning of the word, Monsieur. I think it is the official word for a man who has been sent to spy. Gauguin is astounded and furious; he restrains a cold incredulous laughter as he looks from one man to another.

PANNING SHOT—REVERSE ANGLE
Face by face we watch Lecascade and his officials as, always with one interested, neutral exception, they exchange glances and watch him with utter suspicion.

CLOSE SHOT—GAUGUIN
. . . looking them over.

GAUGUIN (musingly) What a—cesspool, you gentlemen must have to hide. What a pity I'm *not* a spy!
We pull back into a FULL GROUP SHOT as he rises abruptly and most of them shrink back a little.

GAUGUIN Gentlemen: Monsieur: your Capital is a small-town Paris, and you, gentlemen, are just like the French—*including* the Ministry of Public Instruction. (he makes a mock bow) Good day: I shan't trouble you again. Cooly and insultingly, noting and then ignoring the taboret beside his chair, he plants his damp glass on the official desk, turns, and stalks out as we PAN. As he slams the door,   CUT TO

GROUP SHOT—CENTERING LECASCADE
As they react to the loud slam, o.s., in startlement or anger, again the exception looks after Gauguin with neutrality, interest, even a touch of liking.   DISSOLVE

EXT. PAPEETE—DAY
Throughout the scene, o.s., faint then steadily louder, a blatant mechanical piano plays the same tune as at Mme. La Rosa's.

REFLECTION CLOSEUP—GAUGUIN—PULL SHOT
His face, reflected in a shop window, shows sardonic contempt. We PULL AWAY to show the whole window: tasteless European clothes, corsets, etc., for women. Native and European women pass, dressed thus; then a nattily dressed man, over whom we   LAP DISSOLVE

FULL SHOT—ANOTHER SHOP WINDOW
Gents' Haberdashery. The Shopkeeper hustles out to hook Gauguin who snubs him and looks sharp to o.s. sound of a carriage.

FULL SHOT—THE CARRIAGE
An overdressed European couple and native coachman rattle past in a smart carriage, with high disdain for the foot-borne peasants.

CLOSE SHOT—GAUGUIN
His eyes follow with amused disgust and lift to

CLOSE UP SHOT—CROSSED STREET SIGNS
Against lazing palms, they name two great boulevards of Paris.

CLOSE PANNING SHOT—A SHOP WINDOW
The worst kinds of bourgeois art and bric-a-brac.

REFLECTING DOWN SHOT—ANOTHER WINDOW
Religious objects, sacred chromos, wire-flowered *pompes funebres,* etc.; and, reflected in the windowpane, a street scene in which we epitomize the transient, sleazy vanity and bustle of this little civilization—culminating in a magnificent native woman in native dress, epitomizing the old and incorrupt Tahiti. Gauguin is sick to see her in this mess.

By now Gauguin has had it. He turns, as we PAN, following the loud o.s. piano, and enters the Cafe Bougainville; thirsty.

INT. CAFE BOUGAINVILLE—MEDIUM SHOT—REVERSE—GAUGUIN, OTHERS
Gauguin enters; a bit blinded by the sudden shadow. He nearly collides with TITI, a half-caste girl. They swap experienced once-overs and are interrupted by

DOCTOR'S VOICE (o.s.) Gauguin! Monsieur Gauguin!
Gauguin looks towards him, pleased.

FULL SHOT—REVERSE—CENTERING DOCTOR
He beckons from a corner table, beyond several habitues and sons of same.

TWO SHOT—GAUGUIN AND TITI
They exchange a look of unfinished business and Gauguin leaves.

TWO SHOT—GAUGUIN AND DOCTOR
Gauguin enters shot as Doctor turns a chair, and sits.

DOCTOR Well; this is luck; I couldn't find you, and my ship leaves sooner than I expected.

GAUGUIN When?

DOCTOR I must be aboard within an hour. . . . Garçon! Two absinthes! . . . How do you like Papeete by now?

GAUGUIN With very little persuasion, I'd come back aboard too.

DOCTOR (amused) Oh?

GAUGUIN So *this* is Paradise!
The drinks are brought; the Doctor starts pouring, over a sugar lump.

DOCTOR I tried to warn you.

GAUGUIN Why, it's nothing but the meanest kind of French provincial town, with delusions of grandeur because it's a Capital; and with a bone in its nostrils!

The Doctor laughs.

DOCTOR My good friend, give it a try. Back in the country it isn't so bad . . . unless you expect too much.

GAUGUIN Expecting too much is my business.
Titi lounges across b.g. with an eye for Gauguin.

DOCTOR One fair warning: don't expect too much of Titi.

GAUGUIN Is *that* her name. I rather like her looks.

DOCTOR Oh, charming. But she's a human slaughterhouse.

GAUGUIN You have to take your chances.

DOCTOR Do you? *I* don't.

"NEUTRAL" VOICE (o.s.) Monsieur Gauguin.
They look around; the "Neutral" Officer enters shot.

GAUGUIN (not friendly) Well, Monsieur?

"NEUTRAL" If you please, don't jump to conclusions; I would like to help you.

GAUGUIN (rising) Please join us, Lieutenant.

"NEUTRAL" Thank you; there's no time. . . . I thought that as a traveler—an artist—it might interest you: the King has died.

GAUGUIN The King?

DOCTOR Pomare Fourth; the last Tahitian King.

"NEUTRAL" Yes; with his death, there is no longer even a nominal monarch; France takes over entirely.

GAUGUIN Hm . . . I seem to have arrived a bit late.

OFFICER I must go, Monsieur; if you'd care to come with me to the Palace.
Gauguin is hesitant; he really wonders whether to leave Tahiti.

DOCTOR I'd go with him, if I were you; there'll always be other ships.
Gauguin still hesitates.

DOCTOR After all, it's the end of Maori history.
The "Neutral" Officer nods, gravely. Pause.

GAUGUIN (to Officer) Thank you. I'll come with you.
The Doctor, looking at him, knows he's going to stay a long, long time
in the Islands. DISSOLVE

NOTE: The funeral sequence is to be cut rigidly to the music of Chopin's
Funeral March. I will indicate the cuts and shots exactly, but serve warning that without the melody to key it to, it will be hard to read, or to
imagine the effectiveness of. I will write out and enclose the melody, as
a key; the scoring, and performance, should be those of a French deep
provincial military band of the period: rather shrill and squeaky, and not
very well played; yet with genuine solemnity.

INT. PALACE—CLOSE UP SHOT—FACES—DAY
A moving frieze of faces, which look down virtually into the lens, as at
a corpse in its coffin. Queen's flowers in b.g., luminous white in this light.
First the face of the Governor, hanging like wet washing at this angle;
then assorted dignitaries, clergy, top merchants: the slightly sour cream
of the European Colony. They are here out of official politesse; secondarily,
in some, a mildly contemptuous curiosity or sympathy. The last of them
is Gauguin's very different face.

Four opening bars to this UP SHOT; the music is distant, o.s., from outdoors.
CUT TO

B. VERTICAL DOWN SHOT—KING POMARE IV
An old, bloated man, booze and sadness and tragic apathy still clear in
his face, he lies in state in his open coffin, in a French Admiral's uniform.
Two bars. CUT TO

C. UP SHOT—A MOVING FRIEZE OF NATIVE FACES
They too look down: The Queen; her brother; the King's niece (a
Princess); then a series of old and younger faces, inferring deeper and
deeper primitiveness, and pastoral quality. 3 and 3/4 bars to this shot.
CUT TO

D. MED. SHOT—EXT. OUTSIDE THE PALACE DOOR—DAY
A squad of pigeon-breasted apathetic French soldiers, to one side; to the
other, a squad of tall solemn native troops; both squads present arms, as

the coffin emerges on shoulder. Hearse or horse-drawn catafalque in center f.g., band to right. Now the music is much louder; last quarter note of foregoing bar.

E. MED. SHOT—NATIVES—REVERSE ANGLE
Along a crowd of natives squatting in courtyard, as, with a solemn and thrilling unison, they all stand up and look towards us. First beat of next bar; also very loud, percussive and brassy.   CUT TO

F. LONG SHOT—OPEN COUNTRY
Forlornly rich in midday sun. We see approaching front of the funeral train, through the dust it raises on a country road. Distant music.

MED. CLOSE AND CLOSE SHOTS—WITHIN AND NEAR THE CORTEGE
The music is close and loud. One shot to each beat, for 4 bars, except as indicated.

G. (1) SHOT FROM THE DUSTY GROUND, FROM DEAD IN FRONT: THE PROCESSION, ADVANCING

H. (2) FRONTAL SHOT OF PLUMED HORSES AND HEARSE OR CAISSON OR CATA-FALQUE

I. (3) CLOSE TWO SHOT: QUEEN, UNCLE, PRINCESS
in a buggy; solemn, absurd and splendid.

J. (4) CLOSE TWO SHOT: GOVERNOR AND HIS WIFE
doing a boring duty with ill-concealed patronage.

2nd Bar:

K. (1) A RANK OF NATIVE TROOPS
aloof and fine.

L. (2) A RANK OF UNDERSIZED, SLOPPY FRENCH SOLDIERS

M. (3) CLOSE SHOT—GAUGUIN
walking; the Officer beside him. Gauguin is deeply but complexly moved; eyes darting every which way.

N. (4) CLOSE GROUP SHOT: A CROWD OF NATIVES,
walking: some in native dress, others European; all deeply grave; tears on the faces of a few.

O. ON ROLL OF DEEP DRUMS: Start with FRONTAL PULL SHOT of marching drummers. After a half-beat,   CUT TO

P. CLOSE SHOT—THE QUEEN, IN HER JOGGLED CARRIAGE

Q. FIRST HALF OF SECOND BEAT: CLOSE SHOT—GAUGUIN, WALKING

R. SECOND HALF-BEAT: CLOSE FRONTAL UP SHOT: GRIEVING NATIVES

S. FIRST HALF OF THIRD BEAT: CLOSE UP SHOT—THE GOVERNOR IN HIS CARRIAGE

T. SECOND HALF BEAT: CLOSE DOWN SHOT: HIS CARRIAGE WHEELS, grinding.

U. FIRST HALF OF FOURTH BEAT: MOVING SHOT—ADVANCING TOWARDS THE HORRIBLE MONUMENT OF CORAL AND CEMENT

V. SECOND HALF: GAUGUIN, SEEING IT, APPALLED

4th Bar: Now, except at start, and as indicated, 8 shots to a beat: on second roll.

W. FIRST BEAT: On first half-beat, CLOSE DOWN SHOT OF NATIVE FEET making small explosions in the dust.

W.I THIRD QUARTER-BEAT: FIRST OF A SERIES OF FLUTTERING SHOTS: SYNCHRONIZED WITH DRUM ROLL:
  a) FULL FACE HEAD CLOSEUP: GAUGUIN
  b) DITTO: GOVERNOR
  c) DITTO: QUEEN
  d) DITTO: ROYAL BROTHER

X. SECOND BEAT:
  a) PRINCESS
  b) GOVERNOR'S WIFE
  c) HIGH-CLASS FRENCHWOMAN
  d) HIGH-CLASS NATIVE WOMAN
  e) FRENCH SOLDIER
  f) NATIVE SOLDIER
  g) NATIVE CITIZEN
  h) NATIVE WOMAN

The above shots are so similar in frame that, at this fluttering speed, they form a composite.

THIRD BEAT:

Y. CLOSE MOVING GROUP SHOT—NATIVES, MARCHING, FAVORING ONE, WHO EPITOMIZES NATIVES HERE

FOURTH BEAT:

Z. CLOSE MOVING GROUP SHOT—FEATURING GAUGUIN, whose face sums up from his v.p.

NEXT BAR:

A. FIRST BEAT: CLOSEUP SHOT, THE PLUMED, PASSING HEARSE
B. SECOND: CLOSE MOVING SHOT:
We advance on the ugly monument and the open grave.
C. THIRD: CLOSE SHOT—CARRIAGE WHEELS GRIND PAST
D. FOURTH: FEET PASS IN MARCHING STEP, EXPLODING DUST

NEXT BAR:

E. FIRST BEAT: MED. LONG SHOT FROM BEHIND PROCESSION
F. SECOND: LONG SHOT FROM BEHIND THE PROCESSION
G. THIRD BEAT, and a FOURTH, SILENT: FULL GROUP SHOT, WIDE-ANGLE LENS: AT THE GRAVE

Features are native and European dignitaries; Gauguin; the polloi crowds b.g. On the silent beat, the shopkeeper we saw this morning discreetly picks his nose, and someone gives out a loud *sssshhhh.*

NOW REST, A FULL EXTRA BEAT OF SILENCE, OVER A GROUP SHOT OF THE BAND
We feature a little guy, lipping up for a flute solo; and on the next beat, swing into the sentimental, second section of the march, rather shrilly and mushily played, with mooing, inept horns doing the bass. Again as before, cut rigidly to the music:

a) TWO BEATS OF FIRST BAR:
We stay on the flutist and friends, playing softly and con amore.

b) THROUGH BALANCE OF BAR AND WHOLE OF SECOND BAR: MED. CLOSEUP SHOT: THE GOVERNOR
Silent, ad lib, with gestures, he delivers a little funeral oration. During the six beats we center him we flash cut MED. CLOSE GROUP reactions: Europeans with parasols and simpering pseudo-attention; natives grave, polite, not deceived or impressed by him; the Governor desultory, patronizing, bored. By beginning of his last beat he bows out and the Royal Uncle takes his place.

c) NEXT BAR: MED. CLOSE SHOT: THE UNCLE SPEAKS
(silent, ad lib, music continuing). He speaks gravely, slowly, with dignity and sincerity. By gestures to Pomare, the Queen, the Governor, the Tricolor, himself, he makes clear the final ceding of power from Tahiti to France. During this bar, which he dominates, we again FLASH CUT reactions ad lib: Europeans like tourists or scarcely listening; natives listening hard, aware of the moment in their history. By the start of his last beat he is through and a Protestant Missionary steps in to replace him, wearing the long-tailed coat, etc., of old cartoons of Mr. Prohibition.

d) NEXT BAR—MED. CLOSE SHOT—THE MISSIONARY
He reads the burial service from his book. He is a dry, good enough
man, fantastically out of place. Intercut, ad lib, shots of Queen, Princess,
Uncle, natives, and dirt cast onto the coffin and into the grave. There are
three shots of the grave: (1) dirt thumps on coffin (with subdued sound);
(2) it's better than half full; (3) on the end of this bar, a spade pats the
finished grave (with sound) and, in mid-phrase, the music ends abruptly
as we   CUT TO

FULL TABLEAU—THE BURIAL PARTY—DEAD SILENCE—CLOSE SHOT—GAUGUIN
The silence continues. Then we hear a faint, mysterious, hair-raising
sound, to which he reacts and directs his eyes, astounded. It is the beginning of an unimaginably alien and powerful and ancient native dirge.

FULL SHOT—VARIOUS EUROPEANS
They too, vaguely stirred and disturbed, glance at each other and look
towards the o.s. music.

FULL SHOT—NATIVE SINGERS AND MUSICIANS
They sing in the native tongue, solemnly and magnificently, meanwhile
doing a subdued kind of seated dancing. Enter in f.g. Gauguin later in
the dirge. He is deeply stirred. Officer then enters. Gauguin whispers to
Officer.

GAUGUIN If Beethoven could hear it!
The Officer politely nods, but doesn't get it. Abruptly the music ends. All
stay briefly quiet under its spell. We hear o.s. the slashing of a whip.
Gauguin startled turns to see . . .

MED. SHOT—GOVERNOR'S CARRIAGE—GAUGUIN'S POINT OF VIEW
Governor heads briskly for Papeete, through startled natives.

FULL SHOT
The buggies are hurrying away; gentlemen help ladies into others; soldiers
stroll off, ranks broken; native men and women coalesce, chattering,
linking arms, walking, arms around waists, the women swinging their
hips, the bare feet splashing up dust; a whole epitomizing of swift dis-
integration, and relaxing.

MED. CLOSE SHOT—GAUGUIN AND OFFICER
Strolling homeward, amid the cheerful mishmash.

GAUGUIN It's like "The Return From The Races".
The Officer smiles. Gauguin, seeing something ahead, registers interest
and pleasure.

MOVING SHOT—NATIVES
Native men and women, walking back-to-us, bridge in b.g.

MOVING TWO-SHOT—GAUGUIN AND OFFICER

GAUGUIN They *walk* so beautifully, don't they!
Now he looks *really* interested; and our PULL SHOT brings a bit of the bridge into the frame.

FULL SHOT—A LITTLE STREAM
Some women are descending the bank beside the bridge. Other women, concealing themselves among rocks in the water, lift their skirts to the waist, and squat in the water, cooling off.

CLOSEUP SHOT—GAUGUIN
He looks down at them, touched and entranced.

FULL SHOT—THE STREAM
Some women clamber out towards us, their skirts clinging to their wet bodies; they break flowers from bushes and, putting them over the left ear, approach us, smiling and easy.

OFFICER'S VOICE The *tiare*. Over the left ear, it means desire.

GAUGUIN'S VOICE They're like perfect young animals.
The young women are quite near us now; smiling, pleasant.

CLOSE SHOT—GAUGUIN AND OFFICER
The young women come nearer, and pass. At their nearest, Gauguin sniffs unabashedly, smiling at them.

GAUGUIN Their smell is so touching; so alive; the perfume of the flowers, and of their blood.
Overhearing, these two women laugh sweetly.

WOMAN (to Gauguin) Teine mahari noa noa.
Smiling, they look back over their shoulders as they start to cross the bridge.

OFFICER (translating for Gauguin) Now we are very fragrant.
Gauguin, looking after them, remembering the word, feels a tender exhilaration.

GAUGUIN (smiling; to himself) Noa noa.
The two men turn as we PAN, and walk away from us, among the natives, across the bridge. After a moment, and after o.s. sound, everyone has to stand tight against the rail as, briskly, a carriage-load of Europeans passes.

FADE OUT

FADE IN

INT. GAUGUIN'S HUT—MATAIEA—CLOSE SHOT—GAUGUIN—NIGHT

He sits writing, by lamp or lantern light, in a swirring whirl of insects (SOUND) which only bother him casually, ad lib. In b.g. a bed; an easel; the b.g. is barely visible; dim gold. We hear the scratching of his pen. He, like the scene, looks extraordinarily peaceful.

GAUGUIN'S VOICE (as he writes) King Pomare's funeral filled me with sadness. It was indeed "the end of Maori history". It was the Tahiti of older times—that I loved. But how was I to find traces of this past. (he begins to smile, remembering) I soon made up my mind. I would leave Papeete. I felt that by living intimately with the natives in the wilderness, I would by patience gradually gain their confidence, and come to know them. DISSOLVE

FULL SHOT—SILENT (or subdued sound)—EXT. PAPEETE—MORNING

He helps Titi into the carriage, gets in himself, nods thanks to the Officer (LaPlace) and starts off.

GAUGUIN'S VOICE And so, one morning, I set out in a borrowed carriage, in search of a "hut" I might rent. DISSOLVE

MOVING TWO SHOT—GAUGUIN AND TITI

SOUNDS of locomotion under. Titi, dressed to kill as described in *Noa Noa*, p. 19, is pleased, proud; an underlying fierceness. In an experienced yet vain way, she takes Gauguin's arm. He smiles, pleased but aloof.

GAUGUIN'S VOICE My *vahina,* Titi by name, accompanied me. She was of mixed blood. She was proud to be in a carriage; to be so elegant; to be the *vahina* of a man whom she believed to be important and rich.

MOVING TWO SHOT—FULL AHEAD—CARRIAGE VIEWPOINT, SOUND UNDER

GAUGUIN'S VOICE The journey was soon accomplished . . . inconsequential talk; a rich, monotonous country.
PAN right, bring in sea sounds, waves sheeting and spraying on coral reefs and rocks.

GAUGUIN'S VOICE On the right there was always the sea . . .

PAN left, more slowly; continue carriage and sea sounds.

GAUGUIN'S VOICE . . . to the left, the wilderness, with its perspective of great forests.

The shot enlarges what he says. LAP DISSOLVE

FULL MOVING SHOT—CARRIAGE VIEWPOINT
Slower moving, and sound o.s. And over Gauguin's next lines

CUT TO

TWO SHOT—GAUGUIN AND TITI
He gets down from the carriage and offers his hand; she stays up. In the FULL SHOT, above, we enter a loose palm grove; a few huts at various depths in it; people appear, shy and candid; we first see the Landlord, the "Olympia" woman; Jotefa.

GAUGUIN'S VOICE By noon, we arrived at the district of Mataiea.

FULL SHOT—TITI IN B.G.
Gauguin talks (silent) with Landlord; the woman and Jotefa watch, curious and friendly, in b.g.; Gauguin is aware of them. There are gestures towards a new hut, and an old.

GAUGUIN'S VOICE I soon found a suitable hut, which the owner rented to me. He was building a new one nearby, where he was already living.

TWO SHOT—GAUGUIN AND TITI
Others in b.g. She pantomimes to get down; smiling, he shakes his head. He climbs into the carriage, waves to the Landlord, turns the carriage and starts away from us back towards Papeete as we

CUT TO

MOVING TWO SHOT—NEW ANGLE
Titi looks sore as a boil; Gauguin looks pleased, convinced, kindly.

GAUGUIN'S VOICE (over the two above two-shots) There and then, I decided that Titi shouldn't live with me here. It wasn't her terrible clinical reputation; it was her half-white blood.

LAP DISSOLVE

CLOSE SHOT—GAUGUIN
writing. Remote night sound o.s.

GAUGUIN'S VOICE (as he writes) I felt she could not teach me any of the things I wanted to know. I told myself that here in the country, I would find what I was seeking; it would only be necessary to choose. Thus at last I have begun to cure myself of civilization, and initiate myself into savagery.

He draws a short elegant line under this; then, very tired and content, leans back in his chair; then blows or blots the ink dry; and closes the large notebook.

INSERT: TITLE OR COVER PAGE OF MS. VERSION: READING: "NOA NOA"

Over this, with sound, the lamp is blown out.

FULL SHOT—THE MOUNTAIN

. . . as described in *Noa Noa,* behind his hut. It is drowned in night.
SLOWLY PAN around, passing the open grove, to a

FULL SHOT—OVER GAUGUIN—INCLUDING WALL OF HUT

He is just outside the hut; smoking; in deep stillness. He looks out over
the moonlit sea, whose sound of calm crumpling reaches us. He looks
through regularly spaced bamboo reeds. After a sufficient pause to establish
the stillness we bring on, pianissimo, on one reed instrument, the Peruvian
melody. (It bears some rough relation to the melody of the dirge for
Pomare.) Early within this melody he retires into the hut and out of the
shot. We hold the shot. The melody completes itself. The night sound
dies. Silence.   DISSOLVE

IDENTICAL FULL SHOT OF THE SEA

Earliest daybreak.

FULL SHOT—REVERSE ANGLE—THE MOUNTAIN

TWO MORE, SMALLER, MORE INTIMATE LANDSCAPES

Here seek rough approximations of some of the casual landscapes in *Noa
Noa.*

MED. SHOT—GAUGUIN

He is at his easel; his back is to us; a landscape.

CLOSE SHOT—GAUGUIN

From front, at work. Moving light and shadow dapple his face and the
whole shot. He works freely, happily, as a newcomer.

CLOSER SHOT—GAUGUIN

Aware of being watched, he turns to look.

CLOSE DOWN SHOT—HIS VIEWPOINT

A charming adolescent face, half hidden among rich leaves, vanishes. The
leaves collapse together and nod.

CLOSE SHOT—GAUGUIN

Smiling but shy, he resumes work. Again a little self-conscious, he glances
ahead to his right.

LONG SHOT—HIS VIEWPOINT

Deep in the open grove, beside two huts, natives stand quiet, watching
him.

CLOSE SHOT—GAUGUIN

He works a little more.

JOTEFA'S VOICE (o.s.) Ia orana.

A little startled, Gauguin looks behind, to his left. Jotefa, a charming and finely made young man, crosses the shot, with nets and fish.

GAUGUIN (shyly) Ia orana.

Jotefa smiles with arresting sweetness as he goes by. Gauguin looks again to his work; then, with shy interest up ahead to his left-of-center.

MED. SHOT—REVERSE ANGLE

The "Olympia" woman approaches, her eyes on him, face calm.

CLOSE SHOT—GAUGUIN

Really interested, and really shy, he finally manages:

GAUGUIN Ia orana.

MED. SHOT—REVERSE—OVER GAUGUIN

She crosses, close, amused, lowering her eyes, and leaves the shot. He looks after her. Her laugh o.s. embarrasses him, and he quickly gets back to work . . . Pause . . . then Gauguin looks around again; sees someone o.s. and again to work. Jotefa strolls into the shot back to camera, without his fish, and watches Gauguin.

CLOSE SHOT—GAUGUIN

His painting, on which he is intent in b.g. Gauguin is aware of Jotefa, turns his head away from us to him. We infer his smile by Jotefa's bright smile in return. Gauguin returns to his work. Jotefa gets up and walks forward just behind him and to one side. Gauguin pretends not to notice . . . Pause.

JOTEFA Good morning.

GAUGUIN (working) Ia orana.

JOTEFA What are you doing?

GAUGUIN What are *you?*
Jotefa laughs a little, charmingly.

JOTEFA Watching you work.

GAUGUIN (smiling; working) Don't *you* have work to do?

JOTEFA (comfortably) No more, for today.
Silence. Gauguin keeps working.

JOTEFA What are you making?

GAUGUIN (After each statement Jotefa nods) You know how to fish; to dive; to hunt; to build a hut; to pray; to make love . . . (emphatic nod and nice smile) You like what I'm doing. (nod) Why don't you see what *you* can do?

JOTEFA (sincerely) Monsieur, I am an ignorant man, who knows only how to stay alive and be happy.

This, of course silently wows Gauguin.

JOTEFA *You* know how to do something *useful.*
Gauguin is profoundly surprised and touched.

GAUGUIN (with moved irony) *Useful;* you think so?

JOTEFA O yes, Monsieur; you give men everything, beyond their just staying alive. You make them know that it is a great wonder to be alive; a great joy; a mystery and fear; an honor. *What else* could be so useful! Pause.

GAUGUIN (moved and tender) Jotefa; my friend; nobody has ever said that to me before.

Jotefa looks puzzled, surprised, friendly.   DISSOLVE

INSERT: GAUGUIN'S HAND, WRITING
The handwriting is exceptionally elegant, virile, self-critical. Fleet shadows in whirling insects, and their o.s. sound. We watch him finish a sentence as he says:

GAUGUIN'S VOICE It was thus that I won my first friend. I was soon to find how ready they *all* were, for friendship.   DISSOLVE

A SERIES OF DISSOLVES
. . . at the pace of the following narration, which will illustrate, inflect and extend Gauguin's lines.

GAUGUIN'S VOICE Getting to know the world I wanted to paint, was not so easy. I made all kinds of notes and sketches. But the landscape, with its violent, pure colors, dazzled and blinded me. Golden figures in the brooks and on the seashore enchanted me. Why did I hesitate to put all this glory of the sun on my canvas—to paint things as I saw them—to put without special calculation a red close to a blue? Oh, the old European traditions! The timidities of expression, of degenerate races!

SHOOTING NOTES:
Through the "landscape" line, concentrate on landscape and "violent, pure color", briefly cutting in Gauguin at work. The "golden figures" line: nude children, medium distant, play on the shore; the "Olympia" woman,

dripping water, looks calmly at an abashed Gauguin, her nudity masked by brook-side leaves. From there on, center on Gauguin, disturbed; cutting in the things that inhibit him. On the "traditions" line, DISSOLVE him back to the writing table; a rueful, self-contemptuous smile.

INT. GAUGUIN'S HUT—GAUGUIN WRITING
A change of expression and voice as he continues writing and speaking:

GAUGUIN'S VOICE There was another difficulty; I was very lonely. Titi, and all that she meant, I had outgrown.   DISSOLVE

A SERIES OF DISSOLVES
Illustrate again and extend his lines o.s. simultaneously.

GAUGUIN'S VOICE The women of our neighborhood were willing—even eager—to be "taken", brutally; but I was not capable of that brutality. In Europe, where such matters are frowned on, or made into a fetish, I had never been backward;—but here, where it was as simple and as casually approved as friendship, I was as shy as a schoolboy. I decided to leave home for a while; to make a tour of the Island.

SHOOTING NOTES:
We shoot, here, the kind of Tahitian communal evening, described in *Noa Noa,* showing at least three very attractive girls who are much interested in Gauguin; featuring the calm "Olympia" woman, who is *always* too much for him; indicating the benevolent interest of the older people, that he be well-provided in this way, and their friendly bewilderment at his backwardness; and concentrating on his deepening shyness and his ironic amusement at himself. The mood is essentially "lyric" and quietly comic: we are giving a glimpse of the white man's "ideal" of South Sea life—and of his inadequacy to it.

From a CLOSE SHOT of Gauguin's rueful, inadequate face
                                                                DISSOLVE

A SERIES OF DISSOLVES
Two or three maximally fine landscapes from the interior—mountains, valleys, etc.—one involving people, fairly close, the others showing Gauguin walking, almost foolishly small in the magnificent solitude. Over these; his line about leaving home.

EXT. TARAVAO (OR ANY SMALL SHORE VILLAGE—MED. SHOT—GAUGUIN—DAY
Silently thanking a uniformed gendarme, whose wife is in b.g., he rides towards us on a horse.

LONG SHOT—GAUGUIN
He rides away from us along a deep, quiet vista of shoreline.

GAUGUIN'S VOICE At the far end of the Island a gendarme loaned me his horse, and I set out along the east shore, seldom visited by Europeans.

FULL SHOT—GAUGUIN
He rides up to MEDIUM CLOSE through this tiny village in an open glade, and we see a man speaking to him (silent).

GAUGUIN'S VOICE In the tiny district of Faone, a native invited me to have dinner.

Nodding thanks, Gauguin dismounts, the man ties his horse, and we PAN IN a nearby hut in front of which, in pleasant shade, food is cooking, men and women sit about smoking, and children play. In shady b.g., in profile, sits a black-clad old woman like the one in Gauguin's THE SPIRIT OF THE DEAD WATCHES. She never speaks or moves throughout the scene, but we feel she sees and hears everything.

GROUP SHOT—NEW ANGLE
As Gauguin and the man join this group.

MAN (to all) Yes, he is the man who makes human beings.
Gauguin bows shyly; various gracious nods.

MAN He will eat with us.
A beautiful woman of forty, his hostess, speaks.

WOMAN Monsieur, you are welcome. Why do you come to our part of the Island?
All watch him, courteously.

CLOSE SHOT—GAUGUIN
He considers briefly—then almost by reflex:

GAUGUIN I am looking for a wife.

WOMAN There are many pretty women here at Faone. Do you want one?

GAUGUIN Yes.

WOMAN Very well. If she pleases you, I will give her to you. She is my daughter.

GAUGUIN It is well. Let me see her.
The woman rises and leaves, disclosing her "chair"—a hat-block. Gauguin notes and reacts. Silence. Two women get food from the cooking pit. Gauguin and a man exchange tobacco and light up. All watch Gauguin courteously but disconcertingly. He is curious and a bit uneasy about the silent old woman. A lovely child comes near him, watching him gravely.

Too shy at first, he then meets the child's eyes and the child smiles beautifully and everybody smiles.

WOMAN'S VOICE (o.s.) Monsieur . . .

He looks to the voice, and his eyes alter; he is moved. CUT TO

GROUP SHOT—CENTERING TEHURA

She should stop our breath in this first shot: vide Gauguin's description in *Noa Noa:* golden skin through almost transparent rose-colored muslin, etc.; her hair, in the sunlight, "an orgy in chrome". A little girl with her, carries a small bundle.

WOMAN . . . My daughter, Monsieur; her name is Tehura.

CLOSE SHOT—GAUGUIN

GAUGUIN (rising) I am happy to meet you, Tehura. My name is Paul.

MED. CLOSE SHOT—TEHURA

She smiles, and starts toward him. CUT TO

GROUP SHOT—GAUGUIN AND TEHURA

. . . as she calmly sits down beside him. The natives are courteously interested.

GAUGUIN How old are you, Tehura?

TEHURA Thirteen years.

GAUGUIN I have a daughter that age, but she lives far in the cold north. She is still almost a child. But you are already a young woman.

Tehura gives a sensuous, mocking little smile, which all but scares Gauguin.

TEHURA How old are you, Paul?

GAUGUIN Forty-three.

She darts a look at him, then smiles to herself again.

GAUGUIN (clearly scared of her; "projecting") Aren't you afraid of me?

TEHURA No.

GAUGUIN Do you wish to live in my hut for always?

TEHURA Yes.

GAUGUIN You have never been ill?

TEHURA No.

She gets up and brings him food on a banana leaf. They eat.

Honestly concerned for her, he glances uneasily towards her mother.
Tehura catches the worried glance and her sensuous, mocking little smile
makes him realize he'd better be concerned for himself. He glances up.

GROUP SHOT—CENTERING OLD WOMAN
A girl puts food before her; rigid and silent, after pause, she starts eating.

CLOSE TWO-SHOT—GAUGUIN AND TEHURA
Amused and relieved that the old woman is alive and human, Gauguin
smiles more easily at Tehura. She looks at him deadpan; then a smile of
mocking tenderness. He's hooked bad.

MOTHER'S VOICE (o.s.) In a week, Monsieur . . .
Both look to her, "dutiful children".

GROUP SHOT—NATIVES, CENTERING MOTHER

MOTHER . . . if she is unhappy, she will come back to me.

FLASH CUT
her daughter and son-in-law, nodding; DISSOLVE on Mother,

DISSOLVE

EXT. TARAVAO IN FRONT OF GENDARME'S HOUSE—CLOSE SHOT—GAUGUIN,
TEHURA, GENDARME
Gauguin turns over the horse to its owner.

GAUGUIN I am very much obliged to you, Corporal.
The courteous gendarme shrugs; he's fascinated by Tehura.

WIFE'S VOICE (o.s.) What! You bring back such a hussy?
All look to her as she enters the shot—a bleak woman, heavily corseted.
With her eyes she "undresses" Tehura, who is wholly indifferent.
Gendarme is embarrassed.

CLOSE SHOT—GAUGUIN
He looks them both from head to foot, silently reacting.

CLOSE TILTING SHOT—THE WIFE
We tilt slowly, from head to foot; then PAN to Tehura's bare feet and TILT
slowly up from feet to head. FADE OUT

FADE IN
MED. CLOSE SHOT—GAUGUIN
(NOTE: The following scene, mainly pantomime, is so played that we
can't mistake it for mere honeymoon playfulness: Tehura has very mixed
feelings about Gauguin—until the end of it; she really likes to tease and

torment him. And Gauguin is really badly on the hook. So, we here see him win her over, as he hasn't till now.)

Gauguin sits facing us. He works at a small wood sculpture. Tehura lounges on mat in b.g., watching him; she slits a palm leaf with her fingernails. Bored, she strolls up behind him; aware of her, he pretends no attention. She watches him work. No attention. She tickles the nape of his neck with the palm leaf. No attention. She leans and blows softly in his ear. He reacts with annoyance and delight, but no attention. She stands so close she virtually touches him, the length of her belly and his back. By his reaction we strongly realize her fragrance and physical emanation and his excitement, but he pretends no attention. Then, unable to resist, he looks back and up at her, smiling, and reaches to embrace her hips. With a look of cold mockery she eludes him. He feels really badly rebuffed, and pretends indifference. She saunters behind and past him and then along a wall ahead of him as he pretends not to watch her and we PAN with her, losing Gauguin as she examines photographs of paintings. She stops before Manet's *Olympia*. Pause.

GAUGUIN'S VOICE (o.s.) What do you think of her?

TEHURA (after pause) She is very beautiful.

CLOSE SHOT—GAUGUIN
He is touched and amused.

CLOSE SHOT—TEHURA

TEHURA Is she your wife?

CLOSE SHOT—GAUGUIN
Short pause; he nods.

CLOSE SHOT—TEHURA
A long, appraising look at him; a shrug of dismissal; she moves to further art as we PAN—and stops again, special charm in her posture as she studies an Italian Primitive.

CLOSE SHOT—GAUGUIN
He quickly gets a sketch-pad, sits again, and begins to sketch.

INSERT—THE PAD
Gauguin's hand, with charcoal; swift, expressive strokes.

CLOSE PANNING SHOT—THE PRIMITIVE PHOTO
Then PAN IN her contrasting yet related face. On a grating of charcoal o.s. she glances to him, then as we PAN, strolls towards him, comes behind him,

looks down as he works. She cuffs him sharply and runs out the door. He looks after her, startled, amused, dismayed; resumes statue.

She re-enters in a high dudgeon, hiding something, and vanishes behind a screen or curtain in b.g. Sharply interested, he pretends no attention.

Busy sounds behind the curtain; some native cuss-word: then she emerges, beautifully dressed, a flower behind her left ear; proud and ironic. She walks in slow behind him as we DOLLY IN CLOSE; then, with a *moue* for his unawareness (we can see he is intensely excited and curious), she walks past him and out of the frame.

TWO-SHOT—GAUGUIN AND TEHURA
. . . over Gauguin, who faces away from us. She walks nobly into the shot, takes a chair, swings it into place and sits down, facing him—with a look into his eyes, of slight humor, deep expectancy, and immense challenge.

TWO-SHOT—REVERSE ANGLE—SHOOTING PAST TEHURA
Quite as amused as excited, Gauguin accepts the challenge. He takes the sketch-pad and, looking at her, gravely smiling, tears off the sketch of her and crumples it.

MED. CLOSE—TEHURA
Over the sound of crumpling she looks straight at him o.s. in a kind of amused scornful challenge.

MED. CLOSE—GAUGUIN
He looks at her very hard, wholly grave and intent now; and carefully as a surgeon, makes his first line.

INSERT: THE PAD
His hand describes a beautiful, opulent line—perhaps of the whole rondure of her head, plus the line of open cheek and chin.

TWO-SHOT—GAUGUIN AND TEHURA
. . . from the side, facing each other rigidly, like two contestants.

CLOSE SHOT—GAUGUIN
Working intensely. He looks up to her studying, cold; wholly free, of course, of "flirtation".

MED. CLOSE—TEHURA
She watches and accepts his cold studying; she is *all* sex, but with dignity.

CLOSE SHOT—GAUGUIN
Working in wide, quiet sweeping lines: in fact, we here see him deeper and better at work than ever before; he is "finding himself" as we watch. In a purely aesthetic way he is deeply moved by what he sees, and is

doing and learning; this emotion is "cold, sad, impersonal, tender": it also carries in it gaiety and a curious kind of anger or delight.

CLOSER SHOT—GAUGUIN
Watching her, very sharp and grave. TIGHTEN SHOT A LITTLE.

INSERT: THE SKETCH—VERY CLOSE
His hand, careful yet swift, draws her mouth.

CLOSE SHOT—GAUGUIN
The face is tight; as much erotic as aesthetic or workman. He glances up from work to her, deeply excited and uneasy.

MED. SHOT—TEHURA
We DOLLY VERY SLOWLY in as her face fulfills Gauguin's lines; STOP DOLLYING; pause.

CLOSER SHOT—GAUGUIN
His face is intense, his forehead damp, his eyes brilliant as he looks to her o.s.; now, less as an artist. He receives something from her, o.s., which causes him to get slowly and shyly, yet confidently, from his chair, and to advance.

CLOSE SHOT—TEHURA
Resume the SLOW DOLLYING IN, coming first INTO EYE CLOSEUP. Pause, then TILTING DOWNWARD TO MOUTH CLOSEUP. The mouth opens . . .

DISSOLVE

A BRIEF SERIES OF DISSOLVES AND MELTS
. . . in which, indirectly, we epitomize erotic and emotional release and through them, the release and clarifying of the senses and the creative faculties—and link these, further, to Gauguin's painting. These will be ultra-sensuous detail shots, almost orgiastically rich in form and color, of flowers, foliage, fruit, portions of faces and bodies of men, women and children; and of the most voluptuous of Gauguin's paintings of that period . . . in that order. We lead with perhaps five seconds of visual.

GAUGUIN'S VOICE (very quiet) Now that at last I had won my new wife, it was through her that I began to understand this Island and its mysteries. She opened for me a childlike world;—the perfect candor and courage of the senses. I began to know how to live—and how to paint.

INT. GAUGUIN'S HUT—CLOSE SHOT—GAUGUIN, WRITING—LAMPLIGHT

GAUGUIN'S VOICE She came into my life at the perfect hour.

He feels so happy and so moved that he gets up and, as we PAN, softly crosses to the bed, past a whole new array of his own paintings, dim but rich in the lamplight.

CLOSE PANNING TWO-SHOT—GAUGUIN AND TEHURA
Gauguin comes to the mosquito-netted bed and gazes down in deep happiness and gratitude. We PAN DOWN to Tehura, asleep, beyond the net—very powerful, both woman and child.

GAUGUIN'S VOICE (tender and grateful) I was permeated by her fragrance—Noa Noa.   FADE OUT

FADE IN
INSERT: THE OLD WOMAN
. . . in his painting, The Spirit of the Dead Watches. We start maximally close to her long white sinister eye.

GAUGUIN'S VOICE It was through Tehura, too, that I began to understand the *soul* of Tahiti.

PULL BACK to frame the old woman's profiled head.   DISSOLVE

EXT. TAHITI—MOVING SHOT THROUGH WOODS—NIGHT
The ominous, ghostly night—trees, whispering leaves, deep sound of surf o.s.

MOVING SHOT—GAUGUIN WALKING THROUGH DARK WOODS
He is awed but not frightened; then looks uneasy.

FULL SHOT—HIS DARK HUT
He walks away from us to the hut, carrying supplies. In above shots lead with visuals, then

GAUGUIN'S VOICE One day I had to go to Papeete for various supplies—we were out of light, for one thing. I was late getting home; long past midnight.

CLOSE PULL SHOT—GAUGUIN
Seeing the dark hut—uneasy—he speeds up, carrying his supplies.

CLOSE SHOT—GAUGUIN
Back-to-us, he opens the door and looks in; we DOLLY PAST HIM. The hut interior is pitch dark; only the vaguest outlines.

CLOSE SHOT—GAUGUIN
He feels the place is empty; and is badly worried.

GAUGUIN (softly) Tehura?
He is still more worried: is she *really* gone?

GAUGUIN (louder) Tehura?

No answer; only the continuing sound of surf o.s. Looking suddenly really agonized, he advances out of shot, striking a match   CUT TO

CLOSEUP SHOT—GAUGUIN

... as the match flares and, seeing her, he reacts with fright and shock.

CLOSE SHOT—TEHURA

She lies belly-down, diagonal on the bed, in the matchlight. We TIGHTEN THIS DOWNSHOT from her nude back, waist-up, to a head CLOSEUP. In this light her eyes, enlarged by fear, look phosphorescent, and deeply animal. She looks up at him but seems not to recognize him. She is tremendously beautiful; wholly different from ever before. We hear her stifled, terrified, animal breathing.

CLOSEUP SHOT—GAUGUIN

He is afraid to move, for fear of scaring her worse. As his match goes out we begin to hear a low moan from Tehura o.s.

CLOSE SHOT—TEHURA

We see only her gleaming eyes.

CLOSE SHOT—GAUGUIN

He gets a candle from his luggage and lights a match and the candle; and now, from her viewpoint, we see him clearer.

TEHURA (very strange o.s.) Paul?

Touched and scared, he stoops towards her into TWO-SHOT of Gauguin and Tehura. He takes her head gently between his hands, and gazes into her eyes.

GAUGUIN (gently) Tehura, child: it's only me; did you take me for a demon? A ghost? A Tupapau?

TEHURA (after pause) Never leave me again, so alone, without light.

DISSOLVE

DETAIL SHOT—TEHURA'S FACE—IN PAINTING

Much as we just saw it, but now in the painting, Spirit of the Dead watches. Gauguin's brush applies last touches. Then as Gauguin speaks we PULL BACK to frame the whole painting; then MOVE IN to frame the old woman and bear down on her white eye.

GAUGUIN'S VOICE Now that through Tehura's fear I came to the source —to the gods themselves—I became a full savage.

From the white eye,   DISSOLVE

BRIEF SERIES OF LAP DISSOLVES

... in, or near, pure black-and-white. We derive our apparitions from such mysterious monotypes as *Oviri* and *The Creation of the World*. The figures are more formless and mysterious than his pictures of them. They loom and threaten and vanish, luminous in absolute blue or black darkness. The mood we work for is abrupt and frightening; compact of the primordial, cryptic, and terrifying. Music o.s. (Using negatives might work well here.) We end with INTER-DISSOLVES of his monotypes and paintings, which figures in the foregoing have clearly suggested.

CLOSE SHOT—GAUGUIN, WORKING
There is new maturity, calm, and intensity in the face; he is far more deeply busy, sure and productive than before.

GAUGUIN'S VOICE Only now that I knew how to paint Tahiti, I began to realize how deeply I differed from a true "savage"; for now, I had time for nothing except work.

We PULL OUT AND AWAY into a FULL SHOT, showing other new paintings —genre, as well as cryptic and religious. We also see Tehura and Jotefa in b.g., loafing like nice but restive children. Gauguin works, oblivious of them. Silence. Then he stops work, struck for the moment, and steps back, looking at the painting, and working very hard in his head. Tehura and Jotefa glance at each other. Finally she speaks:

TEHURA Paul . . .

GAUGUIN (absently) Shut up.
He gets back to painting and looks only to that till further notice.

TEHURA Jotefa has come.

GAUGUIN Good morning, Jotefa.

JOTEFA Good morning, Monsieur Paul.

TEHURA (after pause) He has been here a long time, Paul.

GAUGUIN (working) Has he?

TEHURA He is thirsty.

GAUGUIN (vaguely) Well . . . (he forgets about them)

TEHURA Can we drink some rum?

GAUGUIN I thought you finished it.

TEHURA Almost . . . Paul . . .
He turns, annoyed.

GAUGUIN Well: what *is* it!

TEHURA May I buy more from the Chinaman?

GAUGUIN More what?

TEHURA Rum.

GAUGUIN So soon? No. I can't afford it.
He goes back to work and immediately forgets about them.

TWO-SHOT—TEHURA AND JOTEFA
They glance at each other, puzzled; likewise at him; again at each other. Tehura is clearly a little griped and bored. Between her and Jotefa we see liking; a world in common; a first glimmer of sexual interest.

DISSOLVE

TWO-SHOT—GAUGUIN AND TEHURA—INT. HUT—LATE AFTERNOON
In f.g., Tehura mopes, rolling a pandanus-leaf cigarette. In b.g. Gauguin, tired and satisfied, finishes cleaning brushes. Other new work of the period in b.g. Then he turns, and sees her sulking. A look of weary indulgence; then he comes to her. She pretends not to notice, but there is a spasm of sullenness. Pause, as she lights her cigarette.

GAUGUIN Tehura?
No answer.

GAUGUIN You are not happy?
She drags on her cigarette.

GAUGUIN What is it, child?
Silence; she smokes.

TEHURA You no longer like me.

GAUGUIN *Like* you? You know I— (he cuts it off)

TEHURA You no longer make me happy.
This is a kick in the belly. Pause.

GAUGUIN (quietly) I'm busy, Tehura. I'm *very* busy.

TEHURA You were not always so busy.

GAUGUIN But I am now. I know how dull it must be for you, but—I must work.

TEHURA Why?
He chews that one over, sad and sardonic, watching her tenderly.

DISSOLVE

INT. HUT—A RAINY DAY—TWO-SHOT—GAUGUIN AND JOTEFA
Since Gauguin is merely stretching a canvas, he is free to talk.

JOTEFA Why do you work so hard, Monsieur Paul?

GAUGUIN You work, too. We all work.

JOTEFA Enough to live; yes. But you: all of every day, waking to sleeping.

GAUGUIN I came here to work.

JOTEFA When I first knew you—

GAUGUIN I was finding how to do my work, then; now I *know* how.

JOTEFA But, Monsieur!
Gauguin looks enquiry. Jotefa struggles with a hard concept.

JOTEFA You—*like* us here. The way we live.
Gauguin nods.

JOTEFA And—you do not like your countrymen. Or the way *they* live.

GAUGUIN (amused) No.

JOTEFA But when you work, you work harder even than any Frenchman. Harder even than the Chinese.
Gauguin smiles, sardonic.

JOTEFA If *I* work hard, I am not *happy*. If I would work so hard as you, I would be so unhappy—I think I would wish to die.
Gauguin leaves his work and sits down beside Jotefa.

GAUGUIN Look here, Jotefa: I have just two hundred francs left in the world.

JOTEFA Two hundred francs? You are a rich man, Monsieur Paul!

TEHURA'S VOICE Two hundred francs!
They glance over.

CLOSE SHOT—TEHURA
She lies on the bed, bored and griped and beautiful.

TEHURA No rum; no absinthe; not even good food from the Chinaman. (she sniffs contemptuously)

GROUP SHOT—NEW ANGLE—TEHURA IN B.G.

GAUGUIN We can't afford it any more, Tehura; not until more money comes from France.

TEHURA (contemptuous) Can't *afford* it!

JOTEFA (with authority) Be quiet, Tehura. (On Gauguin's startled reaction, as he realizes the intimacy the bossing infers, Jotefa is a bit embarrassed.) Forgive me, Monsieur. (Gauguin nods, a little hurt, but amused. Jotefa tells him, very reasonably) Money is not needed, Monsieur Paul, except for—drinks, tobacco, the pleasures. For food? The sea is full of it. The mountains. The trees.

GAUGUIN But if I work to get my food, Jotefa, there is no time for my own work. That's why I must have money.

JOTEFA (with perfect generosity) I will get food, for all of us.

GAUGUIN (with kindly, perfect understanding) You would *mean* to, my dear friend; but I know you: to get even your own food, is quite enough work for you. As you said, hard work makes you unhappy. Jotefa thinks it over, realizes it; his smile of admission is so charming that Gauguin smiles too.

GAUGUIN In fact, I'm not a Tahitian, as I wish I could be: I have too much work to do.

Silence. Jotefa ponders deeply and sympathetically.

JOTEFA It is such a pity, Monsieur Paul. I wish that you could be happy.

GAUGUIN I am always happy when I work well.

JOTEFA No, Monsieur; you frown so. You worry. What could make you happy.
Gauguin seriously reflects a moment, then, with deep irony:

GAUGUIN Money.
Gauguin smiles bitterly as he reflects on this ineluctable fact; Jotefa watches him with gentle concern and interest.

GAUGUIN'S VOICE There came a time, though, when I took a day off from my own work to join in work of a more popular kind . . .

FADE OUT

FADE IN
EXT. BY THE SHORE—NATIVES WORK AROUND TWO LARGE CANOES—FULL PANNING SHOT—NATIVES AND CANOES—DAYBREAK
Two men test lines and hooks. Two women cross to canoes with a tub of live bait. As we center canoe prows the Canoe-master and others lash them together. We PAN ON GAUGUIN, keenly interested.

PANNING SHOT—NEW ANGLE
Gauguin helps launch the lashed canoes. After they lunge past us into
the water we see Tehura and Jotefa among those who stay ashore,
smiling and waving.

MED. SHOT—THE CANOES
Gauguin, as he gets aboard, smiles and waves like the others. Then like
them mans an oar (or paddle: CK). O.s. we hear the loud crowing of
a rooster. In unison the men dig in their first stroke, setting the canoes
in motion. On next beat of oars,   CUT TO

MOVING SHOT—FROM CANOES
We look back, from the prow, at the people on the dwindling shore,
in brightening light. On the next beat,

GROUP SHOT—CENTERING ON GAUGUIN
He works with pleasure; he looks down into water. Next beat:

MOVING VERTICAL SHOT—THE WATER
The fantastically colored corals and sea-plants and small fish at the
bottom of the lagoon. Next beat:

FULLSHOT—THE SHORE—OVER CANOES
(NOTE: the beat of oars, when not seen, will be heard, o.s.: and in this
early stage, is leisurely.) The shore dwindles; light is brighter; people
straggle away. On next beat we TILT DOWN and glimpse the fanged
dangerous reefs as we pass through narrowly. On next beat,
                                                                   CUT TO

FULL SHOT—ALONGSIDE THE CANOES
As they pass they are lifted and then let down on the long, low swell
of the open sea. Next beat:

FULL SHOT—GAUGUIN AT WORK
among a long rank of oarsmen—there are eleven to each canoe. Amused,
he watches something they are passing—o.s. Next beat:

MED. MOVING SHOT—A SEA TURTLE
Huge and ancient, body lolling, head above water, he turns his head
watching them as they pass, with sound, o.s. Next beat:

FULL SHOT—THE CANOE—GAUGUIN'S VIEWPOINT
For three beats we watch, from his viewpoint, the "Homeric" quality
of the oarsmen; and the gear, all ship-shape—the hooks, the cleanly
coiled lines, the long rod and its leverage arrangement. A fresh breeze
stirs all light and loose things. Cries of sea-birds begin o.s.

MED. SHOT—CENTERING GAUGUIN

. . . in quiet and happy reaction to this. TWO BEATS: cries of sea-birds louden o.s. and Gauguin glances toward the sound.

MOVING FULL—THE "TUNA-HOLE"

Medium distant, ahead and to the side, many birds hover and cry out; some dive like plummets, and emerge with strips of flesh. Canoe sounds o.s.

MED. SHOT—GAUGUIN

. . . with a gesture of his head towards the birds.

GAUGUIN There must be many fish *there.*
Others hear; the Master of the canoe replies:

MASTER (nodding) That, we call the "tuna-hole". The sea is very deep there. But we cannot fish there.

FULL MOVING SHOT—THE HOLE

We are nearer, passing it broadside. The birds are very clamorous.

MED. SHOT—CENTERING GAUGUIN

GAUGUIN Why not?

MASTER (gravely) Because that is the dwelling place of Ruoa Hatou; the God of the Sea.

Gauguin reacts to this, and looks again to the hole.

FULL MOVING SHOT—THE HOLE AND THE BIRDS

They list off behind us, now; quiet sea between; the bird cries are distant.

MASTER (o.s., after pause; quietly) Now.

CLOSE FLASH CUT—GAUGUIN

Alert and interested in everything.

FULL SHOT—BOTH CANOES

In unison, every man in both canoes stops paddling, and ships his paddle; the canoes swerve gently, bringing in the magnificent peak of Morea, luminous blue in the distance. There is a sudden deep stillness over everything; including the faces of the fishermen.

INSERT: THE BAIT-TANK

We glimpse the crowded live-bait, all swimming circular in the same direction like a nervous galaxy; then a strong brown hand reaches in and selects and seizes a fish. PAN or   CUT TO

INSERT: A HOOK
The living bait is affixed to this vicious hook. TILT UP or

CUT TO

FULL SHOT—THE ROD
Two men thrust the very long rod far out past the prow; we see that by means of two lines, at the butt, it can be abruptly raised. (same action in second canoe in b.g.) The canoe's Master nods to a fisherman; he casts out the baited hook. As it hits water we   CUT TO

CLOSER SHOT (FREE OF THE CANOES)—THE ROD AND LINE HANG QUIET

GROUP SHOT—FACES, INCLUDING GAUGUIN'S
. . . they watch and wait.

CLOSER SHOT—ROD AND LINE
After a still moment, a strike; the rod bends deep.

CLOSE SHOT—TWO MEN
. . . pull with full strength on the lines which control the rod.

CLOSER SHOT—THE TUNA
. . . surfaces under the bending rod; he is a big one; a shark dives for him and rends him. INTERCUT as need be with men in boat and with Gauguin's reactions as they struggle for the fish. When they bring it in, only the head is left on the hook.

GROUP SHOT—INCLUDING GAUGUIN AND MASTER
The Master nods to Gauguin.

MASTER Now you.
A man hands Gauguin the baited hook and he stands up into:

CLOSE SHOT—GAUGUIN
. . . and feeling his mettle, makes a strong cast.

MED. WATER SHOT—ROD AND LINE
as the bait hits the water and sinks.

CLOSE SHOT—GAUGUIN
All his interest and ego are focused. By his sudden reaction we know of a strike.

CLOSE AND MED. SHOT—MEN AND THE FISH
. . . as, Gauguin helping with all his strength, they bring in a magnificent tuna. As a man clubs it on the head we see, in a CLOSE SHOT, that it is hooked in the lower jaw; then TILT to show its whole length and splendor as it quivers, dying, in the bottom of the canoe.

CLOSE SHOT—GAUGUIN
Looking down at it with a sportsman's pride. We hear laughter and whispering o.s. and Gauguin glances to his companions, mildly perplexed.

FULL SHOT—HIS VIEWPOINT
Men snicker and whisper ad lib, looking to Gauguin; no meanness in it, but real amusement.

CLOSE SHOT—GAUGUIN
The uncertain smile of one who doesn't get the laugh but realizes it may be on him.

THE MASTER'S VOICE (o.s.) Again, Monsieur.
Gauguin glances down surprised and pleased.

CLOSE DOWNSHOT—THE MASTER NODS
Past him, the newly baited hook is handed to Gauguin who, AS WE TILT UP, casts again.

FULL SHOT—THE MEN
They watch Gauguin and the line, silent and intent.

CLOSE WATER SHOT—A HARD STRIKE

CLOSE SHOT—GAUGUIN
He reacts to this big strike with fierce joy and pride.

CLOSE SHOT—THE FISH
. . . as they get its head up alongside the gunwale; he too is hooked in the lower jaw; a burst of loud laughter o.s.

FLASH CUT—THE MASTER
A look of polite concern. Laughter continues o.s. but also sounds of pleasure and congratulation ad lib.

GROUP SHOT—GAUGUIN IS CENTERED
. . . as they congratulate him ad lib.

MASTER (smiling) You bring us good luck, Monsieur.

FISHERMAN (frivolously noisy) O yes! Monsieur is a lucky man!

ANOTHER FISHERMAN A *very* lucky man!
But the laughter and whispering persist, and Gauguin is puzzled.

DISSOLVE

LATE AFTERNOON LANDSCAPE—TILT CAMERA DOWN TO ROUGHLY SAME GROUP SHOT
favoring Gauguin and young fisherman. The line is coiled, rods are stowed, bait is dumped. Gauguin still puzzled. After a moment he touches young fisherman's arm.

GAUGUIN (quietly) Why am I a "lucky man"?

YOUNG FISHERMAN (reluctant) . . . It was the fish. (embarrassed; regretful) *Both* fish, Monsieur.

The others, politely dead-pan, are listening sharply.

YOUNG FISHERMAN (delicately) Forgive me, Monsieur.
He leans close to Gauguin as we   CUT TO

CLOSE SHOT—GAUGUIN AND YOUNG MAN

YOUNG MAN (quietly) If the fish is caught with the hook in the lower jaw—and both yours were, Monsieur—it means that—I am so sorry, Monsieur—that the *vahina* is unfaithful while her *tane* is away.

Gauguin looks at him, amused. The youth feels lousy.

YOUNG MAN (miserably) Forgive me, Monsieur.
Gauguin smiles incredulously; yet it worms at him a little. Now o.s. a command from the Master, ad lib, in native tongue; and a second of great stirring in the canoes.

YOUNG MAN (quick and quiet) Now we must make haste, Monsieur; for unless we cross the reef before dark, we are in great danger.

He sits down in his own place and picks up his paddle.

FULL SHOT—THE TWO CANOES
In the late light, twenty-two oars are readied in unison at the same angle and, at an ad lib cry, are dug into the water; the canoes are turned, and begin to move homeward.

CLOSE GROUP SHOT—FAVORING GAUGUIN
Like the others he digs hard and fast. Someone begins an ancient native rowing-song and the others—except Gauguin—pick it up. During the singing we INTERCUT:

FULL AND CLOSE AND GROUP SHOTS
. . . as may best be shot at the time, TO POINT UP:
1) The race against darkness, to the reef:
2) The timeless beauty, power and unself-consciousness in all that we see and that which is being done.
3) Gauguin's reactions.

NEAR THE REEF, we clamp down with all that can best convey life and death race with darkness; suspense; and skill in crossing the reef. By now, no singing, natural, sound ad lib.

AFTER CROSSING REEF we move, as near as possible in one shot from the prow, triumphantly up to shore, on which some people run, shouting, with great torches; others just sit.

DUSK OR DARK—FULL SHOT—BEACHING THE CANOES
... in the fierce torchlight the men leap overside and, while their craft still has momentum, beach her with all their strength and, as we PAN, hurry to the shore people, who hurry to them ... among them, Gauguin and Tehura. Din of ad lib voices o.s., and in b.g., some are already unloading the catch.

CLOSE TWO-SHOT—GAUGUIN AND TEHURA
... as they meet. She greets him with such special warmth that he becomes really suspicious.

CLOSE SHOT—GAUGUIN
He smiles, but is rather cool in returning her greeting.

CLOSE SHOT—TEHURA
She wonders what's wrong. He walks past her and puzzled, she follows.

CLOSE GROUP SHOT—CENTERING GAUGUIN AND TEHURA
They stand in line. She watches him; he watches the fish.

GROUP SHOT—NEW ANGLE
The whole catch is laid out on the ground in torchlight; the Master is dividing the catch and people walk away with big chunks. Gauguin and Tehura move next in line.

CLOSE SHOT—GAUGUIN
His eye catches that of Jotefa o.s.

MED. SHOT—JOTEFA—AMID A GROUP
Jotefa smiles charmingly and gestures greeting.

CLOSE TWO-SHOT—GAUGUIN AND TEHURA
Gauguin returns the gesture, sad and suspicious. The Master's hand holds up a big chunk of fish to him. Gauguin is unaware at first, then rather absently takes it, and they start for home, Tehura watching him closely.   DISSOLVE

INT. HUT—NIGHT—CLOSE TWO SHOT—GAUGUIN AND TEHURA
She is eating her fish raw; his is cooked. They are silent. He does not look at her. She steals a glance at him; he turns; their eyes meet; silent, smiling a little, he stares her down; then looks away and goes on eating.
                                                              DISSOLVE

INT. HUT—NIGHT

Lamplight at first; then moon only. CAMERA PANS as Tehura sits on the edge of their bed in HEAD CLOSEUP, watching Gauguin o.s. We can hear him moving about. We PAN him in losing her, at far side of room as he comes to his table, back to us. He lights a cigarette and reaches for a notebook.

CLOSE SHOT—GAUGUIN

He stands at his table by the lamp, glances at the top notebook—For Aline—and with a little constriction of the jaws, puts it aside; then opens the next book, flat on his table; a sad and complex smile. Tehura watches in b.g.

INSERT—TITLE PAGE OF "NOA NOA"

He leafs through his book a bit, lingers with the last page of writing, then riffles blank pages.

CLOSE SHOT—GAUGUIN

Sad and bitter, shuts the book, kills his cigarette, blows out the lamp and, in moonlight walks towards Tehura.

CLOSE PANNING TWO-SHOT OF GAUGUIN AND TEHURA

We PAN HIM IN CLOSE to bed. She is very still. He sits beside her, then looks hard into her eyes.

GAUGUIN (quietly) Have you been sensible?

TEHURA (very quietly) Yes.

GAUGUIN (quietly) And your lover today; was he to your liking?

TEHURA (as before) I have no lover.

GAUGUIN (as before) You lie. The fish has spoken.

As Tehura raises her head and straightens her back,   CUT TO

CLOSE SHOT—TEHURA

An extraordinary look of mystery and grandeur. She stands up very slowly.

TWO-SHOT—GAUGUIN AND TEHURA

Both stand up into it; he looks awed.

HEAD CLOSEUP—TEHURA

She seems on the verge of inexpressible speech.

HEAD CLOSEUP—GAUGUIN

Awe deepening, his eyes follow her o.s. . . . (Directing note: "I felt," he writes, "that something sublime had risen between us.").

PANNING SHOT—TEHURA

She walks to the door, with great dignity; closes it; walks to center of room; pauses as if in deep prayer; then, eyes to Gauguin's o.s., walks into a CLOSE SHOT and on, as we PAN, into a CLOSE TWO-SHOT. Her eyes are full of tears.

TEHURA (quiet and pure) You must strike me.

Her beauty and words impale and astound Gauguin.

TEHURA You must strike me many, many times; otherwise you will be angry for a long time and you will become ill.

Gauguin is profoundly moved. She looks up into his eyes and suddenly and passionately he kisses her. The kiss and emotion become deeper as we start   A VERY SLOW DISSOLVE

INT.—PARIS—MONFRIED'S STUDIO—NIGHT

THE ABOVE TWO-SHOT IN TAHITI BEGINS TO GO STRANGELY GRAY. THE COLORS GO INTO A VAGUE PASTEL SHADE. MEANWHILE:

IMAGE GROWS BEHIND IT PRINTED AT FIRST VERY DARK THEN FADES GRADUALLY LIGHTER. IT IS A CLOSE DOWNSHOT—GAUGUIN three years older, NOW IN PARIS. His head lowered as he reads; we see mostly his forehead. Gauguin's head is so close that IT COVERS BOTH OUTFADING HEADS IN TWO-SHOT OF TEHURA AND GAUGUIN.

NOW THE TWO-SHOT DIES OUT AS CLOSE SHOT IS IN FULL DOLLY BACK SLIGHTLY

He is seated reading in an older voice aloud from his *Noa Noa.*

GAUGUIN And now that I love without suspicion, I murmur these words of Buddha: "By kindness you must conquer anger: by goodness, evil; and by the truth, lies."

Pause. WE TIGHTEN A LITTLE:

GAUGUIN That night was more miraculous than any of the others; and the day rose radiant.

He now remembers vividly and with emotion.   LAP DISSOLVE

INT. GAUGUIN'S HUT—MORNING—CLOSE TWO-SHOT—GAUGUIN AND TEHURA

(NOTE: This shot is printed very light.)

They look up smiling to Jotefa o.s. They are at breakfast; glowing; happy as clams. We PAN TO Jotefa, the open door, carrying ripe fruit; he enters and we PAN HIM INTO CLOSE GROUP SHOT as he presents his fruit and sits down with them.

GAUGUIN'S VOICE (o.s.) Early in the morning, Jotefa came to see us. He said to me, "You went fishing yesterday. Did everything go well?"

Jotefa says it, silent, under Gauguin's Voice. Gauguin speaks (silent too) under his own, older voice, looking straight at Jotefa, smiling.

GAUGUIN'S VOICE I replied: "I hope to go soon again."
Jotefa glances at Tehura; blithe and charming. She returns his smile as Gauguin watches, purely with love; she looks to Gauguin, smiling; his love increases. They all thoroughly understand and are fond of each other.

LAP DISSOLVE

CLOSE SHOT—GAUGUIN IN MONFRIED'S STUDIO—PARIS
He sits quiet now, eyes unfocused, remembering, smiling. The 3-shot slowly dies. He shuts his MS. as we PULL OUT TO

FULL GROUP SHOT—IN A POOR MAN'S STUDIO
Gauguin, Monfried, Charles Morice, Anna, Strindberg. They all watch Gauguin. Silence.

STRINDBERG But—*were* they lovers?

GAUGUIN (shrugging) How do *I* know. I out*grew jeal*ousy . . .
A rather interested silent reaction; just a stirring and exchange of glances.

MONFRIED You continued to live with her.
Gauguin nods.

GAUGUIN O yes; in fact we have a child. (grin) O, he's *mine*—(he touches his large nose)

ANNA You left them.

CLOSE SHOT—GAUGUIN

GAUGUIN My dear Mademoiselle Anna; on Tahiti there are thousands of loving and willing foster-parents. Is that not true in Java?

CLOSE SHOT—ANNA

ANNA (with dignity) I am a mulatto, Monsieur.

CLOSE SHOT—MONFRIED

MONFRIED (quickly) You wrote no more, Paul?

CLOSE SHOT—GAUGUIN

GAUGUIN (ironically) Only a page or two, to explain that . . . "imperative *family* matters called me back to France."

CLOSE SHOT—MORICE

MORICE Why didn't you write more, Paul?

CLOSE SHOT—GAUGUIN

GAUGUIN For the next year, Charles, I was much too busy painting and much too hungry.

CLOSE SHOT—MORICE

MORICE I want to explain, Paul, about that money . . .

CLOSER SHOT—GAUGUIN

GAUGUIN (with increasing poisonous bitterness) It's a bit late in the day for that, don't you think? Do you know what I lived on, most of that second year? Breadfruit and tea; and the alcohol I cadged in the barrooms of Papeete. Do you know what happened to me, late in that year? I began to vomit blood. Too much strain on the heart, the Doctor thought—too much work, with too little food.

TWO SHOT—MORICE AND MONFRIED
Monfried looks shocked; Morice just looks sick.

MONFRIED (aghast) *No,* Paul!

CLOSE SHOT—GAUGUIN

GAUGUIN *Yes,* Daniel. However don't *you* feel badly; you did everything for me *you* could.
An icy glance at Morice; then the glance softens.

TWO SHOT—MORICE AND MONFRIED
Morice is *really* wretched by now.

CLOSE SHOT—GAUGUIN

GAUGUIN (genuine kindness) As for you, Charles, forget it. It's worked out all right; after all, rich uncles don't die *every* day.

CLOSE TWO-SHOT—ANNA AND STRINDBERG

ANNA Rich uncles?
Strindberg shoots her a glance full of poisonous irony.

GAUGUIN'S VOICE (o.s.) As a playwright, you'll appreciate it, Monsieur Strindberg . . .

CLOSE SHOT—GAUGUIN
He parodies cheap theatrical style.

GAUGUIN . . . it's like the sleaziest kind of melodrama. I arrive in Paris, penniless, a pariah, to find that a rich relative has left me 13,000 francs.

FLASH CUT—STRINDBERG
He claps his hands and laughs.

CLOSE TWO-SHOT—ANNA AND STRINDBERG

ANNA (sharply interested) Why did you return to Paris, Monsieur? Strindberg knows her kind.

GROUP SHOT—FAVORING GAUGUIN

GAUGUIN (sardonic) I was starving, Mademoiselle.

ANNA Do you plan to return to the islands?

GAUGUIN I have no plans whatever, Mademoiselle: beyond the exhibition of my paintings.

MORICE (aglow) *That's* going to change your plans—*permanently!*

CLOSE SHOT—GAUGUIN

GAUGUIN (ironic) You think so?

CLOSE SHOT—MORICE

MORICE *I know*. You've never done such work before. Nobody has.

CLOSE SHOT—GAUGUIN

GAUGUIN (quietly) That's why I have no hope of this show.

CLOSE SHOT—MONFRIED

MONFRIED I think you're right, Paul. Good work sometimes sells; but not if it seems to come from another planet.

MORICE'S VOICE (o.s.) You're *both* mistaken. I *know* you are!

CLOSE SHOT—MORICE

MORICE Forgive me, but I know Paris.

CLOSE SHOT—GAUGUIN
We DOLLY VERY SLOWLY IN ON HIM, as he listens and begins to catch fire—though his look is one of bitter contempt which we may suppose is for Morice.

MORICE'S VOICE (o.s.) Paris is worn-out with fads. Paris wants something *new* to go daft about. Paris won't like it for the right reasons. But

Paris will gobble it up. The morning after your show opens, you'll have all Paris at your feet!

CLOSE SHOT—MONFRIED
Monfried watches Gauguin quietly; concerned.

MONFRIED Do you care, Paul? Those silly swine?

CLOSE SHOT—GAUGUIN
Pause. Then he speaks quietly, looking at no one, with mounting intensity, bitterly.

GAUGUIN *Care?* I care *this* much: I've given up a great deal for my work; and I've worked under—difficulties. Now, I'm going to show this work. Fame, and money: let's say they'd—facilitate my work. Fame, and money: my life in order. My family again. And I make idiots of those who think *I'm* one. I think I'd like a bit of fame and money for their *own* sweet sakes: after all, I've got them coming to me. As for those "silly swine," nothing would delight me more than to see them "at my feet." (casual; throwing it away) No, Daniel; if my show's a success, I think somehow I'll be able to endure it. (with fearful bitterness) Why do you suppose I came back!

SIDE DOLLYING SHOT—THE GROUP
They are shocked; he hardly seems sane.

MONFRIED (quietly) My dear friend, you came back out of poverty, and desperation, with two years' magnificent work. That's all. I implore you: Don't forget: Your show may fail.

WE PAN ALONG TO GAUGUIN, INTO CLOSEUP. Pause.

GAUGUIN (hateful, irony) You think so? (with burning, bitter arrogance) We'll see.   DISSOLVE

PANNING SHOT—MUSIC UNDER
(a light-scored conflicting of French and Tahitian motifs.)

We PAN ACROSS a corner of the dark studio, and past a window to a couch where Gauguin lies asleep. En route we glimpse his ratty luggage, some Tahitian curios, and, through a window, the sleeping glow of Paris. We DOLLY IN on Gauguin whose dreaming face works a little; than a
                                              SLOW, WELTERING DISSOLVE

CLOSE DOWNSHOT—THE SURFACE OF CALM SEA-WATER
Music throughout. To be shot in tank and lagoon.

Fully to detail the shots for this sequence would type out deceptively long, so the action—which involves a maximum 40 seconds—is only outlined here.

Gauguin stands, proud and uneasy, in a Tahitian canoe. The Canoe-Master (from fishing sequence) tells him: "You may dive only once." Looking about him, Gauguin meets the eyes of others in the canoe: fine native types; then Mette, Aline, Vincent. All, looking at him, politely doubt his competence. With an air of bravely facing the ultimate he draws a deep breath and dives.

We follow him down to a sea-floor so deep it is semidark in crystal water, and among the strange and marvelously colored sea-plants and corals he searches out shell-fish, for their pearls. He opens the first two with a knife and puts the pearls in his mouth. Thenceforth he is too short of breath to open the shells; he just cuts them loose and tucks them into his *pareu* —which he wears almost as a G-string. Suffering for air, he sights still more shells. We intensify to maximum the conflict between lack of air, exertion, and greed for more pearls. Carrying all the shells he can in each hand, plus his knife, and half-asphyxiated, he stands upright, settles his feet against knife-edged coral, and with all his strength springs upward, his cut feet trailing blood. We milk the ascent for maximal suffering and will-he-make-it, especially during the last few feet. Our last shot plunges upward rapidly from below-surface and as camera bursts through we

CUT TO

INT.—THE DURAND–RUEL GALLERY—PARIS—DAY—PAN AND TRACK SHOT—GALLERY-GOERS

Fashionable Parisians enter the Gallery through a sumptuous door and disperse as we PAN across-corner to wall, picking up a Gauguin painting, beyond other gallery-goers. We DOLLY IN through their sauntering and past a Fashionable Couple, facing away from us, examining the painting; and we frame the painting itself.

Over this shot, from the instant of the Cut, we hear two sounds: the genteel babble of a gallery crowd; and the terrible, agonized breathing of the diver. Both sounds are replaced by music as we frame the painting; into which we continue moving closer and   DISSOLVE

SERIES OF LAP DISSOLVES—PAINTING AFTER PAINTING

... some we have glimpsed before, or uncompleted; others are new to us. In this scene and the scenes following we epitomize two years of inspired work.

CLOSE SHOT—GALLERY-GOERS

Now the Camera stands still at average head-height and, in series, people pass us, looking almost at the lens, as at a painting, in the same beat as we set up in the track shot of the paintings. (Other gallery-goers buzz and glance about them and greet each other and move around in b.g.) Now one person fills our closeup; now a couple; again (and at most) three people; and a couple of times the superficial wash over a lingerer, like water over a stone. Some are courteous and a very few are appreciative, but our general average is a horrifying contrast with the quality of the paintings. We don't caricature; the effect is merely to hold up fashionable Paris against this man's work.

IN ROUGH SERIES

THE FASHIONABLE COUPLE seen FROM FRONT. The expression is one of bewilderment. The woman starts twittering. The man looks pained; then an indulgent little smile. Taking her elbow, he leads her along.

AN OLD GENTLEMAN (similar to Cocteau's wicked drawing of "THE PUBLIC," which he epitomizes as a mustached baldhead) is a very correct wholly stumped old bourgeois doing his damndest to look polite and to "understand" and "enjoy." He looks merely, rather constipated. He stands low in our frame and glances at his program; tries again; shakes his head and is supplanted by:

A TWEEDED ENGLISH GOVERNESS AND A JEUNE FILLE BIEN ELEVEE
The governess begins with an Open Mind; the girl, with startlement. Then the governess starts glaring at the girl who looks interested. The student would like to linger but meekly obeys her boss.

DEGAS, not yet identified, lifts his tinted spectacles visor-like from his weak eyes and peers intently here and there over the painting, with keen interest and growing recognition. As Degas stands there . . .

TWO EPICENE YOUNG MEN, taller than he come in behind him, extreme sophisticates who respect everything and can see nothing. A quick once-over and they exchange a glance of utter disdain; then one points out Degas, whom they interestedly recognize with his chin. Both take on gestures of, "Mercy how can he be interested!" One gestures with a toss of head. They exit . . . Degas is pleased and exits as . . .

TWO ACADEMICIANS—elderly, whiskered, well-to-do men, with ribbons or rosettes, etc., as research may justify. They take one good hard look with open faces; then one scowls with real anger and disgust, while the other looks "sad" and "hurt."

In the b.g. Morice and Monfried stroll, looking worried. We PAN PAST the Academicians and DOLLY IN CLOSE to a critic. Critic jots in his notebook with a tight, mean little smile, as he overhears . . .

GAUGUIN'S VOICE (smooth o.s.) Monsieur, I would say rather that the critics are like bats.

We CONTINUE PAN LOSING CRITIC AND CENTERING ON GAUGUIN, amid a group, now in MEDIUM SHOT. We DOLLY SLOWLY TOWARDS HIM as Degas enters the shot, strolling towards Gauguin. We PAUSE, behind Degas, at edge of group. Gauguin continues the above without a break. He is rigidly self-possessed and smiling.

GAUGUIN Throw them a handkerchief full of sand and they will rush for it.

MAN I find more *drama* in your work than painting, Monsieur; there's a wonderful opera to be made out of Tahiti. You should be a dramatist.

GAUGUIN (polite) You ask me to exchange a great art for a lesser one, Monsieur.

WOMAN How can you paint such *ugliness?*

GAUGUIN (polite) The ugly can be beautiful, Madame; the pretty, never.

MAN But—it isn't real. It doesn't exist.

GAUGUIN Yes, it exists, Monsieur; when one must express the grandeur and mystery of Tahiti on a canvas of one square metre. That's the reason for these fabulous colors, and for making my air fiery and yet softened . . .

WOMAN I can understand Puvis de Chavannes, but . . .

GAUGUIN (interrupting) Of course, Madame, I *quite* understand. You see, Puvis *explains* his idea, but he does not *paint* it. He is a Greek; I am a Savage. Puvis will call a picture Purity, and in order to explain it, he will paint a young virgin with a lily in her hand. To represent purity, I would paint a landscape with limpid waters, without any taint of civilization. (gently) But I don't expect civilized ladies to understand.

After each of these exchanges, the interlocutor leaves in something of a huff. We MOVE IN TO CLOSE TWO SHOT. Now Gauguin, his smile smooth and desperate, his eyes hard and brilliant, looks around for the next comer.
CLOSE TWO-SHOT—GAUGUIN AND DEGAS

DEGAS (quietly) Monsieur Gauguin.

GAUGUIN (ready for the worst) Monsieur Degas.
They shake hands.

DEGAS You have arrived, Gauguin.
Gauguin does a bitterly sardonic little take.

DEGAS Not with the public; but with yourself.

Gauguin, profoundly moved and gratified, presses the hand warmly and drops it.

GAUGUIN Thank you, Monsieur.

Monfried and Morice come up.

GAUGUIN (a grim smile) Thanks, my friends. I wish you were crutches . . . After today I know how the Indian feels, who smiles as he is burned at the stake. (he looks about) Just a moment. (he calls out) Monsieur Degas!

FULL SHOT—REVERSE ANGLE

The gallery is emptying; Degas, in distance, about to go, turns startled, and waits. Many watch curiously as Gauguin all but trots to the wall, takes from it a richly-sculptured cane, and hurries toward Degas and into a:

CLOSE TWO-SHOT—GAUGUIN AND DEGAS

Gauguin comes up, a little out of breath.

GAUGUIN Monsieur Degas; you have forgotten your cane.

He offers it, and Degas, as touched and deeply pleased, accepts it as their eyes meet in fraternity and understanding.   DISSOLVE

EXT. A SIDEWALK CAFE—DAY—PULL SHOT—A GROUP AT A TABLE

We PULL AWAY from Morice who reads from a newspaper, to GROUP SHOT:

Gauguin, Monfried, Anna, Strindberg; all are dejected; Gauguin is shattered, and tight.

MORICE (reading) ". . . landscapes treated in an intentionally clumsy, almost wild manner."

GAUGUIN That's what's called an *intelligent* critic; he knows art is *intentional*.

He drinks; Morice reads from another paper.

MORICE (reading) "Your children will amuse themselves before the colored images of four-handed females, human apes, stretched out on a billiard cloth, under a shower of exotic words."

GAUGUIN That's an even greater critic; he's *clever*.

He snaps his fingers, a waiter comes, he gestures for drinks.

GAUGUIN I'm a great *commercial* success, too.

MORICE At least you have the 13,000 francs—and a little more, from what you sold.

GAUGUIN Ah yes; every artist should manage to kill off an uncle every six months.

MONFRIED It's security, Paul; be thankful.
Gauguin looks contemptuous.

MORICE (excited) It's better than that: it's your trump card.
Gauguin looks interested enquiry at Morice and Monfried.

MORICE (intense) Rent a fashionable studio. Get a bizarre mistress. Set yourself up as a sensation—an outrage. Throw big parties. You know these idiots: they'll come running, to see the circus—and to buy from you.

GAUGUIN (a bitter smile) Show them what I *really* think of them, eh?
Anna looks interested, Strindberg watches her and Gauguin.

MONFRIED Do you *want* that kind of buyer, Paul?

GAUGUIN I want *any* kind.

MONFRIED *Save* your money.

GAUGUIN Since when have I played safe?

MONFRIED You could even—rejoin your family.

HEAD CLOSEUP—GAUGUIN

GAUGUIN (ferociously bitter) O yes, always *at a price*: the usual price of bourgeois domestic bliss. No thanks. I'll support my family as an artist, or not at all. Meanwhile, I think your advice is excellent, Charles. If they can't understand art, they can surely understand vulgarity.

PANNING CLOSE SHOT—GROUP
In order: Monfried, Gauguin, Morice, Strindberg, Anna.

MONFRIED Paul, you know better; art isn't showmanship.

GAUGUIN Daniel, *you* know better. I'm not an artist. I'm a showman. I'll bring them to me; I don't care how.

Morice looks pleased; Anna looks avid; Strindberg watches her sharply and bitterly; we PAN BACK to Anna, wetting her lips.   DISSOLVE

DOWNSHOT—A STAIRWAY—DAY
Monfried comes up into a CLOSE SHOT and, as we PAN, knocks on a door, on whose glass panel Gauguin has done a sexy painting.

MAN'S VOICE (o.s.) Don't bother us. The rent is paid.
He knocks again. Pause. The door is opened by a venomous young man—

the ultimate criminal pseudo-artist. Past him we glimpse part of an anteroom crowded by a bed, and a segment of Gauguin's bright yellow studio.

MONFRIED I would like to see Monsieur Gauguin.

YOUNG MAN Who are you?

MONFRIED A friend of his, Are you?

YOUNG MAN As a friend of his, you must know that he is away for the summer.

MONFRIED I haven't heard from him in some time.

YOUNG MAN (insolent) Oh?

ANOTHER MAN'S VOICE (o.s.) Who is it, Claude?

YOUNG MAN Someone looking for Paul.

VOICE Paul's in Brittany for the summer.

YOUNG MAN Shut up, you fool. (a nasty smile) Well, Monsieur . . .
He starts to close the door. Monfried blocks it, with foot and shoulder. A virulent look from the young man.

MONFRIED What are you doing here?

YOUNG MAN What business is that of yours?

MONFRIED M. Gauguin is my friend.

YOUNG MAN M. Gauguin is my patron.
Another young man appears—as silly as the first is vicious.

MONFRIED (with irony) Is he your "patron" too?

2ND MAN Paul? Of course.

MONFRIED (to both) Why?

BOTH (sniffily) Monsieur, I am an artist.
Monfried laughs in their faces. Both look dangerous. He doesn't even bother to put up his guard. He waits; they subside.

MONFRIED (quietly) Get out.
Both look at him, very still.

MONFRIED Give me your keys and get out.
One, with hating eyes, gives a little *rire jaune,* the other wets his lips. The First Man speaks to someone o.s.

YOUNG MAN Put your clothes on.

DOWNSHOT—NEW ANGLE—THROUGH DOOR AND OVER THEM ALL
A sluttish girl, naked, half-covering herself in pseudo-modesty with the
bedclothes, reaches for a chemise and looks up at us with hatred.

DISSOLVE

CLOSE SHOT—A VILLAGE WOMAN
Elderly, rugged, she wears Breton headgear. She turns, gaping, to look
after someone. Her wonder becomes disapproval. Shrill voices of children
o.s. Other starers in b.g.

FULL SHOT—REVERSE ANGLE
Medium distant, Gauguin, Anna, an Artist, and a Monkey, promenade
away from us. All who meet them turn and gawk. Children follow,
fascinated.

FULL SHOT—GAUGUIN AND COMPANY
Full length, they come towards us, gaining slowly into maximal:

GROUP CLOSEUP
followed by children. Gauguin is loudly and fantastically dressed; Anna
wears orange; the monkey on his shoulder sports a fez; the Artist is just
dressed like "an Artist." Gauguin walks in a cold travesty of a Grand
Seigneur; contemptuous disregard of gawkers; making way for nobody.
A few steps in GROUP CLOSEUP, then, through the shrill children:

SAILOR'S VOICE (o.s.) Hey you! . . . You in the baby-blue coat! . . . *Who's
the monkey?*

Gauguin and Company stop cold. He looks calmly to the voice. The
children hush and bystanders freeze.

FULL SHOT—THE STREET—GAUGUIN'S VIEWPOINT
Across the street stand half a dozen French sailors.

SAILOR (shouting) Where's your hand-organ?
The others laugh; and wait.

CLOSE GROUP SHOT—GAUGUIN AND COMPANY
He looks fixedly towards the sailors; his smile grows icy.

ARTIST (low) Paul. Please. There's a *woman* involved!
Gauguin, icily happy, starts towards the sailors; they come, too.

FULL DOWNSHOT—NEW ANGLE—THE STREET
Gauguin and Company cross leisurely; the sailors coalesce and stiffen,
then wait; townspeople coalesce more slowly; a few run.

CLOSE GROUP SHOT—OVER SAILORS, CENTERING GAUGUIN
. . . as they converge.

GAUGUIN (quiet and cold) My hand-organ is in hock. But I didn't quite hear that, about the monkey.

ARTIST (low) Paul. I implore you. No violence.

CLOSE GROUP SHOT—REVERSE—SAILORS, OVER GAUGUIN
Spectators thicken in b.g.

SAILOR (cool) I asked: which one is the monkey? The thing on your shoulder? Or the thing on your arm? Or you?
The sailors smile as one; expectant.

CLOSER GROUP SHOT—FAVORING GAUGUIN
He hands the monkey to the Artist.

GAUGUIN (quietly) Take care of my mistress, please.
A flash of wild hatred from Anna. He hands along his fancy cane. The monkey absurdly encumbers the Artist.

ARTIST (desperate) Paul! Remember Tolstoy!

GAUGUIN Keep out of this; it isn't your affair.
The Artist flashes him a look of pure gratitude.

CLOSE SHOT—GAUGUIN
He just smiles, looking the sailors over.

CLOSE GROUP SHOT—THE SAILORS
They're interested now, even puzzled; but not scared. Mainly watching Gauguin, they exchange little glances.

HEAD CLOSEUP—GAUGUIN

GAUGUIN (with cold mock-amiability) You know, I'm a sailor myself.

HEAD CLOSEUP—THE MAIN SAILOR
He looks Gauguin over, slow and cold, from head to foot; then smiles with contempt. Suddenly Gauguin's fist explodes like a bomb against his jawbone.

FLASH CUT HEAD CLOSEUP—GAUGUIN
. . . as he follows through. The face is demoniac; and happy.

MED. PANNING SHOT
The fight is mainly ad lib but along these general directives:

Gauguin is a good boxer; the sailors are plenty tough, but less skilled. They box with feet as well as hands. Gauguin boxes only by hand, but he doesn't scruple to viciously twist a foot he catches; or to kick the heads and/or bellies of men who are down; he makes free with rabbit-punches and such; and he delights in breaking a nose. Gauguin's effort is to stay against a wall; the sailors try to get him into the open. They fight ad lib from wall to street and back as we PAN. Anna is exhilarated and neutral; the Artist is horrified; the monkey is just wild; the villagers are dead silent. We cut these reactions in a bit.

Gauguin takes hard punishment but is doing more than all right until a sailor (in PICK-UP SHOTS) gets a wooden shoe Gauguin has shed, creeps behind him and, with one savage hatchet-like blow; breaks his ankle. With a scream of agony Gauguin drops his guard and they chop him down to the cobblestones with fists and feet. O.s. we hear a gendarme's whistle. The sailors scatter as the cops come running. We cut in bits of this exploded action, and back to Gauguin as he is lifted onto a wheel-barrow, fantastically messed-up and bloodied. He lights his pipe and clenches it in agony between his teeth. A Doctor briefly examines the ankle and gives him a hypodermic. (We point this a little: Gauguin's first anguish, and narcotic.)

GAUGUIN (to Artist) Where's Anna?

ARTIST (bewildered) Perhaps . . . back at the hotel?

GAUGUIN I doubt it. (he shrugs) Good riddance.
A cop trundles him off, with painful jolting. Someone tosses into the wheelbarrow his devastated hat; another, his shoes; another, his fancy cane. He grasps the cane, and smokes. DISSOLVE

INT. GAUGUIN'S STUDIO—PARIS—DAY—PANNING SHOT—THE STUDIO—GAUGUIN'S VIEWPOINT
The golden yellow walls are hung with Gauguin's paintings and with Polynesian trophies and curios; on a mantel, beautiful shells and stones. Here and there, a conspicuous gap. Along the floor, broken china, torn books, old clothes. In the middle of the room, on an easel, we PAN past the nude portrait of Anna with the monkey. We PAN BACK to it.

GAUGUIN'S VOICE (o.s., sardonic) Well, well, well! She took everything she could lay hands on, didn't she!

CLOSE GROUP SHOT—FAVORING GAUGUIN
He's just inside the entrance; Morice and Monfried in b.g. They nod sadly.

GAUGUIN That is, everything she thought was *valuable*.

The monkey chatters o.s. All glance down surprised as we TILT DOWN. The monkey holds about its shoulders some vivid glad-rag of Anna's. Gauguin detaches this and drops it and picks up the monkey as we TILT BACK to normal. He holds the animal on his wrist and strokes it absently, quieting its chattering, as they talk.

GAUGUIN I appreciate her taste, for the first time. With what she was kind enough to leave me, I can dig myself out of my grave.

They wonder what he means. He turns to them and smiles.

GAUGUIN I've made a fool of myself. But I believe that's over. I had a great deal of time to think, during those weeks on my back. I'm finished with Europe, Daniel: as finished, as Europe is with me. I'm going to auction off everything I have; and I'm going back to the Islands. And this time I won't come back.

Silence. He looks all around the room. It is good-bye. Then he remembers the monkey. He looks at it, brooding a moment; almost tender. Then he lowers it, chattering, below-frame. An abrupt twist of one arm and the o.s. chattering is cut off by an o.s. sound of crunching; then, an o.s. thud. Gauguin's friends are speechless with horror and shock.

GAUGUIN (gently) Come on, let's get out of here.

He turns and hobbles ahead of them through the little anteroom bedroom; they follow. He shuts the door after them; as we DOLLY IN on the reverse side of the painted glass panel, we hear it locked.   FADE OUT

FADE IN

INT. LIVING ROOM—DAY

Mette is distinctly older; an odd, brittle dryness.

CLOSE TWO-SHOT—GAUGUIN AND METTE

GAUGUIN There's 12,000 francs from the auction; and a dealer has promised me that no matter how long it takes to put my work over, I'll always have the necessities.

METTE You have that on paper?

GAUGUIN I have his promise.

METTE And you were once a businessman!

He is silent; then, very shy:

GAUGUIN My dear . . . there's something much more important I came here to speak about.

METTE Yes?

GAUGUIN We've all been apart too long. Let's never be apart again. No matter what happens.

She is deeply, piteously stirred.

METTE (level) What are you trying to say, Paul?

CLOSE SHOT—GAUGUIN
He hesitates; then bravely jumps off the precipice.

GAUGUIN Come to Tahiti with me.

CLOSE SHOT—METTE
She just looks at him: blend of hope, hopelessness, heartbreak.

CLOSE SHOT—GAUGUIN
Passionate and gentle, he wants all this so desperately he has lost all sense of reality. Cut in her silent listening.

GAUGUIN *All* of us! . . . Oh, I know how strange the idea must seem at first, but *think* of it a moment! What do you have ahead of you here! Your parents. No husband. Translating Zola, of all bores. See what it has done to you already. What kind of a life is that, for a woman like you! Let's have the *rest* together, anyway! And what about our sons? What can they learn in Europe except cowardice and respectability? There, they'll turn into *men!* And Aline, Mette. This climate is slowly killing her. Can you begin to imagine how strong she'll be after a few years there —and how beautiful? Besides, she needs me. She needs a father.

SILENCE: PULL AND PAN into CLOSE TWO-SHOT

METTE (quiet; moved) And how do you propose to support us?

GAUGUIN My dearest Mette, those are the worries of a climate like this. You've no idea how much less is needed there, to live comfortably . . . For one thing, there's hardly any housework.

METTE How would you even pay our passage: six of us?

GAUGUIN If you sold your furniture . . .
Cold outrage grows so strong, it brings her to her feet. He gets up too, using his cane.

METTE Have you *entirely* lost your mind?

GAUGUIN Mette!
O.s., the front door opens.

METTE (louder) You can *dare* . . .

GAUGUIN Sshh.

She quiets; both look to door; Gauguin smiles, loving, pleading.

MED. SHOT—ALINE

Lovely but frail, 16, she stands in the doorway, sparkling with snow, very shy. A self-conscious smile and curtsey.

HEAD CLOSEUP—GAUGUIN

Quietly, smiling, he realizes he has lost her and them all forever.

DISSOLVE

INT. A SMALL PARIS CAFE—NIGHT—GROUP AND INDIVIDUAL SHOTS

A group of a dozen or less; friends of Gauguin; sit at the tagend of a little farewell dinner. Plenty of bottles; an atmosphere of pleasant squiffiness. We see Monfried, Morice, possibly Degas, also the sillier young man whom Monfried kicked out of Gauguin's studio. Monfried is proposing a last toast to Gauguin—

MONFRIED—tomorrow, he leaves us—leaves Europe—*forever,* according to his plans. But in my heart I believe that we'll be seeing him again. (applause) So, gentlemen . . . (suddenly raising his glass he speaks very quietly and sincerely) Good-bye, Paul. God-speed. And God willing, you'll come back.

All rise and drink, in quiet emotion. Gauguin is much moved.

GAUGUIN There is nothing I can speak of: except my gratitude to my friends. Good-bye.

He drinks and Monfried helps him on with his coat.

YOUNG MAN (drunk) Just a moment, please.

He raises a full glass. As he speaks we pick up Gauguin and others, listening. A few think it rather charming; the wiser, quietly sick, wonder what Gauguin will do or say.

YOUNG MAN (very fancy) Let us drink, Gentlemen, to a man who knows the prerogatives and obligations of Genius. To a man, who knows what money is good for: to enjoy; and to lavish upon young artists, as a Prince of Artists should. To a man who knows what women are good for: to be enjoyed when when they are enjoyable; beaten when they are bores; and kicked aside when they interfere with one's *serious* pleasures. To a man who knows what one's *children* are good for: to be ignored, as a gentleman ignores any *other* social error. To a man who knows that the one thing worth any serious attention, is Art and Art alone. Gentlemen, I give you M. Paul Gauguin!

Two or three applaud uneasily; the wiser friends are stunned; even more so when, as the Young Man drinks, Gauguin, smiling and bowing, takes wine in his own mouth. Then he spits it all in the Young Man's face; bows again, smiling, all around; puts on his hat, takes his cane, turns his back, and limps out, still smiling.

We shoot from near the front door as he comes towards us; in b.g. they stand appalled, watching him, wondering whether he will turn; but he doesn't turn or look back or pause. He walks into and past a CLOSE SHOT, still smiling, and we watch the Group watch him as we hear the door open and close o.s. FADE OUT

END OF PART TWO

Part 3

INT. A DOCTOR'S OFFICE—PAPEETE—CLOSE SHOT—GAUGUIN'S FEET—DAY

One is bandaged, the Doctor finishes bandaging the other. As we PULL AWAY into TWO-SHOT Gauguin painfully draws on loose Russian-leather boots. Gauguin is smoking. He's shockingly aged.

DOCTOR Are you *using* the arsenic?

GAUGUIN What good is it?

DOCTOR Well . . . at least there's no deterioration.

GAUGUIN What about my heart?

DOCTOR That's your affair.

GAUGUIN It's either my heart or my work.

DOCTOR Plus smoking like a chimney, and living on rice and water.

GAUGUIN Tobacco's my last luxury, Doctor—unless we count morphine. As for eating: paint and canvas cost money.

DOCTOR Haven't you heard from Paris *yet*?

GAUGUIN (a bitter smile) My dealer? . . . Ah, my friend, I'll be a long time paying *you*.
Silence.

DOCTOR (quietly) Tell me, Gauguin: do you want to live?

GAUGUIN Is this an offer?

DOCTOR It's a warning. In less than five years, you've aged a good twenty. Get out of the tropics. You were a fool to come back; you'll be a madman, if you stay.

GAUGUIN Sorry: that seems to be my trade.

DOCTOR It'll be the death of you.

GAUGUIN We all die.
The Doctor shrugs, turns to desk, and as Gauguin gets up, hands him parcels.

DOCTOR (weary irony) Very well: . . . for the feet; the heart; the blood; the stomach; the eyes; the pain . . .
Silence; their eyes meet.

109

GAUGUIN Thank you, Doctor.

DOCTOR Next month, then . . .
Gauguin nods.

DOCTOR Perhaps there'll be mail, this boat.

GAUGUIN If there is, you'll be the first to know—if I can afford to tell you.
They grin; nod good-bye; Gauguin limps out.   DISSOLVE

INT. THE POST OFFICE—CLOSE SHOT—GAUGUIN—DAY
Heading a line at the barred window, he is given a letter.

INSERT—THE ENVELOPE—CLOSE SHOT—GAUGUIN
Postmarked Copenhagen; addressed in Mette's hand. Transfigured, he
props himself against the wall, opening and reading the letter with painful eagerness; his eyes are weak now. He slows down; a slow take; he
holds it closer, rereading as we DOLLY IN to HEAD CLOSEUP.
His eyes strain; his lips shape silent words; he is incredulous. As we PULL
AWAY AND PAN he lifts stunned eyes and blindly walks out, unaware of
watchers.   LAP DISSOLVE

EXT. GAUGUIN'S HOME—MED. PANNING SHOT—GAUGUIN AND FAMILY—DAY
A new, more solid home; new location. As he painfully gets down from
his buggy a LITTLE BOY (half-caste) runs out and hugs this thigh and a
NATIVE WOMAN (more mature than Tehura,) pleased, appears in doorway.
Gauguin absently hugs the boy to his thigh as he limps towards the door,
then thrusts him away. His mother takes him. Gauguin walks blindly
past them.

INT. GAUGUIN'S HOME—FULL SHOT—GAUGUIN AND FAMILY—DAY
In b.g., some of the best paintings of the second Tahitian period.
He walks straight to his writing table into CLOSEUP and sits; woman and
child in b.g., puzzled and scared. He gets out his little book to Aline
(INSERT) opens to last written page, and in ink draws a brutal line below
the last writing.

INSERT—THE PAGE
. . . as the pen breaks the paper. Then his shaking hand begins: *I have
just lost . . .*

GAUGUIN—CLOSE SHOT—WRITING

GAUGUIN'S VOICE (o.s.) I have just lost my daughter, Aline. I no longer
love God.

In b.g. the child whimpers, the mother shushes. Desperate, half-mad grief
seizes Gauguin and he turns to them, screaming:

GAUGUIN Get out! Get out!

Appalled, they leave; he turns back to us, eyes streaming, as we DOLLY

INTO EYE CLOSEUP.

GAUGUIN (whispering) *Where do we come from! What are we! Where are we going!*

The obsessed, grief-driven eyes become visionary. LAP DISSOLVE

A SERIES OF LAP DISSOLVES

Music Over.

Here, as in the earlier fight and dream sequences, a full detailing of shots would be deceptively long: this silent sequence is climactic on Gauguin strictly as an artist. Its main drive: to involve us deeper than ever before in films, in the work of painting a masterpiece, and in the picture itself—always with the further drive, not yet explicit, of suicide. The painting is Gauguin's "Where Do We Come From? What Are We? Where Are We Going?"

The general line:

At a Chinese store, then at a European, Gauguin bums burlap sacks and piles them in his buggy. They think he's nuts.

At home, alone, he sews them together with care.

By lamplight he stretches this "canvas" over a huge frame—15 feet by 6; then applies sizing to this "canvas."

By earliest daylight he begins to lay out the master outline, with charcoal. Further DISSOLVES develop this.

By night he lies sharp awake, thinking; gets up; turns up a low lamp; and makes an improvement.

By early light and by DISSOLVES through the day he begins using color, improving on the sketch as he goes. Through LAP DISSOLVES we show corrections; and how a new color brings startling harmony to two others.

We see him standing on a chair; his feet suffering. He clambers down, considers using arsenic, hoards it; uses hypo; back to work.

We see him absently eating rice, with his fingers, staring at the canvas; too absorbed to eat; back to work.

We see him wash out his sick, hurting eyes and examine them closely in a mirror; disgusted with himself; back to work.

We watch him size up his virtually finished painting, check on the remaining light (late afternoon,) and add a few final touches, in deep exaltation and exhaustion.

By last daylight, finished and "emptied," he lays down his palette, lights a lamp, and sits down at his table. He begins to write. As he writes, and reads o.s.:

CLOSE MOVING SHOT—THE NEW PAINTING
We prowl slowly and closely over this vast canvas, linking major relationships, still building up to, rather than giving, a first full view of it. The daylight fades. Later on we see it by lamplight as Gauguin returns to it; then PULL OUT into MEDIUM SHOT of him, facing away from us. Meanwhile:

GAUGUIN'S VOICE (o.s.) Before dying, I wanted to paint a big canvas I had in mind; and for a month I have worked day and night in an unheard-of fever. By God, it isn't the ordinary thing—studies from nature, preliminary cartoon, and so on: it's all boldly done, directly with the brush, on a sackcloth full of knots and rugosities, and so, it looks terribly rough . . . They'll say it's loose . . . unfinished. But I believe not only that it outdoes all my earlier paintings, but also that I shall never paint a better one.

Now we bring on moving lamplight and, midway in the following, very slowly PULL AWAY.

GAUGUIN'S VOICE (cont.) I put into it, before dying, all my energy; such a painful passion under terrible circumstances, that the haste disappears and the life gushes out. I really do admire it. I realize the enormous mathematical mistakes and I wouldn't retouch them for anything. It must stay as it is—in a sketchy state, if you want to call it that.

He is now examining his work, back to us, lamp held high. After adequate silence:

WOMAN'S VOICE (o.s., softly) Paul?
He turns and sees her o.s.

GAUGUIN What are *you* doing here?

MED. SHOT—HIS WOMAN AND CHILD
They stand just inside the dark, open door. It is night. They are dressed their best—blend of native and European clothing. They advance and we

PAN them into MEDIUM CLOSE 3-SHOT.

WOMAN Don't be angry with us anymore.

GAUGUIN I was never angry with you . . . Where have you been?

WOMAN With my mother . . . Paul: come with us.

GAUGUIN Come where? . . . Hello, boy. Why are you dressed in *this* rig?

WOMAN Come with us to Mass.

GAUGUIN At this time of day?

WOMAN To *Midnight* Mass.

GAUGUIN (surprised, then ironic) It's Christmas Eve? . . . *Hm*—a great Feast for artists. No thanks, Paura; I have my own Communion to make. They watch him, sad and uneasy.

GAUGUIN (gently) Goodnight. (he touches the boy's hair) Goodnight, my son. . . . A Happy Christmas to both of you.

They go out.

CLOSE SHOT—GAUGUIN
He watches after them with a certain impersonal tenderness; then, as we

PAN, goes to his medicines.

CLOSE SHOT—GAUGUIN—NEW ANGLE
He opens the box of arsenic. He gets three other boxes from a table drawer. He empties all into one box.

PANNING SHOT—GAUGUIN
Throwing a cloak about him and carrying the box he comes close to us at the open door, then turns for a last look at painting.

HEAD CLOSEUP—GAUGUIN
He looks to the painting, proudly. A strange smile.

GAUGUIN (very quiet) "Where are we going?"
He turns and goes out, leaving the door open.

CLOSE PANNING SHOT—A CRECHE
We PAN across the innocent figures: the Holy Family, the Beasts, the Shepherds, in trembling candlelight. Crude singing, o.s., of the *Adeste Fidelis,* in Latin, French and native voices.

MED. LONG SHOT—EXT. A SMALL CHURCH—NIGHT
Beyond palms, the windows glow with beating candlelight. The hymn continues distant o.s. Gauguin climbs uphill across the shot, MED. CLOSE. We HOLD on Church after he has gone.

MED. LONG SHOT—EXT. AN ANCIENT TERRACE—NIGHT
A kind of paved, truncated pyramid, such as was used in the old days for coronations and human sacrifices. At one edge, the silhouette of a stone god. Gauguin's silhouette limps towards it.

CLOSE SHOT—GAUGUIN—PAST THE GOD
Arriving, he looks up to it; takes off and spreads his cloak.

CLOSE PANNING DOWN SHOT—THE CLOAK
As it settles we PAN past the feet of the god to a large anthill; and begin to hear o.s. sound of brook.

CLOSEUP SHOT—THE GOD
At this angle he is less terrifying than ominous.

CLOSE SHOT—GAUGUIN
He sits on his cloak; considers smoking a last pipe; tosses it aside; opens his box of arsenic; and, without dramatics, swallows the contents. Tosses box away; lies down below-frame.

CLOSE DOWN SHOT—GAUGUIN
Lying flat he looks into the sky and waits. We hear his heart beat ever more strongly and bring up sound of brook.

UP SHOT—HIS VIEWPOINT—THE STARS
. . . in maximal quiet and magnificence; but heart and brook continue. Hold; then TILT DOWN TO

HEAD CLOSEUP—THE GOD
He is demoniacally terrifying. *Sounds of heart and brook louden;* then a hideous wrenching, retching groan and a thrashing sound o.s. TIGHTEN IN. Pause.

CLOSE DOWN SHOT—GAUGUIN
He is beastlike on hands and knees and has clearly just finished vomiting. He cocks his head up and sidelong into CLOSEUP of face, wet with agony and nausea; also clear, is a furious will to live. He slants his head, listening sharp; hears the water; and crawls towards it through thick foliage.

CLOSE SHOT—GAUGUIN
We shoot across the little brook as he reaches it and buries his face in it, frantically drinking. He shoves a finger down throat.   DISSOLVE

CLOSE SHOT—THE GOD'S HEAD—DAYBREAK
In this light he looks terrifying yet gentle.

FULL SHOT—EXACTLY FRAMING GAUGUIN'S PAINTING—DAYBREAK
At last we see this painting whole and in the purest daylight. We hold on it in silence long enough to begin really to take it in; then weak, dragging footsteps o.s.; then Gauguin appears, his back to us, as much dead as alive. He stops; he stands looking up at his painting.
                                                                FADE OUT.

FADE IN

EXT. DOCTOR'S GARDEN—CLOSE SHOT—GAUGUIN—DAY
PULL OUT to MEDIUM CLOSE TWO-SHOT WITH DOCTOR. Both sit smoking.

DOCTOR (partly o.s.) You overdid starvation; and you overdosed on poison. Your stomach couldn't hold it. That's all that saved you. . . . That, and the fact that you helped yourself get it out. That's the only reason you *deserve* to be alive.

GAUGUIN (haggard, amused) I do seem to be condemned to live, don't I!

DOCTOR A man who's fool enough to say that is fool enough to try it again.

GAUGUIN I would like very much to be dead; but when you bring yourself as close to death as I—and survive—you learn the *value* of life; no matter how much you hate it.

DOCTOR Hm . . . Then I guess you'll live out your time, anyhow.

GAUGUIN I have to.
A tinkling doorbell o.s.

DOCTOR Come on; I've patients who want to *live*.
They start for his back door.

PANNING SHOT—INT. DOCTOR'S OFFICE
As rear door closes and they cross, the Doctor gives him a parcel.

DOCTOR Here's your—arsenal, once more.
He opens door to waiting room and stands aside for Gauguin.

INT.—A SMALL WAITING ROOM

CLOSE SHOT—GAUGUIN AT DOOR
. . . Doctor in b.g. Gauguin halts, a little shocked.

MED. SHOT—THE ROOM
It is crowded with sick, patient natives, who glance touchingly towards Camera. We feature a mother, who doesn't look up, but sharply nips her inert baby's scalp.

CLOSE SHOT—GAUGUIN AND DOCTOR AS BEFORE
The Doctor looks worried. Gauguin keeps watching the mother.

GAUGUIN (undertone) What's *she* doing?

DOCTOR (same) Trying to raise the dead.
In Tahitian he tells the natives he'll be right back; then beckons Gauguin into office and shuts the door.

CLOSE TWO-SHOT—GAUGUIN AND DOCTOR

DOCTOR Where are your woman and child?

GAUGUIN At the far end of the Island.

DOCTOR Keep them there. And keep to your house. This is a particularly virulent type of influenza.

GAUGUIN I had influenza, in the Canal Zone.

DOCTOR This kind? I doubt it; you're alive. Now please go; I've got work to do.

GAUGUIN You mean, an epidemic.

DOCTOR Exactly; and a handful of doctors. Poor *fools* . . . Now please get out. And keep away from them.

GAUGUIN I'd like to help you.

DOCTOR Don't be an idiot: there's very little *I* can do.

GAUGUIN In that case even I can learn what little there is.
Pause.

DOCTOR (curious) You know, Gauguin, I rather like you. You may be a crackpot, but you've got courage; and God knows you're stubborn. But I'd have sworn that for pure selfishness, you took all prizes. Why do you want to do this?

GAUGUIN (smiling) You said it: they *want* to be alive.
Their eyes meet. The Doctor thumbs open a big book and gives it to Gauguin.

DOCTOR Well . . . at least it's a *respectable* suicide.
Both smile grimly, in mutual respect.   DISSOLVE

INT.—A NATIVE HUT—GROUP SHOT—GAUGUIN AND NATIVES—NIGHT
He squats beside a dying old woman and soothes the ancient forehead with his hand. He is terribly exhausted, and sick. We are in CLOSE SHOT. She speaks a few dim words in Tahitian; he doesn't get it; she repeats with great urgency; she dies. As we PULL AWAY into GROUP SHOT he gets up. Natives beside him and in b.g.

GAUGUIN What was she trying to say?

A NATIVE She said you are the first kind white man she has ever known.

CLOSE SHOT—GAUGUIN

He is so moved his mouth trembles; then his teeth rattle.

GAUGUIN (stemming tears) There . . . there are others.
The Doctor enters hut in b.g. and turns Gauguin by one shoulder.

DOCTOR Now you rest.

GAUGUIN Oh no. There are others.
The Doctor examines him sharply.

DOCTOR You're going straight to the hospital. You're a very sick man.

GAUGUIN (vaguely) Am I? . . . *Am* I!
Wavering away to the door he starts laughing and crying; he collapses as
Doctor and Natives catch him and we   DISSOLVE

EXT. HOSPITAL—CLOSE TWO-SHOT—GAUGUIN AND DOCTOR—DAY

We identify the Hospital by its door. Gauguin comes to threshold, Doctor
in b.g. He looks around happily; his face darkens.

FULL SHOT—REVERSE—NATIVES IN SUNLIGHT

A comically demure shot: they are dressed like a Missionary's dream;
women in black mother-hubbards, men in shirts and pants. All walk
decorously. In b.g. some bow to a Priest, others to linked Nuns. The proud
beautiful woman who epitomized the best of Tahiti early in Part 2, passes
near us. She is in black from chin to toe. Catching Gauguin's eye o.s. she
quickly looks down.

GAUGUIN'S VOICE (old) In the Name of all that's . . .

TWO-SHOT—GAUGUIN AND DOCTOR

GAUGUIN What has *happened!*

DOCTOR (amused) The Shadow of Death. (Gauguin is puzzled) The
epidemic has made thousands of converts.

GAUGUIN Why—the cowards! The fools!

DOCTOR Oh, I wouldn't be too harsh: most people, in the face of Death,
look for God.

GAUGUIN Where am I going to find models? I used to have to give them
rum, or love. What do I give them now! Testaments?

DOCTOR (chuckling) I wouldn't worry about that for a while, Gauguin.
Just—take the best possible care of yourself.
We TIGHTEN on Gauguin.

GAUGUIN (a low growl) Oh, I'll *take care* of myself!   DISSOLVE

INT. CAFE BOUGAINVILLE—PANNING PULL SHOT—TITI, THEN GROUP—CENTERING
GAUGUIN—DAY

O.s., we hear Gauguin's ranting; so does Titi as we follow her practiced
stroll. She looks older, shopworn, diseased; and she is amusedly contemptuous of Gauguin. So are the white men at the table with him—to
whom we TILT DOWN as she saunters past, and off, in b.g. We PAN PAST
THEM CLOSE, to Gauguin, then PULL AWAY TO GROUP SHOT. Gauguin is very
drunk, and talks violently. From the start, till further notice, dissonant
electronic sounds imitate dizziness like a slow lopsided wheel.

GAUGUIN (o.s.) Pigs! Fools! Traitors! The loveliest best people on the
face of the earth and frighten them a little and what do they do! They
turn into so many deaconesses! And the filthy missionaries, just biding
their time, to fill them with sin and nonsense and guilt and shame.!

A MAN Hah! Listen to Cokey!

GAUGUIN (o.s.) Don't call me Cokey. I take that for pain not for pleasure.

ANOTHER What Cokey wants to do is save their souls from Christianity.

GAUGUIN (on, now) You put it in a nutshell, my friend. Only it's too
late. They're ruined. Done for . . . How about a little drink?
Some one claps palms, then gestures for it.

GAUGUIN Ruined! From the day we set foot here! This place is no longer
fit for decent human beings.
An elderly wild-looking Sea Captain has kept out of the kidding.

CAPTAIN If this is too tame for you, why don't you go where they're still
wild and woolly?

GAUGUIN I don't like that kind of talk.
The drinks are brought; he snaps his down fast.

GAUGUIN Thanks.

CAPTAIN I know islands so far out of the regular runs that you can buy
out a whole village for a keg of rum. You can get a girl for a bag of
candy. Why, you could be a *King* there, if that's what you want.

GAUGUIN (bleary) I don't like Kings. I'm too old for candy. But I'd sell
my house and my land and everything I have on earth to find a place
where—where—That hasn't been ruined by white men or yellow men for

that matter. Where there are people who'll never give in to all this . . . this . . . *You* know!
Unaware it isn't his, he snaps down another man's drink.

GAUGUIN Thanks.

CAPTAIN (touched) Of course I know. And you sell your land—if you've got any . . . Get yourself a little stake . . . and I'll sail you there for— a lot less than I would anyone *else* here.

GAUGUIN (wildly eager) Would you? Will you? *You do:* Because you know what I'm looking for.
The electronic sounds stop. We DOLLY IN as, in heartsick clairvoyance, he blurts:

GAUGUIN I'm looking for a place fit to die in.
The Captain's voice o.s. is gentle but strange, as if heard under ether.

CAPTAIN I know old boy; I know just what you mean.

GAUGUIN (childlike) Where are you taking me?

CAPTAIN'S VOICE (magical) To the Marquesas.

SWIFT DOLLY IN TO HEAD CLOSEUP OF GAUGUIN TO STOP ON HIS EYES AND HOLD, as simultaneously he nods happily looking forward to it. We see in his face as we close in on his eyes, the homestretch and his death. EYES HOLD as we: SLOW DISSOLVE

EXT. MARQUESAS ISLAND—LONG SHOT OF CLIFFS—LATE AFTERNOON—Sort of a gun metal overcast. This shot DOUBLE EXPOSED with EYE CLOSEUP as
                               MEDIUM DISSOLVE

FULL SHOT—WAVE RUSHING TOWARDS CLIFF—as it smashes against the cliff in a burst of splendor, EYE SUPERIMPOSED OVER LONG SHOT OF CLIFF; DISSOLVES OUT;   FAST DISSOLVE

FULL IN ON BURST OF SMASHING WAVE: CUT TO

CLOSE SHOT—GAUGUIN AT SHIP'S RAIL
. . . reacting as to the greatest music. His eyes lift . . .

FULL SHOT—CLIFFS OF FATU-HIVA—LATE AFTERNOON
They spring sheer out of the ocean to an incredible height, and thousands of birds swarm the late sunlight like shattered foam. This is Gauguin's "Gateway to Death."

CLOSE SHOT—GAUGUIN
Still deeper reaction: awe, sadness; savage joy. The Captain comes up beside him at the rail.

CAPTAIN Is that what you're looking for, my friend?
Gauguin turns away to conceal his sudden tears; smiles grimly; nods hard, twice.

CAPTAIN A place fit to die in, eh?
The knowledge enters Gauguin; the smile hardens. As the Captain watches him, with liking, and wave explodes o.s.   DISSOLVE

EXT. THE DOCK AT HIVA-OA—FULL SHOT—A GANGPLANK—DAY
. . . as it is lowered from the sailing vessel to land. Then Gauguin, with luggage, starts limping ashore. What he sees makes him pause.

HEAD CLOSEUP—GAUGUIN
. . . as he pauses and looks sharp o.s., his face complex and ironic—reading the end of his life. Then he starts down.

FULL MOVING SHOT—HIS VIEWPOINT—GROUP AND NATIVES
The background is a corrugated-iron shed, against which natives loaf, eyes sullen and hostile. Salient is Tioka, the oldest, wisest and least friendly. All look straight to Gauguin o.s., as do the men in foreground: the Lieutenant (i.e. "The Gendarme"); LeMoine (The Painter); The Trader (American); Vernier (The Protestant Pastor); The Priest. As we move down the gangplank into CLOSE GROUP SHOT these silent members of our Prologue, against a backdrop of grim natives and iron, read like a sentence of death.   DISSOLVE

INT. MISSION HOUSE—GROUP SHOT—GAUGUIN—PRIEST—LIEUTENANT—BISHOP—EVENING

GAUGUIN (earnestly—briskly) I understand, Monsignor, that it is only through you that I can buy land; only *you* can persuade these savages to work.

GAUGUIN (cont.; Bishop nods) Permit me to inform you, Monsignor, that I am a passionately devout Catholic. I gather that the natives are still far from won over, and that the Protestants are making inroads. Permit me, Sir, to use my poor powers as an artist, to lead them to you. That is my life's hope; and without your help, all my long voyage is but a fantasy.

BISHOP Monsieur Gauguin: it may be that God has sent you among us for His own inscrutable purposes. You shall have your land, and your builders . . . See to this, Lieutenant:

GAUGUIN Oh Sir!

He goes on one knee and kisses the Bishop's ring.   DISSOLVE

EXT. MOVING SHOT—GAUGUIN WITH HORSE AND WAGON—MORNING

VERNIER'S VOICE Good morning, Monsieur.

Vernier, politely salutes, Gauguin returns an unfriendly nod. Vernier is hurt, he stops and looks after Gauguin.

MOVING SHOT—TRADER'S STORE

The Trader, at his door, lifts a hand.

TRADER 'Morning.

GAUGUIN'S VOICE (across) Good morning.

TRADER Keeping tabs on your workmen?

GAUGUIN No; I want to see a bit of the Valley.

A "well, you'll see" look from Trader, watching after him.

MOVING SHOT—GAUGUIN'S HOME—TIOKA'S HUT

The home is just begun; Tioka squats outside his hut, nearby.

GAUGUIN (friendly) Good morning.

MOVING SHOT—TIOKA

His eyes meet Gauguin's in silent dislike.

CLOSE MOVING SHOT—GAUGUIN

Hurt; without pleasure he salutes workmen o.s.

MOVING SHOT—HOUSE AND WORKERS

They bow and scrape as we pass.   DISSOLVE

CONTINUE MOVING SHOTS—DEEPER WOODS

Also reaction shots, passing shots, etc. Since they are generally self-evident, and depend on location, only the broad description is indicated here.

A palm grove opens like a vast accordion. Outside a hut, natives squat; they hardly look up. Gauguin is disturbed by their apathy. Then o.s., distant, he hears paroxysmic coughing of t.b. Another hut: a family sits outside, looking deaf; the coughing comes from indoors. Another cough begins o.s., a third, more distant.

Three huts in sequence. Some natives are out, others come out with sound of wagon. Some show mere apathy. Some are hideously ill: flagrant symptoms of smallpox; syphilis; elephantiasis; leprosy. From the last hut a native emerges with the "lionlike" face of leprosy. Gauguin's reactions are cut in, always in moving shots; this is a death-parade.

Distant, o.s., a weird increasing keening. Gauguin, curious, gets from his wagon and limps towards it through deep woods. He peers through leaves, stealthy and horrified.

A native sits in his coffin; others sing. He is given a fruit and eats it; seizes his middle in pain; and calmly lies down in the coffin. Natives put the lid on, lower it into a ready grave, and shovel in earth. Others wave good-bye.   DISSOLVE

EXT. TRADER'S—TWO-SHOT—GAUGUIN AND TRADER—LATE AFTERNOON
They smoke and sip.

TRADER He knew he was done for; so why wait around?

GAUGUIN What was it he ate?

TRADER They call it the "Eva-Apple."

GAUGUIN (furious) Missionaries, again . . .
This bores the Trader.

TRADER Finishes you off in a few minutes.

GAUGUIN (still shocked) All day, I hardly saw one human being who showed any interest in being alive.

TRADER (placid) What have they got to live for? (noting Gauguin's shock) The man you ought to talk to is Vernier.

GAUGUIN (contemptuously) *That*—sky pilot?

TRADER He knows more about the natives than any *other* white man here —cares more too, I'd guess.

EXT. VERNIER'S FRONT PORCH—TWO-SHOT—GAUGUIN AND VERNIER—EVENING
Gauguin smokes; Vernier rocks and fans himself.

VERNIER (quiet) Do you know what is means, where we live—the Valley of Atuona? "The Valley of Unfading Flowers."

GAUGUIN (bitter) The Valley of the Shadow of Death . . .
Vernier is silently interested.

VERNIER You see, they're much less charming than the Tahitians: prouder, fiercer, more religious, more primitive. So they have taken defeat much harder. They fought back very bravely; that's how many of them died. They still fight back in the only ways they have left—through apathy; refusal to work; a hatred, most of them, for any form of Christianity.

GAUGUIN (hotly) Good!
Vernier's ignoring of this interests Gauguin.

VERNIER But civilization brought deadlier things than bullets: they had never known disease; so they were hopelessly vulnerable. A Peruvian ship brought smallpox; the Chinese brought leprosy; an American sailor was put ashore who was dying of consumption, and the natives were kind to him; of course, the whole civilized world brought venereal disease.

GAUGUIN And France brought Law and Order and Taxes and Money-grubbing and Servility and Hard Work: and you and the good Fathers brought Christianity. And that was the deathblow. You Missionaries killed all joy and courage in the soul itself.

VERNIER (quiet) God willing, we have *saved* a few of those souls. . . . But by and large I feel much as you do, at what I see: this was a great people; now it is sick unto death.

GAUGUIN I know what they're dying of: heartbreak.
Vernier, moved, nods.

VERNIER (gently) Then perhaps you can understand why, as a Christian, I want to bring them the consolations of my Faith.
Gauguin looks at him hard; then a hard smile.

GAUGUIN No, Vernier: you're not a bad sort; but we will never be friends. (with fury) They don't need "consolation": what they need is someone to *fight* for them!

Vernier, silent, realizes the hopelessness of this.   DISSOLVE

EXT. GAUGUIN'S HUT—CLOSE PANNING SHOT—GAUGUIN—NIGHT
He stands outside his half-made home, moved by the day's sights and the deep night, and the silence. Then, o.s., we hear the terrible coughing. He looks up to his left. We PAN to the sublime peak of Temetiu, drowned in starlight. The coughing intensifies; echoes begin; a second cough; the echoes multiply. We PAN BACK to Gauguin: his face is clenched like a fist in anger, sorrow, love, resolve.   FADE OUT

FADE IN
INT. GAUGUIN'S NEW COMPLETED HOME—FULL SHOT—GAUGUIN AND A MODEL—DAY

A spacious, comfortable studio. She is a native girl, savagely beautiful. She wears a lace and muslin chemise; pineapple-eyes wreath her hair. We PULL BACK from a CLOSE SHOT of her, posing, past Gauguin, painting her. Her eyes drift to an open bottle.

GAUGUIN Don't move! . . .
He limps to her with the bottle as we DOLLY IN to CLOSE TWO-SHOT. She takes a big slug fast and he recorrects her pose, using his hands on her body. His impersonality interests her. Then with a little cry she hides behind him. He looks back; sore.

MED. SHOT—REVERSE—OVER GAUGUIN AND GIRL—THE BISHOP
He stands at the open door. He is not amused.

GAUGUIN (angry) Don't be afraid of *him!* . . . Well, Monsignor: what brings you here?

The Bishop glances about, averts his eyes, and walks forward. We PULL AND PAN into MEDIUM GROUP SHOT.

GAUGUIN (nasty) Make yourself at home.

BISHOP No, thank you. . . . We have noticed, Monsieur, that you haven't attended Mass recently.

GAUGUIN I was missed?

BISHOP (significantly) Not, in fact, since your house was finished.

GAUGUIN Exactly, Sir.

BISHOP (quietly) I see. . . . It was not—honorable of you, Monsieur.

GAUGUIN I find it quite a task, Monsignor, to be honorable even according to my own lights.

BISHOP No doubt. . . . I must apologize for that.

BISHOP (cont.; sharply, to girl) Tetua: you must leave this house. You must never come here again.

The girl tries to hide her wreath.

GAUGUIN Tetua: stay where you are.

BISHOP In the name of your Faith I command you: leave at once.

GAUGUIN In the name of your own good sense I invite you: make yourself welcome here.

Finding an unexpected champion, the girl becomes excited. In calm, insolent mischief, staring at Bishop, she replaces wreath.

BISHOP You know it is forbidden to adorn yourself.

GAUGUIN Enjoy your beauty, child.
She goes ahead. The Bishop, defeated, walks closer to Gauguin.

BISHOP (deeply sincere) Monsieur Gauguin, I must implore you: don't corrupt our women here, our natives.

GAUGUIN Haven't you managed that already?

BISHOP (ignoring this) Please, Monsieur: can't you paint only the glories of Nature, like M. LeMoine?

GAUGUIN I'm afraid I didn't come half around the world to submit to the artistic advice of a clergyman.

BISHOP I shall preach against you, Gauguin; I'll forbid the natives to have anything to do with you.

GAUGUIN Preach away. I have my house and my deed to it. And I can promise you that I will do my best to "corrupt" the natives back into their innocence.

BISHOP (quietly) Monsieur: I fear that you are possessed of a devil.

GAUGUIN Nobody possesses me, Monsignor; or ever will. Good day, Sir.
The Bishop turns and walks out as we PAN. Down past him, beside his hut, Tioka looks up.

TWO-SHOT—GAUGUIN AND GIRL
Excited by Gauguin and ready for fun, she is disconcerted when he coolly gestures her to resume her pose. He resumes work. She looks to door, o.s. Annoyed, he looks around and then shows deep pleasure. He starts for door.

GAUGUIN (almost gloating) *Come in,* Sir!

CLOSE SHOT—TIOKA
Shy at the door, he smiles charmingly.

TIOKA Kaoha, Monsieur.

GAUGUIN'S VOICE (o.s.) What does that mean, Sir?

TIOKA Love.
Smiling, he advances.   DISSOLVE

TWO-SHOT—GAUGUIN AND TIOKA

Two unreconstructible old men, they smoke and drink on Gauguin's steps, making friends, as daylight fades.

TIOKA (mildly) Oh, there are worse things than the Christians; I hate them only because I am a religious man. . . . You see, I remember the old days.

GAUGUIN Where are your gods? Their images?

TIOKA They have all gone. The French took them away, to the Paris exhibitions.

GAUGUIN Tell me about the old days, Tioka.

TIOKA In the old days. . . . Ah, then we were well. In the hour of a child's birth we planted breadfruit, and blew great cries on a shell. . . . In those days, Monsieur, all work was honorable and beautiful, as yours is. A boy became a carver of wood, or a carver of stone, or a master of tattooing, or a master of legends. . . . In those days the boys and the girls would stain their bodies with saffron and wander day and night through the Valley, enjoying each other, and singing the songs which the Christians say are indecent. They forbid us to sing those songs, Monsieur. Also the *Rari's*, the sad songs.

Silent, he sighs, and gestures towards the beach.

FULL SHOT—THE SURF—AS LIGHT DECLINES

TIOKA'S VOICE (o. s.) There, in the old days, hour after hour, all day, we played in the water, from the young to the very old. You cannot know, Monsieur, how good it is: for all people: to play together in the water. . . . The body, touching another, is smooth as a fish; yet so warm, so full of liking.

TWO-SHOT—GAUGUIN AND TIOKA

TIOKA But now, we are so heavy in our hearts, not even the children play. See!

FULL SHOT—THE EMPTY BEACH AND SURF

Through surf noise we hear a multitudinous shouting and laughter. It dies. Pauses.

TIOKA'S VOICE (o. s.) All gone.

TWO-SHOT—GAUGUIN AND TIOKA (resumed)

TIOKA How we laughed! *Kakata-kakata;* that was our name for the laughter of true happiness. And how we talked. It is good to talk at this hour of the day, Monsieur, and you are the first I have talked with in many years. But then it was not sorrowful talk. We spoke of the things and of the people of each day, and we spoke of the stars; of how this world began. Our talk was all laughter or reverence, one or the other. . . . But who speaks like a man, today?

Pause.

GAUGUIN (deeply stirred) Tioka: if you will allow me: if you will tell me how: I will make you an image of a god to worship.

TIOKA You are kind. . . . I will tell you how; and we will hide it in my hut; where those who are true to the old ways may come.

GAUGUIN Shall I make it of stone, or wood?

TIOKA Of sandalwood, Monsieur: stone has such a cruel fragrance.
Pause.

GAUGUIN What were you, in the old days, Tioka?

TIOKA I was a sorcerer. . . . If you like, I will make your house sacred to my people; and there will never be thieves.

GAUGUIN I would be very grateful. (pause) Did you ever taste human flesh?

The lids lower and the dry lips part as Tioka remembers.

GAUGUIN Tell me about it.

TIOKA (dreamily) The man was tied by a rope for two days, alive, in a swift stream, which would throw him about. His head was above water so that he could not drown; the bones of his arms and thighs were broken, so that he could not escape. This made the flesh even more tender than pork. Then he was killed, and roasted, and eaten.

He notices Gauguin's speechless horror.

TIOKA (tranquil) Yes, Monsieur, it must surely have been painful; but. . . . (he shrugs) . . . . not to us; they were always from a hostile valley.
Pause.

GAUGUIN Tioka, I want to do everything in my power to bring back the old days. Not the—man with his bones broken; but the best of it. Will you help me?

TIOKA Let us first try to make better, the days we suffer now.

GAUGUIN The Church?

TIOKA The Lieutenant; the Administration. O Monsieur, if you will fight for us . . .

GAUGUIN Tell me.

TIOKA I will bring them to you.
Ka-Hui appears behind them in the doorway.

KA-HUI Monsieur: it is ready.

GAUGUIN Have supper with me. Tioka.

TIOKA (incredulous) You will really help us?

GAUGUIN You *know*. Have supper with me.

TIOKA No, thank you. I have messages to send.

INT. GAUGUIN'S HUT—FULL SHOT—A LARGE GROUP OF NATIVES—DAY
They sit on chairs and mats, scared, but excited.

FULL SHOT—GAUGUIN AND TIOKA—OTHER NATIVES
Gauguin sits at his writing table which has been pulled into the middle of the floor; papers and pen before him. Tioka sits beside him.

CLOSE TWO-SHOT—GAUGUIN AND TIOKA
Gauguin looks them all over.

GAUGUIN Now I shall read from the notes I have taken, for we must be very sure of the truthfulness of our testimony.
He looks to a man in the front row.

GAUGUIN It is true that the Lieutenant and his assistants. . . .
(no pause)
CLOSE TILTING SHOT—THE BRUTALLY BRUISED LEGS OF A NATIVE

GAUGUIN'S VOICE . . . stomped and trampled upon your bare legs with their police boots?

TILT UPWARD to the man's face. He nods.

GAUGUIN'S VOICE And this was because you refused to work on the roads?
The man nods.

GAUGUIN'S VOICE And this is true of many others as well?
The man and others nod.

CLOSE TWO-SHOT—GAUGUIN AND TIOKA (resumed)
Gauguin looks to his papers and up again, to another, o.s.

GAUGUIN And to you, he applied the thumbscrew?

CLOSE SHOT—A NATIVE
He merely lifts his horribly mangled thumbs.

GAUGUIN'S VOICE And this was for refusing to raise hay for the Lieutenant's horse?
The man nods.

TWO-SHOT—GAUGUIN AND TIOKA (resumed)

GAUGUIN And it is true that several of your friends prefer jail, to this forced labor?

FULL SHOT—THE NATIVES

GAUGUIN'S VOICE It is true that a native, if accused, always pleads guilty?

TIOKA TRANSLATES (o. s.)
Several nod.

GAUGUIN'S VOICE And this is for fear of the thumbscrew?
Many nod.

GAUGUIN'S VOICE This was true of you, and in fact you were innocent?
A man nods.

GAUGUIN'S VOICE And of you?
A woman nods.

GAUGUIN'S VOICE It is true that, rather than risk court proceedings. . . .
He waits, Tioka translates o.s.

GAUGUIN'S VOICE . . . you will give him your chickens, pigs, even the favors of your daughters?

Many nod.

GAUGUIN'S VOICE It is true that drink is forbidden; (general nods) how many of you have bribed the Lieutenant, in order to drink? Please raise your hands.

GROUP SHOT—FAVORING GIRL

GAUGUIN'S VOICE It is true that twelve men here violated you?
She nods.

TWO-SHOT—GAUGUIN AND TIOKA (resumed)

GAUGUIN (with pitying irony) And your complaint is: that none of them paid you?

GROUP SHOT (resumed)
She nods. PULL AWAY TO FULL SHOT.

GAUGUIN And now of the Judge. It is true that when he visits this Island, he makes a practice of deflowering the schoolgirls who come to him to sign their graduation diplomas?

Many nod, especially women.

GAUGUIN And you, Tioka: it is true that when you sold your copra, you were fined 1,000 francs for being drunk in your own house?

TIOKA It is true, Monsieur.

GAUGUIN And that that was more than the value of your whole crop?

TIOKA Yes, Monsieur.
Gauguin looks happy; he shuffles together his papers.

GAUGUIN (to all) Then everything that has been told here has been corroborated as true. When these abuses are brought into court . . .

FULL SHOT—THE NATIVES

GAUGUIN'S VOICE . . . will you promise to appear as witnesses, and to testify as you have testified here?

Silence. They all exchange uneasy glances. Tioka translates. Even more uneasy glances.

TWO-SHOT—GAUGUIN AND TIOKA
They look deeply sad and troubled. They look to each other, and again at the natives. Gauguin rises, puts his fists on the table, and gets ready to talk to them gently, but very firmly; and o.s. we hear the sound of hard boots on the outside stones.

FULL SHOT—OVER GAUGUIN AND TIOKA—THE NATIVES
They are in deep alarm, and when the Gendarme and two assistants appear at the doorway, they all, in rustling frightened unison, turn away to hide their faces.

GAUGUIN (angry) Don't *hide!* Don't be *afraid* of him! He can't *touch* you, after this!

CLOSE SHOT—GENDARME AND FRIENDS

GENDARME After *what*, Monsieur? Don't trouble to tell me; I have already been told.

CLOSE TWO-SHOT—GAUGUIN AND TIOKA

Tioka is standing too, now. He is badly scared but brave.

GAUGUIN Then you understand, Monsieur, that you are finished here.

CLOSE SHOT—GENDARME

GENDARME You think so?

CLOSE SHOT—GAUGUIN

GAUGUIN You will be quite sure of it, when the Judge and the Governor, and the Colonial Inspectors receive my letters.

CLOSE SHOT—GENDARME (resumed)

GENDARME We shall see, Monsieur.

DISSOLVE

INT. GAUGUIN'S HOME—EVENING

Gauguin, Vernier, Trader LeMoine, Peyral. Gauguin finishes reading a long letter:

GAUGUIN (reading) . . . respectfully yours, Paul Gauguin. (a satisfied pause) Now, gentlemen: will you add your signatures to mine?

Silence; two or three exchange glances.

TRADER There's no use sending them, Gauguin.

GAUGUIN Oh? Why are you so sure of that?

TRADER Well: The Judge long ago made up his mind never to believe anybody except the Lieutenant.

Vernier nods sadly; LeMoine looks scared at hearing such open scandal; Peyral looks drunkenly wise.

TRADER The Lieutenant sends the Governor the prettiest girls in the Valley. (same reactions) And the Colonial Inspectors; they get the *cream* of all the graft. Can you see *them* robbing their own pockets? (same reactions) So you see. What's the use.

Silence.

CLOSE SHOT—GAUGUIN

GAUGUIN Then it's all the more important that these letters be signed by every responsible white man on the island. Now. (to Trader) Will you sign?

CLOSE PANNING SHOT—BEGINNING WITH TRADER
Pause.

TRADER Come right down to it, I wish I could; but, you've got to understand, I haven't got much of a foothold here. I'm not a National you see.

GAUGUIN'S VOICE And you, Monsieur Peyral?
We PAN TO A CLOSE SHOT of PEYRAL, a heavy sleepy drunkard.

PEYRAL (wise and sleepy) You take a very narrow view, Monsieur. In any administration, it requires a little graft and corruption, to make the wheels turn without squeaking.

Pause.

GAUGUIN'S VOICE Monsieur LeMoine?
We PAN TO CLOSE SHOT of LEMOINE, a little smug, timid man.

LeMOINE As an artist, Monsieur, I'm sure you will understand. I'm not a wealthy man as you and I've a wife and children to support. It's possible for me to live here and work only through my appointment as a schoolmaster.

Pause.

GAUGUIN'S VOICE Monsieur Vernier.
We PAN TO CLOSE SHOT of Vernier. Long pause; he is deeply troubled.

Finally (and he's the only one to meet Gauguin's eyes):

VERNIER I can't sign. It could mean my removal. My life's work.

Hold a silent moment on his deep regret and shame; then PAN in Gauguin, CLOSE. Gauguin looks from man to man o.s. in sick contempt. Then:

GAUGUIN (quietly) Good evening, gentlemen.

FULL GROUP SHOT
They all look at him; he rises.

GAUGUIN I said, "Good evening."
They get up. He goes to door and opens it as we,   CUT TO

MED. CLOSE SHOT—GROUP AND GAUGUIN AT DOOR
They stand looking at him.

GAUGUIN (quietly) I'll thank you not to come here again; and not to speak, if we should chance to meet. Please don't regard this as personal dislike; or even just as the effect of your cowardice. The matter is much simpler than that: I despise the sight of white men.

Pause; then one by one they file past him and out; Vernier last, with dignity and with pained eyes. Vernier pauses.

VERNIER Monsieur Gauguin. . . .
Their eyes meet.

GAUGUIN Good evening, Monsieur.
Vernier lowers his eyes; a little nod and a mumbled "good evening;" exit. Gauguin quietly shuts the door.   FADE OUT

FADE IN
INT. POST OFFICE—FULL PANNING SHOT—GROUP—DAY
Gauguin, Vernier, Priest, Trader, LeMoine, a Chinese, others. Some lounge in semi-privacy, eagerly reading their mail; others stand in line at the window. Gauguin hobbles in. Our men glance up; he meets their eyes in dead silence; they watch with interest as he takes his place in line, trying to conceal his desperate eagerness. Nothing for him. Looking at nobody, he goes out. Trader and Vernier look after him, then resume reading. The Chinese, who follows him in line, gets mail. We PAN to door, through which we see Gauguin painfully clambering into his wagon.
                                                         DISSOLVE

PANNING AND DOLLYING SHOT—PAINTINGS AND GAUGUIN
In an elaborate, wandering shot we examine, in this order, Gauguin's *Contes Barbares, The Idol, The Apparition, The Appeal,* and *Group With Angel* . . . always in their context in the studio of a man at work: i.e., many, too, are hung but not framed, others lean against a chair or wall; the last is wet on the easel with a blemish at the middle. We tighten on the blemish, then PAN to a rear shot of Gauguin, standing at a mirror.

EXTREME CLOSE REFLECTION SHOT—GAUGUIN'S EYES
He examines one with the greatest care, holding the lids open with thumb and forefinger: a sad and ugly sight. Then he steps back and just looks at himself.

CLOSE SHOT— GAUGUIN—REVERSE
The graven face of a man who realizes he may be going blind.
                                                         DISSOLVE

CLOSE SHOT—GAUGUIN
He puts aside his hypodermic, takes up his pipe, limps to easel.
                                                     LAP DISSOLVE

CLOSE PROFILE SHOT—GAUGUIN AT EASEL
Smoking, blinking, he works intently; studies canvas; then looks to his
palette (towards us)—and stops dead.

INSERT—THE PALETTE
Caught in the fresh paint is a frail, elaborate tropical insect.

CLOSEUP SHOT—GAUGUIN
Transfixed, amused, moved, he considers briefly—then AS WE TILT, lifts
the bug free with the butt-end of his brush and with a match and turpentine starts helping him.   DISSOLVE

CLOSE SHOT—SUNFLOWERS AND PEARS
. . . arranged as for Gauguin's painting.

CLOSE SHOT—GAUGUIN
He leans far towards the flowers, studying hard, eyes sore and weak: he
cares deeply for this memorial. As he works he remembers Lear's lines
to Cordelia, with their strange appositeness to him, Vincent, and all
artists. Now and then he mutters a bit aloud but mainly his "inner voice"
speaks. By the end he is crying quietly.

GAUGUIN'S VOICE No, no, no, no! *Come, let's away to prison; We two
alone will sing like birds i' the cage: When thou dost ask me blessing,
I'll kneel down, And ask of thee forgiveness: And we'll live, And pray,
and sing, and tell old tales, and laugh At gilded butterflies, and hear poor
rogues Talk of court news; . . . and we'll talk with them, too; Who loses
and who wins; who's in, who's out; And take upon us the mystery of
things, As if we were God's spies; and we'll wear out, In a walled prison,
packs and sets of great ones That ebb and flow by the moon.*

Brief pause; then behind him, silently, the Trader appears; waits a
moment, then, quietly:

TRADER (quietly) Gauguin. . . .

CLOSE SHOT—GAUGUIN, TURNING
His face fills with contempt.

GAUGUIN (quiet) Leave here.
In fury he wipes away his tears.

TRADER I've got something to tell you.
Gauguin surges up, clutching on chair. Trader still in b.g.

GAUGUIN Leave or I'll *throw* you out.
The Trader, touched, has the courtesy to back off a bit.

TRADER This time there was an answer! The Judge will be here in three days. You have been asked to appear in person . . .

Gauguin perplexed, then:

TRADER (kidding) You plan to accept this invitation?
Gauguin gives him a look of fight and determination.

TRADER (affectionately) Good luck, you old buzzard.
Gauguin, a look of fire in his eyes, pounds fist on easel and determinedly rises as we, DISSOLVE

INT. GOVERNMENT HOUSE—DAY—MED. SHOT—LIEUTENANT
flanked by two officials, one of whom hands Judge some papers. We PAN to Judge and PULL BACK to included Gauguin back to camera. He stops before Judge's high table. The Judge is rather distinguished in blue and gold uniform, always dignified. On PULL BACK ON RIGHT TOP FRAME is an engraving of Delacroix' Revolutionary painting, to the left a tricolor-draped photo of the President of France over the judge.

JUDGE Monsieur Paul Gauguin?
We must believe in Judge until the payoff. Gauguin back to camera, in highest spirits, wears new bandages, a scarlet *pareu,* and green beret with silver ball.

GAUGUIN (mock respect) Your Honor!

JUDGE You will step forward, please.
Gauguin limps forward away from camera, concealing intense pain.

JUDGE (showing it) You are the author of this letter?

GAUGUIN (slight bow) I am.
Lieutenant, enters left frame border, reacts to this.

LIEUTENANT You accuse the Chief Gendarme of dishonesty. You have been making a nuisance of yourself for quite long enough. Under the Code of July 1881, for fomenting rebellion among the natives, you are sentenced to a fine of one thousand francs and to three months in prison.

GAUGUIN (shaken) This—this is an outrage!

JUDGE (placid) You may appeal to Tahiti.

Gauguin back to camera, turns profile, then head on into camera, dazed, starts for door, CAMERA PULLS BACK SLIGHTLY, Judge ignores him. Gauguin looks years older: he can hardly stand. He flicks an almost humble glance to the Lieutenant and others. They meet Gauguin's eyes smugly. CAMERA

PULLS BACK MORE FOLLOWING GAUGUIN IN MAXIMAL CLOSE SHOT. Older and older as he approaches toward camera and o.s. door, Gauguin exits shot in EXTREME EYE CLOSEUP. After exit, CAMERA SWOOPS IN with Lieutenant and others who converge toward Judge. Door slams. Lieutenant and Judge smugly congratulate one another on their victory over Gauguin as CAMERA MOVES SWIFTLY IN ON EXTREME CLOSE SHOT OF DELACROIX' REVOLUTIONARY ENGRAVING AND TIGHTENS CLOSE ON MARIANNE'S SCREAMING MOUTH. Judge and Lieutenant o.s. are heard laughing heartily. On MOUTH CLOSEUP, Gauguin's voice.

GAUGUIN'S VOICE (o.s., shouting) *Appeal?* ...   CUT TO

INT. GAUGUIN'S HOME—DAY—DISTORTED CLOSE DOWNSHOT—GAUGUIN

GAUGUIN I'll appeal it all the way to *Paris* if I have to!
We PULL OUT JAGGEDLY into CLOSE PROFILED TWO-SHOT of Gauguin and Tioka, sitting knee-to-knee. (All Camera motions in this single-shot scene follow Gauguin's chiefly violent mood.)

GAUGUIN (reflecting; wretched) Only it means my ruin ... money, and my health ... It won't go well with me in Tahiti: the Governor will see to that. I'll have to carry it over *his* head: ... and what *that'll* cost! Desperate pause; new idea; a sudden hand on Tioka's knee.

GAUGUIN Tioka! How will your people feel about it? Would they follow me and storm the Government House—the Bastille?
Terribly sad, Tioka shakes his head.

GAUGUIN (bitterly) They've lost their—
Silence; new thought.

GAUGUIN (sweetly) Just our darling Lieutenant, then ...
He looks sharp to one wall.

FLASH CUT—GAUGUIN'S VIEWPOINT
Crossed fencing swords on the wall.
Resume TWO-SHOT—GAUGUIN, TIOKA.

GAUGUIN (ferociously) I'll *challenge* him!
He starts to get up fast and collapses in agony, hissing through clenched molars. Tioka extends a hand which trembles with sympathy.

GAUGUIN (through teeth) Just—leave me alone.
Pause; he recovers; thinking hard.

GAUGUIN Money. That's the trouble. As usual. All my filthy dealer owes me—all these months—Not a *word* from him, Tioka! *Not a word!* (with fearful bitterness and rage) *Hahhh,* the *letter I'll write him!*

Again, more slowly, he rises. Halfway up, he is transfixed by a terrific pain in the heart and we DOLLY FAST into HEAD CLOSEUP. His eyes seem to look into great distance; the face freezes in amazement at such agony. He holds very still as if listening. PULL AWAY TO CLOSE TWO-SHOT: Tioka is on his feet.

TIOKA Koke . . . Koke!
A frozen pause.

GAUGUIN Help me to the bed.
We PAN with them; it is very careful going; we DOLLY AND TILT DOWN to CLOSE TWO-SHOT. Gauglin lies down flat on the bed, staring straight up, breathing as lightly as possible.

TIOKA Koke . . . what harms you?
Gauguin taps his breastbone with fingertips; a long breath; then:

GAUGUIN Bring me pen and paper, Tioka . . . We'll win this yet.
As Tioka goes for them we TIGHTEN on Gauguin; smiling grimly; brewing new plans. DISSOLVE

CLOSE SHOT—GAUGUIN
In angled mirrors he studies his profile and bends to work.

INSERT—THE "OVIRI" SELF-PORTRAIT . . . just finished, in clay.

CLOSE SHOT—GAUGUIN (RESUMED)
He studies it with weak eyes, with an artist's total detachment; then a small, snorting grimace: it's neither very good nor very bad. DISSOLVE

INT. GAUGUIN'S HOME—LATE AFTERNOON—MED. CLOSE TWO-SHOT—
GAUGUIN AND VERNIER

In this scene we go light on CLOSE SHOTS, which are not indicated here; we mainly keep the scene intimate yet detached and neutral. Light slowly fades, throughout. Vernier, hat in hand, sits down shyly as Gauguin discards a book and fills a pipe. Gauguin is propped up in a cot in middle of room. He has a couple of days' beard.

GAUGUIN (quiet) Thank you for coming, Vernier.

VERNIER I'm thankful you sent for me. I've been wishing I could tell you how beyond words I'm outraged, by the Judge's action.

GAUGUIN (calm) It's no matter.
Vernier gives him a look of mild surprise.

VERNIER You'll appeal it, of course.

GAUGUIN I won't live to, Monsieur; that's why I asked you to come.
Vernier is not a man to be "shocked" by this but he is surprised and moved.

GAUGUIN I shall be dying, I believe, very soon.

VERNIER (quietly) What is it, Gauguin?

GAUGUIN My heart.

VERNIER Is there anything I can do?
Gauguin smiles thanks and shakes his head.

GAUGUIN (calmly) Nothing.
Vernier glances at Gauguin's feet, as Gauguin starts lighting up his
tobacco.

VERNIER Are you suffering much pain?
Gauguin forgets the unlighted match . . .

GAUGUIN (smiling gently) I'm afraid I've become an addict, Vernier;
used up my tolerance. I doubt that all the morphine in this world would
entirely cover the pain. But, the feet are—child's play, compared to the
heart seizures.

Silence. Gauguin strikes a match and makes to light his tobacco.

VERNIER You are a very brave man.
Gauguin, who proudly knows it, bows slightly, smiling; then:

GAUGUIN If I were sufficiently brave, I'd have said nothing about it.
A silence. Gauguin's forgotten match burns his fingers; he shakes it
out, throws it away, reaches for another.

GAUGUIN I wanted to see you to ask if—after all the—unpleasantness—
you would grant me a favor.

VERNIER You know I'll do anything I can.

GAUGUIN Thank you . . . Will you see to it that I'm given a burial, with
civil rites only?

VERNIER Of course I will.

GAUGUIN (smiling) You see, much as I'd like to be, I'm not really a savage; I can't leave it to Tioka . . . And God knows I'm no Christian . . .
Much as I regret it, I'm a civilized man. Even worse: I'm a citizen of
the French Republic. So I'll leave my carcass for France to deal with—
so long as I can be sure there's no religion.

VERNIER (shy) Gauguin: in some way you're a religious man, in caring at all.

GAUGUIN Yes. Perhaps in many ways.
He starts to make with the second match.

VERNIER You have kept faith with yourself. You have made great sacrifices.
Pause. Gauguin forgets the match.

GAUGUIN (vague and old) Yes. . . .
He muses; then begins gently to laugh. Still laughing a little.

GAUGUIN (wonderingly) If I'd known the whole cost of it—if I'd ever dreamed! I wonder whether I could ever have done it. Ever dared begin!

Vernier curbs a comment; he listens close. Gauguin talks as much to himself as to Vernier. He "learns" as he talks.

GAUGUIN (smiling) You see, essentially I'm a very limited and stupid man. When I left my family I was sure *that* was temporary. And so it has gone, straight through: a steady *stripping away,* like the taking apart of an onion to its center. I used to have a very good opinion of myself. I was foolish enough to suppose I could become a savage. But in Tahiti I was just a sympathetic tourist; and here I've become just a crank. I was foolish enough to hope that I might have fame during my lifetime; and foolish enough to care; and foolish enough to try to win it through vulgarity and arrogance. I learned better. I lost a beloved daughter. I lost the desire to live. I lost the delusion that I had the right to take my own life. I may have lost my sanity, at times; and it's quite clear that I'm losing my sight. I've lost even the faith in myself as an artist; and the desire to be one. Some of my work is good; some is very good. Some may change the course of Art, ever so little; some may give a vision of possibility to men who suffer in a time even worse than ours. All of it is honest. But beside the vision, it is only a glimmer; and beside the sublime works of art . . . (he smiles and shrugs) And now, I am going to lose my life. And yet in all this lifetime's accounting of losses, I feel a kind of peaceful joy I had never dreamed could exist for me. I've always tried to be true to my vocation, come what might. But I begin to realize that—if I could properly use your language—the real effort has always been, simply, to be true to my own soul. And that I have been and now I know the price.

Vernier, moved, nods slowly. Silence.

GAUGUIN You're a good man, Vernier. It has meant a great deal, to talk to you about this. (shyly) All my life I have been very lonely.

Eyes suddenly damp, Vernier lightly touches Gauguin's shoulder.

VERNIER So have I. That's why I became a Christian.

GAUGUIN (musing) Hm. . . Perhaps it's why I became an artist.
They sit very quietly in the deep twilight.

GAUGUIN (gently) I'm quite tired, now.
Vernier stands up.

VERNIER Where is your boy?

GAUGUIN Ka Hui? Since this Court trouble he's afraid to be associated with me.

VERNIER I'm afraid a storm is coming up; you may need help. I'd be very glad to stay.

GAUGUIN No, thank you. . . I'm quite used to taking care of myself.
He gets up.

VERNIER (across it) Please don't get up.

GAUGUIN I'd like to look out, before dark.
Hiding his pain, he walks Vernier to the door.

TWO-SHOT—EXT.—GAUGUIN AND VERNIER AT DOOR

VERNIER (shyly) I'd like to come soon again, if I may.
Gauguin knows they will never see each other again.

GAUGUIN (kindly) I would always be happy to see you.
They shake hands.

VERNIER Good night, then. . . God bless you.

GAUGUIN Good-bye.
The word enters Vernier; he meets Gauguin's eyes, much moved. Aware of it too, Gauguin smiles warmly; his look gently forbids words. Vernier smiles with a curious shyness and exits, down the steps. Gauguin watches after him; a rising breeze moves on him. He draws in a deep breath and looks towards the shore.

FULL SHOT—THE SHORE AND THE SEA—(GAUGUIN'S VIEWPOINT)
In the twilight the wind is rising. The water is slaty; the palms louden. Darken print during the shot.

FULL SHOT—REVERSE—THE PEAK OF TEMETIU—(GAUGUIN'S VIEWPOINT)
Dusk deepens, palms louden; light leaves the peak; sky is smoky.

CLOSE SHOT—GAUGUIN
Looking towards Peak, quietly aware this is the last he will see of the open world; then looks about, and down. Tender smile.

GAUGUIN (calling) *Koaha,* Tioka.

MED. SHOT—TIOKA
Looking very small and old, he hurries towards his hut with a couple of hens. He looks up and grins, in the wind.

TIOKA (calling) *Koaha,* Koke!
He goes in.

CLOSE SHOT—GAUGUIN (RESUMED)
Alone a moment, looking at nothing, in wind and darkening and rising sounds of wind, surf and palms. O. s., the loud, fugitive cry of a storm-scared bird. Gauguin goes in and shuts door.

INT. GAUGUIN'S HOUSE—CLOSE SHOT—GAUGUIN
In the last daylight, sounds o.s., he turns up a lamp, whose light turns his face the dark gold of Marquesan skin.   FADE OUT

FADE IN
CLOSE FULL SHOT—(WIDE ANGLE)—A WAVE-NIGHT
We shoot from shore. It smashes home with great force. Scream of wind and palms o.s.

CLOSE DOWNSHOT—THE GROUND
A "flayed" look, under strong wind; torn palm branches rasp and skate along it.

FULL SHOT—THE PEAK
Barely visible in black storm; immobile as the world.

INT. GAUGUIN'S HOME—NIGHT
From here on, storm sounds continue o.s. but are deeply subdued: a feeling of absolute calm and stillness, indoors, at the center of a storm. Keep strong o.s., throughout—but "shut away," the solemn, bell-like tolling of the surf.

DOWNSHOT—GAUGUIN'S WRITING TABLE
Everything is in perfect order, as never before.

PANNING DETAIL SHOT—UTENSILS, ETC.
Freshly cleaned eating utensils, a still-damp wisp of a towel, soap and brush and razor; a neatly hung face towel.

CLOSE DETAIL SHOT—GAUGUIN'S FEET AND BANDAGES
Also legs of chair and easel. One foot is bare. His hands finish unbandaging the second and with a sigh of relief, as he starts rolling the bandage, he "works" the swollen foot.

MED. SHOT—GAUGUIN
He puts both neatly rolled, very clean bandages on a table beside him. A deep twinge of pain in the feet. He glances at his hypodermic, shrugs at its uselessness, picks up palette and brushes, and resumes work. For the first and last time we see him, at an easel, just peacefully killing time. He is clean-shaven, freshly bathed and combed; he wears a clean *pareu*. A look of calm, patience, solitude—and *waiting*.

A "buffeting" sound of wind o.s. and the lamps flicker; he calmly paints. Another "buffet"; all go out, except one ship's lantern. He gets up, with difficulty, calmly adjusts this light and brings it near; and resumes work. The screaming wind o.s. intensifies. We TIGHTEN VERY SLOWLY on the calm face and the suffering eyes. Suddenly he hesitates; a look of perplexity. He looks harder at his work.

INSERT—THE BRITTANY SNOW SCENE
We see it briefly in full color; then one color dies out.

CLOSE SHOT—GAUGUIN, reacting.

FULL SHOT—GAUGUIN'S VIEWPOINT—HIS SUNFLOWER PAINTING
One color, absent at first, is restored.

CLOSE SHOT—GAUGUIN—NEW ANGLE
He quickly lifts his palette close to his eyes, and the light.

INSERT—THE PALETTE—HIS VIEWPOINT
All the colors at first; then one is lost; a second; then the shot goes dark maroon; then black and white.

HEAD CLOSEUP—GAUGUIN
His silent reaction is "O God, not that, too!" He gets up slowly.

MED. PANNING SHOT—GAUGUIN AND PAINTINGS
He puts down palette and brushes, picks up the lantern, holding it high by his head, and moves weakly towards the walls on which—commingled with older European art and with native art and fetishes—several of his paintings hang.

NOTE: Except in viewpoint shots, everything is in full color.
DOLLY AND PAN him along to one wall, then PAN into a MOVING VIEWPOINT
SHOT over the paintings. We linger over one; then a second; tormenting
waverings between full color, part-color, and black-and-white.

HEAD CLOSEUP—GAUGUIN

Holding the lantern high. With thumb and forefinger he presses brutally
hard against his shut eyes, then opens them and peers very sharp and
close, very "old-looking," with a look of incredulous fury—fury, against
himself.

CLOSE SHOT—THE PAINTING—HIS VIEWPOINT

A last, trembling shimmer and glimmer of color; then dead black-and-
white.

CLOSE SHOT—GAUGUIN

A moment of utter desperation; then his face hardens into a little smile.
Then suddenly, an inward gasp of sheer agony (by "inward gasp," a
violent sucking-in-of-breath); he stands utterly still. Then he moves,
very carefully, a half-pace—and again is transfixed. His free hand, spread,
trembles almost like that of a cellist, an inch from the center of his chest.
He "listens." Then the pain eases sufficiently, and he knows what it is
time to do.

Moving with great care as we PAN and CUT as need be, he assembles
his needs beside the cot in the middle of the floor: . . . brushes, palette,
tubes of color, a fresh canvas; hypodermic; lantern; the family photograph:—and lies down, and gets to work again. (He must of course do this
without an ounce of self-appreciation or conscious dramatics. N.B.: We
never see this painting except in its final chaotic form—in the prologue.)
After a few moments of rapid work his eyes go blank for a moment; he
fumbles for, and gets, the photograph; and tries it at varying distances
from his eyes, straining to see, with all his power. Then a look of immense relief.

CLOSE SHOT—THE FAMILY PHOTOGRAPH—(HIS VIEWPOINT)

In Gauguin's trembling hand. Black and white shot. It comes out of
middling focus into knife-edge; he steadies his hand; he brings it nearer,
through blur, into large image and maximally keen focus. Hold. Then:

GAUGUIN'S VOICE (very quiet and tender) Mette . . . forgive me . . .
child! . . . child . . .

The photographed images welter for a moment between light and darkness; then go dead blank.

CLOSE DOWNSHOT—GAUGUIN, BLIND

He sits-lies for a moment (he has propped himself up with pillows). as deadly still as with the heart attack; then his face hardens with self-contemptuous purpose. With blind hands he again squares off the framed canvas on his knees; gropes for tubes; knows colors by the size and shape of tube; squeezes out color; gets some on his body; with a silent sneer at himself, wipes it into a smear, and gets back to work. But again, brush in mid-air, he hesitates; freezes. Now we begin, along with the heightening storm o.s. the terrifying shuddering whisper (o.s.) of a subsonic organ-pipe, used earlier in his "vision." He "listens," then very slightly nods, twice. He lays the palette and painting to his left and the photo under his right hand, to the right (he pats it as if it were an urgent little child); draws one of two pillows from beneath him to floor; and lies back, staring straight up with blind eyes, waiting. We MOVE VERY SLOWLY DOWNWARD INTO EYE CLOSEUP AND THEN INTO DEAD BLACKNESS. In the dead blackness, sounds of storm and ogan-pipe continue o.s. Images beat darkly and slowly upon the blackness; they are CLOSE SHOTS and we are always moving in on them, and they look as if into Gauguin's eyes, in perfect and inscrutable calm: Mette (blackness); Vincent (blackness); Aline (blackness): Then all sound is cut off sharp except the steadily intensifying organ-pipe. Then after long pause in blackness, that too is cut off sharp. Pause. Then a woman's voice is heard, pianissimo, singing the Peruvian melody. It comes up gradually to the gentle pitch normal to a lullaby. Then slowly out of the blackness, and close to us, using stop-motion, a tremendous white flower (a hibiscus?), opens from the tight bud, spreads, and blooms out to full, into ever-increasing purity of light, at length almost to incandescence; filling the screen with its splendor and freshness and with its all but palable fragrance. The singing stops, mid-phrase: Pause.

GAUGUIN'S VOICE (in a whisper) Noa noa!

THE SCREEN BLACKS OUT. Hold on blackness. Then:

FADE IN
INT. GAUGUIN'S HOUSE—DAY

We PULL SLOWLY BACK OUT OF THE PAINTING of the sunflowers and back between the wrecked feet; a reversal of the shot which closes our prologue; and,   CUT TO

GROUP SHOT—BISHOP, PRIEST, VERNIER, TIOKA, TRADER, LIEUTENANT

Now, many more natives crowd the door in b.g. Gauguin is not in the shot. The natives murmur low, ad lib. One is audible:

NATIVE (softly) Ua mate Koke; ua pete enata! (Gauguin is dead; we are lost!)

The Priest glances questioning to his Bishop—who nods. The Priest steps forward as we TILT DOWN, bringing in lower half of cot. He draws the sheet down to cover Gauguin's bare feet.

CLOSE DOWNSHOT—GAUGUIN
We have a last glimpse of the savagely paint-mangled body and of the enigmatically smiling head; then the sheet is drawn up.

GROUP SHOT—AS BEFORE
. . . as Priest returns from bed to his place beside the Bishop.

BISHOP (quietly) Send Brother Michel down, to prepare him for burial.
Priest nods; Vernier starts a take.

CLOSE SHOT—VERNIER, OVER BISHOP
He steps towards the Bishop.

VERNIER Excuse me, Monsignor; Monsieur Gauguin asked for a burial with civil rites only.

The Bishop turns into a TWO-SHOT.

BISHOP (quietly) Civil rights? I'm afraid that's out of the question; Monsieur Gauguin was a Catholic. Not a very—faithful Catholic, to be sure; but . . . one of us.
Vernier's silence is powerful.

BISHOP (gently) Surely you can see, Monsieur Vernier, that we must do the best we can for him . . . for him above most people. We must return good for evil.

Silence. Tioka quietly appears in b.g., much interested.

VERNIER (quietly desperate) Monsignor: it was my last promise to him.
Vernier's eyes, and the Bishop's hold hard; we may infer that Vernier's life-work is at stake. The Bishop fully realizes the gravity of Vernier's conflict.

BISHOP (quiet and compassionate) I am so very sorry, Monsieur; you were mistaken to make such a promise. (pause; eyes holding; then) Come, Father.

He leaves the shot, towards the door, followed by the Priest. We center a moment on Vernier, and Tioka in b.g., watching after him.

FULL SHOT—THE ROOM
The sheeted corpse, and the Group; as the Bishop and Priest walk to the door and out into brilliant sunlight—the natives making plenty of way.

DISSOLVE

EXT. THE GRAVEYARD—DAY

Now for the first time we entirely dispense with the "gunmetal overcast" I suggested: until further notice we work to enhance, instead, completely hot and vivid, "documentary" noonday sunlight.

CLOSE AND GROUP SHOTS

Quite a few natives are here; few whites—only Vernier, the Trader, the Bishop and the Priest. The Bishop, in a tone of highly experienced reverence, is reading from the Roman Burial Office, in Latin, with a French accent. We hear earth falling o.s. And throughout this scene we hear a strange and tremendously vital sound of humming, identified later.

We spot the clergy, the whites, the native gravediggers as they spade the earth in. A little native acolyte, in cassock and beautifully French-laced cotta, presents his Bishop with a vessel of Holy Water; and the Bishop thrice sprinkles the grave.

That ends it; all except Vernier and Tioka quickly leave our shot and their receding sounds soon die. Pause; they are keenly aware of each other. Then Vernier kneels. Having done so, he prays silently for a few moments. Tioka stands, courteously, in b.g.

When Vernier has finished the silent prayer, he is silent, without prayer for a moment; then:

VERNIER (to Gauguin in his grave) Forgive me. (pause; then to God in Heaven) God forgive me.

Pause; then he gets up—not dusting off his knees—and leaves the shot. Now Tioka is alone. He advances to the grave.

TIOKA (very quiet) *Koaha, Koke; . . . my friend; . . . my King . . .*
Pause, looking down at the grave, in grim sorrow; then looking up and at large (almost to us), as to all heaven and earth.

TIOKA Now there are no more men.

As we TILT DOWNWARD he reverently places upon the raw earth a huge blood-red flower. As soon as he does, a bee dives into it like a bullet (most easily gotten by reversing a shot??) and we begin to understand the strange o.s. humming. Tioka, beginning to understand it, glances to one side and up as we PAN in, close over Gauguin's own, new, nameless, wooden cross, to the foot of a great Crucifix and the snow-white, weather-split feet of a wooden Corpus. Tioka, turning, comes again into the shot, looking: there are a few bees, and the split feet, from inside, sweat and seep out a rich, golden honey. After looking for a moment, Tioka, with sad and elderly childlike curiosity, tips one finger into the honey; licks it; looks up to the face of the Christ o.s.; and walks out of the shot.

Now if we have a crane we RISE STRAIGHT UP the entire bee-dwelt, honey-swollen body of Christ, culminating with the head. Otherwise,

CUT TO

CLOSE SHOT—HEAD OF THE CHRIST

Split and weathered, crowned with thorns, very beautiful, profoundly victorious in utter defeat, the dying Head is fallen to the left, and the dying Eyes gaze out over the Valley of Atuona (o.s.). There are bees here, too, on the face and on the eyes and among the thorns; the sound of their humming is immortally strong; and here, too, the rich gold of the wild honey seeps through. We hold a few seconds; then PAN over slowly to the peak of Temetiu which, on the far side of the Valley, "leaps up like a battle cry." We hold here again a few seconds more and bring on a new sound, strong and fresh o.s.; then TILT SLOWLY DOWNWARD and see the source of the sound.

The graveyard is on a high hill, opposite Temetiu; the Valley between is filled with thousands upon thousands of palm trees. We so use our filters that they flash azure and green and silver. They stand in a strong but not violent breeze which blows directly towards us, and in this breeze, rank on rank in their thousands, they seem to march triumphantly toward us, proudly, yet in tremendous successive lines bowing their heads, like line upon line of surf, flashing the light. We hold again, then TILT DOWN-WARD. . . . Far down the scrubby hill on which the graveyard rests, small and weary in the distance, Vernier, then Tioka, walk away from us.

THE END

The African Queen

"The African Queen"

*The African Queen, based on the C. S. Forester novel,
was written by James Agee in the fall of 1950, with
the assistance and cooperation of John Huston. The motion
picture was made as an independent production in
1951 for Horizon Pictures, with John Huston as director,
and Sam Spiegel as producer. Released through United
Artists, this film script received an Academy Award nomina-
tion in 1952, and Humphrey Bogart, for his portrayal of
Allnutt, was given the Academy Award for Best
Actor.*

EXT. A NATIVE VILLAGE IN A CLEARING BETWEEN THE JUNGLE AND THE RIVER.
LATE MORNING.

LONG SHOT—A CHAPEL

Intense light and heat, a stifling silence. Then the SOUND of a reedy organ,
of two voices which make the words distinct, and of miscellaneous shy,
muffled, dragging voices, beginning a hymn:

VOICES (singing) "Guide me O Thou Great Jehovah . . ."

INT. CHAPEL—LONG SHOT—THE LENGTH OF THE BLEAK CHAPEL PAST THE CON-
GREGATION, ON BROTHER, AT THE LECTERN, AND ROSE, AT THE ORGAN.

BROTHER, a missionary, faces CAMERA near center; ROSE, his sister, is at
side, her face averted. Everybody is singing.

"Pilgrim through this barren land . . ."

MEDIUM SHOT—BROTHER:

middle-aged, rock-featured, bald, sweating painfully, very much in earnest.
He is very watchful of his flock. He sings as loud as he can, rather nasally,
and tries to drive the meaning of each word home as if it were a nail.
He is beating with his hand, and trying hard to whip up the dragging
tempo:

"I am weak, but Thou art mighty . . ."

151

CLOSER SHOT—ROSE

early thirties, tight-featured and tight-haired, very hot but sweating less than Brother.

She is pumping the pedals vigorously, spreading with her knees the wings of wood which control the loudness, utilizing various stops for expressiveness of special phrases, and rather desperately studying the open hymnal, just managing to play the right notes—a very busy woman. She, too, is singing her best and loudest, an innocent, arid, reedy soprano; and she, too, is very attentive to the meanings of words:

"Hold me with Thy powerful hand."

INSERT—HALF-WAY THROUGH THE FOREGOING LINE, AN EXOTIC AND HORRIBLE CENTIPEDE-LIKE CREATURE SLITHERS INTO VIEW BETWEEN TWO OF THE ORGAN KEYS. WITHOUT INTERRUPTING HER PLAYING, AS METHODICALLY AS SHE WOULD PULL OUT A NEW STOP, ROSE SWIPES IT AWAY.

ROSE—AS BEFORE—

completes "Thy Powerful Hand"; o.s. voices of singers. Unperturbed, Rose finishes her casual disposal of the bug and pulls out a new stop.

MISCELLANEOUS SHOTS—

Through rest of hymn, SHOOT and CUT against its lines for meaning, irony and pathos, roughly as follows:

FULL VIEW of congregation past Brother and Rose. They are all Negroes and nearly all are dressed in glaring white—the women in garments like camisoles, the men in pants which reach about to their shins: splayed, bare feet. Some of the faces bear the marks of heavy savage ornaments which have been removed, or of tatooing and scarring rituals which have been outlived—torn nostrils, lips and ear lobes, a neck curiously thin and weak from the enormously heavy metal bands which used to surround it. Some of the children are naked or near-naked. Nearly everybody dutifully shares open hymnals, but it is obvious that few, if any, can read. The singing of most of them is weirdly shy and inchoate—a little like that of a neighborhood audience when a group "sing" is imposed upon them. But on certain high phrases a glad, rich, wet soprano lifts out large and happy, very child-like; and a big male voice bleats forth joyous, jazz-like improvements on the tune, a little off-key. There are very few men present.

We detail or bring into salience, bare feet slapping time and an anklet shimmying; a very earnest young married couple with the wedding ring prominent and an impressive phalanx of children in tow; the owner of the happy soprano, a sweet, contented, pre-moral face; the owner of the big male voice; the inevitable rather effeminate man in every congregation who loves religion because he loves Beauty. He is immensely pleased that he knows all the words (the others just dab at them): he sings them without any knowledge of their meaning: they sound Hawaiian. Also, we SPOT a tremendously old, wrinkled, bent-over woman, dressed in white like a good Christian, but with a bone stuck through the septum of her nose. She croaks, toothless, bleary-eyed.

These things must be disposed of by late in the first stanza, which continues:

> "Open now the crystal fountain
> Whence the living waters flow,
> Let the fiery, cloudy pillar
> Lead me all my journey through."

We close on the old dame with the bone singing—

> ". . . my journey through."

O.S., on ". . . fiery, cloudy pillar", a queer SOUND, steadily louder: the absurdly flatulent, yammering syncopation of a rachitic steam motor. Eyes begin to wander from hymnals: CUT IN Brother frowning and singing harder trying to impose order; attention to the hymn begins to fall apart a little; FOLLOW the white, veering eyes to FRAME, through the open window.

LONG SHOT—THE AFRICAN QUEEN
whose WHISTLE lets out a steamy whinny, then REPEATS it, with great self-satisfaction. She is squat, flat-bottomed—thirty feet long. A tattered awning roofs in six feet of her stern. Amidships stand her boiler and engine. A stumpy funnel reaches up a little higher than the awning.

ON SECOND WHINNY,   CUT TO

MEDIUM CLOSE SHOT—ALLNUTT—ON HIS BOAT
He is in worn, rather befouled white clothes. He is barefooted and his feet are cocked up and he is sitting on his shoulder blades, smoking a bad cigar. He wears a ratty boater, slantwise, against the sunlight. He is attended by two young Negroes so tall, thin and gracile they suggest black macaroni. One is proudly and busily puttering at the engine, which requires a lot of attention: the other is fanning ALLNUTT, who is feeling just fine. Allnutt speaks to the fanner in Swahili. The young man without breaking the rhythm of his fanning, licks out one long, boneless arm and alters the lashed tiller; the Queen begins to swerve toward shore.

O.S., the hymn continues, all but drowned by motor noise.

LONG SHOT—INT. CHAPEL

Rose pulls out all the stops, spreads her knees, and pumps like mad in her effort to drown out the ENGINE SOUND. Brother sweats and sings even harder, scowling, shaking his head. The singing is fraying out half to hell; the congregation is a solid black wall of wandering eyes; a few pious converts frown or nudge at the less pious; a little group is coalescing toward the window. Past it, framed by window, we see the boat tie up and Allnutt lands, booting one of his crew in the bottom.

The hymn, meanwhile, continues:

> "Feed me with the heavenly manna
> in this barren wilderness,
> Be my sword, my shield, my banner,
> be the Lord my righteousness."

Rose's sense of artistic propriety is too much for her. To keep things going, she ought to play loud, but on the next line—

> "When I tread the verge of Jordan . . ."

she shuts down to the vox humana and the tremolo and maintains that through—

> "Bid my anxious fears subside."

On this line, Allnutt appears and lounges against the front door frame still drawing on his cigar. Rose lets everything rip fortissimo on the closing lines:

> "Death of death, and hell's destruction
> land me safe on Canaan's side."

By the time of "hell's destruction," Allnutt becomes aware that a lighted cigar in church is bad manners, and, nodding casual apology to Brother, tosses it away onto the packed dirt, out of our sight. Instantly there is a hell of a hullaballoo o.s., all in gibberish, against which the closing words of the hymn compete stridently.

The less self-controlled of the flock are no longer singing, and are craning their necks and rolling their eyes, but with just enough Sunday-Schoolish discipline to stay in their places. The more pious, with effort, keep their eyes where they belong and SING all the harder. IN QUICK SHOTS, Brother and Rose redouble their efforts. There is a final long-drawn "Aaaa-men," and it is clear this is the closing hymn of the service. Brother closes his book and picks up his service-book; Rose shuts and locks the box-organ and puts the key (which is on two shoestrings) around her neck. Brother strides with decorous alacrity down the middle aisle. Immediately following him, the natives hurry from their benches.

SHOOTING PAST ALLNUTT—THROUGH DOOR
on the cause of the hullaballoo—a squabbling football scrimmage of virtually nude male heathens, battling for the cigar butt. In b.g., if permissible, a couple of equally nude women; a thin, pot-bellied little boy dashing happily toward the fight. Brother and the eager heads of white-clad Christians come into the SHOT, BACK TO CAMERA, watching. One of the heathen fights his way up from the heap with a yowl of supremacy, filed teeth in a great grin, prancing and holding high above them all the frantically busted cigar of vaudeville; others leap after it.

REVERSE ANGLE
Allnutt, seeing the wrecked cigar, looks kind of bleak. As Brother comes out, he meets his annoyed eye with mingled reproach, apology and indifference.

ALLNUTT (to Brother) Hello, Reverend.

BROTHER Mr. Allnutt.

ALLNUTT Here's your mail. Sorry I'm late, but one thing and another kept me in Limbasi. You know how it is, Reverend. (he winks) Or maybe you don't.

Brother clears his throat.

ALLNUTT They gave me a real going over when I got to the mine. They called me all the names they could think of—in Belgian, but I don't mind so much bein' cursed in a foreign language, so I just took it with a smile. They wouldn't fire me, I was sure of that. There ain't nobody in Central Africa but yours truly knows how to get up a head of steam on *The African Queen*. It may sound like bragging, Reverend, but I'm mighty close to being in-di-spensable. Seein's how them Belgians is too damn cheap to buy 'er a new engine.

Rose joins them at the door.

ROSE (indifferently) Good morning, Mr. Allnutt.

ALLNUTT Mornin', Miss.

Rose's prayer book is clamped under her sharp elbow. Her walking is used to country, yet tight and spinsterish.

MEDIUM CLOSE SHOT—ALLNUTT, BROTHER AND ROSE
For a moment Allnutt looks at Rose with utter casualness and indifference;

his eyes leave her even before Brother speaks. Brother is looking through the mail. Past them, the liberated Christians walk into the sunshine.

BROTHER Ah, splendid, At last they've come.

ALLNUTT Huh?

BROTHER My marrow seed.
Behind these lines, the TINY OLD WOMAN with the nose-bone makes herself prominent; she's waiting to speak to Brother, almost plucking his sleeve.

BROTHER (to Allnutt) Yes. (to Grandma) Yes?

OLD WOMAN (in snaggle-toothed, adoring enthusiasm) Oh Mistah Sayuh, I does like how you preach!

BROTHER 'k you?

OLD WOMAN All dat hell-fish!
Brother nods and smiles uneasily.

OLD WOMAN De way yo' neck swell up.

BROTHER (in dismissal) Thank you, thank you. (to Allnutt, without enthusiasm) You'll stop for tea, Mr. Allnutt.

ALLNUTT Don't care if I do.
They start walking TOWARDS AND PAST CAMERA.   DISSOLVE TO

INT. DINING ROOM. MED. SHOT—RIGIDLY SYMMETRICAL, ACROSS DINING ROOM TABLE:
Rose at dead center, Brother at her left, in profile, Allnutt at her right, opposite Brother, in profile. The room is so shaded against heat it is gloomy. The silence, gloom and heat are stifling. Rose is pouring the second of three cups of tea; she pours the third. Brother is deep in the news of a Mission paper. Allnutt sits oppressed by the silence, like a child on his good behavior. A long silence while Rose leisurely pours.

ROSE You take sugar, Mr. Allnutt, I seem to remember.

ALLNUTT That's right, Miss. Couple o'spoonfuls.
She doles them into his cup.

ROSE And cream.

ALLNUTT Right.
Rose passes him his tea.

ROSE Bread and butter?

ALLNUTT (taking some) 'oh obliged.

He picks up his cup an inch to drink and puts it down again. Nobody else is served yet. Rose fixes Brother's tea and plants it beside him. She puts a slice of bread and butter on his plate.

BROTHER (reading) 'k *you?*

Rose finishes fixing her own tea, and helps herself to bread-and-butter. She lifts her cup, not quite crooking her pinkie, and sips. Allnutt still doesn't move; he is waiting for Brother. Brother finishes and turns his page, and, without shifting his eyes, finds his tea with a blind hand and blindly drinks it and sets down the cup again. Allnutt, licensed, takes a big bite of bread-and-butter and picks up his cup and washes it down. By Rose's covered reaction, it is clear that she has been taught never, never to do this, but that she expects no better of such as Allnutt. Allnutt sighs wetly and contentedly. This, too, is bad manners to Rose, but she takes it in her stride.

They go on soberly eating bread-and-butter and drinking tea. The only SOUNDS are those of china, sipping, chewing and swallowing. Nobody looks at anyone else. Brother and Rose are wholly, stiffly reposeful; they are used to this. Allnutt begins to get a little squirmy, like a child in church. The silence makes him visibly uneasy, but he tries not to show his uneasiness.

All of a sudden, out of the silence, there is a SOUND like a mandolin string being plucked. At first the sound is unidentifiable, though instantly all three glance sharply up, each at the other two, then away; in the next instant they recognize what it is and each glances sharply, incredulously, at the other two—and then again, quickly away; then Brother and Rose glance with full recognition at Allnutt, at the instant that he knows the belly-growl is his. At the moment of recognition, he glances down at his middle with a look of embarrassed reproach. He glances up quickly and slyly—hopeful they've missed it—to find the eyes of both still fixed on him. The instant their eyes meet they bounce apart like billiard balls, and fix on the first neutral object they happen to hit. Then Allnutt looks at them again: neither will look at him.

All three lift their cups at the same moment, for a covering, disembarrassing drink of tea. Rose and Allnutt simultaneously recognize what they are doing (Brother is pretending to read, misses it, and goes ahead and drinks his), and both, at the same moment, lower their cups to saucers with an almost simultaneous clink. Both look away from each other. Brother clears his throat rather loudly and turns a page. Rose and Allnutt reach for their cups; Brother beats them to it. When Brother has again put down his cup, Rose—the tail of her eye on Allnutt—picks up her cup

and drinks, her eyes carefully empty above the cup. Allnutt has his cup
again on the way to his mouth when his insides give out with a growl
so long-drawn and terrible that Rose first flinches, then makes a noise
across it with her spoon, stirring her tea. Brother tightens up like a fist,
his first reflex being that this loud one is a calculated piece of effrontery.
Allnutt just endures it, with a look of suffering stoicism. When it is over
there is a tense silence. Allnutt slowly, slyly looks up at Brother; he is
stone. He looks to Rose; she is gazing far off into space. Allnutt is quite
embarrassed, and knows they are. He does his best to relieve his own
embarrassment and theirs.

ALLNUTT (in a friendly, yet detached tone) Just listen to that stomick of
mine.

There is a silence. By their almost invisible reaction, it is clear that to just
listen to that stomick of his, is the last thing they want to do. Allnutt
is a bit chilled by the silence, but he tries again.

ALLNUTT Way it sounds, you'd think I'd got an 'eye-ener inside me.
A silence.

Rose looks at Allnutt; their eyes meet; he attempts a friendly smile.
Her face goes stony with embarrassment and she looks quickly away.
So does he.

ROSE (as soon as she can manage it) Do have another cup of tea, Mr.
Allnutt.

ALLNUTT Thanks, Miss, don't mind if I do.
He passes his cup, while she pours. There is a third growling; not so bad.
Allnutt says nothing. Then, after a pause:

ALLNUTT Scuse me.
Rose looks stone deaf. She hands him his cup.

ALLNUTT Much obliged, Miss.
He drinks some tea.

ALLNUTT Queer thing, ain't it. (a silence) Wot I mean, wot d'you spose
it is, makes a man's stomick carry on like that?

ROSE Bread and butter, Mr. Allnutt?

ALLNUTT Thanks, Miss.
He takes some and eats. After a little chewing, his jaws slow; he is
expecting another growl and listens intently; so does Rose; none comes,
After a little, Allnutt relaxes and Rose relaxes at least to a state of armed

truce. They are both munching methodically, eyes out of focus, when Brother takes a curiously official-mannered gulp of tea, sets down his cup, and breaks the silence.

BROTHER Herbie Morton's a bishop.

ALLNUTT (thinking the remark is addressed to him) Huh?

ROSE Who's that, dear?
Allnutt is pretty embarrassed to have said "huh."

BROTHER Surely you remember Herbie Morton. (Rose looks doubtful) Blond, ruddy-complected chap, a bit younger than me. He sang a solo at the graduation exercises. "Holy, Holy", I believe.

ROSE (dubiously) I think I remember. It was so long ago.

BROTHER Well, he's a bishop now.

ROSE Splendid.

BROTHER I'd say Herbie was a bit younger than I—four or five years. (Rose pours more tea into his cup) Surprising in a way. I mean—well, there was nothing outstanding about him. He was no great shakes as a student and he didn't have any more than his share of the social graces. (a pause; he drinks then eats bread and butter, but with rather less relish than before) No doubt one does get ahead quicker at home than in a foreign field . . . And then, of course, he did marry well.

ROSE Oh!

BROTHER That manufacturer's widow. What was his name? Briggs—Griggs—Briggs—yes, Alfred Briggs. Soap flakes, I think. Yes, Mrs. Alfred Briggs. (pause) Not to take anything away from Herbie. (pause) I am delighted for him.

ROSE Of course.

BROTHER It was "Holy, Holy."

ROSE (pause) Yes.
A silence. Brother isn't even looking at his paper. Allnutt's stomach talks gently. They all accept it stoically.

ALLNUTT (after quite a silence) There ain't a thing I can do about it.
A silence.

ROSE More tea, Mr. Allnutt.

ALLNUTT No, Miss, I reckon not. About time I shoved off, if I'm gonna get back to the mine by tomorra night.

ROSE (insincerely) Don't hurry, Mr. Allnutt.

BROTHER (sure he is safe) Stay for dinner.

ALLNUTT (shaking his head) Thanks all the same.
Brother pushes back his chair. Allnutt pushes back his chair and gets up. Rose pats her lips with her handkerchief, pushes back her chair, and gets up.

BROTHER Mr. Allnutt brought the marrow seed at last.

ROSE Splendid.

BROTHER I must say, though, they were forever getting here.

ALLNUTT Lucky they come through now, cause it don't look like they'll be no more mail for a while.

BROTHER Why not?

ALLNUTT Reckon the Germans'll hold it up.

BROTHER (irate—we sense a background of unpleasant relations with the Germans) In heaven's name *why?*

ALLNUTT Cause it looks like there's a war on.

BROTHER No. Really? Where, Mr. Allnutt?

ALLNUTT Europe.

BROTHER (with the patronizing concern of one who hears of another Balkan brawl) Indeed! Between whom?

ALLNUTT Oh, Germany, England, the whole—

BROTHER AND ROSE (electrified) *England! !*

ALLNUTT Right.

BROTHER (pop-eyed) You mm—you really mean war?

ALLNUTT Wot they tell me. Germans claim the British started it. British claim it was the Germans. In any case, it's war.

ROSE (with great intensity) But what's *happened!* What do you *know* about it!

BROTHER (like a whip) Rose! (she shuts up fast) Exactly, Mr. Allnutt, what has *happened?*

ALLNUTT Well, now, that's about all I can remember. Oh yes—France is in it, too. She's with us, I fink. A lot 'o them little countries are in it too —Austria-Hungary, Spain, Belgium—I forget 'oo's with 'oom. A pause.

BROTHER (quiet desperation) And that is all you can tell us?

ALLNUTT All I know.—I'll try to pick up some more, next trip to Limbasi.

BROTHER I wonder to what extent we here shall be affected.

ALLNUTT None, I shouldn't think.

BROTHER This is German territory.

ALLNUTT Why would they want to bother a poor devil of a missionary and his maiden sister?—beggin' your pardons.

BROTHER We are enemy aliens.

ALLNUTT Wot's the difference—in this God-forsaken place?

ROSE (bridling) God has not forgotten this place, Mr. Allnutt—as my brother's presence here bears witness.

ALLNUTT No offence, Miss.
Another puzzled pause.

BROTHER Really war.

ALLNUTT Looks like it . . . Well, I better shove off now. Many thanks for the tea.

He opens the door and goes through it.

REVERSE ANGLE SHOT—GROUP
as Brother and Rose come through after him.

ALLNUTT Well, take care of yerselves. (he goes down the steps) See ya next month.

BROTHER Goodbye. And thank you.

ALLNUTT (at bottom of steps) 'Bye, Miss.

ROSE Goodbye, Mr. Allnutt.

LONG SHOT—PAST THEM

CAMERA watches them watch him as he shambles towards his boat. He soon lights a stogie; his relief in smoking and in being free of them is eloquent in his back. His boys jump to action; curious villagers make way for him; the engine is going by the time he gets there. The boat backs out and sets its course upstream; Allnutt turns and lifts a hand. Brother lifts a hand; Rose doesn't. The boat soon goes out of sight beyond trees.

OVER the above, back-to-CAMERA, or quarter-profiled from the rear as they idly watch his departure, Rose and Brother talk quietly as follows:

ROSE Shouldn't we perhaps call him back? Get to Limbasi while we can?

BROTHER (with unction, yet with dignity) The good shepherd does not forsake his flock when wolves prowl. (a pause) Besides, I think Allnutt is very probably right . . . I can't imagine any reason why the Germans should trouble us.

ROSE No, I suppose not.

By now, the boat is pulling out; Brother and Allnutt exchange their not very friendly waves. Rose looks idly after Allnutt, in Sunday boredom. Nothing is said for a few seconds after the boat vanishes; the SOUND of the engine dwindles.

BROTHER (awed, and moved) War. England. Just think!

As he speaks, CAMERA STARTS a coldly SLOW PAN, past the chapel, and square onto the jungle, so altering its position behind Brother and Rose that they are held in—l.s. (where before they were in r.s.).

(N.B.: BY MID-PAN the ENGINE SOUND dies.)

An almost nude native explodes from the wall of jungle, running as fast as he can, bellowing breathlessly in Swahili and English. Until they hear his bellowing, Brother's and Rose's heads are still ANGLED AWAY from jungle—not towards river still, but idle and unfocused. With the first sound of his voice, their heads turn sharply, with weary impatience, not alarm, towards the sound.

The native does not pause in the village, though he shouts vague things in Swahili as he runs, setting up a kind of helpless agitation among the villagers; in b.g. we see still more of them coming with lazy interest out of their huts, while the native tears towards the bungalow bellowing, breathlessly.

NATIVE Mistah Sayuh! Mistah Sayuh!

MEDIUM CLOSEUP—ROSE AND BROTHER (FROM RUNNER'S ANGLE) favoring Brother.

NATIVE'S VOICE (o.s.) Mistah! *Oh* Mistah Sayuh!

The eyes of Brother and Rose abruptly lift beyond the runner and come into focus as hard as hawks; almost instantly, their faces become terrible with recognition, despair, and courage—and, for the moment with uncertainty, still, whether such emotions are needed.

REVERSE SHOT—(FROM THEIR ANGLE AND DISTANCE)—GERMAN TROOPS emerge from the somber wall of the jungle, tiny against the wall, but looking very efficacious and professional in their tropical uniforms. Instantly they form ranks before an officer who barks an order in German, just audible to us. The natives are somewhat scared and awed, but mainly immobilized with scare, awe, and curiosity. Upon the order, the Germans promptly break ranks and start swiftly and effectively about their business. One group starts rounding up the natives. Another starts collecting livestock, usable food and supplies. Another covers operations with rifles. Two men light torches and start setting fire to straw huts. One man stands by the officer.

BROTHER'S VOICE (o.s.; as soon as it becomes clear what the Germans are up to, his voice is quiet but harsh) Rose—go indoors and stay there.

o.s., the SOUND of their feet on the front steps. They come swiftly into the SHOT BELOW the CAMERA and walk fast, Rose trailing, towards the officer. After only a few steps Brother begins to trot, ungainly; Rose, still more ungainly, in her narrow skirt, trots too.

CLOSE SHOT—THE OFFICER—
a tired, rather heavy, neutral, thoroughly unmemorable face. He is not as tall as Brother, to whom he is giving the once-over. His look is neither brutal nor humane: just experienced. It seems to say, roughly and humorously: "Well, well, what have I got to deal with here?" His guardian soldier steps quickly to one side and forward; a nonentity with a gun.

LESS CLOSE SHOT—BROTHER—(ROSE IN B.G.)

BROTHER (boiling mad, the innocent courage of a lion) What is the meaning of this outrage!

OFFICER—
centered, but a little less close than before; his guard in extreme r.s.

OFFICER (calmly, in German) Speak German, please; I speak no English.

CLOSER SHOT—BROTHER
the crest of a wave of righteous fury mounting just before breaking; toppling forward; the terrifying face of a man almost ready to murder out of a sense of being right.

MEDIUM CLOSE SHOT—THE FOUR OF THEM—
as close as the CAMERA can frame all four; as, simultaneously, Brother
lunges forward at the officer, Rose lunges forward to prevent Brother; the
officer steps neatly backward and sidewise, and his guardian steps forward
briskly and, sharply but just hard enough to be effective, and with an
ugly SOUND of impact, strikes Brother on the left joint of the jaw with
his rifle butt. Brother goes heavily to the ground with a groaning gasp.

BROTHER (rage, shock, astonishment) No!

ROSE (at same instant, squatting beside him, turning his head; she is
beside herself) Judkins!

CLOSE UP—BROTHER—(SHOOTING DOWN PAST ROSE)
as she turns his head.

BROTHER (semi-conscious; his jaw not broken but bleeding and already
swelling) No. No.

ROSE (across his words) Oh, Judkins. Brother dear. Come, dear. Come,
Brother.

She helps him to his feet; past them, the officer and his guard walk briskly,
aloofly away, and past the whole business, as Brother and Rose get up
and the CAMERA LIFTS to normal eye level with them, a much later stage of
the destruction of the village is visible in b.g. and is implied o.s. by
Brother's eyes.

Brother's eyes, scorched-looking, appalled, all but demented, flick from
horror to horror; he is watching the annihilation of his life's work and, to
his mind, the annihilation of Christian and potential Christian souls; his
head quavers in the negative gesture like that of a paretic; his mouth,
always hard up to this moment, trembles now and looks curiously large
and sensual.

BROTHER No! No, Lord! O no! O no! Lord! No! O no!
Rose is in the SHOT with him; shorter and less favored than he is. Her eyes
are constantly upon his face. Tears come out of her eyes, but she is doing
no vocal crying. She is watching his heart break and, essentially, she is
watching him die, and knows it.   SLOW FADE

FADE IN
LONG SHOT—SAME AS THAT WHICH OPENS THE PICTURE—
the hottest part of the day—most smashing sunlight possible.

There is no village now—only the round scorched marks where the huts
stood; a sketch of debris.

At some distance from the bungalow, and in the middle of a lot of gaping space, Brother is hoeing in his vegetable garden. He is terribly small in the enormous barrenness and light. He hoes long enough to convey great loneliness and a kind of blind perserverance, then straightens and looks rather vaguely around him, mopping his face and bald head with a hand-kerchief. Then, with an abrupt look of purpose, he starts walking, letting the hoe fall where it happens to. He walks towards the bungalow, across the bare ground, not very fast or very steadily, but purposefully. The sunlight makes a near-halation on his bare, bald head. The walk takes him long enough to infer utter loneliness and the destruction of any human sense of time. He starts up the front steps.

MEDIUM CLOSE SHOT—ROSE IN THE PARLOR
She hears him coming up the steps o.s. She continues mending his night-shirt. On SOUND of him coming through front door, she glances up again and her face becomes curious, then concerned.

MEDIUM CLOSE SHOT—BROTHER—(FROM HER VIEWPOINT)
as he advances into room. He is dressed in his Sunday best, immaculate except for sweat-and-dust of immediate garden work. His face is carefully shaven, but it has thinned and he is very pale. The wounded jaw is not bandaged and is virtually healed; stubble around it. There is a streak of garden dust across the temple and up onto the bald head. He is looking hard at Rose, but his eyes can't keep in focus.

BROTHER (sweat pouring from him, teeth rattling) Why aren't you dressed, Rose? It's time for Service.

SIDE ANGLE SHOT—ROSE
gets up, deep concern on her face, comes quickly to him, bringing both into SHOT, and lays a hand against his forehead. Her reaction infers that Brother has a terribly high fever.

ROSE You *must* wear your *hat!*

BROTHER (teeth chattering) Time, *this minute!*
Rose starts to lead and support his obstinacy, CAMERA WITH THEM, towards his bedroom door.

ROSE You must lie down a bit. You're not at all well.

BROTHER (resisting feebly but coming along, shakily) But it's time. It's time.

ROSE You're not well enough. Lie down a bit, dear.

BROTHER Perhaps I should. I feel rather odd.

ROSE I'll help you off with your things.

BROTHER (in a suddenly normal and shriveling voice; quietly) Rose.
She opens his door for him; he starts through.

BROTHER (as he turns to shut his door) 'k *you?*
He shuts the door in her face.

For a moment she stands outside the door as if paralyzed. Then she starts somewhere fast.

CLOSE UP—THEIR FORLORNLY POPULATED BOOKSHELF.
Rose hurries into the SHOT and takes down a large obsolescent-looking Home-Medical Compodium.

CLOSE SHOT—ROSE
SHOOTING LOW across the bleak dining room table as she hustles the big book to it and opens it. She is standing. She is still in a painful rush through the index when o.s. there is the NOISE of a catastrophic fall.

CLOSE SHOT—ROSE (BACK TO CAMERA)
at Brother's door. By reflex, she hesitates and raps timidly. Instantly realizing the idiocy of this, she bursts in.

REVERSE ANGLE SHOT—ROSE
inside Brother's bedroom, SHOOTING FROM LOW as she enters and stands a moment transfixed by what she sees, her face suddenly rigid and masklike with horror and pity.

CLOSE SHOT—DOWN—BROTHER (FROM ROSE'S VIEWPOINT)
He is piteous, absurd and ugly; sprawled out on the floor as ill-shaped as a wounded bat, with his nightshirt partly on, shrouding his head, and his trousers half off, trammeling knees which are grotesquely angled. Between lowered pants and hiked-up nightshirt, a sad, humiliating expanse of long white drawers in this furnace weather. His feet are fouled-up in his suspenders. The SHOT is to be both preposterous and shocking.

CLOSE UP SHOT—ROSE
past Brother from floor.

ROSE (almost whispering) Brother! Brother dear!
She rushes stooping towards him. CAMERA MOVES into CLOSE UP, as she lifts his heavy head clearly into the SHOT and gets it unveiled from the nightshirt. The big face looks ruined, disgraced, dead, but a low mumbling sighing comes from him. He is far gone.

She is about to try to lift him towards his bed when he begins to walk; she waits and listens.

BROTHER (eyes shut; a faint, delirious voice) Smite them, Lord! Smite the Amalekites, hip and thigh!

ROSE (whispering—almost by reflex) Amen. (with a long *a*)

BROTHER So cold and so foggy. My eyes are so tired. Where is Rose? Rose, are you down there in the shop? Rose, bring me a cup of hot tea.

ROSE I'm here with you, Brother dear. Right here beside you.

BROTHER I try to study—so hard. I haven't had the start some have: 'Ebrew; Greek—no—facility. If only there were more *time*. Well, if I can't pass the examinations, I can volunteer. I can be a missionary. Rose, too. Not comely among maidens, but she can become a servant in the house of the Lord. Yes, even for such as she, God finds a goodly use.

There is deep pain on Rose's face. She almost wants to say something, but knows the senselessness of it. She just keeps looking at him and listening.

BROTHER (with calm, resolve, acceptance) I'm going to put my books away, Rose. I'm not going to study any more. If I don't pass, it only means that God has other work for me. Thy will be done. (in a different voice, secret, piteous, impassioned) But, Lord, if it be Thy Will, O let me distinguish myself and give me a call here in England, right here at home, Lord. Mother will be so proud, Lord. Abash and put to shame all them that revile me and persecute me for Thy Name's sake. (whispering; pleading) Lord, I have tried so hard.

He is silent; she is motionless. Slowly LIFT CAMERA, losing Brother, CENTERING ROSE IN CLOSE UP.   SLOW FADE

FADE IN

FULL SHOT—MUDDY WATER—MORNING
The screen is filled with a foamy, strongly sliding floor of muddy water; a strong, serene freshness of water SOUND. The SHOT is VERTICAL onto this water from perhaps three feet above it. o.s., already loud, and loudening, the NOISE of the engine of *The African Queen*.

LIFT CAMERA, picking up the launch unexpectedly close as, slanting into broadside, she draws the letters of her name.

THE AFRICAN QUEEN

large across the SHOT.

CONTINUE LIFTING; as boat passes, we see Allnutt very briefly and see that he is alone.

MEDIUM CLOSE SHOT—ALLNUTT

over SOUND of expiring engine and rattle of anchor chain, reacting to his first sight of the vanished village. He looks a little scared and very cautious; he has seen what was done at the mine, and now even the smell of violence, or the echo of its impact, makes him very uneasy. He is even dirtier and more unshaven than when we first saw him and he looks extremely tired.

LONG SHOT—THE VILLAGE

what we see of it from his angle. Since he is lower than the village, all we can see is a lot of abnormal, empty sunlight.

MEDIUM CLOSE SHOT—ALLNUTT (SAME AS BEFORE)

He is wary, but knows he must investigate. He goes overside, almost out of the SHOT, stepping across a stump to shore. SWING WITH HIM.

As he reaches the top of the low bank, TRUCK with him, MEDIUM CLOSE, as he walks through a little of the burnt-out village. Past him, the scorched circular blotches where the huts were; burned and half-burned little pens and fences; ravaged gardens. He is still careful and uneasy. Unaware of it, he walks through this silence of devastation almost on tiptoe. Now he raises his eyes towards the intact bungalow o.s., and a new kind of carefulness comes into his eyes.

STOP the TRUCKING and PAN with him as he walks past and bring in the bungalow, looking cavernous, very still, and cryptic or menacing in the sunlight, as he walks the last few paces towards it. He hesitates a moment at the foot of the steps. It obviously occurs to him that he may find corpses, or nobody at all. He starts up the steps, still walking a little stealthily.

MEDIUM CLOSE SHOT—ALLNUTT

through the screen door, from inside, as he comes up the quietly creaking steps, sensitive to the mood of a kind of desolation different from that of the village; uneasy. He crosses the porch very quietly, again hesitates, peers through the gray screen door into the dark interior, and raps rather timidly.

ROSE (o.s., a dry quiet voice with the calm of exhaustion in it) Come in, Mr. Allnutt.

Her voice startles him as much as it should ourselves. He peers again, forehead wrinkled like a monkey's. He can't see her. He shyly opens and comes through the door, mumbling something apologetic and subversal.

As he catches sight of her, SWING CAMERA TO RIGHT, losing him, and PICK ROSE UP, MEDIUM CLOSE. She is past the angle of visibility from the screen door. She is in a wicker rocking chair, sitting quite primly, working with those rings on which embroidering is done. She glances up at him with eyes like fused glass—then quickly back to her needlework. It is clear by the over-precision of her motions, and their rigidity and tension, that she is under great strain, but this is to be keyed low and simple.

CLOSE SHOT—ALLNUTT (FROM HER ANGLE)
He watches her; he knows enough to keep quiet; he waits; becomes aware of his muddy feet and quietly tries to clean one against the calf and shin of the other leg.

CLOSE SHOT—ROSE (SAME AS BEFORE)
She does a couple more stitches, obtains sufficient control of herself, and lowers the needlework into her lap.

ROSE (quietly, as before) Thank God you've come.

CLOSE SHOT—ALLNUTT (AS BEFORE)
Nobody has ever thanked God in connection with him before. His reaction is quiet, but clearly this is a surprising and novel experience. He says nothing.

ROSE (o.s.) Sit down, Mr. Allnutt.

ALLNUTT Don't mind if I do.
He walks into:

TWO SHOT—ROSE AND ALLNUTT
He sits on the edge of a chair and jockeys it, shyly, a little nearer her.

ALLNUTT So they got here afore I did, eh?

ROSE Yes, they *got here*. Just after you left.

ALLNUTT No!
She says nothing.

ALLNUTT Couldn't a been more wrong, could I? Bout the Germans.

ROSE (a quieter, remote voice) Burning villages.

ALLNUTT That's to keep the natives from runnin' away. No place to come back to. Been doin' it all over, they told me up at Limbasi. The Germans are gonna train 'em into an army and try to take over the whole of Africa.

ROSE Poor helpless natives!

ALLNUTT It was the same up at the mine when I got back from Limbasi. A clean sweep of everything. Just plain luck I was on the river. They could certainly use my launch and what's in 'er, too. Blastin' gelatine, Miss. Eight boxes of it. An' a lot of canned grub. An' cylinders of oxygen an' hydrogen for that weldin' job on the crusher. Lots o' stuff.

ROSE (same dead voice) Oh, trust them.

ALLNUTT But as it 'appens, *I* got the stuff—*an'* the launch. Only I've got no crew, an' she ain't an easy boat to run single-'anded. Cause them two boys o' mine just skipped in the night. Don't know if they were scared o' me or the Germans.

ROSE (quietly, always) They are fiends out of hell. . . . His whole life's work smashed. Ruined. In a few minutes.

ALLNUTT The Reverend, eh? (Rose nods) Where's 'e now, Miss?

ROSE (pause; quietly) He's dead.

ALLNUTT I say, that's too bad! Pretty rough on you, Miss. (embarrassed; trying to keep the ball rolling) What'd 'e die of, Miss?

ROSE They killed him.

ALLNUTT (really a little surprised and shocked) Well, now that's just awful! If they'll up and shoot a Reverend, who couldn't do 'em a bit a 'arm, there ain't nobody safe.

ROSE They didn't shoot him, Mr. Allnutt. But they are accountable to God just as surely as if they had.

ALLNUTT 'Ow d'you mean, Miss?

ROSE They broke his heart. He didn't take care of himself. He didn't want to live.

She is looking into his eyes as if daring him to doubt or disagree. He is timid, perceptive and kind enough not to argue with her. After a moment, he avoids her eyes.

ALLNUTT Well, Miss that's cert'nly too bad, that's all *I* can say. (both are quiet and he is uneasy in the silence. Making conversation) When'd 'e die, Miss?

ROSE Early this morning. (an odd gesture) He's in there.

ALLNUTT *Hey!*

ROSE I beg your pardon?

ALLNUTT 'Scuse it, Miss. (delicately) Wot I mean to say is—the climate 'n all—quicker you get 'im under ground the better, if you don't mind me sayin' so.

Rose nods.

ALLNUTT (getting up) Got a shovel?

ROSE Behind the bungalow.

ALLNUTT Right.—Tell ya wot. While I'm diggin' the grave, you get yer things together, Miss—all the things ya want to take. Then we can clear out of 'ere.

ROSE Clear out?

ALLNUTT Germans might come back any time.

ROSE Why should they? They left nothing.

ALLNUTT Oh, they'll come back, all right. Lookin' for *The African Queen.* They'd dearly love to get their 'ooks on *'er*. She's the only power boat on the river.

ROSE Where will we go?

ALLNUTT I thought, Miss, 'ow we might find somewhere quiet behind an island. Then we could talk about what to do.

ROSE (a pause; then with quick decision) I'll get my things ready.

ALLNUTT Fine, Miss, I'll be quick's I can.
He starts for the front door.

ROSE Thank you, Mr. Allnutt.

ALLNUTT You'd do the same for me, Miss.
As he thinks it over, he begins to wonder, literal-mindedly, whether she really would. He goes on out.   DISSOLVE TO

TWO SHOT—ROSE AND ALLNUTT—AT THE GRAVE
They stand on opposite sides of the new grave. At its head is an improvised cross, two pieces of wood carefully and securely wired together.
Rose is reading the last lines of the burial service from a Methodist or Presbyterian prayerbook.
She reads rather badly; (i.e., with the Protestant shadings of "expressiveness") yet between the language and the conflict between restraint and deep emotion in her voice, it is quite moving. Allnutt, while she reads,

is trying to pay polite attention; he even says "Amen", and such, in a sheepish kind of way. But his eyes keep sliding uneasily to the jungle; the Germans really do worry him.

When she has finished, she stands very silent, for longer than he can take. He tries reasonably hard, but finally he has to speak.

ALLNUTT Well, Miss, let's get outa here while the gettin's good.

Rose, without looking at him or at the grave, and without speaking, walks away; he picks up his spade and follows.

MEDIUM SHOT—ROSE AND ALLNUTT

at the edge of the porch. Rose pauses, looks over towards Brother's grave for the last time. Allnutt stands beside her, carrying her suitcase, not wanting to hurry her again, but wishing she'd get a move on.

MEDIUM LONG SHOT—ROSE AND ALLNUTT—(SHOOTING PAST THEM, FROM THE INSIDE EDGE OF THE PORCH)

By the turn of her head, our eye is led across the scarified clearing. We see the stunted cross and the overwhelming jungle and, perhaps, a little of the chapel.

ROSE (really meaning it; but very restrained and prim) It was very kind of you, Mr. Allnutt, to think of the cross.

ALLNUTT Shucks. Just seemed like he oughta have one, him a Reverend 'n all.

Rose walks down the steps and towards the river. Allnutt eagerly keeps pace. We SWING the CAMERA losing the grave, and passing and losing the chapel, and centering them getting smaller along the bare ground in the hot sunlight, bringing in the river beyond them.

ALLNUTT'S VOICE (o.s.) Careful now, Miss. Watch your step. That's right.

MEDIUM LONG SHOT—OF AFRICAN QUEEN AT ANCHOR (SHOOTING PAST BOW)

and keeping the noisy SOUND of the water. We pick up Rose and Allnutt as Allnutt helps her aboard. In her long and somewhat narrow skirt she is distinctly old-maidish.

ROSE (with the upward English inflection—a little as if he had passed her a teacup) Thank—*you?*

Allnutt steps aboard.

MEDIUM SHOT—ROSE AND ALLNUTT

Rose sits down at the rear of the boat and looks around her. Her feet are drawn under her and knees close together and hands lightly folded on her knees (perhaps a lady's scrap of handkerchief in one hand), as prim, genteel and ladylike as if, on a holiday afternoon, she were about to be rowed across an artificial lake fifty yards wide. And that is more or less the way she glances about her in her new surroundings—politely and restrainedly, as if a little critical of a parlor somewhat humbler than her own.

(This SHOT, at the very beginning of her voyage, is to be quite touching, delicate and ironical, and through her very genteelism and total unconcern for what she is up against—an unawareness—we begin already to sense her complete intrepidity.)

Allnutt pauses to light up a cigarette before getting to work. He hangs the cigarette inside his upper lip. This cigarette, dead or alive, is a chronic fixture with Allnutt.

Allnutt kneels in the bottom of the boat and addresses himself to the engine. He hauls out a panful of hot ashes and dumps them overside with a sizzle and a splutter. He fills the furnace with fresh wood from a pile beside him, and soon smoke appears from the funnel, and we hear the ROAR of the draught. The engine begins to sigh and splutter, and then begins to leak gray pencils of steam. Allnutt peers at his gauges, thrusts in some more wood, and then leaps forward around the engine, displaying monkeyish agility in handling more tasks than he quite has the hands or the stamina for. With grunts and heaves of the small windlass, he hauls in the anchor, the sweat pouring from him in rivers. We see already that he is physically not a strong man.

Allnutt thrusts mightily at the muddy bank with a long pole, snatches the pole on board again, and then rushes aft to the tiller.

ALLNUTT 'Scuse me, Miss.

He sweeps her aside unceremoniously (she is astonished but quickly reassembles herself) and he puts the tiller over just in time to save the boat from running into the bank.

CAMERA IN on Rose, resettling her plumage, and on Allnutt at the tiller. The river bank starts to swing in square to the stern. Their eyes are past the CAMERA.

MEDIUM SHOT—(MOVING WITH BOAT)—ROSE AND ALLNUTT
Rose is deeply sad and very tired, but a very quiet kind of exhilaration is already growing in her; and still more clearly, her calm and tremendous, unreflecting resoluteness begins to show.

A pause.

ROSE Mr. Allnutt.

ALLNUTT Yerss . . . ?

ROSE What are the chances of our getting out through Limbasi on the railway to the Coast?

ALLNUTT The railway was in German 'ands when I was in Limbasi—and by this time Limbasi is too, I'll bet.

ROSE Then how do we get out, Mr. Allnutt?

ALLNUTT You got me, Miss. (after a pause) We've got 'eaps of grub 'ere, Miss, so we're all right, far as that goes. Two thousand cigarettes, two cases of gin. We could find a good 'iding place an' stay there for months if we want to.

Rose's astonishment at this suggestion keeps her from replying.

ALLNUTT (rattling on) I spose there's goin' to be a fight. If our troops come from the sea, they'll attack up the railway to Limbasi, I spose. In that case, the best thing *we* could do would be to wait round down 'ere an' just go up to Limbasi when the time came.—On the other 'and, they might come down from British East, an' if they do that we'd 'ave the Germans between us and them all the time. Same if they came from Rhodesia or Portuguese East. We're in a bit of a fix, whichever way y'look at it, Miss. (abruptly) Mind takin' the tiller, Miss?

Allnutt stands up and Rose takes over the tiller, holding the iron rod resolutely. Allnutt goes to his engine and is violently active once more. He pulls open the furnace door and thrusts in a few sticks of fuel; then he scrambles up into the bow and stands balanced on the cargo. The river is studded with islands so that it appears as if there were a dozen different channels.

ALLNUTT Port a little, Miss.

CLOSE SHOT—ROSE
She is confused by the command.

ALLNUTT'S VOICE (o.s.) Pull it over this side, I mean.—That's it! Steady!

MOVING SHOT—THE LAUNCH
The boat crawls up a narrow tunnel of leaf and shade. (If color photography is used, the SHOT would be startingly juicy and green—many shades of green reflected in rich brown water.)

Allnutt comes leaping back over the cargo and shuts off the engine; the propeller stops vibrating.

Allnutt dashes into the bow again. Just as the trees (SHOOTING PAST ROSE and her interest in it) begin apparently to move forward again as the current overcomes the boat's way, he lets go the anchor with a rattling CRASH, and almost without a jerk the launch comes to a standstill.

A great silence seems to close in on them—the silence of a tropical river at noon. The only SOUND is the subdued rush and gargle of the water. The sober air is filled with a strange light—a green light.

Allnutt turns from his work at the anchor. He and Rose look about them and at each other, for a moment mysteriously bemused by the stillness and by the beauty of the place. The sudden quietness and the look of the place are richly romantic; the two people are quieted by it, but they are wholly unaware of any such potentiality between them. They are just a couple of oddly assorted derelicts who hardly even know each other, and don't care for what little they know.

A pause.

ALLNUTT So far so good. 'Ere we are safe an' sound, as you might say. (he beams upon his surroundings) Not too bad a spot, is it, Miss, to sit a war out in? All the comforts of 'ome, includin' runnin' water.

He laughs at his joke and is disappointed when Rose does not join him.

ROSE I'm afraid, Mr. Allnutt, that what you suggest is quite impossible.

ALLNUTT 'Ave you got any ideas? (he takes a map out of his pocket and hands it to her) 'Ere's a map, Miss. Show me the way out an' I'll take it.

Rose opens the map and starts studying it.

ALLNUTT (after a while) One thing sure; our men won't come up from the Congo, not even if they want to. They'd 'ave to cross the lake, and *nothin'* won't cross the lake while *The Louisa* is there.

ROSE (blankly) *The Louisa?* What's that?

ALLNUTT It's an 'undred-ton German steamer, Miss, and she's the boss o' the lake 'cause she's got a six-pounder.

ROSE What's that?

ALLNUTT A gun, Miss. The biggest gun in Central Africa.

ROSE I see.

ALLNUTT If it wasn't for *The Louisa,* there wouldn't be nothin' to it. The Germans couldn't last a month if our men could get across the lake . . . But all this doesn't get us any nearer 'ome, does it, Miss? Believe me, if I could think wot we could do. . . .

ROSE This river, the Ulanga, runs into the lake, doesn't it?

ALLNUTT Well, Miss, it does; but if you was thinkin' of goin' to the lake in this launch—well, you needn't think about it any more. We can't and that's certain.

ROSE Why not?

ALLNUTT Rapids, Miss. Cataracts and gorges. There's an 'undred miles of rapids down there. Why, the river's even got a different nyme where it comes out on the lake to what it's called up 'ere. It's the Bora down there. No one knew they was the same river until that chap Spengler—

ROSE He got down it. I remember.

ALLNUTT Yes, Miss, in a dugout canoe. 'E 'ad half a dozen Swahili paddlers. Map makin', 'e was. In fact, that's 'is map you're lookin' at. There's places where this ole river goes shootin' down there like out of a fire 'ose. We couldn't never get this ole launch through.

While he talks, Rose begins to look restive and vague, as well as discouraged. By the time he is through, she has stood up, CAMERA WITH HER; she hardly hears him. She strolls a little aimlessly PAST THE CAMERA, which SWINGS TO CENTER HER BACK as she walks forward. As if half in her sleep, she sidesteps the engine.

REVERSE ANGLE—ROSE (SHOOTING FROM THE BOW)
as Rose sidesteps. She walks toward CAMERA into MEDIUM CLOSE UP, eyes glazing with dreamlike concentration. She sees something before and below her eye-level; stops, focusing on it.

CLOSE SHOT—(FROM ROSE'S ANGLE)—THE GELATINE CASES
not marked or labeled as such.

ROSE'S VOICE (o.s.) Mr. Allnutt—

MEDIUM CLOSE SHOT—ALLNUTT

ALLNUTT Yes, Miss.

MEDIUM CLOSE SHOT—ROSE—(FROM ALLNUTT'S ANGLE)

ROSE What did you say is in these boxes with the red lines on them?

MEDIUM CLOSE SHOT—ALLNUTT—(FROM ROSE'S ANGLE)
lounging and lazy.

ALLNUTT That's blastin' gelatine, Miss.

MEDIUM SHOT—ALLNUTT AND ROSE (SHOOTING FROM BOW)

ROSE (head towards him, away from CAMERA) Isn't it dangerous?

ALLNUTT Bless you, no, Miss, that's safety stuff, that is. It can get wet and not do any 'arm. If you set fire to it, it just burns. You can '*it* it wiv an 'ammer and it won't go off—at least I don't fink it will. It takes a detonator to set it off. I'll put it over the side if it worries you though.

ROSE (sharply, yet absently as she turns into CAMERA) No. We may need it. Allnutt keeps watching her idly, a little amused and very slightly contemptuous. She wanders away from the boxes, eyes downcast in thought, and pauses again.

ROSE (not looking up) Mr. Allnutt—

ALLNUTT Yeah?

INSERT—THE STEEL CYLINDERS IN BOTTOM OF BOAT

ROSE'S VOICE (o.s.) And what are these queer long round things?

MEDIUM SHOT—THE BOW—(PAST ROSE—ON ALLNUTT)

ALLNUTT Them's the oxygen and hydrogen cylinders, Miss. Ain't no good to *us,* though. Next time I shift cargo, I'll dump 'em.

CLOSER SHOT—ROSE

ROSE (sharply, yet still more subconsciously and quietly than before) I wouldn't do that.

She keeps looking down at them, musingly, "subconsciously," while CAMERA CREEPS CLOSER to her.

ROSE They look like—like torpedoes.
"Torpedoes" is spoken over:

INSERT—CYLINDERS—
a new and most deadly possible looking SHOT of the cylinders.

STILL CLOSER SHOT—ROSE
Slowly she raises her eyes from floor angle to normal; a wild light is dawning in her eyes.

ROSE (in the voice almost of a medium) Mr. Allnutt—
She turns very slowly towards him.

MEDIUM CLOSE SHOT—ALLNUTT—(FROM ROSE'S ANGLE)

ALLNUTT (a little bit smug) I'm still right here, Miss, and on a thirty-foot boat there ain't much of any place else I could be.

MEDIUM CLOSE SHOT—ROSE—(FROM ALLNUTT'S ANGLE)
walking slowly and somewhat portentously towards him.

ROSE (full of the wild light) You're a machinist, aren't you? Wasn't that your position at the mine?

MEDIUM CLOSE SHOT—ALLNUTT—(FROM ROSE'S ANGLE)

CAMERA ADVANCING on him at Rose's pace, stopping, looking down, during his last six or eight words.

ALLNUTT (comfortably) Yeah, kind of fixer. Jack of all trades and master o' none, like they say.

CLOSE SHOT—ROSE—(FROM ALLNUTT'S ANGLE)
disconcertingly close.

ROSE Could you make a torpedo?

ALLNUTT'S VOICE (o.s.) Come again, Miss?

ROSE Could you make a torpedo.

CLOSE SHOT—ALLNUTT

ALLNUTT You don't really know what you're askin', Miss. It's this way, you see. A torpedo is a very complicated piece of machinery what with gyroscopes an' compressed air chambers an' vertical and horizontal rudders an' compensating weights. Why, a torpedo costs at least a thousand pounds to make.

He relaxes; his manner is "The State Rests."

SWING CAMERA to center Rose, still perched on the gunwale.

ROSE (after a short pause; unperturbed) But all those things, those gyroscopes and things, they're only to make it *go,* aren't they?

MEDIUM CLOSE SHOT—ALLNUTT—(NEUTRAL ANGLE)

ALLNUTT Uh-huh. Go—and hit what it's goin' after.

ROSE—(AS BEFORE)

ROSE (at the height of her inventiveness; the words triumphant and almost stumbling out) Well! We've got *The African Queen*.

She stands up with these words, CAMERA RISING with her, SHOOTING FROM A LITTLE BELOW; her eager eyes are constantly on Allnutt.

ROSE If we put this—this blasting stuff—in the front of the boat here—and a—what did you say—deno—detonator there, why that would be a torpedo, wouldn't it?

CLOSE SHOT—ALLNUTT

looking up at her, greatly amused, almost sardonically admiring her.

ROSE'S VOICE (o.s.) Those cylinders. They could stick out over the end, with that gunpowder stuff in them and the detonator in the tips where the taps are.

ROSE—(AS BEFORE)

ROSE Then if we ran the boat against the side of a ship, they'd—well, they'd go off, just like a torpedo. (somewhat doubtfully, in a return to her submissive feminine habit) Wouldn't they?

TWO SHOT—ROSE AND ALLNUTT

ALLNUTT (tremendously amused; gravely) That might work. (humoring her along, and a little taken in by his own fondness for makeshift) Them cylinders'd do right enough. I could let the gas out of 'em and fill 'em up with the gelignite. I could fix up a detonator all right. Revolver cartridge'd do. (warming up to it, as an impossible project) Why, sure, we could cut 'oles in the bows of the launch, and 'ave the cylinders stickin' out through them, so's to get the explosion near the water. Might turn the trick. But what would 'appen to us? It would blow this ole launch and us and everything all to Kingdom come.

ROSE I wasn't thinking that we should be in the launch. Couldn't we get everything ready and have a—what do you call it—a good head of steam up and point the launch toward the ship and then dive off before it hit? Wouldn't that do?

ALLNUTT Might work, Miss. But what are we talkin' about, anyway. There ain't nothin' to torpedo. 'Cause *The African Queen's* the only boat on the river.

ROSE Oh, yes there is.

ALLNUTT Is what?

ROSE Something to torpedo.

ALLNUTT An' what's that, Miss?

ROSE *The Louisa.*

ALLNUTT (on mention of *The Louisa,* a blank, silent stare of mock amazement. Then, patiently) Don't talk silly, Miss. You can't do that. Honest you can't. I told you before we can't get down the river.

ROSE Spengler did.

ALLNUTT In a *canoe,* Miss!
Rose looks stubborn.

ROSE If a German did it, we can, too.

ALLNUTT Not in no launch. We wouldn't 'ave a prayer.

ROSE How do you know? You've never tried.

ALLNUTT Never tried shootin' myself through the 'ead, neither. (pause) Trouble with you is, you just don't know nothin' about boats, or water.

A pause. They look at each other, Rose much more fixedly and searchingly than Allnutt

ROSE In other words, you are refusing to help your country in her hour of need, Mr. Allnutt?

ALLNUTT I didn't say that.

ROSE Well then—!

ALLNUTT (sighs deeply) 'Ave it your own way, Miss—only don't blame me, that's all.

Allnutt stands perplexed and inarticulate, his cigarette drooping from his upper lip. His wandering gaze strays from Rose's feet, up her white drill frock to her face; he starts slightly at her implacable expression.

ROSE Very well, let's get started.

ALLNUTT What! *Now,* Miss?

ROSE (impatiently) Yes, now. Come along.

ALLNUTT There isn't two hours of daylight left, Miss.

ROSE We can go a long way in two hours.

Allnutt starts to speak; refrains; limps over to windlass and raises the anchor. Rose watches him. CAMERA PANS after *The African Queen* as Allnutt backs her out into the channel, then turns her nose downstream.

CLOSE SHOT—ALLNUTT AND ROSE

He is at the tiller—back to CAMERA; Rose, standing looking downstream. The Mission clearing on the bank, which they now approach, is unobserved by both of them. Presently pencils of steam begin coming out of the engine. Allnutt, feeling that it requires his attention, signals to Rose, who takes his place at the tiller. Allnutt goes to the engine and begins to tinker.

CLOSE UP—ALLNUTT—(ROSE IN B.G.)

ALLNUTT A lot o' the time I'm going to 'ave more than enough to do, keepin' the ole engine goin'.' So you might as well start learnin' to steer right now.

Rose nods. Her hand takes a firmer, more authoritative hold on the tiller.

ALLNUTT (continuing) She ain't no one-man boat, the Queen. Not in the shape she's in.

Rose again shifts her hand a little; and she sits up very straight with her new sense of responsibility.

ALLNUTT Know port from starboard, Miss?

ROSE I've heard of them.

ALLNUTT Well, that's port—(gesturing)—an' that's starboard.

ROSE Isn't that a bit—well, silly? Why not just say left and right?

ALLNUTT Well, spose yer facin' the other way in the boat an' I say "to the left." You might think I meant to *your* left, see, an' move to starboard. It's the boat ya gotta think of, see? So port's *always* that side—(gesturing) —an' starboard, that—an' forrard's always up there an' aft is where we are right now—no matter what way we're turned around or the boat is headed.

ROSE Why yes, I *see*. It's really quite—sensible, isn't it?

ALLNUTT Uh huh. Okay. Now go easy, Miss—light on the tiller. Now steer her just a little to starboard.

Rose puts the tiller to starboard; the launch swerves a little to port. She looks at Allnutt, bewildered. Allnutt is quietly amused.

ALLNUTT Okay, Miss, just straighten her out again. (using flat hands to demonstrate) Now looky here. Here's yer tiller. (he extends his right hand) Here's yer rudder. (he extends his left hand, below and beyond his right) They're joined. Tiller sets the rudder, rudder steers the boat. (he slants both hands rigidly to one side) ·

ROSE (eagerly) Oh, *I* see!
Rose lifts her own hand from the tiller to show; the boat yaws abruptly.

ALLNUTT *Tiller,* Miss!
Rose, startled, grabs the tiller and rights her course.

ROSE (blushing) Sorry.

ALLNUTT 'S all right, just don't never do that, 's all.

ROSE Why, the water—well—pushes against the rudder, where it turns, and—sort of drags the boat *that way. Turns* it.

ALLNUTT You're catchin' on fine, Miss.
Rose looks as pleased as if she had personally invented the rudder.

ALLNUTT Now a little to starboard, Miss. Easy now. (Rose does it right) Fine. Now a little to port. (Rose does it right)

ROSE Is *that* all there is to it?

ALLNUTT Well, ya gotta know how to read the river.

ROSE Read?

ALLNUTT Ya gotta know the water an' what's under it, that ya gotta steer clear of.

ROSE Steer clear of. Why, *that's* where that expression comes from.

ALLNUTT (uninterested) Uh huh. Mostly ya can tell it by the surface o' the water. Now ya see that long thing out there like a "V" kinda?

LONG SHOT—ACROSS THE LINE
a long, quiet "V" on the water.

ALLNUTT'S VOICE (o.s.) That always means a snag. Limb stickin' up from a dead tree; likes o' that.

TWO SHOT—ROSE AND ALLNUTT

ALLNUTT Stay off them "Vs," they're murder.
Rose looks very seriously, almost reprimandingly, towards the "V."

LONG SHOT—A DIFFERENT PART OF THE RIVER
The higher light shows it is later in the morning. In the distance, past smooth water, a choppy patch.

ALLNUTT'S VOICE (o.s.) Now all that little choppin', them's shallas, Miss.

TWO SHOT—ALLNUTT AND ROSE
Rose's eyes move from the shallows to steering; she shifts course a little, and a long "V" trails past.

LONG SHOT—FORWARD ALONG THE BOAT
as she resets her course.

MEDIUM CLOSE SHOT—ROSE
her eyes to starboard. Again the light is later. Rose's face is a shade more pleased and in bloom than before.

ROSE (pointing) What's that queer flat place, Mr. Allnutt?

MEDIUM LONG SHOT—ANOTHER PART OF THE RIVER
at medium distance off starboard bow, an odd flat turbulence in otherwise easy water.

ALLNUTT'S VOICE (o.s.) That's a rock. An' it ain't only a few inches under water. The Queen's got a shalla draft, an' that's where we're lucky. 'Cause anythin' ya can't read on the surface, we're safe to go right over it.

TWO SHOT—ROSE AND ALLNUTT—(HIGHER LIGHT)
The BEAT of the engine alters a little.

ALLNUTT Only thing to worry us is much of a breeze. I reckon you know why.

The BEAT of the engine alters still more.

ROSE It makes us—it—pushes the boat around?

ALLNUTT Naw. It chops the water so—
He rushes forward to the engine.

MEDIUM SHOT—THE ENGINE—ALLNUTT
starts rapping the boiler's safety-valve smartly with a wrench. After a few socks, it blows off steam.

WIDE SHOT—THE AFRICAN QUEEN

ALLNUTT (loud, over his shoulder, while steam blows off) Chops it up so bad ya can't see no signs to warn ya.

ROSE (louder) Oh. Of course.

Allnutt is intently busy at the feed pump—this time, a brief operation. Rose watches him out; he does a little refueling. (Wood is piled high in the waist now, drying in the sun.)

(NOTE: From here on until indicated, no TWO SHOTS. Allnutt is amidship, in hot sunlight; Rose, at stern, in cool, breezy shadow of awning.)

ROSE What was the matter, Mr. Allnutt?

ALLNUTT Feed pump choked. An' one o' my boys dropped sumpin in the safety valve; can't count on it, ya gotta hit it.

ROSE What happens when the feed pump chokes?
He finishes fueling and sits down and dries his sweat.

ALLNUTT Whole boiler can blow up. Specially the shape she's in. This water's awful muddy. Rots the tubes, plugs 'em up with scale. 'Sides that, the pressure gauge is kinda on the blink. Can't count on it fer sure, but ya can't forget it, neither. Bring 'er higher'n fifteen pound, the whole engine starts fallin' apart. An' much less'n that, she quits. Oh, come to think of it. Know why I got to keep the engine goin'?

ROSE Why, so we can go, of course.

ALLNUTT That ain't wot I mean.
Rose looks blank, and interested.

ALLNUTT (cont'd) 'Cause if the engine dies ya ain't got enough—

ROSE Oh. The water doesn't push against the rudder hard enough to—

ALLNUTT (nodding approvingly) That's right. No steerage-way. An' in bad water that's life or death.

Rose looks at him, for the first time aware that he is as important to navigation as she is.

ALLNUTT If you steer wrong we're goners; if I let the engine die, we're goners, too.

He adds another couple of pieces of wood. Rose nods, and takes on both a sense of dignity and a sense of interdependence.

ALLNUTT (proudly) Oh, she's fulla tricks, this ole engine. Even the fuelin'. Ya gotta fuel 'er light an' steady, keep the pressure right. An' that ain't so easy as it sounds, Miss. 'Cause wood makes an awful lotta ash an' chokes yer draft. Ya gotta plan it all very careful. Empty the ash pan, ya

gotta figure 'ow it'll change yer draft. Ya got 'alf a dozen different kinds
o' wood an' every one burns different. Got to figure on wot the heat o' the
sun does to the boiler, different times o' day. An' that safety valve. An'
the water pipes keep springin' leaks, an' the water gauge just works when
she's a mind to. (he looks over the whole engine with affection) You got
to know 'ow she's feelin', Miss—keep a step ahead of 'er. Right now she's
got 'er best foot forrard 'cause there's a stranger aboard. But don't be took
in, Miss. Wait till you see 'er in a mean streak.

He puts on a little more fuel, and lights a cigarette.

MEDIUM SHOT—THE BOILER AND ENGINE HEAD-ON
like an altar. Allnutt lounges in one side of the SHOT like an acolyte, and
quietly watches toward Rose, steering.

CLOSE SHOT—ROSE
steering. There is something regal about the way she sits holding the tiller,
as though it were a scepter.   FADE OUT

FADE IN

EXT. THE RIVER—TWILIGHT

MEDIUM LONG SHOT—THE PROW OF THE LAUNCH
as it noses upstream along a narrow channel. A swerve and a steadying;
the prow advances into MEDIUM CLOSE UP; the anchor starts to drop.
Before it hits the water:

MEDIUM SHOT—THE FAÇADE OF THE ENGINE
with SPLASH and RATTLE of anchor and chain o.s., as Allnutt rushes into
the SHOT and shuts off steam. The pencils of steam abruptly fade and
drift.

MEDIUM CLOSE SHOT—ALLNUTT
standing very attentively. PAST HIM, a wall of leaves shows that the boat,
after a couple of inches of drift, stops gently. He still stands attentive, as if
he were listening in the abrupt new silence. He is much more grimy and
sweaty than before.

ALLNUTT It's 'ot work, ain't it, Miss? I could do with a drink.

TWO SHOT—ROSE AND ALLNUTT
He goes to the locker beside Rose, produces two dirty enamel cups.
Watching him, Rose frowns slightly. Then, from under the bench he
drags out a wooden case. From the case he brings out a bottle. He opens
the bottle, proceeds to pour a liberal portion into one of the cups.

CLOSE SHOT—ROSE
watching with a kind of fascination.

CLOSE SHOT—ALLNUTT
as he makes a movement with the bottle toward the second cup.

ALLNUTT 'Ave one, Miss?

CLOSE SHOT—ROSE

ROSE (horrified whisper) What is it?

ALLNUTT'S VOICE (o.s.) Gin, Miss. And there's only river water to drink
it with.

ROSE (appalled) No!

MEDIUM CLOSE UP OF ALLNUTT—(ROSE'S VIEWPOINT)
He dips the empty mug overside. He turns back straight and, with care,
decants the water into the gin.

CLOSE SHOT—ROSE
She is in conflict between her intensifying fascination, and her sense of
actually watching something forbidden and even outrageous. Impulses
play through her, covertly suggested in her face, to protest, to appeal to
his better nature, even to snatch the drink from him. And now a new
shading enters her face. All she has seen up to now as mere *preparation*
for sin: now she is witnessing Sin itself. Something related to fear begins
to enter her face.

CLOSE SHOT—ALLNUTT—(FROM ROSE'S ANGLE)
He slaps casually at a mosquito, and lifts the mug for a second swig.

CLOSE SHOT—ROSE
eyes still more fixed, fascinated and full of wild doubts and suppositions.

CLOSE SHOT—ALLNUTT—(FROM ROSE'S ANGLE)
Allnutt lowers the mug. Happier now than before, he glances at Rose
in an impersonal way; looks away; looks back in doubt at her, mildly
puzzled by what he sees, but not interested.

STILL CLOSER SHOT—ROSE
as she watches him very sharp. She is puzzled by how quiet and peaceable he is, but she knows better than to trust him. She is waiting for the
trouble she is sure is bound to come. O.s., Allnutt hiccups slightly. She
tightens and withdraws a little more, then comes to a standstill.

CLOSE SHOT—ALLNUTT (FROM ROSE'S VIEWPOINT)
He looks up again, a little more puzzled.

ALLNUTT Somethin' the matter, Miss?

CLOSE SHOT—ROSE

ROSE (shortly) No.

ALLNUTT—(AS BEFORE)
Still a bit puzzled, he raises his mug and finishes his drink off. Across this nice, long drink:

TWO SHOT—ROSE AND ALLNUTT
Rose's whole body and posture is as withdrawn, pinched and tense as her face.

ALLNUTT (setting down his cup) Now, Miss, 'ow 'bout some tea?

CLOSE SHOT—ROSE
By the way she lets out a long, long-held breath, we realize for the first time the extremity of tension she has been under.
PULL AWAY TO INCLUDE ALLNUTT, as Rose relaxes all over, all but trembling, between relief and her ravenous need for tea.

ROSE (able to speak now) Ohhh! Yes!

CAMERA PANS with Allnutt as he goes over to the boiler. He draws hot water into the two cups, then places them on the bench before her and makes tea.

ALLNUTT (stirring) 'Course it tastes a bit rusty, but you can't 'ave everything. (a little formally) Sugar, Miss?

ROSE (also a little formally) 'k you?

ALLNUTT (a little bit caught by her tea-party manner; bashfully) don't mention it.

Allnutt brings out a lantern and lights it. They both drink.
She takes a ladylike trial sip; then really guzzles as never before. Sweat starts out on her forehead and she shuts her eyes. Across her bringing down the cup:

ROSE (in a tea-wet voice, more relaxed and female than at any time before) It's *simply delicious!*

TWO SHOT—ROSE AND ALLNUTT

ALLNUTT (surprised, and somewhat pleased) Not *'alf* bad, *is* it!

He tastes his again. Living to himself, he has not been much interested in taste and such.

Rose sets down her cup and, angling her sharp, long-sleeved elbows high, extracts a long pin from her hat, lays it beside her and lifts the big, dark hat from her head and lays that beside her too, and carefully thrusts the pin back into the hat and briefly tidies her tight hair. Then, picking up her cup again, she drains the last of her tea.

ROSE (holding out her cup) If you please?

ALLNUTT Right. (he starts the business of making tea again) 'Ow long you been out 'ere, Miss?

ROSE Almost ten years.

ALLNUTT You're from the midlands, ain't you?

ROSE Manchester.

ALLNUTT Ever get 'omesick?
He goes over and gets crackers and tinned meat out of the locker.

ROSE Every day of my life.

ALLNUTT I'd give my eye teeth to be back on a Saturday night, rubbin' elbows like they say—all the jostlin' an' the noise an' the music—ain't nothin' can touch it for cheering a chap up.

ROSE It's always Sunday afternoons I think of—the peace and quiet.
They are eating the meat and crackers as they talk.

ALLNUTT I don't remember very much about the Sundays. I was always sleeping it off.

They finish eating. For a few seconds they listen to the quiet soliloquy of the water.

ALLNUTT (continuing) Didn't see no crocodiles in this arm, Miss, did you?

ROSE Crocodiles? No.

ALLNUTT No shallas for 'em here. An' current's too fast. (he coughs, a little self-consciously) I could do with a bath, 'fore supper.

MEDIUM CLOSE SHOT—ROSE

ROSE (spontaneous, unconsidered) I'd like one too.
She is a little surprised at herself, but not troubled.

MEDIUM CLOSE SHOT—ALLNUTT

ALLNUTT (getting up) I'll go up in the bows an' hang onto the anchor chain. You just stay back 'ere an' do what you like to, Miss. Then, if we don't look, it won't matter.

MEDIUM CLOSE SHOT—ROSE

She is semi-aware of a change in herself, but still irresistibly spontaneous.

ROSE Very well.

MEDIUM CLOSE SHOT—ALLNUTT—(PAST ROSE)

ALLNUTT (hesitant) Well. . . .

ROSE (coolly) Very well, Mr. Allnutt.

He walks towards the bow, sidestepping the engine. Bring up SOUND of water a little.

REVERSE ANGLE—ROSE

Rose looks after him, checking the six-inch width of the funnel which will stand between them; not much concerned. While she watches, she is undoing her dress at its cuffs and at its high neck. She stands and takes it off over her head with a voluminous motion. She starts to remove an undergarment and hesitates, frowning a little; compresses her lips and, clearly, decides not to remove the garment.

CLOSE SHOT—THE FUNNEL

centered, in the lamplight. The water SOUND rises another fraction; other SOUNDS fade a little.

CLOSE SHOT—ROSE'S FEET IN THE WATER—

not more than shin-deep. (She is sitting on the gunwale.) The water distorts and drives and sways them a little and she is moving them gently.

CLOSE UP—ROSE (HEAD AND SHOULDERS)

Her head bent forward, she is watching and quietly enjoying her feet in the water.

There is a little NOISE o.s.; her eyes slip a little in the direction of the bow.

TAIL-OF-THE-EYE SHOT—PAST ENGINE AND FUNNEL

A dim grayish-white shape lowers itself over the bow.

ROSE—(AS BEFORE)

eyes not too quickly forward. She is not shocked, excited, or self-conscious; just calmly interested. (O.s., prodigious KICKINGS and SPLASHINGS and WHOOSHINGS as Allnutt takes his bath.) Slowly her head goes lower in the SHOT and her head and shoulders begin to twist as she turns to cling to the gunwale. Bring up WATER SOUND a little. As she lets her body loose into the water, CAMERA SWINGS loose along it; it is clear as she lengthens out and submerges that she is wearing bloomers and camisole.

CLOSE SHOT—ROSE'S FACE—(PAST HER HANDS)

clinging to the low, stern gunwale, as her arms stretch. There is a deep and delicate sensuous enjoyment in her face; her body lifts out full length behind her, a dim and water-addled blur. Then she pulls herself up towards the boat as strongly as she can; her wet, strapped shoulders rise, and one elbow clamps over the gunwale.

VERTICAL INSERT—SUITCASE

Over SOUNDS of her vigorous drying o.s., the insect- and moisture-proof tin suitcase or box in which Rose has packed all her worldly goods. It is open. By lantern light some of its contents are visible; a few garments and undergarments, neatly folded; her prayer- or service-book and her Bible; and a group photograph of Rose and Brother and their family, in which the intention is to anchor Rose deep in English puritanism. Perhaps eight seconds are allowed for a look at this photograph; then Rose's thin, cleansed hands lay in the dark dress in which she began this voyage; it is neatly folded; it covers not only the picture but also the religious books.

MEDIUM CLOSE SHOT—ROSE

Her head emerges from the white drill dress into which she is shuffling herself; the head, with its slightly dampened hair (which is still pinned up, but strands are loose) looks so refreshed and integrated in the lantern light that it is as if it were brand new. With somewhat freer motions than she has made before, she pulls, straightens and pats the dress, and buttons it at the bosom.

ALLNUTT (o.s.) Are you ready, Miss?

ROSE Yes.

She glances past her shoulder towards him as she wrings out a damp undergarment, overside. Allnutt comes past the engine out of the shadows, into SHOT, carrying a couple of rolled rugs.

ALLNUTT You better sleep 'ere under the awnin', Miss, 'case it rains. 'Ere's a coupla rugs. There ain't no fleas in 'em.

ROSE Where will you sleep?

He unrolls a rug and spreads it on the bottom of the boat as he talks.

ALLNUTT Forrard, Miss. I can fix up a sorta bed outa them cases.

ROSE The—explosives?

He spreads the other rug.

ALLNUTT Sure, Miss. Won't do 'em no 'arm.

The idea is queer to Rose, but everything is now.

ROSE (a little curtly) All right.

ALLNUTT Be sure you cover up good. Gets a bit chilly on the river, towards mornin'.

ROSE All right.

Allnutt returns into the bow. SWING and HOLD CAMERA a couple of seconds on the shadows; he is vaguely visible and there are the SOUNDS of his arranging the gelatine cases.

CLOSE SHOT—ROSE

finishing her hair into the second of two short, tight braids. She reaches into the tin box and under the dark dress and brings out the folded spare clothing. SOUND of the picture rattling against the bottom. With one hand she puts her hat and her comb in on top. She closes the box. HOLD on the closed box a moment.

CLOSE SHOT—ROSE—(ANOTHER ANGLE)

On one rug and beneath another, in her dress, Rose arranges the spare clothes as a pillow and settles her head; from the instant it settles she is immensely but not unhappily tired. Over Allnutt's line, o.s., her eyes focus and follow his sentence, sleepily in the lantern light.

ALLNUTT'S VOICE (o.s.) I'll turn out the light if you're ready, Miss.

ROSE Quite ready.

The light on her face begins to dwindle.

CLOSE SHOT—ALLNUTT—(FROM HER ANGLE)

at the lantern. He turns it down. He neither looks at Rose nor takes squeamish care not to.

ALLNUTT (quietly, impersonally, when the light is very low) 'Night Miss.

ROSE—(AS BEFORE)

in the lowered light.

ROSE (as quietly and impersonally) Good night, Mr. Allnutt.

O.s., the SOUND of his blowing out the lantern; darkness.

The darkness is almost total for a second; then there is faint visibility. O.s., very subdued, the brief SOUNDS of Allnutt's settling-down; then silence from him.

Deeply subdued, the SOUNDS of water slowly dwindle and die entirely, and Rose's eyes are closed. Her mouth softens a little and opens a little; in sleep her face is even more deeply virginal than when she is awake. But now in her sleep one hand moves up to her throat and slips inside her dress, next the skin.

CLOSE SHOT—ALLNUTT
in a similar hovering SHOT, asleep in his nest of explosives-boxes. He is not snoring, but with each exhalation his lips blow out lightly, with a small SOUND of "Puhhh"—"Puhhh . . ." In his sleep, comfortably, his fumbling hand scratches his haunch. There is no sound of water.

FADE OUT

FADE IN
CLOSE SHOT—ACROSS TOP OF AWNING—(NIGHT)
It is raining, quietly but firmly.

CLOSE SHOT—VERTICAL—OVER ALLNUTT
It is raining into his face. Not quite waking, he pulls his blanket over his face.

CLOSE SHOT—VERTICAL—ALLNUTT'S FEET
as the pulled-up blanket exposes them to the quietly increasing rain. They pull up under the blanket like a touched snail into its shell.

CLOSE SHOT—ALLNUTT'S FACE
He is peering disconsolately from under the torn blanket. The rain is increasing. He glances aft.

MEDIUM SHOT—ALLNUTT—FULL-LENGTH
The rain is bristling meanly all over the hunched blanket; he gets up, wrapping it around him, and walks past CAMERA.

MEDIUM SHOT—ALLNUTT—(PAST ROSE)
He comes in under the leaky awning and on into a

CLOSE SHOT—ALLNUTT
as he comes under the awning as quietly as he can, clearly trying not to wake up Rose. He lies down beside her, CAMERA TILTING and bringing ROSE IN CLOSE UP, and rising into VERTICAL TWO SHOT above them.

Rose is asleep. He is being just as discreet and careful as he can, but the margin of dryness is narrow; in avoidance of leakiness, and efforts to settle himself comfortably, he jostles her awake. She wakes up, facing him (his head and body are turned from her) and instantly assumes the worst of him. In profound shock and outrage, she sits up and clutches her rug about her—though she is wearing a dress.

ROSE *Mr. Allnutt!*

ALLNUTT (turning, murmuring) Sorry I woke you, Miss.

ROSE (across his line; her eyes cold blaze) *What are you doing here?*
He meets her eyes and understands what she thinks of him. He is very
much astonished and embarrassed.

CLOSE SHOT—ALLNUTT

ALLNUTT Blimey, Miss!

CLOSE SHOT—ROSE

ROSE (measuring her words, with her really terrifying quiet anger) Get
out—this instant!

CLOSE SHOT—ALLNUTT

He feels an explanation is hopeless and is beyond words anyhow. He gets
up out of the SHOT.

CLOSE SHOT—ROSE

settling down prostrate again. Her eyes follow him in cold fury.

CLOSE SHOT—ALLNUTT—(FROM HER VIEWPOINT)
as he walks humbly out into the rain.

A splendid outburst of THUNDER and LIGHTNING blinds and deafens the
SCREEN, and the rain really cuts loose.

CLOSE SHOT—ROSE
The thunderbolt makes her leap like a salmon; spray from the rain gets
at her face, even under the awning. Now she understands and she is a bit
embarrassed and sorry; her changed eyes look at Allnutt.

CLOSE SHOT—ALLNUTT—(FROM HER VIEWPOINT)
He is sitting, hunched, in the open, patiently adjusting the blanket over
his head. He is facing away from her.

ROSE (o.s.) Mr. Allnutt.
Her voice is barely audible in smashing rain. He does not hear.

CLOSE SHOT—ROSE

ROSE (calling loudly) *Mr. Allnutt!*

MEDIUM SHOT—ALLNUTT—(FROM HER VIEWPOINT)
He turns his head sadly towards her.

ROSE (loud, o.s.) You may come in out of the rain, Mr. Allnutt!

He looks unsure of himself, but gets up and comes towards her. He stumbles against an awning stanchion and gets a cataract down his neck and comes along under the profusely leaky awning towards Rose, stooping, then lying down and adjusting his bedding; he is whimpering gently.

ALLNUTT Thanks, Miss.

CLOSE SHOT—ROSE—(PAST ALLNUTT)

ROSE Certainly, Mr. Allnutt.

VERTICAL TWO SHOT—ALLNUTT AND ROSE

ALLNUTT (after a pause) Miss . . .

ROSE Yes, Mr. Allnutt?

ALLNUTT Sorry I give you such a turn.

ROSE That's quite all right, Mr. Allnutt.

ALLNUTT Thanks, Miss. Night.

ROSE Goodnight, Mr. Allnutt.

He turns away from her and tries to make himself comfortable. A quick drop-drip-dropping of water starts directly into his face. He miserably pulls his head out of the way and it drops loudly onto the boards beside him. Back to her, Allnutt huddles into the dry space, doing his best not to touch her, yet to stay dry.

As CAMERA DESCENDS INTO CLOSE UP OF BOTH, he has already dropped off. Upon one elbow she hovers over him, watching him, with a strange cool virginal tenderness. Splatterings of rain which have hit the bench above them, spray his sleeping face. Gently but inhumanly, as if he were an ugly little doll, she draws a corner of her rug across him, to protect him.

FADE OUT

FADE IN

FULL SHOT—THE AFRICAN QUEEN

moving down the river. The water is almost painfully bright in the midday sun.

MEDIUM CLOSE SHOT—ROSE

at the tiller. There is a new shading of pleasure and confidence in her expression. She is almost smiling.

CLOSE SHOT—ALLNUTT

in the killing sunlight, and beside the devastating heat of fire and boiler (an extreme shimmering of heat waves); he is half-drowned in sweat, yet his face is unconcerned as he oils the cylinders.

TWO SHOT—ROSE AND ALLNUTT

ROSE What a frightfully strong smell, isn't it! I suppose it's bound to be at its worst in the middle of the day.

ALLNUTT What smell?

ROSE The river. I never realized before how very *strongly* it smells.
Allnutt sniffs at it, curiously.

ALLNUTT Hmm. So it does, now I notice it. Guess I'm on the water so much, I forget all about it.

ROSE It's like marigolds. Stale ones.

ALLNUTT (tries again) Don't guess I ever smelt no marigolds.

ROSE Well, they smell just like this.

ALLNUTT Do, huh? Not a very good smell for a flower.

ROSE They're very pretty, though. Marigolds.

ALLNUTT Are, eh?
He puts on some more fuel. O.s., a NOISE of soft ROARING begins. Allnutt's eyes hear it and look mean and happy; he starts aft.

TWO SHOT—ROSE AND ALLNUTT
as he sits down, with cruel and secret pleasure, the ROAR loudens.

ROSE Mr. Allnutt.

ALLNUTT (all innocence) Yes?

ROSE What is that *roaring* sound?

ALLNUTT (licking his chops) Oh, that? Rapids, Miss.

ROSE Really? So soon?

ALLNUTT Just around the bend. (pause) Kind of dangerous. (pause) P'raps I better take over, Miss.

ROSE You be *ready* to—but I'd like to try it.

ALLNUTT (gloating) Well—maybe that's a good idear at that, Miss. (malicious) Learn by doin', like they say.

MEDIUM SHOT—THE RAPIDS

Shooting against the prow of *The African Queen,* which is charging downstream quite rapidly. The NOISE of water is joltingly louder.

CLOSE UP—ALLNUTT

Past him, wild water, rocks, a swiftly moving, ragged shore. He is pretending to tinker with the engine, in order to leave Rose alone with her fear. He is a little scared, knowing that Rose is a neophyte at steering and being a woman, may get rattled—but mainly he is feeling fine—by God, *this*'ll big rapids. He takes time off for a quick glance back at her (o.s.); turning back to his tinkering, his face is even more satisfied.

ROSE—MEDIUM CLOSE SHOT—(FROM HIS ANGLE)

Her face is extraordinarily chiseled and tense; her eyes are hard as diamonds. We can easily suppose her expression to be one of cold terror, as Allnutt does.

NOTE:

This SCENE is to last about thirty seconds. The rapids are to be rough enough to excite and to give a considerable sense of hazard, but they are mild compared to what will be seen later on. A fair amount of the SCENE is just racing through loud, ragged water, but there are to be perhaps three real hazards. They might, for instance, be: the two rocks the scene opens with; a buried rock, just spotted and avoided in the nick of time, scaring the daylights out of Allnutt and tightening Rose's face still more into this simulacrum of fear (he is comforted out of his own fears, seeing this face); and, caught between rocks, jutting into their only available channel, a large jagged tree-limb, bony-looking as antlers. There's no way out: Rose drives dead against it with an instinct for the angle which will bring against it the most powerful leverage: it hits hard and there is a tremendous NOISE of CRACKING and BREAKAGE. Within another couple of seconds they are in quieter water; within a couple more, the water is almost normal, the ROAR is fading. The boat has slowed down. The ENGINE SOUND is near normal balance; Rose distinctly relaxes, and sits down; Allnutt relaxes at his tinkering, and finishes it off with a bit of a flourish. (From the breaking of the branches, SHOOT FROM AMIDSHIPS, sternward, on Rose past Allnutt.)

While he stands, back to Rose, finishing his tinkering, Allnutt looks happy as a clam and thoroughly smug. Everything's the way he wants it, now. He checks his gauges, o.s., and turns away, and strolls back towards Rose with something of a swagger.

TWO SHOT—ROSE AND ALLNUTT

as Allnutt seats himself a little too smugly on the sternbench at right angle to Rose. He sizes her up for a couple of seconds, greatly relishing the moment.

ALLNUTT (quietly gloating) Well, Miss, had enough?

ROSE Enough? Of what, Mr. Allnutt?

ALLNUTT White water. Rapids. Now ya got a taste of it, how d'ya like it? Huh?

ROSE Very much indeed. (Allnutt's eyes change; his mouth falls open a little) I'd never dreamed that any—any mere—er—*physical* experience could be so—so *stimulating*.

He just keeps looking at her. He begins to need a cigarette. Without taking his eyes off her he gets one out. Rose is quite unaware of what she is doing to Allnutt—much friendlier in her tone than ever before.

ROSE (cont'd) (fishing up the *mot juste*) So— *exhilarating*.
Allnutt puts the cigarette between his lips, and gets out a match; he is still watching her; every moment, he is more and more deeply aghast.

ROSE (cont'd) I notice that near rocks, the water seems to *push away* from the rock. One must take that into account in steering, mustn't one? Allnutt scratches a match; it fails to light. He gets another.

ROSE (cont'd) You know, I've only known such—excitement a few times before.

His look inquires of her. He gets a match lighted.

ROSE (cont'd) A few times, in my dear Brother's sermons, when the Spirit was really upon him.

Allnutt raises the match to light his cigarette. His eyes leave hers for the lighting. His eyes look bruised and sick; his hands are shaking. He stands up, in quiet desperation, to beat it into her thick head.

ROSE Tell me, Mr. Allnutt.
He looks up at her hopelessly.

ALLNUTT (just managing to shape the sound) Yes?

ROSE I steered rather *well* for a beginner, didn't I?

ALLNUTT (without spirit) Not so bad, Miss, considerin'. But that wasn't such bad water—nothin' compared to what's farther on.

ROSE I can hardly wait! (Allnutt looks as if he could wait quite a while. A pause) Now that I've had a taste of it I don't *wonder* you love boating!

He gives her one last flabbergasted, hopeless look, wheels abruptly and walks away—CAMERA SWINGING, losing Rose—and sits near the engine, turned away from her, looking crumpled and beaten. He is still shaking his head. O.s., blithely, Rose hums the opening bars of *Guide Me, O Thou Great Jehovah.*

Allnutt shifts a little as if to look at her; hasn't the heart to; shudders faintly; and stretches his shaking hands toward the furnace.

DISSOLVE TO

DETAIL SHOT—GIN BOTTLE (TWO-THIRDS FULL)
as Allnutt pulls out cork, with luscious SOUND.

TWO SHOT—ROSE AND ALLNUTT (AT RIGHT ANGLES IN STERN SEATS)

SHOT slightly favors Allnutt. Late twilight; the boat is moored near a bank. Rose is taking a swallow of steaming tea; she lowers her cup. Allnutt's full mug of tea stands beside him on the bench, untouched.

Rose watches him with interest. Allnutt lifts the bottle to drink; he raises his eyes and meets hers; sullen and defiant. He puts the bottle in his mouth, cocks it up and drinks deep of neat gin; past the bottle, the hostility of his eyes increases.

Rose looks perplexed.

The rum gin burns him; he has a brief spasm of the gasping shakes. He tries not to show this, and avoids her eyes.

Genuine concern blends with her perplexity.

ROSE (gently) Is something the matter, Mr. Allnutt?
He meets her eyes again, sullen, a little bitter. His eyes still on hers, he raises the bottle, cocks it up showily, and drinks again—looking at her past the bottle. The gin makes sweat start out on his forehead. He keeps on, though, taking a deep drink, watching her all the time. Finally he brings the bottle down. His eyes go out of focus, against his will. And against his will and pride, he wipes the sweat off his forehead with the palm of his hand, and the sweat from his hand onto his shirt.

ROSE (gently, again) Tell me.
He looks at her with angry reproach. A pause.

ALLNUTT (already affected by the gin; proud and sullen) Nothin'.
A pause. He raises the bottle; lowers it.

ALLNUTT (cont'd) Nothin' *you'd* understand.
He drinks.

ROSE (after waiting him out) I want to understand. I just can't *imagine* what's the matter. It's been *such* a pleasant day. (pause) What is it, Mr. Allnutt?

Allnutt looks at her bitterly. Suddenly he looks mad and stands up. Just as suddenly he sits down again. This makes him sore at her.

ALLNUTT (bitterly; after a pause) All this fool talk about *The Louisa.* Goin' down the river. . . .

ROSE What do you mean?

ALLNUTT I mean we ain't goin' to do nothin' of the sort.
He needs a drink on this, but Rose interrupts.

ROSE Why, *of course* we're going! What an absurd idea!

ALLNUTT (feeling his oats and his gin; mimicking nastily) What an absurd idea! What an absurd idea! Lady, I may be a born fool, but you got ten absurd idears to my one, an' don't you forget it! (pause. Speechless with scorn and resentment) Huh!

He drinks. A pause.

ROSE (with a glimmer of tact) Why don't you want to go, Mr. Allnutt?

ALLNUTT What do *I* want to blow up sumpin' for? You tell *me*. Yeah. *You tell me. That's* all!

ROSE (quietly) Why don't you want to go?
A pause.

ALLNUTT (sullenly) Already come further'n I ever meant to. Don't hardly even *know* the river, this far down. (bitterly and a little incoherently) Only come *this* far 'cause there you was all by your lonesome, lost your brother and all—wot you get for feelin' sorry for people.

ROSE (quietly) *Why,* Mr. Allnutt?

ALLNUTT This river. That's why. An' Shona.

ROSE Shona!

ALLNUTT (mimicking her tone, nastily) Shona! (pause) If there's any place along the whole river the Germans'll keep a lookout, it'll be Shona. 'Cause that's where the old road ferries over from the South.

ROSE But they can't do anything to *us!*

ALLNUTT Oh, they *can't,* eh? They got rifles, maybe machine guns, maybe even cannons, an' just one bullet in that blastin' gelatine an', Miss, what's left of us would be in bits and pieces.

ROSE Then we'll go by at night.

ALLNUTT Oh no, we won't!

ROSE (with asperity) Now why not?

ALLNUTT 'Cause the rapids start just a little ways below Shona, an' they ain't nobody in his right mind 'ud tackle 'em even in daylight, let alone at night.

ROSE Then we'll go in daylight. We'll go on the far side of the river from Shona, just as fast as ever we can.

ALLNUTT (a sudden realization. Boozily, sorely)—Say, *who do you think you are,* all this *we'll* do this an' *we'll* do that? 'Oose boat *is* this, any'ow? 'Oo asked *you* aboard? *Huh? Huh?* You crazy, psalm-singin', skinny old maid.

CLOSE UP—ROSE

In the first phase of realization, her lower lip thrusts out like a shovel or like the lower lip of a baby within a stone's throw of crying, and her eyes look soft with dampness. Then she catches her lower lip between her teeth in her effort to restrain herself, and her eyes harden with self-discipline. Then she doesn't need the teeth any more. Her lips are tight and thin. Her whole face is edgy. Her eyes are hard with bitter resentment and with hatred. Slowly, without moving her head or altering her face, she lifts her tea into the SHOT and drinks, and lowers the cup out of the SHOT. Her face grows still harder and more immovable.

Against this, o.s., mostly in breathy, lonesome undertone, on one or two phrases loudly and assertively, Allnutt is singing, rottenly and inchoately, some part of the following:

ALLNUTT'S VOICE (o.s.; singing)

> Gimmy regards ter Leicester Square
> Sweet Piccadilly an' Myefair,
> Remember me to the folks darn there
> They'll under-sta-and.

SLOW FADE on Rose as first daylight begins to appear.   SLOW FADE.
FADE IN

EXT. RIVER AND THE AFRICAN QUEEN—MEDIUM CLOSE SHOT—ALLNUTT

He is prostrate beside the engine in early morning sunlight. Except that his eyes are closed, he looks as if he had been dead for about a day.

O.s., the HARSH SCRAPING of broken glass against wood and the happy shouts of early birds; also the quiet gurgling of river water.

For a few seconds, these sounds don't even register. Then they reach into him and he winces profoundly. (NOTE: Suddenly and painfully exaggerate all SOUNDS.) His dry mouth works a little. His eyelids twitch. The eyes open—and shut fast; light is painful to him.

O.s., the SOUND of a small avalanche of broken glass being thrown overside and hitting the water.

Rose's hand reaches down past the far side of his head and picks up an empty bottle and an almost empty bottle, and withdraws from SHOT. Allnutt registers vague awareness that someone is near, but doesn't open his eyes.

O.s., again painfully exaggerated, the SOUND of the gin case being DRAGGED along the deck. His eyes still shut, Allnutt suffers intense pain. He opens his eyes, squeezes them tight shut (which hurts him badly), opens them again, and gazes up past CAMERA in listless, uncomprehending horror.

ROSE—(FROM HIS VIEWPOINT)
She is in painfully bright, early sunlight, and she is wearing white. She has lifted the bottles and the case to the bench beside her. She kneels on the bench, aloof to the CAMERA. She tosses the empty bottle astern. She is on the verge of disposing of the gin in the nearly-empty bottle; on second thought she sniffs at it with mistrustful curiosity; her reaction indicates disgust with the smell, with Drink, and with Allnutt. She turns the bottle upsidedown and lets the contents pour overside into the river, and tosses the bottle contemptuously astern.

ALLNUTT—(SAME ANGLE AS BEFORE)—A LITTLE CLOSER
His eyes are bloodshot and are swimming with tears induced by the light. He doesn't quite take in what he sees.

ALLNUTT (a whimpering moan, pure misery; not for what he sees) Oh. . . . Oh. . . !

Allnutt shuts his eyes. O.s., the GLUG-GLUG-GLUGGING of a full bottle. He looks again. He begins to comprehend and what he sees is, to him, terrible and almost unbelievable.

ALLNUTT (with deeper feeling but quietly; reacting now to what he sees) Oh. . . !

O.s., the SOUND of another flung bottle hitting the water, and of another being opened. Allnutt, using all his strength, manages to lift his head from the floor. The effort is so exhausting and the pain so excruciating that he just lets it fall; the bang is even more agonizing. He licks his dry lips with his dry tongue and tries speaking.

ALLNUTT (in a voice like a crow) Miss.

ROSE—(FROM HIS VIEWPOINT)
She is emptying gin and pays him no attention.

ALLNUTT'S VOICE (o.s.) *Miss?*
She pays him no attention except to turn the inverted bottle to absolute verticle.

ALLNUTT—(AS BEFORE)—A LITTLE CLOSER

ALLNUTT Have pity, Miss! (pause; SOUND of "glug-glug" o.s.) Miss? ("glug-glug") Oh, Miss, you don't know what you're doin' . . . I'll perish without a hair o' the dog.

SOUND, o.s., of bottle hitting water.

ALLNUTT (continuing) Ain't your property, Miss.

SOUND, o.s., of a new bottle being opened. CAMERA CREEPS CLOSER on Allnutt, whose eyes become those of a man in hell who knows, now, that his sentence is official, and permanent. With terrible effort, he lifts his head and shoulders.

MEDIUM CLOSE SHOT—ROSE—(NEUTRAL ANGLE)—NORMAL EXPOSURE
She is emptying gin. She hears the SOUNDS of Allnutt's moving o.s. Her hard face hardens still more. She glances towards him, continuing to pour.

MEDIUM SHOT—ALLNUTT—(FROM HER VIEWPOINT)
He is with great pain and effort getting himself to his knees and his arms onto the side bench. It may seem for a moment that he is going to try to come at Rose and make a struggle for it, but no: he now gets his knees to the bench and hangs his body far out over the gunwale and drinks ravenously of the muddy water. He overhangs so far that he is in clear danger of falling in.

ROSE—(SAME ANGLE AS BEFORE)—A LITTLE CLOSER

She is watching him. SOUNDS, o.s., of the gin emptying, and of his drinking. She is aware he may fall in and she doesn't care.

ALLNUTT—(AS BEFORE)

He finishes drinking and tremulously pulls himself back, and turns, and collapses into a sitting position on the bench.

ROSE—(AS BEFORE)

She is opening another bottle and casually watching him, and as casually looking away. She is pitiless, vengeful, contemptuous, and disgusted.

ALLNUTT—MEDIUM CLOSE SHOT—(NEUTRAL ANGLE)

His head hangs between his knees; his hands hang ape-like beside his ankles. After a little he is able to lift his head. He props his temples between his hands and his elbows on his knees. He is so weak that one elbow slips, letting his head fall with a nasty jolt and a whimper of anguish. He sets himself more carefully solid and gazes ahead of him at the floor.

ALLNUTT Oh. . . !

ROSE—(AS BEFORE)

She ignores him completely; she lays the flap back from some canned meat.

ALLNUTT—(AS BEFORE)

He gets out and fumblingly lights a cigarette; his hands are shaky. He takes a deep drag and it gives him a dreadful fit of coughing. He glances toward her piteously.

ROSE—(AS BEFORE)

She is slicing bread; she ignores him. His coughing is loud, o.s.

ALLNUTT—(AS BEFORE)

Recovered from his spasms, he timidly tries a lighter drag. This time he can taste it. It tastes foul. He puts it out, carefully, for later use, takes one look at it, and disconsolately tosses it overside. He looks again towards Rose. He looks away again. He sighs deeply and buries his face in his hands.

O.s., their SOUND abnormally sharp, the birds are singing like mad.

DISSOLVE TO

MEDIUM SHOT—ROSE—(MID-AFTERNOON)

She is sitting on a side-bench in the shade of the awning, calmly reading her Bible. She is in a clean white dress, exactly like the one she wore yesterday. Not a hair is out of place in her tight hair-do. Her bare feet are crossed demurely at the ankles. She sits up straight. She looks very cool, considering the weather.

PULL BACK, bringing in her day's work: up past her left, pinned to the edge of the awning, hang her newly-laundered dress and undergarments, full of sunlight. There are a few ineradicable streaks of grease in the dress. On the bench to her right, her sewing-basket and some evidently finished sewing chores.

O.s., the steady GURGLING of river water among the treeroots of the bank; the nervous SCRAPING of a razor.

FORMAL SHOT—THE ENGINE
It looks much cleaner than ever before. (Same SOUNDS o.s.) The CAMERA IS RISING as the SHOT OPENS. It soon brings in Allnutt's head, past the engine, very hot-looking in strong sunlight. He is shaving.

SLOW PANNING DETAIL. A welter of wet footprints and splashed, soapy deck, Allnutt's clean bare heels glistening high in the SHOT as he stands shaving. CAMERA TILTS and brings in a drowned sliver of soap. Allnutt's filthy clothes, a wet and arrestingly filthy towel.

Same SOUNDS o.s., razor-scraping a little UP.

Past the back of Allnutt's head on his close reflection in a small mirror, hung from a funnel-stay; past that, Rose.

Allnutt is shaving; Rose, in b.g., is reading. It is painful to take off as much beard as Allnutt has been carrying, and he is not a man who takes pain easily; but he does his best to keep his reactions private, and by now he is nearly through. He is whistling softly against his teeth, and frowning at his reflected work with the concentration of a surgeon. He knows, however, that he is visible to Rose, and unwisely keeps glancing towards her (she never looks up once); thanks to this, he lets the razor slip.

ALLNUTT Ow. . . . cut myself.
He glances sharply at Rose to see if she has taken any notice. She does not glance up. Allnutt resents this bitterly. He finishes shaving, and strokes his smooth cheeks with satisfaction. Rose turns a page. With a Rembrandt's patience and concern, he perfects, with his comb, the ideal coiffure, with an artistic quiff along the forehead. His eyes go vain. He treats himself, in reflection, to his idea of what the Lord of Creation should look like. Then he glances towards Rose, who keeps on reading. His look is aloof, miles above her.

CLOSE UP—ROSE

SOUND o.s., of Allnutt's entrance past the engine. She does not glance up, but her eyelids flicker.

ALLNUTT—(PAST ROSE)

He walks a couple of steps towards her in the brilliant sunlight, swaggering a little. Then he stands still, the Stag at Eve, looking at her with a certain high contempt. He is obviously challenging response and recognition. He gets none.

ALLNUTT (after a pause; scornfully) *Huh!*

He walks in under the shade of the awning and into

MEDIUM CLOSE UP—(CAMERA SWINGING PAST AND OPPOSITE ROSE)

As he sits down. After another silence, he decides on a new approach. He arranges his face to express high good humor.

ALLNUTT (brightly) Well, Miss, 'ere we are, everything ship-shape, like they say.

PULL AWAY to TWO SHOT of Rose and Allnutt, as he awaits her reaction. No answer.

ALLNUTT (continuing) Great thing to 'ave a lyedy aboard, with clean 'abits. Sets me a good example. A man alone, 'e gets to livin' like a bloomin' 'og. (no answer) Then, too, with me, it's always—put things orf. Never do todye wot ya can put orf till tomorrer. (he chuckles and looks at her, expecting her to smile. Not a glimmer from Rose) But you: business afore pleasure, every time. Do yer pers'nal laundry, make yerself spic an' span, get all the mendin' out o' the way, an' *then,* an' *hone-ly then,* set down to a nice quiet hour with the *Good*-Book. (he watches for something; she registers nothing) I tell you, it's a model for me, like. An inspiration. I ain't got that ole engine so clean in years; inside an' out, Miss. Just look at 'er, Miss! She practically sparkles. (Rose evidently does not hear him) Myself, too. Guess you ain't never 'ad a look at me without whiskers an' all cleaned up, 'ave you, Miss? (no look) Freshens you up, too; if I only 'ad clean clothes, like you. (huh-uh) Now you: why you could be at 'igh tea. (no recognition from Rose) 'Ow 'bout some tea, Miss, come to think of it? Don't you stir; I'll get it ready.

Rose does not stir. Allnutt is running low. A little silence, now. He watches her read.

ALLNUTT (continuing) 'Ow's the book, Miss? (no answer) Not that I ain't read it, some—that is to say, me ole lyedy read me stories out of it. (no answer; pause) 'Ow 'bout readin' it out loud, eh, Miss? (silence) I'd like to 'ave a little spiritual comfort m'self. (silence; he flares up) An' you call yerself a Christian! (silence) You 'ear me, Miss. (silence) Don't yer?

(silence; a bright cruel idea. Louder, leaning to her) *Don't yer?* (silence. Suddenly, at the top of his lungs) *HUH??*

EXTREME CLOSE UP—ROSE
In spite of herself she flinches; but swiftly controls it.

LONG SHOT—FROM OTHER SIDE OF THE RIVER
A half mile of hot, empty water, then jungle, silent on a dream of heat. On the far side the tiny boat and the two infinitesimal passengers.

After two seconds, Allnutt's "HUH?" is heard.

EXTREME CLOSE UP—ROSE
In her face are victory, cruelty, and tremendous secret gratification: a Jocasta digesting her young.

The ECHO comes. Over it—   CUT TO

EXTREME CLOSE UP—ALLNUTT

A second, further echo comes, and dies.

ALLNUTT (yelling) *Heyy!!*
Watchful, listening, he walks out of SHOT; CAMERA LOWERS to Rose, whose quiet, pitiless eyes—wholly unamused—follow him secretly. The ECHO returns to her; she resumes reading.

TWO SHOT—FAVORING ALLNUTT (PAST ROSE)
He wanders all over the boat, CAMERA ALWAYS CENTERING him, always shifting past the statue-like reader. He barks like a dog; he yowls like a tomcat; he roars like a lion; he bleats like a goat; he crows like a rooster. Finally he sickens of it and walks back past her to his old seat at right angles to her.

MEDIUM CLOSE SHOT—ALLNUTT
as he sits. Clearly now he is going to try silent decorum, in imitation of her. He crosses his ankles in imitation, and settles his hands in his lap, and even holds his head primly, watching her. But something itches him under the arm and he scratches—first covertly and insufficiently, then to his heart's content. His exertions have worked up quite a sweat; the midges of late afternoon convene enthusiastically about his head. He looks bitterly towards Rose.

MEDIUM CLOSE SHOT—ROSE
There isn't a bug near her. Taking her time, she finishes the last page and, not hurrying, but without pause, starts right in on *Genesis.*

SWING CAMERA, losing Rose, bringing Allnutt into CLOSEUP. He hates her and the Good Book.

PULL AWAY into TWO SHOT—of Rose and Allnutt. After a few moments of silent, motionless tableau, Allnutt hating, Rose reading, he speaks.

ALLNUTT Feller *takes* a drop too much once in a while. T's only yoomin nyture.

ROSE (remotely) Nature, Mr. Allnutt, is what we are put into this world to rise above.

ALLNUTT Miss, I'm sorry. I 'pologize. There. What *more* can a man do than say he's sorry. Eh? (no answer) You done paid me back, Miss. Didn't even leave me a drop. (no answer) Come on, Miss. 'Ave a 'eart, can't ya? Fair's fair. (no answer) Miss, I don't care *wot* ya say, long 's you say *somepin*. (no answer) I'll be honest with ya, Miss: I just can't *stand* no more of it. I ain't used to it, that's all.

A pause.

ROSE So you think it was your nasty drunkenness I mind.
A foolish, helpless gesture from Allnutt.

ALLNUTT (bewildered) Well—wot else?

ROSE You lied to me.

ALLNUTT (with earnest dignity) Lied? Oh *no*, Miss. Lyin's one thing I don't *never* do. Not unless there's *no* way out.

ROSE You promised we'd go down the river.
He is so honestly flabbergasted, this brings him up on his feet, goggling at her. When he can find words:

ALLNUTT Why, *Miss!* Is *that* wot it's all about?

ROSE Of course.
He draws a deep breath and sits down closer to her than before. He begins quietly, with great patience and reasonableness.

ALLNUTT Now for the last time, Miss. Just try and listen, won't you? Try to understand. (Rose looks at him coldly; her jaw is set) It's sure death a dozen times over down this river. I 'ate to disappoint you, Miss. But don't blyme *me*. Blyme the river.

ROSE You promised.

ALLNUTT (shouting) Well, I'm takin' my promise back!

He gets up and strides away, CAMERA CENTERING HIM, and walks past the engine.

CLOSE UP—ROSE

She watches after him. She is not a hundred per cent sure of victory; only ninety-five or so.   DISSOLVE TO

CLOSE UP—ALLNUTT—(DAWN)

He is asleep on his box of high explosives. O.s., SOUNDS of early birds—and of Rose's bustling, and of a strong breeze, and of leaves. Presently he stirs, groans and opens his eyes. After a moment he glances in her direction.

CLOSE SHOT—ROSE

She is readying the fire for tea.

ALLNUTT—(AS BEFORE)

After a little, Allnutt gives up. He creakily, painfully rises from his bed and gets up into:

MEDIUM SHOT—FROM OUTSIDE THE BOAT—(ON LINE WITH ENGINE AMIDSHIPS)

He walks towards CAMERA into CLOSE UP and passes engine, CAMERA SWINGING INTO TWO SHOT of Rose and Allnutt.

Rose is thrusting a saucepan of water into the crackling furnace. Allnutt pauses shyly.

ALLNUTT (a pitiful effort to sound casual, and dignified) G'mornin', Miss. Rose straightens up and doesn't even see him, and turns and walks away, CAMERA on her, losing Allnutt.

She sits on the stern bench and gets out bread and one mug and a can, and starts opening the can. He does not exist.

After a few seconds, he walks into the SHOT, BACK-TO, and sits down on a right-angle bench, a few feet away from her.

She continues opening the can. He lights a cigarette from the open tin; it is damp and swollen from the night air, lights slowly, and tastes poorly, but he tries to make the best of it.

O.s., the SOUND of hot water joins that of the crackling fire. Rose gets up with a cloth for the hot handle and walks up past Allnutt into CLOSE UP and OUT OF SHOT.

SOUNDS, O.s., of her getting out the water and shutting the door. Allnutt's eyes follow her, wretchedly, wherever she goes.

She reenters the SHOT, BACK-TO, and returns to her place, still ignoring Allnutt, and starts fixing tea for herself.

CLOSE UP—ALLNUTT—NEUTRAL ANGLE
He is watching her; the last of his staying-power is dissolving.

MEDIUM CLOSE SHOT—ROSE—(FROM HIS VIEWPOINT)
She is stirring her tea and now she drinks some.

ALLNUTT—CLOSE SHOT—(NEUTRAL ANGLE)
He is watching her and thorough despair is in his eyes, and unconsciously his head begins to shake a little.

ROSE—(AS BEFORE)
Now she is eating bread and canned meat.

ALLNUTT—(AS BEFORE)
He stops shaking his head and just looks.

ALLNUTT (quietly) All right, Miss. You win.

CLOSER SHOT—ROSE—(AS BEFORE)
She meets his eyes, immediately, but says nothing.

ALLNUTT—(FROM HER ANGLE)

ALLNUTT (accepting utter defeat) Down the river we go.
He turns to the engine.

TWO SHOT—ROSE AND ALLNUTT

ROSE (quietly) Have some breakfast, Mr. Allnutt.
He is so moved by this line that he is on the verge of tears.

ROSE Or, no. Get up steam. Breakfast can wait.
He reacts with the quiet hopelessness of a slave; one beaten look at her, gets to his feet and walks towards CAMERA and engine, filling SCREEN.

                                                              DISSOLVE TO

SHOOTING FORWARD ALONG PORT SIDE OF BOAT—(ABOUT NINE IN THE MORNING)
The boat is going along at full speed. Boat fills most of r.s., a downstream vista of the river, and the bank, l.s. The breeze is strong now; two-foot waves; clear sunlight. A calmly exhilarating NOISE of water and, o.s., strong, the SOUND of the engine.

STRAIGHT ACROSS THE BOAT—ON ALLNUTT
He is sitting on the starboard bench, back to the sun, transferring canned meat to bread.

The floor of the SHOT is a high stack of firewood. The left wall of the SHOT is the engine.

ROSE (o.s., calling something not fully distinguishable, as) Which bank is Shona on?

ALLNUTT (shouting; leaning his ear towards her) *'Ow's that?*

ROSE—FROM SAME POSITION OF CAMERA—(DIFFERENT ANGLE)
She is at the tiller but in spite of cross-bucking the waves she now has the casualness of experience. Except for much more difficult steering, she doesn't have to think much about it now. Her hair is done up, but has blown part free. Her dress is flecked with the dampness of blowing water.

ROSE (shouting) *Which bank is Shona on?*

ALLNUTT (loudly, o.s.) *Left.* On a hill.

ROSE (shouting) Good. The sun will be in their eyes.

ALLNUTT (o.s.) Huh?

ROSE (louder, gesturing) The *sun.* Will be in their *eyes.*

ALLNUTT—(AS BEFORE)
It is becoming more real to him now. He glances towards her. He sets his breakfast aside, gets up, and goes past the engine into the bow section.

ROSE—(AS BEFORE)
Her eyes strain curiously after him.

MEDIUM SHOT—ALLNUTT—(IN THE BOW SECTION)
He walks in among the boxes of blasting gelatine, his face troubled, and looks down at them.

THE BOXES—(FROM AN ANGLE OPPOSING THAT OF HIS EYES)
They are disposed irregularly in the sunlight; their red lines look sinister.

MEDIUM CLOSE UP SHOT—ON ALLNUTT
as, with face still more troubled, he bends over and lifts a box.

REVERSE ANGLE—ALLNUTT—(SIDE TO CAMERA)
The prow and river beyond him; he is stacking the boxes along the port bow. He has stuck a rug between them and the hull. Now he stacks the last box and covers it with a rug. He stands and looks at the rug a moment, rather helplessly, then turns to CAMERA and into MEDIUM SHOT; his face is still more badly worried. He glances back towards Rose. He

stoops and drags the heavy cylinders into the starboard bow, trimming ship. He walks back towards the engine, mopping his forehead.

ROSE—(AS BEFORE)
She is watching him curiously.

ALLNUTT—(FROM HER ANGLE)
as he comes past the engine, he meets her eye, and looks away. He goes towards his bench and breakfast.

ALLNUTT—MEDIUM CLOSE SHOT
as he sits down. He glances towards his gauges and resumes eating. But his appetite is not so good now.

ROSE (o.s., not quite distinguishably) Don't worry, Mr. Allnutt.

ALLNUTT If a bullet hits them boxes, there'll be no *time* to worry.
Taking his knife to use it eating, he suddenly goes still and wary with a new idea. He glances secretly at the knife, and secretly towards the engine.

INSERT: A PIECE OF ROTTED RUBBER HOSE, PART OF THE WATER LINE.

ALLNUTT—(AS BEFORE)
His face gets still darker with guile. With a clumsy imitation of concern for the engine, he gets up and walks out of the SHOT, the open knife in his hand filling the SCREEN.

TWO SHOT—PAST ENGINE—FAVORING ALLNUTT (CLOSE)

ROSE STANDING IN BACKGROUND. As he pretends to tinker with the engine below SHOT, his eyes flicker towards the hose and the knife and think, obviously, of danger and of Rose, of whom he is painfully aware.

It is clear by his eyes and face that he is trying desperately to make up his mind to cut the hose; and delays because he so dreads the consequences with Rose, who is watching him with mild curiosity. The decision is taken out of his hands.

Past him, Rose looks with interest ahead, off the port bow.

ROSE (shouting and pointing) *Mr. Allnutt!*
She shifts course sharp to starboard. Allnutt hears her and looks around and sees her pointing, and quickly turns and looks ahead and to port. Great fear comes into his face, but also some excitement unrelated to fear.

LONG SHOT—PAST ALLNUTT AND THE ENGINE
As a curve opens, the walled hill-town of Shona is disclosed. Above one building of corrugated iron, a German flag flies.

EXTREME CLOSE UP—ALLNUTT
Besides the fear and excitement in his face, indecisiveness reaches the point of agony. Past him, the right bank of the river approaches, moving more and more swiftly.

MEDIUM CLOSE SHOT—ROSE
She is near the bank. She straightens her course.

EXTREME CLOSE UP—ALLNUTT
He glances desperately toward the rubber hosing.

INSERT: RUBBER HOSING

ALLNUTT—(AS BEFORE)
He glances desperately towards Shona. Shona is swinging wide into view. People are seen, including two men apparently in uniform. Allnutt glances desperately towards his knife.

INSERT: He closes the knife and slips it into his pocket.

ALLNUTT—(AS BEFORE)
His face is committed helplessly to catastrophe. He turns his head to call to Rose.

REVERSE ANGLE—MEDIUM CLOSE—ALLNUTT

ALLNUTT (over his shoulder, as he crouches) Keep as low as ya can, Miss.

ROSE—(FROM HIS ANGLE)
She nods, and crouches below the benches, her hand still high to steer.

INSERT: THE RUBBER HOSE
as it bursts; a strong spume of water.

CLOSE UP—ALLNUTT
eyes to SOUND.

CLOSE UP—ROSE
eyes to SOUND.

INSERT: The WATER GAUGE slowly drops.

ALLNUTT—ANOTHER CLOSE UP
as with frantic speed he gets tape and a piece of flat rubber out of his tool-box.

INSERT: RUBBER HOSE, as Allnutt claps the rubber to the burst hose and starts taping; water still escapes abundantly.

CLOSE UP—ALLNUTT—(FROM ANGLE OF HOSE INSERT)
His desperate face as he works.

INSERT: The PRESSURE GAUGE, sinking.

INSERT: The WATER GAUGE, still lower.
O.s., the engine SOUND slows and fades to a lugubrious CLANKING, then stops altogether.

From here on, very quiet but in all shots on the boat, steadily LOUDER, a faint RUMBLING ROAR, o.s., the rapids.

MEDIUM SHOT—ROSE
anxious and much interested, but no fear.

ALLNUTT (o.s.) Just turn 'er loose, Miss. Let 'er drift.
Rose looks uncomprehending.

MEDIUM SHOT—ALLNUTT—(FROM HER ANGLE)
He is hard at work. There are no pencils of steam any more.

ALLNUTT (over shoulder; bawling desperately in the silence) Let 'er drift! All we can do!

ROSE—(AS BEFORE)
She nods. She releases the tiller. O.s., the SOUND of a bullet; followed, seconds later, by the REPORT of a rifle. Rose looks towards Shona and towards Allnutt.

ALLNUTT—(AS BEFORE)
He is working. Water is still splattering.

ALLNUTT (over shoulder) 'Cross our bows, I reckon. Didn't 'it us any'ow.
He ducks still lower to his work.

LONG SHOT—THE AFRICAN QUEEN
and its occupants, through field glasses, from high bank. Even so, they are small, on the far side of the river.

1st OFFICER (o.s. in German) But why didn't they put in?

2nd OFFICER (o.s. in German) Probably they're making for the lower landing.

Across this: CUT TO

LONG SHOT (NOT THROUGH GLASSES)—LOWER LANDING

Deep in l.s., the lower landing, which is small.
High in r.s., *The African Queen.*

MEDIUM SHOT—1ST AND 2ND OFFICERS AND SWAHILI TROOPS

on hard, bare ground, corrugated iron building, and German flag, and a portion of the town, in b.g.

1st Officer is a moderately stupid German. 2nd Officer is a moderately intelligent German. The Swahilis, in their whites, with their elderly Martini rifles, are all eyes and teeth and excitement—and eagerness to use their weapons.

1st OFFICER (in German) Fire twice more across their bows.
2nd Officer raises rifle, with telescopic sight.

LONG SHOT—THE AFRICAN QUEEN—(THROUGH CROSS-HAIRED SIGHT)
raked from stern to stem.

2nd OFFICER (o.s. in German) She is adrift.

1st OFFICER (o.s. in German) Fire.
The shot moves ahead of the boat. A little kick in the SHOT as the rifle fires; SOUND o.s. The boat advances into the SHOT.

1st OFFICER (o.s. in German) Again.
The shot again leads the boat safely. Some kick, SOUND o.s., and advance of boat as before.

MEDIUM SHOT—THE OFFICERS AND THE NATIVES

1st OFFICER (in German) She's not turning.

LONG SHOT—THE BOAT
is opposite the lower landing, still at far shore.

2nd OFFICER (o.s. in German) She can't. She is adrift.

OFFICERS AND MEN—(AS BEFORE)

1st OFFICER She could anchor.
2nd Officer has no answer for that.

1st OFFICER (cont'd) (quietly, to Swahili corporal, in Swahili) Order your men to fire.

The corporal clicks heels and salutes with enthusiasm, and about face, to his men.

CORPORAL (happily and bossily, in Swahili or in Swahili-esque German) Fire!

The boys are all eagerness and delight. They hurry forward into:

A TRUCKED FRIEZE OF MEDIUM CLOSE UPS
Some fall prone to fire as they have been trained; others stand; several squat where they take aim. It is clear by their handling of their weapons that they are all farcically lousy shots.

A SHOT ALONG THEIR RAGGED LINE—
some prone, some standing.

CORPORAL (with a sweeping gesture) Fire!
They fire a ragged volley, rifles at all sorts of angles.

MEDIUM SHOT—ALLNUTT—(PAST ROSE)
Allnutt is still hard at work. The boat is moving faster, near the bank. There is a peculiar multiple NOISE in the air, like bees in a violent hurry, accompanied by the SOUND of tearing paper.

ALLNUTT (crouching still lower at his work) They got us!

ROSE—(FROM HIS ANGLE)
curious about the sound. Now comes the straggling REPORTS OF RIFLES; a volley echoing back from cliff to cliff.
INSERT: Allnutt completes his taping.
ALLNUTT—(FROM ROSE'S ANGLE)
stepping away.

ROSE (o.s.) Finished?

ALLNUTT Yes—if we can get up steam in time, an' the boiler'll stand that much cold water, an' the mend holds.

He puts on a lot of wood, and he gets the pump going, cautiously. There is a dangerous straining and CRACKLING SOUND from the boiler as the cold water rushes in. Across it, there is another BUZZING of bullets. Some speckle the water; some hit the heightening rock cliff above and past the boat; the reports arrive and ECHO.

ALLNUTT (continuing; he has been cringing and mute during the buzzing; he speaks across the reports) If only we don't drift into the back eddy.

ROSE—(AS BEFORE)
She nods. She is watching anxiously, helplessly.

ALONG STARBOARD—(SHOOTING FORWARD FROM HER ANGLE)
The fast current in which they drift, and the slow back-eddy, and their dividing line, are visible. SWING SHOT to CENTER along axis of boat and on Allnutt. O.s., there is the SOUND of a much faster bullet, and suddenly, causing Allnutt to leap like a stricken faun, the whole boat RINGS like a harp.

INSERT—THE WIRE FUNNEL-STAY
on portside has parted, close above the gunwale. It hangs loose by the funnel.

ALLNUTT—MEDIUM CLOSE SHOT
noting and reacting. He turns to Rose, CAMERA SWINGING into TWO SHOT. She has noticed it too, but is not particularly frightened. O.s., there is a METALLIC SMACK. They glance up sharply.

DETAIL SHOT—(FROM ALLNUTT'S ANGLE)—A HOLE
high in the funnel.

DETAIL SHOT—(FROM ROSE'S ANGLE)—ANOTHER HOLE
on the far side of the funnel.

INSERT: WATER GAUGE, rising.

CLOSE SHOT—ALLNUTT
checking gauges, working hard.

INSERT: PRESSURE GAUGE, rising.

CLOSE SHOT—ALLNUTT
crouching. He adjusts pump to let more water in. The straining SOUNDS intensify. He opens the furnace door.

LONG SHOT—THE BOAT (THROUGH TELESCOPIC SIGHT)
O.s., the rifle FIRES; the shot kicks.

CLOSE SHOT—ROSE
as a bullet WHINES past overhead. O.s., the furnace door CLANKS SHUT and there is an increased SOUND of fire. She looks reprimandingly towards the bank. We can scarcely see the figures of the officers and men. The rifle REPORT comes through.

MEDIUM SHOT—THE OFFICERS AND MEN
The men are sheepish and downcast in b.g. The 1st Officer, who fired, lowers his rifle. The 2nd Officer has field glasses. They look at each other. The 1st Officer shrugs.

1st OFFICER (in German) Give it to me.
He takes the rifle and takes careful aim.

LONG SHOT—THE BOAT—(THROUGH THE TELESCOPIC SIGHT)
He is leading Allnutt just a trifle, and leisurely trying to perfect his aim. While he takes his time, the boat crosses the path of the full glare of the sun. He mutters some German expletive under his breath, and FIRES into blind glare.

DETAIL SHOT—GELATINE BOXES
A corner of one of the gelatine boxes flies apart in splinters.

MEDIUM CLOSE SHOT—THE TWO OFFICERS
as the 1st Officer lowers the rifle, his eye hurt by glare, he hands it back
to the other.

1st OFFICER (in German) Fire at random.

CORPORAL Everybody shoot.
Everybody happily starts shooting at random. The natives love it.

FULL SHOT—ALONG THE FULL LENGTH OF THE BOAT—ON ALLNUTT—PAST ROSE
Ahead, the escarpment looms, the right bank narrows, a deep shadow between them. The ROAR is by now almost deafening.

ALLNUTT (shouting as loud as he can) Man the tiller now—*we'll try.*
She doesn't understand; she does nothing. He gestures—the manipulation
of a tiller. Rose takes it.

The SINGING of the bullets is all but inaudible, but three hit the boat.
Allnutt starts the engine. It stammers and gulps and dies. The boat swings
with great speed into deep, cool shadow as he tries again. It stammers
and catches, and dies.

SHOT PAST ALLNUTT—AND THE PROW
The water is terribly swift, but not yet stony; but within a hundred yards
ahead there is a terrific cataract.

EXTREME CLOSE UP—ALLNUTT—(PAST HIM, ROSE)
There is terrific tension in his face, but he is much too busy to be frightened. Rose's face is a sharpening image of her face among the easier
rapids. Now that they have come within close, high stone banks, the ROAR
is prodigious.

Allnutt, below SCENE, is working on the engine.

THE CATARACT—(FROM HIS ANGLE)
twice as near.

ALLNUTT—(AS BEFORE)
The engine catches and rises, just AUDIBLE ABOVE the ROAR OF WATER.

CATARACT—(FROM ALLNUTT'S ANGLE)
They swallow ten of the last twenty yards before the cataract.

CLOSE UP—ROSE
standing, looking intensely ahead, hand firm on tiller.

THE BOAT—(FROM ALLNUTT'S ANGLE)
as it enters upon the cataract.

CLOSE UP—ALLNUTT
as he drops onto his bench next the engine.

ALLNUTT Our Father Who art in Heaven . . .
The African Queen bucks like a bronco. The air is full of spray and of the ROAR of rushing water. Allnutt serves the engine with panic in his soul. Out of the tail of his eye, he glimpses rocks flashing past.

CLOSE UP—ROSE
She rides the mad tide like a Valkyrie, weaving a safe course through the clustering dangers.

There comes a place where the river widens and the sweep of the current takes *The African Queen* over to the opposite bank, as if she were no more than a chip of wood. Rose tugs at the tiller with all her strength. The bows come around. It looks for a space as if the stern would be flung against the rocks. The boat just manages to hold her way.

Then a backwash catches her, flinging her out again into midstream, so that Rose has to force the tiller across with lightning swiftness. Hardly are they straight again when the banks close in upon them and Rose must instantly pick out a fresh course, through the rocks that stud the surface in flurries of white foam.

FULL SHOT—THE AFRICAN QUEEN
plunging down a narrow ribbon of water between vertical faces of rock.

CLOSE SHOT—ALLNUTT
as he waves at the engine and shouts something that is drowned out by the ROAR of the waters.

CLOSE UP—ROSE
She shakes her head and her lips form the words: "I can't hear."

CLOSE SHOT—ALLNUTT
gesticulating frantically. He moves forward into a CLOSE UP and shouts:

ALLNUTT (shouting) *Need fuel! We got to get fuel!*

CLOSE SHOT—ROSE
She nods, to show her understanding of their plight.

FULL SHOT—THE AFRICAN QUEEN
There is a natural dam ahead, only broken in the center, and there the water piles up and tumbles over in a vast green hump. The launch puts

her nose and heaves up her stern as she hits the piled-up water; then she shoots down the slope, landing with a crash on the high green waves beneath the waterfall.

MEDIUM SHOT—THE AFRICAN QUEEN—(SHOOTING PAST ROSE)
Green water comes boiling over the port deck and into the boat. Allnutt must hold onto the engine to keep from being swept off his feet. It seems as though *The African Queen* is doomed to put her nose deeper and deeper into the torrent until she will submerge entirely—but at the last possible moment she shakes herself loose and comes clear.

CLOSE SHOT—ROSE
as she throws her weight on the tiller

ROSE (shouting) *Stop the engine!*

CLOSE SHOT—ALLNUTT
as he obeys dazedly.

MEDIUM SHOT—THE AFRICAN QUEEN
The maneuver was nicely calculated; the launch's momentum carries her through the edge of the eddy into the slack water under the lip of the dam. She comes up against this natural pier with hardly a bump, and instantly a trembling Allnutt is fastening painters to rocks.

ALLNUTT Whew!!!

FULL SHOT—ROSE
as she starts to rise, but finding herself weak in the knees, sits back momentarily. Despite an empty feeling in her stomach and a pounding heart, she wears a smile of satisfaction.

She looks around. They are moored in what must be one of the loveliest corners of Africa. There are numerous shelves on the high banks bearing flowering plants which trail shimmering wreaths down over the rocks. A beam of sunlight reaches over the edge of the gorge and turns its spray into a dancing shadow. The NOISE of the fall is not deafening, but rather a pleasant musical accompaniment to the joyful SINGING of the river.

ROSE How lovely!
Allnutt enters the SHOT from BEHIND CAMERA. She turns her smile on briefly. then raises her eyes again to the hanging gardens above.

ROSE (continuing) Lovely, isn't it.

ALLNUTT (following her gaze) It is at that. (he laughs suddenly) We sure pulled it off, didn't we, Miss? Sucked the Germans in proper. They were so surprised to see the ole *African Queen*—they didn't think of shootin' at us till we were almost past. They didn't believe anybody'd try to get down these gorges. Didn't believe nobody *could*. Well, we showed 'em, didn't we? (Rose nods) Not that I'd like to do it every day of the week. We took on enough water to sink anything else that floats.

He reaches for the pump and goes to work.

ROSE (coming out of her reverie) Here—let me do that.

ALLNUTT (protesting) Oh, no, Miss.

ROSE Please let me.

ALLNUTT All right—but don't wear yourself out. . . . I'll pick up some wood.

Rose applies herself to the pump. It takes her a little while to get into the right rhythm, and when she does, even so small a thing as this brings a thrill of achievement.

ROSE I hardly know what happened after Shona. Everything's a jumble. I have no idea how far we've come or whether it's morning or afternoon or—

MEDIUM SHOT—ALLNUTT AND ROSE
as Allnutt gathers wood on the bank.

ALLNUTT I guess you were too busy, Miss, to pay attention to anything but what you were doing.

ROSE (hesitantly) Did I—do all right?

ALLNUTT (with deep feeling) Better'n all right, Miss. . . .

CLOSE UP—ROSE
Her face flushes with pride.

PAN SHOT—ALLNUTT
as he goes back onto the boat carrying an armload of wood. He is limping a little. He lets the wood fall by the engine, then sits down and begins to unlace his canvas shoe.

ALLNUTT Picked up a thorn on the bank, I guess. Went right through the rubber sole.

ROSE Let me.

On her knees, she slips the shoe off; she takes his slender, rather appealing foot into her hands. She finds the place of entry of the thorn and presses it with her finger-tips while Allnutt twitches and jumps with absurd ticklishness.

ROSE No, there's nothing there now.

She lets his foot go.

ALLNUTT Thank you, Miss.

He lingers on the bench, gazing up at the flowers, while Rose lingers on her knees at his feet.

ALLNUTT (a certain awe in his tone) It is pretty at that.

Rose looks up at his face. There is something appealing, almost childlike about the little man as he looks wonderingly around. Her expression grows tender; she would like to pet him. He looks down at her. She averts her eyes.

ALLNUTT It reminds me—that waterfall does—of—

Allnutt never tells what it reminds him of. He puts out his hand toward Rose. She catches it—to hold it, not to put it away. Allnutt comes down to his knees and they are in each other's arms.   FADE OUT

FADE IN

LONG SHOT—AFRICAN QUEEN—(EARLY MORNING)

as a few slanting rays of the sun strike her funnel. Vapors still cling to the surface of the river. Over the SOUND of the waterfall, comes the tuneful SINGING of a bird. Presently Rose's figure is revealed moving about.

MEDIUM SHOT—ROSE

as she pours tea into two cups, and moves with them toward the stern, CAMERA PANNING WITH HER as she crosses to the sleeping Allnutt. CAMERA MOVES into CLOSE TWO SHOT as she kneels beside Allnutt and puts one teacup down close to his outstretched hand.

ROSE (softly) Mr. Allnutt. I mean—dear.

ALLNUTT (opening his eyes) Well now—blimey! This is more like it. Breakfast in bed.

ROSE Two spoonfuls of sugar is right, isn't it?

ALLNUTT (nods) Fancy your building the fire and all—while I slept.

Rose regards him tenderly for a long moment; then, with a birdlike movement, she kisses him on the cheek. Allnutt puts his arms around her.

ROSE Dear—there's something I simply must know.

ALLNUTT What's that?

ROSE (after a blushing interval) What's your first name?

ALLNUTT Charlie.

ROSE (to herself like a schoolgirl) Charlie . . . Charlie . . . Charlie . . .

ALLNUTT Give us another kiss.

ROSE (her arms around him, kissing him) Charlie! Charlie dear . . .
They hold each other for a while. Then she slips out of his arms, hands
him his cup and they begin stirring their tea. Rose looks at the beauty all
around them.

ROSE (her eyes suddenly wet) This must be one of the loveliest places in
all Africa.

ALLNUTT I've been around a bit and I must say I never seen no place to
compare with it in the whole world. Kinda hate to leave it. (hastily, as
though he fears being misunderstood) Not that I ain't all for goin' on,
Y'unnerstand. (she gives his hand a squeeze) Do you spose that last big
cataract coulda been Ulanga Falls? As I remember the map, it was just
a little way down from Shona. And if it *was* Ulanga, there ain't no more
big cataracts between us an' the lake.

ROSE How much farther is the lake, Charlie?

ALLNUTT Oh—'bout two 'undred miles.
They are quiet a moment. Abruptly, Rose gets final, and energetic—
swallows the last of her tea in that manner and stands up, a touching
blend of spinsterish ediginess and blossoming female softness.

ROSE Well, I suppose it's time we were on our way.

FULL SHOT—DECK OF BOAT
Rose takes her place at the tiller and Allnutt goes forward in unquestion-
ing obedience. He is boss of the family, but she is boss of the boat and the
voyage. He casts off, and starts up the engine. Again *The African Queen*
is under way.

CLOSE SHOT—ROSE
at the tiller. She looks back, drinking in the place with her eyes. She wants
never to forget a single detail. Allnutt enters the scene—puts his arm
around her, and stands looking back at the loveliest place in the world.

MEDIUM SHOT—AFT—PAST THEM
We see the waterfall and the flowers withdraw. The SOUND of the waterfall still dominates—a SOUND of serene, inexhaustible vitality like that of
their bloodstream.

ALLNUTT (in a broken voice) Give us another kiss, old girl.

They kiss, as the boat is swept into motion.   DISSOLVE TO

FULL SHOT—THE AFRICAN QUEEN

The river is smooth, swift and fairly straight. The launch passes some hippos bathing in the shallows. The deep, swift-running channel carries her to within a few yards of the great beasts.

Allnutt and Rose shout at them and wave their arms. The hippos squeal like pigs. Allnutt imitates the SOUND, a feat which Rose finds to be funny beyond words. She laughs until it is painful and she has to hold her side. Allnutt laughs too, between squeals, hugely delighted with the success of his imitation. Just as Rose is about able to control her laughter, he squeals once again, which sends her off into fresh peals of mirth.

ROSE Stop, Charlie—stop it!

Their laughter begins to die down, then starts up again. Finally comes a moment of silence while they struggle to regain breath, and during that moment Allnutt hears a SOUND which is not at all funny.

ALLNUTT Rosie, listen . . . You 'ear wot I 'ear?

OVER the SOUND of the engine, comes a distant ROAR.

ALLNUTT I guess that wasn't Ulanga Falls, after all.

ROSE (soberly) I guess not.

Allnutt applies himself to the boiler, putting more wood in, adjusting the draft.

The speed of the river increases, as does the DIN of the approaching cataract. *The African Queen* begins to heave among the first waves of the race.

CLOSE SHOT—ROSE

staring forward as she braces herself once more to hold the tiller steady.

LONG SHOT—THE RIVER AHEAD—(FROM ROSE'S VIEW)

as the waterfall comes into view, Allnutt in f.g.

He throws her a swift, backward look.

CLOSE UP—ROSE

scared, but game.

ROSE (calls) Goodbye, Charlie.

CLOSE UP—ALLNUTT

shouting an answer; his voice is lost in the UPROAR.

FULL SHOT (MOVING)—THE AFRICAN QUEEN

as she rears up and hangs for a moment at the crest of the waterfall. Then she shoots forward and down, finally to crash in a tangle of currents below the waterfall. She shakes with the impact. Water flies back, high over the top of the funnel, then she surges on.

There is a TEARING SOUND beneath, followed by a horrid vibration which seems as if it will shake the boat to pieces.

CLOSE UP—ROSE

ROSE (screams) *Keep her going, Charlie!*

CLOSE SHOT—ALLNUTT

opening the throttle. The devastating vibration increases.

CLOSE SHOT—ROSE

as she fights to keep the boat in mid-current, but something is wrong with the steering.

ROSE (screams) *Charlie!*

CLOSE SHOT—ALLNUTT

He points toward the bank where a big rock juts out into the river.

CLOSE SHOT—ROSE

fighting the tiller. The boat swings around crabwise toward the rock, and it looks for a moment as though the stern will surely crash into it. Rose keeps the tiller hard over. Sure enough, *The African Queen* comes all the way about, her bows to the shore, grounded; but the maneuver is not completely successful. Instantly she heels and rolls. A mass of water comes boiling in over the gunwale. The boiler fire is extinguished and a wild flurry of steam pours out.

CLOSE SHOT—ALLNUTT

Grabbing a painter, he leaps like an athlete into the whirling eddy, gets his shoulder under the bows and heaves.

MEDIUM SHOT—THE BOAT

The bows slide off and the boat rights herself, wallowing, three-quarters full of water. Instantly the current pulls her downstream.

CAMERA PANS as Allnutt leaps up the face of the rock, clutching the painter. He gives it a turn around an angle of the rock and braces himself. His shoulder-joints crack as the rope tightens, but slowly the boat swings in to shore. Five seconds later, she is safe, and Allnutt is making painter after painter fast to the shore.

CLOSE SHOT—ROSE

standing on the bench in the stern, the water slopping at her feet. She manages a smile at Allnutt. She feels a little sick and faint now that it is all over.

CLOSE SHOT—ALLNUTT

He sits down on a rock and grins back at her.

ALLNUTT We nearly done it that time, didn't we, Rosie.

CLOSE SHOT—ROSE

as she sits on the gunwale. She doesn't wish to let her weakness be seen. She forces herself to be matter of fact.

ROSE I wonder how much we've lost.

CLOSE SHOT—ALLNUTT

ALLNUTT Let's get this water out and see.

He swings himself aboard, splashes down to the waist and fishes about for the pails.

CLOSE SHOT—ROSE

as she tucks her skirt up into her underclothes as though she were a little girl at the seaside. CAMERA PANS with her to Allnutt. She takes a pail and the two of them go to bailing, and conversation ceases with the effort.

DISSOLVE TO

MEDIUM CLOSE SHOT—ALLNUTT—(SHOOTING DOWN OVER ROSE'S SHOULDER)

He has gotten up a couple of floor boards in the waist, and is down on his knees inspecting the planking.

ALLNUTT It's better than we coulda hoped for. We 'aven't lost nothin', far as I can see. 'Aven't damaged 'er skin worth mentionin'. I shoulda thought there'd been an 'ole in 'er somewheres, after wot she's been through.

ROSE What was all that clattering just before we stopped?

ALLNUTT We still got to find that out, old girl.

ROSE How are we going to do that, dear?

ALLNUTT I'll 'ave to go underneath and 'ave a look.

He is out of his shirt and trousers in a jiffy. His drawers are the old-fashioned kind reaching to the knee and tying up with a string behind. He picks up a rope and ties one end around his middle and gives the other end to Rose.

ALLNUTT There ain't no other way. You stay 'andy with that rope—case there's a fancy current down at the bottom. . . . 'Ere goes!

And over the side he goes. His feet remain in view for a moment; then, kicking, they disappear.

UNDERWATER SHOT—THE PROPELLER SHAFT OF THE LAUNCH
Allnutt swims into the picture, giving forth with bubbles. He inspects the shaft.

CLOSE SHOT—ROSE
leaning far over the stern, trying to glimpse what is happening beneath *The African Queen*. Presently, Allnutt's head breaks the surface of the water.

ROSE (hovering anxiously over him) Could you see anything, dear?

ALLNUTT Yes.

MEDIUM SHOT—ALLNUTT AND ROSE
With her help, he climbs back aboard, sits down on the bench. Rose sits beside him and waits for him to regain his breath. She puts out her dry hand and clasps his wet one.

ALLNUTT (dully) Shaft's bent to blazes like a corkscrew, and there's a blade gone off the prop.

ROSE We'll have to mend it, then.

ALLNUTT Mend it! (he laughs bitterly) Not likely.

ROSE Why is that, dear? (he doesn't answer) What shall we have to do before we go on?

ALLNUTT I'll tell ya. (savage despondency in his tone) I'll tell ya what we could do if we was sittin' in the landin' slip at Limbasi. We could pull this old tub out an' take the shaft down an' 'aul it over to the workshop where they'd forge it straight again. An' then we could write to the makers and get a new prop. They might 'ave one in stock 'cause this boat ain't over thirty years old. An' while we was waitin' we might clean 'er bottom an' paint 'er. Then we could put in the shaft an' the new prop an' launch 'er an' go on as if nothin' 'ad 'appened.—But this ain't Limbasi, an' so we can't.

ROSE (after a pause) Can't you get the shaft out without pulling the boat on shore?

ALLNUTT I dunno. I might. Means workin' underwater. Could do it perhaps.

ROSE Well, if you were able to get the shaft up on shore, could you straighten it?

ALLNUTT Ain't got no hearth. Ain't got no anvil. Ain't got no coal. Ain't got nothin'. An' furthermore, I ain't no blacksmith.

ROSE (tapping her memory) I saw a Masai native working once. Using charcoal . . . on a big hollow stone. He had a boy to fan the charcoal.

ALLNUTT Yes, I've seen that, too! But I'd use a bellows, myself—make *them* easy enough.

ROSE Well, if you think that would be better.

ALLNUTT (the engineer in him taking over) There's 'eaps an' 'eaps of driftwood up on the bank.

ROSE Why don't you try it?

ALLNUTT (suddenly shying) No. It ain't no use, Rosie, old girl. I was forgettin' that prop. There's a blade gone.

ROSE Can't we go on the blades that are left?

ALLNUTT There's a torque. Prop wouldn't be balanced. Wouldn't take five minutes for the shaft to be like a corkscrew again.

ROSE We'll have to make another blade. There's lots of iron and stuff you could use.

ALLNUTT (ironically) And tie it on, I suppose.

ROSE (missing his irony) Yes, if you think that will do. But wouldn't it be better to—weld it? That's the right word, isn't it? *Weld* it on?

ALLNUTT You're a one, Rosie. Really you are. (laughs)

ROSE Isn't weld the right word, dear? You know what I mean even if it isn't, don't you?

ALLNUTT Oh, it's the right word, all right.
He laughs again. At first, Rose is afraid that his laugh is caused by desperation, but when she sees that it is not, she laughs with him.
Directly they are in each other's arms, kissing as two people might be expected to kiss on the second day of their honeymoon.

DISSOLVE TO

UNDERWATER SHOT—ALLNUTT
working on the shaft. Now and then he bangs his hammer on the hull of

the boat. Apparently he and Rose have a system of signals. Just as he succeeds in loosening the bracket supporting the shaft, a whim of the river expresses itself in a fierce underwater swirl. Allnutt is turned upside down, but he holds onto the bracket like grim death.

ROSE—IN THE STERN

pulling in on the rope. Allnutt comes to the surface, drops the bracket into the boat.

ALLNUTT (gasping) Swallered about half the river that time.

ROSE You were down there an awfully long time. I got scared.

ALLNUTT Shaft is ready to come out now. It'll be too heavy for me to swim up with. I'll 'ave to walk with it in to shore ... Well, 'ere goes—for the last time, I 'ope.

ROSE Charlie.

ALLNUTT Huh?

ROSE Let me help you.

ALLNUTT 'Ow do you mean?
She begins to peel off her clothes.

ALLNUTT Wot d'you think you're goin' to do?

ROSE Go down with you.

ALLNUTT An' get drownded? You don't know wot it's like, Rosie. Them currents is just fierce. (he shakes his head) Wot'll you be thinkin' of next! (he takes two deep breaths) Well, 'ere goes. (After a third and deeper breath, he is gone.)

CLOSE SHOT—UNDERWATER—THE SHAFT

Allnutt swims into view, slides the shaft out through the bearings and begins to carry it toward shore. The current catches him. He loses his footing, regains it, only to fall again. The heavy shaft is too much for one man to handle.

He is struggling vainly with it when into the SCENE swims Rose. She takes one end of the shaft, Allnutt the other, and together they walk under water toward shore   LAP DISSOLVE TO

CLOSE SHOT—MAKESHIFT FORGE—NIGHT

Rose is working the bellows while Allnutt hammers patiently. Presently he lays aside the hammer and, using a taut string, judges the straightness of the shaft. Apparently he is pleased with his work, for he grins at Rose and nods briefly.

ALLNUTT If my old dad 'ad put me to blacksmithin' when I was a kid, I don't think I should never 'ave come to Africa. I might've—(a faraway look comes into his eyes; he is thinking about Charing Cross on a Saturday night; finally he shakes himself)—But then I shouldn't never 'ave met you, Rosie old girl. (he goes back to hammering) I wouldn't trade you for all the fried fish shops in the world.

ROSE (protesting this accolade) Oh, Charlie!
He slips a ring of wire over the end of the shaft and moves it up and down its length, testing the diameter.

ALLNUTT (finally) Well, I guess it's just about as good as I can get it—And it didn't take so long a time, neither.

ROSE Only a week.

ALLNUTT The blade's a different proposition. I'll 'ave to make it.

LAP DISSOLVE TO

INSERT: THE NEW PROPELLER BLADE (DAY SHOT)
held in place on stone anvil with a pair of pliers; it is beginning to take shape under blows of Allnutt's hammer. The pliers carry it over the other two blades, which are its models, and turn it this way and that for purposes of comparison.

DISSOLVE TO

UNDERWATER SHOT—ALLNUTT AND ROSE
getting the shaft, with its new propeller, back into position.

DISSOLVE TO

CLOSE SHOT—THE PROPELLER (UNDER WATER)
turning. SOUND of the engine, O.S. CAMERA TILTS UP. Allnutt is leaning over the stern, watching. In the b.g. stands Rose, with her hand on the throttle.

ALLNUTT It turns right enough. But that don't prove nothin' much. Will it stand up under a full head of steam, that's the question. We'll get our answer out there—and Lord 'elp us if it ain't the right one.

ROSE Let's find out right now.

ALLNUTT Why not?

TWO SHOT—ROSE AND ALLNUTT
Rose comes back and takes the tiller in hand. Allnutt casts off the moorings. As the bows come out into the current, he gently opens the throttle.

CLOSE SHOT—ALLNUTT

ALLNUTT Goodbye, darling.
He bends over the engine.

CLOSE SHOT—ROSE

ROSE Goodbye, darling.
Neither she nor Allnutt hears the other; neither is meant to; there is a high courage in them both.

FULL SHOT—THE AFRICAN QUEEN

CAMERA PANS with boat as she surges out into the stream. She spins around as her bows come into the river, and Rose puts the tiller across. Next moment she is flying down the stream once more.   **FADE OUT**

FADE IN

EXTERIOR—THE RIVER—LONG SHOT

In the foreground, a spray of jungle foliage in sharp and exotic contrast to the upland pines of the last sequence. *The African Queen* comes into view, and CAMERA PANS with her. A flock of ibis in the path of *The African Queen* rise on great snowy wings, only to settle again when she has passed.

CLOSE SHOT—ALLNUTT AND ROSE
looking about them.

ALLNUTT Well, we done it, old girl. We got down the rapids all right. I didn't think it could be done. If it 'adn't been for you, sweetheart, we shouldn't be 'ere now. Don't you feel proud of yourself, dear?

ROSE (indignantly) No, of course not. Look at the way you made the engine go. Look how you mended the propeller. It wasn't me at all. (with even greater emphasis) I don't think there's another man alive who could have done it.

ALLNUTT (wryly) I don't think anyone's likely to try.

LONG SHOT (MOVING)—A TURN IN THE RIVER

Her waters widen and a dreary, marshy, amphibious world is revealed; tree trunks and little creeper-entangled islands take the place of the foaming rocks of the upper river.

MEDIUM SHOT—ALLNUTT AND ROSE

ALLNUTT Looks like this old river got tired of all that runnin' an' jumpin' she did an' decided to lay down an' rest for a while. . . . 'Ow about our doin' the same, Rosie—seein' as 'ow the sun's goin' down.

Rose nods. She edges *The African Queen* in towards the shore. Allnutt gets his boat hook into the stump of a large tree which, still half alive, grows precariously on the edge of the water with half its roots exposed.

Rose goes to the boiler and starts making tea, while Allnutt gets a line around a root. There is hardly any current. The light is fading.

ALLNUTT It must be right 'bout 'ere the river changes her nyme from Ulanga to Bora. (he slaps at a mosquito) Not that it matters. Nobody lives between 'ere and the lake. Unless you call monkeys people.

He slaps again. There is the high frequency SOUND of mosquitoes which fill the air.

ROSE (slapping) How much farther do you think it is to the lake?

ALLNUTT Oh—not so many miles, but—
He slaps his arms and legs, get up and stands and makes swift passes in the air, as though shadow-boxing.

ROSE (slapping) But what, Charlie?

ALLNUTT (a note of hysteria in his voice) I got a feelin' that before long we'll wish we was shootin' the rapids again . . . Ow! . . . Ow!

DISSOLVE

CLOSE SHOT—ROSE AND ALLNUTT
It is nightfall and the mosquitoes have left their homes in the mud, under leaves, on stalks of reeds, to hunt flesh and blood. They close in on Rose and Allnutt; they bite through clothes—they crawl under clothes; some of the smallest creep into nostrils and under eyelids. Rose and Allnutt are used to ordinary attacks, but this is beyond all experience. They slap ever more wildly; they begin to show panic.

ROSE Oh!

ALLNUTT This is awful!

ROSE (pulling at her dress) I'm going in! I'm going to get under the water!

ALLNUTT Yes! That's it!
But looking past Rose toward the river, he sees something that makes him grab her wrist.

ALLNUTT No!

ROSE But I'm being eaten alive!

ALLNUTT (pointing) Look.

MEDIUM SHOT—LARGE CROCODILE

on the bank.

ALLNUTT (o.s.) What'd you say 'bout bein' eaten alive?

And now we see that it is not one crocodile but several submerged and partially submerged. Two slide into the water from the bank.

CLOSE SHOT—ROSE AND ALLNUTT

After their first start at the sight of the crocs, they go back to fighting the cloud of mosquitoes that, hungry for blood, fill the air with their WHINING.

ROSE Get me out of here, Charlie! I'm going mad!

MEDIUM SHOT—ROSE AND ALLNUTT

Allnutt runs to the engine, tries to start it.

ALLNUTT Ain't no steam. Can't start engine.

ROSE (wails) I can't stand it, Charlie!

ALLNUTT 'Ere! Lay down! Get under the canvas there! I'll get us out into the channel.

She obeys. Allnutt casts off, and seizing a deckboard begins to paddle. The space between the launch and the bank slowly widens till at last they are in the channel. Rose peeps out from under the canvas.

ALLNUTT Right, Rosie. We got away from 'em. You can come out.

ROSE (crawling out) I'm ashamed, Charlie, acting like that—but I couldn't help it. I was going mad.

ALLNUTT Me, too.

ROSE You're so bitten!

Even in the faded light, his face and body show innumerable bumps.

ALLNUTT The bites themselves ain't so bad; it's 'avin' them all round you. I've 'eard of them sendin' buffaloes an' native cattle stark starin' mad—an' they run an' run till they fall dead.

ROSE (after a pause) What are we going to do, Charlie?

ALLNUTT Now you're asking!

ROSE Will they be like that wherever we tie up?

ALLNUTT Can't say.

ROSE We can't just drift all night.

ALLNUTT If the river keeps straight an' deep an' slow, there ain't nothin' much can 'urt us—I know! I'll let the anchor out a ways. She'll stop us before trouble gets too near.

He lets the anchor chain out, then sits on the bench. Rose leans against him. He puts his arm around her.

ALLNUTT (after a long silence) What a time, Rosie—what a time! We'll never lack for stories to tell our grandchildren—if we live to 'ave any.

The launch seems to be floating in space, solitary as any one of the stars that are now beginning to shine and twinkle overhead.

DISSOLVE

EXT. DELTA—DAWN
The river ends in a five-mile-wide pool, fringed all the way round with reeds. These reeds extend as far as the eye can see.

The boat comes down into the pool, nosing along the edge, looking for an opening. Allnutt and Rose are talking as she steers and he feeds the furnace.

ALLNUTT Look—maybe that's a channel. (it isn't) No.
A herd of hippopotami suddenly surface and scatter. Plunging through water, mud and reeds just ahead of the boat. Behind them is left a faint indication of a channel.

ROSE What about there? (pointing) That looks like a way through.

ANOTHER ANGLE
showing a very doubtful passage into the reed bed.

ALLNUTT Could be. (worried) I dunno. (pause) Once we get in, an' these 'ere reeds close up be'ind our stern—we'd never get back, you know, Rosie.

ROSE We can't stay going round and round out here.

ALLNUTT If anything goes wrong a few 'undred feet in there, we're 'eld in a trap, you know—till we starve or go orf our 'eads. I dunno! (loudly. decisively) All right. Put 'er over.

Rose swings the tiller and the boat charges at the little opening in the reeds.

FULL SHOT—REEDS
looking from outside. We see the boat nose into the opening. In front of her the reeds part. Others are pressed under water. But as soon as her

full length is inside, the reeds she has parted or submerged close together again, or rise slowly from under water. As they close, they form an increasingly solid barrier behind her wide stern. Very soon *The African Queen* is completely hidden from us except for the top of her tall funnel, which moves more and more slowly as she goes on into the reed bed.

EXT. REED BED
seen from a few feet above. A view of the endless miles of papyrus reed. At one place we see the top of the funnel of *The African Queen*.

EXT.—THE LAUNCH
the engine choking and gasping, shaking the launch. CAMERA PANS DOWN TO:

CLOSE—BOW OF LAUNCH
pushing ineffectually against the knotted roots of the reeds, which have piled up under it. There is almost no water—just the tangled roots and an inch of liquid mud.

MEDIUM SHOT—ALLNUTT
shutting off steam. The corners of his mouth tighten. He is badly frightened. He tries to keep the fear out of his voice as he tells Rose; but we can see that Rose is desperately scared too.

ALLNUTT It's the propeller, I think. It won't work in this mud.
Allnutt looks down over stern. He gets up.

ALLNUTT Where's the boat-'ook?

ANOTHER ANGLE
Allnutt finding boat hook and moving forward.

ALLNUTT Maybe we can pull 'er along.

MEDIUM SHOT—BOWS OF LAUNCH
Allnutt reaching forward with boat hook, hooking it into strong clumps of reeds, pulling desperately. The clumps resist; it seems as if the boat is about to move. Then the clumps give way.

MEDIUM SHOT—ROSE
amidships, watching Allnutt.

ROSE Here! Wait a minute!
She finds a long pole or plank, chooses a good spot and begins to push. After a couple of ineffectual attempts, Allnutt hooks an especially strong clump at the same time as Rose finds a solid spot against which to push.

The boat heaves and shakes, and, with a final heart-breaking effort on the part of Rose and Allnutt, it moves forward a couple of feet.

ANOTHER ANGLE—ROSE AND ALLNUTT
gasping for breath, hope flickering up again.

ALLNUTT Come on—again!
As they resume their efforts, CAMERA DRAWS BACK, RISING TO

FULL SHOT—REED BED
from twenty feet above. We see the funnel of the launch inching slowly and painfully through the reeds.   DISSOLVE TO

FULL SHOT—THE AFRICAN QUEEN
in the reeds. Rose and Allnutt are poling with their boat hooks. Even through the masks of mud they are wearing, we can see that they are both terribly haggard and exhausted.

ALLNUTT We've come along under steam, and we paddled an' pushed 'an' pulled the ole boat along with the 'ook. Wot we ain't done yet is get out an' carry 'er. I spose that'll come next.

ROSE Hard to breathe!—the air is so wet and heavy.

ALLNUTT Can't 'ardly tell water from land—or for that matter, day from night.

ROSE The whole thing is like a fever dream, isn't it?

ALLNUTT All the channels we've lost—an' the twistin' we've done—we may come back out where we started—if we come out at all.

ROSE We've always followed the current, dear—what little there is.

ALLNUTT That don't mean nothin'—with *this* river. This river's crazy. Crazy as I am!

ROSE (gently) Charlie. (she touches him) We must try to keep hold of ourselves.

ALLNUTT Sorry, old girl.
Allnutt starts pushing all the more energetically on his pole.

ALLNUTT Best thing to put the roses back in *our* cheeks is to get out o' these reeds.

Allnutt's exertions carry them into the shallows. The boat touches bottom. Not all of their strivings with the boathooks serve to move it an inch further.

ALLNUTT (finally) What I said a while back about 'avin' to carry the boat was meant for a joke—but as it turns out, I wasn't jokin'.

Taking the painter, he goes over the side and starts pulling like a draft animal. Slowly, ever so slowly, the boat begins to move, until at last she is floating again.

Rose helps him back in. Suddenly she gives a cry of horrified surprise.

ALLNUTT What's the matter?

Rose can only point. As he sees what it is, Allnutt's face contorts with panic and disgust. He makes a kind of growl of horrified surprise, across which:

DETAIL SHOT—ALLNUTT'S ARM, CHEST OR BELLY

A couple of leeches hang to him, visibly swelling with his blood.

QUICK PULL AWAY TO TWO SHOT—ROSE AND ALLNUTT—Over his line; we see 20 or 30 leeches on him.

ALLNUTT Augh, the little beggars— (a cracking voice) Pull 'em off me, Rosie—no, the heads stay—poison yer blood.

ROSE (sudden remembrance) *Salt!*

She rushes to get their tin box of it.

EXTREME CLOSE UP—ROSE AND ALLNUTT

eyes on what she is doing below SCREEN.

DETAIL—DAMP SALT

applied to a leech. It flinches, elongates, bunches and swells, and drops off.

TWO SHOT—ROSE AND ALLNUTT

She dabs salt on the last two or three, while he stands like a partly calmed, still shocked horse.

ALLNUTT Anythin' I hate in this world it's leeches—filthy *devils*.

He stands trembling quietly, the triangular bites still bleed freely. Rose dabs tenderly at one of the sinister little wounds.   DISSOLVE

TWO SHOT—ROSE AND ALLNUTT—AT BOWS (SHOOTING FORWARD FROM STERN)

They hook the boat with great effort slowly along. The hull grazes something. They work still harder. There is a rumbling SCRAPE. Then, also, a sludgy GRINDING.

With the grinding, Allnutt moans as if in his sleep and tries desperately to reverse direction.

ALLNUTT (gasping) Back! 'Old 'er back—

ROSE (imitating him) Mud?

ALLNUTT Yes.
There is too much momentum for them.

ALLNUTT (reversing his dragging) Let's try an' get 'er over it, then. Give 'er all you got, Rosie.

They strain enough to half kill them; the sludgy grinding intensifies.

ALLNUTT (gasping) Good girl— we're still makin' 'eadway—All you got now—

Abruptly the boat comes to a dead stop.   DISSOLVE

VERTICAL SHOT—THE MOTIONLESS GUNWALE AND MANGROVES
and the just perceptibly moving slime on the water between.

ROSE AND ALLNUTT
They sit by each other, she holding his forehead; he is in a dry nausea of exhaustion.

ROSE There, there, dear. There, there. There, dear.
Able to speak, ashamed, he tries to joke.

ALLNUTT Fine specimen of a man *I* am, ain't I!

ROSE You're the bravest man that ever lived.
He is silent, slowly and rather inanely shaking his head; she watches him.

ROSE (like a very old wife to a very old husband) Lie down, dear. *Rest.* Both of us.

He keeps on shaking his head.

ROSE You just over*do, that's* all. You *must take care* of yourself! You're not one bit *well.*

ALLNUTT *Well!* We're both of us half dead.

ROSE (ignoring this) Besides, it's high time we had our supper. It'll be dark before long.

ALLNUTT You 'ave some. I ain't up to it yet.

ROSE Or a nice steaming cup of tea.

ALLNUTT You fix yourself some.

ROSE Not just yet, thank you. (she gets up, taking his hand) Come now. (she helps him weakly up) *Lie*-down.

CAMERA STAYS WITH THEM, MOVING INTO VERTICAL TWO SHOT—
Rose helps Allnutt to the floor, and nurse-like, puts bunched rags under his head.

ROSE *There* now. All comfy?
He tries to smile.

ALLNUTT You rest, too.

ROSE Indeed I *will.* (she lies down beside him and smiles at him) That's all we need, a good long rest, and we'll be on our way in a *jiffy. You'll* see.

ALLNUTT (managing a smile) Sure.
She turns her back to him because she can't meet his eyes. Both lie with eyes wide open, obsessed.

ROSE (after a pause) Try to sleep, dear.

ALLNUTT (pause) Sure. You too.

ROSE Of course.
She reaches a hand behind her and pets him. He clearly has, and resists, an impluse to take her hand.

She withdraws her hand. A pause.

ALLNUTT Rosie.

ROSE (pause; with quiet dread) Yes, Charlie.

ALLNUTT You want to know the truth, don't you?

ROSE (pause; very quietly) I know it.
His eyes show deep pain.

ROSE We're finished.

ALLNUTT That's right.

ROSE Even if we had all our strength we'd never be able to get her off this mud.

ALLNUTT Not a chance in this world.
They are silent a while; everything is in their eyes. As suddenly and swiftly as her weakness allows, she turns to him; their faces are close.
CAMERA DROPS NEARER.
She looks into his quiet eyes; her own eyes are fiery, not with tears but

with passionate, incredulous despair; speechless, trying to speak; a sort of palsy.

ROSE So *use*less!

He puts a hand along her cheek. Slowly he realizes, and enhances for us, her only concern with dying.

ALLNUTT They don't come no better'n you.

They lie still, looking at each other.

Within about 15 seconds, their faces profoundly alter; by changes of makeup, every couple of seconds, the motionless faces become years older, and take on a kind of worn majesty; and gradually lose consciousness; by the end of the seconds, the eyes are closed. The CAMERA meanwhile very slowly withdraws upward. In the last we can clearly see of their faces, they are quite possibly dead. As CAMERA RISES, we see them at full length, as prostrated and flattened as grasses pressed in a book; then, their static boat and the crawling water; the CAMERA RISES among the overhanging mangrove branches which obscure and trap them; and, as it rises, the SCREEN slowly darkens.

The CAMERA STOPS RISING. The dead silence is broken by an infinitesimal SOUND OF RUSTLING. By eye and ear, after a few seconds, it becomes recognizable as the stillest, slenderest kind of rain, splintering downward, very gradually increasing in volume and in richness of SOUND as the darkness deepens, to an immense, peaceful, steady, flooding downpour. The darkness pales into full daylight and the downpour continues, and through it we can dimly see the boat and the prostrate bodies, and after perhaps ten seconds of the new daylight (after maybe fifteen of darkness), the rain begins to abate and the CAMERA BEGINS VERY SLOWLY TO DESCEND.

It gets down through the branches. The bodies are motionless; so is the boat; but the slime on the water, though still slow, moves with a distinct new kind of energy.

THE CAMERA STOPS DESCENDING. A couple of seconds later, the boat stirs, just perceptibly; motionless again; then stirs again, more distinctly.

At height of PULL UP OF CAMERA and darkening, a quiet rich CRUMPLING OF THUNDER. (Throughout this short sequence all sounds, even those recorded at full blast, are held way down on the track—as if heard in a dream or in imagination.)

Across MUTTERING OF THUNDER—   CUT TO

SHOT—SKY AND MOUNTAINS

Low in foreground, a sharp watershed peak; all foliage is fiercely ruffled, showing pale undersides: beyond, a tremendous valley, a dim streak of river through it; beyond that, magnificent peaks: but most of the SCREEN is sky, in which (sped up by SLOW CAMERA) prodigious black and white clouds bloom, explode and wrestle. Over all, a solemn, ominous light. A moment of absolute stillness; then first huge drops of splattering rain; then SCREEN is blinded and deafened with simultaneous THUNDER AND LIGHTNING, over which CAMERA TILTS DOWNWARD along the line of enormous columns of rain which take over SCREEN.

SHOOTING UPSTREAM, to breadth of a swollen river, in heavy rain:

PAN DOWNSTREAM, past Mission clearing.

Possible CUT IN: Mission bungalow screen door flapping and banging in wind; or porch rocking chairs' ghostlike cradling:
PAN ON DOWNSTREAM flooding water.

LONG SHOT across roaring river on Shona, PANNING DOWNSTREAM; one tiny figure struggles miserably through mud:
Possible CUT IN: the drowned German flag, clinging disconsolately to its pole.

END PAN on water at mouth of rapids; bring up ROAR
From high and to one side: where the rapids enter the Basin: (greatly augmented water NOISE.)

PULL CAMERA DOWN and to right to VERTICAL SHOT over the Rose-Allnutt waterfall, much more water than before, plunging into pool; bringing up SOUND sharp.

TILT CAMERA UP to right, to center on where rapids leave the pool; the whole pool, dark and calm on first trip, is now boiling white. TILT A LITTLE FURTHER and CUT OFF SHORT.
The rock behind which they sheltered for the welding; it is so overwhelmed with water it is no longer visible; there could be no anchorage here now. QUICK PAN DOWNSTREAM.

Where the river enters the pre-Delta broadening: the water is markedly slowed, but there is much more movement than when we were here before; TILT UPWARD across a solid floor of calmer, rain-marked water, lighter rain and THUNDER, overcast; SOUND of calm, steady rain on miles of water; the reeds where Rose and Allnutt entered: lighter rain; its SOUND among reeds; the water is distinctly higher on the reeds and broken reeds distinctly move on it; LIFT towards mangroves past reeds.

Mangroves and shadow; and the infinitesimal splintery whisperings of light rain. TILT CAMERA DOWNWARD and resume the vertical SHOT on which we faded from Rose and Allnutt, and SLOWLY BRING THE CAMERA TOWARDS THEM, through and beyond mangrove tanglings, to MEDIUM CLOSE. The boat shines with wetness and they are drabbled with it. Nothing moves except the slime-flecked water and that moves slowly, but with a new kind of energy. Neither Rose nor Allnutt is conscious.

At MEDIUM CLOSE, halt CAMERA. A couple of seconds after it stops, there is a first, scarcely discernible shifting motion of the boat. They are still unconscious. Bring up the SMALL SOUNDS OF RUNNING WATER a little; another little shifting of the boat; a little more distinct. They are still unconscious.

ROSE—IN EXTREME CLOSE UP
She looks as if she had cried herself dry, and she looks as if she might quite possibly be dead.

ALLNUTT—EXTREME CLOSE UP
His face is crumpled and distorted against one elbow; in his face, too, there is the look of incredible sadness and defeat; and he, too, could be dead.

(In both faces, also the epitome of utter weariness and of rest after weariness.)

DETAIL SHOT—Allnutt's emaciated hand, motionless, caressing her shoulder, and involved in her hair.

ANOTHER—Her own hands, motionless; they are folded—quite unconsciously—in her automatic gesture of prayer.

TILT CAMERA UPWARDS from this—past gunwale, we see by quiet motion of mangrove roots, that the whole boat is cradling gently in the rain.

FROM BENEATH BOAT—DETAIL SHOT—past bottom of hull, dim daylight opens just discernibly as boat lifts from muck.

PAST PROW—ON MANGROVES

Prow is just perceptibly rising.

UNDERWATER SHOT—BENEATH THE KEEL
a real, gaping light now, visible in motion of boat and of water and of muck-flakes in water.

PAST PROW—ON MANGROVES
The prow really moves forward now.

ANOTHER SHOT—PAST PROW (UNDERWATER)
A new obstruction looms; a thick, dark root; prow (and CAMERA) come right up against it but hit it slowly, a little to one side, and the whole boat, with a hollow SCRAPING, glances along past.

Across the glancing   CUT TO

MEDIUM SHOT—BOAT (FROM DOWNSTREAM)
silently floating towards CAMERA in rustling rain, pointing slantwise, beginning to straighten.

ABOARD—(PAST ROSE AND ALLNUTT)
who are still unconscious; athwart the boat; the quiet movement past the mangroves.

THE ENGINE—(SHOOTING FORWARD FROM STERN)
The engine approaches a low and dangerous-looking branch; it just clears

BOAT—(SHOOTING PAST PROW)
The boat nears a splitting of waterways. Both look bad, but one looks far worse; prow nudges a mangrove mass and for a few seconds everything is at stalemate; then stern begins to swing forward.

BOAT STERN
as it begins to swing forward. It looks as if everything would jam; and with soft bumpings and subdued underwater scrapings and near-misses above water too, the boat does a slow, somnambulistic broken-field crawl during which the light becomes stronger and the rain less, and its SOUND less.

TWO SHOT—ALLNUTT AND ROSE
The strengthened lights and shadows move on their faces and their closed eyes. Rose registers nothing. Allnutt's face and his slow, weak, negative hands both convey that he is dreaming something and doesn't believe it. His face goes inert again. There are fewer shadows now, brighter light, and there is a deep quiet scraping SOUND which makes him open his eyes. Still unable to believe what he sees, he turns his face up toward CAMERA.

MEDIUM SHOT—THE MOVING, THINNING OVERHEAD TANGLE OF MANGROVES—
(FROM HIS VIEWPOINT)
and the sun-touched last of the rain.

ALLNUTT (o.s., softly; an almost incapable voice) Rose. Rosie.

TWO SHOT—ROSE AND ALLNUTT
He is half-up, hands on her, trying to stroke and pat her awake.

ALLNUTT Darling. Dear.

He takes her head gently between his hands and turns her face up to him.

ALLNUTT Look at us, Rosie! My God just *look!* We're movin', dear! We're movin'!

She opens her eyes and looks up. All she sees at first is Allnutt's face, close to her. She looks at it with devotion and with terrible sadness.

ROSE We did our best, dear.

He grabs her quite roughly into his arms and kisses her several times, rapidly and without passion.

ALLNUTT (talking through this) No, *look,* Rosie, just *look* at us! We're movin', don't you see? Movin', that's what!

And with this, as we catch her first realization and reaction, we leave the last of the mangroves and are among the reeds, gliding slowly yet freely; with a RUSTLING of reeds against the boat reminiscent of the rustling of the finished rain, and the late afternoon sunlight moving through the reeds as though they were harpstrings, and casting an almost rustling of slender light and shadow across their faces. Her face becomes quietly transcendent. She gets with great difficulty to her feet (she is very weak; so is he) and, reaching over the gunwale, begins grabbing reeds and with what strength she has, tries to help them along. As soon as he realizes, he gets up weakly, too, and hurries and gets the pole, crying:

ALLNUTT Easy, Rosie dear! You just rest, old girl. Easy now.

Meanwhile, with what strength he has, *he* is poling.

Past them and past prow, we see light beyond the high reeds which steadily, slowly part for the prow and sweep past the flanks of the boat.

ANOTHER ANGLE—ROSE AND ALLNUTT

Both continue working; their incredulous eyes are fixed past the prow. Behind them, reeds partly close back, dark mangroves recede. Their eyes intensify.

PAST PROW—FROM THEIR VIEWPOINT

The last few feet of the reeds part and the boat drifts free and clear onto a horizonless floor of golden light (or if in black and white, a kind of unearthly silver); a low group of wooded islands in the distance.

TWO SHOT—MEDIUM CLOSE—ROSE AND ALLNUTT

as they still drift, a soft breeze on them, looking around.

He sits down, obviously because he feels too weak to stand. Rose, still standing, looks towards him, waiting his authority to believe what she already knows. They speak quietly, as if someone were asleep.

ROSE It—*really is?*
He reaches out his hand to her.

ALLNUTT Come on—sit down, old girl. Yer tremblin' like a leaf.
But she gets down quietly onto her knees and bows her head. He looks at her a few moments, then a little uneasily and shyly, gets down onto his knees. She begins to cry very deeply and silently; we don't see her face. Allnutt puts his arm around her, and she hides her face against him and cries, audibly now but quietly, taking his free hand in her own.

ALLNUTT (very quietly) There, there, Rosie. There, old girl. We're all right now, dear. There, there.

ROSE It's like Heaven.
By Allnutt's face, it is better than that, but he knows what she means.

ROSE (in a queer voice) God let us live.

ALLNUTT Musta been 'Im, all right—'tweren't nothin' in *our* power.
A pause.

ROSE (quiet, charged voice) It wasn't for our sakes, either.

ALLNUTT (pause; carefully) 'Ow you mean, Rosie?

ROSE He brought us here to do His work.
She gets to her feet and walks past CAMERA towards bow.

ROSE—(PAST BOW)
as she comes up, Allnutt following. She is looking all around, and past her we see only empty water and empty sky. She begins to look impatient.

ALLNUTT (quietly) Rosie, this lake's an 'undred miles long; forty wide, at the biggest. It might be days afore she comes our way.

ROSE Then start the fire. We'll go find her.

ALLNUTT No, Rosie, we won't 'ave to go out of our way. She'll come to us.

ROSE *Come* to us?

ALLNUTT Patrolin' the lake. She's bound to come by, don't *you* never worry. An' when she does, we want to be well 'id.

ROSE Hmmm. Perhaps you're right.

ALLNUTT Sure I am. So let's just cruise about a bit till we find a good 'idin' place, an' then we'll lay in wait fer 'er. Right?

ROSE Right.

They go back towards engine.

TWO SHOT—ROSE AND ALLNUTT
as, Rose watching almost with reverence, Allnutt strikes a match and touches it to the carefully prepared wood.

They watch:

THE CURLING SMOKE—(FROM THEIR VIEWPOINT)
and catching flame and the SOUNDS—an image almost of resurrection.

ROSE AND ALLNUTT—(FROM FIRE'S ANGLE)
their faces revitalizing, as light of flame works on them over increasing SOUND of fire; he gently shuts the furnace door, and adjusts the draft; the fire begins a really happy ROARING. Allnutt looks up and around across the water, clearly figuring where they might cruise around.

ALLNUTT (murmuring) Let's—see. We might, uh—

His eyes sharpen into great intentness on something very distant.

All of a suddden he picks up a bailing pail, dips it full, and douses the fire.

TWO SHOT—ROSE (PAST ALLNUTT)
Rose looks at him amazed. He gestures silently with a jerk of his head. She walks towards CAMERA and looks.

LONG SHOT—THE LAKE
Almost invisibly small on the horizon, a small black smudge, a gleaming white speck, which sharpens like a fresh star as we look.

ALLNUTT'S VOICE (o.s.) That's *The Louisa*.

CLOSE SHOT—ROSE AND ALLNUTT
He gets up on the gunwale.

ALLNUTT Yes, that's *The Louisa* all right.

ROSE Which way are they going?

ALLNUTT They're comin' this way.

ROSE (forcing herself to be calm) They mustn't see us here. Can we get far enough among the reeds for them not to see us?

ALLNUTT Got to work fast.

Pulling and tugging with the boat hooks, they swing the launch around and head her into the reeds.

ROSE We'll have to cut some down. How deep is the mud?

Knife in hand, Allnutt goes over the bows among the reeds.

WIDER SHOT—ROSE AND ALLNUTT

as he goes over the bows. He sinks in the mud until the surface of the water is up to his armpits. Floundering about, he cuts every reed within reach. Then, pulling on the bow painter, he is able to work the launch up into the cleared space.

ROSE There's still a bit of her sticking out.

She throws a desperate glance towards *The Louisa,* which is making good time, and is less than half the former distance away.

Allnutt splashes back among the reeds and goes on cutting and hauling. Rose helps him to get back on board. He is in a state of near collapse from his exertions. He lies on the deck panting while Rose cranes her neck over the reeds.

LONG SHOT—THE LOUISA

ROSE (o.s.) She's coming right toward us, Charlie!

CLOSE SHOT—ROSE AND ALLNUTT

Groaning, Allnutt staggers to his knees, then to his feet. Together they watch the approach of *The Louisa.*

LONG SHOT—THE LOUISA

white, spotless, beautiful. At her stern floats the flag of the Imperial German Navy. On her foredeck, we can pick out the six-pound gun which gives the Germans command of the lake. We can see the figures of sailors moving about on the deck.

Over the SOUND of her engines comes a smartly given order, following which *The Louisa* alters her course by a point or two.

CLOSE SHOT—ROSE AND ALLNUTT

Allnutt groans again, this time from relief.

ROSE They're going a different way now.

ALLNUTT I thought they'd seen us.

LONG SHOT—THE LOUISA

heading toward some little islands in the middle of the lake.

ROSE AND ALLNUTT—AS BEFORE

ALLNUTT They're makin' for them islands to anchor for the night. They'll go on in the mornin'. But don't you worry. They'll come 'ere again. You just see if they don't. You know 'ow Germans are; they lays down systems an' they sticks to 'em. Mondays they're at one place. Tuesdays somewheres else. Wednesdays p'raps they're *'ere*. Same ole round, week after week. *You* know.

LONG SHOT—THE LOUISA
as the SOUND of her engines ceases.

ALLNUTT'S VOICE (o.s.) Look! Wot did I tell ya! She's droppin' 'er anchor.

CLOSE SHOT—ROSE AND ALLNUTT

ROSE (nods) How long will it take to get the torpedoes ready?

ALLNUTT I can get the stuff into the tubes in no time, as you might say. Don't know 'bout the detonators. Gotta make them up, you see—devise something. Then we got to cut 'oles in the bows. Might 'ave it all done in three days. Depends on them detonators.

Rose receives this information in silence. Her eyes remain on *The Louisa,* now lying at anchor.

ALLNUTT Rosie, old girl—Rosie—

ROSE (a faraway note in her voice) Yes, dear.

ALLNUTT I know wot you're thinkin' 'bout doin'. (he takes her hand and presses it)

ALLNUTT You're thinkin' 'bout takin' *The African Queen* out at night next time *The Louisa* comes 'ere, ain't you, old girl? (Rose nods) We ought to manage it.   DISSOLVE TO

PAN SHOT—ALLNUTT'S HAND
as it takes one of the packages out of the box and carries it to one of the cylinders and places it inside. A wrench and the cylinder head are in view lying on the deck.

Allnutt's face comes into the SCREEN. He puts more packages into the cylinder.

CAMERA PULLS BACK to include Allnutt and Rose in TWO SHOT. Leaning over the side, Rose brings up handfuls of mud from the bottom and dumps it on the deck. Allnutt carries the sticky stuff to the cylinder and drops it in.
                                        DISSOLVE TO

INSERT: A DISC OF WOOD IN ALLUTT'S HAND.

Three holes have been punched through it. Allnutt's fingers fit cartridges into them. Then a second disc of the same diameter is placed over the first. The second disc has three nails in it. It is turned so that a nail point rests on the percussion cap of each cartridge.

ALLNUTT'S VOICE (o.s.) Ought to work all right.

He begins to screw the pair of discs together. CAMERA PULLS BACK revealing Rose and Allnutt intent upon his handiwork.

ALLNUTT Can't put them into the cylinders yet. They're a bit tricky. We can put 'em in when we're all ready to start.

ROSE It will be dark then, of course. Will you be able to do it in the dark?

ALLNUTT Case of have to. . . . (he puts the detonators away in the locker) Better get the cylinders into place now.

With Rose's help he drags and pushes one of the cylinders forward.

DISSOLVE TO

CLOSE SHOT—THE BOW

The cylinders in position, projecting like cannon through two holes on either side of the stem just above the waterline. O.s., the SOUND of hammering.

The CAMERA RAISES and DOLLIES FORWARD TO:

CLOSE SHOT—ALLNUTT—SHOOTING at him over Rose's shoulder. He is nailing the cylinders solidly into position with battens torn from provision cases. Finally, the work done to his satisfaction, he tosses the hammer aside.

ALLNUTT Well, old girl—I done it all now. Everything. We're all ready.
It is a solemn moment. He shakes his head.

ALLNUTT (reminiscently) You know I been thinkin'. There ain't no need for us both to—to do it. Now I've 'ad time to study it, I can plainly see it's a one-man job.

TWO SHOT—ROSE AND ALLNUTT

ROSE You couldn't be more right, Charlie dear.

ALLNUTT Glad you agree, Rosie. When the time comes I'll put you ashore on the south side of the lake and you wait for me while I attend to *The Louisa.* . . .

ROSE (interrupting) Certainly not! You're the one to be put ashore.

ALLNUTT Me . . . ?

ROSE Of course, you. This whole thing was my idea, wasn't it? . . . I'm the logical one to carry it out.

ALLNUTT Why, Rose! I'm surprised! You're a very sensible woman as a rule. Now we won't 'ave no more talk along *those* lines.

ROSE I can manage this launch every bit as well as you, Charlie Allnutt, and you know it!

ALLNUTT Rosie, you're cracked!

ROSE Didn't I steer going down the rapids?

ALLNUTT Oh, you steered well enough. But you don't know nothin' about the engine. Spose she broke down on you out there in the middle of the lake? Where would you be? But me, I'd leave the tiller and go and do a thing or two to the engine—you know, spit on 'er or kick 'er in the belly—an' she'd go right to work again. She knows 'oo 'er boss is, you bet, that ole engine does.

ROSE (defeated) All right, Charlie. I guess you have to be there.

ALLNUTT Well, now, that's more like it. I'll dive off a second or two before the crash and swim over to where you'll be waitin' on the north shore.

ROSE Charlie . . .

ALLNUTT Yes.

ROSE No need of our pretending.

ALLNUTT I don't know wot you're talkin' about.

ROSE Oh, yes you do. There's got to be a hand on that tiller right up to the last.

Allnutt would like to protest; he opens his mouth to do so, but no words issue. He falls into a stricken silence.

ROSE (continuing) Don't you understand, dear? I wouldn't care about going on to Nairobi—without you.

Having no words, Allnutt can only nod.

ROSE (continuing) We'll do it together. It will be you at the engine and me at the tiller, as it has been from the start.

ALLNUTT (in a choked voice) Right.

ROSE When you come to think of it, we're a very lucky couple, really.

ALLNUTT Aren't we just.

ROSE Charlie.

ALLNUTT Yes, dear.

ROSE Let's make *The African Queen* as clean as we can. Let's scrub her decks and polish her brass.

ALLNUTT (in quick agreement) I've got a can o' paint for 'er mast. She ought to look 'er best. 'Er very best. Representin' as she does the Royal Navy.

MEDIUM SHOT—THE AFRICAN QUEEN
Quite a transformation has taken place in her appearance. Her decks are clean, her brass polished. Rose is engaged in painting her stumpy mast. Her old boiler shines like a mirror. In fact, Allnutt is using it as such while he shaves.

ALLNUTT (between strokes of the razor) I wish I 'ad somethin' clean to put on. It don't seem right for the ship's captain to be without pants.

ROSE Charlie. . . .

ALLNUTT Yes, dear.

ROSE I have a pair you can wear.

ALLNUTT You mean a pair o' yours?

ROSE What's the difference?

ALLNUTT Well, you're the one'll have to look at me.

She gives them to him. Getting into them, Allnutt begins to laugh. When he reveals himself to Rose, it is with obvious embarrassment. He assumes a position rather like September Morn's.

ROSE Here. Put this on, too. (she displays one of her singlets)

ALLNUTT Ain't that goin' a bit too far?

ROSE Don't be silly!

He takes it and puts it on. He looks intently at Rose, expecting ridicule. Her eyes are not on him; they are on the horizon.

LONG SHOT—A PUFF OF SMOKE AND A WHITE DOT
The Louisa.

TWO SHOT—ROSE AND ALLNUTT
as she stares at the horizon. His eyes follow hers.

LONG SHOT—THE LOUISA

DISSOLVE TO

CLOSE SHOT—A CYLINDER—(NIGHT)
as Allnutt's hands finish fitting a detonator into its fore-end, tapping around its edges with a hammer. He is in the water. CAMERA PANS with him around the bow to the other cylinder. Rose passes down the second detonator. Allnutt puts it into place and pulls himself up over the side. He goes to the boiler which casts a red glow on the surrounding deck, and inspects the gauge. Steam is up. He looks across the waters of the lake toward the little group of islands.

LONG SHOT—THE LOUISA
A bundle of faint lights in the distance.

TWO SHOT—ROSE AND ALLNUTT
as a sudden gust of wind strikes the surrounding reeds, causing them to bend and toss. Allnutt takes Rose in his arms. Clinging to one another, they kiss; try to speak; fail—then separate.

ALLNUTT Blowing up a bit. We better get started. All right?

ROSE All right.
He unfastens the side painter, then takes the boat hook and thrusts it against a clump of reeds. *The African Queen* moves slowly out into the fairway. Allnutt lays the boat hook down, feels for the throttle valve and opens it. The propeller begins its beat and the engine its muffled clanking.

FULL SHOT—THE AFRICAN QUEEN
coming out of the reeds into the lake.

TWO SHOT—ALLNUTT AND ROSE
Allnutt is staring at the bows, scowling.

ROSE (observes his expression with anxiety) Is something the matter, dear?

ALLNUTT 'Er bows are ridin' awful low for this kind o' water. Them 'eavy cylinders are what's doin' it.

A wave splashes over the bows into the boat, so that her decks swim in water.

ALLNUTT Got to get 'er nose way up 'igh or we'll be in trouble.

He begins shifting ballast into the stern of the boat, which is swaying and staggering about in haphazard fashion.

ROSE We've been through worse.

ALLNUTT Rivers is one thing—open water another. She ain't built for it. Not when it's rough.

He goes to the engine, begins to tinker with it for a moment.

CLOSE UP—ROSE
steering. She is calm, resolute. Allnutt comes back into SHOT. His brows are working.

ALLNUTT Rosie.

ROSE Yes, Charlie.

ALLNUTT This 'ere storm is messing things up a bit. 'Er bows 'ave got to ride 'igh or we'll be swamped before we get 'alf way to *The Louisa*. On the other 'and, they've got to be low when we 'it 'er, so' the explosion will be down at 'er waterline.

ROSE Can anything be done?

ALLNUTT (nodding) Just before we 'it, I'll bring the ballast back forrard.

ROSE Goodbye, darling.

ALLNUTT Goodbye, sweetheart darling. . . .
A wave breaks over the side, drenching them both.

ALLNUTT Blimey!

FULL SHOT—THE BOAT
It rolls extravagantly as a wind of incredible speed whips down on the lake and rouses the shallow waters to maniacal fury. A series of waves come crashing against the flat sides. Then suddenly the darkness is torn away by a dazzling flash of lightning which reveals the wild waters around them. Thunder follows with a loud BANG like a thousand cannon fired at once. Then comes the rain pouring down through the blackness in solid rivers.

The wind abates momentarily, but the surface of the lake still heaves. The boat begins to pound, raising her bows high out of the water and bringing them down again with a shattering CRASH.

Allnutt seizes a pail and begins to bail furiously, but to no purpose.

Now the wind strikes from a new quarter, laying its grip on the torn surface of the lake and building it up into mountains.

CLOSE SHOT—ROSE
numbed and stupefied, but struggling to maintain her hold on the tiller. Suddenly Allnutt is at her side, putting her arm through a life buoy. They totter and sway for a long moment, then the stern of the launch is engulfed by a heavy wave, and they are up to their waists in water. *The African Queen* is swamped. Very slowly she capsizes. In the distance we see the lights of *The Louisa,* safe at anchor.   FADE OUT

FADE IN
INT. CAPTAIN'S CABIN—THE LOUISA
The CAPTAIN and FOUR of the SHIP'S OFFICERS constitute the court in a proceeding against a small man dressed in woman's bloomers and a ragged singlet. The latter stands, chin on his chest, gazing dully at the carpet.

The CAPTAIN is President of the court, of course. He is a corpulent man with whiskers, groomed in imitation of von Triplitz. Behind him on the wall is a portrait in oils of the Kaiser. He keeps his eyes closed throughout the proceedings.

To the Captain's right, stands the ship's FIRST OFFICER, who is acting as prosecutor. He is clean-shaven, dark, with pale blue eyes; his manner is rigidly correct. To the Captain's left, sits the ship's SECOND OFFICER, who is serving as defense counsel. He is a sleepy, stupid looking man with a big scar on his cheek. All three members of the court are in snowy ducks with gold buttons, white gloves and decorations.

1st OFFICER (in broken English) What is your nationality?
Allnutt does nothing to indicate he hears the question.

1st OFFICER French? . . . Belgian? . . . English?

ALLNUTT (thickly) English.

1st OFFICER Your name?

ALLNUTT Charles Allnutt.

1st OFFICER What were you doing on the island? (Allnutt remains sullenly silent) The punishment for not answering the court is hanging.

ALLNUTT All right. 'Ang me. 'Oo cares?

1st OFFICER What were you doing on the island?

ALLNUTT Nothing.

1st OFFICER How did you get there?

ALLNUTT Swam.

1st OFFICER Do you know that you are in an area prohibited to all but members of the forces of His Imperial Majesty, Kaiser Wilhelm II?

ALLNUTT 'Oo cares?

1st OFFICER What is your rank.

ALLNUTT 'Ow's that?

1st OFFICER You are a soldier, are you not?

ALLNUTT (disgustedly) Naaa!

1st OFFICER What are you then?

ALLNUTT I ain't nothin'.

1st OFFICER (in German) The prisoner is obviously here to spy on the movements of the *Königin Luise.*

The Captain, without opening his eyes, turns to the Second Officer; nods to him to proceed. The latter is completely at a loss. He rises, stammers a few words in German.

2nd OFFICER (in German) No proof of criminal intent—

He stops, tongue-tied; then throws up his hands in a final gesture, sits heavily and starts wiping his face with a handkerchief.

CAPTAIN (to Allnutt in English) What were you doing here, if you were not spying? (Allnutt doesn't answer) The Court sentences you to death by hanging. (then in German to the others) Not from the yard arm, but when we reach port.

At this moment, there is a bustle outside the tiny crowded cabin. Then the door opens and a colored Petty Officer comes in and salutes them.

PETTY OFFICER (in Swahili) We are about to pick up another one. A woman.

The Captain rises and goes to the door.

LONG SHOT—ROSE
FROM HIS VIEWPOINT

She is sitting on one of the small barren islands, a little way up from the beach; the dinghy manned by native oarsmen with a white officer, is already half way there.

CAPTAIN' VOICE (o.s.) She looks like she's white.

INT. CAPTAIN'S CABIN—AS BEFORE

CAPTAIN (to Allnutt in English) Was there a woman with you?

Allnutt drops his mask of sullen stupidity and turns quickly to the door, but the Captain's bulk is blocking his view. He tries to push him aside. The First Officer hits Allnutt a hard blow across the face. Allnutt runs to a porthole and looks out in time to see:

LONG SHOT—ROSE
FROM HIS POINT OF VIEW

She is struggling with the WHITE OFFICER who is trying to make her enter the boat.

CLOSE UP—ALLNUTT
frantic with excitement.

ALLNUTT (calls, shouting) Rosie! Rosie!

LONG SHOT—ROSE
She stops struggling,

ROSE (calling back) Charlie!

INT. CABIN—AS BEFORE
The First Officer, who seems to enjoy hitting Allnutt, now delivers a second blow, this time knocking him down. He remains standing over Allnutt while the Captain and Second Officer resume their seats.

CAPTAIN (to Allnutt) Who is that woman?

ALLNUTT (rising unsteadily) I don't know.

CAPTAIN But you just called her by name.

ALLNUTT I thought it was somebody else.

CAPTAIN (in German) Maybe I'll change my mind and hang you from the yard arm after all.

o.s., the SOUND of approaching steps; then Rose, followed by the WHITE OFFICER, enters the cabin. She stands staring at Allnutt for a long time.

ROSE Charlie dear!

ALLNUTT 'Ello, Rosie.

CAPTAIN Aha! You *do* know her!

ALLNUTT I calls all the girls Rosie.

The WHITE OFFICER swings into view a life buoy on which is printed "The African Queen".

WHITE OFFICER (in German) She had this with her.

CAPTAIN (to Rose, in English) Who are you?

ROSE Miss Rose Sayer.

CAPTAIN English?

ROSE Of course.

CAPTAIN What are you doing on the lake?

ALLNUTT I ain't told 'im nothin', Rosie.

1st OFFICER Silence!

CAPTAIN Answer the question!

ROSE We were boating.

CAPTAIN Last night? In such weather?

ROSE We were not responsible for the weather.

CAPTAIN And why were you boating?

ROSE That is our affair.

1st OFFICER As your fellow-prisoner has already learned, the penalty for not answering the court is death.

ROSE (slow take) You mean he—
She gets it. She goes swiftly close to Allnutt.

ROSE Charlie! Are they telling me . . .

CAPTAIN (in German) Order!
The First Officer lays a restraining hand on her shoulder.

ROSE (wheeling in fury and slapping him hard across the face) *Stop that!*
He goes cold and smiles yellow.

ROSE *Are* they, Charlie? The truth?
Allnutt looks back at her; his chin begins to tremble; with heroic effort he masters it. He nods.

CAPTAIN Fraulein Sayer, you will come to order and answer the questions of this court.

Rose wheels and faces him; she is all cold fire.

ROSE Ask your questions.

CAPTAIN What were you doing on the lake?

ROSE We came here to sink this ship, and—

ALLNUTT (in a loud voice) Rosie!

ROSE —and we would have, too, except for—

ALLNUTT *Rosie!*

ROSE Let's at least have the fun of telling them about it, Charlie.

ALLNUTT Don't you believe her, yer Honor. She's touched with the fever.

ROSE (impatient) Oh *stop* it, Charlie, we've been through all this. (primly) I'm not going to outlive you and that's all there is to it.

CAPTAIN (a bit amused and skeptical) Just how, Fraulein, did you propose to sink—the *Königin Luise?*

ROSE We were going to ram you.

CAPTAIN With how large a vessel?

ROSE With torpedoes.

CAPTAIN AND 1st OFFICER (look at each other; in unison) Torpedoes!

2nd OFFICER Torpedoes?

CAPTAIN AND 1st OFFICER (in unison; tossing bones to a dog; in German) Torpedoes.

2nd OFFICER (gaping) Nein! (foolish enough to believe Rose and Allnutt, he looks at them with awe)

1st OFFICER (interpreting, smooth and sardonic) I think it is safe to assume, Miss Sayer, that the British Admiralty did not entrust *you* and *this* —gentleman—with the torpedoes. Will you be so good as to tell us precisely where and how you acquired them?

ROSE *Acquired?* Mr. Allnutt made them.

First Officer and Captain exchange a significant glance: she is obviously nuts. (All through this, the Second Officer, who no spik English, is like a puzzled observer at a tennis match.)

1st OFFICER (a little like a warden in a loony house) How *very* interesting.

ROSE I don't think you even believe me. Tell him how you did it, Charlie. (Over Allnutt's lines, the officers exchange glances which mean: "He's loony, too".)

ALLNUTT (100% the engineer) Well—wot I did was take the 'eads off two cylinders of oxygen an' fill 'em up with 'igh explosive—'bout two 'undred weight. That was easy enough—it was the detonators took some hinge-nooity. Know wot I used? Cartridges, an' nails, in blocks o' soft wood. A pretty job. Then I mounted the cylinders so they stuck through the bows of *The African Queen,* near the water line, so when we rammed you—

CAPTAIN (half believing what he can't believe) Where is *The African Queen?*

ROSE She sank in the storm.

CAPTAIN How did you get onto the lake?

ROSE We came down the Ulanga—the Bora, you call it down here.
All three officers look at each other—even the Second Officer catches this—and back at Rose.

CAPTAIN (in English) **1st OFFICER** (in English) **2nd OFFICER** (in German) (together) But that is impossible!

ROSE Nevertheless!

CAPTAIN Everybody knows the river is unnavigable.

ROSE (proudly) We came down it, though—didn't we, Charlie?—on *The African Queen.*

CLOSE SHOT—THE DERELICT AFRICAN QUEEN
floating keel up. She is under water except for the two cylinders which stick up like the antennae of a snail.

CAMERA DOES LONG PULL BACK, to show *The Louisa* approaching.

EXT. DECK—THE LOUISA
MEDIUM SHOT—ROSE AND ALLNUTT

as they come out of the cabin surrounded by the ship's officers. The company stops near the main mast where a crew member has finished making a hangman's noose of one rope and is now tying a knot in another.

1st OFFICER (to Captain) The man first.

ROSE Please—hang us together.

CAPTAIN Very well.

He nods to the First Officer to proceed with the execution. Allnutt and Rose exchange a look of satisfaction.

ALLNUTT Rosie, I ain't gonna say goodbye again. It's gettin' to be an old story.

ROSE Darling!

The next moment, the deck heaves upward. There is a rush of air and a frightful ROAR. Smoke and flying debris fill the SCREEN.

MEDIUM LONG SHOT—THE WATER

where those who were on deck are now struggling. There is something ludicrous about the Germans in their ducks with the gold buttons and decorations trying to keep above water.

CLOSE SHOT—ROSE AND ALLNUTT

ALLNUTT Wot 'appened?

ROSE We did it, Charlie, we did it!

ALLNUTT But *'ow?*

Rose points to a piece of wreckage floating on the water in the near distance.

ALLNUTT Well I'll be. . . . Are you all right, Rosie?

ROSE Never better. And you, dear?

ALLNUTT Bit of all right.

ROSE I'm all turned round, Charlie. Which way is the south shore?

ALLNUTT The one we're swimming towards, old girl.

CAMERA MOVES TOWARD the piece of wreckage, losing Rose and Allnutt, into CLOSE SHOT showing the printed words "African Queen" on the wreckage. When the name fills the SCREEN— FADE OUT

THE END

The Night of the Hunter

"The Night of the Hunter"

In 1954 James Agee wrote the film script of The Night of the Hunter, *based on the Davis Grubb novel. The motion picture, directed by Charles Laughton, and with Paul Gregory as producer, was released, in 1955, through United Artists. Agee, who died in May, 1955, never saw this picture in which leading roles were played by Robert Mitchum, Lillian Gish and Shelley Winters.*

FULL SHOT—THE STARLIT SKY

VOICE *And He opened His mouth and taught them, saying. . . .*
FADE sky to day. LAP DISSOLVE TO

LONG SHOT—HELICOPTER—OHIO RIVER COUNTRY
High over the country, CENTERING the winding river.

VOICE *Beware of false prophets. . . .*

LOWER LONG SHOT—HELICOPTER—RIVER COUNTRY
We approach a riverside village.

VOICE *. . . which come to you in sheep's clothing . . .*

A CLOSER, LOWER HELICOPTER SHOT
We descend low over a deserted house; CHILDREN in yard run and hide; we hear "IT" counting *"five, ten, fifteen, twenty. . . ."*

VOICE *. . . but inwardly they are ravening wolves.*

MEDIUM SHOT—"IT"
He finishes his count with a loud *"Hundred"* and turns, then:
"IT" what's wrong?

263

We PAN as he comes towards a little boy, beside an open cellar door, who gestures towards the open door. "IT" looks down.

"IT" (a low gasp) Heyy! (then he shouts to all and to us) Heyy!

We DOLLY IN fast to, and TILT DOWN into open cellar, into:

CLOSE SHOT—A LEG
A skeletal leg in a rotted fume of stocking and a high-heeled shoe. We HOLD a moment, then PULL UP and AWAY over the converging heads of several CHILDREN. A CHILD whimpers softly.

HELICOPTER SHOT
The yard and the CHILDREN, same angle and height as the last descending helicopter shot. We PULL BACK and AWAY.

VOICE *Ye shall know them by their fruits.*   DISSOLVE TO

HIGH LONG SHOT—HELICOPTER

CENTERING the river.

VOICE *A good tree cannot bring forth evil fruit. . . .*

LOWER LONG SHOT (HELICOPTER)

CENTERING on open touring car, as it drives along a river road.

VOICE *Neither can a corrupt tree bring forth good fruit.*
We STOOP LOW towards the car.

VOICE *Wherefore by their fruits ye shall know them.*   CUT TO

CLOSE SHOT—PREACHER
He is the driver of the car. Pleasant river landscapes (PROCESS) flow behind him. He is dressed in dark clothes, a paper collar, a string tie. As he drives he talks to himself.

PREACHER What's it to be, Lord, another widow? Has it been six? Twelve? . . . I disremember.

He nods, smiles, and touches his hat. We see a farm couple in a poor wagon.

PREACHER You say the word, and I'm on my way.
                                                    LAP DISSOLVE TO

CLOSE SHOT—PREACHER DRIVING
He brakes his car in a small riverside town; then proceeds.

PREACHER You always send me money to go forth and preach your *Word*. A widow with a little wad of bills hidden away in the sugar-bowl.

LAP DISSOLVE TO

CLOSE SHOT—PREACHER DRIVING
He shifts into second gear, climbing a steep little hill.

PREACHER *I am tired*. Sometimes I wonder if you really understand. (pause) Not that you mind the killin's . . .
The stones of a country graveyard gleam in the last daylight.

PREACHER Yore Book is *full* of killin's.
He starts fast and noisily down a steep hill.

PREACHER But there *are* things you *do* hate, Lord: perfume-smellin' things —lacy things—things with *curly hair*—

CUT TO

INT. A BURLESQUE HOUSE—MEDIUM CLOSE SHOT—A DANCER
She is hard at work, to music o.s.

FULL SHOT—AUDIENCE—CENTERING ON PREACHER, IN AISLE SEAT
Among the members of the sad burlesque audience, he is in strong contrast: a sour and aggressive expression. Music o.s. We MOVE IN fast to a HEAD CLOSE-UP.

MEDIUM CLOSE SHOT—THE DANCER

INSERT—PREACHER'S LEFT HAND
Labeled H-A-T-E in tattoo across four knuckles, it grips and flexes.

INSERT—HIS RIGHT HAND
Before we see the lettering he slides it into his pocket.

EXTREME CLOSE SHOT—PREACHER
His head slants; a cold smile; one eyelid flutters.

INSERT—RIGHT HAND AND POCKET
We hear the snapping open of a switch-blade knife and the point of the knife cuts through his clothes.

LESS EXTREME CLOSE SHOT—PREACHER
He seems to "listen" for something.

PREACHER No, there are too many of them; you can't kill a *world*.
A hand descends firmly onto his shoulder. He glances up behind him as we

TILT TO

CLOSE SHOT—A STATE TROOPER
He bends down and speaks quietly next PREACHER's ear.

TROOPER You driving an Essex tourin'-car with a Moundsville license?

LAP DISSOLVE TO

INT. COURTROOM—CLOSE THREE-SHOT—JUDGE AND CLERK, OVER PREACHER

JUDGE Harry Powell, for the theft of that touring car you will spend thirty days in the Moundsville Penitentiary.

PREACHER (correcting Clerk) *Preacher* Harry Powell.

JUDGE A car thief! Picked up where *you* were! A man of God? (to Clerk) Harry Powell.
LAP DISSOLVE TO

FULL SHOT—MOUNDSVILLE PENITENTIARY—DAY (HELICOPTER)
A grim stone turretted façade; an American flag idles at top center.

LAP DISSOLVE TO

CLOSE DOWNWARD TWO-SHOT—JOHN AND PEARL HARPER
They sit in the grass, a sentimental picture. JOHN is nine; PEARL is five. They are working together on PEARL's doll; PEARL is dressing her, while JOHN gets on a difficult shoe.

PEARL Stand still, Miss Jenny!

JOHN (across her) There! What's so hard about that!
He proudly exhibits the shod foot.
They hear the sound of an auto engine o.s. They look o.s. and get up, PEARL dangling the doll.

LONG SHOT—OVER THE CHILDREN—BEN HARPER'S FORD
A Model-T Ford approaches at maximal speed on uneven dirt road.

PEARL (to John, happily) Daddy!
The car careens towards us; then swings into the sideyard as we PAN, and stops.

They run towards their father fast; then JOHN looks puzzled and they stop short.

BEN HARPER half-falls out of the far door, his shoulder blood-stained, his eyes wild. A hefty, simple man of thirty. He looks at them, dazed, across the car.

MEDIUM SHOT—BEN HARPER

BEN Where's your Mom?

JOHN Out shopping—you're bleeding, Dad—

BEN Listen to me John.

On this he comes around clear of the car with a revolver in one hand and a bloody roll of banknotes in the other.

CLOSE SHOT—JOHN

He screams. BEN slaps him with the back of the money hand, leaving blood on JOHN's cheek.

CLOSE GROUP SHOT—JOHN, BEN, PEARL

PEARL, and the house, are in BACKGROUND. PEARL just clutches her doll. During BEN's next lines, JOHN touches his cheek and looks at the blood on his fingers and at the bloody money—of which we FLASH-CUT an INSERT.

BEN (rushing) Listen! This money here! We got to hide it before they get me! There's close to ten thousand dollars. (his eyes dart wildly) Under a rock in the smokehouse? Ah no. Under the bricks in the grape arbor? No, they'd dig for it.

CLOSE SHOT—BEN

BEN (sudden triumph) Why *sure! That's* the place!

He moves forward and OUT and in his place we see two police cars, small in distance, coming fast. We hear sirens.

INT. FRONT POLICE CAR—THROUGH WINDSHIELD

. . . and OVER TWO STATE TROOPERS. They move at high speed, with sirens.

BEN and his CHILDREN, tiny in the distance, dilate.

TROOPER (driving) That's him.

2ND TROOPER (over his shoulder, as if to us) He prob'ly still has that gun.

CLOSE GROUP SHOT—BEN AND CHILDREN

. . . police cars approaching in BACKGROUND. PEARL hugs her doll. JOHN is dazed. BEN stands, pistol in hand.

BEN Here they come.

JOHN Dad, you're bleeding. . . .

He grabs JOHN's shoulder and stoops as we TIGHTEN IN.

BEN Listen to me son. You got to *swear. Swear* means promise. First swear you'll take care of little Pearl. Guard her with your life, boy. Then swear you won't never tell where that money's hid. Not even your Mom.

JOHN Yes, Dad.

BEN You understand?

JOHN Not even her?

In b.g. the TROOPERS get out of their cars and fan out cautiously to surround BEN: guns in hand.

BEN You got common sense. She ain't. When you grow up that money'll be yours. Now *swear*. "I will guard Pearl with my life . . ."

JOHN (fumbling) I will guard Pearl with my life. . . .

BEN . . . . "and I won't never tell about the money."

JOHN And I won't never tell about the money.

PEARL You, Pearl. You swear too.

CLOSE SHOT—PEARL

PEARL (giggling) Who's them Blue Men yonder?

HEAD CLOSE-UP—JOHN

JOHN (under breath) Blue men.

GROUP SHOT—TROOPERS IN BACKGROUND

A TROOPER Ben Harper!

BEN I'm goin' now children. Goodbye.

BEN backs away from his CHILDREN, raising his hands, gun in one hand. We PULL BACK a little, enlarging the GROUP SHOT and the role of the TROOPERS in it.

TROOPER Drop that gun, Harper. We don't want them kids hurt.

TWO TROOPERS approach BEN from behind.

BEN Just mind what you swore, son. *Mind,* boy!

GROUP SHOT—JOHN

He runs forward and clasps his stomach, with his mouth open.

MEDIUM SHOT—BEN AND TROOPERS—JOHN'S VIEWPOINT

One TROOPER smacks the back of BEN's head with a pistol barrel.

CLOSE SHOT—JOHN

JOHN (shouting; a sickly smile) Don't!

MEDIUM SHOT—BEN AND TROOPERS—AS BEFORE

Another TROOPER, with a pistol barrel, knocks the pistol from BEN's lifted hand.

CLOSE SHOT—JOHN

JOHN (shouting) Don't!

BEN sinks to his knees as both men, and two others from the front, close in on him.

HEAD CLOSE-UP—JOHN

JOHN Dad!

He takes in the GROUP with his mouth open.

O.s. we hear the slamming of car doors, and car starting away.

FULL SHOT—JOHN'S VIEWPOINT—THE CARS

They drive away fast in road dust.

THREE-SHOT—THE CHILDREN AND WILLA HARPER

Carrying a shopping bag, their mother, WILLA, runs up from BACKGROUND between the CHILDREN, looking always to cars o.s.

CLOSE SHOT—WILLA

She has a rich body.

RESUME THREE-SHOT

PEARL comes to her and she picks up PEARL and the *doll*; JOHN, laden with his oath, walks quickly into the house. WILLA does a bewildered take, then looks again towards the cars o.s.   LAP DISSOLVE TO

INT. COURTROOM—CLOSE THREE-SHOT—JUDGE AND CLERK, OVER BEN

JUDGE Ben Harper, it is the sentence of this Court that for the murder of Ed Smiley and Corey South, you be hanged by the neck until you are dead, and may God have mercy on your soul.   LAP DISSOLVE TO

FULL SHOT—THE MOUNDSVILLE PENITENTIARY

SAME VIEW AS BEFORE; BUT NOW IT IS NIGHT.   LAP DISSOLVE TO

INT. BEN'S CELL—NIGHT—CLOSE DOWN-SHOT—BEN

He lies on his back, chuckling and murmuring indistinctly in his sleep.

BEN I got you *all* buffaloed! You ain't never gonna git it outen me; not none o' you!

PREACHER'S VOICE (o.s., very low) Where, Ben? Where? Where?

BEN (distinctly) And a little child shall lead them.

CLOSE TWO-SHOT—NEW ANGLE—BEN, THEN PREACHER

BEN lies in profile. From the bunk above, the face of PREACHER stretches down into the SHOT, upside down, snake-like.

PREACHER (softly) Come on, boy: tell me.

BEN wakes, sees PREACHER, and hits him so hard in the face that he falls from bunk to floor. PREACHER collects himself into a squat, nursing his face. BEN sits up in bed.

PREACHER (with wholesome dignity) Ben, I'm a Man of God.

BEN Tryin' to make me talk about it in my sleep!

PREACHER No, Ben.

BEN What'd I say? (he grabs Preacher's throat and shakes him) What? What? What? What?

PREACHER (choking) You was quotin' Scripture. You said—you said, "And a little child shall lead them."

BEN Hm!
He lies back, amused. PREACHER sits on the bedside; manner of a parson visiting the sick.

PREACHER (gravely) You killed two men, Ben Harper.

BEN That's right, Preacher. I robbed that bank because I got tired of seein' children roamin' the woodlands without food, children roamin' the highways in this year of Depression; children sleepin' in old abandoned car bodies on junk-heaps; and I promised myself I'd never see the day when *my* youngins'd want.

PREACHER With that ten thousand dollars I could build a Tabernacle that'd make the Wheeling Island Tabernacle look like a chicken-house!

BEN Would you have free candy for the kids, Preacher?
He picks up and wads a sock.

PREACHER Think of it, Ben! With that cursed, bloodied gold!

BEN How come you got that stickknife hid in your bed-blankets, Preacher?

PREACHER I come not with Peace but with a Sword.

BEN *You,* Preacher?

PREACHER gets and pockets the knife.

PREACHER That Sword has served me through many an evil time, Ben Harper.

BEN What religion do you profess, Preacher?

PREACHER The religion the Almighty and me worked out betwixt us.

BEN (contemptuously) I'll bet.

PREACHER Salvation is a last-minute business, boy.

BEN (sock near mouth) Keep talkin', Preacher.

PREACHER If you was to let that money serve the Lord's purposes, He might feel kindly turned towards you.

BEN Keep talkin', Preacher.
He wads the sock into his mouth and lies back, sardonic.

PREACHER (his voice fading into Dissolve) You reckon the Lord wouldn't change his mind about you if . . .   DISSOLVE TO

EXT. PENITENTIARY COURTYARD—NIGHT   DISSOLVE TO

INSERT—PREACHER'S HANDS
They rest on sill of cell window, the lettered fingers legible. The right hand is lettered L-O-V-E. The hands open, disclosing his open knife. They close over it.

CLOSE SHOT—PREACHER, AT CELL WINDOW
His eyes lift from his hands, heavenward. Moonlight on his face. He prays, quietly.

PREACHER Lord You sure knowed what You was doin' when You brung me to this very cell at this very time. A man with ten thousand dollars hid somewheres, and a widder in the makin'.   DISSOLVE TO

EXT. PENITENTIARY COURTYARD—NIGHT
Same SHOT as before, but now, prison lights are on; and a man, a prison GUARD, waits close inside door. BART the HANGMAN joins him with a silent salute. BART wears a hard derby.

EXT. PENITENTIARY—THE DOOR—(REVERSE)
They walk in silence into MEDIUM, MOVING SHOT, the GUARD talkative, BART reluctant to talk.

The Penitentiary recedes in b.g.

GUARD Any trouble?

BART No.

GUARD He was a cool one, that Harper. Never broke.

BART He carried on some; kicked.

EXT. BART'S HOUSE—MEDIUM SHOT—BART AND GUARD
On porch, by door, is a doll's perambulator. BART and GUARD walk into the SHOT.

GUARD stops, BART starts up his front steps.

GUARD He never told about the money.

BART (walking up steps) No.

GUARD What do *you* figure he done with it?

BART (turning, at door) He took the secret with him when I dropped him. The GUARD leaves the SHOT; BART goes in.

INT. BART'S HALLWAY—CLOSE SHOT—BART
He hangs up his coat and hat. Across this his wife speaks o.s.; a lighted door is ajar at rear of hall. A clatter of dishes and pans o.s.

BART'S WIFE (o.s.) That you, Bart? Supper's waitin'.

BART just nods, and, tiptoeing, walks into a door next the kitchen and snaps on a light and turns on water o.s. His wife comes out of the kitchen and goes in.

INT. BART'S BATHROOM—CLOSE TWO-SHOT—BART AND WIFE
He is washing his hands in thick lather. Passing, she pecks his cheek and, as we PAN, looks into the next room. He looks past her, and we see two small CHILDREN asleep in a big brass bed. BART registers, turns again to the basin, and we PAN them back into the original TWO-SHOT.

BART (low) Mother: sometimes I think it might be better if I was to quit my job as guard.

His WIFE's eyes go sharp and quiet.

WIFE (low) You're always this way when there's a hangin'. You never have to be there.

BART rinses his hands. A sigh; he takes up the towel.

BART Sometimes I wish I was back at the mine.

WIFE And leave me a widow after another blast like the one in '24? Not on your life, old mister!

He looks at her a moment. She goes out. He looks o.s. towards his CHIL-DREN. He goes into their room on tiptoe.

MEDIUM SHOT—BART
He approaches his children, across whose bed WE SHOOT without yet seeing them. He comes into MEDIUM CLOSE-UP. As he leans and we TILT DOWN, he extends his large hands.

CLOSE DOWNWARD TWO-SHOT—HIS CHILDREN
Two rose-and-gold little GIRLS lie in sleep; BART's hands enter the SHOT and gently rearrange the covers so that their mouths and throats are free. We watch, for a moment more, the two sleeping faces.

LAP DISSOLVE TO

HEAD CLOSE-UP—BART, HOVERING HIS CHILDREN
CHILDREN'S VOICES (o.s. chanting) Hing, hang, hung. See what the Hangman done!

LAP DISSOLVE TO

EXT. CRESAP'S LANDING—DAY
We are in *Peacock Alley*. The tree-shaded dirt street of a small, one-street river town; a picturesque, mid-19th-century remnant of the old river civilization, which general Progress has left behind. Chiefly we see, in this order: A *schoolhouse* (on far side of street); *Miz Cunningham's second-hand shop*; a *Grange House* sporting a poster for a Western movie; *Spoon's Ice Cream Parlor*. At the end of this street, down the river-bank, is a brick wharf and UNCLE BIRDIE's *wharf-boat*. In b.g. and in passing, suggestions of sleepy small-town life.

From the HEAD CLOSE-UP of BART the *Hangman* o.s. chanting, we

LAP DISSOLVE TO

HEAD CLOSE-UP—JOHN HARPER
Chanting VOICES o.s. complete *"see what the Hangman done!"*

PULL BACK TO

CLOSE PULLING TWO-SHOT—PEARL AND JOHN
They stroll barefoot down the empty dirt sidewalk. They look towards the voices, PEARL friendly, JOHN hostile.

MEDIUM SHOT—THE CHILDREN, OVER JOHN AND PEARL
Several, within the door of the *Schoolhouse*, stick their heads around the edge. They chant at the HARPER CHILDREN. Another, next the door, is drawing something on the wall.

CHILDREN (chanting) Hung, hang, hing! See the Robber swing!

OVER these lines we CUT briefly to—

CLOSER SHOT—THE CHILDREN
. . . chanting, drawing. The ARTIST completes in chalk, a large simple sketch of a man hanging from gallows. As the verse ends we CUT TO:

MEDIUM SHOT—THE CHILDREN, OVER JOHN AND PEARL
They look towards OUR CHILDREN; JOHN pays them no attention. The drawing is revealed. JOHN takes PEARL's hand. The other CHILDREN giggle.

CHILDREN (chanting) Hing, hang, hung! Now my song is done!
Between lines one and two JOHN turns away from them into—

CLOSE TWO-SHOT—JOHN AND PEARL—THROUGH WINDOW
We SHOOT them through the window of MIZ CUNNINGHAM's second-hand store. The back of a watch is silhouetted large in FOREGROUND; JOHN's eyes instantly fix on it; in b.g. the SCHOOL-CHILDREN finish their song and vanish, giggling, into the schoolhouse. We hear the ticking of the watch.

INSERT—THE WATCH
A watch with a moving sweep-hand, ticking.

CLOSE TWO-SHOT—JOHN AND PEARL

PEARL Are you goin' to buy it, John?
No answer. JOHN's eyes are fixed on the watch. OVER a shop-doorbell we hear:

MIZ CUNNINGHAM'S VOICE (o.s.) Uh-Hawwww! (They glance toward her.)

MEDIUM SHOT—MIZ CUNNINGHAM
Fantastically dirty and fantastically dressed, she hustles to them and we PAN her into a THREE-SHOT. She talks like a Tidewater Cockatoo.

MIZ CUNNINGHAM (continuing) So your Mommy's keepin' you out of school! Poor little lambs!

PEARL watches her; JOHN, the watch.

MIZ CUNNINGHAM And how is your poor, poor mother?

JOHN She's at Spoon's Ice Cream Parlor.

MIZ CUNNINGHAM (she snuffles) The Lord tends you both these days!

JOHN doesn't take his eyes off the watch.

CLOSE SHOT—JOHN

His eyes are fixed on the watch o.s.

MIZ CUNNINGHAM'S VOICE (o.s.) Didn't they never find out what your father done with all that money he stole?

Eyes as before till *"money,"* then he looks up towards her.

MEDIUM SHOT—MIZ CUNNINGHAM

MIZ CUNNINGHAM When they caught him, there wasn't so much as a penny of it to be seen! Now what do you make of that! Eh, boy?

She grins horribly.

TWO-SHOT—OVER JOHN AND PEARL

JOHN Pearl and me, we have to go.
He walks off fast as we DOLLY BEHIND THEM; he leads PEARL, who hugs her doll.

PEARL (chanting) Hing, hang, hung.

JOHN You better not sing that song.

PEARL Why?

JOHN 'Cause you're too little.
A few paces in silence; now they come to the big window of *Spoon's Ice Cream Parlor.*

PEARL Can we get some candy?
WILLA's face is seen within; serving a customer, she sees them and waves them away.

JOHN No.
He keeps her strolling. WALT SPOON, comes out, proffering two lollypops.

WALT Howdy, youngins.

PEARL drags at JOHN's hand but JOHN, pretending not to see or hear, drags her out of the SHOT, shaking his head. We DOLLY IN on WALT, who looks after them, surprised and touched, then goes inside.

INT. SPOON'S PARLOR—GROUP SHOT—WALT, WILLA, ICEY SPOON
We PAN WALT across a little of his Parlor; he plants the lollypops back in a jar on the counter and leaves the SHOT as we TIGHTEN IN on WILLA and ICEY. WILLA slides used dishes into wash-water; ICEY jaws down her back, from first moment of shot.

ICEY Willa Harper there is certain plain facts of life that adds up just like two plus two makes four and one of them is this: No woman is good enough to raise growin' youngsters alone! The Lord meant that job for two!

WILLA Icey, I don't want a husband.

CLOSE SHOT—ICEY

ICEY (fiercely) *Fiddlesticks!*   LAP DISSOLVE TO

FULL SHOT—EXT. STREET—NIGHT

The weekly movie audience is letting out, next door to SPOON's. Some start cars or wagons, others stroll to SPOON's.   LAP DISSOLVE TO

INT. SPOON'S PARLOR—EVENING—TWO-SHOT—ICEY AND WILLA

We start with a CLOSE SHOT as ICEY's hands slap together a gooey banana split; TILT UP to TWO-SHOT, favoring ICEY; finish on WILLA, on "it's a *man* you need," etc.

Murmur of CUSTOMERS O.S.

WALT'S VOICE (calling o.s.) One solid brown sody, one Lovers' Delight.

ICEY 'Tain't a matter of wantin' or *not* wantin'! You're no spring chicken, you're a grown woman with two little youngins; it's a *man* you need in the house, Willa Harper!   LAP DISSOLVE TO

LONG SHOT—NIGHT—A TRAIN

A short, lighted, toy-like train departs the town along the river-bank, whistling. The whistle TIES OVER the previous DISSOLVE. STARLIT SKY.
                                                                  LAP DISSOLVE TO

FRAMING SHOT—EXT. HARPER HOUSE—NIGHT

A square, HEAD-ON SHOT, river water below and vibrant starlight above; featuring a gas-lamp by the road; a tree; and pretty tree-shadows which work across a window.

INT. HARPER CHILDREN'S BEDROOM—NIGHT—TWO-SHOT—JOHN, PEARL, SHADOWS

PEARL lies in their bed, her doll snug on her shoulder. JOHN sits on the edge of the bed, in his underwear.

PEARL Tell me a story, John.

JOHN Once upon a time there was a rich king . . . (he sees the shadows on the wall and gets up and looks at them) . . . and he had him a son and a daughter and they all lived in a castle over in Africa. Well, one day this King got taken away by bad men and before he got took off he told his son to kill anyone that tried to steal their gold, and before long these bad men come back and—

PEARL The Blue Men?

He moves, and as his shadow moves away we see the shadow of PREACHER, motionless. PEARL sits up and points at it. JOHN notices her and sees it. We PAN JOHN to the window. He looks out.

FULL SHOT—PREACHER—THROUGH WINDOW, JOHN'S VIEWPOINT.
He stands motionless.

RESUME PREVIOUS SHOT—JOHN AT WINDOW
He turns and we PAN him to bed.

JOHN (casually) Just a man. (he climbs into bed and pulls up the covers) Goodnight Pearl, sleep tight; and don't let the bedbugs bite.

PEARL (to doll) 'Night Miss Jenny; don't let the bedbugs bite.
As they settle down we hear PREACHER's singing, sweet and quiet o.s.: *"Leaning on the Everlasting Arms."*   DISSOLVE TO

EXT. RIVER AND TOWN—MORNING—FULL SHOT—A GINGERBREAD SIDE-WHEELER
She steams around a bend towards a toy-like small town. PREACHER's song, o.s., ties over. People are waving from shore and boat.

FULL PANNING SHOT—THE BOAT, FROM SHORE
We PAN her into frame UNCLE BIRDIE STEPTOE's toy-like little wharf-boat. As she passes broadside we CUT TO:

MEDIUM SHOT—BIRDIE, THEN JOHN
. . . as boat passes. BIRDIE's head sticks through a porthole. He is a wiry old river character. The boat whistles. As BIRDIE speaks we PAN JOHN, and foundered skiff, into TWO-SHOT with BIRDIE.

BIRDIE She don't put in at Cresap's Landing no more, but she still blows as she passes. Come on in and have a cup of coffee.

JOHN (starting towards him) Ain't nobody stole Dad's skiff.

BIRDIE Ain't nobody goin' to neither, long as Uncle Birdie's around.
He vanishes from the porthole. We PAN JOHN from skiff to wharf and Birdie's door.

BIRDIE'S VOICE (calling o.s.) First day my jints is limber enough I'll haul her up and give her a good caulkin'.

INT. BIRDIE'S BOAT—TWO-SHOT—JOHN AND BIRDIE

JOHN enters and sits on a box. BIRDIE, in a ramshackle rocking chair, pours coffee. BESS's photograph on chest near BIRDIE.

BIRDIE Ain't seen you in a coon's age, Johnny.

JOHN I been mindin' Pearl.

BIRDIE Pshaw now! Ain't it a caution what women'll load onto a feller's back when he ain't lookin'?

He gives JOHN a cup of coffee.

BIRDIE 'Scuse me, Cap, while I sweeten up my coffee.
He fetches a liquor bottle from beneath the rocking chair; about to pour he does a take at BESS's PHOTOGRAPH.

INSERT—THE PHOTOGRAPH
It stands in a cabinet frame: A fine-looking young woman in archaic dress, with sharp, accusing black eyes.

BIRDIE'S VOICE (o.s.) Dead and gone these twenty-five years and never takes her eyes off me.

CUT OVER his line to—

CLOSE TWO-SHOT—JOHN AND BIRDIE
He turns the picture away and splashes liquor into his coffee.

BIRDIE (pouring) Man o' my years *needs* a little snort to get his boiler heated of a morning.

They drink. BIRDIE, satisfied, sighs and rocks.

BIRDIE This mornin' I was talkin' to this stranger up at the boarding-house. He knowed your Dad!

CLOSE SHOT—JOHN

JOHN looks cautious.

JOHN Where did he know Dad?

CLOSE SHOT—BIRDIE

BIRDIE's face falls; he takes another drink.

BIRDIE Well, boy, I'll not hide the truth; it was up at Moundsville Penitentiary.

CLOSE TWO-SHOT—NEW ANGLE

JOHN puts his cup down and gets up.

JOHN I got to go now, Uncle Birdie.
He heads for the door.

BIRDIE Why shucks boy, you just got here.
He follows JOHN to the door. JOHN runs up the bank, not looking back.

JOHN (running) I told Mom I'd be back to Spoon's for Pearl.

EXT. STREET—MEDIUM SHOT—JOHN
He runs up the street close to Spoon's and stops dead.

CLOSE SHOT—JOHN
He is horrified by what he sees.

INT. SPOON'S ICE CREAM PARLOR

GROUP SHOT through door-glass, from JOHN's VIEW POINT

PREACHER, WILLA and PEARL surround a little table. WALT stands by, puffing his pipe. ICEY in BACKGROUND, stirs fudge at a little soda-fountain stove. WILLA looks both moved and pleased. PEARL, shyly flirting with PREACHER, all but hides in WILLA's skirts. PREACHER dandles PEARL's doll on his knee as he talks. All the grownups are avid for his words, which we don't hear through the glass.

CLOSE SHOT—JOHN
We SHOOT THROUGH the DOOR; he quietly enters.

GROUP SHOT
They look casually to JOHN, and continue talking.

ICEY (stirring; with a meaningful glance at Willa) God works in a mysterious way, His wonders to perform.

OVER this JOHN ENTERS the SHOT and stands at the fringe of the GROUP, staring at PREACHER's hands and at the doll.

PREACHER I was with Brother Harper almost to the end; . . .

GROUP SHOT—NEW ANGLE—FAVORING JOHN AND PREACHER

PREACHER (continuing) . . . and now that I'm no longer employed by the Penitentiary it is my joy to bring this small comfort to his loved ones.

FLASH-CUT CLOSE-UP—JOHN
On "Penitentiary" he glances quickly at PREACHER's face; then back to his hands.

GROUP SHOT—ICEY

ICEY (sniffing) It's a mighty good man would come out of his way to bring a word of cheer to a grieving widow!

CLOSE SHOT—WALT

WALT So you ain't with the State no more?

GROUP SHOT—FAVORING PREACHER AND JOHN

PREACHER No, Brother; I resigned only yesterday. The heart-renderin' spectacle of them poor men was too much for me.

He becomes aware of JOHN's staring.

PREACHER Ah, little lad, you're staring at my fingers.
He hands the doll to PEARL. JOHN's eyes follow the doll. PREACHER holds up both hands to JOHN. JOHN looks back at his hands.

PREACHER Shall I tell you the little story of Right-Hand-Left-Hand—the tale of Good and Evil?

JOHN stands still. PEARL, with her doll, crosses to PREACHER and twines about his knee.

CLOSE SHOT—JOHN

He looks on, in dumb alarm.

CLOSE SHOT—PREACHER

PREACHER H-A-T-E! (he thrusts up his left hand) It was with this left hand that old brother Cain struck the blow that laid his brother low! L-O-V-E! (he thrusts up his right hand) See these here fingers, dear friends! These fingers has veins that lead straight to the soul of man! The right hand, friends! The hand of Love!

GROUP SHOT—ICEY, WALT, WILLA—OVER PREACHER'S HANDS
They are impressed in their different ways.

PREACHER (o.s.) Now watch and I'll show you the Story of Life. The fingers of these hands, dear hearts!—They're always a-tuggin' and a-warrin' one hand agin' t'other. (he locks his fingers and writhes them, crackling the joints) Look at 'em, dear hearts!

MEDIUM SHOT—JOHN—OVER PREACHER'S HANDS
He looks on with unseeing eyes.

PREACHER (o.s.) Old Left Hand Hate's a-fightin' and it looks like Old Right Hand Love's a goner!

GROUP SHOT—WALT, ICEY, WILLA, OVER HANDS

PREACHER (o.s.) But wait now! Hot dog! Love's a-winnin! Yessirree!

CLOSE SHOT—PREACHER

PREACHER It's Love that won! Old Left Hand *Hate's* gone down for the count! (he crashes both hands onto the table)

FULL SHOT—THE WHOLE GROUP
Slight applause from the ADULTS. PREACHER takes PEARL, with her doll, onto his lap.

ICEY I never heard it better told. I wish every soul in this community could git the benefit. You jest *got* to stay for our church pick-nick Sunday!
PEARL offers PREACHER the DOLL to kiss. PREACHER complies.

CLOSE SHOT—JOHN'S REACTION

RESUME GROUP SHOT

PREACHER (finessing it) I must wend my way down River on the Lord's work.

ICEY You ain't leavin' in no hurry if *we* can help it!

WILLA John: take that look offen your face and act nice.

PREACHER He don't mean no impudence; do you, boy? (no answer) Do you, boy? Ah, many's the time poor Brother Ben told me about these youngins.

JOHN What did he tell you?

CLOSE SHOT—PREACHER
He does a little take. His eyes twinkle palely.

PREACHER Why, he told me what fine little lambs you and your sister both was.

GROUP SHOT

JOHN Is that all?

CLOSE SHOT—PREACHER
Something new enters his eyes; a game has begun between them.

PREACHER Why, no, boy; he told me lots and lots of things. Nice things, boy.

A tight silence. ICEY pours fudge into a buttered pan.

PREACHER *My,* that fudge smells *yummy!*

CLOSE SHOT—ICEY

ICEY (with horrid archness) It's for the pick-nick. And you won't get a *smidgen of my fudge* unless you stay for the pick-nick!

Over her line, o.s., hymn-singing begins and now, OVER her "the case rests" smile we bring up the singing and   LAP DISSOLVE TO

EXT. THE RIVER BANK—CHURCH IN BACKGROUND—FULL SHOT—THE SINGING PICKNICKERS

A pleasant, grassy river-bank. Few men in proportion to women and children. We CENTER PREACHER. They are singing *"Brighten the Corner;"* PREACHER sings conspicuously well. The women watch him and admire him. He gives WILLA the eye as we PAN TO CENTER WILLA, who looks wooed and self-conscious. ICEY enters the SHOT and whispers and beckons WILLA and, as the singing continues, they leave the group and start towards a shade tree in MEDIUM GROUND, which we PAN TO CENTER.

FULL SHOT—WILLA AND ICEY
They walk; singers in BACKGROUND.

ICEY Don't he have the grandest singin' voice?

WILLA nods. ICEY, looking ahead, is displeased.

MEDIUM SHOT—THE TREE, JOHN AND PEARL
They sit on the bench, their backs to us, partly concealed by the tree trunk.

ICEY'S VOICE (sharp) John! Pearl!
They look around. ICEY and WILLA enter the SHOT, their backs to us.

ICEY Run along and play, you two.

JOHN Where?

ICEY Down by the river. My goodness!
Docile, they leave the shot as WILLA and ICEY approach the bench.

CLOSE TWO-SHOT—WILLA AND ICEY
They sit on the bench, their back to us. The CHILDREN recede towards the river in BACKGROUND. WILLA meekly keeps her head down. Singing continues o.s.

ICEY That feller's just achin' to settle down with some nice woman and make a home for himself.

WILLA It's awful soon after Ben's passing.

ICEY If ever I saw a Sign from Heaven!

WILLA John don't like him much.

ICEY Pearl *dotes* on him.

WILLA The boy worries me. It's silly, but it's like there was something still between him and his Dad.

ICEY What *he* needs is a dose o' salts!

WILLA There's something else.

ICEY What?

WILLA The money, Icey.

ICEY I declare, you'll let that money haunt you to your grave, Willa Harper!

WILLA I *would* love to be satisfied Harry Powell don't think I've got that money somewhere.

ICEY You'll come right out and *ask* that Man of God! (turning and yelling) Mr. Paow-well! (to Willa) Clear that *evil mud* out of your soul!

PREACHER starts towards her. ICEY pivots and we PAN OVER her to CHILDREN by river.

ICEY (yelling) John! Pearl!

CLOSE SHOT—PEARL AND JOHN

JOHN looks up from pebble-skimming and loosens his tie.

ICEY (yelling o.s.) Come along *hee-ere* and get some *fuu-udge!*

JOHN (calling) I don't want no fudge.
His brow is furrowed. He skims another pebble.

ICEY (shouting o.s.) *You'll do what you're told!*
They unwillingly get moving.

RESUME TWO-SHOT—ICEY AND WILLA

ICEY You go set down by the River.

WILLA (getting up) Oh, Icey, I'm a sight!

ICEY Get along with you.

Both women set off, WILLA to River, ICEY towards GROUP. We TRACK after ICEY. PREACHER approaches. ICEY, crossing him, gives him a little shove towards WILLA and a coy—

ICEY *You* ! ! !

We FOLLOW her to the women who are busying themselves with the fudge.

CLOSE GROUP SHOT—ICEY AND WOMEN, FAVORING ICEY
. . . a few men in BACKGROUND, and, beyond them, PREACHER sits down by WILLA at water's edge. JOHN and PEARL approach. As ICEY starts yammering the men, WALT among them, shyly withdraw.

ICEY That young lady'd better look sharp or some smart sister between here and Captina's a-gonna snap him up right from under her nose! (they nod and agree, ad lib) She's not the *only* fish in the river! (more agreement. John and Pearl join Icey. Icey speaks to John) Now you two *stay put!*

CLOSE SHOT—JOHN
He looks hard towards WILLA and PREACHER O.S.

ICEY (o.s., to women) Shilly-shallying around . . .

LONG SHOT—WILLA AND PREACHER
. . . from JOHN's VIEWPOINT in tableau of decorous courtship, framed by heavy domestic bodies.

ICEY (o.s.) A husband's one piece of store goods ye never know till you get it home and take the paper off.

CLOSE TWO-SHOT—WILLA AND PREACHER
They sit by the water; drooling willows; almost in travesty of a romantic scene. WILLA dabbles one hand in the water.

WILLA (very shy) Did Ben Harper ever tell you what he done with that money he stole?

HEAD CLOSE-UP—PREACHER
His head goes slantwise and he smiles oddly.

PREACHER My dear child, don't *you* know?

CLOSE SHOT—JOHN
He watches intently towards his mother; PEARL holds his hand. ICEY's voice O.S.

GROUP SHOT—WOMEN, JOHN AND PEARL

ICEY She's moonin' about Ben Harper. That wasn't love, it was just flap-doodle. (agreeing nods and murmurs) Have some fudge, lambs. (she hands some down to John and Pearl. Pearl smears her mouth with it; John, watching always towards his mother, takes one nibble and throws the rest away). When you're married forty years, you know all that don't amount to a hill o'beans! I been married to my Walt that long, and I'll swear in all that time I'd just lie there thinking about my canning.

In BACKGROUND WALT looks sheepish.

WILLA'S VOICE (calling o.s.) John! John?
All look towards her.

LONG SHOT—OVER GROUP
WILLA is standing, beckoning JOHN

MEDIUM TWO-SHOT—JOHN AND PEARL
They start towards their mother.

GROUP SHOT—ICEY AND WOMEN—NEW ANGLE

ICEY A woman's a *fool* to marry for that. It's something for a *man*. The good Lord never meant for a decent woman to want *that*—not *really* want it! It's all just a fake and a pipe-dream.
The others agree with her. She puts a piece of fudge in her mouth.

CLOSE GROUP SHOT—PREACHER, WILLA, CHILDREN
. . . as JOHN and PEARL (with DOLL) come shyly up. WILLA is seated again. She is radiant.

WILLA John, Mr. Powell has got something to tell you.

PREACHER Well, John, the night before your father died, he told me what he did with that money.

CLOSE SHOT—JOHN
He desperately conceals his reaction; he thinks BEN has betrayed him.

RESUME GROUP SHOT

PREACHER That money's at the bottom of the river wrapped around a 12-pound cobblestone.

CLOSE SHOT—JOHN AND PEARL
He now conceals his *new* reaction.

RESUME GROUP SHOT

WILLA touches PREACHER's hand, warmly.

WILLA Thank you, Harry.
She looks all around her, glowing, and stands up, hands to hair.

PEARL John . . .

JOHN Sshhh . . .

WILLA I feel clean now! My whole body's just a quiverin' with cleanness!
She walks away towards ICEY and the WOMEN.

CLOSE SHOT—PREACHER

PREACHER John: here.

CLOSE SHOT—JOHN AND PEARL

JOHN moves to stand in front of him; PEARL, to stand beside PREACHER,
with the DOLL.

CLOSE SHOT—PREACHER AND CHILDREN
From JOHN's eye-level; as JOHN steps in front of him and PEARL beside
him.

PREACHER Your tie's crooked.

HEAD CLOSE-UP—JOHN
The hand named LOVE and the hand named HATE come in to straighten the
necktie. JOHN looks down. He looks up and sees:

GROUP SHOT—JOHN'S VIEWPOINT

PREACHER, in close-up, hands busy o.s.; PEARL, with doll; and between them,
in BACKGROUND, WILLA. She is now running fast towards ICEY, who walks
towards her with arms outstretched. Behind them, the group of WOMEN.
BIRDIE's guitar music begins o.s.   DISSOLVE TO

EXT. BIRDIE'S BOAT—EVENING—MEDIUM SHOT—BIRDIE, JOHN AND SKIFF
Birdie sits beside his open door, strumming a guitar and singing. The
scene is lamplighted from within. Ben's skiff is inverted on trestles in
FOREGROUND. At start of scene we see only JOHN's feet; he's under the
skiff, examining it. After three lines of song he comes out from under, and
lounges against the skiff, tracing a tarry seam with his forefinger.

BIRDIE (singing) 'Twas down at Cresap's Landing, Along the River Shore,
Birdie Steptoe was a Pilot in the good old days of yore. Now he sets in
his old wharf-boat . . .

JOHN (across him) When'll Dad's skiff be ready?

BIRDIE Can't hear ye, boy. (singing) . . . So the big boats heave a sigh, They blow for Uncle Birdie . . .

JOHN (across him) When'll the skiff be ready?

BIRDIE (singing) And the times that are gone by. I'll have her ready inside of a week; and then we'll go fishin'. How's your Maw?

Through rest of scene, Birdie picks lazily at his guitar.

JOHN O, she's all right.

BIRDIE How's your sister Pearl?

JOHN Just fine.
He gets up.

BIRDIE Leavin', boy?

JOHN Yep; gotta watch out for Pearl, Uncle Birdie.

BIRDIE Well goodnight, boy. Come again—any time.

JOHN leaves the SHOT.

BIRDIE And mind now—I'll have your Paw's skiff in ship-shape, 'side of a week.

MOVING SHOT—JOHN
As he runs past SPOON's, looking in, he is curious.

MOVING SHOT—SPOON's, HIS VIEWPOINT

ICEY embraces WILLA or waltzes her around; WALT looks on, pleased.

FULL SHOT—JOHN
He hurries away from us towards home.

FRAMING SHOT—THE HARPER HOUSE
In the otherwise dark house, one window is lighted. JOHN enters the SHOT, his back to us. Seeing the lighted window, he hesitates.

JOHN (softly) Is somebody there?
Silent pause, listening; then he walks cautiously towards us.

FULL SHOT—JOHN
A tall, narrow shooting-frame; right and left thirds of screen are black.

We SHOOT from inside the screen door. JOHN crosses the porch and softly opens the door and enters on tiptoe and pauses, close to us, in the dark hallway, listening sharp.

JOHN (softly) Is anybody here?

Silence. Relieved, but puzzled, he tiptoes along towards the rear of the hallway in CLOSE-UP as WE PULL AWAY. We bring in the bottom of the stairs.

PREACHER'S VOICE (o.s.) Good evening, John.

JOHN gasps, peering, and looks up.

TWO SHOT—JOHN AND PREACHER—NARROW SCREEN

PREACHER looks at JOHN; JOHN sinks onto the edge of a chair. PREACHER sits opposite. A bar of light from door falls across PREACHER's face.

PREACHER I had a little talk with your mother tonight, John; and your mother decided it might be best for *me* to—let you know the news.

From JOHN, just a questioning helpless reaction.

PREACHER Your mother told me tonight she wanted me to be a daddy to you and your sister. We're going to get married, son.

JOHN is still.

PREACHER Did you hear what I said, son?

JOHN Huh?

PREACHER Married! We have decided to go to Sistersville tomorrow, and when we come back—

JOHN (just breathing it) You ain't my Dad! You won't never be my Dad!

PREACHER (obsessed, disregarding him)—and when we come back, we'll all be friends—and *share our fortunes together, John!*

JOHN (screaming) You think you can make me tell! But I won't! I won't! I won't!

He gawks at his own folly, covers his mouth with his hand and looks up at PREACHER.

PREACHER (softly) Tell me *what,* boy?

JOHN Nothin'!

PREACHER Are we keeping secrets from each other, little lad?

JOHN No. No.

PREACHER stiffens, relaxes, and chuckles softly.

PREACHER No matter, boy, we've got a long time together.

CLOSE TWO-SHOT—JOHN AND PREACHER

JOHN starts for the stairs.   DISSOLVE TO

EXT. HARPER YARD—MORNING—CLOSE SHOT—BEN'S FORD
It stands vibrating, then moves out of shot with receding engine sound o.s., disclosing:

TWO-SHOT—JOHN AND PEARL

ICEY's skirts in BACKGROUND. They are awfully spic-and-span; they even wear shoes.

ICEY (o.s.) *Wave yer hands!* Great *sakes!*
They wave after the car, bewilderedly.

ICEY (o.s.) You wait here while I get your night-things.
She hustles out of shot.

PEARL *Now* can I tell?

JOHN Hm?

PEARL When Mr. Powell's our Daddy then I can tell him about—
His hand clamps over her mouth. She struggles and whimpers.

JOHN You *swore*, Pearl!

PEARL (across him). John! Don't!

JOHN You promised Dad you wouldn't *never* tell!
He takes his hand away but holds it ready.

PEARL I *love* Mr. Powell *lots* and *lots*, John.

JOHN grabs her by the shoulders and glares.

JOHN *Don't you tell! Don't you* NEVER DARE *tell!*
Over them we   LAP DISSOLVE TO

SHOULDER CLOSE-UP—WILLA
She is caressing her shoulders.

FULL SHOT—WILLA
Her back is to us. She is in a pathetic night dress; she stands before a mirror in a hotel bedroom in Sistersville. She walks to the door.

INSERT WILLA'S HAND
It hesitates on the doorknob.

CLOSE SHOT—WILLA
Shooting OVER her as she opens the door, we see PREACHER in bed, his back to us. Beyond him, a window. The drawn shade rustles quietly.

CLOSE SHOT—THE DOOR
... from within the room. WILLA closes the door, on which PREACHER's coat hangs. The closing brings a knocking sound. WILLA feels the outside of the coat; feels something hard; takes out the knife and looks at it.

INSERT—THE KNIFE IN HER HAND—CLOSE SHOT—WILLA
A moment of perplexity; then a little smile.

WILLA (whispering) Oh! It's ... uh ...
She puts it back in the pocket and gives the pocket a pat. She starts towards the bed.

TWO-SHOT—WILLA AND PREACHER
We SHOOT OVER PREACHER as she approaches modestly and stands by the bed.

WILLA (softly) Harry ...
His hand comes up; she puts out her own, expecting a loving hand-clasp; but PREACHER points to the window.

PREACHER Fix that window shade.
Startled, then again tender, she moves to:

CLOSE SHOT—WILLA AT WINDOW
She adjusts the shade, looking always towards the bed. She smiles maternally. As we PULL BACK and PAN into FULL SHOT OF BED she comes to the bed and sits on the edge and slips off her mules. PREACHER's back is to her.

WILLA (softly) Harry!

PREACHER (cool and clear) I was praying.

WILLA Oh, I'm sorry, Harry! I didn't know! I thought maybe—
With a sounding of bedsprings PREACHER turns. His voice is quiet and cold.

PREACHER You thought, Willa, that the moment you walked in that door I'd start in to pawing you in the abominable way men are supposed to do on their wedding night. Ain't that right, now?

WILLA No, Harry! I thought—

PREACHER I think it's time we got one thing perfectly clear, Willa. Marriage to me represents a blending of two spirits in the sight of Heaven.

He gets out of bed. WILLA puts her face down to the pillow and moans.

PREACHER snaps on a harsh bare bulb at center of room.

PREACHER (quietly) Get up, Willa.

WILLA Harry, what—

PREACHER Get up.
She obeys.

PREACHER Now go and look at yourself yonder in that mirror.

WILLA hesitates.

FULL SHOT—OVER PREACHER—CENTERING A STAINED BUREAU MIRROR

PREACHER Do as I say.

WILLA walks to meet her image in the mirror; her eyes on PREACHER.

PREACHER LOOK at yourself.
Her head drops, facing the mirror.

CLOSE SHOT—WILLA, PREACHER, BULB

WILLA is in HEAD CLOSE-UP; bulb hangs at center; PREACHER, in his nightshirt, is beyond it.

PREACHER What do you see, girl?
Her mouth trembles; she can't talk.

PREACHER You see the body of a woman! The temple of creation and motherhood. You see the flesh of Eve that Man since Adam has profaned. That body was meant for begetting children. It was not meant for the lust of men.

WILLA just opens her mouth.

PREACHER Do you want more children, Willa?

WILLA I—no, I—

PREACHER It's the business of our marriage to mind those two you have now—not to beget more.

WILLA Yes.

He stands watching her for a moment; then he snaps off the light and gets into bed.

PREACHER You can get back into bed now and stop shivering.

WILLA, in the darkness, does not move. She folds her hands in prayer and lifts her eyes.

WILLA (whispering) Help me to get clean so I can be what Harry wants me to be. LAP DISSOLVE TO

INSERT—A TORCH OR RAILROAD FLARE

VOICES (o.s.) AAA-MEN!

GROUP SHOT—CONGREGATION
A dozen country men and women in religious ecstasy.
(NOTE: No set necessary for this scene. Flare, or flares, in every SHOT. Faces lighted by flares.)

CONGREGATION AAA-MENN!

WILLA (o.s., very loud) You have all sinned!

CONGREGATION Yes! Yes!

HEAD CLOSE-UP—WILLA

WILLA But which one of you can say as I can say: I drove a good man to *murder* because I kept a-houndin' him for clothes and per-fumes and face paint!

GROUP SHOT—CONGREGATION

WILLA (o.s.) And he slew two human beings and he come to me and he said: *Take* this money and *buy* your per-fumes and paint!

FULL FIGURE SHOT—WILLA, STANDING; PREACHER STANDING IN B.G.

WILLA But Brethren, that's where the *Lord* stepped in! *That's where the* LORD *stepped in!*

PREACHER Yes!

CONGREGATION (o.s.) Yes! Yes!

GROUP SHOT—CONGREGATION

WILLA (o.s. screaming) And the Lord told that man—

CONGREGATION Yes! Yes!

CLOSE SHOT—WILLA

WILLA The Lord said, Take that money and throw it in the River!

CONGREGATION (o.s.) Yes! Yes! Hallelujah!

WILLA Throw that money in the River! In THE RIVER!

CONGREGATION (o.s.) IN THE RIIV-ER!   CUT TO

EXTREME CLOSE DOWN-SHOT—PEARL'S DOLL

It lies face down on arbor bricks, its back wide open; money spilling out.
A little breeze toys with the money. HOLD, a moment, in silence. Then
we hear a snipping sound o.s. TILT UPWARD into—

CLOSE SHOT—PEARL

She sits at the end of the grape-arbor. She finishes cutting a skirted paper-
doll out of a hundred dollar bill and lays it down beside a male hundred-
dollar paper-doll. She pats the dolls.

PEARL Now! You're John—and you're Pearl.

JOHN'S VOICE (o.s. calling) Pearl? . . . Pearl?

PEARL starts guiltily and looks towards him, scrambling money together.
JOHN's footsteps o.s.

PEARL You'll get awful mad, John. I done a Sin!

CLOSE SHOT—JOHN—PEARL'S ANGLE

JOHN You what?
He hears the frantic rustling of paper—

JOHN (aghast) Pearl! You ain't—

CLOSE SHOT—PEARL, OVER JOHN

PEARL John, don't be mad! Don't be mad! I was just playing with it! I
didn't *tell* no one!

FLASH CUT CLOSE-UP—JOHN

. . . as he stoops toward her, dumb with horror.

CLOSE SHOT—PEARL

She continues to gather the money together.

PEARL (pleading) It's all here.

CLOSE TWO-SHOT—JOHN AND PEARL

JOHN Pearl! Oh, Pearl!
She's stuffing bills back into the torn doll. They slide through her fingers.
He helps.

FLASH INSERT—PREACHER'S FOOT
... as he plants it, with sound, in damp grass.

CLOSE SHOT—THE CHILDREN

JOHN freezes.

PREACHER'S VOICE (o.s.) John?

JOHN Oh—yes?

LONG SHOT—PREACHER—CHILDREN'S VIEWPOINT
He stands at far end of arbor.

PREACHER What are you doing, boy?

LONG SHOT—CHILDREN—PREACHER'S VIEWPOINT

JOHN Getting Pearl to bed. I—

PREACHER What's taking you so long about it?

FLASH INSERT—THEIR FRANTIC HANDS, MONEY, THE DOLL

JOHN (o.s.) It—she—

CLOSE SHOT—PREACHER—PEERING TOWARDS THEM

PREACHER What's that you're playing with, boy?

LONG SHOT—CHILDREN—PREACHER'S VIEWPOINT

JOHN Pearl's junk. Mom gets mad when she plays out here and don't
clean up afterward.

PREACHER *Come on,* children!

INSERT—JOHN'S HANDS PIN THE DOLL TOGETHER

FULL SHOT—CHILDREN STAND UP, LOOK TOWARDS PREACHER, AND SLOWLY START
TOWARDS HIM. THE TWO FORGOTTEN PAPER-DOLLS ARE BLOWN TOWARDS HIM TOO.

MOVING SHOT—PREACHER—JOHN'S VIEWPOINT

PREACHER'S watch-chain gleams. The shot SLOWLY CLOSES DOWN on it and
becomes still. We see the paper-dolls blow past him.

PREACHER'S VOICE Now, up to bed with the both of you.

CLOSE SHOT—JOHN AND PEARL

JOHN starts to laugh uncontrollably. We PAN them past PREACHER's stomach into FULL SHOT.

PREACHER'S VOICE Come here, John.

PREACHER'S VOICE Run along, Pearl.

PEARL goes, JOHN comes towards PREACHER.

PREACHER—JOHN'S VIEWPOINT

PREACHER Your mother says you tattled on me, boy. She says you told her that I asked you where that money was hid.

JOHN (o.s.) Yes. Yes.

PREACHER That wasn't very nice of you, John. Have a heart, boy.

CLOSE SHOT—JOHN
His helpless reaction. Pause.

PREACHER'S VOICE Run along to bed.
As JOHN turns away we   LAP DISSOLVE TO

CLOSE SHOT—WILLA IN PROFILE
. . . and PULL AWAY showing JOHN as he turns to her. (PEARL's head is turned away; she's asleep.)

WILLA Were you impudent to Mr. Powell, John?

JOHN Mom, I didn't mean—

WILLA What were you impudent about?

JOHN He asked me about the money again, Mom.

WILLA You always make up that lie, John! There *is* no money, John. Can't you get that through your head?   LAP DISSOLVE TO

CLOSE SHOT—A GAR, UNDERWATER

CLOSE UPWARD TWO-SHOT—JOHN AND BIRDIE
They look down into the water.

BIRDIE Meanest, orneriest, sneakinest critter in the whole river, boy! A gar!

CLOSE TWO-SHOT—JOHN AND BIRDIE
They sit up into it.

JOHN Here's your can o' hooks, Uncle Birdie.

BIRDIE There hain't nary hook in the land smart enough to hook Mister Gar. What a feller needs is mother-wit—and a horse-hair.

Over this, he pulls horse-hair out of his hatband. He sets to work rigging his noose.

JOHN Won't he bust it, Uncle Birdie?

BIRDIE Shoot, a horse-hair'll hold a lumpin' whale.
He puts over his line. Pause.

BIRDIE Do you mind me cussin', boy?

JOHN No.

BIRDIE Tell you why I ask—your step-pa being' a Preacher an' all . . .

JOHN's lips go like string. BIRDIE sees it.

BIRDIE Never was much of a one for preachers myself. I dunno what's wrong up at your place, but just remember one thing, Cap—if ever you need help you just holler out and come a-runnin'. Old Uncle Birdie's your friend.

A powerful strike. BIRDIE lands the gar. The air is full of sparkling water.

BIRDIE There! You slimy, snag-toothed, egg-suckin', bait-stealin' so-and-so!

QUICK INSERT—THE THUMPING FISH IN BOTTOM OF BOAT

FULL SHOT
He beats the fish with the heel of an old shoe.

BIRDIE (beating) Mind what I told you. If ever you get in a crack, I just come a-runnin'.

Now there is no sound of thumping or beating.

CLOSE SHOT—JOHN
Admiring BIRDIE, he squares his shoulders, full of confidence.

JOHN Can we eat him, Uncle Birdie?

BIRDIE If you got an appetite for bones and bitterness.

On this, he flings the dead gar in a wide arc out into the river.

LAP DISSOLVE TO

INT. CHILDREN'S BEDROOM—NIGHT
The children are ready for bed.

CLOSE SHOT—PREACHER
Smiling, quiet, awaiting an answer.

CLOSE SHOT—JOHN

JOHN I don't know.

TWO-SHOT—JOHN AND PREACHER

PEARL plays unconcernedly in background.

PREACHER (intimately) She thinks that money's in the river, but you and me, we know better, don't we, boy?

JOHN I don't know nothin'!

PREACHER The summer is young yet, little lad. (he turns away from John) Pearl?

He holds out his hands to her; she comes to his lap, dropping her doll at his feet. JOHN turns his back and looks out the window beside bureau.

PREACHER John's a feller who likes to keep *secrets*.

PEARL Mm-hm.

PREACHER I'll tell *you* a secret.

PEARL Yes?

PREACHER I knowed your Daddy. (PEARL frowns) And do you know what your Daddy said to me? He said, "Tell my little girl Pearl there's to be no secrets between her and you."

INSERT—JOHN'S HAND COMES TO REST BESIDE A HAIRBRUSH

RESUME TWO-SHOT—PREACHER AND PEARL, JOHN IN B.G.

PEARL Yes?

PREACHER Now it's *your* turn.

PEARL What secret shall I tell?

PREACHER How old are you?

PEARL That's no secret. I'm five.

CLOSE SHOT—JOHN—PREACHER AND PEARL IN B.G.
A look of impotent hatred.

PREACHER Sure, that's no secret.

RESUME TWO-SHOT

PREACHER (continuing) What's your name?

PEARL (giggling) You're just foolin'! My name's Pearl.

PREACHER Tst-tst! Then I reckon I'll have to try again! Where's the money hid?

JOHN throws the hairbrush, striking PREACHER's head.

JOHN (screaming as he throws) You swore you wouldn't tell! (he beats the air with his fists) You swore! You swore! You swore!

CLOSE SHOT—PREACHER
He is sure now PEARL knows.

THREE-SHOT—PEARL, PREACHER, JOHN

PEARL (awed) You hit Daddy with the hairbrush!

Another silence.

PREACHER (cheerfully) You see? We can't have anything to do with John. (light off) You and me will go down to the parlor.

PEARL Miz Jenny! Miz Jenny!
She gets the doll. We PAN them through the door.

TWO-SHOT—PREACHER AND PEARL
Outside door as he closes it.

PREACHER John's just plumb bad through and through—

CLOSE SHOT—PEARL
As PREACHER's hand locks the door.

PEARL (at door) Yes, John's just plumb bad.   CUT TO

INT. SPOON'S ICE CREAM PARLOR—THREE-SHOT—WILLA, ICEY, WALT
We shoot over ICEY as WILLA opens the door to leave. WILLA is in outdoor clothes and is not dressed for work in the parlor.

WILLA That boy's as stubborn and mulish as a sheep!

ICEY It's a *shame!*

WILLA's face shines like one possessed.

WILLA Goodnight.

WALT enters shot, his back to us.

ICEY Goodnight, honey.

As WILLA starts away we DOLLY THROUGH DOOR and PAN her to deserted street. There is a river mist.

TWO-SHOT—WALT AND ICEY

WALT is ill at ease.

RESUME SHOT ON WILLA

ICEY (o.s. calling) Plan on a longer visit next time.

WALT (o.s.) You don't hardly get settled till you're frettin' to git home again.

Again WILLA pauses and turns.

WILLA (with sweet radiance. To Walt) I'm needed to keep peace and harmony between them. (to Icey) It's my burden and I'm proud of it, Icey!

She walks off into the mist.   LAP DISSOLVE TO

EXT. HARPER HOME—NIGHT—MEDIUM SHOT—LIGHTED PARLOR WINDOW; REST OF HOUSE DARK
Distant muffled sound of river-boat whistle.

PEARL (o.s.) John's bad.

WILLA enters, her back to us; she stops.

PREACHER (o.s.) Yes; John's bad.

PEARL Tell me another secret about my Dad.

CLOSE SHOT—WILLA
She smiles benignly.

PREACHER (o.s.) *O* no! *Your* turn!

PEARL All right.

PREACHER Where's the money hid.

WILLA keeps smiling.

PEARL John's bad.

PREACHER Where's the money hid? Tell me, you little wretch, or I'll tear your arm off!

Still smiling, shaking her head as in disbelief, WILLA makes for house as PEARL screams.

INT. HARPER HALLWAY—TWO-SHOT—WILLA AND PREACHER
Narrow screen, same set-up as in earlier corridor scene, PREACHER and WILLA. Their eyes meet. Pause.

PREACHER (stunned) I didn't expect you home so soon.

CLOSE SHOT—WILLA
She still smiles; her eyes turn to sound of PEARL's sobbing.

TWO SHOT—AS BEFORE

PREACHER stands still; WILLA in BACKGROUND opens closet door where PEARL sobs. CUT TO

TWO-SHOT—WALT AND ICEY
. . . washing and drying glasses. ICEY is washing briskly, WALT is drying slowly.

WALT Icey, I'm worried about Willa.

ICEY How do you mean?

WALT I'm figurin' how I can say it so's you won't get mad.

ICEY Say *what*, Walt Spoon!

WALT There's somethin' wrong about it, Mother.

ICEY About *what*!

WALT About Mr. Powell. All of it!

ICEY Walt!

WALT Now, Mother, a body can't help their feelin's.

ICEY May the Lord have mercy on you, Walt Spoon!

WALT Mother, I only— CUT TO

INT. WILLA'S AND PREACHER'S BEDROOM—FULL SHOT—WILLA ON BED— PREACHER IN BACKGROUND

WILLA lies in profile on the bed along the bottom of the frame. A prim, old woman's nightdress makes her look like a child. Her hands are clasped.

PREACHER, fully dressed, stands at the window, which is in BACKGROUND towards foot of bed. His coat, hung over a chair, is in silhouette. River mist outside window halated by exterior gas-lamp. The window shade is up. She is mumbling in prayer. She stops.

PREACHER (his back still turned) Are you through praying?

WILLA I'm through, Harry.

He turns. WILLA is calm and immobile with the ecstasy of a martyr.

PREACHER You were listening outside the parlor window.

WILLA It's not in the river, is it Harry?

PREACHER *Answer me!*

WILLA Ben never told you he throwed it in the river? Did he?

PREACHER hits her across the mouth. A pause.

WILLA (continues, unruffled) Then the children know where it is hid? John knows? Is that it? (a pause) Then it's still here, somewhere amongst us, tainting us?

CLOSE SHOT—PREACHER, LISTENING FOR A VOICE

RESUME TWO-SHOT

WILLA So you must have known it all along, Harry.

CLOSE SHOT—PREACHER, LISTENING

After a moment, the river boat whistle blows, nearer. HOLD CLOSE-UP a moment after whistle.

CLOSE DOWN-SHOT—WILLA, SAINT-LIKE

WILLA But that ain't why you married me, Harry. I know that much. It couldn't be that because the Lord just wouldn't let it.

RESUME TWO-SHOT—WILLA

WILLA He made you marry me so's you could show me the Way and the Life and the Salvation of my soul! Ain't that so, Harry?

CLOSE SHOT—PREACHER

He has heard the VOICE and starts to move out of CLOSE SHOT.

RESUME TWO-SHOT

He has moved over to the coat on back of chair.

CLOSE SHOT—COAT

His hand goes into the pocket and brings the knife out. (It is the same coat, and pocket, as in the wedding-night scene.)

RESUME TWO-SHOT

WILLA So you might say it was the money that brung us together.
He pulls down the blind. He moves toward the bed.

WILLA The rest of it don't matter, Harry.

INSERT—PREACHER'S HAND AND KNIFE

It clicks open.

RESUME TWO-SHOT

As he raises his arm to strike:

HEAD CLOSE-UP—WILLA

. . . with foolish, ecstatic eyes.

WILLA Bless us all!   DISSOLVE TO

INT. CHILDREN'S BEDROOM—FULL SHOT—THE SHADOWS ON THE WALL

They are shaped as in earlier scene, but altered by mist. Set-up as in earlier scene. Over them we hear the whinny-and-catch and the failure of the Ford being cranked; once; then again: then JOHN's shadow moves on the wall and on a third cranking which engages the engine, we PAN TO WINDOW, shooting over JOHN, who peers out, into blind mist. The gears of the car shift; the car moves away, unseen; its sounds diminish slowly, and die. A moment of silence; then JOHN turns and we PAN him to the bed. He gets in beside PEARL, who is asleep, and, as we TIGHTEN IN CLOSE, puts his hand across the face of the doll.   DISSOLVE TO

HEAD CLOSE-UP—ICEY

An ominous expression. She looks sharp to WALT, beckoning secretly; through rear screen door of kitchen, onto porch.

ICEY (loud whisper) Walt! Come quick!

FULL FIGURE SHOT—WALT

He is scrubbing out an ice cream container on the back porch. He looks up and moves towards her.

WALT (natural voice) What's wrong, Mother?

MEDIUM CLOSE—ICEY, THEN WALT

ICEY (whisper) Sshhh! He's in there.

WALT ENTERS SHOT with pipe.

WALT Who?

ICEY (whisper) Mr. Powell! (Walt looks enquiry) Willa has run away!

WALT I'll be switched! . . .

They enter the kitchen. We hear muffled sounds of sobbing o.s.

MEDIUM CLOSE TWO-SHOT

WALT Just *went?*

ICEY She took out some time durin' the night,—in that old Model-T—

WALT clucks his tongue.

WALT Is he hit pretty bad?

ICEY All to pieces!

WALT moves towards kitchen cabinet.

WALT There's a little peach brandy—maybe a sip?

ICEY A man of the Cloth?

MEDIUM CLOSE SHOT—WALT
He pours, snaps it down; weak-defiance.

MEDIUM CLOSE SHOT—ICEY

ICEY Walt Spoon, that's for sickness in the house!

MEDIUM CLOSE SHOT—WALT
He looks towards o.s. sobbing.

WALT What can we do, Mother?

TWO-SHOT

ICEY I thought if you went and talked to him—another man—

MEDIUM SHOT—PREACHER
He sits at a table, his back towards us, mumbling over his Bible.

TWO-SHOT—WALT, ICEY BEHIND HIM, ENTERING THROUGH DOOR

WALT Mister Powell?

PREACHER (suddenly loud) A strange woman is a narrow pit!

ICEY (a reverent whisper) Amen! Amen!

PREACHER She lieth in wait as for a prey. And increaseth the transgressors among men.

He closes his Bible and turns to them with weepy eyes and a brave little smile.

PREACHER My dear, dear friends! Whatever would I do without you!

CLOSE SHOT—ICEY

ICEY (wailing) Mister Powell!

THREE-SHOT—NEW ANGLE

WALT Is there anythin'—*any*thin' . . . ?

PREACHER It is my shame—my crown of thorns. And I must wear it bravely.

ICEY What could have *possessed* that girl!

PREACHER (simply) Satan.

ICEY Ah.

WALT sits across from PREACHER. ICEY is at PREACHER's elbow.

WALT Didn't you have no inkling?

PREACHER Yes; from the first night.

WALT The first night?

PREACHER Our honeymoon.

CLOSE SHOT—WALT

WALT How's that?

TWO-SHOT—PREACHER AND ICEY

PREACHER She turned me out of the bed.

ICEY (with pleasure) *Nnnoooo!!*

CLOSE SHOT—WALT
Filling his pipe.

WALT *What* do you figure to do?

TWO-SHOT—PREACHER AND ICEY

PREACHER Do? Why stay and take care of them little kids. Maybe it was never *meant* for a woman like Willa to taint their young lives.

ICEY (hands clasped; with approval) *Mmmmm!*

CLOSE SHOT—WALT

Dabbing at moisture in the corner of his eye.

WALT That's mighty brave of you, Reverend.

TWO-SHOT—PREACHER AND ICEY

PREACHER I reckon it's been ordained this way, Brother Spoon.

CLOSE SHOT—WALT

WALT Didn't—didn't she leave no word?

TWO-SHOT—PREACHER AND ICEY

PREACHER A scrawl. On a piece of notepaper on the bureau.

ICEY smiles sideways.

PREACHER I burned it. (Preacher holds out his hand, stares in disgust, and wipes his palm dramatically on his coatsleeve) I tore it up and burned it— it stank so strong of hellfire.

ICEY *Amen.*

PREACHER The pitcher has went to the well once too often, my friends.

CLOSE SHOT—WALT

WALT She'll come draggin' her tail back home.

CLOSE SHOT—PREACHER

PREACHER She'll not be back. I reckon I'd be safe in promisin' you that.

CLOSE SHOT—WALT

WALT Maybe she's just run off on a spree.

PREACHER'S VOICE (o.s.) No!

WALT Well, there's no harm in hopin'.

TWO-SHOT—PREACHER AND ICEY

PREACHER Ain't no sense in it, neither. I figured somethin' like this was brewin' when she went to bed last night.

ICEY (all woman) How?

PREACHER She tarried around the kitchen after I'd gone up, and when I went downstairs to see what was wrong ...

ICEY (eagerly) What!

PREACHER She'd found this fruit jar of dandelion wine (Icey touches him) that the husband—Harper—had hid somewheres in the cellar. (playing his ace) She was drinking.

CLOSE SHOT—ICEY
ICEY is happy to let her mouth fall open and let out a gasp.

CLOSE SHOT—WALT
Sniffling.

THREE-SHOT—PREACHER, ICEY, WALT

PREACHER I tried to save her.

ICEY I know you did, Reverend. Oh, I know how you tried!

PREACHER The devil wins sometimes!

CLOSE SHOT—PREACHER

PREACHER (eyes upturned) Can't nobody say I didn't do *my* best to save her!   DISSOLVE TO

CLOSE UNDERWATER SHOT (Tank)
We PAN, with slowly streaming weeds, and bring in WILLA in close profile; the current, coming from behind her, drifts her long hair across her throat.

MEDIUM SHOT—WILLA AND CAR
She is in profile as before—

CLOSE SHOT—A BAITED HOOK
It descends, and catches on the windshield, and the line tautens; then tugs. We start to follow the line up.

CLOSE SHOT—ABOVE WATER—THE LINE
We continue to follow the line up, and bring in, close, the stern of BEN HARPER's skiff.

MEDIUM SHOT—UNCLE BIRDIE
He sits back, tugging unconcernedly at the line. Then he leans over to see what's wrong.

CLOSE SHOT—BIRDIE
. . . as he peers over side.

DOWNSHOT—FULL SHOT OF CAR AND WILLA; BIRDIE'S VIEWPOINT

CLOSE SHOT—BIRDIE, HORROR-STRICKEN

MOVING UNDERWATER SHOT—WILLA
We hear PREACHER's voice o.s., singing:

PREACHER (o.s.) *Leaning! Leaning! Safe and secure from all alarms!*
Meanwhile we move vertically DOWNWARD TOWARDS HER FACE, serene in
death. We may or may not glimpse the gashed throat, through drifting
hair.   LAP DISSOLVE TO

EXT. HARPER HOME—FULL SHOT—THE HOUSE AND TREE

PREACHER leans against the tree; he continues singing:

PREACHER *Leaning! Leaning! Leaning on the Everlasting Arms!* (se-
ductively) Children!

CLOSE MOVING SHOT—PREACHER
We start moving before he does. LOW CAMERA; full figure. We TILT to
frame him from the waist downward and follow close behind him. As
he leaves the tree and walks along the side of the house; we TILT DOWN-
WARD and CLOSE IN, to follow only his feet; he steps past a tiny cellar
window and we PAN and TIGHTEN IN CLOSE ON IT, into—

CLOSE TWO-SHOT—JOHN AND PEARL
Their noses are flat against the glass; their cheeks touch; their window
isn't quite big enough to hold both their heads. It is on the ground; we
don't see their chins. They look towards the departed PREACHER.

PREACHER'S VOICE (o.s.) *Chill-dren?*

PEARL, who is on the side PREACHER has left by, turns her head towards
JOHN.

INT. CELLAR—MEDIUM CLOSE TWO-SHOT—JOHN AND PEARL
They are standing on a coal heap, faces at window.

PEARL John, why do we have to hide?

JOHN has taken charge. He speaks very quietly, but calmly and cheerfully,
as to an invalid. He starts down the rustling coal-heap, helping PEARL
down.

JOHN Careful . . .

The following dialogue as they climb down, making as little noise as possible.

We PULL slowly away.

PEARL Where's Mom?

JOHN She's gone to Moundsville.

PEARL To see Dad?

JOHN Yes, I reckon that's it.

They have achieved the cellar floor.

PREACHER'S VOICE (more peremptorily outside) Children!

During the following dialogue we hear, o.s., the opening of a door, and PREACHER's footsteps indoors as he crosses floor, climbs stairs, and opens another door.

JOHN Someone is after us, Pearl.

PEARL I want to go upstairs. It's cold and spidery down here. I'm hungry.

JOHN Now listen to me, Pearl. You and me is runnin' off tonight.

PEARL Why?

JOHN If we stay here somethin' awful will happen to us.

PEARL Won't Daddy Powell take care of us?

JOHN No, that's just it. No.

FULL SHOT—A ROOM UPSTAIRS

PREACHER looks under the bed.

RESUME CELLAR TWO-SHOT—THE CHILDREN

PEARL Where are we goin', John?

JOHN Somewheres. I don't know yet.

o.s., PREACHER's footsteps come down stairs; JOHN leads PEARL carefully past a rake, a hoe, and a shelf-prop and they crouch down into—

CLOSE TWO-SHOT—JOHN AND PEARL
. . . beside an apple barrel. PREACHER's footsteps cross kitchen o.s.

PEARL I'm hungry, John.

JOHN We'll steal somethin' to eat.

PEARL It'll spoil our supper.

PREACHER'S VOICE (o.s.) Pearl?

Both look sharp towards cellar door o.s.

THE CELLAR DOOR—CHILDREN'S VIEWPOINT

The door opens; PREACHER's head, carrying a candle in holder; a white-washed wall and stairs are lighted.

PREACHER'S VOICE I hear you whisperin', children, so I know you're down there. I can feel myself gettin' awful mad, children.

CLOSE TWO-SHOT—THE CHILDREN

PEARL (whispering) John . . .

JOHN claps his hand over her mouth.

CELLAR DOOR

PREACHER'S VOICE My patience has run out, children. I'm comin' to find you now.

He clop-clops nearly to the bottom of the stairs. ICEY's voice cuts cheerfully across his descent.

ICEY (calling o.s.) Yoo-Hooooo! Mis-ter Paow-welll!

He goes up the stairs and vanishes. Light on wall through open door to kitchen.

ICEY'S VOICE Just a little hot supper I fixed for you and the children.

PREACHER'S VOICE Bless you, bless you!

ICEY'S VOICE And how are the children?

PREACHER'S VOICE They're down there playin' games in the cellar and they won't mind me when I call 'em. I'm at my wit's end, Miz Spoon.

ICEY clucks her tongue o.s.

ICEY'S VOICE (yelling) John: Pearl:

She appears at head of stairs. Her voice crackles with authority.

ICEY John! Pearl! Shake a leg! (she claps her hands sharply)

FULL SHOT—THE KITCHEN—OVER ICEY

ICEY (continuing) I won't have you worryin' poor Mister Powell another minute!

A short pause; then the children, covered with coal-dust, emerge into the light and climb the stairs. JOHN's head is hung in defeat. As they enter the kitchen we PULL BACK.

ICEY Just *look* at you! Dust and filth from top to toe!

GROUP SHOT—THE CHILDREN, OVER PREACHER AND ICEY

ICEY Want me to take 'em up and wash 'em good?

PREACHER Thank you, no. Thank you, dear Icey. I'll tend to them. Thank you.

ICEY pats JOHN's head.

CLOSE SHOT—JOHN

ICEY'S VOICE Don't be too hard on 'em, Reverend. Poor motherless children.

JOHN looks to PEARL and we PAN HER IN as PREACHER's hand named LOVE moves through her locks. We PAN with PREACHER and ICEY as they move towards the door.

ICEY Remember now Mister Powell, don't be afraid to call on us. Good night.

CLOSE SHOT—JOHN
He watches ICEY leave, o.s.

PREACHER (o.s.) Good night Miz Spoon, and thank you again.

FULL SHOT—PREACHER AND ICEY
ICEY goes away along path outside. PREACHER, his back to us, watches her a moment, then turns.

PREACHER Weren't you afraid, my little lambs, down there in all that dark?

HEAD CLOSE-UP—JOHN
Wondering what to do next. LAP DISSOLVE TO

CLOSE SHOT—BIRDIE, OVER BESS'S PICTURE
We begin with HEAD CLOSE-UP of BIRDIE as he rocks, and PULL BACK
He is rocking; and drunk. A bottle stands beside the picture. He turns and speaks to the picture.

BIRDIE They'll think it was me! They'll think it was old Uncle Birdie!

CLOSE SHOT—BIRDIE—NEW ANGLE

His hands grip the edge of the chest on either side of the picture, which we now see.

BIRDIE If you'd o' seen it, Bess! I'm drunk as a lord and I know it, but . . .

INSERT—BESS'S PICTURE

BIRDIE'S VOICE (o.s. continuing) Sweet Heaven, if you'd o' seen it!

RESUME PREVIOUS SHOT

BIRDIE picks up the bottle. His hand and the liquor tremble.

BIRDIE (continuing) Down there in the deep place . . . her hair wavin' lazy and soft like meadow grass under flood waters and that slit in her throat just like she had an extry mouth.

INSERT BESS'S PICTURE

BIRDIE'S VOICE (o.s.) And there ain't a mortal human I can tell but you . . .

RESUME PREVIOUS SHOT

BIRDIE (continuing) . . . Bess, for if I go to the Law they'll hang it on to me. The bottle falls from his hand onto its side on the edge of the chest.

CLOSE SHOT—BIRDIE—NEW ANGLE

The reverse angle of the opening shot. BIRDIE rocks heavily; liquor gurgles from bottle to floor.

BIRDIE Sweet Heaven save poor old Uncle Birdie!

LAP DISSOLVE TO

MEDIUM THREE-SHOT—PREACHER, JOHN, PEARL

PREACHER sits at head of table. JOHN stands to PREACHER's right, around corner of table; he remains expressionless and immobile, until he speaks. PEARL stands to JOHN's right, hugging the DOLL. The table is loaded with good food.

PREACHER, well-fed and at leisure, dabs his mouth delicately with his napkin, folds it, puts it in a ring, and folds his hands. He waits.

PEARL (at last) I'm hungry.

PREACHER Why, sure. And there's fried chicken and candied sweets and cornsticks and apple cobbler!

PEARL Can I have my supper please?

PREACHER Naturally.

PEARL Can I have milk too?

PREACHER Yes. But first of all we'll have a little talk.

PEARL frowns and puts her finger in her mouth; she remembers he twisted her arm.

PREACHER (softly) About our secrets.

PEARL No.

PREACHER Why, pray tell?

PEARL Because John said I mustn't.

THREE-SHOT REVERSE—PREACHER, OVER NECKS OF CHILDREN
He slaps the table; his eyes crackle.

PREACHER NEVER—MIND—WHAT—JOHN—SAID!

PEARL starts to snivel.

PREACHER John is a meddler. Stop sniveling. Looky here a minute!

He brings out the knife.

PREACHER Know what this is?

PEARL shakes her head for *no*.

PREACHER Want to see something cute? Looky now!

He touches the spring; the blade flicks open.

PREACHER How *about* that! This is what I use on meddlers.

He lays the open knife on the table.

PREACHER John might be a meddler.

THREE-SHOT—THE CHILDREN, OVER PREACHER
PEARL thinks the knife is a toy and crosses behind JOHN to pick it up.

PREACHER NO—*no*, my lamb. Don't touch it! Now don't touch my knife! That makes me mad. Very, very mad.

She hugs the DOLL and he puts the hand named LOVE on her curls.

PREACHER Just tell me now; where's the money hid?

PEARL (affectionately) But I swore. I promised John I wouldn't tell.

CLOSE SHOT—PREACHER

PREACHER JOHN—DOESN'T—MATTER! Can't I get that through your head, you poor, silly, disgusting little wretch!

HEAD CLOSE-UP—PEARL

Her mouth quivers; a large tear brims in her eyes.

CLOSE SHOT—PREACHER

PREACHER There now! You made me lose my temper!

THREE-SHOT—CHILDREN, OVER PREACHER

PREACHER I'm sorry! I'm real sorry!

PEARL sniffles and wipes her eyes with her free fist.

PREACHER (in a caressing tone) Now! Where's it hid, honey?

JOHN (suddenly and lightly) I'll tell.

THREE-SHOT—PREACHER, OVER NAPES OF CHILDREN

PREACHER (lightly) I thought I told you to keep your mouth shut—

JOHN (light and quick) NO,—it ain't fair to make Pearl tell when she swore she wouldn't. I'll tell.

PREACHER'S EYES CRINKLE and he turns to PEARL, smiling brightly.

PREACHER (chuckling) Well I declare! Sometimes I think poor John will make it to heaven yet!

His eyes snap back to JOHN and his voice is like a whip.

PREACHER All right boy: where's the money?

HEAD CLOSE-UP—JOHN

JOHN In the cellar. Buried under a stone in the floor.

THREE-SHOT—PREACHER OVER CHILDREN

He closes and pockets the knife. His eyes never leave JOHN's.

PREACHER It'll go hard, boy, if I find you're lyin'.

THREE-SHOT—PREACHER OVER CHILDREN

PEARL gapes up at JOHN as he speaks.

JOHN I ain't lyin'. Go look for yourself.

CLOSE SHOT—PREACHER
. . . as he gets up, cellar door in BACKGROUND.

PREACHER All right . . . (he turns towards the door; then glances around)
Come along.

HEAD CLOSE-UP—JOHN

JOHN What?

THREE-SHOT—PREACHER, OVER CHILDREN

PREACHER Go ahead of me—the both of you.

They cross him, towards the door.

FULL SHOT—THE CELLAR STEPS—FROM THE BOTTOM
The CHILDREN precede PREACHER, who carries a candle in holder. PEARL
is gaping at JOHN's lie. JOHN is looking left and right, casing the joint.

PREACHER (continuing) You don't reckon I'd leave you.

JOHN (with forced lightness) Don't you believe me?

PREACHER (sardonically) Why sure, boy, sure.

Now they are at bottom of stairs. JOHN sees PEARL's expression and takes
her hand.

PREACHER Now where, boy? Mind; no tricks. I can't abide liars.

JOHN Yonder.

He squeezes PEARL's hand harder, and points.

FULL SHOT—NEW ANGLE—OVER THE THREE
JOHN points out a place beneath a shelf laden with Mason jars; it is at the
most distant part of the cellar from the stairs.

PREACHER starts toward it, leaving them at foot of stairs, then turns,
catching JOHN's ruse.

PREACHER (sardonic) O no you don't!

He shepherds them ahead of him.

THREE-SHOT—NEW ANGLE
They arrive beneath the shelf.

PREACHER Now: Where?

JOHN (lying magnificently, meeting Preacher's eyes) Under the stone in the floor.

PREACHER sets the candle on a barrel near the shelf-prop and sinks to his knees below shot as PEARL gapes at JOHN and JOHN looks stony. She seems about to speak.

FLASH INSERT—JOHN SQUEEZES PEARL'S HAND HARD

CLOSE SHOT—PREACHER, FEATURING FLOOR
His hands sweep dust and expose concrete. He straightens on his knees and turns to the children in close BACKGROUND.

HEAD CLOSE-UP—PREACHER
. . . as he turns.

PREACHER This is concrete.

CLOSE TWO-SHOT—THE CHILDREN
A moment's silence.

PEARL John made a Sin. John told a lie.

THREE-SHOT—FAVORING PREACHER
PREACHER gets slowly to his feet and puts on his "listening" look. His sincerity is beyond doubt.

PREACHER The Lord's a-talkin' to me now. He's a-sayin', "a liar is an abomination before mine eyes."

He takes his knife out, and springs it open.

CLOSE TWO-SHOT—FAVORING JOHN

PREACHER Speak, boy: Where's it hid? (the knife pricks the flesh under John's ear) Speak, before I cut your throat and leave you to drip like a hog hung up in butcherin' time!

CLOSE SHOT—PEARL
She starts to sob.

CLOSE TWO-SHOT—JOHN AND PREACHER

JOHN Pearl, shut up! Pearl, you swore!

PREACHER You could save him, little bird.

HEAD CLOSE-UP—PEARL

PEARL (crying) *Inside my doll! Inside my doll!*

TWO-SHOT—JOHN AND PREACHER, FAVORING PREACHER
PREACHER is astounded. His hands fall away from JOHN. He leans back against the wall and talks through laughter.

PREACHER In the doll! Why sure! Sure!

HEAD CLOSE-UP—JOHN
His eyes are all over the place.

PREACHER'S VOICE (o.s.) The last place anyone would look!

THREE-SHOT—PREACHER, JOHN, PEARL
PREACHER makes a lunge across JOHN for the doll; JOHN ducking under his arm, pulls PEARL forward with his left hand; he turns backwards and with his free hand, in one movement, knocks over the candle and pulls out the support on the shelf.

CLOSE SHOT—PREACHER
Jars shower over him; one crowns him and breaks, shedding guck, which he wipes from his eyes.

TWO-SHOT—THE CHILDREN
They start up the stairs.

FULL SHOT—PREACHER
He makes one step forward, steps on a rolling jar, and falls.

TWO-SHOT—THE CHILDREN
They are near the top of the stairs. We hear PREACHER below them. JOHN slips and they nearly fall backward. As JOHN recovers, PREACHER enters the shot, his back to us. The children get through the open door as PREACHER reaches top. JOHN slams the door, catching PREACHER's hand. PREACHER screams. JOHN's astonished eyes peer through the crack in the door; the door loosens; PREACHER yanks his hand loose and sucks it, groaning; the door slams to; the bolt is shot home.

HEAD CLOSE-UP—PREACHER
. . . over sound of slamming bolt. He snarls like the Big Bad Wolf.

All the above happens at once.

INT. KITCHEN—CLOSE TWO-SHOT—JOHN AND PEARL, BY DOOR
PEARL, dangling her doll, cries. JOHN panting, leans against wall by door. JOHN is wondering what to do now. Pause.

PREACHER'S VOICE (o.s., sweetly) Chilll-dren?

PREACHER'S VOICE (continuing) The only reason I wanted that money is so's you could have it.

JOHN (to himself; panting) The river. That's the only where! Uncle Birdie Steptoe!

PREACHER'S VOICE (cooing) Puhr-urrl? Want your Mommy back? (Pearl hugs her doll) Want me to get her right now?

PEARL (sharply) John?

JOHN Hush, Pearl. Come on.
They fly out of the house.

PREACHER'S VOICE (bellowing, as they go) OPEN THAT DOOR, YOU SPAWN OF THE DEVIL'S OWN STRUMPET!

FRAMING SHOT—EXT. THE HARPER HOUSE
A pretty, pastoral shot of the house in light mist, as they run across and leave the shot. Before they disappear, we hear PREACHER's fists hammering against the door. We stay on the house at leisure; we hear him lunging, shoulder to door; we begin to hear squeaking of hinges and splintering of wood.

FULL CIRCLE SHOT—FRAMING BIRDIE'S WHARF-BOAT
An ultra romantic image of shelter and peace. Frogs or river noises o.s., then the rattle of running footsteps. The children center, their backs to us, sprinting towards the boat. Light mist as in previous shot.

JOHN (calling) Uncle Birdie! Uncle Birdie!

INT. BIRDIE'S BOAT—GROUP SHOT—BIRDIE AND CHILDREN
We shoot over BESS's turned photograph and over BIRDIE, close, passed out in his rocker. The children run through open door in BACKGROUND and JOHN runs up to BIRDIE.

JOHN Uncle Birdie!

CLOSE SHOT—BIRDIE

BIRDIE (gesturing feebly) Don't!

CLOSE TWO-SHOT—NEW ANGLE—BIRDIE, OVER JOHN

JOHN Hide us Uncle Birdie! He's a-comin' with his knife!

He grabs BIRDIE's shoulder; BIRDIE half-rises, and falls face down on floor.

CLOSE TWO-SHOT—BIRDIE ON FLOOR, OVER JOHN

JOHN It's me! John Harper and Pearl! You said to come a-runnin' if we needed you!

BIRDIE rears on one elbow and looks up at him.

BIRDIE (in friendly recognition) Johnny!

He falls face down again.

CLOSE TWO-SHOT—NEW ANGLE—FAVORING JOHN
JOHN grabs BIRDIE by one ear, turning his face up.

JOHN Uncle—Birdie! Oh—please! *Please wake up!*

CLOSE TWO-SHOT—FAVORING BIRDIE
He looks up earnestly at JOHN.

BIRDIE I never done it, boy. Sweet Heaven I never done such a terrible thing! I'll swear on the Book to it, boy! I never done it! I never!

CLOSE SHOT—JOHN
He is lost; and he becomes a man.

BIRDIE'S VOICE (o.s.) Lord save poor old Uncle Birdie Steptoe that never hurt a fly! (he snores, softly)

JOHN (quiet) There's still the river.—The skiff is down by the willows.

He masterfully takes PEARL by the hand and leads her into the night.

LONG SHOT—THE CHILDREN
We shoot from the river. They struggle through the sumac and pokeberry weeds at edge of river, towards skiff, whose prow, tethered to willow, we see throughout this un-moving shot, at our extreme right. When they come opposite skiff—which is a few yards out from shore—

WE CUT TO

TWO-SHOT—THE CHILDREN
PEARL, frankly bored, dangling her doll, is yawning. JOHN, as he finishes undoing rope from a willow root, looks up and around, checking on pursuit. His eyes fix.

FULL SHOT—PREACHER'S SHADOW
On the bank above, it is huge in the mist. Same camera position as foregoing; new angle.

TWO-SHOT—THE CHILDREN
BACK view: skiff in BACKGROUND. Same camera position; new angle.

JOHN (whispering) Please be quiet—Oh *please, Pearl!*

PEARL (natural voice) John, where are we g—

JOHN Hush.

FULL SHOT—SHADOW, THEN PREACHER
Same position and angle as before.

PREACHER's own figure advances to supplant his shadow. He peers downward, his open knife catching the light.

PREACHER (businesslike) Children?
He starts slashing his way down through the brush-filth.

FULL SHOT—THE CHILDREN
Same camera position as before. They are floundering through mud, half-way to the skiff.

FULL SHOT—PREACHER
Same position and angle as in previous shot of him. He is half-way down the bank. With his knife, he hacks at an entangling vine.

FULL SHOT—THE CHILDREN
Position and angle as before. They reach the skiff. Hacking sounds o.s.

JOHN Get in the skiff, Pearl, goodness, goodness, *hurry!*

PEARL (hesitant) That's *Daddy!*

He picks her up and throws her into the skiff.

CLOSE SHOT—PEARL AND DOLL
. . . as they land, sprawling, in bottom of skiff among fish-heads and bait cans. JOHN gets in after them.

FULL SHOT—PREACHER—CHILDREN's VIEWPOINT
He tears free of brush to edge of river, knife glittering.

CLOSE SHOT—JOHN
With his oar, he tries to push the boat free of mud.

FULL SHOT—PREACHER—CHILDREN's VIEWPOINT
He wades towards them, knee-deep in mud.

CLOSE SHOT—JOHN
He is shoving at the oar even more desperately.

INSERT—JOHN's HANDS
Straining.

FULL SHOT—PREACHER—CHILDREN's VIEWPOINT
He flounders deeper and more heavily through the mud; much closer.

CLOSE SHOT—JOHN
He pushes the boat free of mud.

CLOSE SHOT—PREACHER—CHILDREN'S VIEWPOINT
He hurries much closer through shallow water. Prow of boat in FORE-
GROUND.

PREACHER *Wait*, you little whelps! *Wait!*
Another step forward and he does a pratt-fall and makes a splash.

CLOSE SHOT—JOHN—PEARL IN BACKGROUND

He is trying to feather the boat out to where the current will catch it.
In panic and haste he is clumsy.

JOHN Why can't I do it when I know *how* to do it!

FULL SHOT—PREACHER
. . . as he gets up, at edge of mud.

PREACHER *Wait! Wait! I'll slit your guts!*

FULL DOWN-SHOT—THE SKIFF, THEN PREACHER
The current catches it and spins it round like a leaf. JOHN's efforts with the
oars are useless. PREACHER enters, wading fast. His hands are within an inch
of reaching the helpless skiff; capriciously the current takes it downstream.

TWO-SHOT—JOHN AND PEARL
The skiff is taken steadily by the current. PEARL sits up, doll in arms.
JOHN is almost asleep with exhaustion.

FULL SHOT—THE SKIFF, OVER PREACHER
It is well away from him and getting smaller. Waist-deep, he wades a
couple of steps after it, then just looks.

HEAD CLOSE-UP—PREACHER
He begins a steady, rhythmical, animal scream of outrage and loss.

LONG SHOT—THE RIVER AND LANDSCAPE, FEATURING STARLIGHT; AND THE DRIFT-
ING BOAT—PEARL IN STERN

TWO-SHOT—THE CHILDREN—FRONT ON
JOHN is asleep. PEARL sits sleepily whispering to her doll.

PEARL Once upon a time there was a pretty fly, and he had a wife, this
pretty fly. . . .

MEDIUM LONG SHOT—THE DRIFTING BOAT THROUGH FIREFLIES

PEARL'S VOICE (o.s.) . . . and one day she flew away, and then one night his two pretty fly children . . .

SPECIAL SHOT—THE MOVING SKIFF, THROUGH DEW-JEWELED SPIDER-WEB

PEARL'S VOICE (o.s., continuing) . . . flew away too, into the sky, into the moon . . .

SPECIAL SHOT—A FROG, AND SKIFF

A big frog is profiled; the skiff drifts by in distance; the frog twangs out a bass-note. DISSOLVE TO

INSERT—A PICTURE POSTCARD—A COUNTY COURTHOUSE

As the card is turned to the handwritten side we CUT TO

CLOSE TWO-SHOT—WALT AND ICEY

WALT (reading aloud) Dear Walt and Icey: I bet you been worried and gave us up for lost. Took the kids down here with me for a visit to my sister Elsie's farm. Thot a little change of scenery would do us all a world of good after so much trubble and heartache. At least the kids will git a plenty of good home cooking. Your devoted Harry Powell

ICEY Now ain't you relieved, Walt?

WALT Sure, but you was worried too, Mother; takin' off with never a word of goodbye. I even got to figurin' them gypsies busted in and done off with all three of 'em.

ICEY You and your gypsies! They been gone a week!

WALT Not before one of 'em knifed a farmer and stole his horse. Never caught the gypsies nor the horse. LAP DISSOLVE TO

DESCENDING HELICOPTER SHOT—THE RIVER—DAY

A man is going along a river lane on horseback.

It is PREACHER; he walks the horse away from us. DISSOLVE TO

DESCENDING HELICOPTER SHOT—ANOTHER BEND OF THE RIVER

We descend to a poor riverside farmhouse; JOHN and PEARL tether a boat in front of it.

GROUP SHOT (FROM GROUND) THREE HOMELESS CHILDREN, OVER JOHN AND PEARL

They are eating hot boiled potatoes. A glance at JOHN and PEARL, and they turn away towards lane in BACKGROUND. JOHN and PEARL proceed towards the house.

MEDIUM SHOT—JOHN, PEARL, WOMAN, THROUGH DOOR
We shoot from within open door of kitchen. JOHN and PEARL advance to edge of porch. A TIRED FARM WOMAN stands by door, within. We shoot OVER her.

TIRED FARM WOMAN Hungry, I s'pose. Well, I'll see if there's any *more* potatoes to spare. Where's *your* folks?

JOHN Ain't got none.

Woman leaves shot briefly (we HOLD ON CHILDREN) She re-enters and goes to them with a bowl of steaming potatoes. They take hands-ful, and make to eat.

TIRED FARM WOMAN Go 'way; go 'way.

They turn away and walk towards boat. She looks after them.

TIRED FARM WOMAN Such times, when youngins run the roads!

She leaves the SHOT. We frame them briefly, walking away, then;

DISSOLVE TO

CLOSE SHOT—A PLACARD—NIGHT
It is lit by firelight. It reads:

PEACH-PICKERS WANTED
WEEKLY HIRE

PREACHER'S VOICE (o.s.) An ungrateful child is an abomination . . .

LAP DISSOLVE TO

GROUP SHOT—PREACHER AND MEN
PREACHER stands behind the flames; in FOREGROUND an OLD MAN sits profiled on a box. Other workers, all men, sit around fire.

PREACHER (continuing) . . . before the eyes of God. The world is fast going to damnation because of impudent youngins a-flyin' in the face of Age.

Short silence, as the other men look at PREACHER without liking. Then the old man spits into the fire.

CLOSE SHOT—THE FLAMES
A spurt of steam as spit strikes.

CLOSE SHOT—A HOOT OWL
. . . hooting.

LAP DISSOLVE TO

CLOSE SHOT—A TURTLE—NOONDAY
He comes down to water.

JOHN'S VOICE (o.s.) They make *soup* out of them . . .

LONG SHOT—THE CHILDREN IN PASSING SKIFF
Full landscape in BACKGROUND.

JOHN (continuing) . . . but I wouldn't know how to go about gettin' him open. LAP DISSOLVE TO

LONG SHOT—CHILDREN AND SKIFF, OVER RABBITS IN GRASS
We shoot OVER two sitting rabbits as they watch, their ears up. The skiff passes. PEARL plays with doll JOHN unsnarls line.
LAP DISSOLVE TO

FULL SHOT—THE CHILDREN AND SKIFF, FRAMED BY WILLOWS—TWILIGHT
The skiff passes. Baa-ing of sheep o.s.

MOVING SHOT—FROM RIVER—A SHEEP
The sheep bleats. We PAN in a big barn near the river, then a lighted house; willows along shore.

FULL SHOT—THE SKIFF—FROM THE BANK

JOHN re-sets his oar. They angle towards us for the shore.

JOHN We're gonna spend a night on land.

UP-SHOT—THE CHILDREN, OVER THE MOORED SKIFF
. . . they reach top of the bank. Corner of barn and lighted window in BACKGROUND. Sounds of mouth-organ and girl singing o.s.

FULL SHOT—A LIGHTED WINDOW, THE SHADE DRAWN
A wire bird-cage hangs close to the shade, silhouetted. On the perch, a canary. Lullaby and mouth-organ continue o.s. After a moment the CHILDREN enter, backs to us, and stop, looking.

CLOSE TWO-SHOT—THE CHILDREN
Window-light on faces, song over. A moment.

PEARL Are *we* goin' home, John?

JOHN *Ssh* . . .
He turns, her hand in his. We PAN as they tiptoe towards the big, open door of barn; big open hayloft window above.

INT. ROOM—LOW TRACKING SHOT—THE CHILDREN
As they walk down aisle of barn we shoot them past bellies and legs of row of cows. Sounds of munching and soft lowing o.s. JOHN helps PEARL up a little ladder to the hayloft.

MEDIUM SHOT—THE CHILDREN, WINDOW—TWILIGHT
. . . as the CHILDREN bed down in hay, only legs visible, protruding into frame of window, which frames a middle-distant white lane beyond house, and a landscape. Whippoorwill o.s. A DARKENING OF LIGHT.

LAP DISSOLVE TO

SAME SET-UP
The full moon is half-risen. Whippoorwill o.s.

LAP DISSOLVE TO

SAME SET-UP
The moon is well above the horizon. Whippoorwill o.s.

LAP DISSOLVE TO

SAME SET-UP
The moon is still higher. A pause; the whippoorwill stops in mid-phrase. Brief pause; then John sits up into silhouette.

CLOSE SHOT—JOHN
He listens intently. We hear nothing. His eyes alter. We hear, distantly

PREACHER'S VOICE (o.s., singing) *Leaning, Leaning . . .*
At various distances o.s., we hear dogs barking at the sound of the singing.

PREACHER'S VOICE (continuing; louder) . . . *safe and secure from all alarms;*
The dog from the farm rushes braying to his gate. Other dogs continue o.s. PREACHER appears, astride his walking horse, singing.

PREACHER *Leaning . . .*

CLOSE SHOT—JOHN
Watching; dread and despair. Sounds go.

PREACHER (o.s.) *Leaning; Leaning on the Everlasting Arms.*

FULL SHOT—PREACHER
He approaches and crosses center screen, continuing the hymn. (We do not PAN with him; he crosses the frame of the great window.)

CLOSE SHOT—JOHN
Eyes following PREACHER. PREACHER and dogs continue o.s.

JOHN (to himself) Don't you *never* sleep?

FULL SHOT—PREACHER
He vanishes beyond trees, his singing more distant. Dogs continue.

CLOSE SHOT—JOHN AND PEARL—NEW ANGLE
He wakes her. PREACHER's singing o.s.

JOHN (scared whisper) Pearl, wake up! Come on, Pearl!

FULL SHOT—PREACHER
He vanishes; scuttling of children in hay, o.s.; dogs quiet; his song dies.
Brief silence. The whippoorwill resumes.

MEDIUM LONG SHOT—THE CHILDREN, NEAR BARN
Hand in hand, they hurry out of barn and, as we PAN, along its side,
towards River, o.s. Whippoorwill o.s.

FULL SHOT—A BRIGHT FULL MOON
The whippoorwill's singing continues o.s.

FULL SHOT—CHILDREN AND SKIFF

JOHN steers through turbulent, moonlit water. Whippoorwill continues.
Low moon.

CLOSE SHOT—A FOX, BARKING

CLOSE DOWN-SHOT—CHILDREN ASLEEP IN SKIFF (TANK)
Blank, calm water; the skiff enters and passes full length below us, the
CHILDREN asleep in it; blank water again; again the fox barks.

MEDIUM SHOT—THE SKIFF, DRIFTING SHOT THROUGH RIVERSIDE GRASS
Crickets o.s. The skiff nears a sand-bar.

INSERT—THE PROW, GROUNDING
The prow softly grates against sand.

MEDIUM SHOT—THE GROUNDED SKIFF, AGAIN THROUGH GRASS
Crickets fainter. TILTING UPWARD.   LAP DISSOLVE TO

FULL SHOT—THE STARLIT SKY   LAP DISSOLVE TO

FULL SHOT—RIVER LANDSCAPE—SUNRISE
Distant; medium; the near; roosters crow o.s.

CLOSE SHOT—JOHN WAKING
He looks to PEARL o.s.

FULL SHOT—PEARL, THEN RACHEL, OVER JOHN
PEARL is picking daisies. A fence up beyond her. Beyond the fence, a woman, RACHEL COOPER, appears. She carries a berry-basket on her arm. JOHN scrambles up, grabs an oar, and holds it defensively. PEARL freezes.

RACHEL (loud) You two youngsters get up here to me this instant!

TWO-SHOT—JOHN AND PEARL—RACHEL'S ANGLE

RACHEL (o.s.) Mind me now!

JOHN lowers the oar at the female authority in her voice.

RACHEL (o.s.) Now git on up to my house.
They hesitate.

THREE-SHOT—OVER JOHN

RACHEL I'll git me a willow switch.
They still hesitate. She breaks off a switch and comes for them, squishing through the mud. She surrounds them and drives them like geese up the bank.

LOW FULL SHOT—THE THREE, FROM SIDE
They move across the meadow like a nursery frieze. She tweaks with her switch. As she goes near PEARL's calves, JOHN turns.

JOHN Don't you hurt *her!*

RACHEL Hurt her *nothin'! Wash* her's more like it! (hand to mouth, yelling) Ruby!

FULL SHOT—A TOMATO PATCH
Three crouching figures pick tomatoes beyond a low white fence; Rachel's house in background. RUBY, thirteen, pops her head up like a rifle-target.

RACHEL (o.s.) Clary!
Clary, eleven, pops up.

RACHEL (o.s.) Mary!
Mary, four, pops up.

THE GIRLS (in chorus) Yes Miz Cooper!

GROUP SHOT—RACHEL AND HARPERS, MOVING TOWARDS FENCE
She has JOHN and PEARL by their napes.

RACHEL Bring yer baskets.
The three girls enter, their backs to us, carrying baskets of tomatoes.

GROUP SHOT—THE GIRLS, OVER RACHEL AND HARPER CHILDREN

She holds JOHN and PEARL very firmly, inspecting baskets, across gate of fence.

RACHEL Nicely picked, Clary. Mary; put the big ones on top. Ruby, most o' them ain't fit to go to market. Put them baskets down. Ruby, fetch the washtub and put it by the pump. Mary, Clary, fetch me a bar o' laundry soap and the scrub brush.

GIRLS (in chorus) Yes Miz Cooper!
They hurry off.

RACHEL Come on, now; up to the house.
She opens the gate, pushes the Harper children through, shuts the gate, and walks between them, her back to us. The children hesitate. She turns to them and stops.

THREE-SHOT—THE CHILDREN, OVER RACHEL

She looks them up and down. If we saw her face, her lips would be pursed and working with anger.

RACHEL Gracious! If you hain't a sight to beat all! Where you from?
No answer; their eyes are wide with curiosity.

RACHEL Where's your folks?

CLOSE SHOT—JOHN

RACHEL (o.s.) Speak up now!
His eyes go down to her feet. He, and we, start to examine her from foot to head; for this is our heroine at last.

CLOSE TILTING SHOT—RACHEL

. . . from JOHN's eye-level. We TILT SLOWLY UP her height. She wears man's shoes, heavy with mud; a rough skirt; a shapeless sweater hangs over her shoulders; she is in her middle sixties and wears a man's old hat. Her face says:

RACHEL (sort of roughly) Gracious! So I've got two more mouths to feed!

CLOSE SHOT—JOHN

For no reason at all he feels he has come home.   LAP DISSOLVE TO

GROUP SHOT—JOHN, PEARL, RACHEL, RUBY, DURING WASHING

RACHEL mercilessly scrubs JOHN; JOHN doesn't like it; RUBY washes PEARL with a cloth.

CLOSE SHOT—JOHN
Hating the scrubbing. He breaks away.

FULL SHOT—JOHN AND RACHEL

JOHN dodges behind a bush, RACHEL in hot pursuit.

CLOSE SHOT—THE BUSH; RACHEL

RACHEL's head bobs up and down above the bush; we hear the unmistakable sound of a female hand on a child's bottom.

LAP DISSOLVE TO

FULL SHOT—A SHELF, FULL OF MARKET BASKETS, NEATLY COVERED WITH DAMP MUSLIN

LAP DISSOLVE TO

FULL SHOT—THE CARRIED BASKETS, IN MOTION

EXT. MOUNDSVILLE STREET—TRACKING SHOT—RACHEL AND HER BROOD

All carry baskets. RACHEL charges along at the head of the procession. A CATTLE DEALER strolls the other way.

CATTLE DEALER Howdy Miz Cooper—you goin' to sell me yer hog this year?

RACHEL doesn't stop walking.

RACHEL With the price o' pork what is is?

CLOSE TRACKING SHOT—RACHEL
She keeps walking.

RACHEL (talking to herself) I'm butcherin' my hog myself, smokin' the hams, and cannin' the sausage. (she calls to children over her shoulder) *You*-all have your work cut out!

CLOSE TRACKING TWO-SHOT—JOHN AND CLARY IN MID-PROCESSION

JOHN She talks to herself.

CLARY All the time.

JOHN Your Maw's funny.

CLARY She ain't our Maw. We just live at her house.
They walk in silence.

JOHN Where's your folks?

CLARY Some place.

MARY My Daddy's in *Dee*-troit.

JOHN (to Ruby) Who's *your* folks?

RUBY I dunno.

FULL SHOT—THE STREET

A WAITRESS, wearing an apron labeled EMPIRE EATS, hurries across the street towards the GROUP. We PAN her in to MARY. The procession halts briefly. She embraces MARY.

WAITRESS Mary! Honey! Mornin' Miz Cooper. (to Mary) Guess what! I'm savin' up to buy ye a charm bracelet!

CLOSE SHOT—RACHEL

RACHEL Never mind the gewgaws; don't you miss your visit this Sunday; and come to Church with us.

FULL STREET SHOT

The WAITRESS hurries away. She dodges past a car.

WAITRESS See ye Sunday, love!

CLOSE SHOT—RACHEL

she follows WAITRESS, then LOVERS in car, with her eyes.

FULL STREET SHOT

The car CENTERS, held up in traffic; two lovers in it, sitting close.

CLOSE SHOT—RACHEL

She takes in the LOVERS.

RACHEL Women is durn fools! *All* of 'em!
She sighs, angry at all women, herself included, and turns away. We are at the door of a GROCERY STORE. The GROCER is on his doorstep.

FULL SHOT—GROUP AND GROCERY

RACHEL (to children) Take yer baskets in.
The CHILDREN file in past her and GROCER.

RACHEL (to Grocer) Looky there. (she indicates the lovers) *She*'ll be losin' her mind to a tricky mouth and a full moon, and like as not I'll be saddled with the *consequences*.

She starts into store with the GROCER.

INT. STORE—GROUP SHOT—RACHEL, GROCER, CHILDREN

RACHEL and GROCER come up to counter.

RACHEL (continuing; she takes a list from her bosom and gives it to Grocer) Here's what you owe me. (she counts baskets) One, two, three, four, five . . . where's the other basket? Where's Ruby?

CLARY She went.

RACHEL John: *you* go fetch Ruby. (John goes. As Grocer empties baskets and tots up, Rachel continues:) Big Ruby's my problem girl. She can't gather eggs without bustin' 'em; but Ruby's got mother hands with a youngin, so what're you to say?

EXT. DRUG STORE—FULL SHOT—RUBY
She stands with her market-basket, reacting to wolf whistles o.s.; she is seeking the world.

THREE-SHOT—RUBY, OVER TWO YOUNG LOAFERS

1ST LOAFER How 'bout tonight, Ruby?

RUBY gestures RACHEL's nearness.

2ND LOAFER (to 1st) What gives?

1ST LOAFER The Old Lady's around. (to Ruby) How 'bout Thursday?

RUBY nods.

1ST LOAFER (to 2nd) The old gal thinks she comes in fer sewin' lessons o'-Thursday.

FULL SHOT—RUBY; JOHN IN BACKGROUND

JOHN (calling) Miz Cooper wants you.
He turns and goes; RUBY, with an eye to 1ST LOAFER, turns and follows.

INT. GROCERY STORE—GROUP SHOT—CENTERING RACHEL

GROCER (to Pearl) And will you show me your dolly, little lady?

JOHN has entered in BACKGROUND. PEARL holds the doll to her, and JOHN moves in quietly to her side. They stand together, as so often before.

GROCER See ye got *two* more peeps to your brood.

RACHEL Yeah, and ornerier than the rest.

GROCER How's your *own* boy, Miz Cooper?

RACHEL Ain't heard from Ralph since last Christmas. Don't matter—I've got a new crop. (she laughs. Loudly) I'm a strong tree with branches for many birds. I'm good for something in this old world and I know it, too! We know that she will rout the Devil.

GROCER (a good tradesman) Got a good buy in soap, Miz Cooper.

RACHEL (triumphant) Don't need no soap. I'm boilin' down the fat from my hog.   DISSOLVE TO

INT. RACHEL'S SCREENED PORCH—EVENING—GROUP SHOT—RACHEL, GIRLS, JOHN ASIDE

CENTERING RACHEL as she takes a book from table, and the GIRLS MOVE to set at her seat, and JOHN stands to one side. RACHEL glances at him.

CLOSE SHOT—JOHN

He looks suspiciously to the Book in her hands, for to him it has come to mean only Preacher.

INSERT—THE BIBLE

. . . as she opens it on her lap o.s. we hear a screen door open.

GROUP SHOT—RACHEL, CHILDREN, JOHN IN BACKGROUND

We see the door closing as JOHN goes out. The girls sit on low stools in semi-circle at RACHEL's feet. We CENTER RACHEL. RACHEL, keenly aware of JOHN, pretends to ignore him. JOHN crosses behind her and stands with his back to us. We see the back of his head through the screen. RACHEL, changing her mind about what story to tell, finds the new page she's after, and spreads her hands flat on the pages. She never glances at the text. She is fishing for JOHN.

RACHEL Now old Pharoah, he was the King of Egyptland! And he had a daughter, and once upon a time (louder) she was walkin' along the river bank and she seen somethin' bumpin' and scrapin' along down on a sandbar under the willows.

CLOSE SHOT—THE BACK OF JOHN'S HEAD, IMMOBILE

RACHEL (o.s.) And do you know what it was, children?

RESUME GROUP SHOT

RUBY, CLARY, MARY (excited) No!

PEARL No!

RACHEL (still loud) Well, now, it was a skiff, washed up on the bar. And who do you reckon was in it?

RUBY (confidently) Pearl and John!

RACHEL (still loud) Not this time! It was just one youngin—a little boy babe. And do you know who he *was*, children?

CLOSE SHOT—JOHN'S HEAD
. . . as he turns around.

RUBY, MARY, CLARY, PEARL (o.s. in unison) No!

RESUME GROUP SHOT

RACHEL closes the Bible; she knows the Lord's battle is won. As she continues, she puts aside the book and takes up her mending.

RACHEL (very quietly) It was Moses!—A King of men, Moses, children. Now. Off to bed. Hurry.

On "off to bed," JOHN turns his back again.

CLOSE SHOT—RACHEL; JOHN IN BACKGROUND
She mends for a few moments.

RACHEL (commandingly) John, git me an apple.

JOHN crosses behind her and off, towards door. We hear it open and close.

RACHEL Git one for yourself, too.

MEDIUM SHOT—JOHN
He approaches with two apples. We PAN him into a:

TWO-SHOT—JOHN AND RACHEL
He gives her an apple. She immediately takes a bite. He doesn't bite his. She looks up at him from her apple.

RACHEL (suddenly) John, where's your folks?

JOHN (plainly) Dead.

RACHEL Dead. (she nods with finality)

JOHN starts to eat his apple.

RACHEL Where ye from?

JOHN Up river.

RACHEL I didn't figger ye rowed that skiff from Parkersburg!

JOHN makes a move; he slowly and tenderly reaches out his hand and lays his fingers on her knuckles.

JOHN Tell me that story again.
Our heroine would like to thank the Lord openly, but she knows she must not show her feelings; she speaks gruffly—

RACHEL Story, honey? Why, what story?

JOHN About them Kings. That the Queen found down on the sandbar in the skiff that time.

RACHEL Kings! Why, honey, there was only one.

JOHN I mind you said there was two.

RACHEL Well, shoot! Maybe there was!

CLOSE SHOT—RACHEL
Maybe we see—though JOHN does not—the thanksgiving in her eyes.

RACHEL Yes, come to think of it, there *was* two, John.
O.s., in distance, we hear the whistle of a river boat.   DISSOLVE TO

EXT. MOUNDSVILLE STREET—EVENING—MOVING SHOT—RUBY
Her head and shoulders from behind as she walks down the neon-lighted street; drugstore and loafers in b.g.; jazz music o.s.

FULL SHOT—RUBY, OVER DRUGSTORE LOAFERS
Our two loafers lounge on a bench. RUBY approaches.

2ND LOAFER (to 1st) Hey. Must be Thursday.

1ST LOAFER Here we go.
He gets up and starts towards RUBY, who catches his eye.

RUBY, FROM BEHIND
She turns to a magazine stand and fingers a magazine, awaiting LOAFER, who approaches in BACKGROUND.

INSERT—RUBY'S HAND; MAGAZINES
They are lurid, tawdry fan and pin-up magazines.

PREACHER enters, between RUBY and LOAFER, and turns to RUBY into CLOSE TWO-SHOT. LOAFER pauses in BACKGROUND.

PREACHER You're Ruby, ain't you, my child?

RUBY Can I have this?

PREACHER Surely. I'd like to talk to you, my dear.

RUBY Will you buy me a choclit sody?

PREACHER O' course.

LOAFERS Watch out Preacher! Why, *Preacher!*

PREACHER (sternly) Shet yer dirty mouths!

CLOSE SHOT—RUBY
She looks up at him admiringly; then to LOAFERS; back to PREACHER.

LAP DISSOLVE TO

INT. DRUGSTORE—CLOSE TWO-SHOT—PREACHER AND RUBY
RUBY is finishing her soda.

RUBY Ain't I purty?
This is a familiar clue to PREACHER.

PREACHER Why, you're the purtiest girl I've seen in all my wandering. Didn't nobody never tell you that, Ruby?

RUBY (hoarsely) No. No one never did.

PREACHER (moving in) There's two new ones over at your place, ain't there Ruby?

She nods.

PREACHER What's their names?

RUBY Pearl and John.

PREACHER Ahhh. (whispering) And is there—a doll?

RUBY (nods) Only she won't never let me play with it.

PREACHER Ahh!
He gets up and heads for door. RUBY, dismayed, hurries after him.

PREACHER (firmly) Yes!
He strides through door, RUBY following.

THREE-SHOT—PREACHER AND RUBY ON SIDEWALK, 2ND LOAFER IN B.G. IST LOAFER HAS GONE.

PREACHER comes out fast, RUBY touches his arm, he turns on her. They are in CLOSE TWO-SHOT. RUBY goes on tiptoe. PREACHER inclines his ear.

CLOSE SHOT—RUBY

RUBY Did you ever see such purty eyes in all your born days?

CLOSE SHOT—PREACHER

INSERT—PREACHER'S HAND
It slides into his knife pocket. We hear a click.

2ND LOAFER (o.s.) Don't let him git away, Sugar!

THREE-SHOT—PREACHER AND RUBY, LOAFER IN B.G.

RUBY He ain't like you-all! Next time I won't even ask him to buy me a sody!

She turns to PREACHER, but PREACHER, on "next time," has left the SHOT.

CLOSE SHOT—RUBY
She looks after him, clasping the magazine under her chin.

FULL SHOT—PREACHER
Her hero strides away into darkness.

CLOSE SHOT—RUBY
Gazing after him.

RUBY I been bad! DISSOLVE TO

CLOSE DOWN-SHOT—THE MAGAZINE, OPEN, IN RACHEL'S LAP
We PULL UP and AWAY into:

TWO-SHOT—RACHEL, SEATED; RUBY STANDING BESIDE HER

RACHEL Ruby, you didn't have no money to buy this.

RUBY You'll whip me!

RACHEL When did I ever?

RUBY This man down at the Drugstore . . .

RACHEL The *Drugstore?*

RUBY Miz Cooper. I never went to sewin' lessons all them times.

RACHEL What you been up to?

RUBY I been out with men.
RUBY collapses face down over RACHEL's lap and sobs, as we TRACK IN CLOSE.

RACHEL Dear God, child!

Now RACHEL also weeps. She bends low over RUBY, stroking her hair.

RACHEL You was lookin' for *love*, Ruby, the only foolish way you knowed how. (she lifts Ruby's face cheek to cheek beside her own) We all need love. Ruby, I lost the love of my son—I've found it with you-all.

They weep together.

RACHEL You must grow up to be a fine, full woman; and I'm goin' to see to it you do.

She starts making up RUBY's hair like that of a young woman.

RUBY This gentleman warn't like *them!* He just give me a sody and the book.

RACHEL Now who was this?

RUBY He never asked me for nothin'.

RACHEL He must have wanted *somethin'*, Ruby. A man don't waste time on a girl unless he gets *something*.

RUBY shakes her head.

RACHEL What'd you all talk about?

RUBY Pearl and John.

RACHEL John and Pearl!

RUBY nods.

RACHEL Is he their Pap?

RUBY shrugs.

RACHEL Why hasn't he been to the house?   DISSOLVE TO

FULL SHOT—PREACHER ON HORSE ON ROAD

FULL FIGURE SHOT—RUBY
Seeing PREACHER, she drops two eggs.

RUBY (shouting) Miz Cooper!

RACHEL (o.s. from within house) What?

RUBY The man! The man!

TRACKING SHOT—PREACHER

He tethers his horse and, as we PAN and TRACK on behind him, walks to the bottom of the steps; RUBY moves into side of SHOT: beyond PREACHER, RACHEL stands behind her screen door, hands folded under apron.

PREACHER Mornin', ladies.

FULL FIGURE SHOT—RACHEL, BEHIND SCREEN

RACHEL How'do.

FULL FIGURE SHOT—PREACHER

RACHEL'S VIEWPOINT, through screen.

FULL FIGURE SHOT—RACHEL, BEHIND SCREEN

PREACHER You're Miz Cooper, I take it.

RACHEL (coming through door) It's about that John and that Pearl?

THREE-SHOT—PREACHER, RACHEL, RUBY IN BACKGROUND

PREACHER'S face twitches with emotion. He breaks out into great thankful sobs. He falls to his knees.

PREACHER My little lambs! To think I never hoped to see them again in this world! Oh, dear Madam, if you was to know what a thorny crown I have borne in my search for these strayed chicks!

CLOSE SHOT—RACHEL

She takes him in. He doesn't take *her* in.

THREE-SHOT—AS BEFORE

RACHEL Ruby, go fetch them kids.

RUBY minces off around the side of the house.

CLOSE SHOT—PREACHER—RACHEL'S ANGLE

He wipes off tears with the heel of his left hand, watching her.

PREACHER Ah, dear Madam, I see you're looking at my hands!

CLOSE SHOT—RACHEL

She is.

CLOSE SHOT—PREACHER—AS BEFORE

He holds up the right hand.

PREACHER Shall I tell ye the little story of Right-Hand-Left-Hand—the tale of Good and Evil?

CLOSE SHOT—RACHEL

PREACHER (o.s.) It was with this left hand that old brother Cain struck the blow that laid his brother low—

RACHEL (wanting to know) Them kids is yours?

CLOSE SHOT—PREACHER

PREACHER (recovering from the interruption) My flesh and blood!

CLOSE SHOT—RACHEL

RACHEL Where's your Missus?

TWO-SHOT—PROFILING RACHEL AND PREACHER

PREACHER gets to his feet.

PREACHER She run off with a drummer one night. Durin' prayer-meetin'.

RACHEL Where's she at?

PREACHER Somewheres down river! Parkersburg, mebbe!—Cincinnati!—One of them Sodoms on the Ohio River.

RACHEL She took them kids with her?

PREACHER Heaven only knows what unholy sights and sounds those innocent little babes has heard in the dens of perdition where she dragged them!

CLOSE SHOT—RACHEL

RACHEL Right funny, hain't it, how they rowed all the way up river in a ten-foot john-boat!

CLOSE SHOT—PREACHER
. . . recovering, and by-passing it.

PREACHER Are they well?
He turns his head.

FULL SHOT—RACHEL AND PREACHER, FROM SIDE
All the CHILDREN enter, around corner of house. As they move in, RACHEL replies:

RACHEL A sight better than they was.

By now JOHN is on the top step beside RACHEL. One of his hands holds on to her skirt, as if he were pulling her towards him. His eyes never leave hers. All the CHILDREN freeze, PEARL is on ground, just beyond JOHN. Others in BACKGROUND; RUBY as near PREACHER as she can get.

PREACHER Gracious, gracious! You are a good woman, Miz Cooper!

RACHEL How you figgerin' to raise them two without a woman?

PREACHER The Lord will provide.

PEARL, with a wail of happiness, drops the DOLL on the step and runs to PREACHER, who picks her up. JOHN instantly picks up the DOLL and holds it to him. He looks up at RACHEL.

CLOSE TWO-SHOT—JOHN AND RACHEL

JOHN looks deep into RACHEL's eyes.

PREACHER (o.s.) The Lord is merciful! What a day is this!—And there's little John!

RACHEL What's wrong, John?

JOHN Nothin'. (he smiles)

PREACHER (o.s.) Come to me, boy!

RACHEL What's wrong, John?

TWO-SHOT—PREACHER AND PEARL

PREACHER Didn't you hear me, boy?

TWO-SHOT—JOHN AND RACHEL

RACHEL bends a little over him. She wants the situation clarified.

RACHEL John, when your Dad says 'come', you should mind him.

JOHN He ain't my Dad.

HEAD CLOSE-UP—RACHEL

She takes this in; JOHN has sold her. She looks to PREACHER o.s.

RACHEL He ain't no Preacher neither. I've seen Preachers in my time, an' some of 'em was saints on earth. A few was crookeder'n a dog's hind leg, but this 'un's got 'em all beat for badness.

She starts to turn.

GROUP SHOT
She walks purposefully into the house. PREACHER lunges for JOHN and the DOLL.

CLOSE TWO-SHOT—PREACHER AND JOHN

JOHN ducks under the porch and PREACHER tries to follow him. He can't get under. O.s. we hear the slam of the screen door. PREACHER's head comes up to see and we TILT UP, shooting OVER the back of his head. RACHEL stands there, full figure, with a pump-gun.

RACHEL Just march yourself yonder to your horse, Mister.
Back of PREACHER's head is still immobile.

RACHEL March, Mister! I'm not foolin'.

CLOSE SHOT—PREACHER, OVER GUN-BARREL

PREACHER gets to his feet. The open knife is in his hand. As we see it, the gun-barrel twitches. PREACHER backs away towards his horse, bouncing the knife lightly in his hand.

PREACHER (screaming) You ain't done with Harry Powell yet! The Lord God Jehovah will guide my hand in vengeance! You devils! You Whores of Babylon! I'll come back when it's dark!

As he mounts his horse we   DISSOLVE TO

FULL SHOT—RACHEL'S HOUSE—NIGHT
It is dark. O.s. we hear PREACHER singing *Leaning*.

FULL FIGURE SHOT—RACHEL
She sits in profile, her gun across her knees. Song continues o.s.

FULL SHOT—THE CHILDREN, ASLEEP
. . . in a big bed. RUBY sits up, listening to song o.s.

FULL FIGURE SHOT—RACHEL, AS BEFORE
Song continues o.s. We PAN to PREACHER outside. We see him through window. He sits hunched on a stump.

FULL SHOT—THE HOUSE, OVER PREACHER
He continues singing.

HEAD PROFILE—RACHEL
After a moment we see her mouth open; and either to comfort herself or to drown out PREACHER's voice, she joins in the hymn.

FULL SHOT—THE HOUSE—AS IN OPENING SHOT
A descending candle moves past a window; RACHEL and PREACHER sing O.S.

FULL SHOT—PREACHER ON STUMP
. . . over back of RACHEL's head. The song ends. RUBY enters SHOT carrying a candle. Its light blacks out the window-glass. RACHEL looks up.

RACHEL Moonin' around the house over that mad dog of a Preacher! *Shame,* Ruby!

She blows out the candle. We see through the window. PREACHER has gone.

CLOSE SHOT—RACHEL

RACHEL Merciful Heaven!
She stands up.

CLOSE TWO-SHOT—RACHEL AND RUBY

RACHEL Ruby, get the children out of bed. Bring them all down here to the kitchen.

RUBY leaves the SHOT. RACHEL moves towards window. She puts her hand over her eyes.

RACHEL Women is such fools!
The soft hoot of an owl O.S. RACHEL looks up.

CLOSE SHOT—AN OWL ON A BRANCH, LOOKING DOWN

CLOSE SHOT—A BABY RABBIT

CLOSE SHOT—THE OWL SPREADS HIS WINGS AND SWOOPS

CLOSE SHOT—RACHEL
Still for a second; then O.S., the scream of a rabbit.

RACHEL It's a hard world for little things.

OVER this line we have heard the patter of feet down staircase. She turns.

GROUP SHOT—THE CHILDREN
They look at her with complete trust.

GROUP SHOT—RACHEL, OVER CHILDREN

RACHEL (snapping) Children, I got lonesome. I figgered we might play games.

PEARL and MARY jump up and down, patting their palms. RACHEL extends her hands and they gather close to her.

PEARL Won't you tell us a story?

CLOSE SHOT—RACHEL

RACHEL I might (a swift furious glance into the moonlight) I might tell A Story.

She sits down, the gun across her knees.

GROUP SHOT—RACHEL AND CHILDREN
. . . as MARY and PEARL sit at her feet. RUBY stands beside RACHEL. JOHN stands near RACHEL.

CLARY I'll light the lamp.

RACHEL It's more fun hearin' stories in the dark.

CLARY sits at RACHEL's feet.

CLOSE PANNING SHOT—JOHN
He is alert now. He moves in close beside RACHEL, whom we PAN into

CLOSE TWO-SHOT with him, and presses the whole of his right arm against her arm. RACHEL registers quietly.

CLOSE GROUP SHOT—RACHEL AND CHILDREN

RACHEL Well . . . mind what I told you about little Jesus and his Ma and Pa and how there was No Room at the Inn?

HEAD CLOSE-UP—RACHEL
Her eyes, sharp and glittering, look outside.

FULL SHOT—THE OUTSIDE, FEATURING EMPTY STUMP, RACHEL'S VIEWPOINT

GROUP SHOT—RACHEL AND CHILDREN
She gets up with gun; we PULL AWAY; in BACKGROUND, CHILDREN turn faces to keep watching her. She comes close to window, gun ready, CHILDREN in BACKGROUND

RACHEL Well now, there was this sneakin', no-'count, ornery King Herod! She turns round and walks back to her chair; CHILDREN's eyes always on her.

RACHEL And he heard tell of this little King Jesus growin' up and old Herod figgered: Well, shoot! There sure won't be no room for the both of us! (she sits down) I'll just nip this in the bud.

GROUP SHOT—RACHEL AND CHILDREN, FROM SIDE

RACHEL (continuing) Well, he never knowed for sure which one of all them babies of the land was King Jesus.

HEAD CLOSE-UP—RACHEL

Her eyes glittering as she turns to look towards us.

RESUME SIDE GROUP SHOT

RACHEL gets up, with gun. Again we PULL AWAY, as faces of all CHILDREN in b.g. turn to watch her.

RACHEL And so that cursed old King Herod figgered if he was to kill all the babies in the land, he'd be sure to get little Jesus.

Without speaking, she goes back to her chair.

FRONT GROUP SHOT

RACHEL (more relaxed) And when little King Jesus' Ma and Pa heard about that plan, what do you reckon they went and done?

CLARY They hid in a broom closet!

MARY They hid under the porch!

HEAD CLOSE-UP—JOHN

JOHN No; they went a-runnin'.

TWO-SHOT—RACHEL AND JOHN

RACHEL Well now, John, that's just what they done! *They* went a-runnin! The clock starts striking three. RACHEL looks to sound o.s.

FULL SHOT—CLOCK AND HALL MIRROR, BEYOND DARK KITCHEN
In the mirror, a shadow ducks.

FULL GROUP SHOT—RACHEL AND CHILDREN

RACHEL gets up, gun at port, and faces into the darkness.

PREACHER (o.s.) Figured I was gone, eh?
Eyes on the darkness, she bends low to the CHILDREN.

RACHEL (whispering) Run hide in the staircase! Run quick!
They scatter out of shot; RUBY lingers.

RACHEL (without turning to her) Ruby, git.

RUBY obeys in a trance. RACHEL, gun at ready, looks into the darkness.

FULL SCREEN—DARKNESS
Pause.

RACHEL (o.s.; in a high, steady voice) What do you want?

PREACHER (o.s.) Them kids!

RACHEL (o.s.) What are you after them *for*?

PREACHER (o.s.) None of your business, Madam.

RACHEL I'm givin' *you* to the count of three to get out that screen door; then I'm a-comin' across this kitchen *shootin'*!
A stepped-on cat screams o.s. and PREACHER's satanic face, and his hand lifting the open knife, rise swiftly from floor.

FULL FIGURE SHOT—RACHEL—SAME SHOT AS BEFORE
She fires off her gun.

FULL SHOT—SCREEN DOOR

PREACHER staggers out and runs yelping with pain into the barn. O.s. we hear the zing-zing of a country phone being cranked.

GROUP SHOT—RACHEL, OVER BACKS OF CHILDREN'S HEADS

They huddle on the stairs in reverent silence. RACHEL, her gun slung sportily under one arm, talks into wall phone which hangs just within the box stairway.

RACHEL Miz Booher? Rachel Cooper. Git them State Troopers out to my place. I done treed somep'n up in my barn.   DISSOLVE TO

FULL SHOT—RACHEL AND JOHN

RACHEL sits on the screened porch, awake, gun on knees. JOHN sits on floor, asleep, his head leaning against her. Barn in BACKGROUND. Sunrise.

CLOSE SHOT—RACHEL AND JOHN
Same position. JOHN awakes.

JOHN I'll see to Pearl.

RACHEL I'll make coffee.
They get up and start into kitchen.

GROUP SHOT—THE CHILDREN, OVER RACHEL AND JOHN
They lie huddled in calm sleep. JOHN and RACHEL watch a moment.

JOHN She's all right.
They start for the stove.

TWO-SHOT—RACHEL AND JOHN, AROUND STOVE

RACHEL puts her gun beside the stove, ready to hand, and picks up a coffee-pot; JOHN puts kindling in stove.

RACHEL John, you know? When you're little you have more endurance than God is ever to grant you again? Children are Man at his strongest. They abide.

JOHN looks at her a moment. O.s. we hear police car sirens. They look towards the sound.

FULL SHOT—THROUGH POLICE CAR WINDSHIELD
We SHOOT OVER two TROOPERS. Sirens loud, they rapidly approach RACHEL'S house as RACHEL, without gun, holding JOHN's hand, comes down to fence. Presently, the other CHILDREN hurry out of house behind. The car brakes.

FULL SHOT—RACHEL AND CHILDREN OVER TWO POLICE CARS—BARN IN BACKGROUND
The TROOPERS, fanning wide, advance towards barn. RACHEL and the CHILDREN are grouped a short distance behind them. The barn door gapes black. Short pause; then PREACHER appears.

A TROOPER (shouting) Is that him, Ma'am?

RACHEL (shouting) Yes! Mind where you shoot, boys! There's children here!

TROOPER Whyn't you call us up before?

RACHEL Didn't want yer big feet trackin' up my clean floors.

CLOSE SHOT—PREACHER
He stands, swaying; his left arm is bloody and helpless. In his right hand the open knife hangs apathetic. His eyes are glazed. He does not seem to care whether they come or not.

TROOPER'S VOICE (o.s.) Harry Powell, you're under arrest for the murder of Willa Harper!

MEDIUM SHOT—PREACHER AND TROOPERS—JOHN'S VIEWPOINT

TROOPERS close in on PREACHER, from before and behind, exactly as for BEN's arrest.

CLOSE SHOT—JOHN
The same sickly look, as at BEN's arrest.

MEDIUM SHOT—PREACHER AND TROOPERS—JOHN'S VIEWPOINT
One TROOPER smacks the back of PREACHER's head with a pistol-barrel.

CLOSE SHOT—JOHN

JOHN (shouting) Don't!

RESUME VIEWPOINT SHOT
Another TROOPER, with a pistol barrel, knocks the knife from PREACHER's lifted hand.

CLOSE SHOT—JOHN

JOHN (shouting) Don't!

RESUME VIEWPOINT SHOT

PREACHER sinks to his knees as both men, and two others from the front, close in on him. The tableau is the same as in BEN's arrest.

CLOSE SHOT—JOHN

JOHN (shouting) Dad!

FRONT GROUP SHOT—RACHEL AND CHILDREN

JOHN grabs the DOLL from PEARL and starts to run.

RACHEL John! John!
She starts after him.

FULL SHOT—TROOPERS, JOHN, RACHEL, OVER PREACHER

PREACHER prostrate along bottom of screen. TROOPERS are beating him. JOHN runs up from BACKGROUND followed by RACHEL. JOHN rushes among the TROOPERS, flogging PREACHER over the head with the DOLL. The TROOPERS, astounded, lay off. RACHEL is stopped in her tracks.

JOHN Here! Here! Take it back! I can't stand it, Dad! It's too much, Dad! I don't want it! I can't do it! Here! Here!

The DOLL has burst open and the money has spilled over PREACHER. Now two TROOPERS gently lift JOHN away. RACHEL lifts him in her arms; she turns towards house.

FULL FIGURE PULL SHOT—RACHEL AND JOHN—GROUP IN BACKGROUND
She carries JOHN towards the house. His head hangs back over her arm.
We hear his dry, exhausted sobs.

INT. COURTROOM—DAY—CLOSE SHOT—ICEY

ICEY (yelling) Lynch him! Lynch him!

TWO-SHOT—WALT AND ICEY

ICEY (yelling) Bluebeard!

WALT (yelling at all the men around him) Twenty-five wives!

ICEY And he killed every last one of 'em!

GROUP SHOT—WALT, ICEY, MEMBERS OF COURTROOM AUDIENCE
Perhaps ten faces. Most are frenetic. Our two LOAFERS are having fun.
General hubbub o.s. A gavel o.s.

ICEY (yelling) If the People of Marshall County . . .

LOAFERS (cynically, across her) Bluebeard! Bluebeard!

CLOSE SHOT—JOHN
He looks to sound of gavel. The hubbub and the gaveling stop.

LAWYER (o.s.) Will you identify the prisoner?

JOHN looks over his shoulder in same direction as the gavel.

LAWYER (o.s.) Please, little lad. Won't you look yonder . . . (his pointing
finger enters the shot. John shakes as if he had a cold) . . . and tell the
Court if that is the man who killed your mother?

JOHN looks at the finger. Short pause.

LAWYER (o.s.) It's all right, Mrs. Cooper. You can take the little fellow
away.

The LAWYER's hands gently help him from chair.

GROUP SHOT—RACHEL AND CHILDREN

. . . as LAWYER's hands consign JOHN to RACHEL.

LAWYER Merry Christmas to you and yours, Mrs. Cooper.
The CHILDREN bob and reply, ad lib, "Merry Christmas to *you*." RACHEL
sniffs.

LAWYER (o.s.) And what's Santy Claus going to bring *you,* little man? Above JOHN's head, by winding and holding to ear, RACHEL pantomimes a watch.

LAWYER (o.s.) O-*ho-oo-o!*

ICEY (o.s.) Them is the ones he sinned against, my friends! Gaveling starts.

LOAFER (o.s.) Bluebeard! Bluebeard!

CROWD (o.s.) Bluebeard! Bluebeard!
As RACHEL and CHILDREN turn to go, gaveling and hubbub fade and we
LAP DISSOLVE TO

INT. A CAFE—NIGHT

RACHEL and her CHILDREN sit in two booths, in a corner, next to a big front window. Christmas parcels on bench at RACHEL's right.

FULL SHOT—RACHEL AND HER GROUP, THEN CAFE AND WINDOW
Sound o.s. of approaching crowd. As we PULL BACK we bring in a few other customers and the big window. There are Christmas decorations in the cafe and the street outside is hung with them. Thirty feverish people, some of whom carry torches, enter the scene; ICEY stares in the window and screams.

ICEY (high-pitched) Them's hers!

Everyone in the cafe stands up. RACHEL gathers her parcels. ICEY rushes to door and opens it.

ICEY Them's her orphans!
She turns to crowd.

RACHEL Where's Ruby?

CLARY She went.

ICEY shouts into the cafe.

ICEY Them poor little lambs!

ICEY turns to the street mob. RACHEL hurries her CHILDREN to door.

ICEY leaves door to yell at mob.

ICEY Them's the ones he sinned against, my friends!

CASHIER (across Icey) Go out the back way, Miz Cooper.
As RACHEL leaves SHOT, the CASHIER shuts and locks the door.

EXT. BACK ALLEY—NIGHT—PANNING SHOT—RACHEL AND COMPANY EMERGING
FROM DOOR

MARY and CLARY come out first and start walking to our left. RACHEL comes
out and hurries off to our right, followed by JOHN, holding PEARL's hand.

We PAN to MARY and CLARY.

CLARY Ain't we goin' to the Bus Depot?
No answer. They turn and we PAN with them as they hurry after RACHEL,
and we bring in RACHEL, charging away from us with her brood hustling
to keep up.

GROUP SHOT—FEATURING WALT AND ICEY

ICEY carries a torch. She is flanked by rabid faces and by smiling LOAFERS,
one of whom carries an axe. As she speaks, a MAN rushes up to WALT and
gives him a rope.

ICEY (shouting; high-pitched) Draggin' the name of the Lord through
the evil mud of his soul!

WALT (bellowing) Come on!
They all start marching, in step.

PANNING SHOT—RACHEL AND CHILDREN
Marching and voices o.s. and in BACKGROUND.

Carrying Christmas parcels, they hurry alongside a building and, at
CENTER of PAN, cross the end of a street.

The MOB marches down the street TOWARDS CAMERA; Men run to join it.

ICEY (high-pitched) He lied!

WALT Tricked us!

ICEY He taken the Lord's name in vain and he trampled on His Holy
Book!

WALT String that Bluebeard up to a pole!

ICEY He's Satan hiding behind the Cross!

OTHERS (ad lib) Lynch him! String him up!

We PAN RACHEL and CHILDREN past this street and they hurry towards
RUBY, who stands alone in BACKGROUND, facing the jail.

HEAD CLOSE-UP—RUBY'S ECSTATIC FACE
In BACKGROUND, RACHEL and CHILDREN hurry towards her. MOB noise o.s.
Hearing the approach of RACHEL'S GROUP, RUBY turns the back of her head
towards us. Now there are no mob voices; only the ominous sound of
fifty-odd people marching in step.

RUBY I love him!

TRACKING SHOT—RUBY
Ominous silence.

RUBY He loves me because I'm so purty! You think he's like them others!

SIDE TRACKING SHOT—RUBY, RACHEL AND GROUP
Marching sound o.s.

RACHEL firmly takes RUBY's arm and drags her off in our direction. RACHEL
shoos MARY and CLARY ahead of her. JOHN and PEARL flank RACHEL, clinging
to her wide skirts. RUBY, nearest us, keeps looking back over her shoulder.
We TRACK them along side of JAIL to rear of JAIL.

RUBY (continuing) You took on something awful about him buying me
that there movie book. You was so mad you shot him and the blue men
took him.

On "blue men," we stop TRACKING and, as GROUP leaves SHOT, CENTER a
POLICE CAR, waiting at rear door of JAIL. POLICEMEN start out of door.

MEDIUM GROUP SHOT—POLICEMEN AND PREACHER
They roughly hustle PREACHER into the car. Marching sound o.s.

SHOT—FROM WITHIN CAR—BART

PREACHER and POLICE are in b.g. Through car window we see BART the
HANGMAN come out of his door. He wears his derby. A POLICEMAN puts
head out of window. Marching sound o.s.

MEDIUM SHOT—BART THE HANGMAN
On porch, by door, is a doll's perambulator, but this time there is a Christmas wreath on the door. Marching o.s.

POLICEMAN (o.s.) Hey *Bart!*
Auto engine starts up o.s.

HEAD CLOSE-UP—BART

BART Yeah?

MEDIUM SHOT—BART
Marching o.s.

POLICEMAN (o.s.) We're savin' this bird up fer *you!*

HEAD CLOSE-UP—BART
Marching o.s.

BART This time it'll be a privilege.

FULL PANNING SHOT—POLICE CAR, THEN RACHEL AND GROUP
The car jumps fast out of SHOT and we PAN PAST BART and CENTER RACHEL
and GROUP, walking fast away from us. Mob voices o.s.

A VOICE (o.s., over departing car) Bust the door down!

CLOSE GROUP SHOT—RACHEL AND CHILDREN
Clutching Christmas parcels they hurry away from us into darkness. RUBY,
hanging back, dragged by RACHEL, babbles over her shoulder.

RUBY (happily) They'll git him out. I'll git my things ready—my shawl
and my Mickey Mouse wristwatch that don't run and the straw hat with
the flower, and we'll be married and live happily ever after!

VOICES (o.s. ad lib, cutting across Ruby) Bust the door down! Set *fahr*
to it! Where's that axe! Climb up on the balcony! You six git 'round to the
back!

ICEY (o.s., screaming) *People of Marshall County!*

DISSOLVE TO

FULL SHOT—NIGHT LANDSCAPE—PINE TREES, AND SOFTLY FALLING SNOW

DISSOLVE TO

EXT. RACHEL'S HOUSE—EVENING; SNOWING—CLOSE SHOT—RACHEL AT MAILBOX
She peers into empty mailbox.

RACHEL Nothing!
She slams the box shut and, as we TILT and PAN, walks away from us
through snow towards her lighted house.

RACHEL I'm glad they didn't send me nothing! Whenever they do it's
never nothing I want but something to show me how fancy and smart
they've come up in the world.

She goes into the house.

INT. RACHEL'S KITCHEN
It is decorated for Christmas.

GROUP SHOT—RACHEL AND CHILDREN

Rachel enters; the four girls stand in line, packages ready; JOHN stands in b.g., in doorway to next room.

MARY Can we give you your presents now?

CLOSE SHOT—RACHEL

RACHEL Shoot! You don't mean to say you got me a present!
Their hands hold packages up to her.

RACHEL Shoot now!
She takes a package.

CLOSE SHOT—JOHN

RACHEL (o.s.) Why, Ruby!
Embarrassed, JOHN leaves the shot.

RACHEL (o.s.) A POT-HOLDER!

CLOSE SHOT—JOHN—NEW ANGLE

From a fruit bowl, he selects the biggest apple, shines it on his shirt, wraps it in the doily under his bowl, opens a drawer and gets out a clip clothespin, clips his package, and leaves shot.

RACHEL (o.s., continuing) And much neater than last year's, Ruby!
(Sound of tearing gift-paper o.s.)

RACHEL (o.s.) And Clary! *ANOTHER POT-HOLDER!* Ain't that thoughtful. I'm always burnin' my hands.

FULL SHOT—RACHEL, AND CHILDREN, OVER JOHN

. . . as he enters with present. RUBY and CLARY are standing aside; MARY and PEARL hold up a third pot-holder.

RACHEL And did you two make this *together?*
Both nod.

MARY You hop us, *some.*

CLOSE SHOT—RACHEL, ACCEPTING JOHN'S GIFT
She opens it.

RACHEL (quietly) John, that's the richest gift a body could have. (continued, briskly) You'll find *your* presents in the cupboard under the china-closet.

GROUP SHOT—RACHEL AND CHILDREN

RACHEL You know where, Ruby.

All turn and run through door except Ruby, whom RACHEL detains.

RACHEL Ruby: (she takes a box from her apron pocket) This is yours.
RUBY opens it quickly; it is a cheap costume-jewelry flower-spray. RUBY
and RACHEL kiss like grown women and RUBY goes to join the others.

FULL SHOT—RACHEL

She turns to her stove and is framed by Christmas garland in b.g.; banging
pots about and stirring; praying as she works, which is the best way to
pray.

Appropriate noise, o.s., of opening presents.

RACHEL Lord save little children! (bang) You'd think the world would
be ashamed to name such a day as Christmas for one of them . . . (bang)
. . . and go on the same old way. (she starts stirring) My soul is humble
when I see the way little ones accept their lot. (she pauses in stirring)
Lord save little children! The wind blows and the rain is cold. Yet, *they
abide.*

In BACKGROUND, the girls run upstairs, their new dresses over their arms.
RACHEL glances over her shoulder.

MEDIUM SHOT—JOHN—RACHEL'S VIEWPOINT

JOHN stands in next room, looking at something in his hand.

CLOSE SHOT—JOHN—IN OTHER ROOM

We see he holds a watch. He looks live any boy, rich or poor, with his first
watch.

HEAD CLOSE-UP—RACHEL

RACHEL (whispering, so that he does not hear) For every child, rich or
poor there's a time of running through a dark place; and there's no
word for a child's fear. A child sees a shadow on the wall, and sees a
Tiger. And the old ones say, "There's no tiger; go to sleep." And when
that child sleeps, it's a Tiger's sleep, and a Tiger's night, and a Tiger's
breathing on the windowpane. Lord save little children!

JOHN enters boldly behind her and, with a scrape, masterfully swings a
chair around close to her and straddles it. RACHEL turns her back to us. She
expects him to speak, he doesn't, so she fills in:

RACHEL That watch sure is a fine, loud ticker!

JOHN gives her a burning, proud smile.

RACHEL It'll be nice to have someone around the house who can give me the right time of day.

JOHN finds his tongue.

JOHN This watch is the nicest watch I ever had.

RACHEL A feller can't just go around with run-down, busted watches.
She turns back, face to us, and goes on with her stirring. JOHN goes off towards the staircase to join the girls; then turns back.

CLOSE SHOT—JOHN

JOHN I ain't afraid no more! I got a watch that ticks! I got a watch that shines in the dark!
He turns and hurries to the stairs.

HEAD CLOSE-UP—RACHEL
Over the sound of his running upstairs:

RACHEL (telling us) They abide and they endure.

LAP DISSOLVE TO

FULL SHOT—STARRY SKY

FADE IN TITLE:

THE END

The Bride Comes to Yellow Sky

"The Bride Comes to Yellow Sky"

The Bride Comes to Yellow Sky *was written by James Agee in 1951-1952 for Huntington Hartford Productions. Filmed in 1952, it was released through R.K.O. (combined with another short picture) under the title of* Face to Face. *Because of the light satire and elements of farce,* The Bride Comes to Yellow Sky *represents a departure from Agee's usual scenario techniques. Courage, however, remains its central theme.*

FADE IN

EXT. MAIN STREET OF YELLOW SKY—DUSK

Late summer dusk; SOUND of church bell O.S. PULL DOWN onto Potter's little home, of which the second story is a jail—barred windows. Jack Potter comes out his door, dressed for travel, carrying a bag. He walks a few steps, then glances back around at his house.

PRISONER (in upper window) So long, Marshal. Don't do nothing I wouldn't do.

POTTER Don't you do nothing I wouldn't, s'more like it. You lock yourself in right after mealtimes.

PRISONER You can trust me, Marshal.

POTTER I don't need to. I done tole Laura Lee to keep an eye on you. (pause; shyly) Well, so long. I'll be back in a couple of days.
He walks away.

PRISONER (calling after) Give my howdy to the gals in San Antone!

POTTER You do that when you git out. I ain't no hand fer it.

PRISONER Oh, I doan know, Marshal. They tell me still waters run deep.
Potter doesn't answer. He walks on away.

357

DOLLY SHOT—POTTER AND DEACON SMEED

Deacon Smeed falls in with him. CAMERA DOLLIES along with them. The following dialogue interrupted two or three times by eminently respectable people converging on the church. All treat Potter respectfully but a little remotely.

SMEED Evening, Mr. Potter.

POTTER Evening, Deacon.

SMEED Leaving town so soon again?

POTTER It's been most two months.

SMEED Oh *has* it indeed, indeed. Hm. And what's going to happen to your prisoner, if I may ask?

POTTER Laura Lee's gonna take care of him.

SMEED Mrs. Bates? (Potter nods) She'll bring him his meals?

POTTER He'll let himself out for 'em.

SMEED Do you think that—ah—looks right?

POTTER (quietly) Afraid I ain't worryin' *how* it looks, Deacon. It's the easiest way, and you know as well as I do, he ain't gonna make no trouble.

SMEED I'm afraid you don't care how *anything* looks, Mr. Potter.

POTTER Oh now, Deacon, don't start on that church business again!

SMEED I'm sorry, Marshal, but every respectable person in Yellow Sky agrees with me. If only for appearance' sake, you ought to come to church.

POTTER Looky here, Deacon. We never did get nowheres with that argument, and we never will. I ain't got nothin' against church-goin'; I just don't hold with it fer myself.

SMEED And then all these mysterious trips to San Antonio lately—
They pause in front of church.

POTTER Now looky here, Deacon—if you mean light women and such, you know I ain't a man to fool around with them.

SMEED Oh, you *misconstrue me,* Marshal, *indeed* you do. But . . . Caesar's wife, you know . . .
The church bell stops ringing.

POTTER How's that?

SMEED She must be *above* suspicion.

POTTER Well, who's suspicious? You?

SMEED Of course not, Marshal. Perish the thought. Only you never *say why* you're going to San Antonio.

POTTER (after a pause) Just business. Goodnight, Deacon.

SMEED Goodnight, Mr. Potter.

Potter walks ahead; he blows out his cheeks; his eyes focus gratefully on:

VIEWPOINT SHOT—"THE WEARY GENTLEMAN" SALOON   CUT TO

POTTER AS BEFORE

He checks his watch and speeds up out of shot.   CUT TO

MEDIUM SHOT—DEACON

He pauses at the church door, sees Potter enter the "Weary Gentleman", and goes into church, over SOUND of first hymn.   CUT TO

INT. "WEARY GENTLEMAN"—DUSK

There is a typical western bar, behind which Laura Lee, a woman in her fifties, is presiding as bartender. CAMERA PANS Potter to bar. He leaves his bag on a table near the door.

POTTER Evenin', Laura Lee.

LAURA LEE (behind bar) Hi, Jack.

JASPER Jack.

ED Howdy, Marshal.

POTTER Jasper,—Ed.

ED Leavin' town again?

POTTER That's right.

ED San Antone?

POTTER (nods; drinks) Laura Lee, you tell Frank no drinks, no foolin' around. Just come right straight here and eat and get right back again. 'Cause it's got the Deacon bothered, him goin' out at all.

LAURA LEE Aw, Smeed. I tell you, Jack, when you waded in here and cleaned the town up, it wasn't just a favor you done us. Everything's gettin' too blame respectable.

POTTER It was my job.

LAURA LEE I don't hold it agin you. But if things get too tame around here, you'll up an' quit town fer good.

POTTER Uh, uh. I aim to be buried here. Besides, long as ole Scratchy busts loose now an' then, things won't never get *too* tame.
OVER mention of Scratchy, Laura Lee's eyes focus on something o.s.

LAURA LEE (a little absently) Here's *to* 'im.
Potter's eyes follow hers.

MEDIUM SHOT—ALONG BAR—FROM THEIR ANGLE
A half-finished glass of beer, no customer.

CLOSE SHOT—POTTER
A glance from the beer to Laura Lee, a look of slightly concerned inquiry, meaning, "Is that Scratchy's?"

CLOSE SHOT—LAURA LEE
nodding.

LAURA LEE It don't work holding him to nothing, Jack. I figured maybe beer, on 'lowance . . .

POTTER Don't hear me hollerin', do you? It's worth tryin'. Only thing bothers me is if I'm out of town.

LAURA LEE He ain't due for another tear yet.

POTTER Ain't sure we can count on him hittin' 'em regular, no more. He's gettin' rouncier all the time.

JASPER (breaking a pause) What ye doin' in San Antone, Jack?
Laura Lee gives him a cold glance.

POTTER Just a business trip.
OVER this last, Scratchy comes in through a side door and up to bar, to a half-finished glass of beer.

POTTER Howdy, Scratchy.
Scratchy doesn't answer. Potter and others are quietly amused.

LAURA LEE What's wrong with ye, Scratchy? Cat got yer tongue?
Scratchy drinks glass down.

LAURA LEE (continuing) Yer last one tonight. Rather wait fer it?

SCRATCHY Just draw me my beer.

POTTER Ain't still sore, are ye, Scratchy?

SCRATCHY You know it was all in fun. What d'ye go an' plug me fer?

POTTER 'Tain't fun, Scratchy. Not skeerin' the daylights out o' folks that ain't used to gun-play.

SCRATCHY You're a fine one to talk about gunplay. Mean, sneakin' skunk!

POTTER Sneakin'? It was fair and above board, like it always is.

LAURA LEE He just beat ye to the draw, an' you know it.

SCRATCHY That don't make my leg no happier.

POTTER Mendin' a'right, Scratchy?

SCRATCHY Oh, *I* git around.

POTTER Just mind where ye git *to*, that's all I ask.

SCRATCHY Next time, I'll make *you* dance.

POTTER Better not be no next time. 'Cause next time, instead o' the meat o' the leg, I might have to pop you in the kneecap.

SCRATCHY You wouldn't do that.

POTTER I wouldn't want to. But I might have to, Scratchy, just to learn you. You don't know it but you're gettin' dangersome when you drink, lately.

SCRATCHY Me—dangersome? A good man with a gun's a safe man with a gun, an' I'm the best they is.

LAURA LEE When you're in yer likker, yeah. But you don't drink fer fun no more, Scratchy. You kinda go out o' yer head.

POTTER That's right, Scratchy. One o' these days you're gonna shoot to kill, an' swing fer it, an' then all of us'll be sorry.

SCRATCHY I don't need to kill nobody more—I got my notches, an' to spare—(he pats his gun)

POTTER That was all right, agin the kind o' varmints that used to be around here in the old days—You come in right handy. Sort of a scavenger, like a turkey-buzzard. But you can't go shootin' up law-abidin' citizens an' git away with it.

SCRATCHY (with extreme contempt) Who wants to shoot a law-abidin' citizen!

UNDER the above, Potter finishes his drink, pays, starts out.

POTTER Well . . .

SCRATCHY You leavin' town again?

POTTER 'Bye, Laura Lee. See you day after tomorrow. (to Scratchy) You watch yer drinkin' while I'm gone.

SCRATCHY I'll save it all up fer you, Jack. 'Tain't nobody else is wuth the hangover.

Potter exits.

JASPER Reckon what he's up to, all these trips to San Antone?

LAURA LEE Never you mind, it's his business.

ED You ain't sweet on Jack, are ye, Laura Lee?

LAURA LEE (a cold look at him) Only man I ever was, he's in his grave ten year.

SHE HEARS the train draw out, pours and drinks.

LAURA LEE (continuing) But if I was, that's the only one *man* enough since. CUT TO

INT. DAY COACH—CLOSE SHOT—POTTER—NIGHT

He finishes rolling a cigarette, lights it and, elbow on windowsill, settles into the tired posture of night travel, gazing out of window. CAMERA SLOWLY PANS, losing his face, then his reflected face, squaring on the dark land flooding past. FADE OUT

FADE IN

INT. PARLOR CAR

CAMERA LOOKS SQUARELY through window at fast-moving daylit land, reversing direction of preceding shot; then in a SLOW PAN picks up the reflection of Bride's face in window; then the face itself; then PULLS AWAY into:

TWO-SHOT—POTTER AND BRIDE

For a few moments we merely HOLD on them, as though this were a provincial wedding portrait of the period. (Circa 1895) He has an outdoor clumsiness in his new suit, which is a shade tight and small for him.

Her very new-looking hat and dress are in touchingly ambitious, naive taste.

Between their heads, in the seat just behind theirs, the head of a "sophisticated" man turns slowly, slyly watching, filled with patronizing amusement. Potter, gradually aware, turns and looks him in the eye; the guy shrivels and turns away fast.

HOLD on Bride and Potter a moment. Bride looks at something o.s.

MEDIUM SHOT—TWO WOMEN
watch her, whispering and giggling.

MEDIUM SHOT—CENTERING POTTER AND BRIDE—FROM VIEWPOINT OF WOMEN

The Bride smiles very sweetly, looking straight into the CAMERA, and we HEAR o.s. a more intense giggling and whispering and a few inaudible words.
The Bride looks a little puzzled, her smile fading; then she smiles again, sure there can be no malice toward her; then looks straight ahead of her. Both are glowing and intensely shy. His large, spread hands englobe his knees; hers are discreet in her lap. He stares straight ahead, his eyes a little unfocused. She keeps looking around. With almost the manner of a little girl, she draws a deep breath and utters a quiet sigh of joy, at the same time slightly raising, then relaxing, the hands on her lap. He hears her happy sigh; he looks at her; he watches her shyly and with a certain awe. He slowly shakes his head in the manner of one who can scarcely believe his good fortune. He lifts his own hands from his knees; decides they were where they belong; carefully replaces them. When he finally speaks he tries to be light and tender and it is clear that the loudness of his voice startles and embarrasses him, and in the b.g. heads flinch slightly.

POTTER WELL, MRS. POTTER!

BRIDE (by reflex) Shh!
Both are terribly embarrassed.

POTTER (quick and low) Sorry! Frog in my throat.

BRIDE (ditto) I'm sorry, I didn't mean to shush you. It just made me jump's all.

POTTER You shush me any time yer a mind to.

BRIDE (after a pause; with shy daring) You *call* me that, any time yer a mind to. 'Cause I like to hear you say it. Only not so loud.

POTTER (after a pause, whispering it, very shy) Mrs. Potter . . .
Overwhelmed by his daring, he blushes and looks away. She shivers
with quiet delight; she glances up at him, then all around, with shy
pride; then, as delicately as if it were asleep, she moves her hands in her
lap as to uncover her wedding ring, and slowly, almost unbelievingly,
lowers her eyes and looks at it. Then she looks around again, speculatively.

BRIDE Think they can tell we just got m—— (she speaks the word almost
sacredly) married?

POTTER Don't see how they would. We ain't treatin' 'em to no lovey
dovey stuff or none o' that monkey business.

BRIDE (whisper) Jack!

POTTER 'Scuse me.

BRIDE It's all right.

POTTER No it ain't neither. It ain't fittin' I talk to you like that.

BRIDE Yes it is, Jack. I reckon it just kinda crep up on me from behind.
Silent, they look out the window. They have run out of talk. They have
plenty to think about, but soon he feels he has to make conversation.

POTTER This-yer train sure does gobble up the miles, don't it?

BRIDE My yes. Just goes like the wind.

POTTER It's a thousand mile from one end o' Texas to the other, and it
don't only stop but four times.

BRIDE My land!

POTTER It only stops for water at Yaller Sky.

BRIDE Oh.

POTTER Hope you ain't gonna mind. What I mean, it's a good town, but
it might look awful puny, side o' San Antone.

BRIDE Oh no. I never did like a big town. I like it where ever'body knows
ever'body else.

POTTER You'll like it there then.
They run out of talk again. She looks around with more and more
appreciation of the opulence and splendor of the car. CAMERA PANS around
Pullman car.

BRIDE'S VOICE (o.s.) I just can't get over it! (pause) It's all so handsome and rich-lookin'!

POTTER'S VOICE (o.s.) Yeah. They do it in style, sure enough, don't they?

BRIDE'S VOICE (o.s.) It's just like it was a palace or sumpin'. Even the ceilin'!

MEDIUM SHOT—A FANCY CEILING OIL PAINTING—CUPIDS, ETC.

POTTER'S VOICE (o.s.) Gee. You sure do notice things. I never even seen it.

CLOSE SHOT—POTTER
who has been looking up.

POTTER (continuing) Ever rode a parlor car before?

BRIDE No.

POTTER Me neither. One of these days we'll go on a trip overnight. Both are quietly aghast with embarrassment.

POTTER (struggling) I mean, I always did have a hankerin' to see what them Pullman berths are like.

BRIDE (helping him) This is wonderful enough.

POTTER Shucks. This ain't *nothing*. After a while we'll go forward to the diner and get a big layout. Ever et in a diner?

BRIDE No. I always took me along some lunch.

POTTER Finest meal in the world. Charge a dollar.

CLOSE THREE SHOT—POTTER, BRIDE AND SOPHISTICATED MAN
Sophisticated man registers, "God, what rubes!"

BRIDE A dollar? Why that's too much—for us—ain't it, Jack?

POTTER Not this trip, anyhow. We're gonna do the whole thing.

He swells up, a little like a nabob, and looks away so she can look at him admiringly.   DISSOLVE TO

INSERT:

INT. SCRATCHY'S HOUSE (ADOBE)—DAY

EXTREME CLOSE SHOT
Sighting above the bore of a long-barreled, blue-black revolver, against a raggedly-curtained window.

INSERT:

The smoothly spinning cylinder of the revolver. Scratchy's other hand, with a rag, wipes the weapon clear of cleaning oil; the weapon is turned this way and that, lovingly, catching the light; then is sighted along, aiming it at Indians on a calendar, and is dry fired, with a click of the tongue and a whispered, "Got ye that time, ye dog!"; then it is laid delicately down on a patchwork quilt. CAMERA PANS with Scratchy's hand to a pint whiskey bottle on the floor by the bed. (Next to it is another bottle, empty.) Hand and bottle move out of shot; SOUND of drinking; bottle is returned, a good inch lower; hand unwraps a second revolver from a worn, fine old napkin. Then a rag, then a little can of cleaning oil and a little rod. The hands start cleaning revolver.

OVER THIS ENTIRE SCENE, Scratchy Wilson's voice is HEARD, deeply and still tranquilly drunk, humming as much as singing, "Brighten The Corner". The singing is of course interrupted; by his muttered line; by occasional shortness of breath; by his drinking and a sharp cough afterward; and just as it resumes after the drinking, the voice is raw. But in overall mood it is as happy and innocent as a baby talking to itself in its crib. Over hand cleaning revolver,   CUT TO

INT. PARLOR CAR—DAY
MEDIUM SHOT—CENTERING POTTER AND BRIDE
The dining steward walks through SHOT fast, hitting chimes.

STEWARD Fust call for dinnah! Fust call!
Only Potter and Bride react. A quick exchange of glances and they get up and follow steward out of shot.

INT. DINING CAR—DAY
MEDIUM SHOT

Shooting past waiters ranked ready beside empty tables as Potter and Bride enter the car, registering abrupt dismay at all the service, whiteness, glitter and loneliness.

VIEWPOINT SHOT—THREE WAITERS
solicit them, with knowing glances.

MEDIUM SHOT—DOLLY
The waiter nearest them tries to steer them toward a two-some table. Potter, in a replying spasm of independence, steers Bride to a 4-chair table opposite. The two sit down side by side as CAMERA DOLLIES sidelong into a

TWO SHOT

POTTER (low) Looks like we're the only customers.

Instantly a hand plants a large menu in Potter's hand, blocking off his face, and then the same to the Bride.

WAITER'S VOICE (juicy, o.s.) There you are, sir! An' how're *you*-all today!

Potter slowly lowers menu, looks to waiter. Bride, ditto, looks to Potter.

POTTER Gone up on yer prices, ain't ye?

WAITER'S VOICE (o.s.) Things are costin' more all ovah, these days. (oily) Matter o' fact, though, we can 'commodate folks of more moderate means. (his finger reaches down and points out on menu) There's a nice gumbo, good sandwiches . . .

POTTER (across him) We'll have the dollar and a quarter dinner.

The Bride watches him with admiration.

WAITER Yes indeed, sir. The chicken or the ham, sir? The ham is *mighty* delicious today, sir.

POTTER Chicken.

WAITER Yes, *sir!*

They unfold their napkins. Potter glances about.

VIEWPOINT UP-SHOT

Several waiters pretend not to watch.

BRIDE AND POTTER AS BEFORE

As Bride settles her napkin in lap, he starts tucking his high into his vest.

DISSOLVE TO

EXT. "WEARY GENTLEMAN" SALOON—DAY

DOLLY SHOT

Following the nattily dressed Drummer through swinging doors into INT. "WEARY GENTLEMAN" SALOON, we pause and shoot past him as he hesitates and looks around at Jasper, Laura Lee and Frank. All glance at him casually and resume talking.

FRANK Not even a small beer?

LAURA LEE (sliding a tall one toward Jasper) Not even that, Frank. What's more, it's high time you locked yourself back in. 'Cause Jack Potter's treatin' you white, an' it's up to you to treat him the same. Now git along with ye.

CLOSE SHOT—DRUMMER

Over "lock yourself back in," he registers sharp interest, glancing keenly back and forth between Frank and Laura Lee.

FRANK'S VOICE (o.s.) He'd treat me a whole lot whiter if he'd get back when he said he would.

LAURA LEE'S VOICE (o.s.) He ain't but a day late.

FRANK'S VOICE (o.s.) A day's a long time when you spend it in jail.

Drummer registers curiosity and consternation and looks exclusively at Frank.

NEW ANGLE—LAURA LEE AND FRANK

LAURA LEE Read them magazines he give ye.

CAMERA PANS with Frank as he starts toward door, HOLDING on Drummer.

FRANK Done read 'em four or five times. Git tired of it, all that bang-bang stuff. (to Drummer) Howdy, stranger.

He walks on out.

DRUMMER (belated and odd) Howdy.

CAMERA PANS with his walk up to the bar.

DRUMMER (to Laura Lee) Did I hear that man correctly, ma'am? Is he a *jail-bird?*

LAURA LEE If you want to put it that way.

DRUMMER (looks to Jasper who is wholly neutral) Well! (he looks to both; both are neutral) Well!

LAURA LEE What'll ye have, mister?

DRUMMER Beer, please, a big head on it.
Laura Lee draws and hands it to him, sizing him up.

LAURA LEE Big head.

DRUMMER Nice little town.

LAURA LEE It'll pass.

DRUMMER Oh, I've had quite a profitable morning's work. (he sips)

LAURA LEE That'll be a nickel, mister.
He pays and sips again.

DRUMMER Matter of fact, I'm a Drummer.

LAURA LEE I can see that.

DRUMMER That's right. I travel in stockings. "Ex*quis*ite" stockings. (hustling his sample case to bar) Paris to your doorstep, that's our slogan. Now if you're willing to spare a moment of your time, I can *promise* you, a lady of your taste and refinement, you just won't be able to *resist!*

LAURA LEE (across him) Don't trouble yourself, mister, I don't—
But the drummer is already lifting the lid of the case. She leans her arms on it, nipping his fingers.

LAURA LEE (continuing)—Now, looky here, young feller; I ain't even a'goin' to *look* at them fool stockin's, let alone *resist* 'em.

OVER THIS, two Mexican sheepherders enter quietly by the rear door and sit at a table.

LAURA LEE (to Mexicans) What's yours, Narciso Gulliermo Diorisio Mario?

1st MEXICAN Cervezas
The second Mexican nods.

DRUMMER (sucking his fingers) That hurt, ma'am.

LAURA LEE (drawing beer) Wouldn't be surprised.

JASPER Seen Scratchy around, Laura Lee?

LAURA LEE Not since t'other night.

JASPER Gittin' so ye can't count on him fer nothin'. He was 'sposed to clair out my cess-pool yesterday. Never showed up.

LAURA LEE (pause—quietly) Can't say as I blame him, Jasper; that's a job ye do yourself—and nobody ought to have to do it for him.

JASPER Well—sometimes ye gotta take what ye can git.
She is silent.

JASPER (continuing) All I hope is, he ain't a-tyin' one on.

CLOSE SHOT—LAURA LEE

LAURA LEE If I had to do a job like that fer you, I might tie on a few myself.

CAMERA PANS as she takes beer to end of bar. First Mexican pays and takes them. She sits on her stool, looking at nobody.

A NEW ANGLE—JASPER
He watches her, nettled, and a little malicious.

JASPER Hey, Laura Lee.

LAURA LEE Yeah.

JASPER Reckon what Jack Potter's *up* to in San Antone.

LAURA LEE Reckon what business 'tis o' yourn.

JASPER Just figured he might of *told you*.

LAURA LEE (quiet and stern) Jack Potter ain't tied to *my* apron strings, nor nobody's.   FAST WIPE TO

INT. DINING CAR—DAY
Potter and Bride are finishing their desserts opposite a wooden, middle-aged married couple, (the car is now full of people).

We INTER--CUT CLOSE SHOT as Potter and the man meet glances; Bride and woman do same. Potter glances secretively down at his lapel and, privately as he can, scratches with his thumb-nail at a food stain.

Their voices are low:

BRIDE Don't worry. I can get that off in a jiffy.

POTTER Ain't likely I'll wear it much, nohow.

BRIDE Why, you'll wear it a-Sundays, church an' all.

POTTER (uneasy) I ain't never been much of a hand for church.

BRIDE You don't ever go?
Potter uneasily shakes his head.

BRIDE (continuing; uneasy) I don't know what I'd do, for lonesomeness, without no church to go to.

WAITER'S VOICE (o.s.) Look what I done brung yah both! An extra pot of nice fresh coffee.

VIEWPOINT UP-SHOT cuts into his line.
He leans over, setting down pot, beaming, proprietary, working for a big tip.

NEW ANGLE—POTTER AND BRIDE
Mild embarrassment reactions; they murmur appreciations ad lib.

BRIDE Want some more?

POTTER No thanks.

She pours for herself. The sugar is not in easy reach.

POTTER (formally, to other man) Pass the sugar, please.

MAN (glumly) Certainly.

POTTER Thank you.

MAN Certainly.

POTTER (to Bride) Sugar?

BRIDE Sure you won't have some more coffee?

POTTER All right. Thanks. Thank you.

BRIDE Certainly.

She leans to pour for him, much enjoying serving him, and knocks her napkin from the edge of the table to the floor between them. Both quickly stoop to reach for it.

INSERT:

Their hands touch accidentally and fly apart as if they had struck a spark.

BOTH *'Scuse* me!

TWO SHOT—POTTER AND BRIDE AS BEFORE

As they straighten up quickly, Potter bumps the table making a clatter and the Bride slops a little of the coffee from the pot in her other hand onto their clothes.

TOGETHER: POTTER (to everyone) *'Scuse* me. **BRIDE** (to him) Gee, I'm sorry.

REVERSE ANGLE

The two older people exchange unsmiling glances and pretend nothing is happening.

POTTER AND BRIDE AS BEFORE

He with his handkerchief, she with his napkin, they gently dab coffee off each other; they are embarrassed but not at all at odds.

As the waiter's arm presents the check to Potter, the CAMERA LIFTS AND TILTS, DOLLYING gently in to center his right hand near his trousers pocket. The hand makes the odd, helpless gesture of putting aside a holster which isn't there.

BRIDE'S VOICE (o.s.) What's the matter?

POTTER'S VOICE (o.s.) Just habit I reckon. Fust time in years I ain't totin' a gun.

CAMERA ZOOMS, centering.   FAST DISSOLVE TO

INT. SCRATCHY'S—DAY—CLOSE VIEWPOINT SHOT
Scratchy's loaded cartridge belt lies heavy and lethal across his knees. He thumbs in the last cartridge and lays aside the belt. The CAMERA, as Scratchy rises to his feet, goes into a short SPINNING BLUR IN AND OUT OF FOCUS.

SCRATCHY'S VOICE (o.s.) Whoa there.

CAMERA proceeds into a slow, wobbly DOLLYING PAN, past window and bureau to pegs where Scratchy's hand fumbles among his few clothes. Most of them are old and poor but his hands select and get off the hook a violently fancy pseudowestern shirt on which CAMERA comes into ULTRA SHARP FOCUS. Then one hand, as CAMERA CREEPS IN, FOCUS DITTO, reaches for a real shocker of a necktie, muffs it, and as CAMERA comes into EXTREME CLOSE SHOT, drags it drunkenly, snakily, slithering from its hook. All this time Scratchy is muttering and humming. OVER the slithering tie we

                                                            IRIS OUT

IRIS IN
INT. PARLOR CAR—DAY
Center CAMERA on Potter's more conservative tie. Tense and uneasy, he adjusts it.

TWO SHOT—POTTER AND BRIDE
He is tense; she is content. He takes out and looks at a thick hunter watch. Watching him, she realizes his uneasiness. She checks her own watch with his.

BRIDE Mine's slow.

POTTER Nope: I trust yourn. She's a seventeen jeweller.
Behind them, the "sophisticated" man slopes an amused eye.

BRIDE Gracious.
Potter corrects his watch, pockets it and avoids her eyes. She watches him. An uneasy silence. He looks at his watch again.

BRIDE (continuing) Jack.

POTTER Hmm.

BRIDE Somethin's eatin' at you.

POTTER Me?

She nods—a pause.

POTTER Nuthin' much. Only I wisht I'd sent a telegram.

BRIDE Thought you did, there at the depot.

POTTER I just tore it up.

Silence.

BRIDE (shyly) Was it—about us—gittin' married this morning?

POTTER I oughta told 'um, back in Yaller Sky. That's all. You see, they're so used to me bein' a bachelor an' all. They ain't gonna take it no way good, me never tellin' 'em—an' all of a sudden I come home married—(an inarticulate pause; ashamed)—Reckon I'm just plain bashful.

BRIDE (very shy) Reckon I feel the same.

He looks at her, unbelieving. She corroborates her statement with a little nod. They are so relieved they awkwardly resist an impulse to join hands and both face rigidly front, their tension growing.

                                                            FAST DISSOLVE TO

INT. SCRATCHY'S HOUSE—DAY

A lurching CLOSE PAN to a broken, distorting mirror. The CAMERA is on Scratchy, and the reflection is his. He is wearing a fancy shirt, both revolvers and the cartridge belt and he has to stoop to see himself. He is in a reeling slouch, glaring, stinking drunk. He draws closer, making savage faces which are still more savagely distorted in the mirror. He becomes momentarily fascinated by these distortions. He draws both guns and lurches into EXTREME CLOSEUP, growling low:

SCRATCHY All right, Jack Potter. Yore time has come!

CAMERA PULLS BACK centering hands getting, from his dresser drawer, a newish hat as phony as the shirt. The hands lift this through the shot as valuably as the Holy Grail and CAMERA again LEANS for mirror reflection as he preens the hat on his head.   DISSOLVE TO

INT. "WEARY GENTLEMAN"—DAY

CLOSE SHOT—THE DRUMMER

His eyes fixed almost on the lens in the cold manner of a snake charming a bird. CAMERA PULLS AWAY along his fully extended, shirt-sleeved, and fancily sleeve-gartered arm. It is clothed to the armpit in a super-sheer, elaborately clocked dark stocking.

DRUMMER (soft and almost lascivious) Speaks louder than words, doesn't it! (he shifts his eye o.s.) *You* tell her, gentlemen; in *all your experience,* did you ever meet a lady that wouldn't *swoon* just to look at it? (eyes back to center) Sheer as twilight air. And just look at that clocking! (he points it out, then his subtle hand impersonates a demi-mondaine foot) Nothing like it ever contrived before, by the most inspired continental designers, to give style to the ankle and moulding to the calf. (he runs fingers up his arm to the armpit, his eyes follow) And they run all the way up—opera length. (he casts his eyes down, then returns to off-center and gives his eyes all he's got. With a trace of hoarseness, almost whispering) How about it, madam? (He gives her an homme-fatale smile. A grand pause.)

TWO SHOT—JASPER AND ED
They look toward him with quiet disgust.

TWO SHOT—TWO MEXICANS
They glance at each other and toward Laura Lee.

CLOSE SHOT—LAURA LEE
She gives the merchandise one more cold, fascinated once-over, then looks the Drummer in the eye.

LAURA LEE All right son. I'm still resistin'. So, fork over that dollar.

DRUMMER But madam, you haven't given the Exquizzit—

LAURA LEE (across him) Save yer breath young feller. Why, if my husband had caught me in a pair o' them things, he'd 'a' broke my jaw. You're in the *wrong territory,* son. 'Cause this is a man's country. It's hard country. A young man comes in quickly.

YOUNG MAN Scratchy Wilson's drunk an' he's turned loose with both hands.

Both Mexicans set down their unfinished beers and fade out the rear door. The Drummer views with mystification; nobody pays any attention to him. They're as quick and efficient as a well-rehearsed fire-drill. Jasper and Ed go out the front door and close the window shutters. The young man bolts the rear door. Laura Lee bars the window on her side and goes center, swinging shut one leaf of the plank door. As Jasper and Ed return, Jasper swings the other shut and bars his window and Ed brings from the corner the bar for the main door and helps Laura Lee put it in place. Laura Lee returns to her place behind the bar. In the sudden, solemn, chapel-like gloom, the Drummer is transfixed; his eyes glitter.

DRUMMER Say, what *is* this?
A silent reaction from the men.

DRUMMER (continuing) Is there going to be a gun-fight?

JASPER (grimly) Dunno if there'll be a fight or not, but there'll be some shootin'—some good shootin'.

YOUNG MAN Oh, there's a fight just *waitin'* out there in the street, if anyone wants it.

Jasper and Ed nod solemnly.

DRUMMER (to young man) What'd ye say his name was?

ALL Scratchy Wilson.
The Drummer does a fast multiple take, person-to-person.

DRUMMER What're you goin' to do?
Grim silence.

DRUMMER (continuing) Does he do this often?

More silence.

DRUMMER (continuing) Can he break down that door?

LAURA LEE No: he's give that up. But when he comes you'd better lay down on the floor, stranger. He's dead sure to *shoot* at that door, an' there's no tellin' what a stray bullet might do.

The Drummer, keeping a strict eye on the door, begins carefully removing the stocking from his arm.

DRUMMER Will he kill anybody?
The men laugh low and scornfully.

JASPER He's out to shoot, an' he's out fer trouble. Don't see no good *experimentin'* with him.

DRUMMER But what do you *do* in a case like this? What do you do?

YOUNG MAN Why, he an' Jack Potter—

JASPER AND ED (across him) Jack ain't back yet.

YOUNG MAN (suddenly frightened) *Lordy!*

DRUMMER Well who's he? What's *he* got to do with it?

YOUNG MAN He's Marshal.

LAURA LEE Comes to shootin', he's the only one in town can go up agin him.

Far off, o.s. we HEAR a wild Texas yell, a shot, another yell. Everyone becomes very still and tense.

DRUMMER (half whispered) That must be him comin', hey?
The men look at him in irritation and look away again. They wait, their eyes shining in the gloom. Jasper holds up three fingers. Moving like a ghost, Laura Lee gets out three glasses and the bottle. The Drummer lifts one forlorn finger; she adds another glass. They pour. In unison they snap the drinks down at a gulp and walk to windows to look through chinks. The Drummer quietly puts a coin on the bar. Laura Lee just looks at it, at him, and away.
He shamefacedly takes back his coin. She silently takes a Winchester from beneath the bar and breaks it.

DRUMMER (whispered) You goin' to *shoot* him?
Silence; everyone looks at him bleakly.

LAURA LEE (low) Not if I can help it. I ain't a good enough shot. Might kill him.

DRUMMER Well, it'd be pure self defense if you did, wouldn't it?
No answer.

DRUMMER (continuing) Well, *wouldn't* it? Good riddance *too, I'd* say.

LAURA LEE closes the breech.

LAURA LEE (low) Mister, Scratchy Wilson's an old friend. Nobody'd harm a hair of his head if they's any way out—let alone kill him. You see, trouble is, he's a wonder with a gun. Just a wonder. An' he's a terror when he's drunk. So when he goes on the war trail, we hunt our holes—naturally.

DRUMMER But—why do they allow him—what's he doin' in a town like this?

LAURA LEE He's the last of the old gang that used to hang out along the river here.
A silence. Then nearer, but distant, a howl is HEARD. The Drummer reacts, jittery.

LAURA LEE (continuing) You better come back o' the bar. I kinda fixed it up.

DRUMMER (ashamed) No thanks, I'll—

LAURA LEE (with a peremptory gesture) Come on.

He does. He squats low in the front angle of the bar and examines, with some relief, the various plates of scrap metal with which she has armored it. o.s., nearer, we HEAR another shot and three yowls. There's a shuffling of feet. They look at each other.

MEN (quietly) Here he comes!

PAN SHOT
We DOLLY with Laura Lee, carrying her gun, to look through a chink in the shutter, and through the chink see Scratchy round the corner at the far end of the empty street, yelling, a long heavy blue-black revolver in either hand. We HEAR his words, distant, but preternaturally powerful, as he strides to the middle of the street and stops dead, both guns alert, threatening and at bay.

SCRATCHY *Yaller Sky, hyar I come!*

MEDIUM SHOT—SCRATCHY
He holsters a revolver, extracts a pint bottle from his belt, cocks it vertically and drains it, and tosses it high and glittering into the sunlight, in mid-air; then shoots it into splinters, left-handed, and does a quick 360-degree whirl, drawing both guns, as if against enemies ambushing him from the rear. He raises a small tornado of dust. CUT to a HEAD CLOSEUP into which he finishes his pivot, glaring. His eyes are glittering, drunk, mad, frightening. He is eaten up with some kind of interior bitter wildness.

SCRATCHY (a low growl) Got ye, ye yaller-bellies!
PULL DOWN AND AWAY. He gives a lonely Texas yowl; the echoes die. He glares all about him; his eyes, focusing on something o.s., take on sudden purpose.

SCRATCHY (loud) Jack Potter!

MEDIUM SHOT—WITH STILL CAMERA—POTTER'S HOUSE—FREEZE CLOSER SHOT—SCRATCHY
trying to adjust his eyes to this oddity.

SCRATCHY (louder) Jack Potter!

MED. SHOT—POTTER'S HOUSE—AS BEFORE

SCRATCHY'S VOICE (o.s.) You heared me, Jack Potter. Come on out an' face the music. Caze it's time to dance.

CLOSE SHOT—SCRATCHY
Dead silence.

He is puzzled.

SCRATCHY 'Tain't no ways like you Potter, asullin' there in yer house. You ain't no possum. I treated ye fair an' square. I saved it all up for ye, like I told ye. Now you play square with me.

FRANK'S VOICE (o.s., scared) Hey, Scratchy.

SCRATCHY (puzzled, looking around) How's that? Who *is* that?

POTTER'S HOUSE—PAST SCRATCHY
FRANK'S VOICE Hit's me. Frank.

SCRATCHY Why don't ye say so. Whar ye at?

FRANK'S VOICE I'm up yere in the jail.

SCRATCHY Well *show* yerself! What ye skeered of?

FRANK'S VOICE You.

SCRATCHY Me? Shucks. Only man needs to be skeered o' me is Jack Potter, the yaller hound.

FRANK'S VOICE Jack ain't here, Scratchy.

SCRATCHY What ye mean he ain't here?

FRANK'S VOICE He ain't got back yet, that's what I mean. That's what I was tryin' to tell you.

SCRATCHY Ain't back! Don't gimme none o' that. He come back yesterday when he promised he would.

FRANK'S VOICE No he didn't.

SCRATCHY You lie to *me*. Frank Gudger, I'll give ye what *fer*.

He shoots, striking a bar and ringing a musical note.

FRANK'S VOICE Scratchy! Don't do that! Hit's dangersome.

SCRATCHY Not if ye keep yer head low it ain't.

FRANK'S VOICE 'Tis too. Ye can't tell *whar* them bullets'll *rebound*.

SCRATCHY Don't you dast tell me how to shoot, ye pore wall-eyed woods colt. *Is* Jack Potter back or *ain't* he?

FRANK'S VOICE No he ain't and that's the honest truth.

SCRATCHY Don't you *sass me.*

CLOSE SHOT
Scratchy shoots another bar, ringing a different musical note, which is followed by a shattering of glass.

SCRATCHY (continuing) Is he back?

FRANK'S VOICE Quit it, Scratchy. Ye done busted my lamp chimbley.

SCRATCHY *Is* he back or *ain't* he?

FRANK'S VOICE All right, have it yer own way. He's back if you say so.

SCRATCHY Well, why didn't you tell me so straight off?
No answer.

SCRATCHY (continuing) Why don't he come on out then?

FRANK'S VOICE Reckon he would if he was inside.

SCRATCHY Oh, he ain't inside, huh?

FRANK'S VOICE Not that I know of.

SCRATCHY Well, that leaves just one other place for him to be.
He turns toward the "Weary Gentleman," hikes his trousers, reaches for the bottle which is no longer there.

SCRATCHY (growling and starting) Dad burn it. Never seed it yet I didn't run out just at the wrong time!

He walks fast past the respectable houses, the churches and so on, and DOLLYING, SHOOTING PAST HIM, we see they all have an unearthly quietness. As he walks, he talks, now to himself, now shouting.

SCRATCHY (continuing) But that's all right. Just lay low. 'Caze quick as I wet my whistle, I'm gonna show ye some shootin'!

He stops in front of Morgan's house.

SCRATCHY (continuing) You, Jasper Morgan. Yeah, and that snivellin' woman o' yourn, too! Too dainty to do like ordinary folks. Too high an' mighty! Git yerself a lot o' fancy plumbing, an' ye aint' man enough to clean out yer own cess-pool. "Let Scratchy do it." Ain't nuthin' so low but Scratchy'll do it for the price of a pint.

He glares around for a target. He spies a potted fern suspended from the porch ceiling. He shoots the suspension chain and the whole thing drops to the porch floor with a foomp. There! Clean that up! He turns, Deacon's house is opposite.

SCRATCHY (continuing; a horrible travesty of a sissy voice) *Deacon!* Oh *Deacon Smee-eed!* (he makes two syllables of Smeed) You home, Deacon? Kin I pay ye a little call? *Most* places in town, ye just *knock* an' walk *in,* but that ain't *good* enough for a *good* man, *is* it, Deacon? Oh *no!* No—*no!* Pay a little call on the Deacon, ye got to shove a 'lectric bell, real special. (a hard shift of tone) All right, Smeed, start singin' them psalms o' yourn. You'll be whangin' 'em on a harp, few mo' minutes, you an' yer missuz, too. Can't stop in right now, I'm a mite too thirsty. But I'll be back, Deacon. Oh, I'll be back. (he studies the house) Here's my callin' card.

He takes careful aim, and

INSERT
Hits the doorbell, so fusing it that it rings continuously. We HEAR a woman scream hysterically.

CLOSE SHOT OF SCRATCHY

SCRATCHY Ah, quit it. Don't holler 'til yer hurt.

INT. DEACON'S HOUSE—DEACON AND WIFE
Past Deacon and his wife, through the curtained window, we see Scratchy pass.
The Deacon has an arm around his wife. He is trying pathetically to resemble an intrepid doomed frontiersman in an Indian fight.

DEACON He'll pay for this. By the Almighty, he'll pay dearly. I'm not going to stand for it, I'm simply not going—

MRS. SMEED Oh hush. For goodness sake, stop that horrid *bell!*
He looks at her, goes into the hallway with wounded dignity, and jerks a wire loose. Just as the bell stops, there is a shot and the stinging SOUND O.S. of the church bell being shot at. The Deacon reacts to this latest outrage.

MEDIUM SHOT—UPWARD—CHURCH BELL—FROM SCRATCHY'S VIEWPOINT

CLOSE SHOT—SHOOTING DOWN—SCRATCHY
looking up at bell, both pleased and angry, and shooting again at the church bell.

SCRATCHY (he bellows) Come on out and fight if you dast—only you don't dast.

He starts glancing all around; the revolvers in each hand are as sensitive as snakes; the little fingers play in a musician-like way; INTER-CUT with still facades of details of greater stillness; a motionless curtain of machine-made lace with a head dimly silhouetted behind; a drawn shade, with an eye and fingertips visible at the edge.

SCRATCHY (continuing) O no! You know who's *boss* in *this* town. Marcellus T. Wilson, that's who. He ain't fittin' to wipe yer boots on, no-sir-ree, he's the lowest of the low, but he's boss all same. 'Caze *this* is a boss, (gesturing with a revolver) an' *this* is a boss, (another) an' this is the feller that can boss the both of 'em better'n any other man that's left in this wore-out womanizin' country. An' there ain't hardly a man of ye dast *touch* a gun, let alone come up again a *man* with one. Oh no! Got lil' ole honeybunch to worry about, lil' ole wifey-pifey, all the young 'uns, make ye some easy money runnin' a store, doctorin', psalm-singing, fix ye a purty lawn so Scratchy kin cut it for ye, if ye can't get a Mex cheap enough. Oh, I—(he searches helplessly, then half-says)—hate—I could wipe every one of ye offen the face o' the earth, a-hidin' behind yore women's skirts, ever' respectable last one of ye! Come out an' fight! Come on! Come on! Dad *blast* ye!

He glares all around again. There is no kind of response at all. His attention shifts; his eyes focus on something o.s., he becomes purposeful.

EXT. "WEARY GENTLEMAN" SALOON—BARRICADED—DAY

DOLLY SHOT over Scratchy's shoulder as he advances on door.

CUT TO

MEDIUM CLOSE SHOT—SCRATCHY
He comes to door and hammers on it with gun butt.

SCRATCHY Laura Lee. (pause) Laura Lee. (pause)
Now he hammers with both revolvers.

SCRATCHY (continuing; yelling) *Laura Lee!* (no answer) You can't fool me. I know you're there. Open up. I want a drink. (no answer) All I want's a little drink.

Now he hammers harder than ever. Over SOUND of hammering, CUT INSIDE

TO CLOSE SHOTS IN THIS ORDER

CLOSE SHOT—LAURA LEE
low behind bar, her rifle ready if need be, thumb on safety.

CLOSE SHOT—THREE LOCAL MEN
on floor, watching the door fixedly.

CLOSE SHOT—THE DRUMMER
behind the bar, plenty scared.

CLOSE SHOT—BACK TO SCRATCHY
finishing his hammering. He is rather tired. He glares at the door a moment, then:

SCRATCHY All right then. All right.

He looks around him, sore. He sights a scrap of paper in the dirt, picks it up, and with a vicious and cruel thrust, nails it to the door with a knife. Then he turns his back contemptuously on the saloon, walks to the far side of the street and, spinning quickly and lithely, fires at the sheet of paper.

INSERT
The bullet misses by half an inch.

SCRATCHY AS BEFORE

SCRATCHY Well, I, Gah . . . gittin' old in yer old age, Scratchy.
He takes careful aim and fires.

INSERT
The bullet splits the haft of the knife; the blade clatters down; the paper follows, fluttering; a hole appears in the door.

CLOSE SHOT—INT. WEARY GENTLEMAN
Jasper is on floor, between a chair and a spittoon. Bullet flicks wood from chair, ricochets with appropriate SOUNDS, puncturing spittoon from which dark liquid oozes. Jasper, with slow horror, looks at it.

FROM SCRATCHY'S VIEWPOINT
the paper finishes settling.

CLOSE SHOT—SCRATCHY
He is satisfied; he turns and starts walking grandly away. Suddenly he cries out:

SCRATCHY Hey! (and stops and faces the saloon again) Hey, tell Jack Potter to come on out o' there like a man!

REVERSE ANGLE—OVER SCRATCHY
No answer.

SCRATCHY (continuing; yelling) *Jack!* JACK POTTER?

CLOSE SHOT—INT. SALOON

LAURA LEE Jack Potter ain't here, Scratchy, an' *you know it!* 'Cause if he was, he'd be out thar arter ye.

CLOSE SHOT—SCRATCHY
He hesitates, thinks it over.

SCRATCHY (uncertainly) You wouldn't fool me, would ye, Laura Lee?

LAURA LEE'S VOICE (o.s.) I never did, did I?

SCRATCHY Well don't never you try it. 'Caze I ain' the man'll stand fer it. (suddenly sore) That lyin' no-'count Frank! I'll fix *him!* I'll cook *his* goose!

HE STARTS OUT FAST UP THE STREET—there is the SOUND of a distant train whistle o.s. Over it   DISSOLVE TO

INT. PARLOR CAR—DAY
SOUND of dying wail of whistle o.s. Throughout scene, SOUND of slowing train.

TWO SHOT—POTTER AND BRIDE
Tension and emotion increase in their faces.

POTTER (with desperate finality) Well—
She looks to him anxiously—he meets her eyes briefly and both smile, then lower their eyes pathetically. He gratefully thinks of *something* to do.

POTTER (continuing) Better git down our truck.

With day-coach reflex, he stands up, reaching for the non-existent baggage rack, realizes his mistake, and pretends he is only tidying his clothes.

PORTER'S VOICE (o.s., loud and glad) Don't you bother, mister—
                                                                    CUT TO

CLOSE SHOT—PORTER
grinning.

PORTER (continuing)—I got it all ready an' waitin'!

FULL SHOT
Some amused heads turn.

BRIDE AND POTTER AS BEFORE
He sits down abashed. Train SOUND is much slower. Their time is short.

POTTER (smiling and wretched) Home at last.

BRIDE (uneasy) Mm-hmm.

A silence.

CLOSE SHOT—POTTER

in real desperation. o.s. SOUND of train bell.

POTTER (sweating; rapidly) Say listen. You ain't goana like me fer this an' I don't blame ye, but I just can't face 'em if we can help it, not right yet. What I want, I want to sorta *sneak* in, if we can git away with it, an' make home without nobody seein' us, an' then study what to do about 'em. I figure we got a chance if we kinda skin along the hind side o' Main Street. We got cover 'til about sixty foot from my door. Would ye do it?

CAMERA PULLS AND PANS into TWO SHOT—POTTER AND BRIDE

BRIDE (fervent) Oh gee, if only they don't ketch us!

POTTER (incredulously grateful) You don't hate me fer it?

BRIDE (with all her heart) *Hate* you?

They look at each other with entirely new love. The train is stopping. They get up fast and leave the shot.   CUT TO

EXT. STATION YELLOW SKY—DAY

As trains pulls to a stop, PAN AND DOLLY into CLOSE UP-SHOT of train steps. The Porter descends first and leaves the shot. Potter, with Bride behind and above him, peers anxiously forward along the station platform.

LONG SHOT—HIS VIEWPOINT

The empty platform.

MEDIUM SHOT—PANNING

POTTER (over shoulder) Come on girl. Hurry.

He steps to platform, she follows unassisted. He grabs up both bags and, looking back to her, collides with the untipped, dismayed Porter.

POTTER Oh.

He sets down bags. A fumbling rush for change. He hands out a coin.

POTTER (continuing) Much obliged.

He picks up bags and starts walking, the Bride alongside.

POTTER Let's git outa here.

PORTER (across him) Much obliged to *you*, sir.

Potter walks away so fast that she has to hustle to keep alongside. Both are eagle-eyed—he with anxiety, she with that and with simple interest.

REVERSE ANGLE SHOT

We glimpse an empty segment of street.

BRIDE'S VOICE (o.s.) Gee, I don't see *nobody*.

BRIDE AND POTTER AS BEFORE

POTTER Just the hot time o' day, let's not risk it.

They walk still faster around rear corner of station and out of sight.

CUT TO

CLOSE SHOT—CELL WINDOW IN POTTER'S HOUSE

It is empty; very, very slowly a little mirror rises to eye level above the sill —and jerks down fast.

CLOSE SHOT

between the rear of two buildings toward the vacant Main Street. Potter's head comes CLOSE INTO SHOT, then the Bride's.

POTTER (whispering) All right.

They dart noiselessly across the gap.

POTTER (continuing) Good girl.

They laugh, low and sheepish, and steal ahead. CAMERA PANS WITH THEM l. to r.

POTTER (still whispering) Next corner, dear, an' I can show you our home.

BRIDE (same) Oh, Jack.

She stops. Her eyes are damp. He stops.

POTTER (whispering) Sumpin' the matter?

VERY CLOSE SHOT—BRIDE

BRIDE The way you said that!

POTTER'S VOICE (o.s.) Said what?

BRIDE (moved) Our home!

She smiles very shyly. He is moved and says, in a most embarrassed voice:

POTTER Come on then, girl.—Let's *get* there.

ANOTHER ANGLE
They start walking fast and quiet; we PAN with them, approaching the frame corner of a house.

POTTER (continuing) Now right the next second, you can see it!

They continue. WE LEAD THEM slightly as they circle the corner and come face to face with a CLOSE SHOT of SCRATCHY. He is leaning against the wall, just around the corner, reloading. Instantly he drops this revolver, whips the other from its holster, and aims it at Potter's chest.
A deadly silence.

REVERSE ANGLE—OVER SCRATCHY ONTO POTTER AND BRIDE
The Bride grabs Potter's right arm. He drops both bags and exhibits the desperate reflex of a man whose fighting arm has never before been encumbered. He reaches for the gun that is not there. He sweeps her behind him.

CLOSEUP—SCRATCHY

CLOSE SHOT—THE BRIDE

Her face looks crumpled with terror; she gazes at the gun as at an apparitional snake.

CLOSE SHOT—POTTER
He looks up from the gun into Scratchy's eyes.

CLOSE SHOT—THE REVOLVER

CAMERA RISES SLOWLY TO BRING IN SCRATCHY IN EXTREME CLOSEUP.
His eyes are cold and mad; his face is almost solemn.

SCRATCHY (almost reproachfully) Tried to sneak up on me. Tried to sneak up on me!

TWO SHOT OF THE MEN—THE BRIDE BEHIND POTTER
Potter makes a slight movement; Scratchy thrusts his revolver venomously forward; CAMERA LUNGES FORWARD CORRESPONDINGLY.

CLOSE SHOT OF SCRATCHY

SCRATCHY (he smiles with a new and quiet ferocity) No' don't ye do it, Jack Potter. Don't you move a finger towards a gun just yet. Don't you bat an eyelash. The time has come fer me to settle with you, so I aim to do it my own way, an' loaf along without no interferin'. So if ye don't want a gun bent on ye, or a third eye right now, just mind what I tell ye.
He slowly raises his revolver to eye level, so that it is pointing a little upward, DEAD INTO THE LENS

CLOSE SHOT—POTTER—PAST GUN

He is looking directly down the barrel. He is not at all a cowardly man but he is looking directly into the eye of death. Sweat breaks out on his face.

EXTREME CLOSE SHOT

looking down the pistol barrel.

EXTREME CLOSE SHOT—POTTER

then,

THE BRIDE'S FACE, saying "our home" (without sound) and smiling.

RETURN TO POTTER

His eyes, a little dizzily out of focus, restore to normal.

POTTER (quietly) I ain't got a gun, Scratchy. Honest I ain't. You'll have to do all the shootin' yerself.

CLOSE SHOT—SCRATCHY—PAST POTTER

He goes livid and steps forward and lashes his weapon to and fro.

SCRATCHY Don't you tell me you ain't got no gun on you, you whelp. Don't tell me no lie like that. There ain't a man in Texas ever seen you without no gun. Don't take me fer no kid.
His eyes blaze with light; his throat works like a pump

CLOSE SHOT—POTTER—PAST SCRATCHY

POTTER I ain't takin' you fer no kid. I'm takin' you fer a damned fool. I tell you I ain't got a gun an' I ain't. If you're gonna shoot me up, ya better do it now; you'll never get a chance like this again.

PULL AWAY INTO TWO SHOT—Scratchy calms a little.

SCRATCHY (sneering) If you ain't got a gun, why ain't you got a gun? Been to Sunday school?

POTTER You know where I been. I been in San Antone. An' I ain't got a gun because I just got married. An' if I'd thought there was goin' to be any galoots like you prowlin' around, when I brought my wife home, I'd a had a gun, an' don't you fergit it.

SCRATCHY (says the word with total, uncomprehending vacancy) Married?

POTTER Yes, married. I'm married.

SCRATCHY (a little more comprehension) Married? You mean, *you?* (he backs off a pace; the arm and pistol drop) No. (he studies Potter cagily and shakes his head)

Then literally for the first time, he sees the Bride.

SCRATCHY (continuing) What's that ye got there? Is this the lady?

POTTER Yes, this is the lady.

A silence.

SCRATCHY Well, I 'spose it's all off now.

POTTER It's all off if you say so, Scratchy. You know I didn't make the trouble.

He picks up both valises.

NEW SHOT—SCRATCHY—OVER POTTER
He studies Potter up and down, slowly, incredulously. Then he looks at the ground.

SCRATCHY Well, I 'low it's off, Jack. (he shakes his head) *Married!*

He looks up with infinite reproach, sadness and solitude. He picks up his fallen revolver. He hefts it and turns both revolvers in his hands, looking at them, then puts them with finality into their holsters. Then he again meets Potter's eyes.

SCRATCHY (continuing; almost inaudibly) G'bye, Jack.

CLOSE SHOT—POTTER
He begins to comprehend; he is moved.

POTTER 'Bye, Scratchy.

REVERSE ANGLE—SCRATCHY
He looks at Potter a moment, then turns around and walks heavily away.

TWO SHOT—POTTER AND BRIDE
She emerges from behind him, whimpering, glancing from man to man, hugging his arm. His eyes on Scratchy o.s., he is hardly aware of her.

INSERT
A lace curtain is plucked aside and Deacon's wife looks out.

CLOSE SHOT
A front door opens cautiously, squeakily; and cautiously, a man we don't know emerges.

                                                              CUT TO

INT. "WEARY GENTLEMAN"—DAY
The doors open; Jasper, Ed, the Young Man, and finally Laura Lee, followed by the Drummer, emerge onto the porch, looking up the street.

LONG SHOT—POTTER, BRIDE AND SCRATCHY
through this group as a few people timidly venture into the space between.

REVERSE ANGLE—GROUP SHOT—FAVORING LAURA LEE AND DRUMMER

DRUMMER (smug) You were saying, ma'am—this is a *hard* country?

She gives him a look and looks again toward Scratchy and company.

LONG SHOT—PAST ED AND DRUMMER
The Deacon trots out to Potter, frantically effusive.

PANTOMIME introductions.

ED Drummer: looks like ye got ye a new customer.

Drummer registers certainty and anticipation.

DRUMMER (to Laura Lee) And how about you, ma'am?

CLOSE SHOT—LAURA LEE
She turns on him, colder than ever.

LAURA LEE (in measured tones) I wouldn't wear them things if it killed me.

Then she realizes she is dead. Her eyes fall, tragic and defiant, to a neutral angle. In b.g., Jasper, watching her, realizes a little of the meaning. He is sympathetic.

ED'S VOICE (o.s.) Well look at that!

LONG SHOT—PAST ALL OF THEM
Potter is walking toward home with Deacon and the Bride as if between custodians. They stop. The Deacon, extra effusive, peels off and toddles for home.

CLOSE MOVING SHOT—POTTER AND BRIDE WALKING
She glances back toward the filling, watchful street, which we see past them. Potter is looking toward Scratchy o.s.

BRIDE Sure looks like the cat's outa the bag.

POTTER More like a wild-cat.

He stops. So do Bride and CAMERA.

POTTER (continuing) You know? There's somethin' I always wanted to do.

He sets down the suitcases and looks her up and down, business-like. She is willing but mystified. He picks her up.

BRIDE (surprised and grateful) Oh, Jack . . .

As he carries her forward out of the shot, he looks sadly again toward Scratchy o.s. while she, loving and puzzled, looks at him.

MEDIUM SHOT—FRANK
at the window.

FRANK Howdy Marshal! Proud to know ye Miz Potter! Welcome home!

With the attempted velocity of a fast baseball, he slams down handsful of improvised confetti. PULL CAMERA DOWN. Potter and Bride walk to door amid showering confetti.

CONTINUE PULLING DOWN as Potter shoves door open with his shoe, enters, Bride in arms, and shoves door shut.

DOLLY IN—STILL PULLING DOWN to
CLOSE SHOT showing that Scratchy has shot the lock to pieces.

END PULL DOWN—vertical to the doorstep as last confetti flutters down. Salient are the torn pictures of the murderous faces and weapons of early western fiction.

VERY LONG SHOT—SCRATCHY
Very small, he walks heavily away toward a solitary, still more distant hovel; empty earth and sky all around. A LONG HOLD; then CAMERA PULLS DOWN TO

CLOSE SHOT—the funnel-shaped tracks of his feet in heavy sand.

THE END

The Blue Hotel

"The Blue Hotel"

The Blue Hotel, *based on the Stephen Crane short story,
was written by James Agee, under contract to Huntington Hartford, in 1948-49, shortly after he left* Time,
*where he had served for seven years as a book and
movie reviewer. Although no motion picture of this script
has as yet been made, an adaptation of it appeared
on* Omnibus, NBC *television.* The Blue Hotel *was Agee's
first feature length film scenario.*

TITLE
on black screen above center:

NEAR THE MIDDLE OF THE UNITED STATES
O.s., quiet, but swiftly louder, the humming, then hammering of rails;
then over this, increasing SOUND, the SOUND of a hoarse, old-fashioned train
whistle coming swiftly nearer: two long blasts, one short, one long, which
trails down and out.

Over the fading train whistle and increasing train SOUND

FADE IN

TITLE
below center:

TOWARDS THE END OF THE NINETEENTH CENTURY
Start the rapid SOUND of a train bell. SWOOP SOUND of bell and train up suddenly two seconds before   CUTTING TO

CLOSE SHOT—A TRAIN (NITE)
Instantly bring SOUNDS of train and bell up as loud as the audience can
stand. A transcontinental express-train crosses through r.s. to l.s. at

393

frightening velocity. CAMERA is pulling back from a close shot at medium height of the train. In the train's wake, a long, luminous ruche of snow is raised, filling the screen, and slowly sinking, as SOUNDS dwindle o.s.

As the last snow settles to the ground, and the SOUNDS die o.s., the CAMERA ends its pull-back about 12 feet off the ground in a

LONG SHOT—EXT. A STATION, A SMALL HOTEL, A SMALL TOWN, THE PRAIRIE—IN DARKNESS AND SILENCE

It is not snowing and the night sky is overcast but the snow on the ground gives off enough light—using infra-red if need be—to establish the station (extreme l.s.), the hotel (dead center), the edge of the town (extreme r.s.). Even in darkness the hotel gives off something odd and curdled. Beyond and between these buildings, as our eyes become accustomed to the darkness, we see an immense perspective of snowed land, and a very distant low horizon against a black sky which holds two thirds of the screen.

HOLD THIS DARKNESS perhaps eight seconds

Then, within a maximum thirty seconds, the darkness alters through the lights of pre-dawn, dawn, etc., to the light of late morning. At the proper early juncture, one or two small lights appear in windows, and go out again. At the edge of the town, in the earliest real daylight, a man's tiny figure comes out of a door and walks out of r.s. Little flags of smoke and steam sprout, compact and crisp, in the bitter air. Shading and detail become increasingly clear. The station is coal-black; its sign FORT ROMPER, is just readable. The town is mostly low, mean, frame construction—the drab shades of tired blotting-paper. The Hotel, of a disturbing shade even in darkness, gives off under the changing light an always more and more sinister and unearthly fish-belly glare. Its sign, PALACE HOTEL, is newish, and easy to read. It is a crummy rather frail-looking wooden building of two stories, crowned by florid cornice work.

Beyond these buildings we can see perhaps forty miles. The sky is dull gray; the snow is like rice; there are farms, at lonely distances apart.

When high, shadowless morning light is established, the tiny silhouette of a man—SCULLY—walks briskly out of the Hotel front door and towards the station. O.s., begin and bring up SOUNDS of an overworked locomotive and a train; he walks faster; bring up the SOUNDS; he trots; a somewhat archaic locomotive, crusted and bearded with ice and snow, slowing, drags on from l.s. a baggage car, a daycoach, the first of a string of boxcars; covering SCULLY as he trots; stopping. As quickly as will not be be absurd, SCULLY reappears, walking towards the Hotel, followed by the COWBOY, the EASTERNER, the SWEDE, in single file. At the same moment, the CAMERA, which is centered on the hotel door, starts towards the door at their pace, holding them within left-screen. We get at first only character by silhouette and near-silhouette, then in more detail.

SCULLY is in the lead, half-turning as he walks, to talk; short, chunky, late middle-aged. Next, the COWBOY, size and structure of John Wayne, tight city trousers, a solid block of mackinaw, his best hat; he walks like a horseman and with the stooping, rather diffident stride of a man of his height; he carries a scarred raw-hide suitcase or a splotched Holstein-hide roll-grip. Next, the EASTERNER. He is small, slender, bears himself well and entirely without the bumptiousness of so many small men. Without at all mincing, he is more neat-footed along the icy boards than the others are; he carries a briefcase and a middle-sized, neutral valise, possibly with faded labels on it. Last, the SWEDE: He is above average height but stocky enough to seem shorter than he is, and disturbed and scared enough, as a rule, to sag an inch or two more. A shiny black leather coat to the middle of the thighs, trousers which look as if he had on two suits of long underwear beneath them, a cap of coarse hairy wool, two sizes too small, high on his head, with earflaps which at best cannot thoroughly cover his ears. There is something shaky, equivocal and arythmic about his walking. An outsize new suitcase which looks to be covered by black oilcloth increases his clumsiness at the knees.

As these men grow out of silhouette into detail and size, and we begin to hear their SOUNDS, the CHOWF-CHOWFINGS of the locomotive, o.s., drown out these SOUNDS and the locomotive and the train, gathering speed, cut off the men from view and then fill most of the screen, the Hotel still jutting above. As locomotive makes r.s., the CAMERA is quite close to train and place-names, emblems and names of lines, swinging by, suggest the whole nation and continent in geography and history.

CUT OR LAP

DISSOLVE TO

MEDIUM TWO SHOT—FACADE OF HOTEL—DOOR AT CENTER

The CAMERA is still creeping, lowering quietly to eye height. O.s. SOUNDS of walking on icy boards. The four men enter, in single file and in the same order, at l.s. SCULLY steps a pace past his door and wheels and stops abruptly, bowing slightly and flinging out one hand in a slightly uneasy parody of Mine Host and causing the others to stop or tread water in uneasy courtesy, indulging his spiel. The CAMERA stops creeping at the same moment; they are medium close. The EASTERNER looks quietly and curiously at the strange color.

EASTERNER (politely concealing his faint nausea) I've never seen the shade before, but once.

SCULLY (a little jealous, but very polite) And where might that be, may I ask?

EASTERNER On the legs of a kind of heron; one of the wading birds. It's a very strange color; there's nothing else quite like it in Nature. It declares the bird's position against any background.

SCULLY Declares his——*does* it now! Well now, surely that's a mischievous hue for the Almighty to paint a poor craytcher in this murderin' world. Declare me *position* indeed. Aginst *inny background*. That's nicely put. That's it in a nutshell. You kin see the Palace Hotel for miles up the line, all weathers, and she's starin' like the morning star. Now didn't ye? And do ye truly admire it?

EASTERNER It's a very remarkable shade.

SCULLY Ahh, count on a traveled man for connisewership! But gintlemen, may heaven forgive me an' me guests rattlin' their teeth on me own doorstep. (he hurries to open the door and wave them past him) Come in! Come in! (to Johnnie) One twenty-two three an'—No, line 'em up along the south corridor and don't let the grass grow under yer feet. Hang yer coats in here, gintlemen, unless ye prefer to go straight to yer rooms.

AD LIBS No.—No, thanks.

SCULLY (continuing) Let's thaw ourselves out a bit; ye can sign up at yer layzhure. Not that ev'ry room in me establishment ain't as warm as toast, gintlemen, but in weather the likes o' this, ye should have the binifit o' the lee o' house.

AD LIBS Sure.—Of course, thanks.

SCULLY Now here's something, friends, ye couldn't hope to find in the Waldorf. Ye see? (he pours a slashing tinkle of ice-splintery water into the first basin) What would ye git there? (contemptuously) Shteem! Where fer the chills there's nuthin' on earth to set the blood hummin' agin like a bit o' nice brisk water. (Meantime, he is filling two more basins) Ye don't believe me? (to the Easterner) Don't be shy! *try* it! You'll see. (The Easterner plunges; the instant the water hits his face he utters four sharp coughs, but he stays at it and emerges gasping and groping; Scully produces a towel he grabbed from a shelf under the tub and now says with an air of great graciousness) Yer towel, sir.

SCULLY Yer towel, sir. (same old towel)

DOLLY along to the Swede, eyes downcast and shifting a little; he plants his heavy fingers in the water up to their second knuckles, and quickly withdraws them, quailing profoundly.

SCULLY (handing out the towel, now quite draggled, politely but with less enthusiasm) Yer towel, sir.

The Swede sinks one finger at a time into the towel and twists.

CLOSE UP—THE EASTERNER
He is looking into a mirror. His skin shines as if he had used some kind of metal polish on it; he is quietly surprised and pleased. He glances down casually to see if his nails are clean.

CLOSE UP—THE COWBOY
Also gazing into the mirror. He has the same burnished look of metal polished. Impersonal light eyes, a little bit bovine, very virile and empty, fixed through most of the shot on his hair, which he is tidying with a public comb. His eyes rake down, casually and impersonally across his face at the finish of the shot.

CLOSE UP—THE SWEDE
He is twisting his fingers, one by one, heavily in the towel; by the angle of his eyes and their surreption, it is clear that he is very carefully watching the other three men in the mirror. At the end of the shot, Scully walks into it as the Swede drops the towel beside the basin. The Swede turns for the door, Scully picks up the towel, tosses it into a cardboard box, CAMERA SWINGING as they make for the door.

SCULLY (in re the towel) Thank you. (calling after them) Now just make yerselves comfortable by the stove, gintlemen. It won't be no time till dinner.

They start through the door.

MEDIUM CLOSE—THE MAIN ROOM
Past stove on the FARMER as he glances up and starts to edge back his chair to make room.

FARMER Mean weather.

COWBOY Mean enough.

FARMER Seven below, last night.

COWBOY That a fact.

FARMER Warmed up a leetle, but it's jest makin' fer more snow.

COWBOY Snowin' a'ready.

FARMER Big wind acomin' too, shouldn't wonder.

COWBOY Shouldn't wonder.

FARMER No sir, shouldn't wonder if we git us a real ole fashion' blizzard. If ye don't mind my askin', stranger, where might ye be from?

COWBOY I was down to Omahaw; a little business.

FARMER An' where might ye be headin'?

COWBOY Got me a little ranch, up near the Dakota line.

FARMER That a fact? Stoppin' over fer the Spur train, 's 'at right?

COWBOY That's right.

FARMER Myself, I'm a farmer.

COWBOY That right?

FARMER Yup. That's right. Started as a homesteader, back in seventy-six, but now I own muh land.

COWBOY Uh huh.

FARMER Quarter section.

COWBOY That right?

FARMER Yup. Quarter section. When I come here it warn't nuthin' but a untamed wilderness like you might say. But now I own me a quarter section.

A silence. Farmer spits again, then addresses the Easterner.

FARMER An' what might yer own business be, stranger, if ye don't mind my askin'?

EASTERNER Not at all, sir. I'm a journalist. Newspaper man.

FARMER Now is that a fact? (carefully) Not meaning no offense, you're from the east, ain't you?

EASTERNER (smiling) Yes. (against his natural reticence) A Philadelphia paper.

FARMER Is that right now. Well, not meanin' no offense, I'm *mighty* glad to hear that.

EASTERNER (smiling) Why's that, sir?

FARMER I was skeered ye might be from Noo York City. Not that I've ever laid eyes on one, an' o' course, it could be I heared wrong. But what ye hear tell . . . (a half silent whistling *whew* with a shake of the head) . . . them Noo Yorkers! (Uneasy glance at the Swede; tactful change of subject) But they ain't never nuthin' happens out here, Mister, not that's fer the nooze papers.—Is they?

EASTERNER Well, you see, I'm not after news stories just now. (politely) Back east we're all so ignorant of the rest of the country, that's all. I am too, and I don't like to be ignorant. I just want to learn what things are really like, If I can, and tell others who don't know, you see.

FARMER (chews it over, interested but puzzled) An' they'll pay ye a livin' fer that?

EASTERNER (smiling) That's right.

FARMER But if ye don't mind me askin', why how come ye coms to Rawmpr? Ain't nuthin' *ever* happens here.

EASTERNER (careful and very polite but candid) Frankly I didn't know I was getting off till I got here. Seeing it from the train, I just felt I couldn't go on by without seeing more of the Blue Hotel.

FARMER Blue Hotel! Oh! You mean right where we're sett'n'?

The Easterner nods, smiling.

FARMER Well, I ain't no proper jedge, but the woman, she thinks it's *mighty* purty.

EASTERNER I never saw a color like it. Not on a hotel.

FARMER Is that a fact now? Well I'll be dogged. (pause. To the Swede) An' how 'bout you, Mister, if ye don't mind me askin'? Where might *you* be from?   DISSOLVE TO

MOVING CLOSE SHOT—ALCOVE OF THE DINING ROOM
CAMERA VERTICAL over the dining table, starting at the head, pulling down along the aisle of places moderately slow. Perhaps one or two heads ad lib into the shot, ducking over the plate for a bite, but except for this, heads are not visible—only what is on the table, and the busily eating and reaching hands. Subdued SOUNDS of shy, speechless, hungry eating. The food is all on the table and by evidence of damage done, we are well

on into the meal. Voices are very sporadic and ad lib, possibly recognizable; close to monosyllabic and wholly utilitarian except for the Easterner.

AD LIBS Meat please . . . Pass the potatoes . . . Turnips.

They are passed, used and returned without comment. A hand and fork reach to spear a biscuit.

EASTERNER Could I have the butter, please.

An almost inaudible "Sure," in reply and

EASTERNER (quietly) Thanks.

The voices are o.s., such hands as reach deeper into the terrain than the eating plates, appear at unpredictable angles and rhythms; perhaps two might also collide and spring apart with the almost electric-shock celerity of shy courtesy. Not more than ten seconds to this VERTICAL PULL before we begin to hit barren space, the tundra-like lower reaches of the table, all much-mended, not perfectly clean, white tablecloth, no places set. After just a little of this, CAMERA begins to tilt and settle so that as it reaches the end of the long table, (room for a crowded 14) it is at eye level of a seated man looking up the center of the table at Scully at the head. Along l.s., the Swede (next Scully), and Johnnie; r.s., the Cowboy, (next to Scully) then the Easterner and the Farmer. We pause just long enough to get a glimpse of Scully's character through his eating: a business-like but rather frugal and finicky eater, even a touch of old-maidishness; an old fashioned and rather cute old guy; absorbed in eating, he loses entirely his Mine Host mannerisms, he's just an aging pappy at home, reloading. Rather frail eyelids and stretched neck when he drinks water; an evidently self-taught but deeply habitual care to take small bites and to keep his lips closed over his chewing; dabby with his fork; delicate at harpooning a biscuit; a suggestion of dental plates which don't quite fit.

MEDIUM CLOSE SHOT—THE SWEDE

A big napkin is tied under his ears, its knot-ends make spare ears below his own. He is sweating a little. He uses his fork left-handed and upside down, European style. He eats steadily with heavy square gestures, and we see in his eating and chewing a conflict between the hunger of a fairly heavy eater and his uneasiness. He is intensely silent and his eyes are darting all over the joint with a dog's eating-vigilance plus his own special kind of uneasiness. Elbows wide and clumsy, he usually grazes Johnnie and as CAMERA pulls to the left losing the Swede and picking up Johnnie, the elbows collide rather hard and the first we see of Johnnie's face involves a spasm of annoyance.

MEDIUM CLOSE SHOT—THE COWBOY FROM JOHNNIE'S ANGLE
The Cowboy is winking at Johnnie, amused.

CLOSE SHOT—JOHNNIE
He watches the Swede. A small, sour smile, friendly eyes, in reaction
to the Cowboy. His eating is the normal fast heavy eating of a not very
well mannered, far from meek, kid, exactly on the watershed between
being a boy and a very young man.

CLOSE UP—THE COWBOY
A napkin tucked fairly high into his dark shirt, his large elbows held in
with unaccustomed tightness. His eating system is to mash whatever
can be mashed into malleable material, mix it, load his fork by help of his
knife as heavy as possible, sculpture and trim it with his knife; changes
fork to right hand, brings it up to a mouth which opens for it and closes
over it as efficiently as a steamshovel, then working his full jaws with a
fair amount of SOUND which he keeps reasonably subdued, meanwhile
lowering his fork, changing hands, and starting all over again. He
swallows exactly as soon as the new load is ready and takes a swallow
of water just before shifting the fork to the right hand: solid machine-like
reciprocation between knife, fork, left hand, right hand, mouth and water
glass. Otherwise, as a rule, his eyes are either attentive to his plate, or
out of focus.

PULL CAMERA TO THE RIGHT, losing the Cowboy and picking up the Easterner: his are the ordinary eating manners of a well-brought-up middle-
class Easterner, shaded by his own considerable natural elegance. The
modestly hearty appetite of a small healthy man. Small, strong, fine hands.
As with his way of speaking, he neither obtrudes nor tries to conceal
or modify what is natural to him or to his background. He is a clear
master at seeing everything there is to be seen without appearing to
stare, or to sneak glances, or even to look, or even to be careful not to
look. As the CAMERA leaves him, PULLING RIGHT, he touches his mouth with
his napkin, which has been in his lap.

TAIL OFF briefly on the Farmer, napkin tucked broad over bib of overalls,
hard, heavy-knuckled red-looking hands: looking at nobody; hoeing it in;
an aging, hard working countryman, at home at this table, and unself-
conscious of strangers.

MEDIUM SHOT—THE WHOLE TABLE FROM THE EMPTY END
They are all eating slower, the tail-end of the meal. AD LIB and unob-
trusively behind this, is Scully's daughter moving, waiting on table,
silently. She is a pale, melancholic, pious, once-pretty spinster of about

30. By-play and reaction between her and the diners should be present but minimal, and played ad lib in passing, never pointed up.

Scully rearranges himself to lean back in his chair and puts his hands on the table. A heavy silence as they dab at their food.

MEDIUM CLOSE SHOT—THE SWEDE
His eyes angle sharply to the Cowboy and then to the Easterner.

TWO SHOT—THE EASTERNER AND THE COWBOY FROM SWEDE'S ANGLE
The Easterner catches the Swede's eye, looks quickly down. The Cowboy's eyes up; down. The Easterner looks up again with an inevitable tinge of surreption.

MEDIUM CLOSE SHOT—THE SWEDE
The Swede is disturbed by the Easterner's look; glances sharply to the Cowboy.

TWO SHOT—THE EASTERNER AND THE COWBOY FROM SWEDE'S ANGLE
The Cowboy looks up with inevitable surreption.

MEDIUM CLOSE SHOT—THE SWEDE
The Swede is still more worried. Gives Scully a sharp glance.

CLOSE SHOT—SCULLY FROM THE SWEDE'S ANGLE
He looks up at the worried look, quickly down again; up again, slyly.

CLOSE SHOT—THE SWEDE
Eyes sidelong to Johnnie, very sly and worried, then to the Easterner and the Cowboy, intensely suspicious and deeply worried.

TWO SHOT—THE EASTERNER AND THE COWBOY FROM THE SWEDE'S ANGLE
The Cowboy looks up in flat perplexity; the Easterner looks up in curiosity so veiled it looks almost criminal; then he looks down; then the Easterner and the Cowboy glance toward each other, each rather secretly, checking if the other had noticed anything odd; it looks very much like complicity.

CLOSE SHOT—THE SWEDE
Very deeply bothered, he rakes his glance at each man in turn, then sharply up at the wall above Scully.

INSERT: WALL ABOVE SCULLY FROM SWEDE'S ANGLE
A SOMBER STEEL ENGRAVING OF "THE STAG AT BAY."

CLOSE SHOT—THE SWEDE
The Swede's eyes leave the engraving, quick glances all around again; he is sweating. He looks into his plate and at his heavy hands on either

side of it. He is working hard to brace himself, he begins to get brave and to resolve himself; at last he determines to speak.

SWEDE (to Scully) Me, I come from New York City.

The Swede casts quick somber eyes at the Farmer.

MEDIUM CLOSE SHOT—THE FARMER FROM THE SWEDE'S ANGLE
His fork hesitates a fraction near his mouth and goes in fast. The Farmer looks oven more absorbedly into his plate.

SCULLY (juicily polite) *Do* ye now! Now isn't that *int*ristin'! Isn't that *fascina*tin'! A great city. Ah a *great* city. Well I remember me own arrival.

SWEDE You come from New York too?

SCULLY No, I only seen it fer a matter of days.

The daughter passes behind them; bread pudding to each.

SCULLY (cont) My home was Bahstin Mass.

Every one quietly starting to eat dessert.

SWEDE I lived there ten years.

SCULLY Tin yearrs. Ye don't say. Tin years. A great city.

SWEDE Before that I come from Sweden.

SCULLY Ye don't say. Fine people, the Swedes.

SWEDE In New York I was a tailor.

SCULLY A tayylor! Ye don't say! A tailor ye say. Now isn't that simply fascinatin'. (to the table at large) The gintleman here tells me he was a tailor. Isn't that *int*ristin'!

SWEDE Yah: tailor.

SCULLY Well sir, tailorin' I never learned. Ye might call me a jack of all trades and master o' none, exceptin' hotelkeeping . . . (laughs modestly, glancing hopefully around the table) . . . but tailorin', no, that's a mystery to me . . . It must be a fascinatin' trade.

SWEDE (dead silence)

SCULLY Hard on the eyes, maybe.

SWEDE (More silence; his eyes go again to Scully; a kind of suspicion is in them, and in his voice) How long you been here?

SCULLY Fourteen years this last August I came here and I never had cause to regret it. A good town, sir. Good neighbors.

Scully beams a little nervously, glancing around.

SWEDE What are the crops?

SCULLY Wheat, sir. That's the main crop, ye might say the *only* crop. Wheat. (Eyes and polite gesture to angle of Farmer.) Here's a man kin tell ye all there is to know about wheat, can't ye Henry? Henry's a wheat farmer.

The Cowboy and the Easterner are eating very quietly.

The Farmer nods, saying nothing.

SCULLY Splindid soil. Rich as cheese. Some farms here, the yield is up to thirty-five bushels to the acre. (to the Farmer) Isn't that correct?

The Farmer nods.

SCULLY Last summer at the best it brought 20 cents a bushel. So ye can readily see it's a prosperous community. (A rather wretched smile) Plain but prosperous. (More silence) There are farmers hereabouts who are to be accounted as *wealthy* men. (Silence) *Farmers*, mind ye. (To table at large, almost pleadingly) *Wealthy!*

MEDIUM SHOT—SCULLY FROM THE SWEDE'S ANGLE
Appalled, his glasses wobble on his nose. SOUND of Swede's laughter o.s.

MEDIUM SHOT—COWBOY, EASTERNER AND FARMER—FROM SWEDE'S ANGLE
The Cowboy's jaw hangs open as if he were dead; in the Easterner, a far more sophisticated astonishment and wondering; the Farmer scowls more with puzzlement than anger; all dead silent, hands of all three arrested; continue Swede's laughter o.s.

CLOSE SHOT—SWEDE'S HEAD
Laughing and gleaming and glinting at them in great amusement and a glitter of fear.

GROUP SHOT—FULL LENGTH OF TABLE
Towards Scully. Everyone motionless and silent except the Swede, all heads gawping at him: he is rocking with laughter and quietly raising

his heavy hands an inch from the table and slapping them down again, over and over.   SLOW FADE

FADE IN

CLOSE SHOT—THROUGH THE FRONT WINDOW OF THE MAIN ROOM
Extreme violence of snow and wind, the only visual anchorage is a blanched gate post leaning rigid into it. SOUNDS of strong wind, shut away, and of snow against the window pane. PULL BACK as Scully's aging hand releases a harsh ornate lace curtain he has pulled back, and BACK PAST SCULLY turning his face in CLOSE UP from the window, smiling, and announcing to the room at large:

SCULLY A real old-fashioned blizzard, gintlemen. (Almost proprietary about it.)

FULL SHOT—DOWN THE ROOM FROM SCULLY'S ANGLE
They are all filing in from the dining room past the stove in the profoundly relaxed few moments of shapeless drifting after a satisfying meal. In their whole demeanor and tone of voice there is absolute security; total lack of personal connection with the blizzard except the pleasure of being indoors.

EASTERNER (forward along l.s. and drifting toward the center) I should say it is. (he continues leisurely across the room fishing in his pocket for a cigarette)

The Cowboy is a little behind the Easterner.

COWBOY Sure looks like it.

A little right of center he slowly turns his back, getting out tobacco sack and papers. The Easterner by now is lighting up. The Swede walks much more slowly, beveling almost straight toward the CAMERA, deeper towards us than any of the others, eyes on angle of window; slowly prodding tobacco into his pipe. His comment is a scarcely audible breathing; in his face is already the beginning of a strange excitement as he watches through the window and approaches it.

SWEDE (with a strange, private excitement, almost a whisper) Yaahh!

The Farmer, meanwhile, swings in just behind the chairs at the stove. He utters the quiet gasp of total belly-satisfaction, an "ahhh" not unlike Titus Moody's to Fred Allen, but earthier. He is loosening his belt and contentedly fingering through a gap in his shirt to scratch his belly. Johnnie is in, silent, between the chair and the stove. The Easterner starts glancing at the news headlines; the Cowboy starts slowly toward the stove; the Swede continues very ponderously and slowly toward the CAMERA and the window.

MEDIUM SHOT—PAST EASTERNER TOWARD SCULLY; SWEDE IN B.G.; COWBOY LEAVING R.S.

SCULLY (sharply) Johnnie! Lay on more coal.

MEDIUM SHOT—PAST EASTERNER TOWARD JOHNNIE BACK OF COWBOY AND FARMER

JOHNNIE Want to burn the place down?

The Easterner turns to face the room. CUT IN MID-TURN.

MEDIUM SHOT—SCULLY PAST EASTERNER
Advancing from the window and leaning to peer toward the stove.

SCULLY Sure, it's rid hot now.

He comes down to the middle of the room, the CAMERA with him, losing the Swede, still talking.

SCULLY (continuing) I tell ye, friends, there's nuthin' like a chair beside a stove . . .

MEDIUM CLOSE SHOT—THE EASTERNER
His eyes and head following Scully who is already out of shot toward the stove. The Easterner is lazily and happily observant.

SCULLY'S VOICE (o.s.) . . . to make ye shpit 'n the eye . . .

MEDIUM SHOT—FROM EASTERNER'S ANGLE TOWARD SCULLY and the group coalescing toward the stove.

SCULLY (back to CAMERA) . . . o' the worst weather Heaven kin send.

COWBOY (absently; contentedly) That's right.

The startling SOUND, o.s., of hollowed palms being clapped together.

MEDIUM SHOT—SWEDE FROM EASTERNER'S ANGLE
Pipe clenched, a queer grin on his face, just finishing his handclap of solitary excitement and pleasure.

CLOSE UP—EASTERNER
Much interested, his eyes flick from the Swede's angle to the angle of the stove and the group; the newspaper droops in his hand.

MEDIUM SHOT—GROUP AT STOVE FROM EASTERNER'S ANGLE
They have noticed nothing.

SCULLY Well, I'll be off about me dooties if you'll excuse me gintlemen.

COWBOY Sure. So long.

EASTERNER'S VOICE (o.s.) Certainly.

Scully crosses up the room toward l.s. CAMERA FOLLOWING, losing the group.

JOHNNIE'S VOICE (o.s.) How 'bout it? Ready to get skinned alive again?

GROUP SHOT—FROM EASTERNER'S ANGLE—FARMER AT CENTER

FARMER Son, day I see you skin a gopher I'll deed ye my farm, an' my old woman throwed in.

SOUND of a squeaky hinge across this.

MEDIUM SHOT—SCULLY FROM EASTERNER'S ANGLE
Going through the little swinging gate by the registration desk.

GROUP SHOT—JOHNNIE CENTERED

JOHNNIE Be good thing for your land and a mercy for your wife.

COWBOY Ouch!

FARMER (approaching the table) Jest get busy with that skinnin', son, loud talk never proved nuthin'.

COWBOY (swinging chair into place) I want to *see this*.

The Easterner walks into the shot as they severally arrange chairs, cards and chips and start to settle down.

MEDIUM CLOSE SHOT—FARMER—PAST JOHNNIE
Farmer sits in original position; Johnnie nearest the coatroom and with his back to it. They are cutting for deal and the Cowboy and the Easterner, who are doing the last necessary hiking of chairs, look on.

LONG SHOT—SWEDE FROM SAME ANGLE
His rigid, leaning stance has been four feet or so from the window. He is now very close to the window and is just pulling under himself a small stool.

O.S. THE SOUND of the oily whirr of expert shuffling.

CLOSE SHOT—SWEDE FROM THE SAME ANGLE
The window is beyond him, his eyes are fixed deep into the snow. O.S. SOUNDS of dealing and ad lib bidding. CAMERA PULLS SLOWLY around so that the Swede is in still larger close up, filling most of the screen. He is look-

ing out intensely past the CAMERA, giving tiny, rapid pulls on his pipe; his face showing signs of an inexplicable excitement; eyes becoming almost dreamy. CAMERA SLOWLY TURNS square on the window to focus on what his eyes are fixed on,—the post. Storm SOUNDS UP and card SOUNDS FADING to inaudibility. DISSOLVE to snow higher on post and, almost immediately, A LOUD SLAPPING DOWN OF CARDS and the Farmer's angry voice and the scrape of a chair.

EXTREME CLOSE UP—SWEDE
Deep fright and guile in the face and a strange and malignant smile.

MEDIUM SHOT—FARMER FROM JOHNNIE'S ANGLE
He is just finishing standing up, a look of heated scorn on his face.

JOHNNIE Too bad. Poor feller just ought to leave cards alone. (They nod; they are wholly on his side) Or his temper, *one* or the other.

COWBOY That's right. Ye can't afford a temper, not if ye play much cards.

EASTERNER Or cards, if you have a temper.

COWBOY (chuckles) Mister, ya got sumpn' there.

JOHNNIE How 'bout a whirl at four-handed; or do you reckon *we* can keep from bitin' each other's heads off?

COWBOY (heavy jocosity) Buster, my gun's right on the table so don't try nuthin' fancy.

EASTERNER (smiling with Cowboy) We might draw up a treaty of non-aggression.

COWBOY Reckon I'll throw in with you, Johnnie, you look like a mean man to have agin ye.

EASTERNER (in a low voice) Better make sure the Swede'll play.

COWBOY Hey *buddy*.

JOHNNIE Hey *Mister*.

EASTERNER I beg your pardon.

SWEDE Hehnh?

EASTERNER I wondered if you'd be my par—

JOHNNIE How 'bout a little game?
Uneasy but determined to show everyone that he is not afraid.

SWEDE Yeh? What kind of a game?

JOHNNIE High Five.

SWEDE Never heard of it.

COWBOY'S VOICE Some call it Cinch.

JOHNNIE'S VOICE Ain't no cinch the way that poor Farmer plays it.

EASTERNER'S VOICE Some call it Double Pedro.

COWBOY Never knowed that.

SWEDE *Ohh. Yaah. Double Pedro.* Is *that* it.

JOHNNIE Five o' trumps yer Pedro, five o' same color's yer left, . . .

SWEDE'S VOICE (across him) Yah.

JOHNNIE . . . ranks jest below yer five o' trumps, each count ya ten points.

SWEDE Yaahh. Suure I played it. (sharp pause) For money you mean?

JOHNNIE Either way suits me.

COWBOY'S VOICE Let's just play for fun.

EASTERNER'S VOICE Suits me.

COWBOY (voice up) Just for fun, if that suits you.

SWEDE Fun. Yah. Yah. I play.

EASTERNER'S VOICE (o.s.) Fine.
They all pull up their chairs. The Swede laughs shrilly and strangely.

CLOSE SHOT—EASTERNER FROM THE SWEDE'S ANGLE
He looks up quickly at the Swede (lens)

CLOSE SHOT—COWBOY FROM JOHNNIE'S ANGLE
His jaw drops open, his head and eyes toward the Swede.

CLOSE SHOT—JOHNNIE FROM THE COWBOY'S ANGLE
Not really looking except very quietly, 'as if from under his eyes', holding the cards with still fingers.

CLOSE SHOT—JOHNNIE PAST COWBOY AND EASTERNER
His hands still suspended motionless.

JOHNNIE Well, let's get at it. Come on now!
Faint nods of agreement and shiftings forward as they begin to cut for deal.

CLOSE SHOT—JOHNNIE'S HANDS SHUFFLING THE CARDS
He is a very fast shuffler. We watch him finishing one whirr, and through another, then he puts the cards toward the Swede for the cut, the CAMERA FOLLOWING AND PULLING BACK. The Swede slowly and seriously cuts the deck three ways as the CAMERA RECEDES AND RISES to take in his face and Johnnie's. He is smiling at Johnnie who seems about to speak—not quarrelsomely exactly—but lets it go and starts gathering in the deck.

CLOSE VERTICAL SHOT—OVER TABLE
Johnnie deals very rapidly, three cards to a man at a time, the CAMERA following the cards around and the eyes of the four men following too. The Swede picks up his first three cards as quick as they fall, the others leave theirs on the table. He instantly takes them in so close to his chest that, in looking, he is like a woman looking down the front of her dress.

"CIRCULAR" SHOT
They all pick up their cards and look and arrange them.

CAMERA ON SWEDE—EASTERNER'S VOICE BIDDING

CAMERA ON JOHNNIE—COWBOY'S VOICE BIDDING

CAMERA ON EASTERNER—SWEDE'S VOICE BIDDING

CAMERA ON COWBOY—JOHNNIE'S VOICE PASSING
The Swede's VOICE names the trump suit.

VERTICAL SHOT OF TABLE
The players discard, face up. (They have been dealt nine cards each). They lay them down almost simultaneously: The Easterner 7, the Cowboy 7, the Swede 5 and Johnnie 8. The Cowboy WHISTLES softly.

THREE SHOT—SWEDE CENTERED
Johnnie fills for them. 4 to the Easterner, 4 to the Cowboy and 1 to the Swede.

THREE SHOT—JOHNNIE CENTERED
He robs the deck for 5 cards.

"CIRCULAR" SHOT
The Swede leads, Johnnie lays a card out, then the Easterner, then the Cowboy. The Cowboy lays his first card down quietly but already his face, especially the eyes, have strangely altered. He seems essentially quite a

gentle guy but the usually rather slow eyes are bright and ruthless. THE SHOT CONTINUES to the Swede as he rakes in a trick and leads his next card; past Johnnie for his and the Easterner for his to the Cowboy who, with a face like the Archangel Michael goosing Satan, WHAMS down his card.

THREE SHOT—SWEDE, JOHNNIE, EASTERNER
The instant the card hits the table with its startling noise, the Swede jumps with fright, is mad at being scared and flicks a smoldering, mean eye at the Cowboy.

Johnnie is mildly startled and quietly amused, much aware of the reactions of the other two.

The Easterner flinches with startlement; mildly annoyed; a little annoyed with himself for being annoyed; an automatic and almost successful effort to show nothing.

CAMERA ON SWEDE AND JOHNNIE—THE SWEDE LEADING

CAMERA ON JOHNNIE AND EASTERNER—JOHNNIE PLAYING

CAMERA ON EASTERNER AND COWBOY—EASTERNER PLAYING

THREE SHOT—FROM COWBOY'S ANGLE
As the hand and card WHAM down again, Johnnie's eyes go to the Cowboy, more amused. The two others take care not to look up.

CLOSE UP—COWBOY FROM JOHNNIE'S ANGLE
He is on top of the world.

CLOSE UP—THE SWEDE
SOUND of shuffling. His face has begun to darken, swell and crease; he is looking dull daggers toward the Cowboy from under his brows; sore as a boil. It is clear the Cowboy has busted hell out of his bid.

CLOSE UP—EASTERNER
SOUND OF COWBOY'S VOICE bidding. The Easterner is sizing him up with care; he is a little annoyed and shaken, but a disciplined man.

CLOSE UP—JOHNNIE
He is playing a card, eyes very watchful of his two opponents and still more amused. He knows how sore they are getting and how off-their-game it is putting them.

CLOSE UP—COWBOY
Still more tickled with himself and more ruthless than before. WHAM.

COWBOY Bullet by golly.

NEW CLOSE UP—COWBOY
Still more so than before. WHAM.

COWBOY Reckon that'll learn ye.

NEW CLOSE UP—COWBOY
A card lifted high to wham, then laid out quite gently.

COWBOY Reckon we'll leave um take this-un Johnnie-boy, sure looks like they could use it.

WHAM on CLOSE UP OF SWEDE
By now boiling internally, he sullenly plays his card.

WHAM on CLOSE UP OF EASTERNER
Managing almost perfectly to control his wincing and hide his anger.

WHAM on CLOSE UP OF JOHNNIE
Eyes quick at Swede and the Easterner, just managing to hold in his laughter.

WHAM on CLOSE UP OF COWBOY
Sweat bright on his forehead, his tie and collar loosened, impervious to their anger; happy as a clam.

WHAM on CLOSE UP OF JOHNNIE
He can no longer contain his laughter.

WHAM on CLOSE UP OF EASTERNER
Looking pinched around the nostrils and pretty sick.

CLOSE UP—SWEDE
Ready for the wham; a light card falls.

COWBOY'S VOICE o.s. Reckon we can afford it.
The Swede does a quiet collapse equivalent to that of leaning against a strong wind which suddenly stops; Johnnie's laughter LOUDENS o.s. The Swede, still wearing coat and vest, is in a great state of dishevelment, sweating hard, miserable; by now he is as mad at quiet cards as at whams and as mad at Johnnie as at the Cowboy.

WHAM on CLOSE UP OF THE EASTERNER
His vest unbuttoned, unable to sit up straight any more; he is smiling bitterly; SOUND of Johnnie's laughter intensifies o.s.

CLOSE UP—JOHNNIE
Weak with laughter, but still at it; by now his shirt is unbuttoned down

to the waist and he is sweating with laughter, laughing as much at the Cowboy as at the others.

CLOSE UP—COWBOY
His large, thick, long red neck sprouting enormously from a tie and collar still more awry than before; aware he too is being laughed at but stolidly and hugely pleased with himself: eyes to all three players: WHAM.

The CAMERA lifts and loses his head and shoots over it and the slickening SOUND of the cards, up the length of the room, centering on the window and the wild snowing outside: ordinary full daylight: HOLD, fading the card SOUNDS and the laughter and the beat of *wham* almost to inaudibility and whiffling up the blizzard SOUNDS: CUT TO

SAME SHOT
Well into the beginning of dusk; a melancholy and slightly sinister light through the window, touching everything visible; fade card SOUNDS in and up, and Johnnie's laughter, much more tired and habituated; LOWER CAMERA to take Cowboy's head, the kind of guy who never knows when a joke stops being a joke; another full-sized WHAM;
                    CUT OVER JOHNNIE'S FIRST WORDS TO

MEDIUM SHOT—SWEDE, JOHNNIE, EASTERNER from COWBOY'S ANGLE
Johnnie is practically sick with laughter; the other two are beat-out and sick to death of it. They are almost sorer at Johnnie than at Cowboy and show it in their hangdog glances at him.

JOHNNIE Haahh, Lordy, I could die laughin'!
The Swede, and even the Easterner, flick him bitter glances. Johnnie relaxes still more limp in his chair, tears on his cheeks, catching their hard looks and totally unmoved; just another whicker of laughter at them.

COWBOY'S VOICE (o.s.) Your deal Johnnie, and you'd better give the *other* boys some cards for a change. They sure look like they could use a few.

JOHNNIE Gett'n' chilly in here. (looking up and around) Hey, it's gett'n' dark.

MEDIUM SHOT—FROM MIDDLE OF ROOM
They all look up and around towards the window and realize it for the first time. Johnnie gets up; behind the following lines he puts on coal:

EASTERNER Hmm! (he acts bemused coming out of deep concentration on the cards)

A pause. From mid-room, in the fading light, we watch them watching the darkening, the strange light on their faces, the faces calming, even saddening a little.

COWBOY (quietly) Snow sure does look blue, this time a day.
The Easterner nods; a little surprised that Cowboy notices it.

COWBOY Funny, cause snow ain't blue, it's white. Snow white, like they say.

The Easterner smiles very quietly.

COWBOY Reckon it's the light.

EASTERNER (nods; then all but whispers) Yes.
The Swede, throughout this, is deeply still and withdrawn; his face is preparing, inconspicuously, the strange line on which he will re-enter the conversation.

Johnnie, finished with the stove, crosses between CAMERA and the table to side table o.s., their eyes follow him quietly, light changes on their faces as, o.s., he lights and turns up a lamp.

MEDIUM CLOSE SHOT—FROM SAME POSITION—JOHNNIE
As he finishes with the lamp and leaves the shot, HOLD a moment on the lamp, its light tender and magical in the fading day, and disclosing their faces, still bemused in the ambiguous lightings of the last daylight and of lamplight on in daylight. There is a soft, strange point of light in each eye.

MEDIUM CLOSE SHOT—ON JOHNNIE—PAST EASTERNER AND COWBOY
Johnnie reseats himself, pulls up, and gets the deck ready for shuffling; and their heads turn back from the lamp toward the game. Johnnie, realizing the shift and slowing of mood and influenced by it, dawdles a little, more or less idling and toying with the cards. A deeply pleasant and comfortable silence, tinged with the melancholy of dusk.

SLOW "CIRCULAR" SHOT—
Beginning on the Easterner's quiet face; then the Cowboy's (past him we see the whole room and the darkening window); then the Swede whose strange eyes still catch the lamplight; then Johnnie, ready to resume playing but waiting for them. This shot is to crown and epitomize the mysterious yet peaceful mood—which is now broken by

SWEDE'S VOICE (o.s., quiet and musing) I suppose there have been a good many men killed in this room.

A short, electrified pause.

JOHNNIE (quietly) How's that?

MEDIUM SHOT—COWBOY, JOHNNIE, EASTERNER—FROM THE SWEDE'S ANGLE
All looking at the Swede sharply.

CLOSE UP—SWEDE
His eyes move to the Cowboy and the Easterner, then to Johnnie.

SWEDE I said, I suppose there have been a good many men killed in this room.

CLOSE UP—JOHNNIE—FULL FACE
A short pause.

JOHNNIE What the divil 're *you talkin'* about?

QUICK, CLOSE FULL FACES OF THE COWBOY AND THE EASTERNER astounded and intensely curious.

CLOSE UP—SWEDE

SWEDE (a blatant laugh, full of false courage and defiance) Oh, you know what I mean, all right!

CLOSE UP—JOHNNIE

JOHNNIE I'm a liar if I do!

FAST FLICKED CLOSE SHOTS OF EASTERNER, COWBOY AND JOHNNIE FROM THE SWEDE'S ANGLE

JOHNNIE (very much the son of the proprietor) Now, what might you be drivin' at, Mister?

CLOSE SHOT—SWEDE FROM EASTERNER'S ANGLE

SWEDE (winks at Johnnie, a wink full of cunning) Oh, maybe you think I have been to nowheres. Maybe you think I'm a tenderfoot?

JOHNNIE I don't know nuthin' about you and I don't give a whoop where you've been. All I got to say is I don't know what you're drivin' at. There hain't never been nobody killed in this room.

COWBOY (a sudden swing of his whole head toward the Swede) What's wrong with you, Mister?

ALL FROM SWEDE'S ANGLE, AT SPEED OF FLICKING EYES: Cowboy with the Easterner in the b.g. and slightly blurred focus; Johnnie with the Easterner in the b.g. and slightly blurred focus; the Easterner alone, in sharp focus; all are tightly looking into the Swede's eyes but the Easterner is the only one who looks at all "concerned" or in the least sympathetic.

MEDIUM CLOSE SHOT—SWEDE—PAST EASTERNER, COWBOY AND JOHNNIE
He seems to feel he is "formidably menaced". He sends an appealing glance to the Easterner. Start very quietly, bring up ever louder, o.s. SOUND of "some loose thing beating regularly against the clapboards"—"like a spirit tapping".

SWEDE (mockingly, to Easterner) They say they don't know what I mean!

EASTERNER (impassively) I don't understand you.
Johnnie and the Cowboy exchange glances and look to the Swede.

MEDIUM SHOT—SWEDE—PAST EASTERNER: COWBOY AND JOHNNIE FLANKING

SWEDE (shrugging) Oh, I see you are all against me. I see—
During the shrug, the CAMERA creeps a little to the r. past the Easterner and bores in on the Swede and the Cowboy, the latter in deep stupefaction and rising impatience. By the time of the second "I see", the CAMERA loses the Swede entirely and the Cowboy, in solitary CLOSE UP, slams down his hands on the board:

COWBOY Say, what're you gett'n' at, hey?
WHIP CAMERA TO SWEDE AND TILT UP as he springs up with the celerity of a man escaping from a snake on the floor.

SWEDE (standing in tilted close up from the angle of the center of the table) I don't want to fight! I don't want to fight!

CLOSE SHOT—SWEDE (STANDING)—LEVEL A LITTLE ABOVE THEIR HEADS
They have saved the table from his sudden getting up; their hands clench it. The Cowboy stretches his long legs insolently and deliberately. He jams his hands deep in his pockets. He spits, twisting past his shoulder, into the cuspidor almost at the Swede's feet.

COWBOY (quiet and contemptuous) Well, who in tarnation thought you did?

MEDIUM CLOSE SHOT—SWEDE AND COWBOY
The Cowboy's turned head and jaw in floor of shot at the beginning; slowly CREEP ON THE SWEDE, gaining a little, losing the Cowboy, as the Swede backs rapidly toward the wall near the coat room, in his eyes, "the dying swan look". The TAPPING outdoors is VERY LOUD by now.

SWEDE (voice quavering) Gentlemen, I suppose I am going to be killed before I can leave this house! I suppose I am going to be killed before I can leave this house!

SOUND of door opening o.s.

MEDIUM SHOT—SCULLY, FROM SAME POSITION, NEW ANGLE
He enters from his office near the front door. He pauses in surprise.

MEDIUM SHOT—SWEDE—GROUP IN B.G.—FROM SCULLY'S ANGLE

SWEDE (eagerly and swiftly; head turning to answer Scully) These men are going to kill me.

SCULLY *Kill* you! *Kill* you? What are you talkin'?
The Swede makes the "gesture of a martyr".

SCULLY What is this, Johnnie?

JOHNNIE (sullen, but looking at Scully) *I* dunno. *I* can't make no sense to it. (eyes drifting, he begins to shuffle the cards with an angry snap) He says a good many men have been killed in this room, or something like like that. And he says he's goin' to be killed here too. *I* dunno what ails him. He's crazy, I shouldn't wonder.

SCULLY Kill you? Kill you? Man, you're off your nut.

SWEDE Oh, *I* know. *I* know what will happen. Yes, I'm crazy—yes. But I know one thing . . .

GROUP—FROM THE SWEDE'S ANGLE
An almost lightning quick shot of all of them from the Swede's angle.

CLOSE SHOT—SWEDE

SWEDE . . . *I know I won't get out of here alive.*
HOLD on him, sweating and full of dread, at least three seconds of silence.

CLOSE UP—COWBOY
He "draws a deep breath, as if his mind was passing into the last stages of dissolution".

COWBOY (whispering almost to himself) Well, I'm doggoned.

MEDIUM CLOSE SHOT—SCULLY
Wheeling suddenly on Johnnie.

SCULLY You've been troublin' this man!

MEDIUM CLOSE SHOT—JOHNNIE—PAST COWBOY, SCULLY IN L.S.

JOHNNIE (loudly; with grievance) Why *good night, I* ain't done nothin' to 'im!

MEDIUM CLOSE SHOT—SWEDE—PAST EASTERNER AND COWBOY, AND PAST SCULLY, STANDING, JUST BEYOND COWBOY

SWEDE (one step forward; stops) Gentlemen, do not disturb yourselves. I will leave this house. I will go away, because—

He accuses them dramatically with his glance.

CLOSER SHOT—SAME ANGLE

SWEDE—Because I do not want to be killed.

SCULLY (wheeling, furious, to Johnnie) Will ye tell me what's the matter ye young divil? What's the matter, annyhow? Speak out!

JOHNNIE Blame it! I *tell* you I don't know. He—he says we want to kill him, and that's all I know. I can't tell what ails him.

SWEDE Never mind Mr. Scully; never mind. I will leave this house. I will go away because I do not want to be killed. Yes, of course, I am crazy—yes. But I know one thing! I will go away. I will leave this house. Never mind, Mr. Scully; never mind. I will go away.

SCULLY You will *not* go away. You will not go away until I hear the reason of this business. If anybody has troubled you I will take care of him. This is my house. You're under my roof, and I will not allow any peaceable man to be troubled here.

SWEDE Never mind, Mr. Scully; never mind. I know *you* don't want trouble, but *you* can't stop them. *N*obody can stop them, not God Himself. (sad wag of head) No Mr. Scully, I will go away. I do not wish to be killed. I'll get my baggage.

The screen is empty for a moment, then Scully darts into the shot, half across the screen.

SCULLY (peremptorily) No, *no!*

MEDIUM SHOT—SAME POSITION
Angle for the Swede's "beyond words" backward glance at Scully, and his sad and deliberate exit.
Scully still transfixed in c.s., looking after the Swede; SOUND of a door closing and the Swede's slow feet on the stairs. He holds, slowly turns,

walks slowly and very impressively back toward the table, CAMERA with him.

SCULLY Now. What does this mane?

CLOSE SHOT—THE THREE FROM SCULLY'S STOOPED, INVESTIGATORY ANGLE

JOHNNIE AND COWOY (rather loudly and almost in unison) Why, we didn't do nuthin' to him!

CLOSE SHOT—UP AT SCULLY—FROM EASTERNER'S ANGLE
So close that Johnnie and the Cowboy are not in the shot.

SCULLY (coldly) No? You didn't?

CLOSE SHOT—JOHNNIE—FROM EASTERNER'S ANGLE

JOHNNIE Why this is the wildest loon I ever see. We didn't do nuthin' at all. We were jest sett'n' here playin' cards, and he . . .

SCULLY'S VOICE (o.s., interrupting) Mister—

CLOSE SHOT—SCULLY—FROM EASTERNER'S ANGLE—LOOKING STRAIGHT INTO LENS

SCULLY (solemnly) Mister: what has these boys been doin'?

CLOSE SHOT—EASTERNER—FROM SCULLY'S ANGLE

EASTERNER (slowly, after a long, careful pause) I didn't see anything wrong at all.

PULL BACK to frame in Johnnie and the Cowboy; vindicated and a little smug.

CLOSE SHOT—SCULLY
Miserably and desperately chewing that one over: a sudden outburst.

SCULLY (howling) But what does it *mane?* (to Johnnie) I've a good mind to lather ye for this, me boy!

CLOSE SHOT—JOHNNIE—FROM SCULLY'S ANGLE

JOHNNIE (frantic) Well what've *I* done?

CLOSE SHOT—SCULLY—FROM JOHNNIE'S ANGLE

CLOSE SHOT—COWBOY—FROM SCULLY'S ANGLE

CLOSE SHOT—EASTERNER—FROM SCULLY'S ANGLE

MEDIUM CLOSE SHOT—SCULLY—PAST THE THREE

SCULLY (scornfully) I think you are tongue-tied.

He looks at them 1-2-3 again, turns on his heel; walks toward the stairway door and out of shot, CAMERA LIFTING a trifle to follow.

MEDIUM CLOSE SHOT—THE THREE—PAST SWEDE'S EMPTY CHAIR
Over SOUND of closing door and Scully's climbing feet, each looks from one to the other, speechless, dumbfounded.   QUICK FADE

FADE IN

CLOSE SHOT—THE SWEDE'S ROOM (UPSTAIRS)
The Swede's leaning left shoulder; he is strapping his valise. A LITTLE NOISE; he straightens up wheeling with a loud cry, CAMERA following into CLOSE UP; his terrified eyes are fixed just to the right of the lens.

MEDIUM CLOSE SHOT—SCULLY AT THE OPEN DOOR
He is carrying a small kerosene lamp which scare-lights his wrinkled face. He should "resemble a murderer" sufficiently to startle even the audience.

MEDIUM CLOSE SHOT—SWEDE—PAST SCULLY
Still sick with terror as Scully leaves the dark corridor and enters the lighted room.

SCULLY Man! Man! Have you gone daffy?

CLOSE TWO SHOT—SCULLY WALKING INTO SHOT
Carrying his lamp; ordinary lighting of room.

SWEDE Oh, no! Oh, no! (short pause) There are people in this world who know pretty nearly as much as you do—understand?

CLOSE SHOT—SWEDE—FROM SCULLY'S VIEWPOINT
On his deathly pale cheeks are two spots, "as sharply edged as if they had been carefully painted". His eyes brighten almost as if with tears. For a moment his mouth trembles; then he makes it firm.

SWEDE (quiet, solemn, profoundly sad) Just one rule, Mr. Scully, and I learned it young. Don't never trust *nobody*. Be ready for *any*thing.

He looks at Scully, both daring him to contradict, and desperately pleading for assurance that this is not so.

SWEDE My father beat *that* into me. That's why I'm alive today. (his pleading, forbidding look intensifies)

CLOSE SHOT—SCULLY FROM SWEDE'S VIEWPOINT
Scully means well but all this is far beyond him; besides, he is wholly wrapped up in the immediate situation. He is studying the Swede very

carefully, in deep concern and puzzlement. After a moment he puts his lamp on the table and sits on the edge of the bed, CAMERA SWINGING to keep him centered.

MEDIUM SHOT—SCULLY R.S.—SWEDE STANDING L.S.
As Scully sits

SCULLY (ruminatively) By cracky, I never heard of such a thing in my life. It's a complete muddle. I can't for the soul of me think how you ever got this idea into your head. (a short silence) And did you sure think they were going to kill you?

SWEDE (scans him as if he wants to see into his mind. At last, with a great effort) I did.
He turns again to the valise straps, back to Scully. His whole arm shakes, his elbow wavering like a bit of paper.

SCULLY (banging impressively on the footboard of the bed) Why, man, we're goin' to have a line of illictric street-cars in this town next spring.

SWEDE (stupidly, vacantly) A line of electric street-cars. (he gets busy on the other strap)

SCULLY And there's a new railroad goin' to be built down from Broken Arm to here. Not to mention the four churches and the smashin' big brick schoolhouse. Then there's the big factory, too. Why in two years Rrhahmpr'll be a metro*polis*.

SWEDE (he straightens up and politely awaits the termination of the foregoing lines) Mr. Scully, how much do I owe you?

SCULLY (sore; getting up) You don't owe me one red cent.

SWEDE Yes I do. (he takes coins from his pocket and offers them to Scully, who snaps his fingers in disdainful refusal; their eyes rest on the open palm between them, gazing in a strange fashion)

INSERT:
The open palm, very heavy and alive, tailors' marks and callouses on it, trembling faintly; three quarters on it.

MEDIUM SHOT—SCULLY R.S.—SWEDE STANDING L.S.
Their eyes lift from the open palm and meet strangely in silence.

SCULLY (quietly) I'll not take your money. Not after what's been goin' on here.

All of a sudden he begins to look very crafty. The Swede watches the change in his face with deep uneasiness.

CLOSE UP—THE SWEDE
His eyes to Scully, looking still more uneasy.

CLOSE UP—SCULLY—FROM SWEDE'S ANGLE
Looking still more crafty.

SCULLY Here, here! (he turns and picks up the lamp, CAMERA following, and comes back close again, beckoning, guileful) Come with me a minute.

MEDIUM CLOSE SHOT—SWEDE—PAST SCULLY
Recoiling in overwhelming alarm.

MEDIUM CLOSE SHOT—SCULLY—FROM SWEDE'S ANGLE
Pressing closer; wheedling, crafty.

SCULLY Yes! Come on! I want you to come and see a pitcher—just across the hall—in my room.
Swede very close, his teeth shaking like a dead man's; PULL BACK to bring in Scully very close in almost the posture of a Judas about to plant the kiss, eyes slantwise up to the taller man.

SCULLY Come on. There's nuthin' to be afraid of: Come on. (he starts for the door)

PULL CAMERA BACK and lead them out through the door, Scully holding his lamp high, the Swede following with the step of one hung in chains.

CLOSE SHOT—SCULLY'S BEDROOM
The lamp is thrust through darkness high upward against the wall of Scully's room, picking up first a sliding swatch of ornate wallpaper, then a ridiculous photograph of a little girl, the figure graceful as an upright sled-stake. She is the hue of lead. She leans against a balustrade or gorgeous decoration. The formidable bang to her hair is prominent.

SCULLY There, that's the pitcher of my little girl that died. Her name was Carrie. She had the purtiest hair you ever saw.

PULL BACK to take Scully close, looking up.

SCULLY (continuing) I was that fond of her, she—
Scully's eyes to the Swede, SWING CAMERA onto the Swede, Scully beyond him. He is not looking either at Scully or the picture but is keeping keen watch on the gloom at the rear.

SCULLY (continuing) Look, man! That's the pitcher of my little girl that died. Her name was Carrie. (Swede is around, reluctant, scared, uninterested. As his eyes lift toward the picture, SWING CAMERA to lose him, and past Scully, and to new picture as Scully continues) And then here's the pitcher of my eldest boy, Michael ... (graduation shot, cap and gown, a smart, shrewd, ambitious-looking young Irishman) ... he's a lawyer in Lincoln, an' doin' well. I gave that boy a grand eddication an' I'm glad for it now. He's a fine boy. Look at him now.

CLOSE SHOT—SCULLY AND SWEDE—FROM PICTURE'S ANGLE

SCULLY Ain't he bold as blazes, him there in Lincoln! An honored and respected gintleman. (turning to the Swede) An honored and respected gintleman. (he smites the Swede jovially on the back; the Swede smiles faintly, lugubriously)

SCULLY Now, there's only one thing more. (he turns from the wall and the Swede turns his head back to CAMERA to look.)

MEDIUM SHOT—SCULLY
He drops to knees, plants his lamp on the carpet, and burrows under the bed.

SCULLY'S VOICE (muffled) I'd keep it under me piller if it wasn't fer that boy Johnnie.

MEDIUM CLOSE—SWEDE—FROM JUST OFF ANGLE OF LAMP

SCULLY'S VOICE (o.s.) Then there's the old woman—Where is it now?

CLOSE SHOT—SCULLY'S HIGH RUMP AND THE LAMP

SCULLY'S VOICE (from under bed) I never put it twice in the same place. Ah, now, come out with ye.
Scrambling and grunting he backs from under the bed dragging an old coat rolled into a bundle, flecked with lint.

SCULLY I've fetched him!
He starts brushing off flecks of lint.

MEDIUM CLOSE—SWEDE—FROM JUST OFF ANGLE OF LAMP
The Swede, his eye sharpening.

Scully brushes off a last little whisk of lint and carefully unrolls the coat, and extracts from its heart a large yellow-brown whiskey bottle. He holds the bottle against the lamplight. Reassured that nobody has been at it, he thrusts it upward with a generous movement toward the Swede.

MEDIUM SHOT—SWEDE—PAST SCULLY

He is about to eagerly clutch this element of strength but suddenly jerks his hand away and casts a look of horror upon Scully.

Scully gets to his feet, lamp in one hand, bottle in the other, and takes a step toward the Swede.

SCULLY (affectionately) Drink.

MEDIUM CLOSE SHOT—SCULLY AND SWEDE

Lighted only by the lamp. A silence. Scully clamps the bottle under the lamp-bearing arm, twists out the cork, holds out both bottle and cork.

SCULLY Drink!

Suddenly the Swede laughs wildly. He grabs the bottle, screws it into his mouth.

CLOSE SHOT—SCULLY—PAST SWEDE

Small, worried, the beginning even of a look of fright.

CLOSE SHOT—SWEDE

In witch-like lamplight: bottle tilted high, lips curling around the opening, throat working and SOUNDS of his swallowing: his eyes, burning with hatred, fixed upon Scully.   DISSOLVE TO

MEDIUM CLOSE SHOT—COWBOY, EASTERNER, JOHNNIE—PAST SWEDE'S EMPTY CHAIR

A long astounded silence. The Easterner lights a cigarette.

JOHNNIE (almost reverently) That's the dod-dangdest Swede *I* ever see!

COWBOY (contemptuously) *He* ain't no Swede.

JOHNNIE Well what is he then? What is he then?

COWBOY (astutely and deliberately) It's my opinion he's some kind of a Dutchman.

Johnnie is impressed; the Easterner, interested and amused by both of them, covers his amusement.

COWBOY (continuing) Yes, sir, it's my opinion this feller is some kind of a Dutchman.

JOHNNIE (sulkily) Well he *says* he's a Swede anyhow. (to Easterner) What do you think?

EASTERNER Oh, I don't know.

COWBOY Well, what do you think makes him act like that?

EASTERNER Why, he's frightened. (he flicks ash in spittoon)

CAMERA slowly creeps them into close up.

EASTERNER (continuing) He's clear frightened out of his boots.

JOHNNIE AND COWBOY (in unison) What *at?*
The Easterner reflects.

JOHNNIE AND COWBOY (again in unison) What *at?*

EASTERNER (slowly turning the cigarette between his fingertips, scrutinising the coal) Oh, I don't know, but it seems to me this man has been reading dime novels about the wild west, and he thinks he's right out in the middle of it—the shootin' and stabbin' and all. (he looks to the Cowboy and then to Johnnie)

CLOSER SHOT—COWBOY—FROM ANGLE OF JOHNNIE'S RIGHT SHOULDER, EAST-ERNER'S BACK, IN L.S.

COWBOY (deeply scandalized) But this ain't Wyoming, ner none o' them places. This is Nebrasky.

CLOSER SHOT—JOHNNIE—FROM ANGLE OF COWBOY'S LEFT SHOULDER, EAST-ERNER'S BACK, IN R.S.

JOHNNIE (sore and eager) Yeah, an' why don't he wait till he gits *out West?*

CLOSE SHOT—EASTERNER—FROM ANGLE OF SWEDE'S CHAIR

EASTERNER (laughs quietly) It isn't so wild out there even—not in these days. But he thinks he's right in the middle of hell.
He is quiet. Johnnie and the Cowboy muse long.

JOHNNIE (after a silence) It's awful funny.

COWBOY Yeah, this is a queer game. I hope we don't git snowed in . . . (Easterner glances toward front window) . . . 'cause then we'd have to stand this here man around with us all the time. That wouldn't be no good. (he wags his head) No sir ree bob *tail.*

JOHNNIE I wish Pop ud throw him out.

COWBOY Couldn't do that. He ain't done nuthin'. Not edsackly.

JOHNNIE I don't care. I don't like him.

COWBOY You or me neither.

They are alerted by SOUND of loud stomping on the stairs, o.s. Scully's ringing voice ad lib, no words audible; the Swede's laughter. They all look quickly to the stairway door, then "vacantly" at each other.

COWBOY Gosh!

SOUND of door opening o.s.; all look sharply toward it.

LONG SHOT—SAME POSITION—UP ROOM TO DOOR
Scully, flushed and anecdotal, swings into the room and down toward the table like all three musketeers. The Swede follows, laughing bravely.

SCULLY (more or less over his shoulder) An' then he sez, sez, *'Oh',* he sez, 'I've got to bring *thim* along to *hould* the jackass,' he sez: 'He don't *like* it.' (plenty of haw haw from Swede and Scully) *'He* don't *like* it', he sez! Wouldn't that *kill* yez?

SWEDE *He* don't *like* it, huh? Haw, haw,! Durn good!

Scully is almost up to the stove, Swede close behind; CAMERA PULLS BACK to shoot past them at the seated men during Scully's next line.

SCULLY (sharply) Come now, move up and give us a chance at the stove. The Cowboy and the Easterner obediently sidle their chairs to make room. Johnnie, keeping the board on his lap, simply arranges himself in a more indolent attitude.

SCULLY Come, git over there.

JOHNNIE Plenty of room without me movin'.

MEDIUM CLOSE SHOT—SCULLY—FROM JOHNNIE'S ANGLE
SWEDE IN BACKGROUND

SCULLY (roaring) An' you with the warmest spot in the house?

SWEDE (a patronising bully) No, no. Let the boy sit where he likes.

SCULLY (deferentially) All right! All right!

MEDIUM CLOSE SHOT—COWBOY AND EASTERNER
They exchange glances of wonder.

MEDIUM CLOSE SHOT—ACROSS GROUP BETWEEN EASTERNER AND JOHNNIE

SWEDE Anyhow, I don't know as I want to sit with these people.

SCULLY Just suit yourself Mister. We'd be glad of yer company, but just suit yourself. Liberty Hall, ye know. (he laughs nervously)

SWEDE I want a drink of water.

SCULLY (at once) I'll git it for you.

SWEDE (contemptuously) Nahh, I'll get it for myself.
He walks off with the air of an owner toward and into Scully's office.
CAMERA LIFTING TO FOLLOW, shooting past tops of the heads of the seated
men. As soon as he is out of sight Scully and CAMERA lean down quick
and close into the group.

SCULLY (in an intense whisper) Ye know what? Upstairs? I gave him a
little snort o' what's good for yez, an' he thought I was tryin' to *poison* 'im!

MEDIUM CLOSE SHOT—ON JOHNNIE AND SCULLY—PAST THE EASTERNER AND
COWBOY

JOHNNIE (not lowering his voice) Say, this makes me sick, why . . .

SCULLY (finger to lips) Ssh!

JOHNNIE (voice scarcely lowered) . . . why don't you throw 'im out in
the snow?

SCULLY Why, he's all right now. It was only that he was from the East,
and he thought this was a tough place . . .

CLOSE SHOT—COWBOY
Looking with admiration toward the Easterner

SCULLY'S VOICE (o.s.) . . . That's all. He's all right now.
As the Cowboy speaks, the CAMERA SWINGS to include the Easterner.

COWBOY You were straight. You were onto that there Dutchman, dead
to rights.

CLOSE SHOT—JOHNNIE—FROM COWBOY'S ANGLE

JOHNNIE Well, he may be all right now, but I don't see it. Other time he
was scared, but now he's too fresh. Ain't that right?

COWBOY'S VOICE (o.s.) Sure looks like it to me.

MEDIUM CLOSE SHOT—COWBOY AND EASTERNER—PAST JOHNNIE

COWBOY Looks like to me he's bound to fall off one side a th' hoss or
t'other.

The Easterner nods quietly.

JOHNNIE'S VOICE (o.s.) Why don't you kick him out, Pop?

A sharp INTAKE OF BREATH from Scully; all look up sharply.

CLOSE SHOT—SCULLY

PULLING BACK with him as he leans down into group, hands on knees, thundering at him with passionate solemnity.

SCULLY What do I keep? What do I keep? What do I keep? (he slaps one knee impressively; shouts) I keep a hotel! A *hotel,* do ye mind? A guest under my roof has sacred privileges. He is to be intimidated by none. Not one word shall he hear that would prijiduce him in favor of goin' away. I'll not have it. There's no place in this here town where they can say they iver took in a guest of mine because he was afraid to stay here. (he wheels intensely on the Cowboy and the Easterner—to the Cowboy) Am I right?

COWBOY (solemnly) Yes, Mr. Scully, I think you're right.

SCULLY (to Easterner) Am I right?

EASTERNER (solemnly) Yes, Mr. Scully, I think you're right.

CAMERA tilts upward a little, shooting across the group, still HOLDING them in the bottom of the shot; after a second the Swede re-enters from the office and walks toward them, his footsteps heavy, his eyes on them. None of them look up or around at him.

The SOUND of an opening door, o.s.; Scully's eyes toward it.

MEDIUM SHOT—SAME POSITION BUT NEW ANGLE—DINING ROOM DOOR
Past the stove on the dining room door; Scully's daughter is leaning through it.

DAUGHTER (low, inhibited voice) Papa: supper.

CLOSE SHOT—SCULLY

SCULLY (almost under his breath) Supper, gintlemen. (he gestures them up)

They are all up and filing toward the door; still no eye for the Swede who is walking alone toward them.   QUICK FADE

FADE IN
CLOSE SHOT—DINING ROOM—THE SWEDE
His head is against an almost halation-brassy highlight, through glass, on a broad perforated mechanical-music disc and, when we PULL BACK, a mechanical violin or mandolin: stentorian NOISE of the nervous plucking of the perforations and the exact driven rasping screech of the violin (playing some potpourri of Waldteufel waltzes or of early honky-tonk ragtime):

also a NOISE of cranking and of tightening springs. The Swede's stooped round shining malignantly grinning face is on level of disc and much like it. His napkin on, his hair wetted and combed slick but beginning to spike up awry; he laughs low, finishes his cranking and listens a moment with burlesque of connoisseur's or Old Maestro's relish, imitates a would-be-lyrical phrase of the violin with the skreeky humming of a bass humming falsetto and with mock-affected hands mocking those of a violinist and with a look of mock ecstasy; then smacks his hands together loudly and does a peasant dance step on his way back to his chair, which is almost directly in front of the machine so that the turning disc backs Swede's head throughout this scene like a phony halo. He scrapes back his chair as loudly as he can; sits down, and looks triumphantly and cruelly and with an air of great benefaction from man to man, while he shovels down the food in the manner of Henry VIII.

QUICK FLICKING SHOTS, AS FROM THE SWEDE'S EYES: SEATING SAME AS AT DINNER

THE EASTERNER
Looking even smaller than he is, eating rather little; encased in reserve.

THE COWBOY
Staring across at the Swede in wide-mouthed amazement, forgetting to eat.

SCULLY
His own version of the Easterner, shoulders huddled, eyes to plate, trying to pretend to eat as if nothing were happening.

MEDIUM CLOSE SHOT—SWEDE AND JOHNNIE—PAST EASTERNER AND COWBOY
The Swede is leering happily sidelong at Johnnie, who is eating quickly and savagely. PULL AROUND to lose Johnnie and CREEP INTO FULL CLOSE UP on the Swede, losing the Cowboy and the Easterner.

The Swede munches and finishes a huge mouthful, drinks from his tumbler with parodistic extension of thick pinkie, swabs his mouth royally with the apron of the napkin which is tied under his ears; flicks glances from eye to eye.

SWEDE (with brutally mock incredulity) You gentlemen *don't like* a little *dinner music?*

FLICK SHOT OF EASTERNER AND COWBOY FROM SWEDE'S ANGLE
They are even more-so what they were, than before.

FLICK ON SCULLY—FROM SWEDE'S ANGLE
He primly and delicately sips from his glass, looking a little like a hurt old lady.

CLOSE ON SWEDE

SWEDE Or maybe it ain't the *cus*tom in your country? (leans toward Scully)

CAMERA SWINGS to bring in Scully

SWEDE (continuing) Ain't it the *cus*tom Mr. Scully? Am I making a foe pah, like the feller says?

SCULLY (not looking up; mumbling) O, yes, yes. It's a custom. Music or not, it's all the same.

SWEDE (to table at large, talking with mouth full most of the time, CAMERA PULLS BACK to center him, Scully flanking on r., Johnnie and Cowboy's shoulder on l.) Now on the other side, go to a high class restaurant, beer garden, why they wouldn't call it a nice place to eat without they have a feller with a fiddle, pianner, couple a palm trees on a little platform, they play you sweet music while you eat. (bite; gobble) New York City it's the same. Calms you down. Cheers you up. Settles yer stummick good. (drink; bite) But here, (chew) seems like you gentlemen don't *enjoy* it. (bite) Maybe you just don't like *music*. Hehnh? (he giggles low as he looks around)

FLICK SHOT—EASTERNER—FROM SWEDE'S ANGLE

FLICK SHOT—COWBOY

CLOSE SHOT—SWEDE

SWEDE (Takes another big bite) 'Course in a low-class joint—a *domp* . . . (Scully winces) . . . you can't expect no musicians, nor no appreciation, neither. Bunch of ignorant louts is all. Ain't that right, Mr. Scully?

Scully half nods, not speaking or looking; trying to pretend to eat.

SWEDE (continuing) Yah, just a bonch a louts. (flicks his eyes around) *Tough* guys. (flicks eyes and giggles) But *this* ain't no domp! (giggles) *Oh* no. (giggles harder) And *you* ain't no tough guys. (flicks and giggles harder) *Ooohh* no! (laughs outright) *Are* ye Johnnieboy? (he sideswipes Johnnie with his eating elbow; Johnnie swipes back hard; Swede roars with laughter.) *Oh, I beg* yer pardon Johnnieboy! I got to mind my manners I can see that!

INSERT

Vertical over biscuit plate as the Easterner's small, reaching hand is all but impaled by the Swede's fork, reaching for a biscuit.

MEDIUM CLOSE SHOT—EASTERNER—QUICK SHOT FROM SWEDE'S ANGLE
Easterner's reaction, which is to cover up as quick as possible.

MEDIUM CLOSE SHOT—SWEDE
He glints expectantly toward the Easterner, bursts into loud laughter at
his reaction, which he translates as cowardice.

Up through the SOUND of his hard loud laughter and the hard loud music,
comes an enigmatic racket; the chuffing, growling roar, the banshee wail
of wind in the chimney. The Swede's laugh bites off like a hatchet through
a hen's neck: he is transfixed by the profound fright which unexpected
noises cause in some men.

SWEDE (to Scully) What's *that?*

No answer. The ROAR continues. The Swede's fear increases.

MEDIUM SHOT—DOWN THE TABLE PAST SCULLY
Three grateful, happy faces, nobody eating, eyes all lifted to study Swede.

CLOSE SHOT—SWEDE—SCULLY IN AT R.S.

SWEDE *What's that* I said!

CAMERA PULLS BACK a little, equalizing the Swede and Scully

SCULLY (with sardonic relish) Nuthin' to be scared of Mister. Just the
wind. Just the angle of the wind in the chimney.

They all resume eating; little glances to the Swede and each other; plenty
pleased.

CLOSE SHOT—SWEDE
He listens a moment; the SOUND begins slowly to diminish.

SWEDE (coldly, heavily) Who's scared? (he looks around; silence) Who
says so? (looks around again)

CAMERA begins to PULL BACK on his bullying glance to their silence.

SWEDE (continuing; low hard giggle begins) *Me* scared? (giggle) *Me?*

CAMERA arrests pull-out; Swede is centered, Scully and Johnnie and the
Cowboy's shoulder flanking. The giggle breaks into full malicious
laughter.

SWEDE (continuing; finally; to Johnnie) Butter please.
Johnnie acts as if he didn't even hear.

SWEDE (continuing; reaching across Johnnie for the butter just short of brutally enough to require action) Thankk you, son. (he takes a huge hunk of butter, while Scully winces, and loads it onto a split biscuit. In a friendly, chatty manner, to Scully) That's what I like about the hotel you keep Mister Scully. (chomp, chomp) It ain't got no class but they ain't nobody can say you're stingy with the vittles: hah?

On "hah?", a mouthful of buttery biscuit wide open in mock-friendliness; some of it falls out almost on Scully's plate. Swede, in mock embarass-ment, picks it up as prissily as if it stank and puts it on the edge of his own plate.

Scully's daughter enters to clear plates.

SWEDE O *parrdon mee.* Marrdon me paddum this pie is occypewed, allow me to sew you to another sheet, a-har-har-har-har-har, that's a hot one, huh? How do you like that! This pie is occypewed. Huh? Oh *marrdon* me paddum. (the daughter, behind him, is trying to get past his elbow: he makes her have to lean against him) Miss I ought to say. Mardon me . . . (he begins to finish the spoonerism with silent lips, is taken by mock surprise, mock shock, amusement and delight; Scully glances up at him very sharply; to Scully, pleasantly) She *ain't* married is she Mister Scully? (silence; even more honeyed) How *old* is your daughter, Mister Scully? (no answer.—Daughter by now has collected Scully's plate and vanished down the line of Cowboy and Easterner, out of shot) Mardon me sir I mean sardon me mur; that ain't a question a gentleman would ask, is it? *Is* it Mister Scully? (silence) But it's a fair bet she's older than Johnnieboy, huh Johnnie? Could pretty near be Johnnie's mother, huh?

She is coming behind him with dessert and now tries to serve him; again he forces her to lean, twisting and looking up at her with broad mock-admiration; at the moment her face leans lowest he winks into her face enormously and clicks his gums; she shrivels, shoveling his saucer onto the table, and hurries away. Scully is damn near ready to take action but the Swede breaks through a comfortable giggle in a voice of deep and kind concern, genuine-seeming enough to counter Scully.

SWEDE Poor girl. I must of said something that hurt her feelings. You tell her how sorry I am Mister Scully if I don't get a chance to tell her myself, will you? (no answer) Please sir. They ain't nothing a gentleman feels so ashamed of as if he hurts a lady's feelings.
Yes, I tell you, Mister Scully, you're a mighty lucky man, you got a fine girl will stay with you she likes her old Dad so much, when plenty would

just get married and clear outa this town quick as they got the chance. Cuts down the overhead, you don't have to hire no help. Maybe she gives you her tips, hah? Besides, you run a hotel that ain't so much fer class, it makes up fer a lot if you see a pretty girl around the place. Hah? Little services she can do the guests, don't ya know, that need the woman's touch? Yes, sir, my opinion is, you're a mighty lucky man. (but instead of quite getting out "man" clearly, he nurses and relishes along and delivers a slow tremendous growling belch) Now where I come from, a feller that done that, they'd say it was somethin' so awful it ain't any use to make excuses. They'd just say, go on out an' eat with the pigs. That's in Europe. But heere: In *Ameri*cah: Course in China they tell me, why if you don't give a nice big belch why your host his feelings get hurt cause you ain't got no manners. You give a belch to prove you like the eats. Like that. See? But then you ain't no Chinaman, are you Mister Scully. (the low steady giggle and the look around) No sir, it takes all kinds.

(He looks around for something else to say; picking his teeth and talking through it.) Funny thing, you fellers don't *eat* enough. Look hearty, except a course our little friend from Philadelphia, but you don't *eat* enough. Except Johnnieboy here. He'll eat you outa house and home, hah Johnnie? But Johnnie needs it. Gonna make a *man* of him someday hah Johnnieboy? (giggle) If he can eat *enough*. (giggle) Now me: one thing I can say for myself, ain't nothing ever hurts my appetite. I betcha I could eat hearty off my dead mother's coffin. (the look around) Take tonight. Nobody talking hardly but me. Nobody but me trying to be sociable and keep the ball rolling. Lotsa people that'd put um off their feed like it done you fellers, but not me. Like you see it in the papers, the condemned man ate a hearty breakfast. Supper I mean. (pleasant laugh) All it takes now to make it perfect is another little glass of schnapps, uhh? Settle our chow? Put the stummick juices to work? Hehnh?

CAMERA PULLS BACK to bring Scully into TWO SHOT

SCULLY (almost inaudible muttering) No . . . think not . . . moderation . . . save it for medicinal purposes . . .

SWEDE (archly) Oohh, *Miss*-ter *Scu*lly!

Scully pulls back his chair and gets up, CAMERA PULLING BACK to include whole group and table as all pull back and rise with relief. The Swede gets up too; as Scully passes he gives him a hell of a whack across the shoulders, and steps along with him.

SWEDE Well, anyhow old boy, that was a good square meal.

CLOSE SHOT—SCULLY

It looks for a moment as though he might flame out over the matter.

MEDIUM CLOSE—THE GROUP—PAST SCULLY

On their hopeful, expectant eyes.

Scully breaks down into a sickly smile and remains silent. It is clear from his manner that he is admitting his responsibility for the Swede's new viewpoint.

The Swede towers past Scully and past CAMERA toward the door; Scully follows, CAMERA SWINGING with him. As he passes Johnnie, Johnnie plucks at his sleeve and whispers something to him.

SCULLY (in undertone) Why don't you license somebody to kick you downstairs?

They go along toward and through the door, CAMERA following. CAMERA PICKS UP the Easterner and the Cowboy as they come along the end of the table toward the door.

EASTERNER (low) I thing that Swede *had* something.

COWBOY Anything *he's* got he can *keep*.

EASTERNER When he thought Scully was trying to poison him.

COWBOY *Mi*ster!

They go through the door into the main room.

MEDIUM SHOT—MAIN ROOM

CAMERA on dining room door, already swinging, catching them as they file in, stiff and silent with antagonism; swing with them as they pass on the far side of the stove to the crescent of empty chairs; the Swede strides immediately to the best chair, (nearest CAMERA) hand proprietorily on its back; not yet sitting; he wheels on the others as they straggle into the shot. They are all very tense and still with lounging hostility, intensely silent except when speaking. The Swede just keeps looking at them until they are all there, all still standing; as if he were a Chairman, waiting for members of a meeting to assemble.

SWEDE (domineering) Alll *right*: where's them cards?

SCULLY (gently) Oh, I don't think that's such a very good idea perhaps . . .

MEDIUM CLOSE SHOT—THE SWEDE—FROM SCULLY'S ANGLE

SWEDE (with a wolfish glare) Oh *you don't* huh?

MEDIUM SHOT—THE GROUP—STOVE AT CENTER

SCULLY (subsiding; meekly) Well, of course it isn't for me to decide . . .

SWEDE (threateningly; to the Easterner) How about you?

CLOSE SHOT—THE EASTERNER

EASTERNER (tightly) It suits me if you gentlemen want to play.

CLOSE SHOT—THE SWEDE

SWEDE (to Cowboy) Got any objections?

CLOSE SHOT—THE COWBOY

COWBOY (hard and taciturn) Suits me Mister.

SWEDE Looks like you're out voted Mister Scully so where's them cards?

SCULLY (still trying to be pleasant) Well now that's friendly of you but if you gentlemen don't mind I think I'll just look at me paper; here it is night already and all day I haven't . . .

SWEDE (interrupting; to Johnnie) *So?*

For a moment their glances cross like blades. Then Johnnie smiles.

JOHNNIE Yes; I'll play.

CAMERA PULLS BACK to include the whole group as he starts for the table. The Swede nods curtly. The Easterner and the Cowboy swap quiet glances. Scully looks uneasy enough almost to intervene; then purses his lips, shrugs faintly, and drifts out of the group and across shot nearer.

CAMERA SWINGS AND HOLDS on him, back-to, turning up the lamp on the side table for reading.

CLOSE SHOT—JOHNNIE'S HANDS

The purring shuffle, swiftly, twice, PULLING OUT AND UP on second shuffle to take Johnnie, back to stove as before, and Swede at his left—i.e. in r.s.

CLOSE UP—COWBOY—SCULLY IN DEEP B.G. AT WINDOW

SCULLY (turning from window) It's quit snowin' gintlemen.

COWBOY Yeah?

SCULLY (back toward reading table) But a worse wind than ever. Bitter night.

(No comment from anyone)

CLOSE UP—EASTERNER

Arranging his cards. He is absorbed in the tensions rather than the game.

CLOSE UP—JOHNNIE

He is the only one of them well inside the cards. We see also his extreme hatred for the Swede, quietly and rather gracefully borne.

JOHNNIE (to Swede, after a silence) Well, it's your bid.

CLOSE UP—THE SWEDE

His eyes, in a jagged flickering, down to the cards close to his chest, then toward each face in turn.

SWEDE Don't hurry me, boy. (a pause)

He bids rather high: in this game trumps are named only after bidding is finished.

HOLD CAMERA on the Swede as the Cowboy raises, Easterner passes and Johnnie passes.

SWEDE (to Easterner) Couldn't help me out, Huh?

No answer.

SWEDE I pass.

He throws out his discards and picks up his new cards; looks to the Cowboy, expecting, as we do, the usual WHAM.

Move CAMERA into the CIRCULAR SHOT; on the Cowboy as he lays down his card, quite gently for him; on the Easterner's mildly surprised reaction as he plays; on Johnnie playing, his face very quiet and hating; on the Swede as, vindictively, with scarcely any amusement about it, he WHAMS harder than the Cowboy did all afternoon. His hand moves to rake in the trick.

COWBOY'S VOICE (o.s.) That's my trick.

SWEDE (a dead voice) So? I played the ace.

COWBOY'S VOICE (o.s.) That ain't the trump suit.

SWEDE (his hand still on the trick) So?

JOHNNIE'S VOICE (o.s.) Yeah, *so*.

SWEDE It's yours. (he shrugs and tosses trick to center of table)

CAMERA turns on them again, a little more quickly as each plays, picking up their smoldering reactions to the Swede's perversity; on the Swede's play he WHAMS again, even harder than before. Again he starts to rake in the trick.

EASTERNER'S VOICE (o.s.) That's Johnnie's trick.

SWEDE So? What's trumps?

COWBOY'S VOICE (o.s.) Clubs, and besides you didn't only play a trey.

SWEDE My left Pedro.

COWBOY Five o' spades yer left Pedro.

SWEDE Oh, *five*; oh yaah. Five. (shrugs) Okay; it's yours. (he tosses the trick toward Johnnie) It's only in fun.

MEDIUM CLOSE SHOT—THE THREE FROM SWEDE'S ANGLE
Just looking at him.

SWEDE'S VOICE (o.s.) Your play.

Cowboy wonders for a moment whether to go on; then he plays a card quietly.

CLOSE SHOT—THE SWEDE
Watchful and somber. SOUND of Easterner's and Johnnie's playing.

MEDIUM CLOSE SHOT—SCULLY
In his chair, flinching at the SOUND of the Swede's WHAM o.s. Continue card sounds and low voices ad lib o.s. as Scully loads his pipe; lights it; unfurls and arranges his newspaper for reading as the CAMERA creeps very slowly toward him into CLOSE UP; starts reading. Card SOUNDS fade and wind SOUND is brought up a little. Easterner's voice comes as vague as if through ether.

EASTERNER'S VOICE (o.s.) If you'd held onto that Jack we could have busted them you know.

SWEDE'S VOICE (o.s.) Just play your own hand Mister. I'll take care of mine.

SOUND of shuffling o.s., then of dealing; the card SOUNDS FADE OUT completely and the wind fades to a dreaming whine as we slowly FADE on Scully, deeply absorbed in his reading, his lips moving a little.

FADE IN

Just a little soft in focus, faint card SOUNDS, the wind up a little; Scully is dozing; a wind-whicker wakes him with a jerk with which we jerk to pure focus. He glances up at the clock on the wall to his left; it is eight-twenty-seven and for those who noticed it before the fade, was then seven-fourteen: Scully registers an aging man's surprise and mild embarassment at old-age dozing. He clearly reproves himself and determines to wake up thoroughly and stay awake till a fit hour. He brushes spilled ash and tobacco crumbs from his lapel, polishes his glasses, readjusts them on his nose, resets himself to read; realizes the lamp is smoking a little; gets up fussily and adjusts it properly; business with paper again and really settles down to read, with that peering look of an old priest; lips moving, half-whispering what he is reading; a great rumpling turn of the paper, re-settles again, peacefully reading fillers and mumbling to himself.

CAMERA CLOSE

SCULLY (a whispering mumble) "Lake Titicaca in Peru is the highest body of fresh water in the world, altitude a thousand feet. It's depths have never yet been plumbed." Niver yet been plumbed. Fascinatin'. Now isn't that fascinatin'! (he peers) "Some of the Giant Redwoods in California were sturdy saplings in the days of King Solomon (Circa 700 B.C.)". Think o' that! (he clucks his tongue) Sturdy saplings were they! My! (he peers) "The longest railroad tunnel on the North American Continent is—

SWEDE (o.s.) (in a terrible voice) You are cheatin'!

Catch just the beginning of Scully's reaction then

QUICK CUT TO

LONG SHOT

The CAMERA is well toward the front of the room, height of the eyes of the seated men; Scully MEDIUM in r.s., players LONG, down center-to-left.

Scully is half out of his chair at the start of the shot; he stands up fast, his paper floating, forgotten, to his feet, making the only SOUND in the room. His spectacles fall from his nose as he gets up but, by a clutch, he saves them in mid-air; the hand grasping them is poised awkwardly near his shoulder. From the moment he is on his feet, a solid two seconds of frozen tableau: the Swede half crouching out of his chair, a huge fist, (not shaking) in Johnnie's face; Johnnie still seated, looking steadily into the blazing orbs of his accuser. The Easterner, gripping the arms of his chair, sits very still and is very pale.

After this 2-second paralysis, everybody moves as suddenly and simultaneously as if set off by a starter's gun. Johnnie, rising to hurl himself on the Swede, stumbles slightly because of his curiously instinctive care for the cards and table. The loss of this moment allows time for the arrival of Scully (an old man sprinting) and also allows Cowboy time to give the Swede a shove which sends him staggering back. They all find tongue together (ad lib variants and fragments of lines below) and hoarse shouts of rage, appeal or fear, burst from every throat. The Cowboy pushes and jostles feverishly at Swede; Easterner and Scully cling wildly to Johnnie; but through the smoky air, above the swaying bodies of the peace-compellers, the eyes of the two warriors meet each other in glances of challenge which are at once hot and steely.

At the same instant everybody moves, the CAMERA ZOOMS TO CLOSE UP at average shoulder height, arriving just in time to catch them standing up and straining.

CLOSE SHOT—JOHNNIE
Struggling against restraint INTO CLOSE UP

JOHNNIE He says I cheated! He says—

CLOSE SHOT—SWEDE

SWEDE (shrilly) I saw him! He did! I saw him! I saw—

CLOSE UP—SCULLY
Clinging to Johnnie

SCULLY Stop now! Stop I say! Stop now—

CLOSE UP—COWBOY
Holding back the Swede

COWBOY Quit now! Quit! D'ya hear—

CLOSE UP—EASTERNER
Clinging to Johnnie

EASTERNER (to all; unheeded) Wait a moment can't you? Oh, wait a moment!

CLOSE SHOT—SWEDE AND COWBOY
Voices are simultaneous.

EASTERNER (o.s.) What's the good of a fight—

COWBOY Quit it! Quit now! Qui—

SWEDE He did! He did!

CLOSE THREE SHOT—EASTERNER, SCULLY, JOHNNIE
Voices are again simultaneous.

EASTERNER . . . over a game of cards? *Wait* a moment!

SCULLY Stop it now! Stop it I say! St—

JOHNNIE He says I cheated! He—
In a lower tone, o.s., the Cowboy and Swede repeat their lines.

CENTER CAMERA ON JOHNNIE and advance slowly on him into CLOSE UP SHOT
as he continues

JOHNNIE (continuing) . . . he says I cheated! I won't allow *no* man to say
I cheated! If he says I cheated he's a . . .

His lips form whatever most extreme suggestion of obscene or profane
insult can be permitted by inference, covered and silenced by the Swede's
still louder bellowing.

SWEDE (o.s.) He *did* cheat! I *saw* him!

CLOSE SHOT—SWEDE—FULL FACE

SWEDE I saw him! He *did!* He *did!*

CAMERA, starting with a shot past the Swede's head, centering on Johnnie
MEDIUM CLOSE, makes, fairly fast and accelerating, steadily tighter and
faster and closer, the circling movement by which a tethered heifer winds
herself up short around a post. The players meanwhile are all simultaneously repeating their lines as heretofore with only very close ad lib
variations: out of the din of their voices only key words ring out sharply.
The weave of salients is roughly:

Stop n . . .
    Wait a mom . . .
        Quit now . . .
            He says . . .
                He *did!* . . .
                    What's the good . . .
                        Fight . . .

As the CAMERA thus ropes them in they all close tighter and tighter against
one center as if it were literally a rope around them: they come as close
as five people can get. The ROUNDING CAMERA, at shoulder height, SWINGS
through an extreme CLOSE UP of the Swede past Johnnie's head and then
of Johnnie past the Swede's head practically as if they were waltzing, and
comes to a stop, very close in, profiling Johnnie's glaring head at l.s and

the Swede's in r.s. Now there are no words; only the SOUND of excited breathing, then not even that: a sudden great cessation. It is as if each man has paused for breath.

CAMERA PULLS BACK INTO MEDIUM CLOSE—THE WHOLE GROUP as hands relax and there is a cautious unstiffening away from center; even the Swede and Johnnie step back a little way. Then Johnnie steps forward, fairly close in to the Swede and the CAMERA moves in about a foot.

JOHNNIE (less loudly) What did you say I cheated for? What did you say I cheated for? I don't cheat and I won't let no man say I do.

SWEDE I saw you! I saw you!

CAMERA CREEPS very slowly in: Its motion is that of a very slowly winding snake. CAMERA CENTERS ON JOHNNIE

JOHNNIE Well, I'll fight any man what says I cheat!

CAMERA SLOWLY DOLLYING CENTERS COWBOY

COWBOY No you won't. Not here.

SCULLY Ah be still can't you?

CAMERA CENTERS SCULLY AS HE STEPS between Johnnie and Swede

EASTERNER'S VOICE (o.s.; he walks back into shot) Oh, wait a moment can't you? What's the good of a fight over a game of cards? Wait a moment.

A short pause: the eyes of all five are visible. Already the momentum toward war is in them and is already all but irresistible.

Now a series of quick shots, closer in:

SCULLY—HIS EYES TO COWBOY
(His main meaning: How're the chances?)

COWBOY—HIS EYES TO JOHNNIE
(His look means: Boy, will he back down on a man that accuses him of cheating?)

JOHNNIE—HIS EYES TO SWEDE
(His look means: You lying son of a bitch, take that back or fight.)

SWEDE—LOOKING STRAIGHT BACK AT JOHNNIE
(His look means: You know damn well you cheated).

SCULLY—HIS EYES TO JOHNNIE
(His look means: How about it, son?)

EASTERNER—HIS EYES AT JOHNNIE
(His look means: For God's sake let's not have a fight.)

MEDIUM CLOSE SHOT—JOHNNIE
The others flanking: quick, steady glances at Scully, Cowboy, Easterner. From each face we can see from Johnnie's face that he gets fuller and fuller confirmation toward fighting.

Johnnie steps from behind Scully and walks slowly forward. He looks very quiet and brave.

JOHNNIE (quietly) Did you say I cheated?

MEDIUM CLOSE QUICK SHOT—EYES OF SCULLY, EASTERNER AND COWBOY TO THE SWEDE
Intense silence.

MEDIUM CLOSE SHOT—JOHNNIE
Very gallant and graceful, waiting.

SWING CAMERA SLOWLY to lose Johnnie and bring in Swede who is standing still.

A short silence. The Swede looks like a liar sticking with his lie. Even after he finally decides, he waits a moment: when he speaks his monosyllable it is as if he finally jumped off a high building.

SWEDE (showing his teeth) Yes.

MEDIUM CLOSE SHOT—THE GROUP
Johnnie in l.s., the Swede in r.s. For a moment everyone is very still.

JOHNNIE (very quietly) Then we must fight.

SWEDE (instantly; roaring) *Yes, fight!*

CLOSE UP—SWEDE

SWEDE (roaring like a demon) *Yes fight!* I'll show you what kind of man I am!

CAMERA PULLS AWAY slowly to include the three noncombatants.

SWEDE (continuing) I'll show you who you want to fight! Maybe you think I can't fight! Maybe you think I can't! I'll show you, you skin, you card-sharp! *Yes, you cheated! You cheated! You cheated!*

By the last sentence CAMERA also includes Johnnie, who stands cool and quiet. A pause.

JOHNNIE (coolly) Well, let's get at it, then, Mister.

All five stand very still. Then Cowboy, catching Scully's eye, beckons him aside with his chin. The others stay still as they move apart toward the middle of the room.

CLOSE SHOT—PULLING SLOWLY BACK—COWBOY
He walks slowly, stooping next to Scully.

COWBOY (just above a whisper) What ya goin' to do now?

CAMERA SWINGS to include Scully, the Cowboy watching him closely.

CAMERA LOSES Cowboy by middle of Scully's lines, centering on Scully.

SCULLY (stalwartly) We'll let 'em fight. I can't put up with it any longer. I've stood this crazy Swede till I'm sick. We'll let them fight.

He turns out of shot, toward the coats. In his place, MEDIUM DISTANCE, we see the Easterner, his eyes on the Cowboy, very closely. SWING AND PULL CAMERA so that the Cowboy is again in CLOSE UP r.s., Easterner MEDIUM, watching him closely. In the Cowboy's earnest face there is deep-country blood-lust. He turns from the CAMERA toward the Easterner and the group and walks through them toward the coatroom, not speaking. As he walks and diminishes, the others come into view.

The Easterner holds his eye until he is past. Johnnie, hands hooked in his belt, is looking coolly, studyingly, at the Swede. The Swede, hands open and heavy at his sides, shoulders rounded, a little farther apart from the group than they are from each other, is looking calmly, darkly and a little solemnly, at Johnnie; in a sense he may suggest a chained bear which is about to be baited. It is the Easterner who has especially caught the Cowboy's eye and expression. His reaction is that strange, wavering, uncontrollable smile with which some people, to their astonishment and shame, react to news of catastrophe. Just before the Cowboy gets out of their range the other two glance toward him. Johnnie, with a little smile, looks back into the Swede's eyes. The Swede, looking sweaty, ungainly and bashful, looks at the floor.

The Cowboy walks on between them and toward the coat-corridor: Johnnie is the first to follow him; then the Swede, with a curious lethargic doggedness, looking almost sleepy; then the Easterner, as shakily as if it were he who was going to fight. In the b.g. Scully is already hunching into his coat.

MOVING SHOT

CAMERA PULLS BACKWARD through the coat-corridor (lighted by lamp) past Scully, who is now buttoning up his coat. The only SOUNDS are breathing, carefully controlled, and the SOUNDS of clothes and feet. Johnnie comes up to Scully and past him, for his coat; a silent exchange of glances, the son calm, the father calm and proud: Johnnie slips into his coat easily and gracefully. Only he and Scully are completely calm. The Cowboy, with excited hot eyes is putting on his fur cap with shaky hands. Johnnie meets the Swede's eyes very coolly, almost humorously, as the Swede muscles through for his coat. In this highly charged atmosphere all of the men try their best not to touch each other, but the Swede, in ungainliness, does touch Johnnie as he passes. A cold little smile from Johnnie; Swede tightens his mouth.

As we PULL BACK, and the Easterner works his way in, the Cowboy catches his eye; the Easterner's glance quickly drops. The Swede looks at nobody and nobody looks at the Swede except when they are sure he will not see. The Easterner and the Swede get to their coats at about the same time. The Easterner is very nervous; he has trouble finding the sleeve of his coat but he finally makes it. The Swede wraps a thick knitted muffler high around his throat. He is very thick-fingered buttoning his leather coat and, in spite of his efforts to subdue it, we HEAR him begin to breathe heavily. The Easterner watches his clumsiness; he clearly has a sudden impulse to help and he clearly knows that he must not. The Swede puts on his foolishly small cap and tries to pull the too-small flaps down over his ears; the cap would obviously not stay on in a fight; he takes it off, looks at it for a moment, and hangs it back on a hook.

Those who are already in their coats start drifting away from the CAMERA into the main room and out of shot; the Swede and the Easterner are alone at this last moment. Almost timidly, the Easterner looks up into the Swede's eyes, obviously thinking hard about something; perhaps even about to speak. The Swede walks past without even seeming to see him. The Easterner, with the helpless and fatal look of a piece of foam snapping over the lip of a waterfall, follows him.

LONG SHOT—MAIN ROOM—FRONT DOOR IN DEEP R.S.

The shot is made from the corner opposite the door, inward end of the room, past the stove, including the side table and lamp.

SCULLY (at the door, calling the stragglers who are already halfway up the room) Well, come on.

With their very differing gaits, they all hurry up a little.

Scully opens the door. STORM NOISE. A terrific blast of wind makes the lamp struggle at its wick, a puff of black smoke springs from the chimney-top as the men hurry out; the stove gets the cold wind next: its voice swells to equal the roar of the storm and there is the frightening crackling and hammering of hot metal too abruptly chilled; SWING CAMERA DOWN as some of the scarred and bedabbled cards are caught up from the floor and dashed helplessly against the end wall, (some, including a face card or two, hang flat against the wall a few inches from the floor) with SOUND of closing door, these cards start to fall; before they reach the floor,

QUICK CUT TO

Outdoor violence as, with lowered heads, the men plunge into the tempest as into a sea.

MEDIUM SHOT—PAST FRONT DOOR—EXT. HOTEL (NITE)
The CAMERA is medium close to the door, waist-high, shooting past the door toward the station, as they stumble out. FULL SOUND of a very strong wind, but more compelling than any other noise, a pure electric or electronic SOUND, without timbre, either so high it is just at the limit of audibility or so high that it is just beyond that limit and works purely on the nervous system (experiment will determine which is better used in this context).

There is no falling of snow; the wind is so strong it makes them stagger and stumble; they all bow deep and turn their backs to the wind as promptly as if they saw God; the wind blows great whirls and clouds of flakes, streaming southward with the speed of bullets. Though we have known from inside that a strong wind is blowing, this exceeds all expectation: a solid shrieking roar like flame, plus the supersonic scream, which is on a high dead level.

BOOM SHOT
A little above head-height, leads their floundering along the hotel façade toward the station, (leeward side of the hotel). As they flounder into a thigh-deep drift we hear the shapeless illegible bawling of the Swede,

SWEDE (rough approximation) I haven't got a chance against you bastards.

CAMERA DIPS a little toward them into a fairly CLOSE SHOT as Scully waits, puts a hand on his shoulder, and projects an ear.

SCULLY (shouting: it is just possible to hear him) What's that you say?

SWEDE (bawling) I say, I won't stand much show against this gang. I know you'll all pitch on me.

SCULLY (hits him reproachfully on the arm; yelling) *Tut,* man!

Violent wind.

SWEDE (booming) You're all a gang of. . . .

Wind obliterates the word.

They start again, CAMERA PULLS AHEAD of them all, facing them; brings in
the corner of the hotel and swings swiftly into the lee of the building as
the Cowboy and Johnnie turn in. Immediate and striking diminution of

NOISE: but SUPERSONIC NOISE is not diminished. CAMERA with them, facing
the wall, they walk a few paces in and stand waiting, fairly close to the
wall, Johnnie looking toward the corner, the Cowboy toward the CAMERA.
There is a little light from one first-floor window (coat corridor); its
shade is drawn.

MEDIUM SHOT—DOWN PAST JOHNNIE AND COWBOY
An irregular v-shape of heavily encrusted grass amid this great devastation of snow. A long faint rectangle of light from the window.

SOUND of crackling of feet on grass o.s.; both heads turn sharply.

MEDIUM SHOT—EASTERNER, SCULLY AND THE SWEDE
They come around the corner. CAMERA at Cowboy's distance from the
corner but a few feet farther out from the wall.

SWEDE (still bellowing as they come up) Oh I know what kind of a thing
this is! I know you'll all pitch on me! I can't lick you all!

SCULLY (turning on him 'panther fashion'.) You'll not have to whip all
of us. You'll have to whip my son Johnnie. An' the man what troubles
you durin' that time will have me to dale with!

SWING CAMERA to center on Cowboy, Easterner and Johnnie. The latter is
quiet, noncommittal; a spasm of contempt on the Cowboy's face; the
Easterner's teeth are chattering, he is stomping his feet and is as jittery
with cold as a jumping jack.

MEDIUM CLOSE SHOT—SWEDE
His big head pivoting as he looks from one to another sullenly, still suspicious. Scully takes him by the upper arm and leads him cumbrously,
CAMERA SWINGING and PULLING BACK a few feet, away from the wall and
into shot with Johnnie, who steps forward into shot; Scully grabs Johnnie's
upper arm too. The Cowboy comes in close behind Scully; the Easterner
close behind the Swede, (in l.s.) the Easterner alone among the men, is
still trying to keep himself warm.

SCULLY (in a voice of iron authority) All right now. Fight as ye are: ye'll not strip in this weather. Bare fists to a finish, no holds, no kneeing, no kicks, no gouging. Fight to be ended when ayther man calls quits or at me own discretion. That satisfactory?

Johnnie and the Swede glance at Scully briefly and at each other briefly. The Swede nods.

JOHNNIE Suits me.

They keep on looking at each other, the Swede very pale and still; Johnnie serene yet ferocious. Both are taking care not to blink but the Swede blinks once; on Johnnie's face, noting it, a calm flicker of contempt.

Scully plants a hand on each chest and sets them away from him and apart just out of each other's reach.

SCULLY (as he sets them apart) Now await me signal and abide by me instructions.

They raise their fists, Johnnie with something of the suppleness of a good modern boxer of his time; the Swede bearish and archaic, slightly suggesting early 19th century boxing prints, pumping his fists just perceptibly. He stands solid as rock, very heavy and dead on his feet but looks hard to knock off them. The Cowboy, hands on sprung thighs like a shortstop, face tight, eyes brilliant; the Easterner hugging his arms, looking sick, glancing intently from fighter to fighter. It is while CAMERA CENTERS on him or during his close up that the storm seems to get its long mellow cry.

CLOSER SHOT—SWEDE
The Cowboy and the Easterner are not in the shot unless in the b.g.
Pretty close on the Swede, CAMERA at about shoulder-height: he is pale, motionless, terrible; SWING to Scully, the iron-nerved master-of-ceremony; then to Johnnie, serene yet ferocious, brutish yet heroic; PULL AWAY and CENTER on Scully with the Swede in r.s. and Johnnie in l.s.

SCULLY (after a sharp glance to each of them) Now! (no manual gesture)

(A NOTE ON THE FIGHT: This is to be a sensational fight but not in any traditional melodramatic sense of that. It is extremely violent but spasmodic, full of unskillfulness, and very clumsy—the clumsiness enhanced by heavy clothing and by occasional veerings onto patches of glare-ice. Though the violence is of itself shocking, the chief shock or sensational element is getting the shock of two essential amateurs, non-fighters, in something close to mortal combat: almost as disconcerting as if one saw a couple of clergymen trying to beat each others' brains out. This can be arrived at through the ice, heavy clothes, ungainliness and lack of skill. It is also clear that you can kill a man whether you know how or not. Both soon learn that in such heavy clothing practically all that's worth trying to hit is the head; though Johnnie, assuming that the Swede is soft in the middle, tries pumping them into his belly with hard loud smacks of fists against leather. The fight is not shot in detail or from either fighter's angle, but as the spectators see it—not very clearly. SOUNDS of blows and breathings are way up. Insofar as possible, the best fight would come of ad libbing it, barring a few junctures necessary to the story.)

The two men crash together like bullocks and there is a perplexity of flying arms. We so exaggerate the SOUND of the crash that the audience feels it like a kick in the belly; and instead of any sparring or fooling around they instantly start socking with all their speed and strength. Both are evidently trying for instant and pulverizing victory; also it is very thoroughly a hatred-fight. They work with this intensity as long as their first wind and strength holds. They veer side to side and back and forth enough in this first phase that the CAMERA has to waver back and fill a little, but nothing special—except that it should not frame them too carefully or neatly. The spectators, moving slightly when they need to, get into and out of shot ad lib. As they first crash and sock, a squeezed curse,—it is indistinguishable from which fighter. (For 'curse,' try saying the first 2/3rds of "God" and "Christ" simultaneously, from between tight teeth).

CLOSE SHOT—THE EASTERNER
His pent-up breath explodes with a pop of relief from the tension of the preliminaries.

COWBOY (o.s., a sort of Texas yowl)

CLOSE SHOT—THE COWBOY
In mid-yowl and in mid-air; he lands on his feet again and, hands on knees, looks intently.

CLOSE SHOT—SCULLY
Immovable as from supreme amazement and fear at the fury of the fight which he himself had permitted and arranged.

SOUNDS of fight are strong o.s. over all these shots.

CLOSE SHOT—SWEDE AND JOHNNIE
and as suggested above; till they draw away to get their wind; and they now come at it more cautiously. After some sparring and some wild misses, the Swede becomes impatient and tries to be a bulldozer; by his sudden drive toward the CAMERA, the fighters all but knock it over, and

the CAMERA has to "step" quickly aside, mindful for a moment only of its footing, as the fighters pass in a blur.

MEDIUM SHOT—REVERSE ANGLE
The fighters are past the CAMERA which now, reversed on former position, shoots away from the hotel wall; the three spectators come slowly into the shot, flanking and back-to. The drive continues though Johnnie is now giving near as good as he gets; but retreating a little and wheeling. Wheeling, they almost simultaneously hit glare-ice. Johnnie, surer-footed, keeps his feet, the Swede falls heavily backward, to some extent saving himself with one hand. Scully comes up to them fast, the CAMERA nearly as fast; he needlessly stays Johnnie with one hand for Johnnie is standing a little too close over the Swede.

JOHNNIE (with what breath he has, but not jumping him) *Get* up. *Get* up and fight. *Get* up.

Scully has lifted his other hand as if for a count but the Swede grunts:

SWEDE I ain't out.

JOHNNIE Don't lay there all night then you yellow . . .

SCULLY Shut up Johnnie it was no true fall. The man's got a right to . . . But already the Swede lumbers to his feet, dukes ready.

SCULLY (staying the Swede) Git back off the ice both o' yez.

He leads them in toward the hotel, the CAMERA PULLING BACK with them, and steps back to the edge of shot, skidding a little himself.

A second's hesitation, the Swede seeming a little slow and stunned, then Johnnie drives in on him with terrible intensity, the Swede covering up clumsily, Johnnie working mainly on the head.

CLOSE QUICK SHOT—THE COWBOY
Looking much more excited than before.

Johnnie is delivering hard, fast blows against the Swede's hands which are trying to guard his head, and is then hammering clublike wrists on the bowed nape of the Swede's neck.

COWBOY (yelling and springing forward into the shot) Go it Johnnie! Go it! Kill him! Kill him!

Scully comes into shot quickly.

CLOSE SHOT—SCULLY AND COWBOY

SCULLY (barring him) Kape back.

By his glance the Cowboy can see that this man is Johnnie's father. Scully's manner in this must be something to respect.

MEDIUM SHOT—THE FIGHTERS
Johnnie is still hammering but has grown wholly careless of his guard. Suddenly the Swede uncorks a sonofabitch to the belly which doubles Johnnie, and misses a lulu to the head as Johnnie ducks and backs off, getting his guard up; then the Swede lands a wild one to the head which Johnnie sufficiently covers and glances off that they are now again somewhere near even. The Swede rushes it, taking as much as he gives, which is plenty.

CLOSE QUICK SHOT—THE EASTERNER—WATCHING

MEDIUM SHOT—PAST THE EASTERNER
A monotony of unchangeable fighting which is an abomination. Both horribly skid but stay on their feet. As soon he has his balance, the Swede closes and pours it on; Johnnie regains equality; they lurch so near the Easterner that he has to scramble hastily backward and we HEAR them breathe like men on the rack.

CLOSE SHOT—THE EASTERNER
His sickened face, wishing it would end, no matter how.

COWBOY'S VOICE (o.s., bellowing) Kill him Johnnie! Kill him! Kill him!

CLOSE SHOT—THE COWBOY
By the middle of the foregoing line. His face is contorted like one of those agony masks in museums.

CLOSE UP—SCULLY

SCULLY (icily, to Cowboy) Keep still.

The Cowboy leans into the shot, puzzled and offended, looking at Scully and Scully at him.

SOUND O.S., of a sudden loud grunt, incomplete, cut short; their eyes toward the fight.

MEDIUM SHOT—FROM ANGLE OF SCULLY AND COWBOY
Johnnie's body swings away from the Swede and falls with sickening heaviness. The Swede, with a kind of wild animal snarl, (roughly, *Arghrgh*) is obviously about to swing himself headlong on Johnnie.

UPWARD SHOT—ACROSS JOHNNIE

SOUND O.S., of running as the Swede hovers. The Cowboy runs into MEDIUM CLOSEUP and interposes an arm.

COWBOY (to the Swede) No you don't! Wait a second!

Scully hurries into the shot, nearer us, standing but leaning over his son like a mother to a crib.

SCULLY (tenderly) Johnnie! Johnnie, me boy! Johnnie! Can you go on with it? (he is looking anxiously down)

Bring CAMERA down into a CLOSE SHOT, almost upside down from our angle, of Johnnie's bloody, pulpy face.

Scully squats and his head returns into the shot, close above Johnnie's. A moment of silence.

JOHNNIE (in his ordinary voice) Yes, I . . . it . . . yes.
Scully's arm under his nape and then his shoulders, tenderly, nearest to us; clumsy, humiliated and piteous getting-up and helping-up, mostly back-to the CAMERA. CAMERA LIFTING to level of the standing men, brings in the Cowboy and the Swede in b.g.,

COWBOY (still rumbling) You *wait* a second.

The Easterner steps into the shot at r.s., a hesitant hand toward Scully's sleeve.

As Johnnie gets fully to his feet, the CAMERA PULLS AROUND his left shoulder; Scully still has an arm across his back; the Easterner comes closer into the shot on the far side of Scully. But the moment he gets his footing, Johnnie moves to throw off his father's arm and veers toward the Swede, fists readying, but obviously weak.

SCULLY Wait a bit now till you get your wind.

COWBOY'S VOICE (o.s.) You *wait* a second.

EASTERNER (a hesitant hand at Scully's sleeve, a low sick voice, pleading) Oh, this is enough! This is enough! Let it go as it stands. This is enough!

During this speech, the CAMERA has PULLED AROUND so that Scully is in full face CLOSE UP, the Easterner a pinched profile at the side. Scully acts exactly as if he hadn't heard except that his face gets hard as iron. We hear the SOUND of Johnnie's wavy breathing but his face is not in the shot.

SCULLY (coldly) Bill.

MEDIUM CLOSE SHOT—COWBOY—FROM SCULLY'S ANGLE—SWEDE BEHIND HIM
The Cowboy says nothing; an enquiring look.

MEDIUM CLOSE SHOT—SCULLY AT CENTER, EASTERNER AND JOHNNIE

SCULLY (still more iron in his voice) Git out o' the road.

SOUND o.s. the Cowboy's backward step.

MEDIUM SHOT—FULL FACE, FULL LENGTH—THE SWEDE
Cowboy one more step back and at side. The Swede, fists coming up, starts slowly, stonily forward.

MEDIUM SHOT—FULL FACE, FULL LENGTH—JOHNNIE
Scully stepping out of shot toward the CAMERA. Johnnie is more cautious and much less arrogant than before: still half stupid from weakness.

After Johnnie's advance is started, the CAMERA PULLS OUT, facing the wall and opposite the referee's position (the three spectators pull close into a bunch), HOLDING Johnnie in the shot in r.s., the Swede coming in from the left. The Swede aims a lightning blow that carries with it his entire weight. Johnnie, despite his daze, miraculously dodges. His (Swede's) fist sends the overbalanced Swede sprawling (far side of Johnnie, almost fouling up his feet) a brutally heavy fall to shoulder and a hog-like grunt; a burst of cheering from the three onlookers. The Swede cuts it short by scuffling agilely to his feet and coming in berserk abandon at his foe. Another blinding perplexity of flying arms and again, not from any particular blow we can distinguish, Johnnie swings away and falls, even as a bundle might fall from a roof. The Swede staggers out of l.s. as the three others, and the CAMERA, hurry to Johnnie.

The CAMERA fetches up opposite Scully as he stoops, shooting from a little above him, down on his face and on Johnnie. Johnnie is lying on his face, the bloody backs of his unfisted hands, are near his head, rather like a sleeping baby's, on the snow. LOWER CAMERA CLOSER on to him, to height of Scully's stooped head; TILT TO CLOSE UP of Scully's heartbroken face.

MEDIUM CLOSE—AT HEAD-HEIGHT—COWBOY AND EASTERNER
They are standing but leaning. The Cowboy is looking down, past Scully, at Johnnie; so is the Easterner at first; then he looks out l.s. toward the Swede.

MEDIUM SHOT—THE SWEDE—FROM EASTERNER'S ANGLE
He is leaning heavily against a little wind-waved tree, breathing like an engine, while his savage and flame-lit eyes roam from face to face . . . a mysterious and lonely figure, waiting . . . a splendor of isolation in his situation.

CLOSE SHOT—EASTERNER

His sad but awed reaction, still looking toward the Swede; his eyes turn to Johnnie.

CLOSE THREE SHOT—JOHNNIE, SCULLY AND COWBOY

Almost vertical over Johnnie as Scully and the Cowboy (who has come opposite Scully) gently turn him onto his back, their arms sustaining his head and chairing his shoulders a little off the ground. The faces of Scully and the Cowboy are hardly visible at this angle, and are drastically fore-shortened, so that the upper face of each looks like some kind of gro-tesque mourning mask. Johnnie's face, cradled up toward nearly vertical CAMERA, is also somewhat foreshortened but much less so. It is ghastily beaten, bloodied, cut and swollen, eyes shut, neck limp; head far backward and point of chin highest at start of shot, then up through normal view into aforementioned foreshortening; then again to normal view. Blood has matted his dark hair to his forehead and over one eye. Ice and snow are on his face like a broken mask.

SCULLY Are you any good yet, Johnnie?

Nothing from Johnnie.

With his free right hand, tenderly as a woman, Scully smooths back the clotted hair from the smeared, smooth, very young-looking forehead, and wipes away the ice and snow.

Johnnie gasps and opens his eyes languidly.

JOHNNIE (after a moment) No . . . I ain't . . . any good . . . any . . . more. (he begins to cry) He was too . . . too . . . too heavy for me.

As Scully gets to his feet, PULL CAMERA up and back to center on him in MEDIUM CLOSE UP from the Swede's angle. Cowboy and Johnnie low in r.s., the Easterner still closer in l.s., watching Scully. Scully straightens up.

SCULLY (evenly) Stranger, it's all up with our side.

The Easterner's eyes to the Swede, quickly back to Scully.

CLOSE UP—SAME ANGLE—SCULLY

SCULLY (quietly tragic) Johnnie is whipped.

MEDIUM SHOT—SWEDE

Without replying, he leaves his tree, walks toward and past them, CAMERA keeping him centered, the Easterner's eyes following him, Scully not moving or looking at anything: CAMERA SWINGS with the Swede (who passes between it and the hotel wall) and HOLDS ON HIM as he passes out of the lee of the house to where the wind hits him like a Mack truck and tears at his clothes; he disappears bowed-over deeply, back-to the storm.

CLOSE SHOT—EASTERNER
His eyes return from the Swede, absently and indifferently, toward Johnnie. He is chiefly aware that he is freezing. Bring up SOUND of storm strongly.

CLOSE SHOT—COWBOY
His crumpled, leaning face, from Johnnie's angle.

COWBOY (whispering) Tsah-right Johnnie. Tsah-right kid. We'll *fix him.* We'll sure *fix him.*

CLOSE SHOT—SCULLY
His eyes are still on the Swede's face but are out of focus. He has not moved since his surrender. His face has changed only in looking still older, more stern, more sad, more tragic. He lowers his eyes and stoops toward Johnnie.

CLOSE THREE SHOT—CENTERED ON JOHNNIE
The Cowboy has him half-sitting; Cowboy's profile r.s., Scully's comes into shot at left; Johnnie's eyes are avoiding everything. Scully puts out a hand toward an instinctive caress and quickly withdraws it.

SCULLY Johnnie, can you walk?

JOHNNIE Did I hurt . . . hurt him any?

SCULLY Can you *walk,* boy! Can you *walk!*

JOHNNIE (with robust impatience) I asked you if I *hurt* him any!

COWBOY Yes, yes, Johnnie, he's hurt a good deal.

SCULLY (to Cowboy) Let's get him up, Bill.

CAMERA PULLS SLOWLY BACK and up with them:
They get well under him and lift; he winces and gasps in spite of himself.

SCULLY Aisy does it. That's the ticket.

COWBOY How's 'at now?
Johnnie savagely shakes off their hands, totters toward the CAMERA, quickly gets his bearings and turns, walks between them and leads them, back-to the CAMERA, toward the corner of the hotel. Scully and the Cowboy fall in, timidly guardian-like, just behind each shoulder; the Easterner, who has not moved since the Swede left, falls in behind them.

BOOM SHOT—THE GROUP

From just above and ahead of them as they flounder along past the façade of the hotel toward the door. Storm SOUNDS up.

The Swede's staggering, shapeless tracks are still conspicuous in the difficult snow; Johnnie, in the lead, avoids making use of them. After a few paces he flounders badly in the drift near the door: the Cowboy and Scully, flanking him, are alert but still shy to touch him. They are all practically blinded by the blowing snow. After another couple of steps Johnnie is about to fall: the Cowboy comes swiftly to him, obviously shouting something the screaming wind tears away from us; Johnnie fights him off furiously and lunges ahead, CAMERA stooping swiftly as he falls: the Cowboy swiftly to him; Scully's heartsick face is disclosed as the Cowboy stoops, and Easterner's frozen face behind him as Scully leans; the CAMERA on down to the Cowboy and Johnnie as the Cowboy picks him up as if he were a child and staggers with him up the drifted steps, Johnnie protesting violently, Scully hurrying ahead to get the door open.

FULL SHOT—MAIN ROOM—INT.

From same position of last interior shot, from deepest indoor corner. For perhaps a half-second, SOUND of ferocious crackling of the stove and the wrestling trouble inside the lamp in l.s., then the door closes; we hear the SOUND of falling cards; the lamp rights itself and burns steadily.

The Cowboy, painfully embarrassed, is just setting Johnnie on his feet; the Easterner has just got inside; Scully is shutting the door. The Cowboy is slow, embarrassed, careful not to walk ahead of Johnnie; Johnnie, rubber-legged and intensely humiliated, wobbles toward the stove; Scully is at his shoulder, taking great care not to touch him or say anything; the Easterner, the last in, walks as fast as he can past them and up to the stove—CAMERA ADJUSTING to center on him—almost as if he would embrace the stove: he is desperately cold and his face looks like ice. We look past the stove at his face and past that as the CAMERA DOLLIES into position where all the chairs will be visible, MEDIUM CLOSE. As the others come up, the Easterner quits hogging the stove, moves aside to l.s. chair nearest the wall; Johnnie sinks into a chair and, folding his arms on his knees, buries his face in them.

MEDIUM CLOSE SHOT—SCULLY

Standing, Scully warms one foot and then the other at the rim of the stove; he shakes his head quietly, looking down at the hot shoe, making tst-tst-tst with his tongue.

SWING CAMERA to the Cowboy, also standing; removing his cap with a dazed, rueful air, running one hand through his tousled locks. SOUND o.s., of the floor creaking and a heavy step; he glances toward the ceiling sadly and grimly.

MEDIUM CLOSE SHOT—SCULLY

SOUND of another creak or step. He doesn't look up; his head bows a little.

MEDIUM CLOSE SHOT—GROUP

On the stove, and beyond it, the dining room door. CAMERA at standing height shooting downwards across Johnnie's bowed head (he is back-to us); the Easterner's subtle, melancholy profile; the slack hands and bodies, not the heads, of the two standing men. O.s. the SOUND of another creak or footstep; minimal reaction from the men; then a sudden bursting SOUND, the noise of a door flung open, (we can see a little of this and of those who enter, past the stove in b.g.): the Easterner listlessly raises his eyes as the CAMERA lifts swiftly past the bovine head of the Cowboy and the resigned, caught-with-pants-down head of Scully, to catch the wife and daughter swarming in, oh-ohing and ad libbing brogue lamentations.

Mrs. Scully shoulders swiftly past the men toward Johnnie; CAMERA closes onto her in CLOSE UP, at her speed, above Johnnie. She is a wiry, fierce, worn-out woman of 55.

MRS. SCULLY (crossing to him) Did he hurt ye child did he hurt ye so bad? (she squats in front of him) Lookit me Johnnie let me see yez.

(Under this Johnnie, from his first hearing of them, has been shrinking into himself and now mutters across her line)

JOHNNIE (muttering) Cut it out Ma . . . (a couple of half-whispered words, covered by loud talk from her . . .) . . . sake cut it out!

But she is tugging at his wrists and putting a hand under his forehead to lift his face while he still groans, head muffled in hands,

JOHNNIE Please! Please! Quit it! Le' me be!

But he knows there's no use and she gets his face up (away from us) and gives a close quick look and then a low keening wail as tears spring out of her and she turns loose of his stubborn humiliated head to bring her hands incompletely toward the primordial gesture of tearing her hair at the temples.

MRS. SCULLY (hands distrait in the uncompleted gesture: a wailing sob) Ohh, me boy! Me little boy! And him sitchy charmer! Lookit 'im Katy! Jist lookit that! Ohh ain't it dreadful, did you ever see sitch a starin' horror!

With "and him sitchy charmer," CAMERA PULLS BACK and up a little; through the rest of her lines and, the CAMERA, from the same position, does quick flicking shots like glances of the eye, centering reactions of one or another of the men in turn and of the daughter—shots A, B, C, et seq. The daughter meanwhile is horning in ad lib with "Ohh," and "Aww" and "Johnnie dear," "ain't it just awful," "it's a sinful shame," etc., and by a violence of gesture and voice, Mrs. Scully drags CAMERA (by quick cut and a shade belated) back to MEDIUM CLOSE UP of herself past Johnnie's bowed head.

MEDIUM CLOSE SHOT—MRS. SCULLY
As she flings herself on her knees before Johnnie, catches his face between her hands, already talking loudly.

MRS. SCULLY (in a mixture to her son and the room at large) *Crazy* ye are, jist outa yer mind, an' him a man twice his age an' size, the great bullyin' murderer . . .

JOHNNIE (across her lines, in rage, humiliation and disgust) Get away, cut it out, quit it I tell ya, I ain't hurt bad, I'm all right . . .

SCULLY (leaning weakly into shot, aghast with disgust and sympathy for Johnnie; in a weak voice) Molly! (she neither hears nor sees him) Molly! Please! Molly! Hush now! Molly! Not here. Molly!

Mrs. Scully does a slow take on him when she finally hears him, cuts off her former lines and whips her head at him.

MRS. SCULLY (with cold fury) Shut up an' keep outa this, you! Haven't ya done enough, standin' by while a man half kills my baby boy? (her eyes rake all of them) Crazy *men! Bloodthirsty brutes!* (her daughter echoes her less noisily, ad lib)

Mrs. Scully starts bustling up from her knees, CAMERA RISING with her.

MRS. SCULLY (rising) Poor darlin'! *Crazy boy,* brawlin' young fool, now jist come with mother, *gently* darlin', *come* darlin', kin ye walk, son? *Come* on, let's bathe the poor blood off an' fix 'im up comfy.

Johnnie meanwhile is still protesting ad lib and is trying at least to walk alone, as he had with the men, but not a chance; they wholly disregard his gestures of pride, his efforts to shake them off. With ad libs of "Silly boy," and such, they cling to him like limpets, helping him out past the stove and thence toward the dining room door.

CAMERA meanwhile, SLOWLY TRACKS crabwise, parallel with the wall opposite the coatroom, so that until they get past the stove they are in a kind of Recessional from the CAMERA.

They reach the far side of the stove from the CAMERA

MRS. SCULLY (straightening; reproachfully) Shame be upon you, Patrick Scully! Yer own son, too! Shame be upon you!

DAUGHTER (ad lib) Shame, shame.

Scully has huddled meekly out of their path but now comes close to the stove as if he needed the warmth.

SCULLY (gently, almost inaudibly, meeting no eyes) There, now! Be quiet now!

MRS. SCULLY Shame, I say. Shame.

They turn toward the door on the far side of the stove; the CAMERA continues its crabwise glide and stops when stove centers and blanks out screen, but SWINGS to HOLD them as they half-carry Johnnie back through the dining room door, side and back-to the CAMERA; the door closes.

MEDIUM CLOSE SHOT—THE THREE MEN
Over the SOUND of the closing door cut to a new angle, from the same position, MEDIUM CLOSE of the survivors. The Easterner, l.s., is in near profile; a crescent of empty chairs; the Cowboy is standing behind between two chairs; Scully is all but hidden by the stove. Scully walks slowly into the shot, sits down slowly and sadly in the chair next Johnnie's (next the Easterner, it stays empty); hangs his hands between his knees. His head is bowed; he wags it slowly, sighs very deeply; head still.

The Cowboy, deeply sad and embarrassed, walks slowly around a farther chair and sits, facing the CAMERA, staring at the stove. The Easterner just looks at the floor.

SCULLY (after a long pause) Tst-tst-tst.

The Cowboy exhales a deep damp breath through o-ed lips.

The Easterner's hand is on his knee, flat and limp except for the forefinger, which he slowly raises and brings down, repeatedly.

The Cowboy gets his sack and papers part way out, puts them back.

SCULLY Tst-tst-tst.

SOUND O.S. of the creaking board in the Swede's room. From Scully, a short sharp intake of breath, no raising of the eyes. The Cowboy's eyes don't raise but they harden. He glances with shy calculation at Scully and at the Easterner and again at Scully.

COWBOY (carefully) I'd like to fight this here Swede myself.

The Easterner's hand goes still, forefinger up in the air; no change in his eyes.

SCULLY (tempted for a moment, then, wagging his head sadly) No, that wouldn't do. It wouldn't be right. It wouldn't be right.

COWBOY (knowing why but making him say it) Well why wouldn't it, I don't see no harm in it. (he looks to Easterner whose eyes do not change) The Easterner's finger is lifted a little higher; motionless again.

SCULLY (with mournful heroism) No, it wouldn't be right. It was Johnnie's fight, and now we musn't whip the man just because he whipped Johnnie.

The Easterner's finger relaxes and stays flat.

COWBOY Yes, that's true enough, but (hopefully) he better not get fresh with me, because I couldn't stand no more of it.

SCULLY (commandingly) Ye'll not say a word to him.

Under Scully's line, the SOUND of the Swede's heavy tread on the stairs. Hearing it, Scully makes his last couple of words all but inaudible. None of them look up or register hearing, but all go very still. The Swede enters "theatrically," his cap on, sweeps the stairway door shut with a bang, and swaggers to the middle of the room. He is dressed to go and carries his valise in his hand. He has washed his face but even from here we can see that it is bleeding again in two or three places. Nobody looks at him, or even looks up. All sit side or back to him, facing the CAMERA.

SWEDE (loud and insolent, to Scully) Well, I spose you'll tell me now how much I owe you?

SCULLY (no move or look; stolidly) You don't owe me nothin'.

COWBOY (turning slowly to look at Swede) Stranger, I don't see how you come to be so gay around here.

SCULLY (shouting across the last words, a hand forth almost in Cowboy's face, palm out, fingers straight up) Stop! Bill, you shut up!

COWBOY (spitting carelessly into the cuspidor) I didn't say a word, did I?

The Swede has been watching this, his body tightening like a fist, but quite unfrightened; as he sees there will be no fight, a sour spasm of smile.

SWEDE (interrupting Cowboy) Mr. Scully, how much do I owe you?

SCULLY (imperturbably; as before) You don't owe me nothin'.

SWEDE Huh! I guess you're right. I guess if it was any way at all, *you'd* owe *me* somethin'. That's what *I* guess. (he pivots fast and rigidly and takes two paces toward the Cowboy; then, leaning forward, stiff-legged from his heels, and mimicking even the Cowboy's agony-mask, screams) *Kill* 'im! *Kill* 'im! *Kill* 'im! (he guffaws victoriously) *Kill* 'im!

He is convulsed with ironical laughter. He watches them with great interest and delight all the time he laughs. He bites it off sudden and cold. There is an arrogant and expectant silence.

But the three men are immovable and silent. As throughout this act of the Swede's, they stare with glassy eyes at the stove. They hold it while he waits for trouble, and while he walks leisurely to the front door and, with one last derisive glance at the still group, passes into the storm.

After the door closes (omit all former STORM EFFECTS except a moment's howl of wind while the door is open) hold a few seconds of absolute stillness. Then the Cowboy and Scully jump up and begin to tramp around. The Easterner stays very still in his chair, hardly, if at all, even looking at them; but listening.

COWBOY (whipping from his chair; fist hard into palm) Unh! *Byg! Golly!*

MEDIUM CLOSE SHOT—REVERSE ANGLE—COWBOY
He circles behind his chair; he is finishing the above line; the first words of Scully lines, o.s., come over this shot; Cowboy's eyes to him.

MEDIUM CLOSE SHOT—SCULLY—PAST COWBOY
His fists are shaking with great intensity near his temples; he is working his way out between the chairs and toward the Cowboy.

SCULLY *Oh,* but that was a hard minute! That was a hard minute! Him there leerin' an' scoffin'! (he is pretty CLOSE now, WHEEL CAMERA for TWO SHOT, still favoring Scully) One bang at his nose was worth forty dollars to me that minute! How did you *stand* it, Bill!

The Cowboy and Scully are equal in the shot now.

COWBOY (a quivering voice) How did I stand it? How did I stand it? OH! (a violent fist through the air)

CAMERA PULLS BACK a little, follows Scully. Scully begins paddling back and forth in front of the Cowboy (who stands sort of treading water, making hard little shadow-boxing jabs); Scully's hands are close together; his shoulders are hunched, he is rapidly hammering fist into palm and wailing in deep brogue:

SCULLY Oi'd loike to take that Swede and hould him down on a shtone flure and bate 'im to a jelly wid a shtick!

COWBOY (up to him and almost groaning in sympathy) I'd like to git 'im by the neck and h-ha-aaammer 'im . . . (speechless, a hand down on a chairback with a SOUND like a pistol shot) . . . hammer that there Dutchman till he couldn't tell himself from a dead coyote!

Toward the end of the Cowboy's lines, CAMERA favors Scully's reaction.

CLOSE SHOT—SCULLY
Eyes to the Cowboy leaning into upper l.s., Scully is almost crying with the lust of this kind of self-abuse.

SCULLY I'd bate 'im until he . . .

CLOSE SHOT—COWBOY
Past Scully's round little head.

COWBOY (tries to speak; unable)

CLOSE SHOT—SCULLY—FROM COWBOY'S ANGLE
He looks grateful, even loving—and as if he could hardly wait, and as if he wants to prompt him like a stutterer.

CLOSE SHOT—COWBOY

COWBOY (he looks loving too) I'd show *him* some things . . .

CLOSE SHOT—SCULLY
Satisfied, nodding very rapidly but curtly; almost the masculine equivalent of an old-maid gossip's 'yes-yes-yes.'

CLOSE TWO SHOT—COWBOY AND SCULLY
Faces contorted, a kind of gloating; as if embracing in operatic duet, they look almost straight into the lens.

COWBOY AND SCULLY (almost in unison: a yearning, fanatic cry) *Oh*-o-OH! If we only could . . .
They look at each other with breathless and terrible yearning and again speak almost in unison.

COWBOY YES!

SCULLY YISS!

The CAMERA SWINGS to lose them, bringing in their inane shadows on the wall opposite the lamp, chasing each other in circles.

COWBOY'S VOICE (o.s.) An' then I'd . . . (a sock)

SCULLY'S VOICE (o.s.) Yis, an' I'd . . . (more socking)

COWBOY'S VOICE (o.s.) Yeah, an I'd . . . (a terrific blow on the air; four hard fast jabs, a gigantic uppercut, hard breathing)

SCULLY'S VOICE (o.s.; a fierce grunt of hatred and effort; he kicks something which is prostrate)

COWBOY'S VOICE (o.s.) A-aaahhh! (he jumps up and down on it)

SCULLY'S VOICE (o.s.) Oh-o-OH!

COWBOY'S VOICE (o.s.) Oh-o-OH!
Over Scully's grunting and kicking   CUT TO

MEDIUM CLOSE SHOT—THE EASTERNER
He is staring at the stove, hands slack on his knees; he is listening keenly. As contempt and self-contempt increase in his face beyond silence, CREEP CAMERA INTO CLOSE UP.

EASTERNER (quiet but piercing) Oh, *stop* it!

MEDIUM SHOT—SCULLY AND COWBOY—NEUTRAL ANGLE
They are as arrested by his words as in a stopshot. They look toward him, more surprised than offended.

COWBOY How's that, pardner?

SCULLY (at same time) Eh?

MEDIUM SHOT—EASTERNER—SAME POSITION, NEW ANGLE

EASTERNER (quietly contemptuous) I said, *stop* it. (he gets up and walks toward CAMERA and out of shot toward the front of the room. Over his next line, CAMERA SWINGS across Cowboy and Scully, watching him, astonished; loses them and again picks up Easterner as he nears the stairway door.) Surely there's *some* limit to childishness and cowardice and shame!

COWBOY'S VOICE (o.s.) What's eatin' you, Mister?
The Easterner pauses abruptly at the door.

EASTERNER That's all. I'm going to find that Swede and try to make up for what we've done to him.

He goes through the door and starts upstairs.

MEDIUM SHOT—SCULLY AND COWBOY—FROM ANGLE OF DOOR
Slowly, dumbfounded, they turn and look at each other. O.S. SOUND the Easterner's footsteps and, just audible, a train whistle.

LONG SHOT—EXT. (NITE)
Shooting down the narrow boardwalk from the corner of town (edge of a building in r.s. toward the hotel and station. Minimal lighting. Same SOUND of shrieking wind and blowing snow as before; same SOUND of storm and high, timbreless scream at the edge of audibility. The line of the boardwalk is marked by a little line of naked, gasping trees. In the deep distance, when blowing snow allows, we see the small, single, stinging light of the station.

The Swede is about halfway between the hotel and the edge of town, coming toward us floundering, struggling into the eye of the wind, with terrifying spirit and energy—carrying his big valise and now and then clutching his cap almost like Harry Langdon. Within a few seconds (see note below for method) he comes a full hundred yards. CAMERA shoots him at shoulder height, a little upward toward his face. As he gets nearer an ordinary CLOSE UP the CAMERA PULLS BACK. For a moment he just wags his head a little, fast, almost paretically, looking all around; growing in his face is a hunger for enormity, violence, bragging, love, glory, something, anything so long as it is huge enough to meet him half-way. Suddenly he opens his mouth and yells at the top of his lungs—then stands, like an idling locomotive, breathing quiet and fast through clenched teeth. Then his hands begin to move; fists hitting the air. Becoming aware of the suitcase, heavy in his right hand, he mingles grinning and weeping and moaning and hits it as hard as he can with his left fist, and drops it and kicks it twice, three times, as hard as he can. It isn't enough for his desperation and joy; again he scans the darkness; and suddenly, with his right fist, he hits himself as hard as he able on the joint of the jaw. He reels a little with the blow and whispers something, and stoops and picks up his valise (CAMERA adjusts to these violences). As he straightens and starts down the street into the middle of the town, he is smiling with a strange peacefulness and hope and sweetness—a tired Pilgrim on the homestretch to Paradise.

The CAMERA PANS as he passes closer, and centers on him as he plods down the middle of the snow-foundered, lightless street.

(A NOTE ON THIS SHOT): It is to be heightened above realism, during the Swede's advance up the boardwalk. When he is still in the deepest distance, we use only every third frame; then every second; then cut every third frame; then every fourth; meanwhile slurring the CAMERA speed a little, fewer frames per second, so that his speed of approach is at all time super-human and grotesque, but becomes smoother as he approaches. By the time his features become distinct no frames are skipped but the motion, though regular, is fast and dry rather than silky; it is at this time and pace that the train is run through. As he comes into full close up, shade back to normal speed, omitting no frames. The SOUND runs smooth, not clipped; it is not recorded on the spot.

MEDIUM SHOT—MAIN ROOM—INT.
The staircase door; o.s. the SOUND of the fast train quickly dies. The Easterner comes through the door with his traveling bag, ready to go. His eyes meet Scully's o.s., and he pauses. He is quiet and grave.

MEDIUM SHOT—COWBOY AND SCULLY—FROM EASTERNER'S VIEWPOINT
They stand waiting for him in the middle of the room and looking at him with a kind of mystified grimness.

SCULLY (quiet and reasonable) Now Mr. Blanc, what's all this about?

MEDIUM SHOT—THE EASTERNER
He walks toward them, extending his hand

MEDIUM CLOSE THREE SHOT—SCULLY, COWBOY, EASTERNER
As the Easterner walks into the shot, offering Scully coins,

EASTERNER (quietly) Here's what I owe you Mr. Scully.

SCULLY (not accepting) What's your complaint? I thought we was friends here.

EASTERNER Please. Take it. There's no time to waste.
Scully makes no move to accept the money.

COWBOY (incredulous) You *fer* that Dutchman?

SCULLY Yes, what *is* this about the Swede?
A brief pause: the Easterner's feeling conquers his aversion against going into it. They watch him judicially.

EASTERNER (quietly) We've done him a great wrong.

COWBOY (astounded) *Huh?*

SCULLY *Wrong!* We couldn't treat him fairer—we never touched a hair of his head!

EASTERNER (quiet but feeling it strongly) Ah you don't know the *meaning* of fairness. Either of you.

They move nearer him; he stands his ground. CAMERA SLOWLY CREEPS CLOSER.

COWBOY Now you look here, Mister . . .

SCULLY (Solemn and quiet; slowly tapping Easterner's chest with his forefinger) See here, Sir: guest or no guest, nobody can tell Patrick Scully he ain't a fair man.

EASTERNER Suppose I prove it.

SCULLY Try, just. Fair enough. But Mister: ye better make it shtick!

COWBOY That goes for me too.

EASTERNER Very well.
He sets down his bag as the CAMERA stops advancing: A CLOSE THREE SHOT, favoring the Easterner. He looks coldly from one to the other as he talks. They watch him judicially.

EASTERNER When the Swede said Johnnie was cheating, and Johnnie called him a liar, it was one man's word against another. Am I right?

They nod, with a look, "of course."

EASTERNER That was all we had to go on to prevent a fight. Correct?

SCULLY Correct.

EASTERNER All right. (very quiet and cold) Did it occur to either of you that the Swede might be telling the truth?

CLOSE TWO SHOT—COWBOY AND SCULLY

COWBOY AND SCULLY (together; vaguely) *Truth?*

CLOSE SHOT—EASTERNER
He is watching them mercilessly.

EASTERNER (icy; just audible) Mm-hm. That's the word.

CLOSE TWO SHOT—COWBOY AND SCULLY

COWBOY AND SCULLY (gaping, incredulous, innocent) *HIM?*

CLOSE SHOT—EASTERNER
He watches them a moment very tensely, then abrupty relaxes.

EASTERNER (throwing it away) Thank you, gentlemen: there's your proof. (again trying to pay) Now please . . .

CLOSE THREE SHOT—EASTERNER, COWBOY, SCULLY

CAMERA circles, favoring each man as he speaks.

SCULLY (intensely) Are you accusin' Johnnie of . . .

EASTERNER (quiet, cold) I'm accusing nobody. I'm proving you don't know the a-b-c-'s of fairness.

COWBOY But that Dutchman, he's crazy.

EASTERNER (biting the words out) Stick to the point.

SCULLY If he ever *did* tell the truth—an' that I beg leave to doubt—it'd be the *first* time in his life.

EASTERNER That would make it a lie?

COWBOY Good as a lie.
Scully nods.

EASTERNER Fine. Splendid.

CAMERA, shooting past the Easterner, favoring the Cowboy, stops circling.

COWBOY Why, *that* bird, if he did tell the truth, *I* wouldn't keer.

CLOSE SHOT—EASTERNER

EASTERNER (to both) You've proved my point several times over; don't strain yourselves.

His eyes glide quietly from man to man.

CLOSE TWO SHOT—COWBOY AND SCULLY
A pause. They are cornered; half-comprehending, deeply resentful. They are in some degree trying to face it.

CLOSE SHOT—EASTERNER
In deep stillness he watches them.

CLOSER TWO SHOT—COWBOY AND SCULLY
The effort to face it weakens; they glance toward him almost reproach-fully and look quickly down; they glance toward each other but their eyes don't meet. Each does his equivalent of a shrug.

LESS CLOSE SHOT—THE EASTERNER
He looks at them in silence a moment.

EASTERNER (quietly) That's right; shrug it off; it's a small matter. It's why wars are fought; why a great nation can fall apart like rotten meat.

COWBOY'S VOICE (o.s., booming) Yeah? Well what're *you* . . .

CLOSE SHOT—COWBOY

SWING CAMERA to bring in Scully, reacting.

COWBOY (continuing) . . . talkin' so high and mighty about, *I* want to know! *You* was there too, but I didn't notice *you* sayin' nuthin'!

The shot now favors Scully.

SCULLY (eager, vindictive) Now how *about,* yes how *about* that! Tarred with the same brush, ain't you?

They look to him in bitter triumph.

CLOSE SHOT—EASTERNER
A pause as he returns their gaze.

EASTERNER (with calm self-loathing) *Oh* no. A blacker brush. (still quieter) You see: *I knew.*

CLOSE TWO SHOT—COWBOY AND SCULLY
They are held in a strange, prescient pause.

CLOSE SHOT—EASTERNER

EASTERNER (very quietly) Yes: Johnnie was cheating.

CLOSE TWO SHOT—COWBOY AND SCULLY

COWBOY AND SCULLY (blankly) Johnnie . . .

CLOSE SHOT—EASTERNER
He nods, watching them closely.

CLOSE TWO SHOT—COWBOY AND SCULLY
A silence. We can almost see their wheels go round. Finally, relief and pleasure dawn in the Cowboy's face. As he starts to speak he makes a foolish, rather pathetically helpless gesture, and CAMERA PULLS AND SWINGS to bring in the Easterner.

COWBOY Why, no. We wasn't playin' fer money. It was just in fun.
Scully nods, hopefully. The Easterner's reaction to the word "money" is quiet, sick, ineffable contempt.

EASTERNER (unconsciously; just audibly) Oh, yes!
The MOVING CAMERA now favors the Easterner in the THREE SHOT

EASTERNER Fun or not, Johnnie was cheating. I saw him. I know it. I saw him.

A pause.

SCULLY (solemnly) Mister: I don't believe you.

EASTERNER Why would I lie to you?

COWBOY That's for *you* to tell *us*.
In spite of everything, there is a flicker of amusement in the Easterner over this lulu.

SCULLY (shrewdly) Ye lied before *or* now, by yer own admission. I'll take me pick.

EASTERNER (mildly) I lied when I kept quiet.

SCULLY *Why? If* ye saw what ye claim?
A pause. CAMERA moves into CLOSE SHOT of the Easterner, losing them.

EASTERNER (quietly) Cowardice.

CLOSE TWO SHOT—SCULLY AND COWBOY
They can't comprehend or believe such an admission.

CLOSE SHOT—EASTERNER

EASTERNER That's all. (his eyes show us they still can't understand; with self-contempt and weary patience) We hated the Swede; you believed Johnnie; you liked me. I wasn't man enough to make enemies of you. I let that poor fool fight it out alone.

He looks from man to man in silence.

CLOSE TWO SHOT—SCULLY AND COWBOY
They are silent a moment.

SCULLY (quietly) Then why're ye tellin' us now?

CLOSE SHOT—EASTERNER

EASTERNER Because there's a *limit* to cowardice.

CLOSE TWO SHOT—SCULLY AND COWBOY
A short silence as they ponder that.

COWBOY (solemnly) Mister, if you're tellin' the truth, you're makin' yerself out the *yallerist* coward ever I seen.

CLOSE SHOT—EASTERNER

PULLING BACK, as he speaks, into a CLOSE THREE SHOT

EASTERNER Oh, we're all cowards; that's the *root* of the trouble. Johnnie is behind *us;* you're afraid to face the truth about him and your own unfairness; I'm just the worst of a bad bunch.

A short pause.

SCULLY (bitterly) I s'pose that Swede's your idea of a hero.

EASTERNER He was the only brave man here tonight.

SCULLY *Brave? Him?*

COWBOY *Him? His knees* was knockin'!

CLOSE SHOT—EASTERNER

EASTERNER (new realizations breaking open) Sure; he was scared sick. My bet is, he's been sick all his life, with cowardice. What a living hell! But I guess he reached *his* limit too. He stood up to it tonight—worse fear than we'll ever dream of. And beat it too—sure as he beat up Johnnie. Yes Mr. Scully, he's my idea of a hero. And whatever becomes of him now, it's our fault as much as his.

COWBOY'S VOICE (o.s.) *Our* fault! Why, that feller's just . . .

EASTERNER (catching fire more) Certainly our fault. Good heavens, we flatter ourselves we're civilized men . . . fit to cope with Destiny, Fate, the Devil Himself. And we come up against some puzzling minor disturbance like this Swede, and all we can do is the worst that's in us. (a strange, almost clairvoyant bitterness) Oh, *we declared ourselves,* all right . . . as sure as that blue-legged heron! Yes indeed! *We* made him what he's become tonight. *We're* the ones who've put him in danger!

SCULLY'S VOICE (o.s.; bewildered scorn) Talk sense, man! *Danger!*

EASTERNER Look here. Any man is in danger who has spent a lifetime in fear and humiliation, and then suddenly finds his right to be alive. He's a danger to others, too. He doesn't know any better yet how to handle his power, than a child with a loaded gun.

He studies their baffled, hostile faces with deep intensity as the CAMERA PULLS AWAY into a CLOSE THREE SHOT and, with almost a snarl of impatience over having delayed too long and uselessly, reaches down for his bag. Scully's hand detains him.

SCULLY Just a minute, you: Johnnie's goin' to have a fair hearin'.

EASTERNER Oh by *all* means for *Johnnie!* But don't waste *my* time with it. I've . . .

O.S. SOUND of the dining room door opening. Instantly they all become very still and look toward it.

MEDIUM LONG SHOT—JOHNNIE—NEUTRAL ANGLE
He limps toward them, washed, but cut and bruised; partly undressed; on his way to bed. As he comes nearer the CAMERA SWINGS to bring in the other three, MEDIUM CLOSE, favoring Scully.

SCULLY (quietly) Johnnie . . .

JOHNNIE H'lo, Pop. (to the others, with a sad, brave smile as he starts past) 'Night.

SCULLY (gravely) Johnnie . . .
His tone makes Johnnie stop.

CLOSE THREE SHOT—EASTERNER, COWBOY, SCULLY—FAVORING SCULLY

SCULLY (quietly) Mr. Blanc has something to say to you.

CLOSE TWO SHOT—JOHNNIE—PAST SCULLY
Cutting across the foregoing line.

There is a cold, lightning-like spasm in Johnnie's eyes. Then he is friendly, tired, ingenuous.

JOHNNIE Leavin' us, Mister?

CLOSE GROUP SHOT—FAVORING JOHNNIE AND EASTERNER
The others watch them closely, but watch the Easterner sharper than Johnnie.

JOHNNIE (likably) Well what's up?

EASTERNER (very quiet) You cheated, Johnnie.

JOHNNIE (smiling incredulously) What's that?

EASTERNER I said, you cheated. I saw you.
Johnnie looks at him very hard for a moment; then to Scully and the Cowboy, with the smile of a tired good-guy.

JOHNNIE (to Scully and Cowboy) What *is* this, a joke?
They are silent.

JOHNNIE (dignified, quiet and reasonable) You must of made a big mistake, Mister; 'cause I don't cheat.

SCULLY (with pathetic eagerness) Now how *about* that, Sir!

COWBOY (forgivingly) Anybody can make a mistake.
For several seconds Johnnie and the Easterner look hard and quietly at each other. Then the Easterner turns to Scully, again extending the coins.

EASTERNER (not unkindly) I owe you this, Mr. Scully.
Johnnie surges toward him but is restrained with curious ease by the Cowboy and Scully.

SCULLY Now none o' that, son. There's been enough o' that.

EASTERNER (to Scully) You won't take it?
There is no answer from Scully.

EASTERNER Well I can't keep it.
He quietly lays the coins on the floor at Scully's feet. Then he wipes the coin-sweat from his palms onto his coat and picks up his bag.

EASTERNER (on a queer, wild impulse) I'm sorry it isn't thirty pieces of silver.

He turns and walks away toward the door and out of the shot. They watch after him. The Cowboy is utterly baffled by his remark but Scully calls after him bitterly.

SCULLY So now he's *sacred* into the bargain!

MEDIUM SHOT—EASTERNER—FROM THEIR VIEWPOINT
This shot cuts across Scully's line. The Easterner is still walking away from the CAMERA toward the front door. He stops and turns, looking from man to man and, at one moment, directly into the lens.

EASTERNER (quietly) Sacred enough; he's my conscience. Yours too, if you only knew it.

He turns away and goes out the front door.

MEDIUM THREE SHOT—SCULLY, JOHNNIE, COWBOY

O.S. SOUND of the closing door. They watch after him. A silence.

JOHNNIE (quietly) Matter with that guy? Gone crazy?
No answer.

SCULLY (even more quietly) We can't let him *shpread* it all over town.
While the others start for their coats he squats and, with sad dignity, starts to pick up the coins. ON HIM, as he does so, SWIFTLY IRIS OUT.

MEDIUM SHOT—SWEDE—A STREET CORNER (NITE)
He emerges from almost pitch darkness into faint visibility, into MEDIUM
CLOSE UP, looking right and left as he comes to the new intersection. His
face lights up and he stops in his tracks. He is still transcendent, but
much more tired than before.

The CAMERA wrenches through an almost 120-degree, streaking turn to
the left of him, and stops as abruptly as it started. Slant-wise down the
side street, fairly distant, there is a blur of light through furious snow.
A dim sign reads BAR or SALOON.

CLOSE SHOT— SWEDE
With a weary, grateful air of seeing home at last, he sets down his valise.
Then he bends over deep-below-screen and straightens up again and
his hands are full of snow, with which, with great simplicity and infinite
refreshment, he washes his cut face and hands. Then he flicks and shakes
the wet from his hands, lifts his cap with one hand and rakes his other
hand through his hair, replaces his cap and, his face alight with anticipation and new hope, almost with love, picks up his valise, and bevels off
toward the light in a rigid oblique, regardless of drifts, the sidewalk, etc.;
the CAMERA SWINGING to center on his plodding back.

QUICK FADE

FADE IN
INT. MEDIUM CLOSE SHOT—THE BAR—FOUR MEN AT A TABLE (NITE)
It is a clean, well-lighted place; not big. A table at the rear; four men at it:
a lawyer, a doctor, a merchant and a gambler.

We shoot past the Gambler's left shoulder, MEDIUM CLOSE, on the Doctor
at our left; the Lawyer facing toward the front of bar, the Merchant on
our right. It is self-evident by their looks that the three we can see
are among the most respectable and well-to-do men in town. Smoothest
of all is the Lawyer. Of the Gambler we see nothing yet except the
shoulder of his coat and perhaps a rather fine hand with a wedding ring
on it, and a soberly-jewel-linked cuff, and a sleeve of a suit as sober as
the others, except it is an elegant dove-gray. They are all smoking cigars,
and there are drinks on the table. The Lawyer is doing all of the talking,
quietly, smoothly and earnestly; looking always directly into the Gambler's
eyes. We soon realize he is the spokesman for the rest, by the way the
Doctor gazes into the table, nodding now and then, and the Merchant
gazes at the Lawyer, nodding more often and more sensitively; and
by what he is saying.

LAWYER Of course we hardly need to tell you, Sir, how deeply we regret
it: Even those of us who voted against you on principle . . . and it is in

our honorableness and candor due a friend that I tell you that I was one of them . . . (the Merchant is deeply moved by admiration for all this) . . . even *we* regretted it *most painfully,* perhaps most painfully of all if I may say so. After all, every responsible person in Fort Romper, every self-respecting man in this part of the State, knows you as a *square* gambler. You have never yet been known to take advantage of any man who didn't, in every sensible person's . . . uh . . . in the opinion of every sensible person, richly deserve it, one might say "ask for it". Your family life is exemplary. Your companionship is a pleasure which all of us hope to share for many years to come (even more earnestly and gently) But we do hope you understand, Sir. After all, (his voice all but cracks with earnestness) the *Pollywog* Club is a *pleasure* club. Oh, stakes, perhaps modest stakes, but among amateurs as it were; (a feeble would-be-charming smile) greenhorns. Of course there isn't a single member of our little club who could *imagine* that you would ever . . . ever, well, as it were, uh, well, violate, uh, take advantage of . . . (by now he is thoroughly miserable) . . . I do hope you understand me, Sir. (the invisible man just lets him fry) But a *professional gambler,* after all. It's just the *principle* of the thing you know. The ap . . . the app*ear*ance of the thing. No personal offense in the world. (pause; no help from the Gambler) (miserably but with dignity) I do only hope you understand me, Sir, how very deeply embarrassing this is for me . . . for all of us. How very deeply we regret it.

They wait, eyes as before. A medium pause.

GAMBLER'S VOICE (o.s.; an even smoother, gentler voice, whose icy central irony totally escapes them) My dear sir: friends: I wish I might have saved you this painful embarrassment. It is because I honor you as gentlemen and as friends that I know that you must meet me with candor, however painful that might be for you. I am deeply grateful for that candor. Allow me to meet you with equal candor. I think I need say only this: *If I were* a member of the Pollywog Club, and my own name or that of any other professional gambler were brought to a vote, I would have acted precisely as you have done, for precisely the same reasons, and with precisely the same sentiments, before, during, and after. In a word, I would have blackballed myself from the Pollywog without a second thought.

During this speech the Doctor and the Merchant have turned their eyes slowly to him in wonder and almost in unbelief, and the Lawyer's eyes have stayed on his, burning with a steadily increasing light of deep emotion. By the end of it they are all looking at him practically as if he were Jesus and could cook into the bargain.

The Lawyer's eyes are brimming; he clears his throat but he can't speak yet; the Merchant looks at him and now his eyes brim too. At last the Lawyer rises (the others hurriedly following suit) with his glass.

LAWYER (all choked up; very quietly) Let us stand, my friends, and drink: to a gentleman!

MEDIUM CLOSE SHOT—THE GAMBLER
As he rises quickly; he is elegant, histrionic; quietly dignified, cold as ice.

GAMBLER (with a slight bow) To you: gentlemen: and my good friends.

They all touch glasses and drink with their respective ideas of 18th century elegance. The Merchant, overwhelmed with emotion, clearly has the sudden idea of smashing his glass and makes the start of a gesture toward that end.

BARKEEPER'S VOICE (o.s., gently but alarmed) Hey—*Hey!*
The Merchant shrivels up with humiliation like a spider in a flame; the Gambler's amused delight is beautifully concealed. He doesn't look around at the barkeeper, but modestly at the table. Both others glance sharply at the barkeeper.

MEDIUM SHOT—BARKEEPER
From their angle, about halfway up the bar. His forehead is still wrinkled with dismay; he is awfully embarrassed to have spoken so sharp to such respectable folks.

BARKEEPER (in a low voice) 'Scuse me, folks, it just slipped out.
CLOSE GROUP SHOT
Between the Lawyer and the Doctor, on the Merchant and the Gambler. The Lawyer, by his slight stiff turn of head away from the Barkeeper, does not even deign to grant him pardon. The Gambler is very quiet; an almost tenderly sympathetic smile behind which he is reveling in a cruel delight of ironic amusement. The Doctor's head rugged and quiet, a little more scraggy looking than before. The Merchant, crumpled with embarrassment, is just carefully setting down his glass. The Lawyer saves the situation virtually unimpaired by bowing slightly and formally to the Gambler, who returns it to the table at large; the Doctor bows, and the Merchant, a trifle late; as they sit down, the Lawyer gently, manfully claps the Merchant on the shoulder; a glance from the Merchant of spaniel-like gratitude. Their noble mood is addled but not utterly destroyed: they seek to repair it. By the Gambler's smile we know exactly the smile, from the Lawyer, which elicited it; the Merchant is trying to smile too when there is

the o.s. SOUND of the front door opening and a stamping in the vestibule between the street door and the swinging doors: all glance toward the door
except the Gambler, who watches the Lawyer.

LONG SHOT—THE FRONT DOOR
Top rim of the bar in r.s. The rim of the bar is exactly level in perspective
and sprouts from exact center of the right edge of the screen. An almost in-
stantaneous shot as the Swede starts coming through the swinging doors.

CLOSE SHOT—SWEDE
At head height, as he comes through. He is as high and glowing as before,
though slightly less wild; the sudden warmth hits him like a shock of
peace and good prospect; his face softens and swells; his eyes flick the
joint. Again a very brief shot; he is stepping forward.

LONG SHOT—THE TABLE
Faces and eyes just at the end of casually looking at him; resuming their
private conversation. This shot is as quick as a glance.

MEDIUM CLOSE SHOT—BARKEEPER
At his station near mid-bar. Eyes quick from the table to the Swede, a
quick size-up; underplayed and, again, as quick as a glance.

CLOSE SHOT—DOWN ON THE SWEDE'S VALISE AND RIGHT FOOT
He plants his right shoe on the rail; it is clogged with snow; he stomps
and scrapes rather loudly, trying to clear it.

MEDIUM LONG SHOT—THE TABLE
Quick, gentlemanly glances of annoyed wondering what it is, finding out,
gentlemanly ignoring of the boorishness; back to their muttons.

CLOSE SHOT—BARKEEPER
A sharp little glance toward the table and toward the noise; annoyance; a
tinge of refinement.

CLOSE DOWN SHOT—VALISE AND FOOT
The Swede gets his foot hung comfortably.

CLOSE SHOT—THE SWEDE
He settles his elbows at the bar. He is tired, almost sleepy with the sudden
warmth; glowing like a stove; still on top of the world but becoming
very peaceful.

SWEDE (eyes to Barkeeper) Gimme some whiskey, will you?
The Barkeeper walks quietly into the shot with a high-grade Bartender's
faintly insolent politeness toward a low-grade customer; he plants a bottle
on the bar, a whiskey glass, and a glass of ice-thick water.

The Swede pours himself an abnormal portion and drinks it down in three gulps. While the Swede pours and gulps, the Barkeeper, past him, pretty close in the shot, is making the pretension of blindness which is the distinction of his class, but it can be seen that he is furtively studying the half-erased bloodstains on the Swede's face.

BARKEEPER (indifferently) Pretty bad night.
No answer.

BARKEEPER Bad night. (his meaning is clearly double and quietly discourteous: bad night for *you,* bud, that's clear enough)

SWEDE (pouring more whiskey) Oh, it's good enough for me.
He roots under his coat and deep into his britches-pocket, slaps down a coin, and tosses off the new drink, eyes following the Barkeeper.

MEDIUM SHOT—BARKEEPER—FROM SWEDE'S ANGLE
Putting the coin through a highly-nickeled cash register with a brilliant clanging of the bell.

CLOSER SHOT—SWEDE
As he finishes his second drink; he is heavier now yet still tremendously elated and at peace with himself: he pivots eyes and head in a slow benign sweep down the bar and in the direction of the table, looking toward the men, o.s., with towering benign vanity and self-confidence, and friendly interest. SOUND o.s., of a coin slapped on the bar, rouses him from this boozy musing.

CAMERA "adjusts" about as heavily and clumsily as the Swede does, to get the Barkeeper into the shot.

SWEDE (a wave of the hand) Keep it, keep it.

BARKEEPER (with a tinge of sarcasm; the change is only a nickel) Thank you sir.

SWEDE (grandly; abstractedly) Buy yourself a cigar.
A pause.

The Barkeeper is looking toward the table; the Swede at the Barkeeper. The Swede is trying to cogitate. He's somewhat disappointed; nothing is going as he had wildly imagined it *would* go with people, from now on; but he has just enough sense to realize: after all, this guy doesn't know me for what I am. Better let him in on it a little.

SWEDE No, this isn't too bad weather. It's good enough for me.

BARKEEPER (languidly) So? (he drifts a foot or so away, down bar)
The Swede is sweating a little; the booze is getting to him now; his
breathing is a little heavier.

SWEDE Yes, I like this weather. I like it. (nodding heavy time to his
words) It suits me.

BARKEEPER (after a short pause) So? (he turns to study the bar mirror)

Swede flinches, confused with disappointment and uncertain what to
try next, follows his eye along and down the mirror.

CLOSE SHOT—SWEDE'S REFLECTION IN BAR MIRROR
Eyes glittering in the scrolled mirror, o.s. SOUND of his heavy breathing.
After a few moments of this mirror-gazing, the mirror blurs a little and
comes as if effortlessly back into focus; blurs again:

CLOSE SHOT—SWEDE FROM ANGLE OF HIS REFLECTION
He squeezes his eyes tight shut and opens them; his head is lower than
when we saw it before; he is leaning deep and heavy on his elbows. Evidently triumph, melancholy, fatigue, loneliness, the dismay and disappointment of a dream confronting actuality, all balled up in him, not to
mention the whiskey and the warmth, are all hard at work in him, with
all the liabilities a little outweighing. It is in the need for counterbalance
that he speaks next.

SWEDE Well, I guess I'll have another drink. (he pours, a heavier slug
than before but slower and, raising his glass, needing company bad but
trying to make it seem casual, he eyes Barkeeper o.s.) Have something?

MEDIUM CLOSE SHOT—BARKEEPER PAST SWEDE

BARKEEPER No, thanks, I'm not drinking.
The Swede downs his drink fast but a little more doggedly than before;
no real relish for it; while the Barkeeper studies him more openly.

BARKEEPER How'd you hurt your face? (a tinge of mild insult which the
Swede misses).

SWEDE (loud and blustery; grateful for the chance) Why, in a fight. I
thumped the soul out of a man down here at Scully's hotel.

LAWYER'S VOICE (o.s.) Who was it?
Swede turns quickly.

MEDIUM LONG SHOT—TABLE FROM SWEDE'S ANGLE
They are all looking at him.

CLOSE SHOT—SWEDE—FROM SAME ANGLE—BARKEEPER IN B.G.
SWEDE Johnnie Scully. Son of the man what runs it.

MEDIUM LONG SHOT—TABLE FROM SWEDE'S ANGLE
Their reaction is not one of overjoy.

MEDIUM CLOSE—SWEDE
Seeing they are not as impressed as he is, he tries to better it by making it bigger. He is beginning to squint as if seeing them through a needle eye.

SWEDE He'll be pretty near dead for some weeks, I can tell you.
Again he waits a reaction.

MEDIUM SHOT—SAME ANGLE

SWEDE (talking a little louder) I made a nice thing of him, I did. He couldn't get up. They . . .

MEDIUM LONG SHOT—SWEDE—FROM ANGLE OF TABLE

SWEDE (continuing) . . . had to carry him in the house. Have a drink?

LONG SHOT—ON TABLE FROM BEHIND BAR—PAST SWEDE'S HEAD

The men at the table have in some subtle way encased themselves in reserve.

LAWYER (voice neither pleasant nor unpleasant) No thanks.
Now none of them look at the Swede. The Swede keeps looking at them. A couple of seconds after the "no thanks" he turns his face into the shot, disappointed, mixed-up and a little sore.

SWEDE (to Barkeeper) Come on, have a drink. (he grabs the bottle and holds it out)

CAMERA SWINGS losing table and bringing in Barkeeper

BARKEEPER (shakes his head)

SWEDE What. . . . No? Well, have a little one then. (thick fingers measure a little one) By Golly, I've whipped a man tonight, and I want to celebrate. Whipped him good too. (he turns his head suddenly again into hindside close up of his face. Calls loudly) Gentlemen, have a drink?

BARKEEPER Ssh!
The table is back in the shot now; only a fragment of the Barkeeper as in the start of the shot.

The Doctor looks up.

DOCTOR (curtly) Thanks. We don't want any more.

They all conspicuously pay "no attention" to the Swede.

CLOSE SHOT—SWEDE—FROM ANGLE OF TABLE

The Swede is still looking toward the table, sore as a boil; he ruffles up like a rooster, and explodes.

SWEDE (loudly, wavering in his speech between Barkeeper and table) Well, it seems I can't get any one to drink with me in this town. Seems so, don't it? Well!

BARKEEPER Ssshhh!

SWEDE (leaning toward him, snarling) Say, don't you try to shush *me* up. I won't have it. I'm a gentleman, and I want people to drink with me. And I want um to drink with me now. (hard fist on the bar) NOW! You understand?

BARKEEPER (callous and sulky) I hear you.

SWEDE (louder) Well, listen hard then. See those men over there? (he flings out a thick arm) Well, they're gonna drink with me and don't you forget it! Now you watch!

BARKEEPER Hey! This won't do!

SWEDE (already walking; chops out the words.) Why won't it?

CAMERA is with the Swede, along his right side as he walks. He is in pretty large CLOSE UP, filling the right half of the screen, his angry profile almost pushing the right edge of it; the bar streaking past in left half and the Barkeeper hesitantly hurrying, as he walks fast and drunkenly up to the table. Just as he comes up, lower CAMERA a little to his outlifting hand and speed its SWING a little to bring in a flash of the men at the table, not getting up, but tightening in their chairs.

CLOSE SHOT—SWEDE'S HAND

In a heavy combination of a clap and a fall, hits the gray shoulder of the man who happens to be nearest him—the Gambler's.

CLOSE UP—THE GAMBLER—FROM SWEDE'S VIEWPOINT

A diminutive man, twists his head slowly and looks up into the Swede's eyes. From this angle he is all eyes and forehead; the chin looks weak.

STEEP CLOSE UP—SWEDE—FROM GAMBLER'S ANGLE

From this angle he is all truculent jaw and mouth, little glittering eyes above; apishly small upper half of head.

SWEDE (wrathfully) How about this? I asked you to drink with me. (his eyes flick sorely and quickly toward the others)

DOWN SHOT—ON LAWYER AND MERCHANT—PAST SWEDE AND GAMBLER
Keeping their seats; looking at the Swede in icy disgust.

GAMBLER (coolly; somewhat melodiously) My friend, I don't know you.

SWEDE (roughly; trying to smile and be his idea of "Western" about non-introductions) Ahh, come on and have a drink!

CLOSE SHOT—DOCTOR, MERCHANT, LAWYER
All eyes to the Swede, all registering their respective kinds of well-bred silence

MEDIUM CLOSE SHOT—BARKEEPER
Opposite the table, behind his bar; sprung like a ready trigger; watching *everyone* very carefully.

MEDIUM CLOSE SHOT—GAMBLER AND SWEDE
Gambler very low in screen, the Swede very high, past the Doctor in f.g.

GAMBLER (face still up-turned; coolly and with mock-kindness but very firm; very much the gentleman) Now, my boy, take your hand off my shoulder and go 'way and mind your own business.

ZOOM CAMERA to EXTREME CLOSE UP OF SWEDE, slanting up at him a little.

SWEDE What! You won't drink with me, you little dude? I'll *make* you then! I'll *make* you!

On the first "I'll make you" he is rapidly stooping; STREAK CAMERA DOWN TO

EXTREME CLOSE UP of his hands and the Gambler's face; the hands are already grabbing him by the throat and dragging him from his chair, over noise of scraped-back chairs and rising ad libs of *Hey! stop! Great Scott! Stop him!*   CUT OVER THESE SOUNDS AND WORDS

MEDIUM SHOT—THE GROUP
Past the three men at the table, centering on the Gambler and the Swede, (SOUND of running Barkeeper and his ad libbing o.s.). The three men are rising in their far from rough or halfway ready way, to help; but everything is too fast for them. The Gambler almost instantly stops resisting the upward drag and gets up, throwing the Swede off balance; pivoting as he rises so that he drives the Swede behind the chair toward the wall opposite the bar; getting under the Swede's clumsily placed elbows with his whole left arm and shoulder and lifting as he rises so that the Swede's whole slick

and shiny chest and belly of leather coat bulges taut, swollen and shiny as
a watermelon, catching highlight from the bar light. Just while it can still
be visible before the pivoting hides it, he reaches deftly into his trouser
pocket and pulls out something; the snap of a spring and a long blade
flicks out, flashing the same highlight we have just seen on the Swede's
soft belly. SOUNDS of breath drawn in sharp with horror. The Gambler's
arm straightens back, drives forward; a horrifying SOUND as the blade
enters the leather (on far side of fighters from us), and a deep weird
groaning grunt from the Swede.

CLOSE UP—SWEDE
Almost a head taller than the Gambler, whose back is to the shot. The
Swede's eyes and mouth are amazingly wide: pain in them, but far more,
supreme astonishment: childlike.

Low in the shot the Gambler, not too easily, (SOUND o.s.) extracts the knife
and vanishes out of the shot to the left (we don't see his face) as CAMERA
MOVES IN CLOSER ON THE SWEDE.
The Swede is drawing as deep a breath as his lungs can hold; eyes and
mouth are now even more wide and amazed; then, very long and slow
and gentle, incredulous, downward-trailing to a damp breath, he utters
the Swedish word for "no," which is *"nej,"* pronounced 'nay,' in a tone
almost beyond sorrow and wonder but partaking of both: he begins to
step backward very slowly, CAMERA gently and implacably following, and
gaining on him a little, very gradually; and still more slowly to sink;
CAMERA ditto: at the end of the "Nay" his chin trembles a little, the staring
eyes alter, one tear runs out of each:

As the two tears spring out, a SWIFT THRUST OF CAMERA up to the eyes—
not too close;   THEN CUTTING
                                                 NOT DISSOLVING

and with great rapidity: The supersonic tone used pianissimo at first and
steadily increasing to ultimate unbearable intensity, behind all the shots:
likewise a subsonic tone, same intensification.

In a huge soft radiant CLOSE UP involving munificent crystal and mahogany
and a spray of potted palmleaves, over distant male cheers and discreet
streaming SOUNDS of high grade dinner music, the Swede and the Gambler,
in soup and fish, touch glasses, smiling, courtly; in b.g., the vague-focused
heads of the three other men raise glasses; superimposed for a fraction of
the time it takes him to say it, the Barkeeper in smiling CLOSE UP saying,
"It's on the house, gentlemen."

Over brass disc of music of suppertime, very faint, Scully, Easterner,
Cowboy rush to congratulate him by his tree just after the fight.

Over same music, indoors by the stove, Johnnie, battered and sheepish, nods and grins as he lifts the Swede's hand as the victor's.

Over same music, a little louder, Swede in close up, his arm around Johnnie's shoulders, both faces beaten up, both grinning as Scully, grinning, in l.s., offers the yellow-brown whiskey bottle.

Over the sound of transcontinental express, an unknown good looking well-bred blonde woman of a ripe thirty-five loses a look of hauteur and smiles up at him promisingly.

Over train and disc music a whole parlorfull of floozies in negligee hasten, happily, to swarm around an advancing camera.

A fearsome heavily-mustached blond man in clothes of lower middle-class Sweden (circa 1860,—his father), glaring down into the lens over the sound of whipping and child's crying, suddenly smiles beautifully and benignly: total approval and respect as eyes and lens lift and come level: no whipping sound: then scowls again.

The immense vague tender face of a young woman, shot from the angle and nearness of a baby looking up from the crook of her elbow; over the sound of a warm untrained contralto half-humming a lullaby or folksong in a foreign language, she gazes with infinite tenderness and pity into the lens.

sound of impact of a tremendous blow, exploding 398-H into a white flash and recovering into a close image of Johnnie past his still landing fist.

Easterner, from earlier, his mouth saying, "I don't understand you": but silent.

From the Swede's viewpoint: Johnnie does something shady with the cards.

A long line of hard men in a dark bar look up rather dangerously at the advancing camera over the sound of swinging doors.

close detail-shot of *"The Stag at Bay,"* very dark. (The highsound is by now very strong; no other sounds.) Then sound of child's crying o.s.

A little boy pulverizing the face of another little boy who is crying and not hitting back. louden sound of child's crying; begin lullaby.

Face of the Father, closer and fiercer: same sounds.

Swede in extreme close up at the corner of the town in fullest magnificence. He is not shouting but add the sound of his shout, at a great distance, to the other sounds.

The tigerish reflection in the mirror; continue shout and other SOUNDS.

Same small boy alone, face beaten, crying: SOUND of crying.

Again the huge vague maternal face: silent except for HIGH SOUND which is now at its peak!

EXTREME CLOSE UP—SWEDE

His mouth is almost closed now, his eyes are still wide; he slowly, mournfully, wags his head once to and fro as he sinks: the eyes again alter and slowly freeze into an expression of unutterable horror, dread, recognition and grief. The film, with this change in eyes, very gradually darkens, by darker printing: the eyes remain fixed on the same o.s. spot, just off lens, and it is as if they now die and the rest of him is merely trailing them. CAMERA stops following him: he backs against the edge of a little side table; gropes backward with one hand; fumbles backward between two of the small tables which line the wall and backs between them to the bench and slowly lets himself down and, within a second more, is still. After a second of this stillness (make it a stop shot and stop the HIGH and LOW SOUNDS) his eyes are still fixed on the same spot.

MEDIUM LONG SHOT—THE GROUP
The Swede is just out of the shot beyond r.s. The Gambler stands just where we left him; his knife, point downward is still in his hand. Only the Doctor moves. After perhaps three seconds of immobility he comes through his friends and past the Gambler and over to the Swede, CAMERA SWINGING with him, SOUND of his shoes very quietly crackling on the sanded floor. When he gets to the Swede he stands sufficiently between us and the Swede that we can't see what he's doing, but it isn't much—no need for it to be. Then he straightens up and turns, with desperate eyes, and goes back past the Gambler and his friends, CAMERA SWINGING, same quiet, sandy SOUNDS, and gets his coat. As he lifts it from the coatrack.

MERCHANT (softly) O my Gahhd-uh. O my Gahhhd-uh.
He turns and starts toward his coat and stumbles against a chair as if he were blind. The Lawyer reaches out swiftly, as to catch him should he fall; he doesn't; the Lawyer gently pushes-helps him to the coatrack, a hand against his nearest upper arm; they start getting on their coats. The Lawyer is quick, the Merchant clumsy as a child; the Lawyer helps him; the Doctor, all set, starts toward the front door.

MEDIUM SHOT—GAMBLER
He faces the bar squarely (the Swede is not in the b.g.). He is standing very straight and graceful, almost military, facing the CAMERA, looking to l.s. He is managing this with terrific effort and his knees are just visibly

trembling. SOUND of the Doctor's footsteps; the Gambler's eyes moving steadily with him: he comes across close, l. to r.s.; the Gambler's eyes on his. The Doctor doesn't look at him; he is so scrawny and rugged with shock and distress he looks sick and ten years older. He crosses the shot and out. The Gambler's eyes very quietly to l.s. again: 3 flicks of his eyes, to height of the Lawyer, the Merchant and then the Lawyer again, swinging with them. They enter and cross the shot, side by side; the Merchant on the far side of the Lawyer and almost totally obscured by him.

MERCHANT (half-moaning) O my Gaaahhhdd-uh, my Gaaahhdd-uh.
He says this about every five seconds from the time he starts to his exit, ever more moistly, softly, calflike, never louder. The Lawyer's head, close, high in screen, is desperate icy granite, noble Roman; his eyes, which look straight forward, unseeing as a statue's. The Gambler's eyes follow as they exit right screen.

LONG SHOT—THE FRONT DOOR
The rim of the bar in the middle of the edge of r.s., and level in perspective. The Lawyer very erect, an arm across the Merchant's shoulders; the Merchant caved in and stumbling as a widow. Now they either just avoid stumbling, or stumble brutally against, the Swede's valise; then on, not looking back, and out the door.

MEDIUM SHOT—THE GAMBLER
SOUND of closing door. Very slowly he lifts his knife and looks at it. Again by terrific effort he brings the trembling of the blade down to just perceptible. After a long pause he lifts his eyes toward the Barkeeper, o.s.

GAMBLER (very quietly) May I have your bar-cloth, please.

MEDIUM SHOT—BARKEEPER

BARKEEPER (limply; almost inaudibly) Yes, sir.
He walks unsteadily up the bar for the cloth, toward the edge of the shot, while the Gambler walks even more slowly to the bar; his back, like his front, expressive of terrific shock and incredible control.

MEDIUM CLOSE SHOT—GAMBLER AND BARKEEPER
As they converge at the bar, Barkeeper extends the cloth delicately and the Gambler takes it as delicately. Gambler nods thank you. The Gambler wipes his blade and as he does that his hands and knees start trembling badly in spite of himself. With an almost suicidal effort he controls the trembling and makes the faintest beginning of handing the cloth back to the Barkeeper, who winces very faintly; then, reaching carefully rather than tossing, he puts the cloth on the bar. He folds his knife and puts it in his pocket.

GAMBLER (in an unearthly calm, dry voice with a scratchiness underneath) Charlie, you tell 'em where to find me. I'll be home, waiting for 'em.

The Barkeeper tries to speak; he can't; he nods, then nods again.

The Gambler walks into the shot and past the CAMERA and returns, within a couple of seconds, walking into the shot and away, back-to; his hat is already on; as we first see him he is finishing shrugging into and settling his overcoat; and now, by faint motions of hands and elbows, as he continues, we know he is buttoning it. It must be clear that though he walks very erect, calm, and even, he is scarcely able to stand up. He takes a long slanting line to avoid the valise; rectifies the line the instant he passes it; and so out the door. (Under all these exits use SOUND of feet on sanded floor).

The Barkeeper, who leaned back against the bar as the Gambler went for his coat, stays there very still a moment after the door shuts; then up the bar, knees wobbly, a hand on the bar sustaining him now and then, to the bottle on the bar at the Swede's place. He lifts the bottle and the Swede's glass, puts down the glass and drinks from the bottle, deeply. The inevitable violent reaction of a kind of writhing of his whole interior; a kind of gobbling SOUND. Then a great HUH expulsion of breath: then loud deep breathing, stunned eyes wandering vacantly. Then we see that they must light on the Swede, o.s., for they stop abruptly, and so does the breathing. Then after a couple of seconds the breathing begins again, great HUHs, but this time much more terrible shattering with shock and with a kind of dry sobbing: an off-balance pump: HUH——uhhhhh: dead silence: HUH ——uhhhhh: dead silence. He takes two almost sneaky steps toward the door; hand reaching behind and untying his apron: then sprints ungainly, his apron fouling legs and feet and kicked aside as if it were a snake, with another awful HUH——uuuhhh carrying him at high speed through the door. No SOUND of closing door, but SOUND of the scream of the storm, very far down.

BARKEEPER'S VOICE (o.s.; retreating in the street and muffled in the storm, bawling, bestial) Helllllp! Murrrrrder! Helllllp!

HOLD SHOT ON BARE BAR and perspective of its rim, through these lines.

FULL SHOT—THE WHOLE INTERIOR (ORTHOCHROMATIC FILM)

A formal shot from the dead center of the front of the room: a shot modeled on postcards of 1890—1910: our first full view of the nicest bar in a small town: pathetic but not completely unsuccessful in its efforts at a kind of barren charm and grace. The sand on the floor in the f.g. is swept in pretty curclicues; these are scuffed along the bar and where the fight took place. HOLD three or four seconds, long enough to register fully the Swede and the cash register, dead-opposite each other, at exact middles of their sides of the room. No storm SOUND: pure silence.

EXTREME CLOSE UP—THE SWEDE'S LEFT EYE (ORTHOCHROMATIC)
Occupying the whole screen except enough to show a little of a contused cheekbone and across it, a crooked rill of dried blood and a snailtrack shining of a not yet dried tear. The eye, if technically possible, is glazing as we watch. Silence.

EXTREME CLOSE SHOT—THE CASH REGISTER (ORTHOCHROMATIC)
The ornate cast-iron top of the nickel-plated cash register. Its florid shape recalls the florid cornice of the Blue Hotel. The cash amount is below-screen. The stamped lettering of the legend is fiercely cold, glittering, massive and hard—a little ornate like much of the lettering of the time:

THIS REGISTERS THE AMOUNT OF YOUR PURCHASE

O.S. SOUND of a door opening. HOLD the shot a couple of seconds after it.

FADE OUT

FADE IN

MEDIUM CLOSE SHOT—THE EASTERNER
As he comes through the swinging doors, advances a couple of paces, and stops dead in his tracks as his eyes find the Swede. An impulse to go to him is instantly arrested; it is so clear that he is beyond help. Almost unconsciously, he sets down his traveling bag. A freezing anguish of guilt enters his still face.

After a sufficient pause to make clear they did not come with him, Scully, Johnnie and the Cowboy come in, quietly, but winded. They also look, see, and are silent. They try to subdue their breathing. They have left the street door open and we can see that there is no more storm or SOUND outside.

The Easterner is aware when they come in; we feel that he even knows who they are. But throughout the scene, he never shifts his eyes from the Swede; and they shift theirs only rarely. Throughout, they stand *behind* Easterner.

After a considerable silence:

SCULLY (in a subdued voice) How did it happen?

The Easterner says nothing. A pause.

COWBOY (quietly too) You ask me, that feller was *lookin'* for trouble. An' he sure found himself a plenty.

A pause.

EASTERNER (in a strange, vague voice) Looking . . .? (more firmly, but very quiet) Like all troubled men. (pause) And we helped him find it, and we trapped him into it.

A pause. The three men behind now glance at each other.

SCULLY (a little less subdued) See here, Mister.

The Easterner says nothing.

SCULLY Just one thing.

EASTERNER (quietly) Go home.

SCULLY Just one little thing. Johnnie an' me live in this town. We don't want no stories shpread around that ye . . .

EASTERNER (as quietly) Go home. Stop worrying. Tell whatever story you please.

SCULLY Ye mane ye—ye won't . . .

EASTERNER Your conscience is *your* business. Each one of you. My own is enough for *me* to cope with.

They linger, unsure and weary.

EASTERNER (with deep exhausted bitterness) So just go home now. Leave me alone. (pause) If you please!

A silence.

SCULLY (quietly and solemnly) We didn't have no part in it.
The three shake their heads, but they don't look at each other.

EASTERNER Every sin is a collaboration. Everybody is responsible for everything.

The three look unsurely at each other; they are obscurely abashed.

SCULLY (with a slight gesture and an almost inaudible whisper) Come on. Each looks a last time toward the Swede, each in his own strange way, kind of gloomy, shy, foreboding reproach and resentment; and each, one by one, turns away from the CAMERA and walks quietly outdoors and out of the shot. We hear only the SOUND of the faint squeaking of their shoes on snow, and soon this dies.

With the absolute silence an even more fierce and living quiet intensifies in the Easterner's face and becomes, as well, sorrow, pity, tenderness, a passionate desire for, and hopelessness of, expiation. The face rises on a high wave of realization, almost transfigured, on the verge, even, of mysticism, yet iron, virile, tragic—as, very slowly, his eyes still fixed toward the Swede, he walks into extreme CLOSE UP and PAST THE CAMERA out of the shot.

THE CAMERA HOLDS for a few seconds on the swinging doors, whose subtle breathing stops. Beyond them, through the open door, the air is utterly still.

LONG SHOT—THE BLUE HOTEL—SAME AS THAT WHICH OPENED THE PICTURE
Three tiny figures walk in single file down the home stretch. In the immense silence we can just hear their feet. They go in. Light gapes and vanishes, as the door opens and closes. After a few seconds, light appears in the upstairs windows. After a few more seconds, the downstairs light goes out. Then one upstairs light. Then the other. The sky is emblazoned with a freezing virulence of patterned stars.

Almost inaudibly, deep in the distance, o.s. SOUND of a train whistle.
In the silence after it, the cold stars sharpen; and very slowly, like a prodigious wheel, the whole sky begins to turn.

FADE OUT

THE END

ABOUT THE AUTHOR

James Agee was born in Knoxville, Tennessee and attended St. Andrew's School, outside Sewanee. These two surroundings of his childhood provided the backgrounds for his novels: Knoxville is the scene of *A Death in the Family,* and *The Morning Watch* shows the same boy as an adolescent at school—St. Andrew's. Agee graduated from Phillips Academy, Exeter, New Hampshire. He then went to Harvard where he was Editor of *The Advocate.* He became connected with Time, Inc., first as a feature writer for *Fortune* and later as a book and movie reviewer for *Time.*

While at *Fortune,* he and photographer Walker Evans were assigned to do an article on the sharecroppers in the South. It never appeared in the magazine, but was later published as a book, *Let Us Now Praise Famous Men.*

From 1941 to 1948 he was the movie reviewer for *Time* and from 1942 to 1948 he wrote the film column for *The Nation.* His criticism and comment on the movies during this time is collected in the first volume of *Agee on Film.* In 1948 he began writing scripts for such directors as John Huston and Charles Laughton.

His death of a heart attack in New York City on May 16, 1955, at the age of forty-five, ended the career of this unique writer. Two years later, the publication of *A Death in the Family,* which was awarded the Pulitzer Prize in 1958, brought his work greater recognition than it ever had during his life.